I0831365

SIEGE OF TARR-HOSTIGOS

JOHN F. CARR

Pequod Press

THE SIEGE OF TARR-HOSTIGOS

A Pequod Press Adventure Novel

All Rights Reserved
Copyright © 2003 by John F. Carr
Copyright © 2012 by John F. Carr

An excerpt from this novel first appeared in THERE WILL BE WAR: ARMAGEDDON, edited by Jerry E. Pournelle & John F. Carr, published by Tor Books, under the title "Siege at Tarr-Hostigos" in 1989. Copyright © 1989 by John F. Carr.

This book may not be reproduced or transmitted in whole or in part, in any form or by any means electronic or mechanical, including photocopying, scanning, recording, or any information storage or retrieval system, without prior permission in writing from the author.

The First Edition was published by Pequod Press in 2003. This Second Edition has been revised throughout: the Preface was removed and several new scenes have been added.

Second Revised Edition

Manufactured in the United States of America

V 10 9 8 7 6 5 4 3 2

ISBN: 978-0-937912-18-8

On the cover: Alan Gutierrez, Siege of Tarr-Hostigos, gouache on masonite, 2011 (*www.alangutierrez.com*)

Pequod Press
P.O. Box 80
Boalsburg, PA 16827
www.PequodPress.com

Lord Kalvan Novels

Gunpowder God
The Fireseed Wars
Siege of Tarr-Hostigos
Kalvan Kingmaker
Great Kings' War *(with Roland Green)*

Paratime Police Novels

Time Crime *(with H. Beam Piper)*

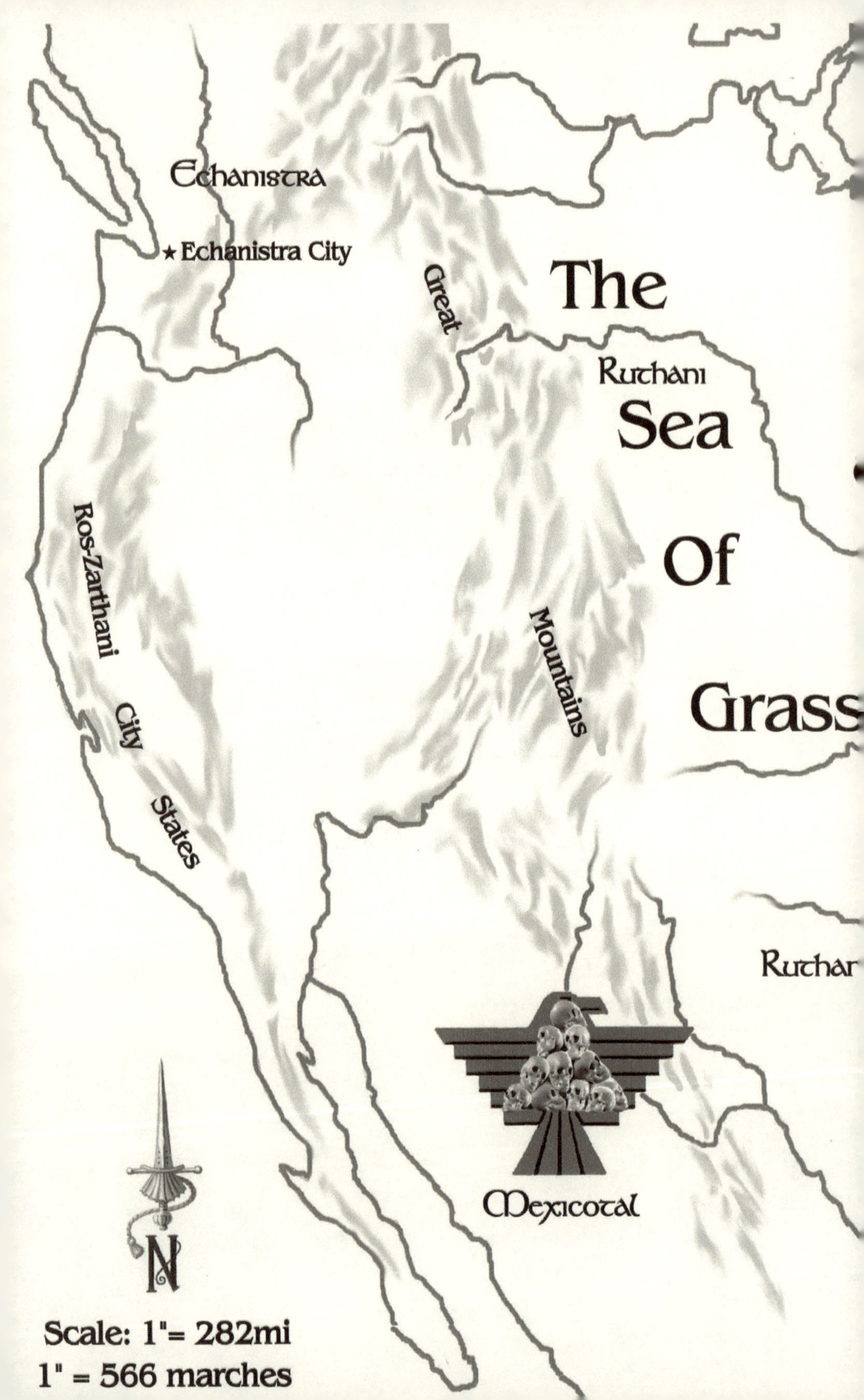
Echanistra
★ Echanistra City
Great
The
Ruthani
Sea
Of
Grass
Ros-Zarthani
City
States
Mountains
Ruthar
Mexicotal
N
Scale: 1"= 282mi
1" = 566 marches

The Great Kingdoms
Hos-Zygros
Saltless Seas
Hos-Agrys
Grefftscharr
Greffa City
Hos-Hostigos
Hos-Harphax
Trygath
Hos-Ktemnos
Balph
Upper Sastragath
Lower Sastragath
Hos-Bletha

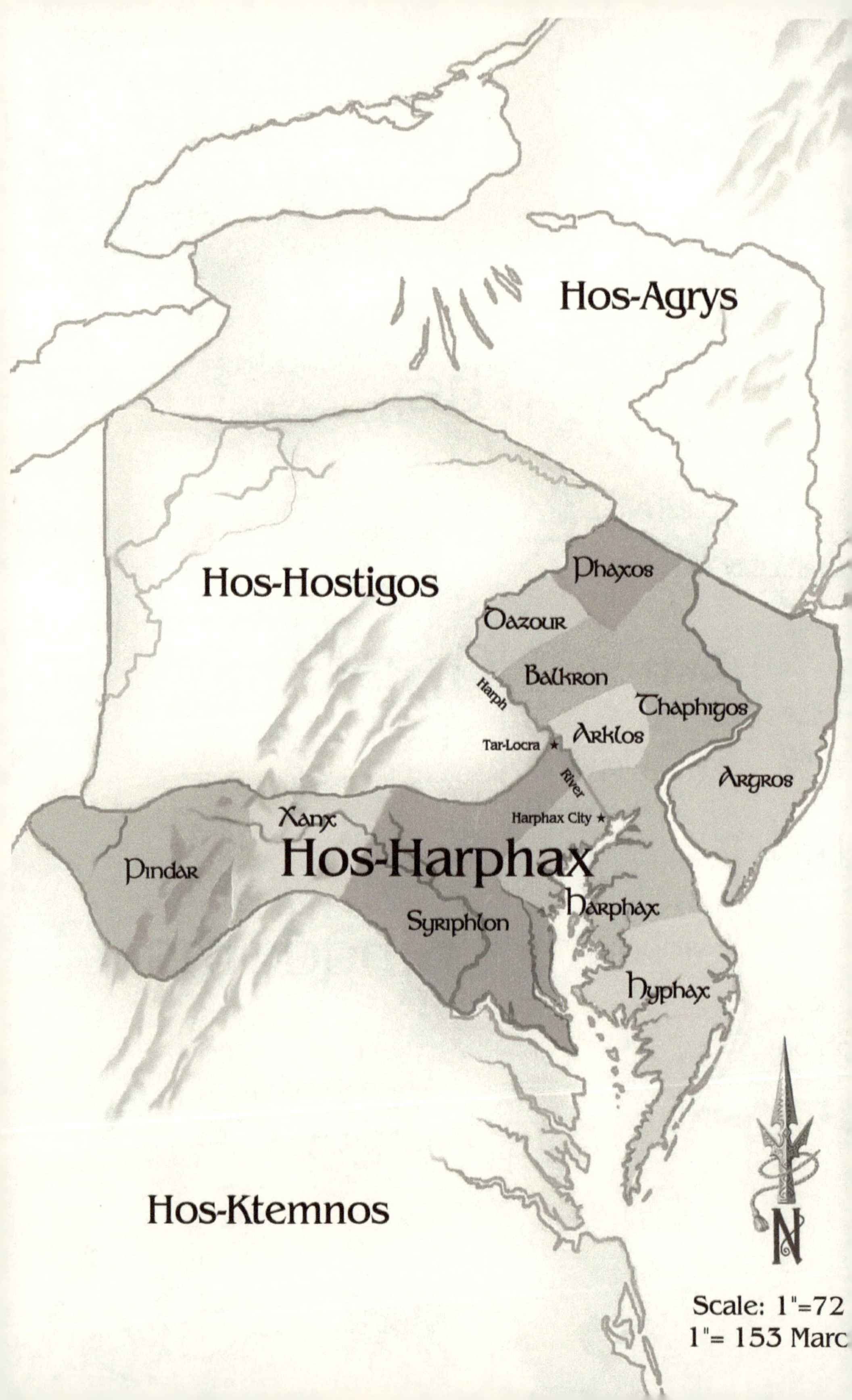

Hos-Agrys
Hos-Hostigos
Phaxos
Dazour
Balkron
Harph
Thaphigos
Arklos
Tar-Locra
River
Argros
Xanx
Harphax City
Hos-Harphax
Pindar
Harphax
Syriphlon
Hyphax
Hos-Ktemnos
N
Scale: 1"=72
1"= 153 Marc

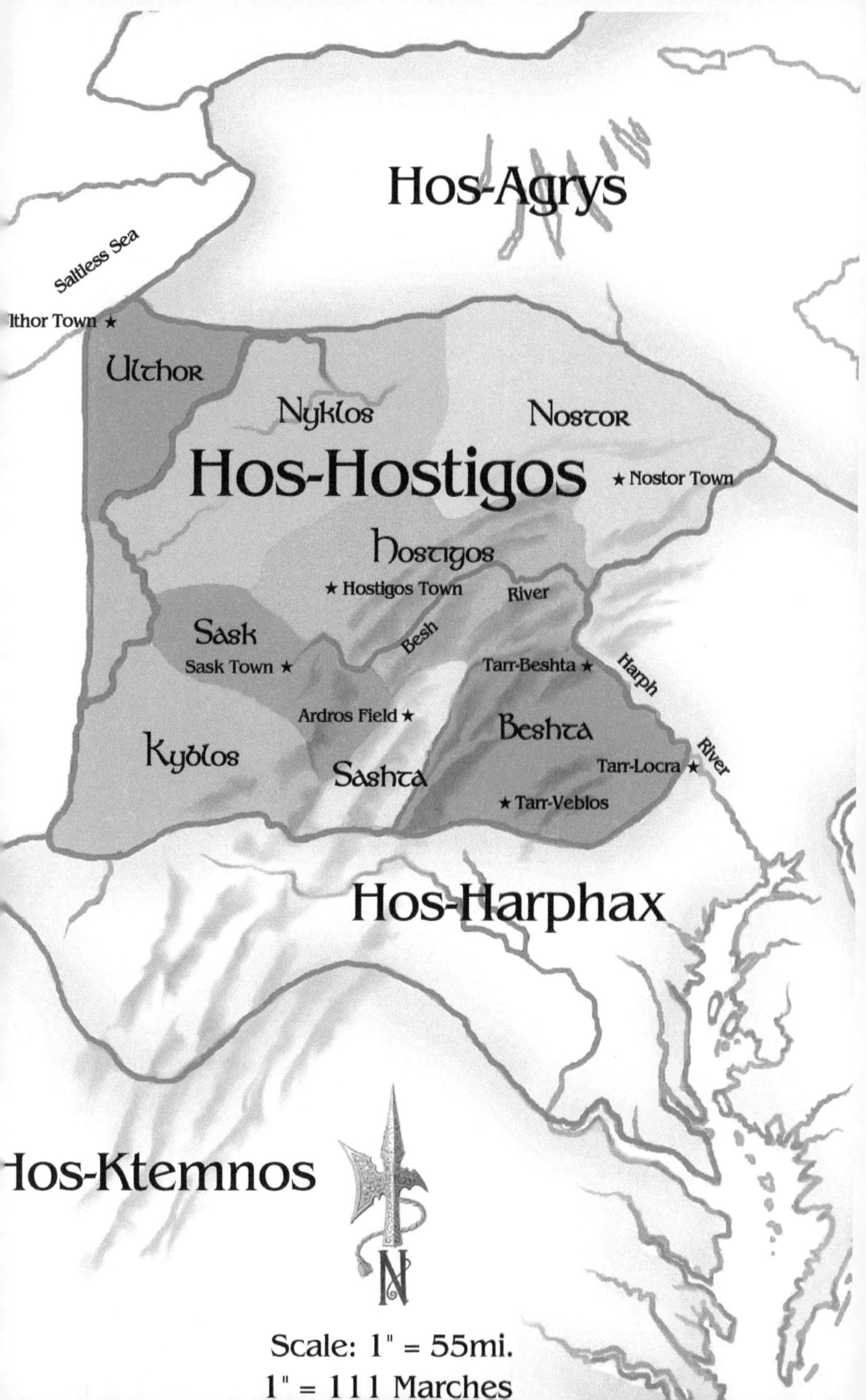

Hos-Agrys
Saltless Sea
lthor Town
Ulthor
Nyklos
Nostor
Hos-Hostigos
Nostor Town
Hostigos
Hostigos Town
River
Sask
Besh
Sask Town
Tarr-Beshta
Harph
Ardros Field
Beshta
Kyblos
River
Tarr-Locra
Sashta
Tarr-Veblos
Hos-Harphax
Hos-Ktemnos
N
Scale: 1" = 55mi.
1" = 111 Marches

DRAMATIS PERSONAE

HOS-HOSTIGOS & ALLIES

Alkides—Artillery general in the Royal Army.
Aspasthar—Commandant of the Hostigos Military Academy.
Armanes—Prince of Nyklos.
Chartiphon—Chancellor of Hos-Hostigos.
Demia—Kalvan and Rylla's daughter.
Ermut—Dean of the University of Hostigos.
Eutare—Prince Phrames betrothed.
Hectides—Scout for the Royal Army.
Hestophes—Captain-General of the Army of Hostigos.
Kalvan—Former Penn. State Trooper and Great King of Hos-Hostigos.
Kestophes—Prince of Ulthor.
Klestreus—Head of Hostigos Security.
Mnestros—Duke of Eubros and Kalvan's ally.
Mytron—Highpriest of Dralm.
Pheblon—Prince of Nostor.
Phrames—Prince of Beshta.
Rylla—Great Queen of Hos-Hostigos, Kalvan's wife and co-ruler.
Sarrask—Prince of Sask.
Skranga—Chief of Hostigos Intelligence.
Tharses—Uncle Wolf and Highpriest of Galzar.
Tythanes—Prince of Kyblos.
Vanar Halgoth—Captain of Kalvan's Tymannian Guard.
Xentos—First Primate of Dralm at the Hos-Agrys Great Temple.
Xykos—Grand-Captain of Great Queen Rylla's Own Horse Guard.

PARATIMERS

Altarn Vor—Deputy Bureau Chief, one of Verkan's trusted advisors.
Aranth Saln—Kalvan Study Team military expert.
Danthor Dras—University Professor and expert on Styphon's House Subsector.
Danar Sirna—Former Member of Kalvan Study Team and Phidestros' mistress.
Hadron Dalla—Verkan's wife and Paratime Police Chief's Special Assistant.
Hadron Tharn—Dalla's power mad younger brother.
Hadron Zinganna—Dalla's adopted Prole sister. Undercover in Greffa as Zinna.
Hasthor Flan—Head of Opposition Party.
Kostran Garth—Head of the Greffan Study Team.
Maldor Dard—Paratime Police Field Agent assigned to Harphaxi Study Team.
Ranthar Jard—Paratime Police Inspector.
Tortha Karf—Former Paratime Police Chief.
Verkan Vall—Paratime Police Chief.
Yandar Yadd—Newsie on First Level.

STYPHON'S HOUSE

Albides—Second in command of Styphon's Own Guard.
Anaxthenes—New Supreme Priest and Styphon's Own Voice.
Aristocles—Grand Commander and second in command of the Order.
Cimon—Inner Circle Archpriest called the "Peasant Priest."
Danthor—Danthor Dras' undercover identity as Styphon's House Archpriest.
Dracar—Archpriest of Inner Circle and Roxthar's puppet.
Drayton—Styphon's House treasurer.
Grythos—Archpriest of the Inner Circle and Military Advisor.
Heraclestros—Archpriest and former Highpriest of Agrys City.
Neamenestros—Archpriest and one of Anaxthenes' allies.

Phyllos—Highpriest of Harphax City Great Temple.
Roxthar—Holy Investigator and Torquemada of Styphon's House.
Sarmoth—Knight Sergeant of the Order of Zarthani Knights.
Soton—Grand Master of the Order of Zarthani Knights.
Timothanes—Archpriest and one of Archpriest Dracar's supporters.
Yagos—Anaxthenes' Special Deputy and spy master.
Xenophes—High Marshal of the Styphon's House Temple Guard.

ALLIES OF STYPHON'S HOUSE

Anaxon—Prince of Ktemnos and heir to the Golden Throne.
Cleitharses—Great King of Hos-Ktemnos.
Demnos—Captain of Lysandros' Bodyguard.
Geblon—Phidestros' friend and General.
Kaphros—Duke in charge of Hos-Harphax while Lysandros is away.
Kyblannos—Phidestros' Chief of Artillery.
Lyphannes—Chancellor of Hos-Harphax and Lysandros' advisor.
Lysandros—Great King of Hos-Harphax and Kalvan's enemy.
Lukthos—Styphon's House's new candidate for Great King of Hos-Ktemnos.
Niclophon—Great King of Hos-Bletha.
Phidestros—Prince of Greater Beshta.
Sopharar—Great King of Hos-Zygros.
Sthentros—New Prince of Hostigos.
Thessamona—Lady of Death and Anaxthenes favorite concubine.

NEUTRALS

Davros—Highpriest of the High Temple of Dralm in Agrys City.
Demistophon—Great King of Hos-Agrys.
Eudocles—Grand Duke of Zygros and Sopharar's brother.

Lavena—Baron Sthentros' daughter.
Nestros—Great King of Hos-Rathon.
Olmnestes—Uncle Wolf Highpriest of the Grand Host.
Pariphon—Prince and heir to the Thorne of Hos-Zygros.
Ranjar Sargos—Var-Wannax of the Sastragath.
Ranthos—Former Paratimer Aranth Saln undercover as a mercenary Captain.
Roldolf—King of Xiphlon.
Ruffulo—Greffan Duke from an old family.
Selestros—Son of former Great King Kaiphranos of Hos-Harphax.
Sopharar—Great King of Hos-Zygros.
Theovacar—King of Grefftscharr.
Varrack—Prince of Thagnor.

FALL

ONE

I

Archpriest Anaxthenes watched as the gulls, following the galleasses' wake, swooped down and dove for fish. This ship was one of the new three-banked galleasses with twelve guns and a beaked prow. The use of a warship to ferry Styphon's House's emissaries was a message to Great King Lysandros about how seriously the Temple took the threat of the Usurper Kalvan. The war with the False Kingdom of Hos-Hostigos was a fight to the death and only one power would emerge victorious from the Fireseed Wars. As First Speaker of the Inner Circle, he meant to ensure that the victor would be Styphon's House on Earth.

Even though they were sailing on the Eastern Ocean, the overseers were pounding the drums to keep the rowers' oar-rhythm synchronized. Anaxthenes' head throbbed as though the blows were striking his skull. The captain was more worried about the dark clouds on the horizon than he was about his rowers' well-being. His yellow robe was sprayed with water when a big wave hit the galleass' bow and exploded over the gunwale. He felt his stomach lurch.

The galleass had left Balph three days before and was still two good weather days away from Harphax City. The Archpriest would have prayed to Lytris, the Weather Goddess, had he believed in any god. Some of the sailors were fingering the emblems hanging from their necks and muttering prayers under their breath to the Weather Goddess. For one of the few times in his life, Anaxthenes envied their gullibility. While their idols would never answer their prayers, the ivory-carved amulets of the eagle-headed goddess offered her believers comfort against the turbulent majesty and raw power of the Eastern Ocean.

Anaxthenes inwardly recoiled at the unexpected touch of a hand on his shoulder. He turned his head and saw Grand Master Soton of the Zarthani Knights in a blue woolen cape with Styphon's Holy Wheel emblazoned on the front in silver thread. The rhythmic creak of the oars, the slapping sail overhead and the sound of waves battering the bow made conversation difficult. Soton took a stubby pipe out of his mouth and pointed the stem to the decks below. Anaxthenes nodded and followed Soton down the companionway to the lower decks into a small cabin that was as devoid of decoration as Roxthar's cell in Balph. The only furniture were two stools and a small table bolted to the floor. Nailed to one cabin wall was a lambskin map of Hos-Harphax—stolen from a dead Hostigi scout at the Battle of Fyk and purchased at great expense—which included within its boundaries the heretic kingdom of Hos-Hostigos now outlined in red.

Maybe, at long last, the Grand Master would explain why he had maneuvered Anaxthenes into taking this journey at a time when even seasoned mariners balked at sea travel. The Grand Master pretended to be indifferent about Temple politics, but Anaxthenes had noticed that for most of Soton's reign over the Order of the Zarthani Knights the Grand Master had gotten everything he'd asked for from the Inner Circle. Anaxthenes had many questions to ask, but knew it was most politic to let Soton open the conversation.

"First Speaker, I wanted to talk to you before we reached the docks at Harphax City away from the ears of your fellow priests." The Grand Master was referring to the half dozen highpriests who had accompanied Anaxthenes on the *Sea King* for the upcoming enthronement of the soon-to-be Great King Lysandros of Hos-Harphax. The Argos River and the Eastern Ocean had been unseasonably calm until today and the landlubber highpriests were busy down in the jakes emptying their bellies of this morning's breakfast.

Anaxthenes nodded.

"I have good reason to suspect that at least one of them is in the Investigator's pay."

"These days Investigator Roxthar has so many informers in Balph that we call them Styphon's Own Ears. Sadly, most of them do it out of fear, since they believe that the Investigator will not turn on his own tools. They do not know him at all—up until last winter I considered him part of my faction. I have since learned a bitter lesson. Once Roxthar sniffs out their corruption, he will dog those priests to their graves."

"I see you know your man," Soton said. "I only hope you know me as well: that I have always been obedient to Styphon's House, that I have always been loyal to the Inner Circle and that I have done Styphon's work, no matter how odious. Also, that I am a believer in Styphon's divinity as well as that of the other True Gods."

Anaxthenes nodded in agreement. Soton was, if anything, a predictable and faithful servant of Styphon's House. He'd always thought Soton's devotion to Styphon was out of character for the Temple's most powerful warlord. Still, the Grand Master was useful and true to his word; he could be depended on. *I only wish the rest of my allies were as trustworthy.*

Soton paused to pull out a stubby corncob pipe and fill it with tobacco. "In the past, while I have not always agreed with the Temple's policies, I have always faithfully carried them out. What I have seen on this past journey from Tarr-Ceros to Balph has convinced me that it is time to change my strategy. The Investigator threatens the welfare of us all with his insane determination to root out the Temple's disbelievers and put Styphon ahead of all other gods!"

"I share your concerns, as well, Grand Master. Since summer, so many of Styphon's underpriests have died or fled from Roxthar's Investigation in Balph that we're running out of priests to hold services in the temples."

"The problems are not only in Balph, Archpriest. Let me share what I have seen with my own eyes on my recent journey from Tarr-Ceros to the Holy City. Roxthar's Investigators have moved the Investigation into the hinterland of Hos-Ktemnos, where there is no one of consequence to observe them and their mischief. On my return from Tarr-Ceros, I passed through villages lying in ruins, with only a few maimed and limping survivors. In some places even the children have died because there are so few adults to care for them!"

Anaxthenes shook his head. More proof that the Inner Circle was too far out of touch with what was happening outside of Balph.

"I learned this from a few survivors who dared talk. When Investigators arrive at a village, usually because of some complaint about the local temple priest, they consider everyone a heretic and subject to Investigation. This is encouraged by the Investigation's confiscation policies. When a man or woman is Investigated, the informer is provided a portion of their earthly holdings—a share of one quarter of the value of the goods and property claimed by the Temple under the Investigator's authority. Another quarter goes to the Investigator questioning the 'supposed' heretic. The remaining half, if there is anything left, goes to the Temple Treasury. As you can see, this procedure has led to corruption and out-right thievery."

"We of the Inner Circle have heard rumors of lesser priests being Investigated, but little else."

"The Investigators leave few witnesses, and those they do leave behind are scared witless or broken in body and spirit. I visited at one village where the peasants had turned on the Investigators, and their Temple Guard, killing them all. They thought I had come with my escort to punish them. Instead I prompted them to tell their story. In this village the Investigators were so corrupt, they started Investigating the more prosperous farmers before anyone had even made a *single* complaint. The local elders took offense, offered them a celebratory dinner, poisoned their wine and cut the throats of all of the Investigators not killed outright by poison."

Anaxthenes shuddered. "Does Roxthar know?"

"I suspect not. He is an honest man by his own lights. The Holy Investigator has eyes only for Kalvan, Hos-Hostigos and the blasphemers of our own Temples which as you know are many."

Anaxthenes nodded, being one himself. The Temple had been built on lies and fakery and had profited handsomely, as had the high priesthood, himself included. Or, at least, until the Usurper Kalvan arrived. Some in the Inner Circle believed Kalvan to be a disaffected highpriest of Styphon's House who had decided to use his knowledge of the Fireseed Mystery to raise himself above the Temple.

"Then you are aware that most of Roxthar's Investigators no more believe in Styphon's divinity than in Allfather Dralm."

"Yes, Grand Master, they are ambitious underpriests who fear that they will not live long enough to advance to the top of the Temple hierarchy where rests an old man of more than ninety winters. They see in Roxthar a path to advancement and are most eager to Investigate any highpriest above their station. Someday Roxthar will discover this himself, and then we'll watch the old wolf devour his own tail and hind parts. Of course, few of us will be alive to witness this satisfying conclusion to this madman's reign of terror."

Soton's calloused hand grasped the Archpriest's shoulder. "I am glad to learn that I am not the only man with eyes in all of Balph. I fear that long before Roxthar discovers the corruption in his own entrails, the peasants, artisans, nobles and kings will have had enough of this Investigation and will kill all of us in an orgy of anger and bloodlust."

Anaxthenes shivered, despite himself, as a vision of townsmen and peasants alike descending upon the temples of Styphon and burning and looting them filled his mind's eye.

The Grand Master's face hardened. "I am convinced that Roxthar is a greater threat to Styphon's House than the Usurper Kalvan himself!"

In lieu of all this information and his own experience of Roxthar, he believed Soton was right. "But how can we stop him? Roxthar holds the Inner Circle hostage like a pigeon in a cat's mouth. Styphon's Own Guard protects him and his Investigators. And he has mobilized the Temple and its allies in the war against the Usurper."

"Very true," Soton nodded. "However, Roxthar is no longer satisfied to watch from the top of the Temple. He has 'assured' me in private that he and his Investigators will join the army now being assembled in Hos-Harphax to re-take the false kingdom of Hos-Hostigos."

"The news of Roxthar's absence will be a relief to the peasants of Hos-Ktemnos and the highpriests of Balph, and every other temple in the Five Kingdoms."

"Yes," Soton agreed, "but it also provides us with a unique opportunity, one which we must take advantage of quickly. It's the primary reason I wanted you to accompany me to Harphax City; the other so that you can gain prestige by officiating over Great King Lysandros' enthronement."

Anaxthenes nodded. It was no secret that his own star had plummeted even as Roxthar's had ascended.

"Furthermore, Roxthar will be joining the command in Hos-Harphax after the Harvest Festival and you will have a one-time opportunity to solidify your position in Balph."

"To what end?" Anaxthenes asked.

"Styphon's Voice. With you in command of the Temple, not even Roxthar will be in a position to Investigate you and the Inner Circle."

Anaxthenes took a deep breath. He had grown accustomed to pulling strings from above, but maybe it was time for him to be on center stage.

"You could even withdraw his Petition of Investigation," Soton finished.

"Not unless the collective body of the Inner Circle has grown a backbone since we left Balph."

Soton laughed, a big booming noise. "Regardless, you would be in a position to direct events and rein in our mad Archpriest."

Anaxthenes nodded. "I am glad to hear you say it out loud. It is true that Roxthar is as mad as a Sastragathi rattlesnake handler. What about old Sesklos? He looks fit enough to live three or four more winters. And what about Dracar, his successor, who trembles at Roxthar's footsteps?"

"If you can't figure out how to take care of a few feeble old priests, then you are not the man I know you to be."

Anaxthenes thought of Thessamona and her little vials—yes, he knew how and what to do. But carefully.... "I agree, it is time to remove some old timbers from the Temple's flooring."

Soton smiled. "Yes, there's already one vacancy. And I have the perfect candidate in mind."

"Who?"

"Archpriest Grythos. He is a former Knight Commander of the Order. Roxthar will not fight his nomination since he has come to believe we need more men of action in the Inner Circle, and Grythos recently distinguished himself as Grand Captain Phidestros' advisor during the successful capture of the Hostigos castle, Tarr-Veblos."

"Will he follow my lead, Grand Master?"

"He is my man and will do as I wish."

Anaxthenes, for the first time that day, felt his spirits lift. "You do your job in Hos-Hostigos, and I will do mine in Balph."

They raised palms. "Agreed."

II

Verkan Vall, Paratime Police Chief, dismounted and walked his horse up to the Royal Foundry outer gate. His wife, Dalla, reins in hand, walked at his side with her long blonde hair blowing in the chill wind. An outtime emergency on Fourth Level Alexandrian-Roman, Seleucid Subsector—where the successors of Seleucus I Nicator had conquered the Nile Delta and kicked out the Ptolemy dynasty—had forced them to cut short their "vacation" on Aryan-Transpacific Styphon's House Subsector by several days. The time had come to return to First Level.

Verkan was pleased to see that the new stone outer walls around the Foundry and living quarters were complete. After the ambush of the Royal Foundry Party en route to Nostor, Verkan had instructed Ranthar Jard to improve Foundry security. There were now watchtowers at each of the four corners of the outer wall and at both sides of the gate.

A guard dressed in a buff jack over a steel back-and-breast called out, "Who goes there?"

"Trader Verkan and Mistress Dalla."

"Welcome, Baron!" The small iron portcullis was lifted, and Verkan and Dalla made their way into a mud-filled courtyard before the stone manor house and the Royal Foundry, which had once been the barn. A few ducks were valiantly trying to swim in the bigger puddles. Gray smoke was pouring from all four of the Foundry's chimneys, and there was the sound of hammering and banging muffled by thick walls. One of the four guards, his morion helmet tilted back jauntily, escorted them to the Foundry door.

The guard banged on the knocker while several peasants gawked. It wasn't everyday that nobility graced the Foundry with its presence. Five or six scrawny turkeys and geese, with obviously clipped wings, pecked at some bushes. While they waited Verkan took off his gloves and rubbed his stiff fingers together. Winter was coming early this year. Dalla's horse, upset at being taken to the livery by a stable boy, neighed loudly; in reply there was a distant wolf howl.

The wolf cry reminded Verkan of two years back, when an unusually hard winter had emboldened the wolves. People in Hos-Hostigos still referred to those times as the Year of the Wolf, just as many were now calling this year—after the nomad invasion of the Trygath—"the Year of the Locust."

The guard turned to Verkan, saying, "No one's answering and my nose is beginning to turn blue!"

Verkan picked up a loose stone, moved the guard out of the way and began to bang loudly on the thick plank door.

The door flew open and a horse-faced woman, wearing a velvet and brocade dress, stuck her head out. "Hold onto your britches!"

After a quick double take, Varnath Lala, the Study Team resident metallurgist, held the door open reluctantly. "Oh, it's you!" There was little love between the Dhergabar University Kalvan Study Team and the Paratime Police, whose duty it was to see to their safety while they studied outtime. They were on Kalvan's Time-Line because it was the Paratime rarity; a time-line identified from the exact point of divarication.

Kalvan, formerly Calvin Morrison, Pennsylvania State Trooper, had been accidentally picked up by a transtemporal conveyer, which sometimes happened when two conveyers temporarily occupied the same space and time, and 'dropped off' on Aryan-Transpacific, Styphon's House Subsector. Most transtemporal 'hitchhikers' were quickly killed, captured or lost. Few of them were able to successfully rebuild their lives in their new environment; Calvin Morrison was one of the few exceptions. He had not only merely survived but was flourishing, having turned the small princedom of Hostigos into the Great Kingdom of Hos-Hostigos.

The inside of the Foundry appeared the same as any other brass foundry on Kalvan's Time-Line, with huge forges and molds. The astringent scent of molten metal and burnt oil filled the room. Two workers were filing the burrs off a newly cast brass cannon barrel. Another group of founders were removing the mold from around a newly cast sixteen-pound gun. Outside, there was a muffled boom from a cannon being proofed.

Despite all the activity in the foundry room, the real heart of the operation was below in the collapsed-nickel shielded basement, where First Level technology, tools and conveyers were kept in hiding to keep Transtemporal Contamination to a minimum. Professor Lala led Verkan and Dalla to the back storeroom where the floor had a well-hidden trapdoor that led to the basement.

No matter what happened to the Foundry in the upcoming war between Hos-Hostigos and Styphon's House, no one without access to a nuclear bomb would ever breach the basement and the transtemporal conveyers hidden inside. Paratime travel was the one inviolate secret of Home Time Line, and anything—including atomic annihilation—would be done to keep it that way.

The stone stairs leading down to the basement were wet and slippery. The collapsed-nickel shielded entryway, a door disguised with steel plates to fool the locals, creaked as it opened in response to Verkan's magnetic key. Inside, there were half a dozen techs, four of them wearing green Paratime Police uniforms. Dalla rushed over to the changing room and shut the door. Dominating the room were two twelve-foot diameter domed silver-mesh transtemporal conveyers.

The room held a desk, some First Level monitoring equipment, a visiplate that almost completely covered one wall, showing an overhead of Tarr-Harphax from the sky-eye above, several racks of muskets and rifles, half a dozen small barrels of gunpowder, a score of replacement gun carriage wheels and hundreds of kegs of barley and corn.

Dalla was returning to First Level and home; while Verkan was on his way to Fourth Level, Seleucid Subsector, so he didn't bother changing. His clothes were those of a prosperous trader and with minor additions would pass muster upon arrival; if not, there would be a change of dress waiting for him. Verkan went over to one of the lockers, opened the door, and put away his sword and scabbard, his powder horn and both pistols, including a little boot gun. Out of one of the drawers he took a Police issue needler and stuck it in his belt.

When Dalla exited the changing room in her Paratime Police greens, he escorted her into the waiting conveyer. Verkan took over the controls and made the proper adjustments. There was a slight lurch, more of a mental—rather than physical—sensation, and after a thirty minute wait they exited into an identical basement on a neighboring Kalvan Control Time-Line ten parayears away, the distance it took a Ghaldron-Hesthor field to build up and collapse. On this time-line no Pennsylvania State Trooper had been dropped off a transtemporal conveyer, which meant there had been no Lord Kalvan to save the small Princedom of Hostigos. Instead the small Princedom had been cruelly conquered, most of the inhabitants slain and the Princedom partitioned off between the neighboring Princedoms of Nostor, Beshta and Sash. This 'Hostigos' was now in ruins and inhabited only by a few peasants, some imported robber barons, turkey thieves, and robbers everywhere.

The Foundry barn had once belonged to one of the local gentry, who had died at the Battle of Fyk on Kalvan's Time-Line. Dying without issue, his property had reverted to the Throne. The noble on this Control Time-Line had died during the sack of Hostigos Town, and in the aftermath his manor had burned to the ground and the barn was abandoned. Occasionally a passing tramp or peasant would spend the night only to hear strange noises and an occasional apparition, courtesy of the Paratime Police. It hadn't taken long for the surviving locals to call the barn haunted. Now it was shunned by all—except the desperate and the ignorant, neither of which were around today according to the local Paratime spy eyes.

As soon as the conveyer had rematerialized inside the basement, the hydraulics of the false floor above began to move, revealing the ceiling of the empty barn. Once the fake floor was recessed, Verkan put the conveyer on anti-grav and let it rise gently until it almost touched the barn's ceiling. Verkan hit the button, which triggered the false floor to move back in place, then eased the conveyer to ground level as soon as the floor was stable. In the early days of transtemporal travel, the conveyer would have materialized within the underlying rock, creating an explosion that would have dwarfed a nuclear bomb. Now conveyers had dead man's switches, and this roundabout trip was much safer than using a conveyer above ground in the Royal Foundry.

Verkan restarted the conveyer and watched flickering glimpses of Fourth Level—airports, buildings, towns, rushing ground cars, water towers and occasionally a raging battle. They were on their way to Fifth Level Paratime Police Terminal, where Dalla would transfer to another conveyer for a journey back to Home Time Line while Verkan took a rocket to Egypt. Once in Alexandria, he would be briefed, assigned a threat team and provided with a larger conveyer for the journey to Alexandrian-Roman, Seleucid Subsector.

Inside the conveyer, Dalla continued the battle they had fought all morning. "I really wish you would have talked to Kalvan. He's behaving like a jerk—to use an appropriate Fourth Level term that even *he* would understand."

"Why, Dalla? Because Kalvan won't sugar-coat Rylla's little massacre in Phaxos Town?"

"You know very well Rylla was only doing what was right by her culture's lights. When an underling insults his overlord—at least on Aryan-Transpacific—it must be met with an appropriate response to ensure it's not repeated. If Rylla had been a man, no one would have said a word. Besides, she didn't massacre the entire town, just killed a few dozen of the local nobility. If they'd been peasants, no one would have cared. You've threatened worse atrocities yourself on the Opposition Party and would have carried them out, too, if you could have gotten away with it. I know that smirk, Verkan, and don't tell me you haven't."

"Maybe in a moment of anger. However, I have no intention of putting Kalvan through what I was subjected to after our divorce. I must have suffered a year of Tortha's advice and fatherly concern—you do remember, don't you? Well, I promised myself I'd never inflict that punishment on another living being, especially a friend!"

Dalla nodded and the temperature dropped. "Good point. I was the recipient of several of Tortha's 'talks' myself. I notice he's refrained from giving Kalvan any of his patented advice."

Verkan laughed. "And who says an old dog can't learn new tricks? Besides, Kalvan and Rylla wouldn't be so angry if they didn't care for each other; we ought to know something about that! Kalvan's already growing bored with his stay at the University and I can tell he misses Rylla and little Demia. He'll rationalize his way back into her arms within another ten-day; after all, Fourth Level Europo-Americans are experts at self-rationalization."

Dalla frowned and picked up her redstone pipe, which was a twin of the one Rylla smoked. "I know Rylla really misses Kalvan and has been in a miserable mood ever since he left. She can't understand why, by her lights, he's so squeamish."

"Kalvan was raised on a Subsector where the shibboleths are Social Security, the Public Good and Welfare. Being force-fed eighteen years of Calvinist guilt might have something to do with it, too. Remember Kalvan's father was a minister, and to hear our researcher tell it, of the fire-and-brim-stone variety. I think Kalvan and Rylla will find a way to get back together; after all, we did—even if it took twenty years and a revolution on an Akor-Neb Second Level time-line to do it. A fracas inspired by my lovely wife, I might add."

Verkan was pleased to note the smile that threatened to break out on Dalla's face.

"Besides," he continued, "they're about to get some help from Styphon's House. Nothing brings a couple closer than a good fight with a determined enemy they both loathe. As I understand it from the Study Team in Balph, Grand Master Soton and Archpriest Roxthar are cooking up a massive invasion force for the coming campaign season—all the soldiers Styphon's gold can buy. They've even got a pretty able commander, if they'll let him actually command the army, in Captain-General Phidestros. He's the general who took the Beshtan castle, Tarr-Veblos, right under Rylla and Phrames' noses."

"That's something else that Kalvan won't let Rylla forget. Vall, he actually had the gall to tell Rylla that the loss of the castle was her fault!"

"Well, of course. It was. If Rylla hadn't pulled most of the Royal Army into eastern Harphax, Phrames wouldn't have had to pull his army off the border to cover her retreat. Then Tarr-Veblos would have had its full complement of soldiers, and Phidestros would still be licking his wounds instead of being hailed as the Great Captain throughout Hos-Harphax and the other Kingdoms."

Dalla shook her head. "If Prince Phrames would have kept his troops where they belonged inside of Beshta, instead of acting paternal, to 'protect'

Rylla, Phidestros would have never taken that castle. Rylla never needed his *protection.* Male bonding—it knows no limits when it comes to excuse making."

"Enough! Let's make a peace treaty before we have our own war. Besides, Kalvan and Rylla will have reasons enough to end their feud when Styphon's House flexes its muscles. Next year is going to be a *doozy,* as Kalvan calls it."

"What can we do to help?"

"Stay out of it. We've got enough problems on Home Time Line. I don't want to give the University Study Team any excuse to blame us for Paratemporal Contamination."

"Are you telling me there's nothing we can do to help our friends, Rylla and Kalvan?" Dalla asked hotly, her green eyes flashing.

Dalla's green Paratime uniform did a lot to highlight those eyes, but Verkan decided that this was not the time to mention that fact. While Dalla was the most competent person he could think of to serve as his Special Assistant, there were times when it would be nice to separate the marriage and the job. This was one of those times.

"I can't see a way to help them without breaking the Paratime Code. That would bring the roof, the rafters and the attic down on our heads. The Opposition Party is unhappy over the re-opening of the Wizard Traders case. They're using my involvement in Kalvan's Time-Line as an excuse to poke into our personal affairs." Verkan didn't bother to bring up the too familiar charge of nepotism in regards to Dalla's appointment to the position of Special Assistant, the second most powerful post in the Department of Paratime Police.

"On top of that the Dhergabar University Kalvan Study-Team is blaming us for Paratemporal Contamination because of the help we've already given Kalvan, while, on the other hand, chastising us for incompetence for not preventing the Phaxi attack on the Foundry Team. The charges won't wash, of course, but they do put the spotlight on what we are doing in Hostigos. Now, thanks to Danthor Dras' book—*Gunpowder Theocracy*—and his genius for self-promotion, we not only have the general public interested in what we're doing, we also have the League to Eliminate Theocracies to contend with."

Dalla made a face like she just caught a bad odor. "Just a bunch of crackpots. They'll go away in a few years, if we ignore them long enough."

"I disagree, Dalla. In a rational society like ours, religious movements are viewed with both fear and fascination. To the average First Level Citizen, religious zealots are either insane or are privy to something the rest of us don't know. Both possibilities scare the average citizen. The majority opinion is that they should be cured or, at the very least, the panderers put out of business. Can you imagine the nightmare the Paratime Police would have to contend with if we had to put every major religion and two-bit theocracy out of business—just on Fourth Level alone? We don't have the manpower and the ammunition to do it on Styphon's House Subsector, much less the billions upon billions of other time-lines we'd have to contend with."

"How could anyone take such a proposal seriously?"

"Study your history. On First Level alone, where religion has been outlawed since the Mystic Rebellion eight thousand years ago, we have had three major outbreaks of religious contagion. The last one cost us half a million lives."

Dalla winced. "I should have remembered. One of my grandfathers was a ringleader of the One God For All Levels Movement. He had to be mind-wiped by the Bureau of Psychological Hygiene. When we were kids, my brother was terrified of being re-adjusted like grandfather."

"It probably wouldn't have been a bad thing," Verkan said, waiting for the inevitable explosion as Dalla defended Hadron Tharn, her younger brother.

She just looked down at the floor. "Vall, what scares me is how much I used to share many of Tharn's views. He still hasn't forgiven me for selling out to the Management Party and their pet stooge, Police Chief Verkan Vall."

Hadron Tharn had been one of several reasons their first companionate marriage had ended so quickly—and bitterly. But Tharn was wrong; Verkan hadn't been the one who had changed Dalla's perceptions. It had been her own realization of how bankrupt her younger brother and the Opposition Party's ideas were what had brought her around to Verkan's point of view. Unfortunately her brother's prejudices were cast in collapsed-nickel and impervious to contrary evidence.

"As long as there are people ready to exploit movements, like the League to Eliminate Theocracies, we have to take them seriously. And the last thing we need is to have observers looking over our shoulder on Kalvan's Time-Line. It's bad enough we've got to deal with the University Study Teams."

"Still, there must be some way we can help Rylla and Kalvan before they're tortured by one of Roxthar's Holy Investigators."

"Aren't you serving dinner before it's been cooked? Kalvan's pulled himself out of some tight places before. Maybe he can do it again. But he's going to have to do it by himself. I've got to make it clear to him on our next visit that there won't be much help from King Theovacar. At least as Verkan the Trader, I can bring him a few more pack trains of arms and provisions."

"If the army that Soton and Phidestros are raising is half as big as our agents say it's going to be, Kalvan's going to need a lot more than a few guns and a dozen wagons full of salted beef. Maybe we could import a few thousand mercenaries from nearby Aryan-Transpacific time-lines. We could even limit the Transtemporal Contamination by bringing them from the Middle Kingdoms where no one's heard of Hostigos."

"To make any real difference, we'd have to bring twenty to thirty thousand mercenaries into Hostigos. We're not equipped to make massive troop deployments. Besides, we could never cover-up an operation of that scale. Someone would talk. And what if Kalvan just happened to question one of the captains, who perchance had just returned from a job in Hos-Harphax and told him how Hostigos was squashed by Nostor and Sask? You think we've got problems now!"

Dalla sighed ruefully. "What's the value of being top cop if you can't even help your friends when they need it?"

"That's a good question. I've been asking myself that a lot lately. Maybe we just need to have a little more faith in Kalvan."

Dalla nodded her head. "Maybe. Still, I'd feel a lot better if we let a couple of those First Level anti-theocracy fanatics loose in Balph with directions to Archpriest Roxthar's quarters."

TWO

I

Kalvan felt a sudden chill, rose up from his desk, and went over to the large fireplace in what had formerly been the baron's bedchambers and tossed several small logs into the hearth. He rubbed his hands briskly over the fire. It was going to be a cold winter this year and he'd better get used to the chill, as well as sleeping alone. Rylla had forcibly ejected him from their bed chambers at Tarr-Hostigos when he had returned from the Sastragath and they'd had their big fight.

Kalvan had elected to move to the University of Hos-Hostigos and into the former baron's living quarters. At the time he was pleased not to have to pretend to an intimacy he no longer felt—at least, for now. Rylla's precipitous attack on the Princedom of Phaxos and the atrocities she'd committed in their name had darkened their relationship almost as much as it had their good name in the Seven Kingdoms. After two weeks of sleeping alone, Kalvan missed Rylla a lot and was regretting the words he'd thrown at her like poisoned darts in the heat of his return.

Back at his desk he turned up the light on his primitive Coleman lantern. The glass still had more green than he liked, but the local glassblower had done a good job with the glass chimney. A new industry was growing up now in

Hostigos Town around the new Glass Works and he was going to have to charter a Royal Glassblowers' Guild before long; he was already getting complaints from the Council of Guilds about un-regulated guildwork. The wicks had been a bit of a problem but they were getting better. The new lamps burned coal oil, which was easier to get than whale oil this far from the Eastern Ocean. The glass lantern threw off more light than three of the primitive whale oil lamps used here-and-now.

Kalvan opened the next packet; inside was a letter from Colonel Simodes reporting progress on the Semaphore Project. Simodes was making good progress building a series of semaphore stations that would link Hostigos Town to the Royal Army of Observation along the Beshtan border with Hos-Harphax. The first semaphore station to be built on Beshtan territory was half completed; the Colonel expected to reach Tarr-Beshta before first snow. The semaphore stations, using a combination of mirrors and flags, would save valuable time for communications between the Harphaxi border and Tarr-Hostigos. Kalvan was sure the stations would be worth their weight in gold once the Army of Hos-Hostigos began its advance into Hos-Harphax.

Captain Waklos, who was in charge of teaching Morse code to future semaphore signalers, had informed him yesterday that he had enough graduates to post two signalers at each semaphore station between Hostigos and Beshta. By this time next year, there would be semaphore lines into neighboring Sask and Nostor, too.

The next dispatch contained disturbing news from Duke Skranga, Chief of Intelligence, about the continuing troop build-up at Tarr-Veblos, Tarr-Harphax and other military centers throughout the kingdom of Hos-Harphax. Maybe Kalvan should have followed his instincts last year and taken his army into Hos-Harphax, while the Harphaxi Army was still in shock after the losses at Phyrax Field and Chothros Heights. This past spring the Harphaxi might have been chased, grounded and defeated with ease. The troop build-up, sponsored by Styphon's House, was getting worrisome. Still, the nomad invasion into the Trygath had been a major problem, one he was able to turn around and spring back upon the Zarthani Knights who'd tried to use the tribesmen as a cat's paw against Hostigos.

Dividing his army might have led to a great victory in Hos-Harphax, but it would have come with a steep cost—a very possible defeat in the west by the Sastragathi horde. The truth was that Hos-Hostigos could not afford a defeat anywhere; the minute he stopped winning battles the people of Hos-Hostigos would stop believing in the Gods'-Sent-Kalvan—then his difficulties would *really* begin. His insurmountable problem was that he was surrounded by enemies who out-gunned him, out-numbered him and everything, but out-generaled him—at least, not yet!

This new Harphaxi Captain-General showed every sign of being a first rate commander, unless his capture of Tarr-Veblos was a fluke. Kalvan knew that pigs might grow wings before fate sent him any more incompetent generals like those who'd led the last Harphaxi invasion force. This Phidestros, from Skranga's reports, was either a fast learner, or a first rate tactician; he doubted he'd face any more witlings like the late Prince what's-his-name who'd led the Harphaxi lancers into a deadly hail storm of lead.

There was a timid knock at the door, which sounded particularly feminine—for a moment his heart hammered like a vibrating drumhead. *Is it Rylla?* Then he heard an unfamiliar voice ask, "May I enter, Your Majesty?"

Where's Cleon when I need him, thought Kalvan to himself. *What's the use of having a body servant if he's never where he's needed.* Then he realized what he was feeling was disappointment; not anger, but disappointment that it wasn't Rylla coming to his chamber to ask his forgiveness. Well, now that he'd thought it out, it didn't seem very likely, but one could hope....

"Your Majesty? Are you there?"

"Come in, please."

A very attractive young lady, of obvious noble birth—her dress and carriage were proof of that—entered the room. "I don't believe we've met before, Your Majesty."

Kalvan shook his head. "Sorry, I kept you waiting, but I was tending the fire." He turned to stir some coals.

"I don't mean to intrude, Your Majesty, but Prince Phrames asked me to intercede."

Ah. This must be the Lady Eutare that Harmakros mentioned the other night, the future Mrs. Phrames. Her father was that rarity on both here-and-now and on his home world; a noble with good business sense. According to Harmakros, he was one of Beshta's richest grain merchants. They were one of the factions that Phrames would need on his side if he wanted to stabilize the Beshtan economy. Now, having seen Lady Eutare, he suspected that Phrames interests were not completely political. He really could use Rylla's take on Lady Eutare and Prince Phrames; it was becoming increasingly more difficult to rule wisely with his best advisor giving him the cold shoulder.

"Intercede in what? Is Phrames having trouble with your parents? If so, I will certainly stand at his right hand—"

"No, Your Majesty," Lady Eutare said, blushing. "I'm Great Queen Rylla's new Lady-in-Waiting. We weren't introduced when you returned. The Queen has sent me to remind you, which I'm sure you haven't forgotten…." She paused to blush an even deeper red. "The Allmother Festival is coming soon—in a moon-quarter."

Kalvan slapped his thigh—he had forgotten. It was almost time for the harvest festival and, with the kingdom-wide bumper crops, their subjects would expect him and Rylla to lead the festivities held in the name of the Goddess Yirtta.

"What does she want now?" he asked too sharply, and Eutare drew back from him as if expecting a slap.

"Excuse me, but I'm not myself these days." He turned to the fire, rubbing his hands vigorously. When he was breathing in measured breaths once again, he turned back to Lady Eutare. "What does the Great Queen have planned for Harvest Festival?"

"A party at her father's palace."

Prince Ptosphes' summer palace, that's good, he thought, *neutral ground.*

"She thought you might want to spend some time with your daughter, since you missed her Name Day."

Yes, I was off killing Zarthani Knights in the Sastragath! Kalvan fought to keep his temper in check. *Don't blame the messenger!*

"Of course, I do," he answered. He wanted to spend all of his time with his little girl, but not with her mother standing over Demia shooting daggers at him with her eyes. "Tell her I'll be there."

"Thank you, Your Majesty," Lady Eutare answered, curtseying. She turned and all but fled the room. That had been happening a lot lately, and not just with the ladies. His being out of sorts with Rylla was not only bad for them, for Princess Demia and for their friends, but hard on the other people around them too. If only there were some way they could turn back the clock, but he might as well wish for another cross-time flying saucer to land, or Styphon's House to declare peace—

II

Myros the Apprentice tightly clenched his chattering teeth, wondering what was more chilling: the screams coming from behind the plank door or the frigid stones he sat upon. Myros had been sawing lumber at the shop of Eranes the Carpenter when the Investigators had arrived to drag off the Master and all his apprentices into the dungeons of the former Balph City gaol. Master Eranes, who was also a secret highpriest of Allfather Dralm, had found Myros begging on the streets of Balph and given him his first job, had even taken him into his home—an act of kindness Eranes was certainly regretting now. *It's not my fault,* he thought, *I'm weak. I can't stand pain.*

The screech of the cell door's hinges set his whole body to shivering beneath the thin tunic he was wearing. The flame from the oil lamp flickered as a shadowy form emerged into the dim antechamber. As the dark figure stepped into the dim light, Myros made out the stark, angular face of the Holy Investigator Roxthar—a devil in human form! The Investigator was wearing a butcher's apron liberally splashed with dried blood; he didn't know what scared him more, Roxthar's glowing red eyes or the blood-spattered apron and all the anguish it promised.

Myros had seen blood before, sometimes copious amounts; after all, he'd grown up on the streets of Balph as the unrecognized bastard son of some temple priest and a tavern drab who'd died when he was seven winters old. In fact, his life would have already been ended had not Highpriest Eranes taken him in as an adopted son. *Allfather Dralm, what have I done?*

"Boy, stand up," Roxthar said in a voice that didn't allow for discussion.

"Yes, Your Holiness."

Roxthar's lips twisted into a small smile that somehow was more frightening than his usual tight-lipped grimace.

"You have done well, boy, giving us the name of this false priest, Eranes. Worshipper of the Daemon Dralm. Unfortunately, he does not bend to my rod. Are you certain that you have given me all the names of the worshippers of the False God Dralm?"

Myros' body writhed in fear. "Yes, Holy One—I have told you everything. I don't know any other worshippers…"

Roxthar nodded for him to continue. A fresh chorus of screams from the hallway outside the chamber punctuated the motions of his long head.

"For a hundred winters, since the worship of the False God Dralm was banned in Balph, the worshippers of the False God have met in secret in the catacombs below the city. Each body of worshippers is kept secret from the others. The Way of the Secret is that only one person from each finger knows anyone else in any other finger. The Highpriest is the one person who knows all the leaders of each finger of Dralm's Hand—as the hidden Temple is called."

"How many fingers are there?"

"Only Highpriest Eranes knows, Your Holiness."

"The Way of the Hand shows more wisdom than I've given these blasphemers credit for. Unfortunately, the false Highpriest Eranes will not talk. Follow me, boy."

Myros walked into a stone room lit by three flickering candles that reminded him very much of the dark tunnels deep below the city streets. Master Eranes slumped from the wall, held upright by the chains on his arms. Eranes' right hand looked strange, and it wasn't until Myros moved closer that he could see that all of the fingers were missing. The stench of burning flesh lingered in the stale air.

"He is a brave man, this false priest," Roxthar intoned. "I'll give him credit for more stomach than my new scribe."

In one corner of the stone cell was a ball of rags that upon closer inspection revealed itself to be a young man in a vomit-stained white robe. The scribe jerked spasmodically and started to choke.

"Boy, drag this sack of excrement out of here. I need an assistant with a stiffer spine for Styphon's Work."

Myros took hold of the scribe's ankles, just above his wooden clogs, and dragged him out of the cell.

"Boy!" Roxthar's voice echoed.

Myros, against his will, returned to the cell like a sleepwalker.

Roxthar grabbed Myros by the front of his tunic, lifting him up into the air with one arm, until he was face-to-face with his former Master and adopted father. Myros' heart beat wildly as Roxthar removed a nasty looking set of long-nosed grips out of an apron pocket and opened them in front of his right eye.

"This is the boy who betrayed you, your family and your assistants. Answer my questions, or I will pluck his eye out like a grape!"

Master Eranes opened his eyes and said, "Spare the boy. He knew not what he was doing."

Roxthar dropped Myros upon the floor like a heap of smelly laundry and loomed over him like the great Golden Idol in Styphon's House Upon Earth. Roxthar nodded to the opposite corner where, unnoticed, a man in black robes, wearing a black mask that covered his entire head except his eyes, stood silently. The man lifted up a piece of wire in both hands, which he held out.

"Boy," Roxthar said, "if your answer disappoints me, my friend here will wrap that wire around your neck and squeeze until your head pops like a boil. Do you understand?"

Myros didn't trust his voice so he nodded.

"Good. What does this false priest value above all things?"

Myros thought quickly and then felt his stomach drop when the answer fell into his mind.

"Speak up, or die."

"His daughter, little Arlass. He always says she is the bright ray of his days."

A tortured "Noooooo!" burst from between Eranes lips.

"You have done well," Roxthar said, nodding to himself. "There may be hope. You have renounced the False God and taken Styphon as your One God. Leave me alone and repent your sins. I will speak to you again after my work in here is finished."

The man in black escorted him out of the cell and back to the cold stone bench. To Myros, having just touched death's face, the stones felt surprisingly warm and comforting. The scribe was nowhere to be seen; it was as if he'd never been. A horrible howl, somehow less than human, echoed down the corridor.

I'm in Regwarn, Myros thought, *and all the gods are dead. If Allfather Dralm can stand aside and let his highpriest be tortured and maimed, what good is this so-called god? And Styphon, what kind of god is he? Only a demon or devil would release a fiend like Roxthar upon the world to do his grisly work. Henceforth, I no longer believe in gods, only in the evil that men do to each other. I will do whatever I must to escape this madman's grasp.*

While his mind pondered the capriciousness of fate and the indifference of gods and men alike, a young girl, her blonde hair cascading down her back in ringlets, was brought into the cell by the man in black. Her entrance was shortly followed by a chorus of shrill screams and a primal growling like that of some beast. Then the cell door slammed shut.

A long time later, when the flame from his oil lamp began to flicker and grow dim, the cell door creaked open, revealing Roxthar, his apron dripping with fresh blood. "Your false priest has given me the names of every blasphemer he knows. We will quickly pluck the garden of Balph of all worshippers of the False God. You have done Styphon's work today, boy. The girl was his weakness."

He threw a handful of bloody, broken teeth at the boy's feet. Some, Myros noted, were quite small.

"Is she…?"

"She rests with her father. I have said a prayer over her body and asked Styphon to accept her in his Hall. She was too young to know Dralm or any other of the false gods."

If only there was a god—somewhere, anywhere—to forgive me for what I have done! Now that I am no longer of use, what new purpose will this monster bend me to now?

"The last apprentice I Investigated informed me that you know your letters. Is this true?"

"Yes, Holy One. Mistress Jomna—" he paused to stop the involuntary circle he'd been about to make around his breast, a sign of the Allfather. Myros gulped. "The false priest's wife taught me well."

"That is what one of the other apprentices, one who was not so cooperative, told us. He will no longer be able to use his right hand, but he has renounced Dralm and accepted Styphon as the True God—as you have."

Roxthar paused to stare into his eyes as though he could peer right through the surface pools and bore into Myros' mind. "Is your faith true?"

"Oh, yes, Your Holiness," Myros said, unable to keep his voice from trembling.

"We will see. For now, you will be my new scribe."

Myros fought the scream that tore at the back of his throat. "Y-y-yes, Holy One."

"First, I must teach you the True Words. How when the Dark God Hadron released the Fireseed Demons upon the Earth, it was Styphon who left the Sky-Thrones to take his message to all the mortals. His words fell upon the Earth like rain, but Dralm's evil worshippers caught them with their hands and swallowed them so no one would realize that their False God was the one who convinced Hadron to release his Fireseed Demons...."

Myros tried to focus his attention on the Evil One's words, because he knew that someday soon he would be called upon to repeat them. Still, he could not escape from the lonely scream that echoed in the back of his skull.

III

The guard to the Great King's private chamber held the ceremonial silver halberd before him with the double-bladed head facing Phidestros. He stomped the butt down on the floor twice and announced, "You may enter,

Captain-General Phidestros! His Majesty, Great King Lysandros is expecting you."

Lysandros sat in his high-backed chair stroking his goatee with one hand while holding a goblet of wine in the other. Lysandros pointed to a shorter chair. "Have a seat, Captain-General."

Phidestros took the seat and tried to will his heart to beat at a measured cadence. This was his first visit to the palace since his return to Tarr-Harphax, after his successful capture of Tarr-Veblos. Soon Grand Master Soton, and whichever temple rat he brought with him from Balph would enthrone Lysandros, Great King of Hos-Harphax, giving him his lifelong wish to sit upon the Iron Throne. Still, Lysandros' temperament was mercurial; one needed a soothsayer to foresee all his moods.

Lysandros lit his pipe, drew deeply, exhaled and then began to speak. "Grand Master Soton had good things to say about your work with the Royal Army before he left for Balph. He believes that you have done wonders with the rebuilding of the Harphaxi Army. As a reward for your efforts and the taking of the Beshtan tarr," Lysandros held up a bank draft, "I present you with this draft on Styphon's Great Banking House for ten thousand golden rakmars. Like Soton, I believe in rewarding success, as well as punishing failure."

"Thank you, Your Majesty!" He was frozen to his seat. Of all the things he had expected, a Styphon's House draft redeemable in gold was absolutely not on the list.

"Keep up the good work and when this Usurper is vanquished you may yet receive the princedoms I promised."

Phidestros was pleased to hear that Lysandros remembered his promise to grant him the Princedoms of Beshta and Sashta after King Kalvan was defeated. Most kings and princes had poor memories when it came to such promises, especially those spoken in private and not put to parchment. As a man and as a Great King, Lysandros had his faults; fortunately, being an oath-breaker was not one of them. If Lysandros' aim was to urge him to win the war, he could not have picked a better incentive.

"The Grand Master did bring up one important point."

Here it comes, thought Phidestros. *The blade between the shoulders!*

"Soton believes that the Army needs to be blooded. Holding them outside of the Phaxi borders while the Hostigi sacked Phaxos Town was not good for morale. True, your siege of Tarr-Veblos was a great victory, but it was the infantry who swept the field. Soton believes that if the cavalry have a taste of victory, they will fall upon Kalvan's troopers like wolves."

"I agree, Your Majesty. It would be very good for morale. But already the Allmother Festival approaches and soon the roads will be impassable." If Lysandros wanted him to recapture Phaxos from the occupying Hostigi, Phidestros would do everything in his power to discourage him. If not, he might be fighting three armies, the Hostigos Phaxi army of occupation, the Hostigos Army of Observation and the Beshtan Army under Prince Phrames.

Lysandros paused to blow out a cloud of smoke. "True. So we must make this campaign fast and hard. I have decided that it is time to clean out that wasp nest in Thaphigos and take the false prince Eltar prisoner."

Phidestros took a deep breath and relaxed. In his heart, Phidestros agreed that the Royal Army needed to take to the field; he just hoped it wasn't too soon. If it was, this bank draft might be his only reward. There was, however, greater consolation in the fact that he wouldn't be facing the Hostigi this time. The Thaphigosi army was neither large nor well armed.

"An excellent choice, Your Majesty. It will also prove our mettle to Great King Demistophon in case he has any ideas of annexing Phaxos, Thaphigos and Argros, while we are fighting the Usurper's army next spring." This was exactly what Phidestros would have done in Demistophon's boots: annex the three Princedoms while the Army of Harphax was in Hos-Hostigos and then station enough troops there that Lysandros would have to live with it—or face another major war. With Phaxos held by a Hostigi puppet Prince and supported by Kalvan's troops, Prince Soligon of Argros sympathetic to the League of Dralm and Thaphigos still reeling from civil war, the entire northeastern corner of Hos-Harphax was ripe for the picking.

Lysandros shook his head with a pained expression. Then in a low voice, as if talking to himself, he said, "I fear you are right. This is why I cannot lead my own Army against the Usurper Kalvan. The greatest campaign of my life and a jumped-up mercenary captain will be fighting my war...."

Phidestros quietly left the chamber with the Styphon's House parchment cradled in his arms. Now he knew for certain that he was not in the King's favor so he would have to win every battle or suffer the consequences. *With great opportunity, comes great risk*, he decided.

He started mentally sorting through the Royal Army, deciding which units would remain billeted at Tarr-Harphax and which ones would be going into the field.

The Princedom of Thaphigos had been leaderless for so long, until Prince Eltar had been invested, he was certain the Princedom's defenses were in shambles. However, Phidestros would have to talk to Grand-Captain Kyblannos who, in his never-ending store of tales, boasted of having been in every tinpot army in Hos-Harphax. If Kyblannos didn't have an answer on the tip of his tongue, he'd know which soldiers to ask.

THREE

I

The moment word reached the Princedom of Eubros that Duke Mnestros had stepped foot on Hos-Agrys soil, outriders were dispatched from Eubros Town to all corners of Hos-Agrys as well as to the border princedoms of Hos-Harphax and Hos-Zygros. The emissaries were sent to call a special session of the Council of Dralm at Tarr-Eubros. News of the battles in the Trygath and beyond were sketchy and rumors had flooded the Northern Kingdoms for the past six moons. Some said that Great King Kalvan had suffered terrible losses at the hands of the Sastragathi barbarians, while others claimed Kalvan had made battle and defeated the Order of the Zarthani Knights and was, even now, besieging the Order's great fortress, Tarr-Ceros.

Mnestros had been told of the Council meeting, but the Duke had not been prepared to speak with the Council before he could shake the dust off his cloak and change his boots. Mnestros took a small cask of Ermut's brandy from his saddle bag, slung his presentation *rifle*—a parting gift from Great King Kalvan himself—over his shoulder by a leather strap and walked through the outer courtyard, past the inner courtyard and into the keep portal.

Inside the keep, Mnestros was immediately ushered into the Great Hall where the assembled princes and noblemen were seated around the great table awaiting his arrival. Every seat at the table was taken, some by noblemen Mnestros had never seen before. Knowing how to stage a dramatic entrance, Mnestros—probably the youngest man in the room—strode into the Great Hall and swept off his high-combed burgonet helmet, handing it to a man servant, and held up his *rifle*. Everyone rose to greet him and pat his back as he made his way to the head of the table where his father, Prince Thykarses, sat.

The old Prince roared, "It's good to see you again, son. I will apologize for not giving you time to sweep the dust off of your breeches and soak your weary bones, but our friends here demand your presence. As a good host, I could not deny them."

Mnestros knew his father would have preferred a briefing in private, impossible under the circumstances, and was trying to put on a good face. The Prince even offered him his seat at the table, but, after four hundred marches of bad road, he chose to stand instead. Mnestros opened with his arrival at Hos-Hostigos, the Great King's Highway—a true marvel, Great King Kalvan's hospitality and his lovely wife, Queen Rylla—the Warrior Queen. "Great King Kalvan holds a grand table and commands some of the best comrades a good fighting man would ever want to guard his back."

There were many nods around the table at these words.

"What is this 'musket' you brought with you that hangs from a strap?" Prince Tryomanes of Thebra asked. Several other lords nodded in encouragement.

"This is one of Great King Kalvan's *rifles*."

There was a sudden silence broken only when one of the dogs outside began to howl.

"Let me see that?" a powerful baron asked. Suddenly everyone was talking at once.

Prince Thykarses silenced them with a bellow. Mnestros then gave an explanation of how the *rifle* worked. He finished with, "Kalvan has some of his *riflemen* ride horses to battle."

One of the younger lords asked, "Does he use these *riflemen* as skirmishers?"

"Sometimes. Other times he places them in the van to fight with the regulars. At the Battle of Spirit Grove they laid waste to the nomad horse archers."

There were *ahs* of appreciation and a score of questions from the more military minded.

After he promised everyone interested, which included all in the Great Council Hall except the serving wenches, a demonstration after the Council meeting, Mnestros was allowed to continue.

He told them about Kalvan's Council of War and how all his commanders had a chance to speak their word. Then he regaled his audience with the story of the march of the Royal Army through Hos-Hostigos and into the Trygath, a place only a few border princes among those present had ever visited. His audience was spellbound as he described the walls of Rathon City and Nestros' great palace. Next, he told the tale of the Battle of Spirit Grove and how Kalvan had defeated the Sastragathi Warlord and then, by his kindness, won him over as an ally.

The Prince of Glarth cried, "Why is the League cooling its heels here when Kalvan offers us all the glory and fighting any prince can ask for?"

There were shouts and nods of agreement.

Mnestros used this pause to drink another tankard of mead. He finished his tale with the flight of the Zarthani Knights, the small mountains of discarded armor and the Burning of the Drynos Mines. "Since Kalvan was honor-bound to vanquish the Knights at Drynos, he posted his ablest commander to chase and harass Soton's retreating forces. While the Zarthani Knights arrived at Tarr-Ceros before the main body of Harmakros' army, the Captain-General's Mounted Rifles acted as skirmishers and inflicted many casualties among the retreating Order horse. Grand Master Soton will not soon forget that trail of blood!"

Many in the chamber applauded and whooped with delight.

"It's Styphon's own luck that Kalvan did not reach Tarr-Ceros before the Knights," the Prince of Orchon cried. "Thanks to those bumbling white-beards who rule the High Temple of Dralm, I missed a chance to fight alongside a real Great King. Were only Great King Demistophon half the solder Kalvan is—be he man or Daemon!"

"Aye, aye," a dozen throats echoed.

Mnestros told the Council how Kalvan and the nomads savaged the land for a hundred marches in every direction around Tarr-Ceros, and taunted the Knights who refused to leave the walls and meet them in honorable battle.

"Styphon's false priests don't know the meaning of honor," the Prince of Argros shouted. "They have Great King Lysandros under their spell, or he would make peace with Kalvan. True, Kaiphranos the Timid almost lost half of Hos-Harphax to Great King Kalvan, yet it was fairly won and Kaiphranos held suzerainty over it in name only. Lysandros is so besotted with Styphon's archpriests I'm surprised he does not dress in a yellow robe!"

The Harphaxi Princes who dared to attend the Council nodded their agreement or studied their wine goblets.

Mnestros hoped for the Prince of Argros' sake that there were no intelligencers in the room, or the Prince would not keep his Princedom—or head, for that matter—once he returned to Hos-Harphax.

Prince Kyphanes of Meligos held up his slender hands. He was a tall man, stooped with care and age. "We cannot commit our forces to Great King Kalvan without the Blessing of the Temple of Dralm." Everyone at the table nodded in agreement. "No one in this Great Hall has any doubts about Kalvan's martial skill and prowess at war. Surely Duke Mnestros' words have proved that beyond dispute. However, if we go without the Temple's blessing, we will be no better than the Styphoni dogs who live their godless lives worshipping both a fraud and hoax!"

As Speaker of the Council, Kyphanes' words carried much more weight than those of a mere Duke, so Mnestros bit his tongue, cursing under his breath all the while.

"You wouldn't be so hesitant, Speaker, if the nomads had come within a hundred marches of Meligos," Prince Clytoss said. "Great King Kalvan did the people of Glarth a great favor when he conquered the nomad horde. My people regard him as a hero. I will tell you this, in all truth, Great King Demistophon would not have sent a single soldier to guard my lands, even though I am sworn to him and he to me!"

"By Dralm, those words ring of truth!"

"Your words border upon treason," Prince Kyphanes shouted. "I will hear no more of such talk at the Council Table as long as I am Speaker!"

Many at the Table looked down at the fine embroidered tablecloth in disgust. Others nodded their heads in agreement. The arguments went back and forth, with Mnestros occasionally bearing witness to Kalvan's character—all were impressed by the Charge of the Two Kings against the nomad Warlord Sargos. The meeting continued for more candles than it was worth, at least in Mnestros' opinion.

Afterwards in private over a goblet of Ermut's brandy, his father said, "I am pleased that you were able to partake of great deeds, rather than jaw about them in endless debate."

Mnestros nodded his agreement. "It was your idea that someone should meet Great King Kalvan. He is a good man and a great captain-general. I would follow him to Hadron's Gates! You would too, Father, had you met him."

"Ah. To be young again. To most of these princes the Fireseed War is far away and most would not be comfortable in the saddle for more than two days on a moose hunt. Unless the whitebeards of Dralm give their blessing to Kalvan and his crusade against Styphon's House, the League of Dralm will limit its warfare to one of words. Maybe some of those of us who are not so afraid of offending the Temple of Dralm will act upon their own, although carefully, since it would be no surprise to find at least one man here today has his hand deep into Styphon's purse."

Mnestros wondered if his father was speaking of the Speaker, who had seemed determined to block every course of action that would aid Kalvan. In his favor, it was also true that one of Kyphanes' sons was a highpriest of Dralm. Furthermore, the Prince was no more a hindrance than the Temple of Dralm itself which was led by the former Highpriest of Hostigos. Meanwhile, his replacement, Highpriest Mytron, was one of Kalvan's greatest supporters. Political loyalties were divided throughout the Great Kingdoms; it was doubtful—though not impossible—that the Temple of Dralm itself was harboring more than one or two of Styphon's intelligencers.

In such times it was no wonder his father was wary of his allies. Mnestros hoped that whatever plan was brewing in his father's mind had a prominent place for him. One way or another, he was going to return to Hos-Hostigos for the war against Hos-Harphax.

II

King Kalvan sat down on the Fireseed Throne, the name given to the magnificent walnut throne with two silver armrests in the shape of musketoon barrels. On the headboard was a gold and mother-of-pearl inlay depicting his first military success at Tarr-Dombra, a border castle he'd captured shortly after arriving in the Princedom of Hostigos. The Fireseed Throne had been commissioned by Rylla as the official throne for the new Great Kingdom of Hos-Hostigos and had been two years in the making by the kingdom's best artificers. Kalvan was waiting in the great audience chamber as Chancellor Chartiphon arranged the order of those supplicants who would be permitted an audience with their Great King.

Last night Kalvan had spent several hours with his daughter and her nursemaid at the Allmother Festival, but Rylla had refused to see him. Kalvan had returned by himself for another lonely evening at the University spent talking with Master Ermut and Harmakros. Now that they had glass suitable for vases and other decorative items, Ermut was attempting to devise a way to get the glass to cool in sheets for window panes. The making of sheet glass was a secret held by the Glassmakers Guild of Hos-Agrys, which kept the price of sheet glass as high as that of gold.

While Kalvan was pleased by Ermut's success, he missed Rylla most of all; her absence was like that of a missing limb. Nor did he like being kept away from his daughter as she learned her way about the world. Already he'd missed Demia's first words and halting steps.

Six Royal Bodyguards marched into the Audience Chamber, holding their ceremonial double-headed poleaxes, followed by Aspasthar, the Royal Page, Harmakros' illegitimate issue. After the Bodyguard had taken their places beside the throne and at the front entrance, Chancellor Chartiphon entered followed by a good-sized crowd, including Rylla's second cousin, Baron Sthentros who was strutting at the head of the party. Kalvan had never liked Sthentros, an arrogant ne'er-do-well who blamed others for his own incompetence.

Kalvan attempted to look regal while searching the crowd for possible assassins and agents of Styphon's House. His crown was solid gold, a simple circlet with a magnificent ruby of forty or fifty carats, set in front. Kalvan had designed the crown himself in an attempt to avoid the traditional overly ornate and weighty crowns worn by the Great Kings.

The Royal Bodyguard stamped their poleaxes twice as the Royal Page announced: "Baron Sthentros of Hyllos Town, for an audience with Great King Kalvan, overlord of the Princedoms of Hostigos, Sask, Nostor, Beshta, Sashta, Ulthor, Nyklos and Kyblos and His Royal Majesty of the Great Kingdom of Hos-Hostigos. You may approach the throne."

Kalvan had finally grown accustomed to the pomp and circumstance that accompanied the position of Great King, but he disliked watching supplicants bowing and scraping as they approached the throne. Still, it was part of the Great King job description and he was stuck with it. However, Baron Sthentros managed to put outrage and injustice into every bow and scrape. Old Chartiphon couldn't keep his hand away from his sword hilt, and the look in his eyes was positively murderous. Kalvan would have to be careful not to show any of the displeasure he felt at dealing with Rylla's slimy cousin; otherwise, the Baron might 'accidentally' trip and fall down a castle stairway some dark night.

It would have been easy for him to believe that Sthentros was someone's bastard and not related to Ptosphes' deceased wife except for the fact that his daughter was almost the spitting image of Rylla, only with flaming red hair and her father's arrogance. Baron Sthentros, who wore a mink robe, looked nothing like Rylla—Dralm be praised. He was tall and thin, with a red goatee and long narrow face, his mouth set in a permanent sneer. Kalvan hadn't liked him the first time they'd met at Tarr-Hostigos, when he had to be ordered by Ptosphes to bring his levy to the Battle of Fyk. Admittedly he'd fought well at Fyk, although with little enthusiasm.

Sthentros hadn't served in the army since Fyk. His only son had died at Tenabra, and Sthentros had blamed Rylla's father for his death. Kalvan wondered if this was another attempt by the Baron to pry guilt money out of the Hostigi moneybox for his son's death. Kalvan would publicly push Sthentros down the stairs from the highest tower in Tarr-Hostigos if he attempted to play on Ptosphes' guilt again!

It was common knowledge that Sthentros was a spendthrift—his summer palace was more ornate than the Prince's—and it was also known that he'd only supported the war against Styphon's House because he owed the Sask regional branch of Styphon's Great Banking House something on the order of fifty thousand ounces of gold. Not that he was the only one in Hostigos—or the Seven Kingdoms for that matter—who was a debtor to Styphon's House. At least, it was a guarantee of Sthentros' loyalty; Styphon's House was far less forgiving of debtors than non-believers.

Chancellor Chartiphon, looking regal in his own blue velvet robe, stared right back into Sthentros' eyes and intoned, in a reasonable voice that little matched the menace in his gaze, "Baron, you may present your petition to His Majesty, Great King Kalvan."

Sthentros made a pained little bow to Chartiphon before clearing his throat. "Your Majesty, I have a complaint to file about my new neighbor, Baron Hestophes."

Sthentros managed to spit out Hestophes' name in a manner that made it sound as if it were a term used to describe something found in an outhouse; little matter that Captain-General Hestophes was the Hero of Narza Gap and one of Kalvan's most valued lieutenants. No doubt, in Sthentros' eyes, Hestophes' first offense was his common origins; his father owned a public tavern. The second, and probably more important, was that Hestophes was now the Baron of Eython, a neighboring domain—just outside Oak Hall, or Eython Village as it was called here-and-now—and a barony that Sthentros had long coveted.

When the last scion of the family had died without heirs during the Year of the Locust, Kalvan had presented the barony of Eython to Hestophes, who had long suffered from an inferiority complex over his humble origins. That the title had given one of his best generals a small measure of happiness had enabled Kalvan to enjoy one of the perks of his own position. He was not about to let this lickspittle turn that pleasure to ashes.

"And what is your complaint, Baron?"

"This Hestophes has been trying to make suit with my daughter Lavena—despite my objections. I have told him repeatedly that she will never be betrothed to a former commoner. He has refused to heed my words and has accosted her in the streets of Hyllos Town. I want an end to his harassment!"

Kalvan found it hard to imagine General Hestophes acting in a manner that would offend any reasonable person, not that anyone who knew Sthentros would ever accuse *him* of reasonable behavior. In the Zarthani lands, nobles, for property or dynastic reasons, arranged their children's marriages. This prohibited him from reading Sthentros the riot act as he would have liked to have done; instead Kalvan swallowed his bile and said, "Baron, Captain-General Hestophes is about to be reassigned to an important post along the Beshtan border so I doubt he will be in a position to continue his suit—if, in fact, there is such a suit."

Sthentros' body went rigid and face turned the color of chalk. However, he was smart enough to keep his mouth shut; two years ago he wouldn't have been able to control his tongue.

"If you have nothing to add, Baron, you may leave. I have important matters to attend to this day."

The Baron leaned back as if slapped, and then wheeled around and stomped out of the audience chamber. Kalvan wished Sthentros had been stupid enough to give him cause for complaint; he would have loved an excuse to have him put in chains and left to rot in the dungeons of Tarr-Hostigos for a month or two—preferably on short rations.

While he was woolgathering Chancellor Chartiphon brought up the next petitioner, announcing, "Guildmaster Dyag, for an audience with Great King Kalvan, overlord of the Princedoms of Hostigos, Sask, Nostor, Beshta, Sashta, Ulthor, Nyklos and Kyblos and His Royal Majesty of the Great Kingdom of Hos-Hostigos. You may approach the throne."

Dyag was a man with an impressive spade-shaped black beard. He wore a black velvet robe that a prince might envy, and carried himself like a baron instead of a Guildmaster of the Goldsmiths Guild. Kalvan had crossed verbal swords with him before and wasn't looking forward to this audience.

The Guildmaster made the slightest of bows and said, "The Hostigos Town Council of Guilds has appointed me as its spokesman." He bowed again and removed a folded parchment from the inside of his robe. "Here is a list of items we would like Your Majesty to address."

Guildmaster Dyag's presumptuous use of the royal we made Kalvan glad Rylla was not seated at her throne, a smaller version of his own Fireseed Throne. Rylla was still unwilling to appear in public with her husband; Kalvan wondered how long her stubborn streak could last—*probably until the rest of Mrs. O'Leary's cows came home.*

"Present your list," he said.

"First, there is the matter of the Royal Guilds appointed by Your Majesty. The Council of Guilds would like to see them disbanded or given to the Council for reform."

This was not the first time the Guildmaster had presumed on Kalvan's good humor and patience. One of Prince Ptosphes' cronies, Count Rogos, had warned him of the proclamation, but Kalvan had thought that the independence of the Royal Guilds was settled. It appeared that someone needed to persuade Guildmaster Dyag of that fact. Maybe it was time to convince Count Rogos to mount a putsch and remove Dyag from the Council of Guilds. However, as Rogos continued to remind him, Guildmaster Dyag had the support of most of the older guardmasters as well as the Quisling faction of the nobility. Maybe it was time to let Rylla thin their ranks.

"That's not a reasonable demand, Guildmaster. The Royal Guilds were created in the first place because the Council of Guilds refused to grant them charters. They are now Royal Guilds chartered by Ourselves, as Great King of Hos-Hostigos, and they will remain under Royal protection until We decree otherwise. This is not negotiable."

Dyag's face contorted as though he were passing a kidney stone. "That is within your prerogative, Your Majesty. But the Council will not sit quietly while its time-honored rights are disregarded and usurped. In the future, you may find that the Council is not as cooperative as it has been in the past upon consideration of items Your Majesty views as important."

Remembering how cooperative the Council had been when he had tried to gain their help to force the gunsmiths to standardize musket bores, Kalvan wanted to laugh in Dyag's face. Instead he reined in his temper, "Are you trying to threaten Us, Guildmaster Dyag? Because if you are, We may find it necessary to sequester the entire Council of Guilds for the duration of the War on charges of treason."

In actuality it was a pretty good idea since it would lead to the creation of new masters and apprentices kingdom-wide, most of whom would be in his debt. He could then appoint Count Rogos as Royal Guildmaster, or some such position. Rogos was mild mannered on the outside, but could make metal weep in a forge. He was also the only nobleman in the Guilds, since Rogos' father had been granted a patent of nobility by Ptosphes' grandfather for designing the molds for the first Hostigos gold Crowns.

This was obviously one response to his demand that Guildmaster Dyag had not anticipated; his face blanched. "That is not at all what I meant, Your Majesty. Perhaps I should advance to the next matter."

"An excellent idea. But first, tell your Council that the Royal Guilds are not taking away jobs or traditional guild privileges. The Royal Papermakers Guild, the Royal Riflemakers Guild, the Royal Alchemy Guild and the other Royal Guilds are making more jobs and work for the other guilds, since much of their materials are made by the Carpenters Guild, the Blacksmiths Guild, the Cordwainers Guild and others. What we have here is an increasing pie with bigger slices for everyone."

"There is much truth to Your Majesty's words; however, this is not our primary complaint. These new guilds do not pay their Council dues, nor are their Masters put to the same rigorous training as provided by our Guilds. After all, it is the people of Hostigos Town we are trying to protect."

Horsefeathers! thought Kalvan. "Are you saying that the Great King of Hos-Hostigos would let unqualified craftsmen work in the Royal Guilds?"

"No, no. Of course not, Your Majesty. It is just that there are certain precedents here and time-tested methods of training, as well as proper observances to Tranth—"

"Balderdash! You can't train people in the traditional time-lengthy matter to do new tasks such as papermaking, soap making or rifle smithing. But enough of this, my time is not endless—nor is my patience. What is your next point?"

"There have been complaints by the Gunsmiths Guild and Fitters and Joiners Guilds that their traditional rights are being usurped by the *teachers* at the Royal University of Hos-Hostigos. They believe that some of their guildmasters should be made Masters of the University faculty and that the students be subject to Guild-sponsored apprenticeships."

Kalvan shook his head. *What happened to those halcyon days when Great King Kalvan could do no wrong?* First it was Chartiphon questioning his military decisions, now the Council of Guilds. Next it would be the midwives going on strike to protest antisepsis. *Is the separation between Rylla and myself, with all the attendant rumors, undermining our rule and lowering morale?*

Or was this just business as usual, as he worked to pull Hostigos out of its Medieval mindset and drag it kicking and screaming into the future?

"We are going to make this quick and very clear," Kalvan pronounced, "because We have more important matters to attend to, Guildmaster Dyag. The Royal University and the Royal Guilds, are under Royal Charter and therefore under complete jurisdiction of the Throne. We will not tolerate any interference in their operation from either you or the Council of Guilds. If you have a suggested list of Masters for faculty positions, send it to the Rector. He will give it serious consideration. That is all We can do, or will do on the matter. This audience is at an end."

Guildmaster Dyag blew himself up as though he were about to launch himself into a harangue, then thought better of it, spun around and stomped out of the room. Kalvan turned to one of his scribes, "Make a note to have Duke Skranga conduct an investigation of Guildmaster Dyag and see if it's possible that he harbors Styphoni sympathies. Also, suggest that the Duke make a listing of reliable persons in the Council of Guilds should we have to make some changes to said body's leadership. Inform the Duke that he can expect full cooperation from Count Rogos and that the Count would make an excellent candidate as Guildmaster should Guildmaster Dyag unexpectedly decide to retire." Remembering Thomas à Beckett, Kalvan added, "In good health, of course—at this time."

If Dyag turned out to be in the employ of either Styphon's House or any foreign overlord, his health be damned!

Kalvan was about to tell Chartiphon to announce the next supplicant, when Uncle Wolf Tharses and a bearded man in a wet traveler's cloak came into the audience chamber. As he drew closer, Kalvan could see that it was one of Harmakros' outriders. *More bad news,* he thought, *it's that kind of day.*

"What is it?" Chartiphon asked waspishly. The Chancellor was probably miffed because he was not allowed to filter the news for his Great King. *Old Chartiphon is getting positively womanish since his promotion.* Unfortunately, he'd already been promoted out of the Royal Army and there was no longer any other worthy position left for the old family retainer, whose talents had been more appropriate to the rural princedom of Hostigos, than the new Great Kingdom.

"Your Majesty, Captain-General Harmakros wanted you to know that we just got word that a large party of Sastragathi have entered Kyblos and appear to be traveling toward Hostigos Town."

"Do they appear hostile?"

"No, although they are led by a fearsome giant of a man, who wears two horns on his helmet. Harmakros said you would be familiar with him as you once saved his life at the Battle of Spirit Grove."

Vanar Halgoth! What brings Warlord Sargos' top henchman all the way from the Sastragath to Hos-Hostigos? Halgoth was the leader of Sargos' personal bodyguard, the Raven Band. It must be important or Sargos would have chosen a different envoy. Maybe he had news from the frontier. Were the Zarthani Knights were planning to attack Hostigos from the rear, while Kalvan's forces attacked Hos-Harphax in the spring? Well, he'd have to rein in his questions for at least a moon-quarter. A large party would have trouble making better time than that traveling across western Hos-Hostigos, over muddy roads and trails, even if they were led by the single most formidable fighting-machine Kalvan had ever encountered.

FOUR

I

Verkan was beginning to feel—and not for the first time—that his time on Kalvan's Time-Line was more and more turning into a job rather than a hobby. The problems there followed him to Home Time Line, just like problems here followed him to Kalvan's Time-Line. The mess on Alexandrian-Roman, Seleuco-Macedonian Subsector had been easy to clean up in comparison. One of the employees of Vendrax Luxury Imports had free-lanced in local dives as a mind reader, using a miniature radio and a local confederate. The problems started when the locals began to take him seriously and word got out that he was in truth the reincarnated Alexander.

By the time Verkan arrived, it was obvious the Paratimer was horrified at the havoc he'd created in his midst and really only wanted to get out of town. It had taken a few days to set the situation straight and he was glad to be home.

He'd returned to his office only to find Kostran Glath, his agent-in-charge in Greffa, absent-mindedly twirling his pipe, sitting across from Verkan's horseshoe desk.

"You're supposed to be in Greffa City representing the House of Verkan—what are you doing here?" Verkan asked, as he sat down.

"Chief, we've run across a real anomaly. Zinganna and myself agreed that you needed to be brought up to speed on what's been happening in Greffa the last couple of days."

I haven't been gone that long, Verkan thought to himself. "What happened? A palace coup?"

"Nothing that bad. We've just verified local reports that a large army from the city-states along the Pacific coast is traveling north across the old Iron Trail. It will be arriving on Grefftscharrer territory in two or three days."

"What? Isn't that the home of the Ros-Zarthani—the supposedly decadent ancestors of the Zarthani populations along the Eastern Seaboard. What are they doing on the old Iron Trail?"

Kostran shrugged. "Their army is too small to be an invasion force, but it's too big for anything but trouble—at least, that's how the Grefftscharri see it. We believe they're from the city-state of Antiphon, but have been unable to verify this since we don't have any agents there. One of our field agents in Balph has heard rumors that they were hired by Styphon's House as mercenaries for next year's campaign against Hos-Hostigos. Which makes sense, since the Fireseed Wars have just about exhausted the supply of available mercenaries in the northern Great Kingdoms. The Grefftscharrers don't have any idea why they're approaching Greffa and many of them suspect that the Ros-Zarthani army is an invasion force. Now all of Greffa City's in an uproar."

"I don't doubt it. The Grefftscharri usually expect their enemies to attack from the east or south, not from the west. What are they going to do about it?"

Kostran stopped twirling his pipe, loaded the barrel and lit up. "The Council of Merchants wanted King Theovacar to raise an army and send them packing. The Assembly of Lords is in full agreement."

"That's a first. I can't remember the last time those two bodies agreed on the color of the sky. I take it that King Theovacar wasn't too anxious to take on this invading army?"

"You're right, Chief. There's no gain for the King no matter what he does. If Theovacar raises an army and defeats the barbarians, so what—they're just a bunch of hicks with spears. On the other hand, if he loses—Theovacar is in a mess of trouble and could lose his throne. Not that either the Council or

Assembly of Lords would shed any tears. Neither body is happy about the way the King has been centralizing his authority throughout Grefftscharr."

"That's a given. So what did Theovacar decide to do?"

"Theovacar told them that as long as the barbarian army did not commit an act of war he was unable to justify attacking them. However, if any of his barons or princes felt threatened, they were free to raise their own army. The Prince Varrack of Thagnor, who's been trying to slip out of Theovacar's leash for years, decided to raise an army on his own. Prince Varrack did a pretty good job; about six thousand of his own levy, three thousand mercenary cavalry and the Army of Thagnor—another four thousand men."

Verkan nodded. "Good move, you've got to hand it to King Theovacar. Even if the Prince wins, he'll lose a lot of troops; if he doesn't win, he might not only lose face but his life as well. How did Varrack get his troops into Greffa without starting a civil war?"

"The Prince is having them ferried over now. They'll be arriving in a few days. If we didn't know better, one might think Varrack had something to do with this invasion."

Verkan nodded. "You're right, but King Theovacar doesn't have our sources of information. I bet he's not sleeping too well these days. After all, it's Theovacar's responsibility, not his nobles' job, to defend his kingdom from invasion whether the threat is classed as 'hicks with spears' or not."

"I think Theovacar's afraid that if he moves the Royal Army away from Greffa City, his enemies will attempt a coup—or start a civil war, while he's out of town. It's the same problem Great King Lysandros faces next spring if he leads the Harphaxi Royal Army and chases after Kalvan. On the other hand, if Theovacar stays in Greffa while his troops march off to fight the barbarians, he's made himself even more of a coup target."

Living in Greffa hadn't slowed Kostran's mental muscles, if anything it had quickened them. "So what's Theovacar's answer?"

"So far, he's not talking. There's lots of grumbling in the streets about kings who don't honor their oaths and obligations—mostly from his petty barons, at this point. The commoners don't care since they feel safe behind the city walls. The merchants are too busy rubbing their hands together over all the profits they're making selling supplies, foodstuffs and weapons to Varrack and his crowd. Meanwhile, Theovacar's most vocal opponents are off playing soldier with Prince Varrack. Maybe Theovacar's hoping they'll get their heads handed to them on a platter!"

Verkan said, "I wouldn't put it past him. I'd like to see Theovacar work the Executive Council."

They both laughed.

"Kostran, realistically, what do you think Prince Varrack's chances are against the western forces?"

"It's hard to tell, Chief. We know very little about the Pacific coast city-states. I've already picked two agents to infiltrate Merinos City. They should be able to find out what's going on since that city is the drop-off point for Ros-Zarthani expeditions along the old Iron Trail.

"I've ordered nighttime aerial surveillance and it appears that this Ros-Zarthani army is a first class operation gauging by the way it's run. It's your typical old-style Alexandrian-Roman army, scale-armored *cataphracti* on heavy horses with lots of heavy infantry and archers. They're not going to be a push-over for the Middle Kingdoms men-at-arms, although they've never encountered firearms before which is their major liability.

"The Grefftscharri are over-confident but don't have a lot of firearms. Plus, Prince Varrack's never been in a battle this size and he's known to be a rash commander. Without more data, Chief, I'd have to call it a tossup."

Verkan shook his head. "I hate to take sides, but I hope Varrack beats the iron-pants off the Ros-Zarthani and sends them back to Antiphon where they belong. Kalvan's got enough problems without another army to worry about."

"You've got that right," Kostran said. "Soldiers from all over the Five Great Kingdoms are arriving at Hos-Harphax now that word of Captain-General Phidestros' success in Beshta is being shouted around to all corners by Styphon's House. You'd think he'd just conquered the entire Princedom of Beshta instead of a border castle. Now, there are rumors of a war against Thaphigos."

"Styphon's House knows they need to counter Kalvan's good public relations. What better propaganda than to show that Kalvan can be defeated on his own turf. This victory has been a big morale boost for Styphon's House.

Maybe they want Lysandros to flex his army's muscles some more. Another unexpected dividend of Rylla's invasion of Phaxos."

"Kalvan's got his work cut out for him next year, all right. He thought he might get some help from the Council of Dralm, now that Xentos is Primate."

Verkan shook his head. He paused to take out his pipe and filled the barrel with tobacco.

Kostran sniffed the air. "That's not your usual blend. It smells like that Kalvan's Time-Line weed."

Verkan laughed, then lit his pipe. "I got used to it—I like the flavor now. But getting back to Xentos, he's both a true-believer of Dralm—which means he can't be trusted to act in a rational manner—and he's very ambitious, which he won't admit to himself."

"Which makes him a good candidate for the Bureau of Psychological Hygiene," Kostran offered.

"Or Roxthar's Investigation! Unfortunately, even Xentos doesn't know which way he's going to blow next, so Kalvan's whistling into the wind if he's depending upon the Primate and the League of Dralm for support to solve Hos-Hostigos' problems. The next round is Kalvan's and it's going to be up to *him* to come up with another one of his 'miracles,' if he plans to knock Styphon's House out of the game."

II

"Welcome, Harmakros," Prince Ptosphes said as he opened the door to his bedchambers. "Sit down and make yourself comfortable."

Since Ptosphes was in a nightshirt, Harmakros sat on a stool and started pulling down his thigh-high black cavalry boots. After he shucked them off, he wiggled his toes for a few moments and sighed. "Damn, that feels good!"

Ptosphes wrinkled his nose, fumbled for his flintlock tinderbox and struck a flame to light his pipe. "Those feet of yours stink almost as bad as my chamber pot!"

"If it bothers you, I'll put my boots back on."

"No, I've been in far too many battles to be offended by the smell of honest feet. You've been in the saddle for almost two days, for Dralm's sake. I wanted to talk to you about something before you fell asleep."

"I'm not very tired. I stopped at the Royal Foundry last night, on the way back from Beshta, and slept there."

Ptosphes smiled. "Any luck with the ladies?"

"No. That wasn't the kind of sleep I had in mind. Not that I didn't steal a few looks at that redhead—Sirna isn't it? I could sleep on her pillows any time!"

Ptosphes laughed and picked up a flask of Ermut's brandy and began to fill two goblets. "Then a few drops of Ermut's Best won't stretch you out on my bedchamber floor. Now, have you noticed any change between Rylla and Kalvan since your return from the Sastragath?"

"Yes, on the few occasions I have seen them together, the air in the audience chamber is as chill as the north wind's breath. Every time the Great King is about to relax, Rylla harrumphs, and his face turns as hard as stone. Where formerly I enjoyed being in their presence, I now find myself looking for excuses to return to Tarr-Locra. Although, Dralm's truth be known, Colonel Democriphon is doing an exemplary job and if I show up unannounced on another of Kalvan's 'fact finding missions' one more time Democriphon will take it as personal criticism of his command."

Ptosphes emptied half his goblet before speaking. "Kalvan is still fretting about the loss of Tarr-Veblos to the Haphaxi. As far as Colonel Democriphon is concerned, he's going to be unhappy anyway; Hestophes has run afoul of Baron Sthentros and his daughter and I've already sent him to take Democriphon's command."

"The vixen?"

Sthentros had been part of the baggage his beloved wife had brought with her from Pygron, a small Hostigi town on the border with Sask, when she'd agreed to be his betrothed. Rumors suggested that Sthentros had been one of Demia's father's bastards, but Ptosphes had never believed them until the Baron's daughter—who was the spitting image of Rylla—was born. The bloodlines in those small border towns were often too close for comfort.

Ptosphes had met Demia when she'd become a Lady in Waiting for his older sister, ten winters deceased now. *Where has all the time gone?*

Sthentros was what Kalvan called a "shirt-tail relative"—the nephew of Demia's much older sister. When he'd married Demia, she had requested that her cousin be given an estate and title. Her father and most of her family had died in one of the border raids that had almost turned into an invasion. Sthentros, although not close, was one of Demia's few surviving male relatives. Ptosphes had never been able to say no to his beloved wife.

He could still remember his first glimpse of Demia—his heart had come to a halt, she was so beautiful—like her daughter Rylla. He wasn't the only one who'd fallen hard for Demia; Xentos, Chartiphon and several others had made court. He liked to think that it was his innate qualities that caused her to choose him as her mate, but she'd always been very ambitious, a lot like Lavena…no, it wasn't right to blemish her memory that way—

Ptosphes felt the stabbing chest pain that Kalvan had told him was *angina*—a strange word that sounded nicer than it felt. Kalvan had also told him that if he had some nitro-something-or-other he could cure the stabbing pains in Ptosphes' chest. Then Kalvan had stopped, laughed wildly, then slapped his forehead. "If I knew how to make *nitro* I wouldn't have to worry about my really big pain—Styphon's House!" Obviously, this nitro-something-or-other was powerful medicine. *Maybe my grandchildren will live long enough to use it.*

"Are you all right?" Harmakros asked.

Ptosphes shook his head. "Just thinking about Demia." Harmakros had been a young man when Demia had died, trying to give birth to his son. Kalvan was right to be worried about fester devils; many women in Hostigos died of childbed fever, but much fewer since Kalvan had come to stay.

"Yes, Lavena is Demia's looking-plate likeness, but only in appearance. She could be Rylla's younger sister as well except for their differences. While Rylla practices at the manly arts of war, Lavena uses the womanly arts of love."

Ptosphes bowed his head. "I fear, I have heard likewise. It's a stain on my dear Demia's memory."

"Has Lavena used these wiles on Hestophes?"

"I know not, Harmakros," he answered. "For the first moon-quarter since his return from Eython, Hestophes acted as if he'd been gut shot. He was distracted, moon-faced; totally unlike his usual self. I believe this new posting, as commander of the Hos-Harphax border army, will occupy his mind and let him break the witch's spell."

"How did this happen?"

Ptosphes laughed. "How does any man fall in love? For me it was as if I saw color for the first time, or had been struck on the side of the head with a halberd!"

Harmakros shook his head in disbelief. "I consider myself fortunate to have missed this curse of love, or war wound as you describe it. I had always considered Hestophes to be a man of stolid temperament, like myself. I've lost respect—"

"Don't make a fool of yourself, Harmakros," Ptosphes snapped. "There's a Demia, if he's lucky; or a Lavena, if he's not, for every man. Apparently Lavena encouraged Hestophes' affections—that's what he told me—and I've never known him to lie. Then dropped him like a hot stone when her father told her about his humble origins."

Harmakros shook his head. "She has a fool for a father!"

Ptosphes paused to knock the bowl of his pipe against the heel of his hand. "I agree. I should have sent Sthentros packing after Demia's death. I've never liked or respected him, that's why I put him in a barony half-a-days' ride from Hostigos Town."

"How is Hestophes taking love's ill wind?" Harmakros asked

"Hestophes has been down in the privy ever since he returned from Tarr-Eython. Kalvan's decided to put Hestophes in command of the Royal Army of Observation to keep him away from his new estate."

"Yes, his barony borders Hyllos." Harmakros shook his head. "As you remarked, Colonel Democriphon will not be pleased."

"Kalvan will soften the blow; he has told me that he will invest him with a title and some lands." Ptosphes paused to refill his pipe.

"Well, that takes care of one romantic misadventure; what about our Royal couple?"

"This fight of theirs is bad for everyone's morale. Even the soldiers' drills have been listless lately."

"This is not any time for slacking now that Captain-General Phidestros is filling Tarr-Veblos to the bursting with stores and arms for next year's campaign season."

"Why hasn't Democriphon been able to stop him?"

"The Colonel doesn't have enough men and the rainy weather we've been having makes it difficult to do proper surveillance. In addition, Phidestros moves his supplies in large trains with lots of military support. Believe me, the Colonel is not happy with the current situation."

Ptosphes finished filling his bowl with tobacco. "Any further intelligence to report, Harmakros?"

"Colonel Democriphon has had more success sending patrols and raiding parties into Arklos, but not enough to do more than slow the flood of victuals and armaments going into Tarr-Anibra and Tarr-Veblos. According to our intelligencers, there are more of Styphon's vessels at the wharves of Harphax than there are harlots in the Sask Army's baggage train!"

Prince Ptosphes laughed.

"The Harphaxi have used the better part of the last two moons to build a new outer courtyard for Tarr-Anibra. They've increased the fort's garrison up to about ten thousand men, most of them untested troops and militia but who are receiving daily drills. To my eye Tarr-Anibra appears to be the staging ground for a major invasion force."

"Harmakros, do you think it would be wise to lay siege to Tarr-Anibra before the first snow? Not only would it upset Lysandros' and Styphon's House's invasion plans, but it would serve to bring Kalvan and Rylla together, united against a common enemy. Who knows, after the siege, they might forget their quarrel."

"There are three problems with that plan. First, while Phidestros has built quickly, he has built well. The new outer walls at Tarr-Anibra are three to four lances thick at the base; we would have to bring our biggest guns into Arklos to make a breach. Secondly, we would have to conquer Tarr-Veblos to protect our rear. Thirdly, Phidestros has two thousand mercenaries billeted at Tarr-Syrax and another thousand encamped outside Arklos Town. Both are less than a day's ride away. We might be stepping into a hornet's nest if we aren't careful, my Prince."

"This is bad news for Hos-Hostigos, especially with my daughter and Kalvan waging their own war. We have to do something to bring those two back together. They are both so desperately unhappy, Dralm-damnit! If Xentos were here, he would know what to do."

"Have you tried to suggest to Rylla that she apologize—"

Prince Ptosphes started to laugh and then began coughing.

"Are you well, Prince?"

"I'm fine, old son. I've just been short of breath lately. Old age is catching up to me." Ptosphes took several deep breaths before he continued. "My daughter believes her actions in Phaxos were completely justified and cannot, or will not, try to understand any other view. Her deepest feelings have been hurt and *nothing* short of a full-blown apology by Kalvan will get her to change her course. Not that my son-in-law is acting any better. You'd think she'd chopped off the heads of Araxes' five children with her own sword the way he is acting. Dralm save us all from their folly!"

Harmakros took a long draw on his pipe and exhaled a cloud of smoke before answering Ptosphes. "As Kalvan says, Dralm helps those who help themselves."

Ptosphes sputtered. "You might be right. The both of them suffer from an excess of pride and stubbornness. What they need is a neutral place and something to take their minds off this mess so that their love for each other can bloom again. Maybe if we can get them talking again, they can sort it out between them. It's that cursed silence of theirs that is driving a wedge between their hearts."

Harmakros leaned forward. "What about Aspasthar's adoption ceremony? I had planned to make Kalvan Aspasthar's godfather—it was his idea that I adopt the boy, surely Kalvan can't refuse. Maybe I can ask Rylla to be his godmother."

"Unusual, but not unheard of, considering you are still unmarried." Ptosphes paused to load his pipe with fresh tobacco. Aspasthar was Harmakros' bastard son, only recently discovered by Harmakros when the boy's mother took ill and died almost two winters ago. "Kalvan won't like it when he's discovered our meddling, but to Regwarn with it! It's time for action, not more talk."

"Good." Harmakros nodded. "I will have my scribe write out a letter in the morning inviting both of them. I know we are doing the right thing. I'll pray for Dralm's Blessing and that our plot works."

"Yes, and soon. Rylla is growing displeased about all the time Kalvan is spending at the University—even if she's the reason he's living there. When she finds out that Kalvan has admitted woman students, she's going to go off like one of Kalvan's *rockets*!"

"Women students?" Harmakros shook his head. "You don't think—"

"No, not yet. But there are days when I feel as if I'm sitting on a barrel of fireseed in the midst of a raging battle. And it's neither Lysandros nor Styphon's House that is holding the match, but my own daughter!"

"Here let me pour us another drink. A toast. To Kalvan and Rylla putting this silliness behind them and getting back to their real work—putting Styphon's Foul Den of Demons out of business!"

They clanked their goblets together to Ptosphes, "Aye, aye!"

FIVE

Kalvan watched as Queen Rylla's Own Bodyguard trailed after the towering Sastragathi warchief, Vanar Halgoth. The Queen's Beefeaters were tall for Zarthani, all over a lance—which was about six foot, two inches, which was as far as Kalvan would venture guessing without a yardstick. Rylla had her recruiters scouring Hos-Hostigos for the tallest and broadest men they could find for the Queen's Bodyguard. They reminded Kalvan of Fredrick the First's, or was it the Second's, Potsdam Guard; now that three years had passed since he'd been snatched from otherwhen, he was beginning to forget such small details. He suspected that in another decade, nothing would remain of his former life as a soldier and policeman except for a few dreamlike remembrances.

The Sastragathi warrior, in his Viking-style horned helmet, stood half a head taller than any of Rylla's Beefeaters except for Captain Xykos. Halgoth approached the throne and bowed, a major concession from any freeman Sastragathi, which Kalvan recognized immediately. "Please, do not bow on Our behalf, Warchief Halgoth. We are pleased to recognize you as a friend."

Kalvan stood up and offered his hand, which quickly disappeared inside a hand the size of a baseball mitt.

Halgoth smiled, showing a mouthful of teeth, in surprisingly good shape for a man in his early forties here-and-now. "Once again, Your Majesty honors me."

Kalvan smiled, appreciating Halgoth's directness and straight shooting; he was sure Halgoth could be a wonderful friend, or a terrible enemy.

"Your Majesty, I have words from my king, Var-Wannax, Ranjar Sargos." Halgoth reached into his cloak to draw out a folded packet.

"High King," Kalvan translated 'Var-Wannax' from the Urgothi/Zarthani bastardized tongue that was spoken in the Sastragath. He'd picked up quite a few Urgothi words in his all night drinking bouts with Sargos, Halgoth and Great King Nestros.

Halgoth grinned. "My king is as much a Wannax as Nestros and can field more warriors."

Kalvan nodded, thinking to himself, *and a much better companion and strategist, too!* "Join me in my private audience chamber where I can read my friend Wannax Sargos' letter." The two of them left the chamber, in a wake of shocked silence from the assembled court. Kalvan was pleased; it would give the court something to think about other than the strained relations between their King and Queen.

Once the two of them were comfortably seated in front of a roaring fire, Kalvan offered the Urgothi giant his tobacco pouch.

Halgoth pulled out a pipe with a bowl twice the size of Kalvan's and filled it to the top. He paused to smell the leaf. "Hmm. This is good tobacco."

Kalvan motioned to his body servant, Cleon, who had unobtrusively followed them into the audience chamber. "Cleon, please bring us a cask of Ermut's Best."

"Yes, Your Majesty."

While they waited for their drinks, they both smoked as Halgoth shared amusing anecdotes about their journey from the Sastragath into Hos-Hostigos. After Cleon had returned and drinks had been served, Halgoth passed Kalvan Sargos' letter.

The parchment was inscribed with Zarthani runes and Kalvan suspected some scribe had improved upon Sargos' choice of phrasing, since it was both wordier and more polite than any words he remembered coming out of the blunt-spoken Warlord's mouth.

To Great King Kalvan of Hos-Hostigos, our Good Friend and Ally from across the Pyromannes:

We hope this letter finds you in both good health and spirits. As my clansman and confidant, Vanar Halgoth, has no doubt already told you, I have agreed to become Var-Wannax of both the Upper and Lower Sastragath. It is my hope to permanently unite both provinces under my rule and leadership. Since our last meeting, I have pondered over your words and have taken actions based on many of them.

You have convinced me that for the outer provinces to survive the Fireseed Wars, we will have to become both united and familiar with the modern warfare as practiced in the Great Kingdoms. The band of fireseed artificers and gunsmiths that you promised have arrived and have been greeted as befits their Great King's friendship and trust. We will guard them well.

Kalvan didn't doubt that for a moment; it was the other stuff, the advice he had given to Sargos in their madcap all-night drinking bouts that worried him.

I have taken heed of your words and greatly enlarged the Clan by granting membership to all Urgothi widows, clanlessmen and children. As you have done with your own mercenary troops in Hos-Hostigos and swelled the ranks of your own Royal Army, so the Tymannes have prospered—even far beyond my wildest imaginings. The Clan now numbers over eighty times a thousand clansmen and three times as many women and children.

Kalvan whistled to himself. If Sargos was not exaggerating, and swelling the truth was not among his faults, the Vannax could field an army better than twice the size of Kalvan's own Royal Army, with his Princes' and liege lords' troops thrown in for good measure!

While taking your advice about taking only fellow Urgothi warriors and womenfolk into the Clan, I did decide to include any and all children left fatherless and homeless by the War of Three Kings. As a result, we now have many thousands of Ruthani children of all ages who I am finding difficult to place among the tribes and women of our Clan.

Kalvan didn't have the least doubt about the truth of his words. The Ur-gothi—descendents of the second wave of Indo-European migrations into the North American hemisphere—were lifelong enemies of the Ruthani from the Sea of Grass, and only the threat posed by the Knights had united these great enemies into a temporary alliance.

So, my great friend, we are asking for your aid in solving our problem. It would bring an end to our temporary alliance with the Ruthani were we not to take care of these orphaned children. Yet they go unwanted—especially the elder children. Thus, I ask for a great boon from my friend, Great King Kalvan. I would like to send many of the children to Hos-Hostigos where they can learn from your people and yourself the new ways that we need to learn if we are to survive the upheavals that the Fireseed Wars have presented us and our world. I am hoping that you will teach these children much of your ways so that they may someday bring your people's wisdom and teaching back to the Sastragath.

Please inform my good friend and councilor of your decision, and listen to his own offer, which may in time prove of great worth.

Your humble servant,
Ranjar Sargos
Warlord and Var-Wannax of the Tymannes and both Upper and Lower Sastragath

For a few moments, Kalvan wasn't sure if he was being presented with a huge problem or a wonderful gift; a little bit of both, he finally decided. First, refusing this 'offer' would both cost him Sargos' friendship and a major ally, with an army larger than both the hosts of Styphon and Hos-Hostigos—an error he was not about to make. He was certain, just from knowing the man, that this *solution* to his clan recruitment had cost Sargos a lot of face; he was not a man to ask for a boon lightly, nor forget one given either.

Sadly, the Ruthani—the descendents of the Great Plains Indians—would be no more welcome in Hos-Hostigos than they were in the Sastragath.

However, Kalvan's power base was far more secure than Sargos' rule over the Sastragath, and Kalvan had the power to make his will be done. Still, he could not order the rank and file Hostigi to 'adopt' foundlings from the Sea of Grass, any more than Sargos could order his clansmen to do the same. Maybe he could set up some kind of orphanage for them. Unfortunately, the Royal Foundling home in Hostigos Town was already filled to bursting with the orphans from last year's war.

He would have to come up with some kind of plan before the children arrived or there would be big problems. He was certain it was only Sargos' kindness that had kept the Ruthani children alive this long.

Kalvan didn't realize how long he'd been contemplating this problem until he drew on his pipe and realized it was dead. He looked up at Vanar Halgoth. "I apologize, but there is much to ponder in this letter."

Halgoth said, "The Wannax is sorely vexed about what to do with the Grasseater cubs. If he treats them less than honorably, our alliance with High Chief Ulldar will go to Wind." The Warchief paused as though reluctant to part with a great secret. "Sargos has a soft heart and would like to see the cubs safely out of the Sastragath where memories are long and vengeance is nursed along with mother's milk."

Kalvan nodded. "I fear they will find no great welcome from my people either. After several years of war, Hostigos has more than its share of widows and orphans. Yet, I have great respect for my friend Ranjar Sargos."

Halgoth nodded as though this were only right. "He has repeated your words to me many times, King Kalvan. And, truth, in over thirty winters I have never seen him so enamored of another man's words."

Kalvan had to repress a shudder. *Which of my midnight drunken monologues will come back to haunt me next?*

"It was your tales of how you had increased the Royal army by making your free companions into Hostigi citizens that gave him the idea to adopt the tribeless men, women and children into the Clan. Now—" Halgoth paused to open his arms in a huge circle. "—the Tymannes number more than all the other Urgothi clans in the Upper and Lower Sastragath. Truth be told, many warriors have left their true clans to join the Tymannes to partake of our good medicine and war glory.

"Wannax Sargos is much beholden to you, Your Majesty, for the success of this plan. In fact, he was loathe to lay this new burden at your feet and, had there been any other solution, he would not have done so."

Kalvan took a deep drink of Ermut's Best. "High King Sargos is a friend and ally; I am pleased that I have aided him in his plans to establish his suzerainty over the Sastragath. I will take these Ruthani children and make them wards of the Royal Throne—"

"Your Majesty! Sargos will be most pleased and thankful."

"Tell him I will do it for our friendship and for the children. I will do my best to train them in our ways in all things."

Halgoth turned slightly red and looked embarrassed, an emotion Kalvan was sure that crossed Halgoth's countenance no more than once every few decades.

"Sargos would not tell this to his scribe, but he would also like to send with the Ruthani some of our own cubs so that they too will learn the ways of Great King Kalvan and Hostigos."

Kalvan slapped the end table next to his chair. "It is done." Sargos might not realize it, but he was putting the next generation of what would become the Sastragathi officer corps right into Kalvan's hands.

"Thank you, King Kalvan, you have lifted a great burden from my head. It is rare that I ask any man for a boon, much less ask for another man's."

"I understand, Halgoth. You are a loyal friend and Sargos is lucky to have you guarding his back."

Halgoth nodded, as though that were his due. "Now that my work is done, I have a request of my own."

"Yes?" Kalvan asked guardedly. What favor might this great warrior ask next?

"When we met at the Spirit Grove and you saved my life, I became in your debt and it is time to settle the account."

Kalvan nodded solemnly.

"I understand that Hostigos is in a great war with the Black Knights and the dung digging priests of Styphon."

"This is true."

"Then you are in need of many warriors?"

"This is also true."

Halgoth squirmed in his seat, looking strangely boyish for a man with sun-darkened skin and weathered wrinkles. "I would like to offer my services and those of the Raven Guard to act as your bodyguard."

Kalvan thought quickly. Halgoth was a man of great honor and pride. He was also Sargos' closest confidant and friend. To deny his request would not only dishonor Halgoth, but Sargos as well. Such an insult might well carry a blood price—or *vergelt* as the Urgothi called it. Kalvan couldn't imagine how he might use such an honor guard of unrepentant Vikings—but the Varangian Guard certainly had done well for their Byzantine masters, at least until Harald Hastrada used his position to virtually empty the Imperial treasury. Nor would it be a bad thing to have such formidable and loyal men as his personal guard. And, who knew how much evil would arise if he refused Vanar Halgoth's request.

"It is done," Kalvan said, as he laid his Sword of State, with a big ruby set atop the hilt, across his lap so that the hilt was placed forward on his right knee.

A smile broke out on Halgoth's face like the sun rising over a bank of purple clouds, then the big man fell down on both knees before Kalvan on the floor and put his right hand under the sword's hilt, while keeping his left arm down in front of him in the most comfortable position, and kissed the King's hand.

"I swear allegiance to Your Majesty and swear, by Thanor's Hammer, to serve Your Majesty with my battle-axe and my life."

Kalvan nodded, saying, "Now that you have seized the sword in the fashion your king desired you would, and are now my sworn liegeman. You may now rise."

They both rose and Kalvan filled the golden goblets to the brim with brandy.

Halgoth lifted his goblet. "A toast to Great King Kalvan and to the Raven Guard."

Kalvan clanked goblets with the massive Urgothi. *Another friend*, he thought, *I can use all the friends I can get.* "Vanar, as your first duty, I want you to return to the Sastragath and bring the war orphans back to Hostigos."

"It will be done, sire. I need to return anyway to gather the Raven Guard. Not all will be old comrades, since some were killed and there are many new tribesmen in the Clan, but all will be proven warriors and loyal paladins. I will put them all under an oath-bond to fight to guard Your Majesty's life with their own. You will not regret this day, my King!"

Kalvan wasn't sure of that, but he knew better than to share his doubts with his new captain. He was going to have to put a truss on both his drinking hand and his mouth before he brought himself any more such good fortune!

SIX

I

Captain-General Phidestros watched as the two Knights, in blackened armor and white capes with Styphon's black sun-wheel emblazoned on the back, brought Grand Master Soton's chair in and then waited at attention while the Grand Master strutted in and took his seat. Phidestros was surprised to note how much Soton had aged; there were sharp lines around his eyes and mouth, and his beard had turned almost completely gray. He wondered what had caused him the most pain, losing thousands of his beloved Knights or having to explain his *retreat* from Kalvan's army to the Inner Circle of Styphon's House. Neither could have been easy, but knowing Soton as he did, he suspected the former.

"Grand Master Soton, can I offer you some winter wine?"

Soton excused one of his Knights, but the Sergeant stayed. "Yes, I could use a drink. I have spent far too many hours talking to nobles with more iron between their ears than in their spines." He sounded weary and a little hoarse.

"We could always meet tomorrow, Grand Master."

"No, I can only stay for a moon-quarter more, and then I have to return to Balph before the first big storms. We have a lot to discuss if the invasion of Hos-Hostigos is to be successful."

"Agreed. Mynoss, serve us some wine." After his manservant had brought them all, including the Sergeant, goblets of red winter wine, Phidestros made a toast. "To Styphon and the fall of the false Kingdom of Hos-Hostigos."

After a long swallow, Soton offered up another toast. "And to Great King Lysandros!"

"To Great King Lysandros."

"Unfortunately, that is about the only good news to come from the Sastragathi debacle."

"I don't just believe it, I know it, Grand Master. If you had not diverted Kalvan's attention to the west, Hos-Harphax would be no more—and Harphax a princedom of Hos-Hostigos! If you still believe, as you did last year, that Hos-Harphax is the anchor of the Five Kingdoms, then your sacrifice was well made."

"I hope you are right," said Soton. "The entire campaign was a nightmare I'd just as soon forget...."

"We have made great progress here."

"Tell me about it."

"By Styphon's Grace and much of his gold, I have completely rebuilt the Army of Hos-Harphax; it now musters over twenty thousand men: two thousand Royal Pistoleers, eight hundred of the King's Royal Lancers, four thousand Royal Foot Guard and four thousand Mobile Dragoons—mounted infantry much like Kalvan's Mobile Force, made up of the best of the City Militia—and a dozen mercenary regiments. I've recently hired another six thousand mercenaries, four thousand foot and two thousand horse; all have agreed to join the Royal Army—for a price. I've formed two mobile batteries of four six-pounders and six four-pounders each and one Royal Rifle Company with seventy-six riflemen.

"Excellent!—Captain-General. You have been busy. But how well trained are these troops?"

"Every third man in each company is a veteran, and we've been drilling them six days a moon-quarter since spring. They're not seasoned yet, but they are in good spirits. I'm paying them twice the usual salary and year-round—"

"So that was how you convinced the mercenaries to join the Royal Army." Soton nodded thoughtfully. "Year-round! I can hear Archpriest Dryton, the Temple's Almoner, screaming all the way from Balph."

"No you won't. I'm not paying them all in gold. Half their salary is paid in iron coin, redeemable in gold *only* when Kalvan's army has been defeated."

"Brilliant." Soton shook his head as he took out a burl pipe with silver inlay. "By what spell do you convince soldiers to accept iron in place of gold?"

"All soldiers are gamblers and see nothing ahead but the piles of gold they will win when the Army of Hostigos has been vanquished. It has also given them a great incentive to work on their drills. Besides, many of the local merchants, ladies of the evening and wagerers accept the iron coins at a discount."

"If that is true, truly you have brought about Styphon's Own Miracle. Styphon be praised! If the local slatterns and sharpers are willing to take these iron rakmars in trade, then even the scum must believe that we will prevail. I wish the Archpriests of the Inner Circle shared their faith."

"They will, Grand Master. They will. The City Militia is now more than ten thousand strong, and are better armed and better drilled than in living memory. Every moon I have a thousand of them sent to Tarr-Anibra where they are drilled from first light to dark. They do much better away from Tarr-Harphax and the city walls. They will not run as they did at Chothros Heights."

"You have made great progress in the past year—even more than I expected. Yet, this shortage of free companies may yet prove our undoing. I had hoped you would have twelve to fifteen thousand mercenaries by this time, but far too many have died in this Ormaz-spawned war against the Usurper—or worse, have taken his colors. Archpriest Anaxthenes has taken means to help us out of our dilemma. Let me present it to you."

Phidestros had to bite his tongue to keep from cursing meddling priests, reminding himself that it was Styphon's House's paychests, not Lysandros' Treasury, that was financing his army.

Soton went on to explain that Styphon's House had merchants and agents who traveled over the old Iron Trail to places as distant as the western settlements at the edge of the world. One of these agents had been authorized by the Inner Circle to hire an entire army of Ros-Zarthani. Word had recently arrived in Balph that they were almost across the Sea of Grass.

"This is interesting news," Phidestros said, his face trying to hide his disappointment. He needed these western barbarians like he needed another regiment of royal lancers. "How do we know they will not break the first time Kalvan's guns fire?"

Soton shrugged. "They may be sounder troops than you suspect. The agent has informed Archpriest Anaxthenes that the Ros-Zarthani, as the barbarians are called, know neither kingdoms nor princedoms as we do. Each city-state acts as its own kingdom—yes, a chaotic system of rule that leads to much fighting. An envoy was sent to 'hire' an army from one of the larger cities to aid in our war against the Usurper Kalvan. The Ros-Zarthani army has marched from their home across the Sea of Grass and soon will pass through Grefftscharr."

"You mean some highpriest, who doesn't know a rake from a ramrod, has hired an unknown army of barbarians in the belief that they will pass unmolested through the Sea of Grass? If they survive the Ruthani tribes, the Grefftscharrers will pulverize them as a grindstone mills wheat. Why not bypass Greffa all together, by going south and taking the—"

"Fighting the Greffa Army will be their test, as I understand it. The Ros-Zarthani have never faced fireseed weapons, and it is well that they do so before they meet the Royal Army of Hos-Hostigos in the field. It will take Styphon's Own Miracle for them to arrive as an intact unit. Yet, Highpriest Prysos believes that these Ros-Zarthani can more than hold their own against the Sea of Grass nomads and Grefftscharrers. At least he has convinced Archpriest Anaxthenes that this is so."

"Anaxthenes may know all there is to be known about running temple services and pulling Sesklos' strings, but he knows nothing of war."

"Don't underestimate Archpriest Anaxthenes. Any Archpriest who has survived for twenty winters in the Inner Circle has more understanding of command than you might think. There is even talk that he will become the next Supreme Priest."

Suddenly all is clear, Phidestros thought. Great King Lysandros might believe the gathering host was *his* army, but Styphon's House had a different opinion. "Since the Temple pays, we cannot lose. What weapons do the barbarians use?"

"They still fight in scale-armor and on destriers, much as our ancestors did and as your Royal Lancers do now."

"Oh no, not more iron hats! Kalvan's artillery will harvest them before they have time to set their lances."

"Not all of them. Many use bows or carry heavy throwing darts."

Phidestros shook his head. "Darts and bows! They will probably run like scalded dogs when the first cannon shot is fired."

"If half of what this Prysos claims is true, they may surprise both you and me—and most importantly—the Usurper. At worst, they will serve as a screen for our own troops."

"For how long has Styphon's House purchased these *soldiers*?"

"Styphon's House has paid their city well; they will fight until they are dead or the Usurper Kalvan is defeated. Scoff if you must, but answer me this: Where else do you intend to find more mercenaries to fight under our banners?"

Phidestros shook his head. "There are no more mercenaries to be bought in the Five Kingdoms, not for gold or glory. No, bring on your iron hats, we will find some use for them—if they ever arrive! If nothing else, they will give the Hostigi guns fresh bodies to fire upon which will allow my men to do more serious work."

II

Primate Xentos still felt uncomfortable greeting supplicants in his official Seat; it reminded him too much of the old Iron Throne he had seen during a visit to the former court of Great King Kaiphranos in Harphax City. The Primate's Seat could just as easily been called the Golden Throne, since it was gilt covered and jewel-encrusted. In Xentos' mind such excess was more appropriate to a Styphon's House temple than Allfather Dralm's chief house of worship. Still, Highpriest Davros of the High Temple of Hos-Agrys, however, had a different view and an answer for every question. Xentos was willing to accept that the Seat's magnificence lent a certain dignity to the High Temple; yet, in his heart, he still wasn't convinced that such opulence was at all proper.

He was temped to turn around and ask the towering statue behind him what it thought, but—unlike Styphon's image in Balph—Allfather Dralm had never spoken to his flock. Xentos wasn't even sure it was proper to use the former Great Hall of Dralm as the Primate's Audience Room. Again, Davros had convinced him otherwise. *Or is it my false pride that has allowed me to be convinced?* There was no comforting answer to that question so he focused upon the merchant asking his intercession with the Allfather.

The supplicant continued to press his case, oblivious to Xentos' state of mind. "I admit, Primate, I bore false witness upon my competitors—even drove some of them out of business. Now the ague strikes almost every night. I awake shivering and lying all night in my own water. Please, ask Allfather Dralm to forgive me—I beseech you!"

The formerly obese merchant now swam in his robes.

Xentos raised his staff. "Leave one hundred gold rakmars as an offering and I will intercede with the Allfather on your behalf."

The merchant fawned all over him, even kissing his ring finger—another custom encouraged by Highpriest Davros. He knew the High Temple needed the gold; what he wasn't sure of was how much good health, if any, it would buy for the suffering merchant. Still, tonight he would make a special prayer to Dralm in the supplicant's name.

The fever-ridden merchant was the last of today's penitents. Next was a meeting with the High Council of Dralm. The Highpriests, led by Highpriest Davros, approached the throne with far less reverence than the previous supplicants. Xentos was beginning to resent their presumption.

Davros looked him straight in the eyes. "Primate, we must come to a firm decision about the Usurper Kalvan. The princes of Hos-Agrys wish to know our policy regarding the outlaw realm of Hos-Hostigos. They are appalled by the slaughter of the Phaxi nobility and are afraid that any alliance with the Usurper might bring them the same fate."

Xentos sighed, as he did not like hearing Great King Kalvan called the Usurper, but unfortunately, that was what he truly was, the head of a self-proclaimed rogue Great Kingdom. "The former prince of Phaxos had been oath-sworn to the Throne of Hos-Hostigos, then he broke his oath. I have previously warned the Council about the impetuousness of Great Queen Rylla. She is willful and has a tendency to take matters into her own hands; however, her actions in Phaxos addressed a legitimate grievance against the traitor Araxes. Had it been Great King Kalvan overthrowing former Prince Araxes, I do not believe this question would have arisen."

Highpriest Davros, his voice filled with lightly veiled impatience, said, "She behaved impetuously and took out her anger on the rulers of Phaxos, many of whom were only guilty of following their rightful overlord's orders. Innocent lords were killed and unnecessary atrocities were committed against Prince Phaxos' family. I propose we put Hos-Hostigos under the Ban of Dralm."

Xentos cried out in righteous indignation, "The Ban of Dralm is always the last resort, particularly in the case of a ruler who has done more of Dralm's work than any Great King in living memory. Before Kalvan's arrival, Styphon's House was about to annex Hostigos and make it their own fiefdom. Without his brilliant military leadership, they would have done so and the Hostigi Temple of Dralm would have been torn down and its priests murdered. The false priests of the Demon Styphon would have then destroyed the Allfather's temples within the neighboring princedoms of Sask, Nostor, Beshta and Sashta. Would anyone care to refute that statement?"

Most of the assembled highpriests were suddenly busy studying their sandals—all except Davros, who stared at Xentos as if he were seeing him for the first time.

He continued, "I believe we have more important work to do than attacking our friends. Am I the only one who has noticed that the Union of Styphon's Friends is not only raising gold for the war against Hos-Hostigos, but troops as well? Well, what do you think they're going to do once Kalvan is deposed or killed?

"If you have no answer, I ask you to turn your eyes toward Hos-Harphax where the Captain-General of the Harphaxi Royal Army recently stormed one of the Beshtan tarrs, Tarr-Veblos. I'm sure it is not news that Captain-General Phidestros took the castle by force of arms even though it is part of the Great Kingdom of Hos-Hostigos."

"A Great Kingdom we do not recognize!" Davros answered back.

"Nor does Styphon's House, which does not mean it does not exist. Prince Phrames of Beshta is a devoted follower of Dralm and has demonstrated his support by sending a thousand rakmars of gold and ten times that of silver for the new Temple. Now, is this how we show our *support* of Phrames?"

Even Davros did not have an answer to that question, nor had Xentos expected one. Xentos was still unsure of Great King Kalvan, where he really came from and whether or not he represented the interests of men or gods. However, he did know one thing for sure: Kalvan was Styphon's House's worst enemy—and that was truth that was worth its weight in gold. Another truth was that Kalvan was the only real counterweight against Styphon's House's expansionism in the Great Kingdoms. Without him, there was no other great king or captain-general who was strong enough or wise enough to stop Styphon's House from greedily gobbling up the Great Kingdoms, one at a time.

If this were true, and Xentos suspected it was, the right thing for Council of Dralm to do would be to throw its support to Kalvan, although he wasn't sure that he could convince the Council to do so. In his mind, Lysandros' ascension to the Throne of Hos-Harphax was far more dangerous to the Temple of Dralm's interests than Rylla's blunder in Phaxos. Especially now that her interference in Phaxi princely succession had provided Lysandros the proof he needed of Kalvan and Rylla's regime changing intentions towards the Harphaxi nobility. Never mind that once Lysandros became Great King he would do his best to remove those Harphaxi princes and nobles who were not already in Styphon's House's pocket.

The next question, and most important one, for the Temple's survival, was: *Do I dare to throw the might and moneychest of the League of Dralm into the coming war?* If he did, he might risk a war of religious persecution should Styphon's House defeat Hos-Hostigos. Or should the Temple continue their policy of neutrality and risk Kalvan's wrath—or certainly Rylla's—if Kalvan won? There had to be a third option. If there was, he meant to find it.

"What do we do, Primate?" the Highpriest of Glarth asked. The old man was actually wringing his hands.

"We dare not openly support Kalvan, for if he loses, it will be laid at our feet and we will face a war of extinction with Styphon's House. A war *they* will win."

"I do not see that," Highpriest Davros stated. "Styphon's House will be busy for many years in Hostigos stamping out heresy and removing all traces of Kalvan."

It was interesting to see how Davros made claims and counter-claims to Xentos' every statement, even if it meant contradicting what he had said before. *Is Davros a Styphoni sympathizer, or merely trying to undermine my rule?* "We have all known for some time that there has always been a strong one-god party within Styphon's House. This party has always been a minority, since most of the archpriests of Styphon's House have been unbelievers. That has changed recently. Archpriest Roxthar has solidified his control of the Inner Circle and he is determined to root out all the non-believers from Styphon's House and elevate Styphon as the only god. He is our enemy, not Lysandros, not Kalvan, not Rylla, not Grand Master Soton. The Holy Investigator has already purged many of Styphon's temples of 'non-believers' throughout Balph and Hos-Ktemnos.

"We must stop Archpriest Roxthar at all costs. We will surreptitiously send funds and soldiers to aid Kalvan, but not openly. This way we will not bind the Temple's fate with that of Kalvan's. Whether we like it or not, we must aid Kalvan." He only hoped it wasn't too little and too late, but he didn't dare start a religious war with Styphon's House that there was almost no hope of winning.

"But Primate, how do we know if this is the will of Allfather Dralm?" a highpriest asked.

"Until this bronze statue speaks, we'll have to assume it is His decision. I do not think that Allfather Dralm would approve of our actions if we stood here wringing our hands while his High Temple fell down around our heads."

Highpriest Davros shot him a look that said, "You may have won this round, but don't count on winning the next one."

For not the first time since arriving in Agrys City, Xentos missed the pastoral peace of Hostigos. However, if Mytron's letters were to be believed, Hostigos was in as much, if not more, turmoil than Agrys City as they prepared for the invasion of Hos-Harphax. If only Great King Demistophon had some of Kalvan's spine, Xentos might be able to offer more than token support to Hos-Hostigos. At the moment, he wasn't sure if he most wanted to aid his former friends, or to do whatever was necessary to halt the advance of Styphon's House.

In truth, the answer was obvious: it was Xentos' duty to do whatever it took to protect Allfather Dralm's House Upon Earth—even if it meant the loss or death of his old friends. Xentos hoped it would not be so, but experience argued otherwise.

III

As Duke Ruffulo walked into King Theovacar's private audience chamber with one of the King's Companions on either side, he noted that it was decorated in marked contrast to the gilded throne room. Theovacar's private inner sanctum contained scrolls and finely glazed amphora with battle scenes from the Western Sea. A large mosaic covered one wall showing the Kingdom of Grefftscharr, outlined in gold, and its vassals Greffa, Brythar, Helmout, Maumue, Rhinnar and even Lyros and Thagnor which were vassals in name only.

The Duke noted that both of the King's Companions, his sworn bodyguard, left the room after a slight nod from Theovacar, an observance signaling both trust and honor to his guest. When King Theovacar rose to touch palms, he noticed the dark circles under Theovacar's eyes and lines of worry that bracketed his mouth. Ruffulo was known in the Assembly to be an occasional ally of the king, but this was the first time he'd been invited for a private audience.

The Duke wondered what Theovacar's price would be since the king never did anything by accident; all was by design, right down to the silver oil-lamps in sconces on the stone walls made in the image of Thanor's hammer, which was Theovacar's personal emblem.

After the expected formal greetings were expressed, King Theovacar asked, "Duke Ruffulo, you are known to be a respected leader within the Assembly of Lords. Is this not true?"

Ruffulo knew this was a question that needed no answer, just as he was certain he wouldn't have been invited to a private audience with the King were it not true. He nodded his head, avoiding the King's direct gaze. Theovacar's eyes were an endless pool of gray ice, like the heart of a frozen glacier. Everyone knew tales of shamans on the Sea of Grass who practiced spells that enslaved free men. He would not be surprised to learn that the King had taken instruction from such magicians.

"I need someone to represent Our interests in the Assembly, someone who is not known to be in Our confidence."

The Duke nodded.

"The Ros-Zarthani army is less than a moon-quarter's march away from our borders. I have heard there is strong sentiment that We should mobilize Our army to stop them."

"I have heard this," Ruffulo said cautiously, careful only to repeat common knowledge. "Prince Varrack of Thangor claims we must punish these interlopers before they reach our Kingdom. Many others agree. Prince Fridrek of Rhinnar believes these Ros-Zarthani are but the skirmishers of a much greater army waiting to fall upon our lands.

"What do you believe?"

The Duke knew this question was as much a measure of him as it was of the Assembly of Lords. "It is my belief that we should escort the Ros-Zarthani army out of our lands with an army large enough to keep them away from temptation. The envoy of the False God Styphon, Archpriest Prysos, tells us that they have engaged this band of mercenaries to fight in the Fireseed Wars against Great King Kalvan, whom they call the Usurper. These false priests of Styphon have lied before, but this tale appears to be truthful."

Theovacar stroked his sable-colored goatee. "This is what We believe, as well. Were this truly an invasion there would be three or four times as many soldiers. Still, We must show the Ros-Zarthani that We are prepared for any misadventures upon their part. Or next time We may be facing a real army of invasion."

Ruffulo smiled. "Since the Trader Verkan brought the fireseed formula to Greffa we have been free of the fireseed priests' demands. Maybe someday we will use this fireseed to return some of our gold to the Treasury."

"Yes, and with interest. We would also like to punish these arrogant priests of Styphon's House who act as if they were still the only source of fireseed. This Kalvan, Thanor be praised, has given us the ability to make our own fireseed and escape their usurious charges and penurious lots."

Ruffulo nodded his accord. Styphon's House had proscribed fireseed sales to the Middle Kingdoms shortly after its discovery. Over the centuries it had been made available in small lots, but only after the price had been raised so high that one pound of fireseed was as expensive as an ounce of gold dust and the supply so limited that the great guns on the City Mole were fired but once a year. Nor was it unusual to find that the fireseed was spoiled. The new Fireseed Works had brought the price of fireseed way down and the City Magazines were full for the first time in Greffa's history.

"However," Theovacar continued, his voice rising, "this is not the time to involve Ourselves in the Fireseed Wars. Let the Ros-Zarthani break their spears on Kalvan's armor, and we will destroy the fleeing Ros-Zarthani should they again dare to trespass upon our lands when they leave with their tails tucked up under their hindquarters!"

The Duke nodded. He agreed with Theovacar's assessment, but the voices in the Assembly of Lords were in opposition to any measured solution. Prince Varrack had them convinced they were honor-bound to oppose the Ros-Zarthani barbarians. He felt differently, as history had shown the Ros-Zarthani were not some loose confederation of tribes from the Sea of Grass temporarily joined together for loot and brigandage. No, the Ros-Zarthani were a disciplined, trained force with centuries of tradition and martial success behind them. True, they lacked arquebuses and bombards, but they made up for that with good morale and training.

"The Assembly is so like-minded that no words of yours, Your Majesty, will change their views."

Theovacar grinned from ear to ear. "I have no intention of stopping those blockheads from rushing to their deaths. In fact, I want you to counsel them to do so."

"But, Your Majesty, your representatives have told the Assembly repeatedly that you oppose attacking the invaders."

"Of course, how else to get Varrack off his endparts!"

"What if Prince Varrack is successful?"

"Then he has lost soldiers to the Ros-Zarthani that might have opposed Us in the future."

Not for the first time this afternoon, Ruffulo regretted being called to attend this private audience with King Theovacar—not that he had a choice. Of one thing he was certain, he did not like the slippery way his King's mind worked and he doubted he would sleep as soundly having found out. Theovacar acted as if his honor were as loose as a slattern's shift. Nor did Ruffulo like serving as the King's tool, but Theovacar was known to punish those who thwarted his will—and their families as well.

Unfortunately, support of the King would cost him the friendship of the very allies that could free him from this trap. Once again Theovacar would use the Assembly of Lords for his own ends; Ruffulo hoped—vainly he suspected—that someday things would not always be such.

"What part am I to play?"

Theovacar's smile was not a pretty thing to watch. "I am going to send five thousand soldiers to Bundt Town, which is our westernmost outpost. This will quiet the opposition and still the cries that I'm not defending Grefftscharrer territory. However, they will be under orders not to attack the Ros-Zarthani unless attacked first."

Ruffulo nodded. "There is little of value in that small town to tempt the Ros-Zarthani, yet it will still the cries in the Assembly that you are ignoring this 'invasion'."

"Yes, and your role will be to encourage Prince Varrack to take his army into the Sea of Grass to fight them."

"He will not bend to *my* will."

"Of course not, or you would not be having this audience. You will encourage him, even if it means ridiculing him on the floor of the Assembly of Lords."

He blanched, looking down. Yes, it could be done; Varrack was hot tempered and impetuous. However, if Theovacar's plan came to fruition, and Varrack suffered serious losses or public humiliation—he would earn himself a very bad enemy. Of course, if he defied Theovacar, he would earn an even greater enemy, as well as one who shared the same city.

When Ruffulo looked back up he could not help but notice the triumph in Theovacar's eyes. Now that the King was in a good mood; it was time for a gamble of his own. "I will need gold, lots of it. I need to purchase some of Varrack's friends, since I am not of their circle. They will not come cheap."

"Yes, We will see that you get your gold. We will give Our Treasurer orders to accept your drafts."

SEVEN

I

Sirna watched with amazement as Baltov Eldra used the limited Zarthani cosmetic palette, mostly rouge, some kind of cornstarch-based whitening powder and charcoal-based mascara to transform her appearance from ravishing to drop-dead gorgeous. Sirna had only sparingly used the lip rouge which tasted of some animal fat that she preferred would remain unidentified. She could see from the polished metal plate that passed for a mirror that her low-cut gown, the obligatory Lady's garment at formal affairs on Aryan-Transpacific, displayed enough of her cleavage to attract far more male attention than she felt comfortable with.

One of the initial attractions of her ex-husband was that he had *seemed* to be attracted to her for her mind instead of her more obvious assets, which thanks to a combination of stays only appeared to be about to flounce out of her bodice. That had been just one of several misconceptions she'd had about Ulvarn Rarth

Her self-confidence had taken a bad beating after the failure of her companionate marriage. To this day she wasn't sure whether Ulvarn had married her because all his friends were getting married, or because he needed an audience for his political lectures. He had certainly spent little time in her company during their decade long marriage, many times disappearing for months as he worked on "special projects" for Hadron Tharn. At the moment Sirna was more interested in personal growth than in attracting an outtime affair with a local that could only end badly.

While she brushed her hair, Sirna said, "This Founders' Day Celebration at the University of Hostigos is the last holiday until Baldar's Feast. It was nice of King Kalvan to invite the Foundry staff. And even better, Lala and Gorath Tran refuse to attend this 'barbaric spectacle' because it condones 'archaic-patriarchal customs'."

Eldra made a laugh that sounded like tinkling bells. "Yes, it is a nice gesture by the King, even if we are under his protection."

"Kalvan is more thoughtful than most men from Fourth Level Europo-American. I wonder if Prince Ptosphes and Rylla will be there?"

Sirna didn't like the twinkle she saw in Eldra's eyes as she answered.

"Ptosphes is supposed to make a token appearance, but it is common knowledge that the Queen won't be attending."

Common knowledge to whom? Sirna wondered. *Does Eldra have someone at the palace on her payroll?* "You'd better be on your best behavior tonight. Rylla might not be at the Celebration, but her eyes and ears will be."

Eldra laughed. "'Palace Intrigues and Assignations' was my minor at the University! I cut my teeth as a student at the Court of the Borgias on Fourth Level Europo-American, Imperial Italian Subsector. A glass of wine with the Borgias on Imperial Italian was as dangerous as one at Archpriest Anaxthenes' table. Did you know that it's Anaxthenes' chief mistress, Thessamona, who prepares his poisons? I learned that from the Balph Study Team's latest report."

Sirna shuddered; that poisonous Fourth Level family had become legendary at the University. In the Imperial Italian Subsector, Pope Alexander VI had managed to consolidate enough power to create a Borgia Dynasty which to this day ruled most of Italy. The poisonous atmosphere of the Borgias had infected all of Europe and spread to the New World where there were scores of competing French, Spanish and Italian city-states. Queen Elizabeth I had lost her head when the Spanish Armada landed and conquered England, returning it to the Papacy as a subject state of Spain and Rome, administered by the Spanish and their Irish allies.

If Archpriest Roxthar and his Investigation kept Anaxthenes from creating another Italian Imperial, then the mad Archpriest's life could be said to have brought about some good! It was certainly true that Kalvan's efforts to improve Aryan-Transpacific were having some unexpected and unpleasant results. None of the other Kalvan Control Time-Lines had spawned a kingdom-wide war, an Inquisition or the beginnings of a religious war.

"I thought marriage was an acceptable practice among Aryan-Transpacific priests. Is Styphon's House an exception?" Sirna asked.

"No, there's no doctrine in Styphon's Way that calls for celibacy. The First Speaker appears to be one of those men who likes multiple partners, but is emotionally unwilling to commit and can afford his own harem of concubines—not an uncommon practice among the top echelons of Styphon's House."

There was a bitter note in Eldra's voice that made Sirna wonder if the professor was speaking from experience when she talked about men who were "unwilling to commit." "What about Anaxthenes' children?"

"None that we know of, which is unusual. There are more than twenty foundling homes in Balph and more street urchins there than in any other city in Five Kingdoms. He either keeps a harem for appearances sake, or has the issues of his couplings left out in the outskirts of Balph to die."

Sirna choked back a gasp, which would have made her look unsophisticated to Eldra, a woman she greatly admired. Sirna had studied enough Outtime Sociology to be familiar with outtime practices when it came to birth control and overpopulation strategies. However, it was one thing to hear a dry lecture, and quite another to actually live on a time-line where these *peculiar* customs were practiced and taken for granted.

The only other member of the Kalvan Study Team attending the Founders' Day Celebration was Aranth Saln, who met them at the stable and drafted a proper escort from among the Foundry guards. Saln was wearing a silvered back-and-breast and a blue and red eagle feather jutting from his finely engraved high-combed morion helmet. The night sky was clear of clouds exposing ribbons of twinkling stars. For the first time since she'd arrived on

Kalvan's Time-Line, Sirna felt alive with the possibilities of life on a more primitive but vital world. She wondered if she would ever meet an outtimer as exciting as Kalvan, and what would happen if she did.

There was no reason for her not to become involved with an outtimer since she had a birth control implant. On the other hand, her emotional well-being was still fragile after the way her ex-husband had coldly abandoned her. Unlike Eldra, she found it difficult to move from one lover to another without a backward glance.

Saln was several horse-lengths ahead while their bodyguards were ranging behind. Sirna's horse riding skills had improved to the point where she no longer felt in danger of being catapulted out of her saddle, but she knew in her heart she would never feel *comfortable* while on the back of any large animal. "Eldra, how can you become intimate with a man without getting...well, involved?"

Eldra's laugh was a little too brittle to be real. "I look at men the same way I do horses. You have to take a new one out, ride him hard and see if he's worth breaking in."

"What happens if you get...say...attached to a horse unexpectedly?"

"You don't ever get attached—that's the rule, Sirna. Not if you want to be free to ride the next one." The next words, "not ever again," were almost inaudible, as Eldra spurred her horse and galloped off to join Aranth Saln.

By the time Sirna caught up, the lights from the University of Hos-Hostigos were visible. This was Sirna's first visit to the University and she found a dozen students volunteering their services to give her a guided tour. Instead, she left with a musician, a big full-bodied man with a limp and a beautiful lyre strapped to his back. His name was Gasphros and when she asked him what his function at the University was, he replied, "I'm the university bumblebee. I watch and listen, stopping at each department to pick up information and ideas, like a bee picks up pollen. Then I share my observations with the Masters of whichever department I think will find them useful. Sometimes they ignore me, but oftentimes they take my advice—and occasionally my ideas work.

"In return they give me a goblet of Ermut's brandy, or few pieces of silver. Sometimes I sing and play for my supper. When things are quiet here, I pack up and visit the Silver Stag or Crossed Halberds in Hostigos Town, tell a few tales and sing a few songs. It's a good living."

Sirna had heard from Aranth that Gasphros the Troubadour was also a spy—or intelligencer, as they called them on Aryan-Transpacific—for Duke Skranga, Kalvan's head of Hostigos Intelligence. He'd left Harphax City with Skranga when the Harphaxi constabulary started to ask too many questions.

"How did you get the limp," she asked, as they viewed the University alchemy laboratory, which was filled with rows of clay cups, green glass beakers and retorts filled with colored liquids.

"I joined the Blethan Army as a lad to escape home. I got shot in the knee with a crossbow quarrel during a rebellion in the Princedom of Artigos. The fester devils set in and I almost lost my leg. In time I recovered the use of my limb, although I still walk with a limp. What I did lose, however, was the last of my youthful idealisms about war."

He gave a deep-bodied laugh. "A few years later I left Hos-Bletha and came north to escape the army. I've sung and told tales, had every kind of adventure known to man, been to every capital city in the Six Kingdoms and a few in the Middle Kingdoms, I've wandered the Trygath and sang in the Sastragath and I hope to live long enough to make a trek to the Great Western Sea and play for the legendary Tyrants."

Sirna laughed. "It sounds like an exciting life. What are you doing in Hos-Hostigos?"

"I was staying with a young lady in Agrys City, which at that time was considered the most civilized city in the world—but only to those in the Northern Kingdoms. The most civilized city in the world has to be Xiphlon, at the mouth of the Mother River. I could tell you stories, but not now." Gasphros paused, gave her a bawdy wink before continuing, "Anyway, when I heard about the new King Kalvan and his miraculous battle against Styphon's House—a thoroughly corrupt bunch of thieves, by the way—I decided that Hostigos Town was the place for me. And I haven't regretted my decision once. This new University is the wonder of the world and is a lodestone for the most wondrous minds and learned men of every stripe. If it isn't happening in Hos-Hostigos, it isn't happening anywhere! Among his many talents it turns out that our Great King is a musician; I've learned some wonderful melodies from him—most inspiring."

Gasphros' enthusiasm was catching, and Sirna found herself in a much better mood as they returned to the Grand Hall, now a temporary ballroom. Had Gasphros not been plucked from her arm by two young girls, she might have been tempted to spend the evening with him. As it was, she was enthralled by the formal dancing to lutes, lyres and some sort of keyboard mechanism in the shape of a cooking stove. The music was pleasant and she recognized the melody *Stardust,* a Hoagy Carmichael standard that had been a hit on First Level airwaves a few decades ago. Another of Kalvan's contributions to Aryan-Transpacific's musical legacy. She was asked to dance by several young men, but she turned them down. She'd been born with two left feet and, unlike Eldra who was dancing every number, it took her ages to learn the steps and motions that made dancing enjoyable.

Then she saw the Great King dancing with Eldra, who was whispering into his ear. *You're out of your league here, Eldra!* She watched as Kalvan shook his head no and went off to talk with a man she recognized as Captain-General Harmakros.

Eldra did not take well to the role of the spurned woman; the look that crossed her face would have frightened a grizzly back into hibernation. Over in the corner the scraggly bearded Duke Skranga watched the attempted assignation play out—missing nothing. Sirna hoped she never caught his eyes; true, the bald and bandy-legged former horse-trader had a charm that defied both logic and good sense, but she'd met more than her share of seedy looking professors and knew that a good kick in the crotch—if all else failed—always restored their good sense.

At first she thought Eldra was coming over to talk with her, but instead she stepped into the open arms of Democriphon, the handsome cavalry colonel who was reported to have broken more hearts in Hostigos Town than even Skranga. The Colonel had returned from Tarr-Veblos in a funk after losing his command to Captain-General Hestophes who was still mooning over that vixen Lavena. She was surprised that he'd bothered to show up, but a few moments in Eldra's arms appeared to have restored Democriphon's good humor. The two of them, as they danced some ritualized piece that defied

Sirna's limited coordination, gazed into each other's eyes as if they'd each just discovered the perfect melody. Sirna looked around for Aranth Saln; she had a feeling she was going to be going home by herself tonight.

II

Verkan was playing catch-up, visiting his various Greffan businesses, which had been flourishing the last year, while he'd been jaunting back and forth between Home Time Line and Hostigos. He hadn't been back in Greffa for half a year and reading over the Verkan Fireseed Works ledger he was amazed at the profit it was making, which was surprising since they were practically giving fireseed away. He'd have to make sure that most of their profits were funneled back to Kalvan as part of their licensing agreement. The Verkan Fireseed Works was selling the *real* Hostigi fireseed. It wasn't his fault that most of the fireseed works that had sprung up in Greffa after Kalvan had announced the gunpowder formula had mangled the instructions! Still, most of it was better than the fireseed Styphon's House was still selling in the Middle Kingdoms, which was powdered—not corned and ground—unlike the fireseed they sold in the Five Great Kingdoms.

For centuries Styphon's House had gotten away with selling an inferior product at inflated prices. No wonder there was so little love for the Temple in Grefftscharr or any of the other Middle Kingdoms.

The goods Verkan was importing from Hostigos, as part of his cover as a pack trader, were also making money—especially the casks of Ermut's brandy. He was going to have to be careful. If he continued to amass this much local wealth, he'd soon become a target of King Theovacar. Verkan had already been targeted by the highly born but tightly-pursed nobility. A gentle knock at the door reminded him he wasn't alone.

"Come in."

His assistant Zinganna, Zinna to the locals, stuck her head in the doorway. "Your afternoon appointment is here, Trader."

"Invite him in and bring a flask of Ermut's Best." She gave him a conspiratorial wink and closed the door. Verkan took his alcodote and removed two of his finest glass goblets from the cabinet behind his hardwood desk. The Grefftscharrers were used to the local mead and ale, but distilled liquor tossed them for a loop. Kalvan's brandy was much easier to administer than a hypnomech and left no traces of First Level *contamination* for the new Greffan Study Team to worry over.

Verkan used his First Level total recall to pull up his mental file on Duke Ruffulo. Ruffulo was in his middle years, married with three children. The Duke was the oldest son of one of Theovacar's grandfather's loyalists. The Duke owned a large estate bordering on Thagnor, which explained his leanings toward Theovacar; Prince Varrack was more openly ambitious than the King. While Ruffulo was nominally an ally of Theovacar, he was reportedly no admirer. He was a man with a reputation of stern integrity and honesty, both in the Assembly of Lords and the Council of Merchants; in other words, a good man to win over to the Paratimer's side.

The Duke's estates were reportedly earning more than he was spending, and he only had one mistress, which was unusual for a noble in Grefftscharr—usually they had a dozen or more. *How much gold is he going to ask for and why?*

It was Kostran's idea to start lending money at a lesser rate than that of the local banking firms and Styphon's Great Banking House to needy nobles. He had been careful not to loan too much, between ten and a hundred ounces of gold. The kind of money a Greffan noble would likely owe to a tradesman, such as a mercer or caterer. Their terms were fair, for Middle Kingdom lenders: interest a flat ten percent—term not to exceed one year—if you put up collateral, or twenty percent if you didn't. Furthermore, Kostran let the grapevine know that the House of Verkan was willing to forgive part of a loan in exchange for political or mercantile favors.

These loans not only undercut Styphon's local influence, but also provided a source of useful intelligence since most of the nobility spent far more than they collected. After a few goblets of brandy and a small purse of gold, many of them were more than willing to talk his or Kostran's ears off.

Duke Ruffulo entered the room, his back straight as a ramrod and with eyes darting around the room as though he expected one of Styphon's fireseed devils to materialize.

"I don't bite," Verkan said in an attempt to lighten the atmosphere.

Ruffulo shook his head. "I apologize, Trader Verkan. I appear to have forgotten my manners. I've heard so many things about the esteemed Trader Verkan in the past two winters, I wasn't sure what to expect. I am Duke Ruffulo and the Warden of Fireside."

Verkan stood up and bowed. "It is a pleasure to make your acquaintance, Your Grace. I hope I haven't disappointed you."

"No, not at all. I was expecting something much more ostentatious. Your office reminds me of my own study back in Fireside."

Most of the successful traders and merchants of Greffa aped the nobility to excess; it was a common phenomenon over all the Levels wherever there were titles, including Home Time Line.

After the required exchange of pleasantries, Ruffulo got to the point of his visit. "I understand that you are able to *arrange* things."

Verkan nodded. He had "helped" a few nobles who had earned Theovacar's ire sell their property and find residences in the countryside, which they could use as boltholes, or even buy estates in Hostigos. Some of the wiser lords were beginning to realize that King Theovacar was not going to be happy until he consolidated his power over the peerage. No one was sure of who might win if it came down to open rebellion, but it didn't hurt to have a hideaway in case events turned in the King's favor.

"I also understand that your word of honor can be trusted."

Verkan nodded, wondering to whom Ruffulo had been talking.

"I recently had an audience with the King. He has charged me with a mission that may well cost me my life, if discovered, and will make me many enemies whether found out or not."

"How can I help, Lord Ruffulo?"

"I will entrust you with ten thousand ounces of gold, which I would like for you to invest for me outside of Grefftscharr. I also have another five hundred ounces of gold for the purchase of a small estate in Dorg. Here is my draft on the Greffan Trader's Bank."

Verkan took the large parchment, which had the seal of the Greffan Trader's Bank. "Many lords are buying estates in Hos-Hostigos. They are inexpensive due to the war—"

"I'm not worried about cost, I want a refuge for my family in case something dire happens to me. However, I don't want to take them out of the raven's beak and drop them into the panther's mouth!"

Verkan nodded, wondering whether the other lords and merchant princes of Greffa shared Ruffulo's dismal view of Kalvan's plight. He'd put Kostran on it in the morning; maybe they knew something the Paratimers didn't. "I will do as you ask, Duke Ruffulo."

"Thank you, Trader. In return, I will pay you a thousand ounces of gold and should the event that I fear take place, I will give you the deed to Fireside."

"But I'm not buying—"

"I know, but if 'people' believe that I have taken loans out from the House of Verkan it will not only explain my visit, but lead them to the conclusion that I am doing less well than they had formerly believed. I will trust in your honor to see that any money realized from Fireside's sale will be held in escrow for my family to do with as they see fit. Less your usual commission—ten percent, I've been told."

"That is correct. You have my oath, Duke Ruffulo." *Nothing wrong with Ruffulo's brain matter,* thought Verkan. It would also allow Verkan to take possession in the event of a Throne takeover and stop Royal confiscation of the Duke's estate.

"I will have your property and possessions assessed. Should some unforeseen calamity happen to yourself, I will see that you are compensated at your new estate—or, in the event you are unable to join them, your family is well-provided for."

For the first time since his arrival, the Duke smiled. "I can see my information regarding your wits was not exaggerated." He picked up the goblet and took a sip. "I can also see that the potency of Ermut's Best was also not over-rated. May both our Houses prosper!"

EIGHT

I

A cloud of dust on the far horizon usually meant a herd of buffalo or cattle were moving across the Sea of Grass. Today Arch-Stratego Zarphu knew it was neither; it was the advancing Grefftscharrer Army. His scouts had already told him the disposition of the enemy army: six thousand infantry, mostly carrying long spears and firesticks, four thousand heavy cavalry and two thousand light auxiliaries, mostly Ruthani cavalry recruited from the grass-lands. He told one of his orderlies to fetch the Highpriest.

Highpriest Arkemanes rode quickly to his side in a very soldierly and un-priestly manner of which he heartily approved. "I see the enemy is closing."

Zarphu ignored the snorts of disapproval from his senior officers; he knew the difference between priests and soldiers even if his officers didn't. "This is not an ideal place for a battle." He paused to indicate the flatlands on all sides. "Nor is it a good place for an ambush."

The Highpriest, who no longer wore his yellow robes, nodded. "If we can defeat the Grefftscharrer Army here, we can perform both a service to Styphon and a disservice to the Usurper Kalvan. The Kings of Grefftscharr only rule as long as they show enough strength to cow both their under-lords and the powerful merchants of Greffa. It has been rumored that arms have been shipped from Greffa to the false kingdom of Hostigos. A win here will be the first victory of next year's campaign!"

Zarphu was impressed with the priest's knowledge of things other than arcane rites and rituals of his trade and wondered if he had served in a military order before putting on his robes. He had learned from the fat merchant, that Styphon's House had two military arms of its own. Zarphu had tried to question Arkemanes about his past; he might have had better success with a stone, could any be found on this endless grassland.

Zarphu was not as convinced as the priest that his army—though greater in size—would be able to seize the battlefield. His knowledge of the enemy was negligible and his own army had no experience fighting against the firesticks. The Highpriest had demonstrated the noisy and smelly "muskets" and they had proved to be capricious. The fireseed had to be dry or they would not fire. However, the muskets were deadly when fired—if they hit their target. Unlike his archers, who could hit the eye socket of an approaching enemy from a hundred paces.

His soldiers were all experienced troops—fourteen maniples of a thousand men each, eight of horse and six of foot soldiers. Plus, two maniples of the Lord Tyrant's own Immortals—heavy armored cavalry who fought with spear and broadsword.

Zarphu turned to Stratego Lyphar and ordered, "The enemy is two marches away. When they are one march, have the foot archers and skirmishers run ahead and engage the enemy. They are not to hold, but fall back and draw the enemy in."

He turned to another general and ordered him to support Lyphar's foot with his light cavalry, mostly horse archers and javelin throwers. Then he addressed Highpriest Arkemanes. "I would have taken the river route that my scouts recommended, but I also thought it might be best to test the mettle of the Eastern ironmen."

Arkemanes looked over in surprise, and even had the grace to blush. It was the first time Zarphu had read any emotion on the priest's face. If these priestly troops of Styphon's were not soldiers at arms, they were soldiers of the heart.

"You must remember Highpriest, our records go back almost two thousand winters. We have traversed these lands and trails more times than there are nomads upon the Sea of Grass. While it is true that trade between us and the Middle Kingdoms has dwindled to a trickle, there are still those among us who trade along the old routes. Several of these are among our scouts. I am as anxious as you are to see how well my men hold against the firesticks. However, I suspect you will be the more surprised."

It was also true that Zarphu sounded more confident about his troops than he felt. His people had heard stories about these fire weapons for centuries, and had obtained more than a few over the years of trading. However, as long as the fireseed was scarce, they were more curiosities than real weapons. One of the former traders had told him that the fireseed mystery was no longer a secret. If this were true, he would take back more than gold from these distant lands. With the firesticks, the Lord Tyrant would be able to complete his conquest of the city-states and expand his reach into the Sea of Grass and maybe even farther.

The light foot soldiers began to run forward and the heavy infantry, with full body shields and long spears, went into double time. The massed heavy cavalry followed to exploit any breaks in the enemy lines. If all went well, the archers and javelin throwers would sting the enemy army, bringing forth the more impetuous cavalry and foot. Then the skirmishers would retreat behind the shield wall and the slaughter would commence; at least that was how it was done in the homelands. Nothing was certain against an unknown enemy—except uncertainty.

II

Prince Varrack, purple plumes jutting out from the back of his burgonet, pointed to the growing mass of men, the sun sparking off their armor, in the distance. "There are the Ros-Zarthani barbarians. We shall ride over them just as the buffalo herds trample the Ruthani tent cities!"

"Your Lordship, I suggest we move to the rear just in case a stray spear comes our way," one of the Barons suggested. "Let the professional soldiers do their work."

"There will be few casualties today, my friend." Prince Varrack said, slapping the Baron on the back with his gauntleted hand. The nobleman, who wore no more armor than a silvered breastplate over his red and black velvet doublet, staggered forward, almost falling off his mount. When he had regained his poise, he gave Varrack a pained expression. "My back hurts!"

Varrack had to choke back a laugh. Such weakness was all too typical of Greffa's decadent nobility. Many of them wore more perfume than his courtesans. *This will all change after the vile dog Theovacar is put in his place. I will return the Middle Kingdoms to their past glory, with Thagnor the king of cities. And, it all begins today with my crushing defeat of these barbarians.*

Another noble, this one with a cultivated lisp, announced, "Please, let us stay at the front, Varrack, so we can watch these creatures die up close!"

A young Count, with a wispy blond beard, cried, "This is so much better than one of Theovacar's Spectacles. One grows tired of pantomime sea battles and bear fights."

Captain-General Errock said with gritted teeth, "Your Lordship, my men need to prepare for battle. We will be hampered if we have to spend our time protecting your guests." The way he stepped on the last word left no doubt about his own feelings concerning the martial ability of Grefftscharrer nobles in general.

"We shall retire, Captain-General. It is your job to win this battle." Under his breath, Prince Varrack added, "And win me the glory I need to challenge Theovacar in his own city."

III

The battle opened almost like a scroll-written exercise out of Arch-Stratego Zarphu's library. It appeared the Grefftscharrer soldiers held his army in contempt, allowing their own front ranks to break as they attempted to chase down the annoying skirmishers. The archers and spearmen quickly pulled back behind the now stationary shield wall and—once the enemy was within bow range—began to fire at will. Several hundred disorganized enemy light cavalry ran into the shield wall; many of them were impaled on spears or shot out of their saddles by arrows. When an enemy fell, a skirmisher would rush from behind the shields and dispatch him with a quick sword thrust.

When enemy cavalry advanced to the shield wall, the surviving skirmishers and light cavalry moved to the wings. Meanwhile the enemy foot soldiers marched forward, setting their long spears and firesticks. The archers continued their steady stream of arrows, with gratifying results as the enemy was forced to close ranks and recoil. With the Grefftscharrer cavalry retreating, they were unable to cover their own advancing infantry. The archers and spearmen killed scores of recoiling of Grefftscharrers, since only the front ranks of their cavalry wore full armor.

The enemy horse, for the most part, retreated to the wings, revealing a large body of firestick men and others carrying short bows with stocks. Suddenly, the firesticks crackled and sputtered, and a cloud of smoke with the stink of brimstone filled the air.

A noise like thunder hammered Zarphu's ears! For a moment he thought his horse would buck him off its back. Several of his officers were thrown, but most quickly re-mounted. For a few moments there were holes in the shield wall, and the entire line buckled, until the rear ranks moved up. Only a few men broke ranks and they were cut down by the swords of their comrades. It appeared to Zarphu that most of the firesticks' force was spent on the shields. Their flight of answering arrows inflicted heavy casualties among the unprotected Grefftscharrer infantry, especially the firestick men who were not wearing steel chest plates.

The firestick men fired several more times, but the shield wall held. The enemy's own lines continued to take casualties from bow fire and javelins.

Out of the cloud of smoke a large body of enemy horse, mostly armored, rushed forward slamming into shield wall. Again the wall held, while the spears points spitted horses that screamed and bucked off their riders. Skirmishers rushed forward with long knives to slash vulnerable horse bellies and the throats of the fallen horsemen. The stalled enemy cavalry milled in front of the shield wall, futilely hacking at it with their swords or firing short firesticks, until their commanders ordered a retreat. When their surviving cavalry were back behind their own lines, the firestick men fired off their firesticks in unison.

One of his chief officers dropped off his saddle, sprouting a red hole just above his left eye. Zarphu cursed and wondered how many more irreplaceable troops he would lose in this battle.

The infantry battle continued, with their arrows inflicting three times as many casualties as the firesticks. The enemy infantry began to bunch up even tighter and the slaughter mounted. The Grefftscharrer foot became bunched together so closely that the enemy cavalry were forced to fight along the wings, where they were sternly rebuffed by the Immortals. Zarphu decided it was time to order forth his own heavy horse.

The horns sounded, and the infantry pulled back into orderly lines. The iron-scaled cataphracti moved forward through the infantry, while the shield wall reformed behind them.

The three maniples of plumbati lead the cavalry until they were within range of the enemy, then took out their heavy darts, casting them into the massed infantry. The enemy infantry were momentarily paralyzed, then forced together so closely that only a few of the firestick men could shoot their weapons. The archers ran forward again, supported by horse archers and began firing point blank into the massed Grefftscharrer foot. The slaughter was horrific, with many of the enemy's long spearmen casting their weapons aside and trying to break rank—only to find there was nowhere to go. The ground ran with streams of the enemy's blood.

The plumbati pulled out their swords and cut their way through the ranks. Suddenly the entire body of enemy foot broke ranks, trampling those who stood in their way. The heavy spearmen now moved forward, cutting and slicing those left behind by the forward movement of the heavy cavalry. The enemy cavalry, spurred by the sight of their own retreating foot, rode over and through their own ranks to reach the plumbati—and died by the score.

Zarphu nodded and another horn sounded. Both left and right wings of heavy cavalry moved out in a flanking pincers movement to surround the enemy army. He was sorely disappointed when the enemy horns suddenly rang out, and the Grefftscharrer horse turned and retreated, leaving behind several thousand foot soldiers. The enemy horse reformed ranks before the wings could close, but the plumbati struck them hard from the rear.

The Grefftscharrer infantry were completely surrounded and disordered; the battlefield was littered with their brightly colored corpses. The cavalry reformed to chase the enemy horse, which fled so hurriedly they even left behind their wounded.

Seeing their own cavalry flee, the Grefftscharrer foot surrendered, putting their helmets upon their swords. The survivors numbered less than half of those who had joined the battle. Zarphu rubbed his hands—a nice ransom.

Highpriest Arkemanes, too, had a big smile. He nodded, saying, "I am impressed, Arch-Stratego." They both watched as the enemy horse, under withering fire, left in a massed but orderly retreat. "Are you going to ride them down?"

"We could grind them into the dust, but they are not cowards. We would take unnecessary losses. Also, another army lies in wait some forty marches away. There is no profit in goading them to attack. Better to let them hide behind their walls and lick their wounds, Highpriest. They will not forget us soon. We have other more important battles to win. And there will be no reinforcements."

"Wisely put," the Highpriest said. "I think many will be surprised by the Iron Men from across the Sea of Grass. None more so than the Usurper Kalvan!"

IV

"What happened to my army?" Prince Varrack cried when Captain-General Errock pulled up alongside, his horse breathing like a bellows.

The Captain-General's face was white and there was blood splattered across his breastplate. "A lot of good men died because we under-estimated the enemy. It's a miracle the Ros-Zarthani didn't decide to chase us to the City walls."

"This is good fortune?" Varrack screamed, looking around at the ragtag collection of horsemen that surrounded him, their finery soiled and their plumed helmets discarded. "We have lost a great battle, and you talk of luck!"

"We will be laughed out of the City," one of the Barons cried.

Varrack punched the Baron in the face with his armored hand, knocking him off his horse and onto the ground, where he was stretched out frozen as if he'd been poleaxed.

"You've killed him, Varrack!" the young Count cried. "This day has been a disaster for all of us."

Except Theovacar, thought Varrack, *who right this moment is laughing himself off his throne!* He ground his teeth until they squealed. *If we'd had King Theovacar's support, this defeat would never have happened. He withheld his soldiers to play us as fools! This disaster is his fault. Theovacar is in the pay of the Usurper Kalvan, as the priests of Styphon's House claim otherwise he would have helped us take the field. Yes, this disaster is the result of Theovacar's treason! Wait until the City learns of it.*

NINE

Kalvan woke with the suspicion that siege bombards were going off beside one of his ears. For the moment, he couldn't decide whether it was the left ear or the right ear.

Finally he decided it was both ears. He groaned and pulled the bearskin coverlet over his head. This movement made the bombards fire salvoes. It also made Kalvan realize that they were inside his ears.

A memory returned—he had been sitting on a bench, watching the All-mother Fires with a jug of wine (a whole jug, not a cup) in one hand and the other arm around a woman. He knew where the wine had gone. *Where's the woman? And who is she?*

Half-remembered fragments of a production of *Midsummer Night's Dream* that he'd seen on stage at the Walnut Stage Theatre in Philadelphia ran through his mind; for a moment, he wondered if some confused here-and-now Puck had turned him into a donkey, because he sure felt like a jackass!

Meanwhile, if it didn't involve too much movement, he could do something about the hangover. Uncle Wolf Tharses had a poultice, which in combination with sassafras tea made a decent headache remedy. Closing his eyes and gritting his teeth, Kalvan reached for the bell pull.

Instead, his hand encountered proof that he wasn't alone in bed. What's more, proof that his companion was definitely female!

Kalvan's gritted teeth couldn't stifle a groan, more of disgust than pain this time. Well, now he knew what had happened to the woman he'd been drinking with. He also knew what would happen to the tattered remains of his marriage, the minute Rylla found out.

Rylla would have right on her side, too—not just her pride. Kings who shared beds with random women were likely to sire bastards. To a precariously seated Great King, a flock of royal bastards would be a real liability. Few of them would turn out to be worthy of admiration, as was Harmakros' son, Aspasthar—

That's what started this nightmare, he remembered. Last night had been Aspasthar's adoption ceremony. Harmakros and Ptosphes had seemed determined to get him drunk on winter wine.

He heard a stifled groan from beneath the bed cover. Kalvan slowly pulled down the bearskin for a look. A thatch of golden blond hair that could only be Rylla's met his eyes. *Dralm be praised!* it wasn't that Greffan vixen from the Foundry—what's her name…Eldra, who'd been making eyes at him and whispered an immodest proposal—at the Founder's Celebration. But how had he ended up in his own bed?

It was months after his return from Hos-Rathon, and many more since they'd fought in the Sastragath, and in all that time neither he nor Rylla had shared a bed—or anything else for that matter.

Yes, the adoption ceremony. Those rascals! Rylla had been there too!

Harmakros had asked her to be Aspasthar's godmother—a custom he had accused Harmakros of inventing on the spot. Then Kalvan vaguely recalled apologizing—for what? —to Rylla, and then taking her weeping in his arms. Shortly afterwards they had both retired to the royal bedchambers….

Rylla had been as drunk as he was. Had to have been. Yes, he saw the hands of *at least* two meddlers in this stirring of the royal stew. *Now what? Should he slip out of the bedchamber before Rylla awakened, so they could both pretend this had never happened? Or should he stay and try to resolve this mess that threatened not only their marriage but the entire realm?*

Kalvan groaned as his head pounded again. Rylla stirred. One lovely arm groped out from under the blankets and pinned Kalvan's hand in place. Sometimes he forgot just how strong she was.

"Kalvan, are you made of iron?"

"Rylla?"

"Or were you expecting somebody else?" Kalvan could hear ice tinkling in those words.

"I was praying it wouldn't be anyone else." He was too hung over to come up with any good lies.

"Are you trying to tell me that you've been faithful ever since your return?"

"Since it's the truth, why shouldn't I tell it?"

"All that time at the Foundry? I know about those Grefftscharri girls and their ways."

"You weren't making our home a very pleasant place, Rylla."

Kalvan felt her arm go rigid as a steel bar. "Well, you made your homecoming something I'm still trying to forget."

"Maybe if you don't forget it, you won't do something stupid like that Dralm-damned invasion of Phaxos again!" Kalvan took several deep breaths and sighed. "I'm sorry, darling. That was not only unnecessary, but unkind."

A long silence, a faint ghost of Rylla's usual hearty laughter. "I'll admit that last night you didn't behave like a man who's found other women." Rylla's head was now on the pillow, blonde hair streaming every which way, eyes red and bleary, her face slowly turning the same color.

Royal dignity demanded that he make a peace offering sitting up. The royal hangover demanded that he stay down. Kalvan finally compromised by raising himself slightly higher on the pillows on his elbows. Rylla did the same, so that the blankets slipped down from her freckled bare shoulders.

Kalvan had the chilling thought that last night he would have gone to bed with any willing woman, and thanked Dralm it had turned out to be Rylla. *No, thank Ptosphes and Harmakros.* His memories of their hauling him up the stairs after he was too drunk to climb them by himself returned; now, it was his turn to flush.

Still, it had all worked out, if not for the best, at least, without doing any more harm.

"And besides, Rylla, you're the most beautiful woman in Hostigos, so what made you think I'd have the bad taste to be unfaithful?"

The smile, like the laugh, was a ghost of its usual self. But some of the old Rylla was still there. Time to see if a peace treaty could bring the rest of it back.

"Rylla, the damage done by your invasion of Phaxos won't be undone. I should have realized that when I came home and said—well, things I shouldn't have said. I went ahead and said them, and now our marriage is—was—almost as dead as the Phaxi Princely House. Our being divided is a gift to Styphon's House. Will you join me in not making us separated anymore?"

The silence this time seemed to last long enough for a man to ride to Ktemnos City with a side trip to Balph on the way. Part of that was the hangover, but Kalvan wouldn't even contemplate servants in the chamber until he had his answer, whatever it might be...?

"Yes." She gripped his hand more tightly. "I won't promise to always take your advice, Kalvan. But by Dralm, Galzar, and Yirtta Allmother, I promise to ask for it. And, I'll even admit, I shouldn't have gone against your wishes—not that I won't do it again—if necessary!"

That was as close to an apology that Kalvan would ever hear out of those lovely lips. Somehow he managed to find the strength to bend over and kiss her on the forehead, which left him so exhausted that it was Rylla who finally pulled the bell cord.

After tea and toast, they held one of their bedroom councils. Neither of them felt quite up to dressing and unfolding a map, but they'd both nearly memorized the Harphaxi frontier. There, clearly, the decisive battle of the next campaign would be fought.

"Well, you certainly took care of the Phaxi problem once and for all."

"I just couldn't stand by and let Araxes continue to defy *our* sovereignty any longer!"

Kalvan bit down on the groan that was about to escape from his lips. "I know, I know. At least, that's one subject we won't argue over again."

"And you did shut the back door against the Knights," Rylla hastily added. "Thank Dralm and Galzar for that. If the Order wants to come against us next year, they'll have to come through Harphax. And Great King Lysandros is no man to give Soton a free passage."

"Not the way he's grooming his Captain-General," Kalvan said. "Maybe Phidestros and Soton will be too busy quarreling to fight us."

"I'm not sure I'd count on that," Rylla answered. "From what Skranga has told me, Great King Lysandros has hocked his lands, his kingdom and his younger sister's trousseau to Styphon's House."

"I'll pray that they do quarrel. I'll even ask a few of Sargos' tame shamans to chant spells. But what I really think I ought to do is visit Agrys City and talk some sense into the League of Dralm. Duke Mnestros will stand behind me."

"Kalvan, no! The Kingdom needs you. Besides, what's to ensure your safety in Demistophon's lands?"

"Great King Demistophon isn't a fool. He knows such treachery would give the League a perfect excuse to turn against him. The ones who aren't against him already, that is. Remember all the Agrysi princes in the League of Dralm."

"I haven't forgotten them, Kalvan. I also haven't forgotten that Great King Demistophon has the shortest temper of any Great King since Pytros the Iron King. Or that he sent an army twelve thousand strong to fight us last summer. If you entered his lands with enough men to keep you safe, he'd suspect it was an invasion. If you kept your guard small to reassure him, you couldn't protect yourself against the Styphon's House's agents. Great King Demistophon and the Archpriests of the Inner Circle wouldn't care who was angry with them, if *you* were dead. It wouldn't matter."

"I suppose not. But—does this mean *you're* not going to be risking your neck in the next battle?"

"The man who fought hand-to-hand with Warlord Sargos in the Battle of Spirit Grove asks that question?" Rylla's laugh was practically back to normal. "An army needs inspiration. You can't give it to them by leading from the back. That silly bunch of old priests in Agrys City needs something that neither kings nor captains can give them."

A firm backbone, Kalvan decided. "I'd counted on Xentos supporting our position in Agrys City. But I underestimated his own ambitions—or, worse yet, his piety."

Rylla looked as if she were holding back tears. "Xentos is no longer the man I grew up with and thought I knew. He believes in his god, maybe too much—"

"Oh, he's sincere, I'll grant him that. But right now hypocrites like Skranga and Baron Zothnes are more useful."

This time Rylla laughed out loud. Kalvan's head still ached too much to let him do the same, but he smiled. There was still a distance between him and Rylla that hadn't been there before. Maybe now, for the first time since his return to Hos-Hostigos, he felt it was no longer too great a distance to cross, with time and love.

TEN

I

Warntha Saln was sitting by the campfire drinking the piss-water the Ros-Zarthani called beer and discussing close-order tactics with an under officer of the 4th Maniple when he felt the vibration from his locater alert. He quickly excused himself from the conversation, using the time-tested excuse of going to the latrine. Instead of going straight to the trenches, Warntha swung around to the northwest where his locater indicated, through increasing vibrations, where the homing signal was originating.

Warntha spotted the silver mesh of the twenty-foot Transtemporal conveyer in a small glade. He had been wondering when Hadron Tharn was going to send someone to pick him up. After their defeat of the Grefftscharrer force, the Ros-Zarthani army had followed the trail to Dorg where water transport was being arranged to ferry the army down river south of Wulfula to Tarr-Ceros, where they would winter. The Dorgi had refused transit down the river until their defeat of the Grefftscharrer army. Now the Dorgers couldn't get the Ros-Zarthani out of their territory on their way fast enough.

Warntha wouldn't have minded staying with the Ros-Zarthani; the company was good—mostly fellow soldiers who had accepted him as one of their own despite his disguise as one of Styphon's highpriests. The possibilities for future fighting seemed endless, so he was content. He was especially looking forward to fighting against Kalvan and his Army of Hos-Hostigos.

On the other hand, things were never dull when Hadron Tharn was around. Warntha was surprised to find he actually missed his crazy boss.

The conveyer door opened to show Tharn with a welcoming smile, flanked by two guards in the black uniforms. "How was your exercise?"

Warntha took a seat inside the conveyer across from his boss and said, "It was a nice vacation. The Ros-Zarthani soldiers are good troops, even without gunpowder weapons. They'll give Kalvan fits, although not enough to be decisive."

Tharn's face changed from welcoming to anger in the blink of an eye. "None of my plans are working. I'm hemmed in on every side by morons and incompetents! The Opposition Party has refused my latest contribution! They claim that Chief Verkan's new policy of phased withdrawal from the Europo-American Sector is workable and acceptable by all parties. So Verkan wins once again!"

Warntha was used to his boss' sudden mood shifts, but this one took him by surprise. He wasn't exactly sure why his boss hated Paratime Chief Verkan Vall, but he suspected it had something to do with his sister Dalla. "So what's our next move, boss?"

"A visit to Fifth Level Base One."

Warntha, as an ex-military specialist, had originally been recruited by Tharn's Organization to help train troops at the Base, mostly proles being trained for military action groups. This had been going on for a decade and Tharn had created quite the private little army. The proles thought Hadron Tharn was a big supporter of the Prole Liberation Movement, the radical branch of the Prole Protection League. Warntha, knowing Tharn's prejudices, seriously doubted that; his boss looked upon proles as little better than beasts of burden. Warntha still didn't know Tharn's plan, but he knew whatever his boss's plans for the proles, they were not going to be in their favor.

Warntha had just finished cleaning his kit when the overhead flickering ceased and the silver mesh began to solidify overhead signifying they had arrived at Fifth Level Base One. The conveyer came to rest in a small room; from there they went aboard a rocket transport which whisked them off to a large island, at the base of the largest southern continental mass. On most time-lines the island served the First Level population as a recreation spot—meaning there was little possibility of a Paratime Police conveyer dropping in unexpectedly.

From there they took an aircar to Base One. Warntha, who was dressed warmly for a higher latitude, felt himself begin to sweat as the aircar arrived at the large military compound. It took a great deal of Tharn's assets to keep this place and the other three bases running, but he had six airstrike teams and fifteen divisions of infantry for his own personal army. To the best of Warntha's knowledge, it was a bigger force than Home Time Line's own military, which primarily existed to put down prole insurrections. The two guards remained in the conveyer.

He followed Tharn into a large conference room with a large visiplate dominating one wall. A dozen proles in military uniforms decorated with gold braid sat around a table. They all stood up as Tharn approached.

"Citizen Tharn, when can we mount our attack?"

"General, the time has not yet arrived. There is still work that needs to be done on Home Time Line. I advise patience."

Warntha choked back a laugh. Hearing Tharn advise patience was like hearing someone advise a friend to take a vacation on Second Level Arzl Dykx, a subsector where the survivors of an ancient nuclear holocaust killed each other for table scraps.

One of the other generals, an older man with a gray beard, said, "With your long life, Citizen, you can afford to wait. I was a young man when I joined the Prole Protection League. Look at me now thirty years later, I'm still waiting for them to do something!"

The other proles nodded their agreement.

"If all goes as planned, you will all get the longevity treatments and you and your children will live a long life indeed."

This promise appeared to settle them down and the generals went back to the business of plotting the overthrow of Fifth Level Force Headquarters.

As a veteran of the Home Force, Warntha knew that the Fifth Level HQ would have to be taken by surprise for this band of half-trained and inexperienced resistance fighters to take them out. *What kind of surprise attack does Tharn have planned?* he wondered. *By definition, as a Hadron Tharn plan, it would be irregular, dangerous and with total disregard to casualties.* He almost felt sorry for the proles.

II

As he and his bodyguard made their way over the narrow cobblestone streets of Harphax City, Captain-General Phidestros was surprised by the large number of gawking onlookers and the occasional applause that greeted their party, which was flying the red and yellow Royal banner of Hos-Harphax and the Iron Band standard. The morale in Harphax was a far cry from that of a year ago, when prosperous merchants and guildsmen were leaving the city in droves for fear of a Hostigi siege train.

The buildings at the center of town were mostly two and three-story white plaster storefronts, but as they drew closer to the city walls these were replaced by ramshackle wood and plaster tenements, timbered warehouses and an occasional stone factory. One of the largest of these factories was their destination, the Royal Artillery Works. The streets were filled with wagons and carriages; it appeared that Styphon's gold had finally brought prosperity to the capital city.

At the Royal Artillery Works Phidestros' ears were greeted by the din of banging hammers, screeching metal and yelling men. He dismounted and walked over to General Kyblannos, formerly head of the Iron Band and now the commander of the Harphaxi Royal Artillery. They touched palms and Kyblannos mouthed, "Follow me" and led him into the cavernous building. As two commanders entered the building, the artisans and helpers who saw them stopped working and they were able to hear each other over the roar of the forges.

"Welcome to my killing ground, Cap'n," Kyblannos said, looking for all the world like a proud father.

Phidestros shook his head. "This is too close to Hadron's realm for my liking."

Kyblannos laughed. He pointed at a brass gun, lying on its side next to a wooden carriage. "This is one of the eight-pounders you brought back from Tarr-Veblos. We're working on some Kalvan-style carriages to mount it on. What's interesting is that it's a Zygrosi cast gun," he pointed to a small proof mark, "but this mark is Hostigi—a keystone, Kalvan's device. Conclusive proof that Kalvan has a band of Zygrosi foundry workers working at the Usurper's Foundry in Hostigos."

"We knew that from our intelligencers, but this proof mark would convince even my father!" Phidestros exclaimed. "It's the Trickster's Own Luck that during your excursion into Hostigos you were unable to capture the Hostigi Artillery train."

"We had a limit on how many men and equipment we could smuggle into Nostor, Cap'n. The countryside is still recovering from the war, but Prince Pheblon has outriders everywhere. Who expected a troop of Hostigi regulars to be escorting the artillery train?"

"Don't fret, Kyblannos, you did well. Leaving the dead behind in Phaxi uniforms was a bit of genius. The Hostigi blamed the entire raid on Prince Araxes who died protesting his innocence." They both laughed, as no one had liked that cowardly fencesitter.

"If Queen Rylla hadn't been so anxious to blame Araxes, things wouldn't have turned out so well," Phidestros said.

"Again, the Lykros' Own Luck, Cap'n. And it didn't hurt that you took full advantage by capturing Tarr-Veblos. Did you ever tell Lysandros or Soton the truth about our raid into Nostor?"

"No. It's our little secret. If word got out, and the Electors of Harphax ever learned that they had been had, well, Great King Lysandros would have turkey feathers in his beard! And you know who he'd take his ire out on."

The artilleryman nodded knowingly.

"So what is it you want to show me?"

Kyblannos took him over to look at a new Harphaxi gun already mounted on one of the Kalvan-style carriages.

"Small isn't it?" Phidestros said, examining the iron tube surrounded by hammered hoops, or metal rings, to give it more strength. As Kyblannos had told him more than once, when the hoops cooled they contracted until they were actually crushing the barrel to a slight degree. This counteracted the tendency of the barrels to come apart when the fireseed charge exploded.

"It's based on one of Kalvan's small mobile guns that the Red Hand captured at Tenabra." Kyblannos pointed to a cannon already mounted on a carriage beside it. "This is the Hostigi gun. Can you tell any difference?"

Phidestros shook his head from side to side.

Kyblannos then pointed to a gun beside it that was bulkier and obviously larger. "This is one of our guns of the same bore. It has noticeably more heft than the Kalvan designed gun." Kyblannos turned back to the Hostigi gun, and said, "I went over it for days until I learned its every secret." He bent over to pat the breech as if it were a favorite dog. "Can you see the difference between Kalvan's gun and our new one?"

"Identical."

"In rough appearance; however, not only are they lighter than the old eight-pounders, Cap'n, but the gun typically only needs four horses to pull it, instead of six, Bless Galzar! This is what gives Kalvan's artillery its mobility."

"Why doesn't Kalvan make the guns even smaller, maybe four-pounders? Then he could use two horses instead of four."

"For a very good reason. It's been my experience with small guns, like four-pounders, that after a few rounds the metal gets so hot that the gun will 'cook off' any fireseed placed in it. I'm sure Kalvan took that into consideration."

Then he led Phidestros over to the corner of the Artillery Works. "See this brass gun?"

"Yes. It's a Zygrosi gun. Only the Zygrosi make brass guns in the Five Kingdoms. Where did it come from?"

"More battle spoils from Tarr-Veblos."

Phidestros nodded, wishing he'd spent more time on the artillery field. The differences between the Zygrosi brass cast gun and the Harphaxi cannon was immediately obvious. Besides being made of brass, the muzzle was thinner and there were no metal rings.

"I don't recall seeing any Zygrosi guns that look like this one. Is this another of Kalvan's designs?" Phidestros asked.

"Yes. The Kalvan gun has much less metal on the muzzle end, which makes it lighter and easier to handle, yet it has even more metal around the breech so that it will take a double charge." He banged on the brass barrel with a hammer, which pinged nicely over the bellows. "That means it will take a double charge of Styphon's fireseed, or a full charge of Kalvan's fireseed formula."

Phidestros nodded. "Remember that gunner who tried to use some Hostigi fireseed in his twelve-pounder at Tarr-Harphax?"

Kyblannos grinned. "They're still finding shards of that gun and the artilleryman's teeth in the outer bailey."

They both chuckled.

"Fortunately," Kyblannos continued, "we've got wagonloads of Styphon's fireseed to burn in our older guns."

"Good, but at some point we're going to have to get better guns or concede the artillery advantage to Kalvan."

"Right, Cap'n. I've got some plans, but it'll take time. And I was wondering if you could use some of those Zygrosi connections of yours to get us some pattern makers and brass casters, so we can cast some of our own cannon."

"I thought you'd already have figured out how to cast your own."

Kyblannos ran his fingers through his curly helmet of gray-streaked brown hair. "I have lots of ideas, but what I don't have is the time to make the molds, train pattern makers and determine the right mixture of copper and zinc for the molten brass. We can cast more guns if you hire Zygrosi brass casters and put them to work, while I spend my time working on the trunnions and gun carriages."

Phidestros reached into his belt pouch to take out his pipe, remembered where he was and quickly removed his hand. "I wish I could help. One problem is that I'm not *recognized* in my birth land. Furthermore, the Zygrosi brass casters who know how to cast hundreds of pounds of brass have never been numerous, not with the shortage of fireseed in Hos-Zygros. Remember how stingy Styphon's House was with fireseed until Kalvan gave away the secret to the Fireseed Mystery. Now, with the fireseed mixture common knowledge, brass founders who can cast guns are worth their weight in gold—and they know it."

Kyblannos nodded. "In Hos-Harphax and Hos-Agrys we've had more fireseed, but never enough to burn wastefully on big guns, so the cannons have kept to the same design for centuries. Until Kalvan."

Phidestros nodded. "Styphon's House has never liked change, but it's unlikely the fireseed mystery will disappear when Kalvan's defeated. Soon every town will have its own fireseed mill, and Styphon's House will go back to healing the sick—if they remember how!"

Kyblannos laughed. "Styphon's House, a plague on it! I've been hearing stories about an Investigation in Balph—and not just of commoners, but highpriests as well!"

"This Investigation is widely known. Even Soton recognized it, but not happily. This rogue Archpriest Roxthar is trying to purge Styphon's House of unbelievers!"

They both roared with laughter, enough that the artillerymen around them gave them funny looks. Kyblannos added, "The streets are full of talk of his Investigation! The Ktemnoi merchants in town talk of nothing else. Has Roxthar actually found any Styphoni faithful?"

"No. He'd have better luck finding a virgin at the One-Eyed Boar!"

They both hooted. When he caught his breath, Phidestros said, "It is wise to watch what your tongue says regarding Styphon, when among strangers. Great King Lysandros appears to be one of the faithful—don't laugh! If he isn't, he gives a very good imitation, attending all manner of Temple rituals and services. Fortunately, being sworn to Galzar means I have no business being dragged to Styphon's House's tedious services. Still, I have to show proper respect to Styphon's images and highpriests."

Kyblannos gave him a look that said better you than me. In a low voice, he added, "By Tranth's Hammer and Galzar's Mace, we live in strange times, when captain-generals are judged by their respect for some piss-ant god!"

"By Galzar's Mace, you speak true words. Soton also warned me that Roxthar wants to join the force against Kalvan—"

"What! So those bedsheet butchers can torture peasants and farm girls?"

Phidestros shook his head. "It's madness, and bad for morale besides. If Styphon's House's paychests weren't paying for the army, I might put my sword into it. It appears Archpriest Roxthar is afraid that the Kalvan heresy might infect the rest of the Northern Kingdoms if not stamped out completely in Hos-Hostigos. I wonder if the lands Lysandros has promised me upon our victory may turn out to be as barren, after this Roxthar's passage, as Regwarn's Caverns of the Dead."

Kyblannos nodded soberly. "In the grog shops it is said that even the Inner Circle fears the Investigation."

"Yes, if Grand Master Soton is worried, the Temple must be quaking right to its very foundation!"

"Then it is up to us to avoid all appearance of heresy."

"Right," Phidestros answered, "which means not mentioning the name Kalvan in association with your new carriages."

Kyblannos spat on the floor. "This is a Dralm-damned funny way to fight a war."

"I agree. Is there anything else you want to show me before I return to Tarr-Harphax?"

Kyblannos nodded eagerly. "I want to show you my latest gun carriages. But first, we have to go out behind the building."

Phidestros followed his old comrade through the Artillery Works moving out of the way of tree-stump sized anvils and forges belching fire. In the back lot amongst broken wagons and second-growth trees were some ten or twelve dismembered carriages, several of them longer than any carriage he'd ever seen before. There was a stone wall twice the height of a man between the Artillery Works and the next building.

Kyblannos pointed to a carriage, which had a long bed for the gun. "This is our new carriage." He gestured to two of the artillerymen following behind and told them to load the gun. "Use sand, we don't want to lose any more neighbors."

It must be artillerymen's humor, thought Phidestros as the gunners all laughed out loud.

"See, that's the counterweight there. Watch and see what happens after the gun goes off."

After putting in powder and ramming it home, the rammer put in a bag of sand wrapped in cloth. When he was finished tamping it down the barrel, another gunner lit the fuse coming out of the touchhole.

"Fire in the hole!"

THWACK!

The ground shook as the gun pushed back to the end of the carriage. The moment the backward motion stopped, the counterweight yanked the cannon back to its former position on the track.

"Galzar's Great Ghost! I'm never seen anything like that before."

All the artillerymen grinned like proud fathers, including Kyblannos. "It means that the crew doesn't have to waste half a candle aiming the gun again."

One of the wheelwrights came forward. "Not even the Daemon Kalvan has these recoil beds!"

"Most impressive. Kyblannos, making you General of the Hos-Harphax Royal Artillery was one of my smartest decisions."

Kyblannos beamed. "Thank you, Cap'n."

"Where did you get the idea for these recoil carriages?"

Kyblannos paused to take his pipe out of a pocket in his apron and stick it in his mouth. "Back when I was younger and a camp follower, I was drafted into the Agrys City Traveling Dramaturgical Theatre Band as a prop artificer."

Phidestros laughed. "I don't know where you get these stories, but you have more of them than a one-eyed Trygathi troubadour!"

For a moment Kyblannos looked hurt, and took his pipe out of his mouth sticking it back into his pocket.

"I'm sorry, old friend. Please, continue."

"I remembered we used to build drawbridges that, when lowered, flew back up again."

"Yes, like the counterweights on a portcullis."

"Exactly, so I used the idea of counterweights on the carriage bed, only with a cannon instead of a drawbridge."

"Ingenious, old friend. I swear by the Wargod's Beard, this recoil gun carriage looks like one of Kalvan's wonders. Now, how many of them can you build by spring?"

Kyblannos looked crestfallen. “I can have eighteen six and eight pounders on Kalvan-style carriages ready by spring, and maybe four more on these recoiling ones.” He held his hands out. “For these new recoil carriages, we don’t have enough time. They take three times as long to build as the Kalvan, I mean, new-style carriages, and we’re still working out the kinks in the rigging.”

“I was afraid of that. Do your best. I’m going to need all the mobile guns you can build for us. The Usurper’s got the edge on us there, but maybe we can show him a surprise or two.”

ELEVEN

I

As Prince Ptosphes followed Cleon into Kalvan's private audience chamber, Kalvan couldn't help but notice how much the Prince had aged since his arrival here-and-now over three years ago. Most of Ptosphes' hair had turned gray and his goatee had gone from rusty gray to silver. His shoulders were no longer bowed, as they had been after the disaster at Tenabra, but his head still drooped. And something new, Ptosphes' breathing was noticeably louder and more labored.

"Have you been chasing after the Princess Demia again?" Kalvan asked. Demia had suddenly gone from tottering to sprinting, and was wearing out the entire corps of Royal nursemaids.

Ptosphes answered his words with a smile that lit up his face. "No, it's those damn stairs. Have you noticed how they just keep getting steeper?"

"I've noticed," Kalvan answered. One of these days the war with Styphon's House was going to end and he would have time to get around to building the long delayed palace he'd been promising Rylla. Kalvan wasn't sure of the design yet, but he'd promised himself no more drafty chambers and high stairwells. Tarr-Hostigos was not only impossible to heat but had staircases that were both too narrow and too steep for comfortable climbing.

As the Prince lowered himself into a chair, Kalvan loaded his pipe, tamping down the leaf carefully so that none spilled. Styphon's House's ban on selling goods to Hos-Hostigos hadn't dried up the flow of trade, but it had raised the cost of most imports, especially those items that were made or grown, like tobacco, in the southern kingdoms. A big tobacco shipment had been confiscated two weeks ago by Hos-Harphax customs agents, which meant that tobacco leaf was temporarily in short supply. Of course, Kalvan could have commandeered all the tobacco he wanted, but he made an attempt to share the lot of his people. He didn't want himself or his Princes to grow insulated the way the Tsars of Russia had; a course of action that had led to their eventual overthrow.

Ptosphes started speaking hesitantly, as though he didn't want to offend his Great King or was embarrassed. "I've gotten letters and visits from several important people who are most unhappy about the Sastragathi children that have been arriving in Hostigos Town by the wagonload for the past few days. They want to know what your plans are concerning these orphans." The First Prince paused, his face blushing. "I think they're afraid you'll settle them here in Hostigos."

Kalvan reined in his temper. The fact that the children were mostly red-skinned was implied but not spoken. The Zarthani had waged a war of ruthless extermination against the native Indians and had succeeded in almost entirely eliminating them in the Five Kingdoms, except in the southernmost Kingdom of Hos-Bletha. The Indians, or Ruthani as they were called here-and-now, flourished on the Sea of Grass and to the south in Mexico and Central America where the cannibal Mexicotál ruled—about South America nothing was known.

Even though the Ruthani had been exterminated several centuries ago in the Northern Kingdoms, there was still residual prejudice against them. Kalvan had anticipated this problem and was having a large former baronial estate that had reverted to the crown refurbished as an orphanage. The Hostigos Town foundling homes and orphanages were already filled to bursting with children whose parents had died in Styphon's invasion in the Year of the Wolf. Any townspeople who wanted to adopt children had more local candidates than were wanted.

Instead, Kalvan had decided to put the children under Royal protection; that would keep the townspeople from pestering them, but it still didn't solve the problem of what to do with what was becoming a wholesale migration of Ruthani children—seven wagons had arrived today alone. In fact, watching the first wagons had reminded Kalvan of stories about the Children's Crusades where the boys and girls who left Europe to fight the Infidel in Acre and Tripoli and retake Jerusalem had been badly used. Most of the children—those who hadn't died of disease or wounds—had ended up in chains and were sold into slavery by either their French and Venetian transporters, or the Byzantines and Latins whom they'd come to protect.

"Let me level with you, Ptosphes. I'm taking these children to help my friend Warlord Sargos out of a bad bind, and because I know that if I don't take them no one else will. That means starvation and slavery for the majority of them. These are the children left behind by the Urgothi and Ruthani clans from the Sea of Grass, many of whose parents were exterminated by our army or the Zarthani Knights. So in a very real sense they are Our problem."

Ptosphes sighed. "I've seen them—a heartbreaking sight—small children, many in rags, who look like they haven't eaten a good meal in moons. Sadly, our townspeople don't share my feelings. Some believe we're harboring an enemy who will someday turn upon us, or invite their kin into Hostigos."

Kalvan nodded, then paused to light his pipe. "About what I expected. I'm only keeping them at the Royal barracks while the army is out on maneuvers. I don't intend to house them in Hostigos Town."

Ptosphes nodded. "Good. That news will take most of the kindling out of the fire. There's no room here, anyway."

"I agree. I plan to house them in the Duke of Northgate's old estate. It's being rebuilt and expanded as we speak."

"Yes, he died in the Year of the Wolf with both his sons. Is it big enough?"

"It will be after I'm finished," he answered. "If necessary, I'll get the Army engineers involved."

Ptosphes nodded. "I would not want to see the children living in tents through the winter like so many new arrivals in Hostigos Town. When does Sargos want us to return the children?"

Kalvan shook his head. "He hasn't said so, but I don't think he wants, or expects them back."

Ptosphes looked as if he were about to make a comment, but instead paused to take his pipe and tobacco pouch out of his pocket. He filled the barrel with tobacco and used his tinderbox to light a wooden splinter. As soon as the tobacco was lit, he drew deeply. Then he exhaled and, through a cloud of smoke said, "I know the Great Gods have given you wisdom beyond mere mortal men, but it will take more than a miracle for the people of Hostigos to understand why we should provide and care for what appears to be an army of nomad children."

"Army—" Kalvan jumped up from his chair and banged his desktop, spilling a clay bottle of ink. "Thank you, Ptosphes! That's it, Janissaries."

"*Janissaries?* What is that?" Prince Ptosphes had a puzzled look on his face.

"A Janissary was an elite soldier, who fought for the Turks—a great people far beyond the Cold Lands."

Ptosphes shook his head as though he had a hard time imagining anything beyond the lands of their ancestors. Zarthani myth cycles variously mentioned the Cold Lands as either a former home or land of the gods.

"Many winters ago the Great Kingdom of the Turks needed soldiers who were both loyal and fierce fighters, so they kidnapped tens of thousands of young children from the Balkan princedoms within their domain that refused to recognize their suzerainty." Kalvan didn't even attempt to go into the religious conflict and the fact that the Muslim Turks were 'kidnapping' Christian children and then raising them to fight in their homelands and abroad. If Styphon's House were ever able to raise fanatical armies of the same caliber as those Muslim armies, his time as Great King of Hos-Hostigos would come to a very quick close. "The Turks raised these children to be among the most feared warriors of their age."

Ptosphes looked horrified. "I do not understand: how could they do this to children?"

The war with Styphon's House was Ptosphes' (and the rest of here-and-now's) introduction to wars of religion, and they were beginning to see that the religious element added a new and much nastier dimension to warfare.

"Our friend Sargos has just dropped into our lap the makings of a loyal army for Our children and your grandchildren. If we treat these orphans right, give them the proper training, We won't have to worry about educating the next generation of titled blockheads who've been trained from birth in methods of warfare that were extinct the day after Tarr-Dombra fell."

"You mean we train these children in your new style of warfare?"

"Exactly," Kalvan said, tossing his pipe aside and rising up out of his chair. He started pacing back and forth in front of the blazing fireplace. "We'll start an academy—we need the right name, too. The Hostigos Royal Academy of Military Studies—"

"For orphans?"

"Yes, it's a tradition in my homeland. Children whose parents are too busy with making money and playing card games send their children to military academies to be raised right and taught discipline."

Ptosphes shook his head. "I would never want to live in such a place."

Kalvan's response surprised even himself. "Neither would I, not even with Styphon's House breathing down my neck!"

"Do you think the war will continue so long that we will still be fighting Styphon's armies a generation from now?" Ptosphes asked tiredly.

"No, I hope not. But that doesn't mean there won't be other threats to Hos-Hostigos. It certainly would be nice to have the nucleus of a powerful army already in place."

"Yes, for my grandchildren."

Kalvan waxed on enthusiastically. "We'll raise the orphans as cadets—junior soldiers—and we'll give these children a life far finer than they would have had even if their parents had not died in the nomad invasions. We'll give them good instructors too, from the Royal Army—"

"We can't pull officers from the Army now, not with Styphon's House breathing down our necks!"

"No I wasn't thinking of active officers," Kalvan said, "but wounded officers and veterans too old for active service. Men who are no longer able to fight for Hostigos with arms, but can fight by molding young minds. We'll make the Academy more than just a training school—it will be a nice place to live, too. The orphans will be Royal charges and we can even leaven the Urgothi and Ruthani children with our own Hostigi orphans. We'll form a special elite corps comprised of our own *Janissaries* and within a generation they'll have earned all the respect they deserve."

Ptosphes shook his head in wonderment. "And solve two problems at the same time. Another miracle, Your Majesty! You've taken a headache and turned it into an inspiration."

Kalvan took two goblets and filled them with Ermut's Best. "To the new army of Hos-Hostigos!"

II

Verkan Vall, in his disguise as Trader Verkan, first saw the checkpoint about half a mile outside of Hostigos Town. He and Dalla rode up on their horses and halted behind two carts, a flatbed wagon filled with barrels and a small party of trappers. It appeared that since their last visit Kalvan had mounted check posts on every road leading into Hostigos Town, including the Great King's Highway. The Iron Curtain was up again.

The guards wore back-and-breasts with tasses and high-combed morion helmets sporting red and blue plumes. Tortha Karf hadn't mentioned the increased security during their talk and Verkan wondered what else had changed since his last visit to Hos-Hostigos.

"It looks like Kalvan's tightening the noose around Hostigos Town," Dalla said.

"Yes, he must have caught some Styphoni agents."

"I hope one of them is Baron Sthentros!"

"You never have liked him," Verkan said, as they waited for the line to move.

"I not only don't like him," Dalla said, crinkling her nose, "I don't trust him, either. He's been far too quiet of late. That's the time to guard your back from a compulsive blowhard like Sthentros!"

Verkan turned his attention to the barricade when one of the merchants, standing beside a towering horse-drawn cart overflowing with baggage, began loudly arguing with the captain of the guards, who had a gold crest at the center of his breastplate in the shape of a keystone—Kalvan's own emblem. The captain suddenly grabbed the merchant's hand, spun him around and frog marched him toward the small hut. When the merchant tried to take out his knife, another guard smacked him in the head with the flat side of his halberd.

As the merchant slumped to the ground, the two men in his party made a sudden dash for their mounts, but came to a quick halt when one of the troopers fired his horsepistol over their heads. "Next time, I won't aim for the sun!"

While his companions had their hands tied and weapons removed, the fallen merchant was trussed up and thrown over a horse. Two of the guards escorted the cart and three prisoners off to what Verkan was sure would be an unpleasant stay in the dungeons of Tarr-Hostigos. One of the trappers muttered, "Plague and pestilence, more Dralm-blasted spawn of Styphon! Hope they boil 'em in oil."

There were nods of agreement from all around, which told Verkan that Kalvan—despite his problems—still owned his subjects' hearts. By the time Verkan reached the head of the line there were about sixty people behind him, some farmers out for a day in town, two rich nobles with dark red velvet robes and a small retinue, several returning craftsmen and various traders and merchant parties.

The captain recognized him at once. "Colonel Verkan!" He all but saluted. Verkan recognized him as a trooper who'd served under him with the Mounted Rifles at the Battle of Chothros Heights. First Level memory enhancement provided him with his name. "Porthos, Captain Porthos now, I see. You've done well since we last served together at Chothros Heights."

"Yes, sir," he said smartly, beaming. "Captain of the Second Squadron, First Royal Horseguard. I'm surprised you remember my name, sir."

"I never forget a comrade," Verkan replied. "Why the guard stations?"

Captain Porthos turned his head and spat onto the muddy ground. "Styphon's privy-rats. We catch two or three every moon quarter."

Kalvan wasn't the only one who was learning, thought Verkan. Styphon's House had proved itself much more resilient than the First Level experts on the Kalvan Study Team had predicted. From the Harphax City Team he'd been receiving reports the Styphoni were not only paying to rebuild the Royal Harphaxi Army, but also bringing in mountains of supplies for the coming spring campaign season. The Inner Circle had even dispatched their top troubleshooters, Archpriest Anaxthenes and Grand Master Soton, to Harphax City to guarantee their gold was well spent.

The cobblestone streets of Hostigos Town were crowded with pedestrians, soldiers and wagon traffic despite the gathering storm clouds. The crack of iron shod hooves on the cobblestones echoed through the narrow streets like musket shots. Verkan noticed that every hitching post at the Red Halberd had a horse, if not two.

When the rain started in earnest, Verkan dropped Dalla off at their townhouse. From there, he went to the nearest livery stable, dropped of his horse and picked out a fresh mount. Then he threaded his way through the crowded streets to Tarr-Hostigos which looked down upon the town from the hills above.

Verkan Vall entered Kalvan's private audience chamber, noticing for the first time a colorful new tapestry commemorating the Battle of the Three Kings—actually two, since at the time of the Battle of the Spirit Grove, Warlord Sargos was neither king nor ally. Things had changed considerably since then. Sargos had crowned himself King of the Sastragath, or Var-Wannax, and was awaiting recognition of his title from Kalvan and Great King Nestros.

Kalvan rose to greet him and shook his hand heartily. Kalvan had introduced the handshaking ritual to Aryan-Transpacific and, after spreading through Hos-Hostigos, it was beginning to appear in the neighboring kingdoms. Up close, Kalvan looked drawn and there were bags under his eyes, as if he hadn't been getting much sleep. Verkan knew it wasn't because of the rift between him and Rylla, since Tortha had told them that the King and Queen had patched up their differences while he'd been shuttling between First Level, Greffa City and the Sastragath—talk about being in three places at once! Despite First Level relaxation techniques and hypno-sleep, Verkan suspected he looked as worn-out as Kalvan.

"It's good to see you again, Verkan. I see you made it back just before winter. Did you bring Dalla with you again? I'm asking now because if I forget,

Rylla will send a courier riding lickety-split over to your townhouse for an answer!"

"Yes, Dalla insisted I bring her along on this trip. We plan to stay a moon-half, maybe more."

"Excellent, the first good news I've gotten in some time." Turning serious, Kalvan paused to light his pipe. "Were you able to bring any field guns from Grefftscharr?"

"Yes, six brass cast eight-pounders. I had them sent by barge from Greffa to Ulthor Port."

Kalvan's eyes lit up and he all but clapped his hands. "We can really use those guns, Verkan. With Captain-General Phidestros stockpiling arms at Tarr-Veblos, our strategy has changed and I, for one, am not happy about it."

"Yes, taking the war to your opponents has always been the best strategy," Verkan commiserated.

"Which is what I'd planned to do before Phidestros circumvented Phrames and took Tarr-Veblos. At last report, he's garrisoned it with several thousand troops with reinforcements nearby. We're still going to go on the offensive, but we will have to marshal our forces more carefully, or face defeat in detail. We'd be much better off if we still held Tarr-Veblos—"

From the grim look on his friend's face, Verkan knew that Kalvan was thinking of Rylla's unanticipated attack on Phaxos which allowed Captain-General Phidestros to establish a beachhead in Hostigi territory the previous year by capturing the Beshtan castle, Tarr-Veblos.

Kalvan shook his head, and continued, "I'd like to end this war on the field of battle in Hos-Harphax this campaign season, once and for all. But, of course, that depends upon what our enemies have up their sleeves. Maybe another attack from Hos-Agrys, or even Hos-Ktemnos…? But enough of this talk, tell me about your visit to the Sastragath. Were you able to meet Ranjar Sargos?"

"Yes, I did, and once Sargos found out I was a friend of Great King Kalvan—there was no end to his hospitality."

Kalvan smiled. "That's Sargos, all right. He's a great friend to his allies, and a holy terror to his foes. It was his idea to burn the Knights out of the Drynos

Mines—the idea came to him in a vision. I could use him and his horde right now—turn them loose in Hos-Ktemnos."

Verkan nodded. "Sargos told me lots of stories about your time together."

"We did have a lot of time to talk and, truth be told, he was a much better conversationalist than King Nestros who quickly proved to be a bore."

Verkan chuckled. "I haven't had the pleasure of meeting Nestros, but I'll accept your judgment. Anyway, Sargos has mulled over your words and come up with some interesting reforms. To solve the problem of all the war orphans, widows and clanless men, from the War of the Three Kings, Sargos has offered to make all those of Urgothi extraction clan members of the Tymannes. He told me he'd liked your 'melting pot' idea, but that the Clan Elders rejected the idea completely. Many of the Tymannes still hate their Ruthani allies—and former enemies.

"Not surprisingly, there were thousands of Urgothi warriors whose clans and tribes were decimated during the Time of Troubles and most of them have flocked to his standard. Being a tribeless man in the Sastragath is a terrible fate, usually ending in indentured servitude or outlawry. To be able to join the Warlord's Clan is not only a great honor, but also a refuge with possibilities of many battles and all the loot and honor that goes along with them. Sargos has added so many clansmen to the Tymannes that they are now the largest clan in the unclaimed territories. Wannax Sargos is personally able to field about fifteen thousand warriors from his own clan, with almost ten times that number of women and children! Altogether, with his closest allies, he can bring together some eighty thousand fighting men under his banner, four or five times that number if he gathers the tribes and clans on the Sea of Grass."

Kalvan paused to knock the heel out of his pipe. "I learned a lot of this from his Warchief Vanar Halgoth, who arrived a moon before your return and he brought me up-to-date. The last time I saw Sargos, all the warriors of the Tymannes didn't number more than a Royal regiment. I do remember warning him about establishing a cult of leadership without sufficient loyal troops."

"Yes, and you also told him about the twenty acres, a mule and ten golden Crowns. Now Sargos is settling his *new* clansmen along the Hos-Ktemnos border. That'll give Great King Cleitharses a few sleepless nights. He told me that your words convinced him that it was time to *civilize* the Sastragath before the Order or the border lords of Hos-Ktemnos did it under Styphon's House's direction."

Kalvan nodded. "I wish I could get Sargos to take his horde into Hos-Ktemnos. After what we did last summer, I doubt that even a Sastragathi invasion would take Grand Master Soton out of next spring's campaign, but Great King Cleitharses of Hos-Ktemnos would think twice before sending any troops north with Soton, what with Sargos and his army knocking on the back door."

Verkan laughed, but the smile quickly vanished. "No one expected Styphon's House to rear up off its hindquarters as if bitten by a wolf! Besides, Sargos might have had to turn you down, which would have meant a blood-debt had gone unpaid—and that might have brought about a real breach between the two of you."

Kalvan finished refilling his pipe with fresh tobacco and nodded. "You're right. Maybe we can get some help from Great King Nestros. I'll have to send an envoy—Prince Ptosphes, maybe Harmakros too, since they hit it off. Anyone with less status than First Prince Ptosphes, Nestros would be sure to see as an insult, damn his thick skull! It's not like I've got so many good officers that I can send some of them haring off on wild-goose chases in Hos-Rathon."

"From what Tortha told me of your Trygathi campaign, Nestros certainly owes you anything you might ask for. As for Sargos, I'm sure he would be more than glad to help out. But he told me that he has already promised his Ruthani allies that he would take a large force into the Sea of Grass to fight against the invaders from the south. Sargos told me that if he can take the war across the Great River that will help settle things in the Sastragath so he will be able to concentrate his future energies on building his new realm. Also, it's been a long time since any Sastragathi Warlord has taken his army into the Sea of Grass and I think that appeals to his vanity. With the firearms he scrounged during the war and the ones you sent him, he'll certainly have more firepower than any Sastragathi army has ever had before him."

Kalvan took a long pull on his pipe. "Sargos doesn't strike me as a man who fights for vainglory; I think he's still establishing his leadership position among the clans and villages of the Sastragath. By taking his warriors across the Great River he's reversing the usual invasion route and proving his capability as Warlord and Var-Wannax. If he's already making the changes you've mentioned, he's going to need all the credibility he can get. Still, we could use his help...."

Verkan said, "Now that the Fireseed Mystery is blown, time is running out for Styphon's House. They must realize that they really need to win this war while they're still in control of the Southern Kingdoms. All you have to do is hold out for two or three more winters, and Styphon's House will collapse from the inside of dry rot."

"It can't happen too soon," Kalvan replied, shaking his head.

TWELVE

I

Archpriest Anaxthenes knew he should be packing for his departure to Balph, but his mind was too crowded with plots and machinations. Great King Lysandros had obviously been pleased that such a high-ranking Archpriest, the Speaker of the Inner Circle, had arrived in Harphax City to officiate at the his coronation. Anaxthenes had met with Archpriest Grythos, Grand Master Soton's candidate for the Inner Circle, and had found him to be a strong potential ally. He'd had several long discussions with Soton and they had found themselves in agreement on most of them. They had even discussed ways to decrease Investigator Roxthar's influence over the Temple Guardsmen. For the first time since Kalvan had begun his conquest of Hos-Harphax, Anaxthenes believed his own star was again on the rise.

Anaxthenes heard the knock at the door, stopped his pacing and turned around. His bedchamber was fit for a prince and recently remodeled by Great King Lysandros for visiting dignitaries to the palace. Former King Kaiphranos had let the palace fall into disrepair and Lysandros had spent a small fortune—mostly borrowed from the Temple—to refurbish it for his coronation. The Archpriest, however, was oblivious to the satin and velvet furnishings, and only had eyes for the door. "Who is it?"

"It's Petty-Captain Fydar. I have *someone* who says he has your permission to call."

Anaxthenes opened the door to see the Royal Bodyguard holding a short, hunchbacked man in a black robe by the scruff of his neck. It must be important or Yagos would never have come directly to his chamber.

"Let him down, Petty-Captain." The bodyguard grimaced but let the little man drop to the floor like a bag of laundry.

"Thank you, Archpriest," the little man said in a surprisingly deep voice, as he scrambled to his feet.

"You may go, Petty-Captain." Anaxthenes passed him a small purse. "I would be most appreciative if you told no one of this visit."

"Yes, Your Sanctity." The Petty-Captain had the look of a man who'd seen all manner of comings and goings in the palace and knew when it was smart to keep his mouth shut.

After the door was closed, Anaxthenes asked, "How did you fare, Deacon Yagos?"

The little man rubbed his hands nervously. "It was more difficult than I expected, Your Sanctity. This mercenary Captain-General commands more loyalty than most of that breed. I had to spend one purse on drinks for these mercenaries that call themselves the Iron Band. Among them, they could drink the Harph River dry were it ale!"

"Yes, yes, go on!"

"They told marvelous and wondrous tales about fighting the Daemon Kalvan and his soldiers, but no one knew much about their captain—other than he makes yearly treks to Zygros City."

"I'm not surprised. His accent is Zygrosi. Go on, Yagos."

"I tried to talk to General Kyblannos, but he is married to his guns and has little interest in anything that doesn't clank or go bang. Grand-Captain Geblon has been with Captain-General Phidestros for eight winters, since he was a petty-captain. The man, besides an unquenchable thirst for drink, has an endless well of stories about his leader. Even falling off his stool, he wouldn't talk about Phidestros' journeys to Zygros City."

"So, then?"

"I found the highest priced madam in Harphax City. For a large purse of gold I was able to purchase the services of a most magnificent harlot."

"I take it you had a plan in mind?" Anaxthenes asked dryly.

"Oh, yes, Archpriest! I paid the Lady Sessadra—she claims to be Prince Selestros' bastard daughter—five golden rakmars, with a promise of ten more were she able to bring me the information I required. I then escorted her to the Red Dog Tavern, with the Temple Guard you loaned me—a wise precaution, Your Sanctity, since the two of us would not have walked six paces before this goddess was spirited away, so lovely is she."

"Please, spare me! The information—what did you learn about our Captain-General Phidestros?"

"Ah. Geblon could not wait to take her to his chambers. I watched from behind a barrel, while she stunned him with beauty like a snake spells a fat bird. Oh, our poor Grand-Captain never had a chance. He told her all about his great Captain-General and how it was rumored in the Zygros City wine shops that he was the get of the Zygrosi royals. Some say he is the spitting image of Grand Duke Eudocles, when he was a young man. Is this the Hos-Zygros connection you suspected, Your Sanctity?"

"You have done well, Yagos," Anaxthenes said, removing a large purse from the cupboard. He turned and tossed it to the little priest. "Here is your reward. Your goddess awaits."

The little man nodded, as the purse disappeared within his tattered robe. "You know me well, Your Sanctity."

"Too well. Just don't mark the *Lady* up too badly; I don't want to have any complaints from the city warden. Great King Lysandros is said to have little patience with lawbreakers. I will not buy your freedom again. And see that you're not too drunk to report to the packet I have arranged for your transport when we leave this barbarous kingdom on the third morning. If you're not at the dock on time, you can walk back to Balph!"

"Yes, Your Sanctity. I will return in time."

"See that you do." Anaxthenes forgot the little man the minute he left the room. So much planning to do. Now that he had his observation verified: what to do? He knew Great King Lysandros would find this information most interesting, but Lysandros was of little use to him. Anaxthenes had taken his measure of Lysandros; he neither trusted the Great King nor his 'ardent' belief in Styphon. Lysandros was a man who loved himself before all things—including men and gods. Nor was he a fanatic like Roxthar, trying to remake the world as he thought it should be.

The question now was: Should he tell the Grand Master? Maybe...Soton might find this information of value in his dealings with Phidestros. Of one thing he was certain, someday this information would be worth much more than a dozen purses of gold coins.

II

Kalvan looked down at the parchment sent to him by his Chief of Intelligence, Duke Skranga. He had spent the day with Master Ermut trying to explain the concept of a lens for the new telescopes, or farseers as Ermut called them. It was too late to return to Tarr-Hostigos, so he was running over some of the day's briefings. One of Skranga's moles at Tarr-Harphax had picked up a very interesting bit of information, a communiqué between Great King Lysandros and Great King Niclophon of Hos-Bletha. The Hos-Blethan King was sending five thousand regulars from the Royal Army and another six thousand irregulars, mostly light cavalry and javelin throwers, under the command of Captain-General Lykron to join the invasion of Hos-Hostigos in the spring. The troops and their mounts would be ferried by Styphon's Great Fleet directly to Port Naphros in Hos-Ktemnos and from there they'd join the Grand Host at Tarr-Veblos.

Kalvan shook his head wearily and poured another shot of Ermut's Best into his new glass goblet, swirling the burgundy spirits around the glass before drinking it all down in one gulp. Suddenly the Styphon's House sponsored invasion force was beginning to live up to its billing as the Grand Host, as Great King Lysandros was calling it, as he rallied his under lords and allies. Captain-General Phidestros already had a sizeable Harphaxi force, five thousand cavalry and six thousand infantry, not counting the City Bands. If Great

King Cleitharses sent the Sacred Square and the other Princely squares, or tercios, Kalvan could be facing another twelve to fifteen thousand Ktemnoi—who were, next to the Army of Hostigos, the best man-for-man army in the Seven Kingdoms.

Kalvan could really use the sixty thousand nomads that had helped chase Grand Master Soton and his Knights back to Tarr-Ceros; unfortunately, they were all irregulars and couldn't be harnessed up and set aside for a rainy day. He had a feeling that Hos-Hostigos was going to be in the middle of a veritable manure storm come spring.

He needed a way to tie down those troops from Hos-Bletha, since there was nothing he could do short of an invasion of Hos-Ktemnos to keep the Sacred Squares out of the war. Maybe it was time to use some of the Confederate guerrilla tactics that his maternal great-grandfather, a former Virginian, used to tell him about as a lad. Winter was approaching and time was running short. Who could he send? Skranga had the brains; once he was given the mission he'd improvise and make it work, if it could be done at all. He'd need a military advisor, but which one? Someone with leadership qualities, like Harmakros—but he needed Harmakros here at home to fight the Styphoni.

If truth be told, Kalvan himself was the perfect candidate to lead a popular uprising. With Verkan's help, they could have the Blethan countryside in such an uproar it wouldn't subside for a decade! It would be fun, too. A sojourn to Hos-Bletha would give him and Rylla some much needed breathing room; unfortunately, without the Gods-Sent-Kalvan to depend upon, the Army of Hos-Hostigos would shrivel up and blow away. *Damn, I'm growing weary of this role of the indispensable man.*

Kalvan poured himself another slug of brandy.

Then it hit him like a flash: Colonel Democriphon. Democriphon was an excellent officer and tactician as long as it was an independent command, but balked at orders when part of a force. Yes, he would be an ideal officer for this kind of campaign, although like Custer before him, Democriphon suffered from a bad case of over-inflated ego. If he pulled this off and took some of the military pressure off Hostigos, he would be welcome to it. It would be best to let him pick his own troops too. He was commander of the Third Royal

Regiment of Horse. No riflemen. That would mark them as Hostigi right at the outset. Democriphon needed some kind of cover story.

Kalvan needed more information about Hos-Bletha, but Skranga was back in Hostigos Town, and the only Blethan Kalvan knew was the troubadour Gasphros who was the University gadfly. For being untutored—although Kalvan suspected Gasphros' childhood station had been higher than the troubadour let on—he had a gift of making interesting connections and asking the right questions. Gasphros had proven to be an asset to the University—enough so that Kalvan had put him on salary as a 'roving' recruiter. Young people flocked after him like the Pied Piper.

Gasphros had also been one of Skranga's best operatives in Harphax City until the Duke's cover had been blown. Gasphros and his lyre had been a fixture at Skranga's legendary soirées and had left, like Skranga, one step ahead of the local gendarmes.

Kalvan had given Cleon permission to retire hours ago, so he went down the stairs into the kitchen where the best of the University's interdisciplinary work took place. He found Ermut in the midst of a deep discussion with Gasphros over the length of the copper condensing tubes for the new distillery that was being constructed on the outskirts of Hostigos Town. Already, the taverns and inns in town were ordering more brandy than Ermut could produce at the University's makeshift distillery. Kalvan, with a huge standing army to support, needed all the revenue he could squeeze—casks of brandy were selling for three times the price of winter wine.

Kalvan was tempted to start distilling corn mash, until he still remembered the horror stories that occurred when cheap gin was distilled from grain and sold in England on the streets by the cupful—"drunk for a penny, dead drunk for two." Alcoholism had hit England's poor with the savagery of the Great Pox. Cheap distilled spirits from grain or corn would come along soon enough, with or without his help, but Kalvan didn't want to be known for bringing this plague into the Seven Kingdoms.

"Gasphros, come into my study. I have some questions about Hos-Bletha I need answered."

Gasphros emptied his tankard of ale and pushed himself away from the table with his more than ample belly. "My information is badly out-of-date, but I'd be glad to share it with you, Your Majesty."

"Good." Kalvan said as he led the way up the staircase.

Gasphros was puffing by the time they reached the study. "I'm out of shape. It's time to go a-wandering again."

Kalvan smiled. "That's just what I had in mind."

Gasphros' intelligent brown eyes peered over his bearded cheeks and into Kalvan's own. Kalvan pointed to a chair, sat down behind his desk and pulled out a pouch of tobacco. Gasphros' long clay pipe was out and filled before Kalvan had time to reach for his own. They both lit up, using Kalvan's Name Day tinderbox, which was made of brass and in the shape of a cannon: a present from Rylla during better times.

Gasphros picked up the heavy tinderbox and examined it closely. "This is a remarkable piece of craftsmanship. It even has a real barrel."

Kalvan pointed to the flintlock mechanism. "Reverse this and you've got a working pistol!" Kalvan reached over and reversed the flintlock to where it would flash into the touchhole of the tiny barrel.

"Amazing! Who made this?"

"Count Rogos, a friend of the family and a wonderful goldsmith. Rylla likes for me to shoot it off whenever we win a battle." He pointed to the baseboard where there were two rows of tiny lead balls sunken into the wood. "Have to be careful of the load or it'll put a hole in the wall." He uncorked the stopper on the decanter of Ermut's Best and asked, "Would you like a drink?"

"Certainly. If I didn't take one, it would be the first one I've ever turned down, Your Majesty."

Kalvan nodded and filled Gasphros' goblet. "From the latest intelligence reports from Harphax City, it appears that Styphon's House is using every bit of influence it has to get all the soldiers in the Five Kingdoms into Hos-Harphax to fight against Hostigos."

"You'll tan their hides, Your Majesty! You always have before."

Kalvan bit down on his pipe stem. "This is going to be a bigger and tougher and more experienced army than anything we've faced before."

"You mean the so-called Grand Host might even live up to its name?"

"Exactly. I just learned today that a sizable army is set to arrive this spring from Hos-Bletha. Delivered to our back porch, lock, stock and barrel, by Styphon's Great Fleet. What I need to do is pick your brain of knowledge about Hos-Bletha."

Gasphros exhaled heavily. "Whew! As I said before, most of what I know is twenty winters past."

Kalvan blew out a small cloud of smoke. "Understood."

"Your Majesty, I've spent most of my life traveling all over this land, and I've learned that Hos-Bletha is completely unlike any of the other Five Kingdoms. Bletha was originally settled by colonists from Hos-Ktemnos around three hundred winters ago. Even today most of the Blethan nobility have links to the noble houses of Hos-Ktemnos. Bletha is also different in that there are large numbers of Ruthani living in the swamplands, which extend for many hundreds of marches almost to lands' end. We call it the Magaouisse Swamp. Only the Ruthani and a few outcast swampmen live in those lands of disease and mud.

"Even Bletha Town is not a true city like Harphax City or Agrys City, but a town the size of Hostigos Town with nearly the same population. Because the lands are sparsely populated, the lords are accustomed to having their own way. The Great King of Bletha is a title little honored outside of the Princedom of Bletha. Several of the major dukes believe they should be Great King and have claims going back a century or more. These are a source of great friction and occasional rebellions. This independence also extends to the freemen themselves, many of whom consider themselves the equal of any noble."

Gasphros looked at Kalvan closely to see how he took to this notion. When he didn't react negatively to the idea, he continued. "This notion of independence among the commoners has long frustrated the Blethan nobility."

"It's an affliction that is common in the Cold Lands, as well."

Gasphros looked at Kalvan shrewdly. "One day you will have to tell me more about your days in the Lands of the Gods."

Not in this lifetime, Kalvan thought to himself. Gasphros was too smart for his own good, and Kalvan wasn't about to let that particular bobcat out of the basket. He'd already told too many stories of his arrival here-and-now and it was an effort to remember to whom he'd told what. Last year the Council of Dralm spent several moons trying to decipher the rumors and facts of Kalvan's arrival; the last thing they needed to hear was the truth, which was far more fantastic than the rumors.

"From what I hear, the present Great King Niclophon is a puppet of Styphon's House and Hos-Ktemnos and has been importing mercenaries to enforce his rule. There have been two rebellions that I've heard about in the last ten winters."

"Do you still have friends in Hos-Bletha?"

Gasphros snorted. "None that I've heard from in fifteen years. I get my information from merchants and peddlers."

"So, no one would recognize you if you were to return?"

"Not anymore." This time there was a note of sadness in his voice. "Why, Your Majesty?"

"I want you to help head up an operation to neutralize the Hos-Blethan Army."

"ME?"

"Yes, you're the only man in Hostigos who knows anything about Hos-Bletha or Blethan politics. Of course, you'll have plenty of help. I want to bring about an insurrection within Hos-Bletha that will cause Great King Niclophon to recall his troops from the Holy Host."

"Is that all?"

"For now, yes."

THIRTEEN

I

Verkan Vall sat at his desk in the Foundry basement, his boots up, cleaning his flintlock hideaway pistol. Thanks to the collapsed-nickel ceiling it was quiet inside the basement: no banging of anvils or endless chatter of Kalvan Study Team intellectuals. The wall-sized visiplate displayed a close-up of Tarr-Hostigos, from the sky-eye above Hostigos Town, showing dozens of carts and flatbed wagons full of provisions and weapons snaking their way up the hills back and forth on the switchbacks to the outer bailey. The rainy season was in full drizzle, but that hadn't stopped the stream of foodstuffs and tools of war from flowing into the castle. The foundry was working night and day to turn out more big guns. The cobblestone streets of Hostigos Town were so filled with wagons a pedestrian wasn't safe on the streets, night or day.

Verkan wished he had the authority to call in an airstrike team and have them hit Tarr-Harphax and Balph. That would settle this war once and for all. The locals might believe it was one of Thanor's bolts, but Kalvan would know better and so would the Dhergabar University Study Team. And that would be the end of his visits to Kalvan's Time-Line as well as his job as Paratime Police chief—the latter he wouldn't mind losing, but he didn't want to give up his visits with Kalvan and Rylla.

He heard the door's hydraulics activate and then creak as it swung open, revealing Inspector Ranthar Jard, still wearing his high-combed morion helmet and back-and-breast. Verkan rose and they clasped shoulders. Verkan noticed fresh cuts on his face and the beginning of a black eye. "What happened to you: A cat fight?"

Ranthar winced. "In a manner of speaking. I got between Scholar Lala and Baltrov Eldra in the middle of their argument over Kalvan's decision to teach the Ruthani orphans 'male pattern bonding and archaic aggressive male behavior patterns' and Professor Baltrov Eldra's rebuttal, which included a detailed description of Sastragathi slave laws. When Varnath Lala couldn't hold her ears tight enough to protect them from Eldra's rather colorful language, she struck out with her nails. I got in the way, only to be on the receiving end of Lala's claws and Eldra's elbow, meant—I believe—for Lala's nose! They were both most apologetic, and it did stop their interminable argument as they went looking for the unguents for my face. Unfortunately, they'll be at it again in another couple of hours."

Verkan laughed. "By then you're going to have one Dralm-blasted black eye. Do you want to use my medpak now, or after our talk?"

"Well, Chief, unless you've got another assignment for me—please, tell me you do—then I'm stuck. Our little contretemps was witnessed by several of the foundry staff, who would think it Dralm's Own Miracle if I were to arrive with anything less than a bruised eye. Thanks anyway boss."

"Well, Ranthar, this may be your lucky day indeed. I had a discussion with Kalvan this morning and he's most impressed by your leadership abilities."

"Likewise, Chief. I think Kalvan could even run this outfit."

"Don't say that within spitting distance of the Kalvan Study Team or you will have another cat fight on your hands!"

Ranthar laughed, holding up his arms, hands flat, in the universal sign of surrender. "Please, say no more. So what's this new assignment?"

"It's a surprise to me. Things are getting bad enough in the war against Styphon's House that Kalvan is taking a few pages from one of his own Europo-American headlines. He wants to start a revolt in Hos-Bletha to force them to withdraw their forces from the Grand Host. He's got a whale of a plan—to use one of his terms—and I think it's more than plausible. Part of it involves a guerilla uprising in the southern provinces starring yourself as none other than Robin Hood—that name's from a common Europo-American myth of a bandit who robs from the rich to give to the poor. Obviously, a fairy tale for children. Kalvan remembers the story and told it to me in great detail. I had to agree that you would make a most excellent Robin Hood."

"Actually, if it will get me away from the Foundry and the Kalvan Study Team, I'd accept an assignment to break into Regwarn."

"Well, you've got it, my friend. And, that isn't all. Guess who else Kalvan wants to *borrow?*"

Ranthar shook his head, then flashed a wicked smile. "He wants to borrow Varnath Lala's head to use for one of his scarecrows!"

"Good guess, but no. He wants to have Baltrov Eldra join his merry little band."

"Baltrov Eldra! Why, Chief?"

"Think. You were at the University Founder's celebration."

"Sure—I got real plastered—left my alcodote pills at home on purpose. Had a good time."

"Do you remember seeing Eldra?"

Ranthar's brow furrowed. "Sure. She was hanging around that skinny horse-trader, Duke Skranga, and Kalvan for the first part of the evening. Then later on she was decorating Colonel Democriphon's uniform—he seemed to like it."

"Well, before she changed dance partners, she approached Kalvan and said something into his ear I'm too polite to repeat in mixed company."

"She tried to seduce Kalvan in public? Does she have a death wish? Sure Kalvan and Rylla are having problems, but Rylla would filet any woman who she saw get within kissing distance of her husband."

"Absolutely. When I heard about it, I was ready to send her packing. But it's not that simple."

"What do you mean, Chief? It looks pretty simple to me. Send Eldra home to First Level 'for her own protection' and let the University of Dhergabar figure out what to do with her. Flirting with Kalvan isn't Paratemporal Contamination, but it more than skirts outtime ethics. University Study Team participants are instructed to act as 'observers only.' Trying to set up a liaison with the primary agent of change on Kalvan's Time Line is bad procedure—even if she wasn't successful. Success could get her killed and who knows what else. She goes home when you give the order. I can escort her out of the Foundry and have her on a conveyer in ten minutes. She'll be back on Home Time Line so fast she'll never know what hit her!"

Verkan shook his head. "Very few people know this, but I was sharing my quarters with Eldra when that Second Level reincarnation fracas came up on Akor-Neb, which led to Dalla and I renewing our marriage contract. You've just witnessed an example of Eldra's temper—how do you think she took that? Or my asking her to leave our apartment?"

"Wow, Chief, you sure can pick them!" Ranthar exclaimed.

Verkan looked down at his shoes.

"Why in Xerpa's Mandibles did you ever pick Eldra as our undercover operative for the Kalvan Study Team?"

Verkan was still studying the floor when he answered. "I owed her one. She could have stirred up a real firestorm for me back then, but she kept it between the two of us. Kept Dalla out of it, too. Eldra heard about the Kalvan Study Team, knew I'd be involved and asked if she could become a member. She had the right credentials so I called one of our *friends* at the University and arranged for her to be assigned to the Kalvan Study Team. It was the least I could do."

"Blackmail?" Ranthar asked with a frown.

"No. Eldra was nice about it. She just reminded me of a promise I'd made to her when she left: I'd told her I'd do her a favor one day if ever she needed one."

"Some favor. Does Dalla know any of this?"

Verkan shook his head.

Ranthar whistled. "Dalla has always had a temper. And jealous! I remember that time she caught you with that prole scarf dancer—"

"You were there. You know it was perfectly innocent."

"Sure, but it didn't look that way to Dalla. It didn't help that the girl had lost all her scarves in the riot—not that it made much of a difference!"

"And, since I've never told her about Eldra…"

"Yes," Ranthar said, trying to keep a straight face. "It would look bad, real bad."

"Eldra even offered, I guess to sweeten the pot, to go undercover and spy on her own cohorts. She's the one who spotted the redhead sending up message balls to Hadron Tharn."

"She's done a good job. After that little tussle I just partook in, no one would ever accuse Eldra of being *our* agent. You should have heard some of the creative language she used on both Lala and me. Still, Verkan—"

"A stupid blunder—I've never even told Tortha. If I had, I'd never hear the end of it. I didn't even want to tell you, but someone needs to know and since you'll be Johnny-on-the-spot, well, Eldra's going to be the party's black widow spider and spy mistress."

"And just when this was sounding like fun."

"It's not that bad. She may not be working with your team. I haven't drawn up the assignments yet."

"Praise Dralm! And, Chief, you'd better think of telling Dalla about your history with our spy vixen soon. If she ever hears it from Eldra, Styphon be damned, it will be a disaster—your disaster!"

II

As his horse came over the rise, Duke Skranga had his first look at the Locra Valley in over a winter. Tarr-Locra was an old fort that was being rebuilt and expanded as part of the war against Hos-Harphax. There was now a small town where there had been a village and it was a hive of activity. Tarr-Locra now covered the entire hilltop and at the base was one of Kalvan's new star forts. Instead of a circular outer wall at the base of the hill, the Great King had Captain-General Harmakros build a large star with about a dozen points that Skranga could see from his position on the opposite ridge. There were eight and ten-pound culverins set at each point.

While his party was stopped at the gate by the guard, Skranga got a closer look at the walls themselves. They were about ten lances tall and about a third that in width. Tarr-Locra would be a tough nut to crack even for the entire Harphaxi Army. Skranga's estimation of Harmakros went up several notches. He hoped that Hestophes could fill his superior's shoes. Skranga mentally reviewed what he knew about Captain-General Hestophes:

First, at twenty-three winters Hestophes was the youngest general on Kalvan's mostly youthful General Staff. His father was a publican; he owned the Silver Stag. Like many other businessmen in Hostigos, his tavern had flourished under Kalvan's rule—war was *always* good for business. Hestophes had been an infantry officer in the Army of Hostigos when Kalvan had arrived.

During the war with Nostor, Hestophes had been the captain who had held the Narza Gap with little better than two companies and two old guns. Hestophes had beaten off ten times his number three times before advancing and forcing the enemy to retreat back into Nostor. Kalvan had been impressed enough to make him one of the first generals in his new Royal Army of Hos-Hostigos.

Hestophes' record during the battles at Chothros Heights and Phyrax was such that Kalvan had elevated him to baron and awarded Hestophes a nice estate and castle at Eython. That was when his rising cloud had begun to stall; Hestophes had met the Lady Lavena, the daughter of Baron Sthentros, whose estate at Hyllos bordered the young Captain-General's. Hestophes had become besotted with Lavena, and he wasn't the first either, so Skranga had learned when he'd arrived undercover as an itinerant peddler in Hyllos to see if there was any truth to the rumors reaching Hostigos Town. While no lady, Lavena was a comely wench and Skranga—had he been a pup like Hestophes—might have followed her dragging his tail behind his legs, too. Still, he knew trouble when he saw it, even if it walked on two lovely legs.

After his report to Kalvan, it had been the Great King's idea to immediately reassign Hestophes to Tarr-Locra and put him in charge of the Great Kingdom's eastern frontier. And from the vigilance of his guards, Skranga would have to say Hestophes had made a good job of it.

While Grand Captain Myklon saw to boarding his horses and seeing to his troopers, Skranga was taken up to the fortress for an audience with the Captain-General. Hestophes was seated behind a large desk that looked as if it were modeled after Kalvan's desk at Tarr-Hostigos. When the Captain-General stood to press palms, Skranga realized just how truly large a man Hestophes was. While not as tall as himself, Hestophes was almost half as wide as he was tall, but without an extra ounce of weight. He was as strong looking a man as Skranga had ever seen.

"What can I do for you, Duke Skranga? I see you brought two companies of reinforcements which we greatly need."

"I'm sorry, Captain-General, but these troopers are but my own personal guards."

"Really?"

"Yes, I've been charged by King Kalvan to leave for Hos-Bletha on a secret mission."

Hestophes' eyebrows went up. "I think you had best tell me just what you're up to."

Skranga pulled out a scroll from his side pouch. "Read this, orders for you from Great King Kalvan."

Hestophes frowned, and for a moment Skranga wondered if he, like Harmakros, were unable to read. Surely no crime, but a disadvantage in the new Hos-Hostigos.

Hestophes picked up the scroll, unwound it and began to slowly and quietly read out loud.

Skranga was able to smoke two bowls of tobacco before Hestophes sighed and set down the paper scroll. "The King says I am to trust you and give you any aid that you require. He does not say why."

Skranga took out his pipe and began to fill it with tobacco again. Kalvan had not said *not* to share his mission with Hestophes, and he might even be of some help. In actuality, he was surprised Kalvan had authorized this mission at all; it was just a sign of how desperate things were getting as Hos-Hostigos prepared to meet the Grand Host. Maybe he could help Kalvan. Now for the hard part, convincing Captain-General Hestophes.

Skranga removed a flask from the inside of his buff jack and presented it to Hestophes. "Some of Ermut's Best."

"Hmm." Hestophes turned to pick up two goblets and fill them with the dark liquid.

"As you may or may not know, Great King Niclophon of Hos-Bletha has been squeezing his Kingdom dry to aid Styphon's House in its war against Hos-Hostigos. The Blethans are relatively poor and, outside Bletha Town, there's little support for either their King or Styphon's House. Now that Niclophon has sent most of his army to Balph to aid King Lysandros, we thought this might be a good time to start a revolt within Hos-Bletha. At worst we might pin down units that would otherwise aid in the fight against Hostigos, while at best King Niclophon might have to recall the Blethan Army."

Hestophes shook his head. "You actually sold this dream story to Kalvan? I'd heard you were silver-tongued enough to sell a dog to an Uncle Wolf, but I didn't believe it until now."

Skranga held both hands to his chest. "Truth: it was Kalvan's idea, not mine. You don't think it will work?"

"Whether it works is of little importance right now since it certainly isn't going to do any good before next spring. Meanwhile, you've got two companies of good troops who could be used in the defense of the realm chasing fireflies...I take it they are former Blethan mercenaries?"

"Most. Some of them are Hostigi who have worked on *special* missions with me before. All the Blethans have families they're leaving behind for this duty to ensure their loyalty. Most have been fighting with Kalvan since Fyk." For half a candle, Skranga continued to explain Kalvan's reasoning behind the operation and their intelligence information on Hos-Bletha.

Hestophes nodded slowly after he finished. "With good soldiers you could stir up serious trouble, if even half of what you say about Hos-Bletha is true. I will admit this idea is not as harebrained as it first appeared; however, it will be your responsibility to see that these soldiers do not end up fighting for Styphon's House against us. So just how is it that you propose to arrive in Hos-Bletha from here?"

"I was planning to go by way of Syriphlon and from there down through the Pirsystros Valley and into Hos-Ktemnos. From there we were going to take a ship to Hos-Bletha."

The Captain-General shook his head. Skranga bit down on his displeasure at being corrected by a man half his age.

"Why not?"

"Soton is hiring every mercenary in Hos-Harphax and Hos-Ktemnos. Do you really believe his agents are going to let two companies of experienced mercenaries, who can't begin to account for their whereabouts for the past two winters, slip through their fingers? You will be up in irons before the moon is up. If you're lucky they'll hang you, if not you'll be up before Roxthar's Investigation."

Skranga paled. There were few things he feared at this point in his long and thoroughly lived life—being Investigated by Roxthar's thugs was one of them. "What do you suggest, Captain-General?"

"First, your men need disguises, and so do you. And a good one at that, something unexpected, yet commonplace. An alias, too. I've got it! You can be Highpriest Sangar from somewhere in Hos-Bletha, the farther distant the better, and your men will be a Temple Band of Styphon's Own Guard."

"You mean disguise ourselves as a Band of Styphon's Red Hand? By Galzar, I love it. Who is going to dare question the presence of a Temple Band with a Highpriest escort?"

"Down south, maybe. But if you take your Band up north through Nostor and the Kratiphlon Pass into Hos-Agrys, you should be home safe. Once in Agrys City, you can probably find a ship to take you down to Hos-Bletha, even this late in the year. That is, if you have enough gold."

Skranga smiled. Besides two score of ingots that had once decorated the roof of Styphon's Temple in Phaxos town, he had his own not inconsiderable fortune. "We are adequately financed. I also have two gunsmiths and six fireseed makers."

Hestophes nodded. "It is true that our Great King sets his sights far into the distance. I am surprised Kalvan let two gunsmiths leave now, though."

"After what he did this summer, we have more riflesmiths than even we need."

"I hadn't heard about his latest dealing with the Gunsmiths Guild. What happened?"

"When they wouldn't increase their production of rifles, King Kalvan started selling smooth bores from the Royal Armory. He sold them for what it cost the gunsmiths to make a musket stock! Whoa, were they unhappy. Then he told them that he would buy all the rifles they could make, but, if they still continued to defy him, he'd give away every arquebus and musket in the Armory. By Yirtta's Dugs, did that put a fire under their arses!"

Hestophes laughed at the idea of such an incongruous sight. "Maybe it *is* possible that our Great King will pull off another of his miracles and vanquish Styphon's Grand Host. I'm just glad I'm on his side."

Skranga's own opinion was that no one should be required to make miracles on demand, because it was human nature that demand for more would quickly outstrip any and all abilities....

"Now, you're going to need the proper uniforms," Hestophes said.

"That's right. The Red Hand dresses in silvered armor and fancy red capes. Do you have anything in the armory at Tarr-Locra we can use?"

"Yes. We have a lot of the armor scavenged from the Battle of Chothros Heights and a room full of Guardsman armor—that is, what hasn't been stolen by the castle staff. I'll see what we have left. You can use some of the other armor. As I recall, your Blethan mercenaries don't believe in armor heavier than boiled leather."

"A few have seen the error of their ways, but you are right. What about capes and breeches?"

"We have lots of seamstresses in Locra Town. If we put a few score of them to work, we should have results. Especially, since you have coin enough to limber their fingers. We also need to have them sew you a yellow Highpriest's vestments. I've got a woman here in Tarr-Lorca that can do that in secret *and* keep her mouth shut. We don't want people thinking we've taken up wearing Styphoni robes."

Skranga nodded, then finished off the last of the brandy. Yes, there was no doubt about it; the resourceful young Captain-General was going to go a long way under Great King Kalvan.

"You're also going to need more men if you're going to pass yourselves off as a Temple Band. Most Styphoni units are under-strength, but not so bad as yours will be. I've got about fifty Blethan mercenaries here, almost all who would jump at a chance to go home. Just one thing."

"What's that?" he asked.

"If I end up facing any of them next spring, Duke, I'm going to personally come after you with gelding shears."

Skranga gulped and tried not to squirm. "It won't happen, Hestophes. Galzar's Oath."

"Good. By Dralm, we've finished off the brandy. Let me call one of my servants and have him bring a barrel of winter wine."

"Yes, by all means. It's been a long and dusty ride."

FOURTEEN

I

That was delicious!" Verkan said as he pushed away from the table. He looked down at his mostly empty plate of turkey, cornbread stuffing, baked potatoes, and succotash and groaned. "I don't think I can eat another thing. . . ."

Dalla agreed.

"I'm sorry, but you're going to have some of Kalvan's *pumpkin pie*," Rylla said. "Kalvan *made* it himself this morning in your honor, and just about drove our cook into a frenzy."

"Where am I going to find the room?" Dalla implored.

"Use your saddlebags if you have to," Verkan whispered sotto voce.

"None of that!" Kalvan said with a laugh, as he came back into the small dining room. "Now, I'm going to have to watch both of you eat. It took me all morning to figure out how to make this pie from scratch, and it's not going to go to waste. The barley crust is more of a shell than a pastry, but it's not bad."

Just then one of the serving wenches brought out a steaming pie.

"Smells good!" Verkan said. "Where'd you learn to make these?"

"In a place far, far away."

"It's all part of what Kalvan calls a proper Thanksgiving Dinner," Rylla said.

"It's probably a bit early for Thanksgiving where I come from, but having our two favorite friends returned to us seems to call for something special. So let's have a toast! To Verkan, to Rylla, and to good friends and good food everywhere."

After everyone had finished their drinks, Rylla ordered their goblets refilled and made another toast. "Praise be to Dralm, we have our heads, our home, and our good friends Verkan, Dalla and Tortha to share this feast with us."

Verkan was glad he had remembered to take his alcodote pill before dinner. Ermut's Best was of high proof indeed.

Tortha Karf looked half-stewed, but he was retired and could afford to enjoy himself. He was attacking the pumpkin pie with real gusto. Verkan, whether or not on leave, was still Chief.

"Great pie," Dalla said. "Kalvan, you'll have to give me the recipe. Rylla, is there anything this man can't do?"

"Other than nursing little Demia, there's not much I can think of right now."

Kalvan blushed to the roots of his beard, and they all laughed.

Another round was poured, and Verkan took the last bite of his pie. *Time to light up a pipe.* Times were few and far between when the Chief of Paracops could relax as comfortably and as thoroughly as this. *I'm going to miss this next year.* A sense of impending doom had been settling around him like a fog. He finished tamping down his tobacco, lit his pipe with the gold-and-pearl inlayed tinderbox Dalla had given him for his first anniversary as Paratime Police Chief, drew deeply, and let loose a great cloud of smoke.

"I see it's time for us to leave," Dalla said, pulling back her chair.

"What! And let them have all the fun?" Rylla asked.

"What fun, Rylla? All they'll do is talk politics and war and get stinking drunk. Let's go to the nursery, play with baby Demia, and then we'll talk politics and war and get properly drunk."

"Let's go."

While the servants removed the plates and unwanted food, Verkan sorted through his thoughts. It was nice to see Kalvan and Rylla getting along again. From what he'd been reading in the dispatches from the University team, he'd half expected them to be using the dinner knives on each other instead of the turkey. In many ways the two of them were a lot like him and Dalla—they both knew how to fight well and make up better.

He wished he could give Kalvan more information about the Grand Host and how fast it was growing, but he couldn't tell him very much without giving away more about his intelligence gathering than he dared to reveal before a man half as sharp as Kalvan. No, he'd just have to keep this to himself. With this new Styphon's House gang Kalvan was going to be both out-manned and out-gunned by a factor of two. And Kalvan didn't even know it yet.

Not that telling him would do much good, as Tortha had reminded him earlier, not with both of Verkan's hands tied as far as help was concerned. Curse and blast all the Paratime Code Regulations that tied a Chief's hands and let his opposition run loose!

"Anything wrong, Verkan? You're awfully quiet."

"Yes," Tortha added. "You have to learn to leave your worries at home."

He gave Tortha a sharp look. Since when had his ex-boss ever left his troubles at home during his tenure as Paratime Chief? "Just digesting this great meal. Kalvan, you really can cook. It's a good thing you don't have a trader's life. If Dalla knew that I could cook, I'd never have any peace."

Kalvan laughed. "There's something to be said in favor of kingship. Although it's not going to be so much fun come this spring."

"Yes, I hear that Hos-Harphax is preparing a counter-strike."

"King Lysandros has moved more decisively than I had anticipated. I see the Inner Circle of Styphon's House and their bottomless moneybox somewhere behind all this. Good thing I hired most of the mercenaries in the Seven Kingdoms before Lysandros and Phidestros learned what I was up to. It looks like I'm going to have to defeat the Harphaxi again. Only this time I'm going to chase them all the way to Harphax City and from there to Hadron's Hall! We're never going to get any peace around here until I do."

"To peace and Styphon's fall!" Tortha toasted, almost dropping his goblet.

After they all had emptied their goblets and gotten them re-filled, Verkan said, "I hear you've been a bit busy, since our meeting."

"I'm still trying to convince the Royal pikemen that an arquebus with a bayonet is superior to any polearm. I made some progress in the last campaign in the Sastragath, but the worst of the hardheads say that was a fight against poorly armed nomads and tribesmen: so it doesn't count. If we didn't have this campaign against Hos-Harphax coming up next spring, I'd fire half the army and start all over again with recruits. I told you both about my Janissaries; they are the future. It's like the old saying goes, 'You buy a man, he owns you; you raise a boy, you own the man.'"

Tortha laughed as he watched Kalvan and Verkan's heads bob in agreement. He rose up. "I can tell the two of you have never raised any children—Ha!"

"You should talk, Tortha. How many children have you sired?"

Tortha sank back in his chair and took another drink. "Well, I've had a lot of nieces and nephews."

"There you have it," Verkan said. He couldn't remember the last time he'd seen Tortha drunk; the last thing he wanted to see was his mentor become emotional. "Not to change the subject, but Kalvan, what have you heard from Great King Nestros?"

"We've exchanged ambassadors and he's asked for more firearms and gunsmiths."

"So far, it sounds like an awfully one-sided arrangement."

Kalvan frowned. He set down his goblet and began to fill the bowl of his pipe. "So far it has been. Nestros keeps coming up with excuses not to commit any troops for our campaign this spring. His excuses are beginning to sound similar to those of the League of Dralm."

"If the Zarthani Knights were moving into the Trygath again, he would be begging you for help."

"I know and I'd probably give it to him, but not because of any affection. Hos-Hostigos is the only Kingdom that recognizes his title which I thought would bind him to us as a natural ally."

"The flip side of that argument," Verkan pointed out, "is Nestros could say that 'Hos-Hostigos would have to be a good ally since my Great Kingdom is the only political body who recognizes Hos-Hostigos as a Great Kingdom!'"

Kalvan shook his head. "I'm sending a delegation under Prince Ptosphes to Hos-Rathon to negotiate with Nestros in person. Maybe he will be more cooperative after he talks with Ptosphes and Harmakros."

"I hope so. Nestros has got to know that Styphon's House would be building an army right now to put Nestros out of business, if Hos-Hostigos weren't their top priority. I know how disappointed you are with the lack of support from the League of Dralm, and now Great King Nestros. With some decent support, they could make your job much easier."

Kalvan set his drink down and shook his right fist. "To Regwarn with the lot of them! After we clean up this Styphon's House racket, I'm going to set some of my neighbors' houses in order as well."

"I often times feel that way about the Greffan Council of Merchants. They're not very happy right now about my virtual monopoly on trade with Hos-Hostigos."

"Then let *them* travel out here and meet with our merchants. I have no quarrel with them. But that brings me to a question I wanted to ask. What does King Theovacar think about this new Great Kingdom of Hos-Rathon that's practically in his backyard?"

"First, you have to keep in mind that King Theovacar doesn't like Great Kings just on principle—the principle being that they can get away with calling themselves 'Great Kings,' a feat his nobles would never let him do. I haven't talked to him about Hos-Rathon, but the word is that he is not unhappy with the arrangement. Prince Varrack of Thagnor is a lot closer to Hos-Rathon and will have to curb his Grefftscharrer ambitions now that he has a new threat in the south. It appears that Prince Varrack's misadventure against the Ros-Zarthani mercenaries neither taught him caution nor slaked his lust for power. In his mind, he lays his loss to the barbarians at Theovacar's feet because King Theovacar refused to come to his aid!

"As long as Great King Nestros doesn't lay claim to any Grefftscharrer territories, which he hasn't done so far, I don't believe there will be any problems coming from King Theovacar."

Kalvan sighed. "There are a few morsels there like Yreth and Ragnar that Nestros would like to devour, but I told him he'd lose my support if he ever threatened their sovereignty."

"Theovacar would like to hear that. I'll see to it that word of this reaches his ears."

"Thanks, Verkan. I don't need any new troubles on my back porch."

"Think nothing of it. I only wish there was more I could do to help until spring arrives. Business is going to keep me in Greffa most of the winter. I'm beginning to think the Mounted Rifles won't even recognize their old commander by the time I return."

Kalvan laughed. "Colonel Ranthar did his best to keep your 'legend' alive before he left for Hos-Bletha. Which reminds me, Baron, it's time I raised your rank from Colonel Verkan to General Verkan. I'll have Captain Mykos, my new adjutant, record it in the muster roll."

"You are too generous, Your Majesty!"

Kalvan made a waving motion with his hands. "No, the Mounted Rifles are a lot bigger these days—a full brigade, not a pumped-up regiment. A lot more rifles, too—almost five hundred. You'll have three regiments under your command, two rifle regiments, the First and Second Mounted Rifles and the Hostigos Mounted Arquebusiers. Your brigade will be the hammer of the Army of Hos-Hostigos."

"Congratulations, Verkan!" Tortha said. "If I were a few years younger, I'd join up with the Royal Army myself."

Kalvan smiled. "You're too valuable in intelligence, Tortha. Especially with my favorite horse-thief, Duke Skranga, off to Hos-Bletha. I need you to run the department."

Kalvan turned to Verkan. "Did you know Trader Tortha was a genius in administration?"

"The family has a lot of names for Uncle Tortha, but genius is not one of them."

Everyone laughed, even Tortha who was turning bright red—and not all from drink.

"In fact, it's time to give Tortha an official rank. Klestreus has been complaining about bringing an 'outsider' into the ranks."

"I'd prefer not to have a title, Your Majesty. As I recall Duke Skranga never had an official rank."

"True, he claimed it would bring him undue attention, and make it difficult, if not impossible, for undercover work."

"A military title might not go over well with the family, after I return to Xiphlon."

"We'll make you the Director of Internal Security: how's that, Tortha?"

"I like it; how about you, Verkan?"

Verkan picked up his pipe and began to fill it with tobacco. "I can't see anyone in my wing of the family having any problems."

"Good," Kalvan said. "Problem solved. Now, Verkan, do you have any more guard commanders of the caliber of Colonel Ranthar? I could use ten or twenty more."

"Sorry, Your Majesty, but I'm having trouble coming up with a new Foundry watchdog. You've stolen my best officer and sent him to Hos-Bletha."

"I agree. Let's just hope that he and Skranga can perform a miracle and convince Great King Niclophon to pull his forces out of the Grand Host."

"Hear, hear," Verkan said, filling their goblets with more of Ermut's Best. "By the way, I can think of one good officer, Captain Porthos. I ran into him at one of your watch stations. I'd use him myself, but he's left the Mounted Rifles for *your* Horseguard." Verkan paused to shake his head. "As soon as I train them, Your Majesty takes them away. Still, I think Porthos will make a good regimental commander. He's cool under fire and has a good grasp of your 'New Model' tactics."

"That's what I like to hear. How old is Porthos?"

"Probably twenty-four, twenty-five winters."

"Good age. Much older and they're mired in the traditional ways of soldiering. I'll have Harmakros interview him for a command position. I've already got more titled nitwits in leadership positions than I can afford. Unfortunately, I won't keep the loyalty of my vassals if I don't give them ranks commensurate with their station. I've scared off the really incompetent with hard work and border duty. Now I need to salt them with good commanders who can keep their head under fire and understand the difference between tactics and strategy."

II

Dalla looked down at the sleeping Demia and sighed. She was so adorable…

"What's the matter, Dalla? Makes you want to have one of your own, doesn't it?"

"Yes… But Verkan would never—"

"To Ormaz with what Verkan wants! It seems to me you think more about what Verkan wants than about what Dalla needs. To this day, Kalvan brags that our daughter was his 'best-executed plan.' The truth is: if I'd let Kalvan set the date for Demia's birth, she'd be arriving about the time Styphon's last priest was blown out of a cannon."

"You mean to say, you had Demia on purpose!"

"Of course. Obviously you have competent Allmother Priestesses in Greffa, or you would be mooning over your own daughter rather than Demia."

"What…? Oh, of course." Even now Dalla was sometimes taken off guard by just how sophisticated outtimers could be. "But Verkan would never forgive me…."

"Listen to yourself. Of course he would, Dalla. Just how angry does Kalvan look to you? He didn't like the idea at first any more than Verkan will."

"You don't know my Verkan…"

"He'll come around, I promise. Did you see him earlier with Demia on his knee? He looked like a proud father."

"You're right, how perceptive." Maybe Rylla had hit on something. *A child, despite all Verkan's complaints, might well give us something to put our lives into perspective.* They were both too career oriented. It wasn't as though they didn't have *plenty* of time. If the baby caused too many problems at work, she'd quit her job.

That would make Verkan's job easier, too. Shut up some of his critics. *Dalla, ol' girl, I think you're on to something.*

"What are you thinking about?"

Dalla looked back down at Demia. "You know. You've given me a different perspective on things. I'll have to talk this over with Verkan—"

"No. That's not the way to do it. He'll just give you a thousand excuses; trust your instincts on this one."

"I will. But what's been happening between you and Kalvan? I've heard some awful rumors. . . ."

"Yes, and they were all true. I did something I really shouldn't have—and wouldn't have, if Kalvan had been here where he belonged! Not that it was all his fault. When the Phaxi attacked the Foundry Party, I used that as an excuse to start a small war."

"But you won, didn't you?"

"Oh, yes. It would have been hard to lose against that gang of incompetents. The trouble is I won a war I should have never started, then I got a little carried away. Sometimes Kalvan acts so squeamish. I wanted to teach him how a rebellious underling was put out of the ruling business for good, so I had Araxes and all of his family put to death."

Rylla showed less remorse than if she'd just drowned a pail full of unwanted kittens. Dalla had to remind herself that in a pre-mechanical monarchy, Prince Araxes' relatives weren't worth as much as a single cat, and held a great more potential for future trouble. "Kalvan doesn't understand how many difficulties deposed princes and their families can bring upon one's House," Dalla said diplomatically.

"Sometimes I believe he truly is too good for this world," Rylla replied. "But in this case he *was* right. The League of Dralm has used this incident to halt all support—what little of it there was—to Hos-Hostigos. Now, if we're not careful we may end up fighting them as well as Styphon's House. I didn't think anyone would miss the little rat!"

"Have you done anything to make the situation right?"

"Kalvan has found a distant relative of Araxes who's sympathetic to Hos-Hostigos and put him on the throne as Prince. He's also given most of Araxes' holdings to those barons sympathetic to our cause. I think he's won their loyalty."

"So it wasn't a complete loss."

"No. But it almost broke up our home. We hardly spoke for almost two moons.… Sometimes, I'm too stubborn for my own good. Kalvan is the only man I've ever loved—but I don't take well to being corrected. Am I wrong, Dalla?"

"Our men wouldn't love us if we tried to be anyone but who we are. A real man doesn't want some cow-eyed wench fawning all over him, but a partner. And sometimes we make mistakes.… One of these days I'll have to tell you about the time Verkan and I split up."

"You and Verkan?"

"That's right. When it comes to blind stubbornness, you don't have any monopoly on that, girl. No, indeed. But we came back together because not only do we love each other, we like each other, too. And we each respect the other, like you and Kalvan."

"It's good to know that Kalvan and I aren't the only ones with this kind of trouble. I'm glad we had this talk, Dalla. I feel much better about things. For a long time I've been feeling that everything that went wrong was all my fault."

"No, no, Rylla. This is no dream castle you have in Hostigos. These Styphoni are really bad people, and they're after you and Kalvan, and nothing either of you do is going to change that. Hostigos earned their unending hate the day Kalvan announced to the world the Fireseed Mystery. Styphon's House will never forgive him for breaking up their monopoly."

"You're right." Rylla shivered.

"What's the matter, Rylla?"

"I was just thinking of what would have happened if Kalvan hadn't come along when he did and saved us all. It would have been bad, wouldn't it?"

"Here, have another drink. You don't want to think about that." *No indeed*, thought Dalla, *I've seen some of those time-lines and it wasn't pretty—not one little bit!*

WINTER

FIFTEEN

I

Danar Sirna took a deep drink of Ermut's Best in the hopes that the spirits would, at the very least, warm some part of her anatomy. Despite a fur shawl and thermal underwear, she was still chilled to the bone. She shivered as the wind blew through the rafters of the Foundry common hall.

There was a roaring fire in the hearth, but Sirna was seated far enough away that its heat was little more than a warm kiss. Like almost everything else connected with University life, seating distance to the fire was a matter of title and seniority—she had neither. Seated closest to the fire were the Study-Team's Director Talgan Dreth, his assistant Gorath Tran and visiting Professor Shalgro, the paratemporal probability theorist. The next circle included the senior faculty, Varnath Lala, Professor Lathor Karv, Doctor Sankar Trav and her friend Aranth Saln, the pre-industrial military expert, who looked as out of place among this crowd as a tomcat in a turkey coop.

Sirna wondered what had convinced the former professor of military science to leave his classes for outtime research. On second thought, Saln was probably more at home here on Kalvan's Time-Line than he ever was back at the University of Dhergabar. The thought of the bald professor with his waxed mustache sitting at a University tea brought a smile to her lips. He was probably as glad to be here, away from University politics and sanctions as she was.

She was beginning to really like living here on Kalvan's Time-Line; it would be a sad day when she had to return to First Level again. She'd have to face herself, her old life and her parents.

Unfortunately, if some of the things she'd just heard about the Grand Host of Styphon were true, going home might come a lot faster than she or anyone else had expected. Grand Master Soton and Great King Lysandros were putting together an army so massive that even King Kalvan would be hard pressed to stop it, much less defeat it as he had done before. Kalvan's problems were legion: the Grand Host; the League of Dralm, which had just rejected his plea for economic and military aid; and then the Princes of Ulthor and Nyklos, who were beginning to worry more about their own necks than the Great Kingdom of Hostigos.

It would take all of Kalvan's military expertise as well as Appalon's Own Luck to survive this spring's invasion; yet, for the Kalvan Study-Team members, Kalvan's success or failure had as much relevance as an academic feud.

"Kalvan is in serious trouble now," Professor Lathor Karv pontificated. "He has severely strained the social and political infrastructure of the Five Kingdoms. The idea of Hos-Rathon being a Great Kingdom is ludicrous. Now the new states are about to revert to their previous forms."

"In other words," Aranth Saln interjected, pausing to drain his tankard, "Kalvan is between a rock and a hard place, as they say on Europo-American."

"If I correctly understand the meaning of your colorful Fourth Level phraseology, yes, Kalvan will be lucky to survive the coming upheavals as the natural social order reforms to its pre-Kalvan boundaries."

"I disagree," old Professor Shalgro interrupted. "Kalvan has done more than disrupt local social and political relations; he has permanently fractured them. Whether or not Kalvan survives the outcome of next year's invasion, his ideas will live beyond his own corporeal existence."

"I beg to disagree, Professor Shalgro. When Archpriest Roxthar's Investigators get through with Hostigos, there won't be anyone who remembers who Kalvan was, much less his so-called innovations."

"That is not true, Lathor," Aranth Saln stated with conviction. "Kalvan's enemies are now using his own tactics and strategies to defeat him—it is still too soon to tell whether or not they will be successful. The reason the Grand Host looks as strong as it does is because the army was put together by the two men, Grand Master Soton and Captain-General Phidestros, who have learned Kalvan-style tactics the hard way. Not even Roxthar is crazy enough to destroy his best generals. And that is to say nothing of the Middle Kingdoms, who now have the fireseed secret and owe no allegiance to Styphon's House or Styphon's priests."

"Then the Middle Kingdoms will be next to fall under Styphon's Grand Host," Lathor Karv declared.

"It's quite apparent," Saln said, "that you know next to nothing about military history. The Grand Host is a fragile amalgamation of not-so-grand allies, who are *only* united in their opposition to Kalvan. The minute Kalvan is defeated or killed, the Grand Host will begin to fall apart. The idea of Captain-General Phidestros leading them into the Middle Kingdoms is a romantic fantasy engendered by too much dependence upon computer programs rather than experience in the field or study of historical analogs. For example, on Fourth Level Europo-American, there was Hannibal, the great Carthaginian general, whose misfortune was that far and away his best student was a Roman named Scipio Africanus the Elder."

"Ha! I see that progress has bypassed by the Military Science Department as well as any coherent theoretical framework," Professor Lathor Karv asserted. "I have personally run over fifty simulations where Kalvan's army is defeated; in every one of them the Grand Host remains united to not only scourge all of Hostigos of Kalvanites, but to invade the Middle Kingdoms—thereby removing all taint of Kalvan's heresies."

"In case you hadn't noticed, there is a difference between computer simulations and real life, which is neither sanitary nor predictable—"

Sirna tuned out the argument, which would probably continue for most of the evening. It was far easier to be concerned about academic debating points when your feet were dry and your nose wasn't tingling from the cold. Besides, it appeared that all of them—even her friend Aranth Saln—had missed the human connection. Kalvan was not a number or equation in the

University database; he was a living breathing human with a will and aspirations of his own. That was something her friend, Baltrov Eldra, would have brought up were she not headed to Hos-Bletha. Not for the first time, she missed Eldra's good sense and humor.

Sirna wanted Kalvan to win. To Regwarn's Caverns with Lathor Karv's theories, or Lala's view of Kalvan as the symbol of unbridled male aggression gone berserk. No, Kalvan was a good man trying his best against almost impossible odds. As far as she was concerned, they ought to be trying to think of ways to help Kalvan rather than dissecting his still warm body.

II

As Kalvan and Rylla rode their horses down the Great King's Highway, he explained his plans for the Hostigos Royal Academy of Military Studies: how he was attempting to create the core of tomorrow's army—today.

"Kalvan, I believe we have enough orphans in Hos-Hostigos for three Great Kingdoms. Use *our* unwanted children for your new army. We don't need to take these Ruthani cast-offs from your *friend* Ranjar Sargos."

"I intend to use the Hostigi orphans like mortar for the building blocks of the next generation's army. The academy can teach the Ruthani our language and customs."

"I still believe it's a mistake to bring these nomads into Hostigos and attempt to teach them our ways. It won't work, darling."

Kalvan knew arguing with Rylla was futile. He expected, knowing Rylla, that once she actually got to see the children and meet with them, her heart would soften as she realized they were only abandoned children who needed a home and some protection.

The royal procession passed a work gang, repairing one side of the Great King's Highway, which had been damaged during a recent thunderstorm. The workers were shoring up the side of the road with boulders and then filling them in with smaller rocks. The men took time off from their work to wave and cry, "Hail, King Kalvan!"

The party crossed a wooden bridge, took the left fork just after Sycamore Creek and followed a winding dirt road through some trees and into a wide pasture which was home to the new Royal Academy. Some of the older children were scampering over the roof, helping to repair the old slate roof of the former baronial estate, while several other large bands were marching in ranks before the assembly grounds. Seeing the Royal Banner, the children were quickly drawn up into files at parade rest. There was a minimal amount of confusion and the small boys looked properly military in their dark green woolen trousers, maroon pullover long-sleeve shirts and dark red stocking caps. The officers wore small morion helmets with maroon and green plumes.

Even Rylla looked impressed.

Harmakros, who as head of the Royal Army had been overseeing their care, told them, "We've already laid the foundation for the new dormitories, and hope to have them built before the first snow."

"You'd better work quickly, then," Rylla admonished.

Harmakros smiled. "We'll get it done in time if I have to impress half the Royal Army. I can do that too, since Kalvan has made the cadets probationary members of the Royal Army of Hos-Hostigos."

Rylla looked over at Kalvan and shook her head.

Kalvan shrugged his shoulders. "They're only kids. We're their parents, *in loco parentis.*

"What's that mean, Kalvan?"

"The throne has taken the place of their parents. And these children are happy to be here instead of working as slave labor in the Sastragath—most of them never surviving to their maturity, the rest haggard and crippled—old beyond their years. It's a rough life in the Sastragath and the slaves I saw there looked badly used."

Since foundations for big buildings here-and-now were built using stone they didn't have to worry about setting concrete. *Portland cement, put that on the to do list,* Kalvan thought, *lots of local limestone.*

"Until the dormitories are finished, most of the older children are living in army tents. We've counted over fifteen thousand children, with more wagons arriving every day." Harmakros paused to shake his head. "If I didn't know better, I'd suspect Sargos was transplanting every child in the Sea of Grass to Hos-Hostigos!"

"Can we feed all these children?" Rylla said, with a disapproving glance at Kalvan.

Kalvan nodded. "We had a record harvest this year, every granary in the kingdom is filled to bursting. If we didn't have all these extra mouths to feed, we'd have to burn some of it to keep the rats and mice out of the surplus."

Colonel Tyral stepped forward and introduced the king and queen to the small cadets, and they spontaneously burst into applause.

Kalvan looked out over the sea of faces, many of them red-skinned Ruthani, while the others were the paler-skinned Urgothi and Zarthani children. "I welcome you all as future subjects of the Great Kingdom of Hos-Hostigos. You may consider Great Queen Rylla and myself as your new parents. And while We will not be able to speak to each of you, the staff of the Academy will take personal charge of your lives in Our behalf."

One of the smaller cadets, about seven or eight years old, came forward brushing the hair out of his big brown eyes. In halting and obviously memorized Zarthani, he said, "We…children all wants to thank the King and Queen Kalvan for give us…a home."

Rylla quickly dismounted and swept the boy up into to her arms to the obvious delight of the watching children. She gave him a big hug and bussed him on the cheek. Some of the other children, ignoring their frantic commandant who was signaling them to remain in their ranks, rushed forward to touch and speak to their Queen.

Harmakros' head swiveled back and forth as he searched vainly for help, "What do we do Your Majesty?"

Kalvan smiled smugly. "She'll be fine. It's only the little ones who are breaking ranks." Meanwhile Rylla was dispensing hugs and caresses to the smallest of their charges, some still stick thin from illness and their lengthy journey. Kalvan was reminded of kittens around a bowl of cream. Even from his saddle, he could see the tears on Rylla's face.

After a few more minutes, Kalvan allowed the colonel to reform ranks and return the children to their drills. Then he dismounted and toured the hastily-repaired manor, although to Kalvan it appeared to be more fortress than estate. The large rooms and great hall had been turned into dormitories, while the kitchen had been enlarged and was full of women and girls preparing barley and mutton stew. Rylla frowned about something, but the facility was surprisingly clean, and the odors wafting from the cooking stew had his stomach churning in hunger. He accepted a spoonful of the rich stew from a young girl and pantomimed 'yummy' to their cheers.

Behind the manor was a veritable tent city of displaced children, many of them dressed no better than beggars. Kalvan had just founded a uniform factory for the Royal Army when the children's army had arrived and had reassigned it to making small uniforms for the newly created cadets. His introduction of the spinning wheel for wool and cotton had vastly increased the factories' ability to manufacture clothing, but they were still lagging far behind the demand created by the necessity to immediately clothe thousands of children.

Already the Council of Guilds was complaining about 'unfair competition' as the spinning wheels spread to residences, and housewives discovered they could spin much more of their own wool with the new spinning wheels than with a drop-spindle.

As they rode back to Tarr-Hostigos, Rylla turned to him and said, "I'm glad you convinced me to visit the Academy. I was wrong and you were right about the children. Under their skin they are all Hostigi. They will be good subjects for Us and Our children."

Kalvan felt as though he were floating on air. But she quickly brought him down to earth with her addendum.

"I just want to know why there weren't any girls marching on the parade ground?"

Kalvan tried to signal Harmakros to keep quiet, but the Captain-General stepped into the breach by himself. "Girls don't soldier, Your Majesty!"

Rylla had her sword point at Harmakros' throat before Kalvan could blink. "What do you mean 'girls don't soldier,' Captain-General?"

Harmakros gulped. "Your Majesty being the exception, of course."

"No, I don't accept that. Girls don't fight because men won't allow them to. I was just lucky that my father had the good sense to give me my freedom."

Kalvan had to bite his tongue. Prince Ptosphes had spoiled Rylla to high heaven and back.

"I know that many girls would choose to be soldiers if they were allowed to make that decision by themselves, instead of by their fathers and brothers."

"Can you remove your rapier, Your Majesty?"

"Sorry, Harmakros. Do you understand what I'm saying?"

"Yes, Your Majesty," he said, rubbing the red spot just below his Adam's apple where the point had rested.

"Then you'll agree that any of the nomad girls who wish to soldier should be given that freedom," Rylla announced.

"It is not my decision to make. I leave all policy matters to Your Majesties," Harmakros answered, giving Kalvan a cat-that-ate-the-carrier-pigeon smile.

Rylla turned her fury upon Kalvan, who held up his hand. "Whoa! I haven't said anything yet!"

"Then you agree with me?"

Kalvan shot Harmakros a look that would have dropped a Sastragathi warrior out of his saddle from fifty paces. He'd read about the Israelis' attempts to integrate line troops and some of the problems, besides the fraternization, they'd had.

"Unlike Our Captain-General, I will not dismiss your idea. But there are certain problems involved in having women in combat positions."

"Yes…?"

"In the Cold Lands we had a few such mixed male and female infantry units, and they had some special problems."

Harmakros looked horrified that Kalvan hadn't dismissed such nonsense out of hand.

"Besides the issue of unwanted births, which was no small problem, they found that male soldiers would not abandon wounded women even under fierce enemy fire. Many men died in futile attempts to save women soldiers, who later died anyway from their injuries."

Rylla nodded. "I could not leave you on the battlefield, wounded or dying."

"Nor would I leave you, my love. This is a real problem because when men and women live together, train together and kill together, deep bonds develop. If we are going to have women in the Royal Army, other than as healers—another tradition from my Homeland—then I suggest we segregate them into all-women units."

"I agree, my husband."

"Also, if we are going to start with the orphans, I suggest we only take determined volunteers. Many of the girls will offer to fight only out of obligation to Us or fear of the future. We only need those who have a burning desire to be warriors, for only then will they make good soldiers."

"I agree in all things. I will, of course, want to have a personal hand in their selection, and insist that in all other ways they be treated as men would be."

Kalvan nodded. Preferential treatment for any special caste of soldier only bred discontent, unless they were elite troops picked for ability alone and thereby had the respect of their comrades. "It shall be done, my love."

Rylla smiled contentedly, while Kalvan wondered how big the ripples from this change might grow in the next few generations. He could already hear the Styphoni propaganda machines working the instant they learned Kalvan was using women soldiers on the field of battle—the ungodliness of it all! The sad part was the people here-and-now, most of whom didn't know any better, would buy it lock, stock and fireseed barrel.

III

Archpriest Anaxthenes found upon his return to Balph that the waterfront was almost deserted, with only a few dockworkers on the wharves. *Where are the transports and merchant ships?* he wondered. Half of the Inner Circle met his party at the Rydos Docks. Archpriest Roxthar was noticeable by his absence.

On the carriage ride back to the Great Temple of Styphon, Anaxthenes was peppered with questions about the coronation of Great King Lysandros and the latest news on the Usurper, and was told of Roxthar's Investigators' latest outrages. His longtime allies, the Archpriests Heraclestros, Euriphocles, Neamenestros and Zemos shared the carriage along with Grand Master Soton.

Anaxthenes noticed that for mid-day the traffic in the streets of Balph was almost non-existent. "Where are all the wagons and carriages? Is the entire City in mourning over Sesklos' illness? I had not thought he was so popular among the people."

"No, Sesklos' illness has been little noticed," Neamenestros answered. "But the Investigation has been going on night and day since you and the Grand Master left. The merchants avoid even the Central Plaza for fear of being caught up and investigated. Roxthar's Investigators have been known to drag a man out of his wagon and take him into the Office of Investigation from which most do not return, for nothing more than failing to doff a hat at a passing Inspector in his white robes. The Holy City hasn't lost so many townsmen since the Great Plague."

"Has Balph now become the City of Butchers instead of priests?"

"Many with impure hearts have fled before the Terror of the Investigation," Neamenestros answered.

"What Neamenestros really means is anyone with any brains has left Balph until the Terror is over." Archpriest Zemos was known for his plain speaking, which had delayed his appointment to the Inner Circle by many winters. "Like most of the Balph's priests, Neamenestros sees white robes in his sleep and is afraid to speak his own mind."

"It pains me to see the Holy City in a state of siege," Anaxthenes pronounced. "It is as though the Usurper Kalvan and his army are at the gates. Only worse, because the enemy has come from within the gates. We must stop Roxthar before he destroys the Temple. Do we have enough votes to stop Roxthar's stooge, Dracar, from being Elected the next Styphon's Voice on Earth?"

"Speaker, we have talked to most of the Inner Circle," said Heraclestros, "and you can count on at least twenty hands raised in your support as Styphon's Voice, as soon as Sesklos makes his journey to Regwarn. True, Sesklos named Archpriest Dracar as his successor, but he would be fortunate to count ten votes, including those of Investigator Roxthar and his supplicants.

"Who else, besides yourself, has enough support to stop that madman Roxthar from imposing his will upon the Inner Circle? While you were absent in Hos-Harphax, the Investigator once again attempted to pass a decree placing Styphon's Own Guard under the powers of his Office of Investigation. Even the most cowardly of the Inner Circle rose up in protest. Roxthar has moved too far and too fast, now all the Archpriests fear his Investigation. Once he has the Guard under his personal command, he will not stop until he Investigates the Inner Circle."

Anaxthenes nodded. *Self-preservation is a good fulcrum,* he thought. "They are not wrong, for Roxthar's ambition knows no limit. Nor his piety, which is even more frightening. We are all allies in this carriage, so I can speak my mind." The other three men looked at Grand Master Soton, who nodded his head in agreement. The archpriests visibly relaxed.

"In the beginning, Roxthar was good for the Temple—a goad to get us up off our hindparts. He forced the Inner Circle to realize that the Daemon Kalvan was the Temple's undoing and if he were not stopped would bring an end to Styphon's House on Earth. It is also true that Roxthar helped prepare us for the upcoming battle against the Usurper. Now, he wastes his time and our blood, thinning the ranks of Styphon's House of its priesthood searching for that which cannot be found—true believers. Other than Archpriest Cimon, they do not exist. Am I right?"

"Yes, Speaker," they all joined in.

"I've been told that there are many true believers among the priesthood of Dralm, but only a few have ever existed among the upper priesthood of Styphon's House. Roxthar might as well search for gold in a privy pit!"

The carriage was filled with nervous laughter.

Anaxthenes continued, "Roxthar is mad, yet he is also our best weapon against the Usurper. We must balance the good of the Temple against our own safety."

"A most delicate balance, Anaxthenes," Soton said. "I do agree with your reasoning. We have to leash this panther and release him upon the Temple's enemies, while keeping ourselves out of his jaws."

"This is true," Heraclestros said. "And Speaker Anaxthenes is the only one amongst us who can restrain this beast in human form. At long last, the Inner Circle has come to see the truth. Too many of us have lost friends and colleagues to Roxthar's ravenous appetite. Even the townspeople are beginning to stir. In the last moon-quarter, four Investigators have been found dead in the City's gutters, with their throats cut. The Investigator's efforts to find the perpetrators have left a thousand dead and Balph in an uproar."

Anaxthenes felt joy in his veins for the first time since Kalvan had arrived to bedevil them from the distant Princedom of Hostigos. "I will accept the Inner Circle's will and promise to do my best to keep this panther caged. But I must have yours and the Inner Circle's complete support—now and in the future. Make this clear to the other Archpriests."

"It will be done," Archpriest Zemos pronounced.

"Good. Now, what other problems have arisen in my absence?"

"Great King Cleitharses..." Heraclestros stammered. "There is talk that he will not commit the Sacred Squares of Hos-Ktemnos to the Grand Host. When Archpriest Roxthar came back from his visit, he was so angry he looked as if he could teethe on musket barrels!"

"The war is lost without the Sacred Squares of Hos-Ktemnos," Anaxthenes said. "They are the largest and best army in the Five Kingdoms. And if they don't join the Grand Host, neither will many of the Ktemnoi Princes and their levy. I will talk to Cleitharses myself and remind him of his debts to Styphon's House. Roxthar knows naught of diplomacy and politics."

He knew full well of Cleitharses, whom many thought the most harmless of men, and his secret vice of taking pleasure with royal pages.

"We will go together," Soton said. "I will convince him that the borders of Hos-Ktemnos will be secure, even if the Order has to take a dozen Lances into Hostigos."

Anaxthenes nodded his agreement. *If Cleitharses won't agree with reason, I will whisper in his ear, and he will do whatever he is told, or risk the wrath of his subjects and Styphon's House.*

SIXTEEN

I

A cannonball smashed into the wall of Tarr-Thaphigos, creating a shower of stone splinters and rocks that cascaded harmlessly down the stone facing. Unlike the rest of the Princedom of Thaphigos, which had fallen into Phidestros' arms like a ripe fruit, this castle was going to take a lot of pounding.

Prince Eltar had not had the time to rebuild Thaphigos' economy and military, after several years of rebellion and the succession wars; however, he had found the time to repair and fortify the seat of his power. Tarr-Thaphigos was an old castle, but stoutly and strongly built; it had repulsed many attacks during the succession wars, but none with as many guns as Phidestros had brought for this investment.

Phidestros knew that within two or three moons the old tarr would fall, either by the cumulative effects of night-and-day bombardment or starvation. Unfortunately, he did not have time to waste; this was supposed to be a quick campaign to stiffen his army's morale, not a stalled siege. In addition it was winter and he had ten thousand soldiers to feed and quarter. They were losing more soldiers to the freezing weather than they were to their enemies' fire.

He motioned Kyblannos over. "How long is it going to take to crack this nut?"

Kyblannos frowned. "It could be a while, Captain-General. I was only able to bring twelve guns, most of them four and eight-pounders—none of them proper siege guns. We only have two sixteen-pound guns. Two moons, if we're lucky...."

He ground his teeth. "That was my own conclusion."

One of his captain's shouted, "Look up, on the wall! A herald holding his helmet up on a spear."

Phidestros looked up and saw a herald. *What's there to talk about?* he asked himself. *Are they going to surrender? Impossible! Or was it?* He signaled Kyblannos to stop firing the guns.

A short while later, after the cannon fire had stopped, the herald was joined by none other than Prince Eltar and his Chancellor.

Captain Lythrax raised his *rifle* and asked, "Head shot, or body?"

His best marksman in all of Hos-Harphax with the new *rifles*, Lythrax could shoot a pigeon off a chimney from three hundred paces. It was awfully tempting.... Phidestros quickly sorted out the obvious scenarios: with Prince Eltar dead the siege would be over by evening, but at the expense of a Ban of Galzar for killing an enemy under the parley sign—which could easily lead to a revolt among his mercenaries. Nor would an assassination, no matter how useful, help his growing reputation as a great Captain-General among the soldiers and folk of Hos-Harphax. "Hold your fire. Let the fool speak."

Lythrax grumbled but lowered his *rifle* barrel.

The Prince shouted, "I challenge you, Captain-General, if you have any honor, to man to man combat. A fight to the death. If you win, my castle and my realm are forfeit. If I win, you will abandon your attack on Thaphigos."

Phidestros could hardly believe his own senses: *what kind of madman would sake the fate of a Princedom on a duel? A desperate man who knows he will lose unless he rolls the dice.*

"Let me take him out, Captain-General."

Phidestros pushed his lanky bodyguard aside and motioned Kyblannos to his side. "What do you know about this Eltar?"

"He's an expert swordsman and a soldier of the old school. You're taller and have longer arms, but he's much more experienced in duels. You will have your work cut out for you if you accept his challenge."

Phidestros nodded. He was good with a sword, but no one had ever called him a great swordsman. On the other hand, the Prince was at least a head shorter than himself and ten winters older. It was a calculated risk that could easily cost him his life. Yet, if he won—"

"I AM WAITING, CAPTAIN-GENERAL!"

"I accept." A great roar rose up from the Army of Hos-Harphax as they shouted their approval.

As the castle gates opened to the Prince and his party, Phidestros huddled with Grand-Captain Geblon and his bodyguard. "Lythrax, bring up the rest of the *riflemen*. If I fall with a mortal wound, shoot the Prince and his seconds. Geblon, prepare a sortie party to enter the tarr if I lose."

"You mean I am to renounce your *oath*!"

"If I'm dead, Geblon, my oath is meaningless. You are my second in command. Your duty is to secure and hold the castle, by any means. Those are *my* orders!"

"What will I tell Uncle Wolf Olmnestes?"

"That the oath died with my body. You have made no promises to Prince Eltar, who by that time will also be dead. So you will not be breaking your word. Galzar will forgive you. Understood?"

Geblon nodded, his face in a scowl, as if he didn't like what he was hearing, but would follow orders anyway.

Captain Lythrax said, "I will avenge you, Captain-General."

Phidestros shook his head in dismay. "This is a contingency plan. My goal is to kill Eltar, not fall on his blade!"

There was a great shout as Prince Eltar pulled forth his sword.

"Time to go. Do as I have ordered."

Phidestros approached the Prince, drawing his own sword, a saber that was half again as long as the Prince's, who suddenly looked dismayed. He'd left his buffalo jacket on since it would offer additional protection from any sword blows that got through his guard. The Prince was shorter, but he was broad-shouldered and heavily muscled.

Before Phidestros could make his first strike, Eltar dashed forward with a powerful sword stroke that he barely deflected. Sweat was already beading on his forehead despite the chill wind. As the Prince pedaled backwards under his counter-attack, Phidestros brought up his sword for a fatal blow and missed when the Prince darted unexpectedly to the left.

Before he could get his sword up, Eltar was moving inside and he deflected a cut that slashed across the armored tasses covering his hips. Only the length of his sword and his greater reach kept the better swordsman from carving him like a side of beef.

It was keeping peace with Galzar's priests that kept Phidestros from drawing his widow-maker and dropping the Prince like an empty suit of armor. He took a glancing blow to his burgonet, making him realize that he'd better use his head before he lost it. Then he saw his advantage: the Prince had the old-style sword with sharp edges but no real point, while he had a Kalvan-style saber.

They exchanged sword blows until both men were drawing deep breaths like bellows. Phidestros was bleeding from a dozen small cuts, when he slipped on a rock. The Prince drew back his sword and Phidestros saw his opening. He thrust upward, ramming his sword point through the chain mail protecting Eltar's right underarm and felt it strike bone. Yanking his sword loose, a stream of blood began to drain from the Prince's armor and Eltar made a savage cry of pain and despair.

The Prince tried to lift up his sword, but it fell from his blood-soaked hands. Before he could take hold of his sword with his left hand, Phidestros rose up to his full height and struck his helm with an overhead blow that sent the Eltar reeling with blood gushing from under his helmet, and finally falling to the ground. A quick stab through the up-raised visor ended the Prince's twitching and his body quickly stilled.

A great cry of triumph came from the Harphaxi Army when Phidestros raised his bloody saber in victory.

His body battered, his limbs numb from the cold wind and his head aching—Phidestros knew that he'd added a bright bauble this day to the legend he was composing.

II

Anaxthenes and his party were met at the door of Great King Cleitharses' private audience chamber by the Chancellor and a distinguished gray-haired Highpriest in yellow robes whom he had never seen before. The Highpriest pulled the door open, bowed and stepped out of the way.

All four walls of the chamber, except for the window slits, were covered with shelves of scrolls in golden cases. The Great King rose out of his chair unevenly, using a cane to gain his feet. Although the Great King's back was bowed by age, his hands were still steady. Out of his cloth-of-gold robes, Great King Cleitharses, with his wild hair and untrimmed beard, could have passed for one of Balph's beggars or vagabonds. Both Cleitharses' eyes were the color of milk, and he was all but blind.

"Your Majesty," Anaxthenes said, "I'm not familiar with your advisor."

"This is Highpriest Danthor who hails from Iylos Town in Hos-Bletha. He was driven from his Temple when the nomads sacked the town. When I asked Archivist Vyros for a new reader for Your Majesty, he recommended Highpriest Danthor. He's done a wonderful job; his voice is magnificent."

Highpriest Danthor made a slight bow, but otherwise appeared attentive. Anaxthenes made a mental note to interview him later. Since the Investigator's purge of the Temple's upper ranks, there was a growing need for highpriests who were not Roxthar's minions. His agents had informed him that Roxthar's tentacles had not stretched as far as Hos-Bletha—for now.

"What can I do for you Speaker? I don't have a lot of time. Danthor has been reading me Plymestros' Chronicles regarding the Second Nomad Invasion."

Everyone looked at Anaxthenes, so he began. "Styphon's House has come to ask for your support for the final war against the Usurper Kalvan."

"Yes, of course, you have my support." He looked back at Highpriest Danthor as if he expected them to suddenly disappear.

"We need more than your moral support, Your Majesty. We need the Sacred Squares and the princely armies of Hos-Ktemnos for the coming battles."

"No, Speaker. You and your generals," Cleitharses paused to look straight at Grand Master Soton. "You used the armies of Hos-Ktemnos badly last time in this Dralm-blasted war. Now, We have two new barbarian provinces, which dare to call themselves kingdoms, to protect Ourselves against. Use the Armies of Hos-Harphax and Hos-Agrys."

"They are not large enough to win this war, Your Majesty. We must have the Sacred Squares to defeat the Usurper Kalvan in his own lair."

"Kalvan, what has he ever done against Us? Kalvan, in his letters to Us, asks for peace and tells Us he has no animus against Our subjects. He does not attack unless provoked. No, I will not make the same mistake a second time against Our neighbor. Let this ruthless King Lysandros, who steals his nephew's inheritance, spend *his* men to regain his lost princedoms. It is not Our fight and We will not countenance it!"

Anaxthenes was taken aback. "It's not a request from me, but from Styphon, your God."

"Styphon is no longer my god, or that of my people. We have many gods and goddesses, and none are as ruthless and heartless as Styphon and his so-called Investigators. Your priests have badly used Our subjects. We will not aid you or Styphon's House any farther in your endless wars."

Anaxthenes cursed Roxthar and his bloody ways under his breath; this was a side of Cleitharses he had never seen before. Since Cleitharses was not moved by this wind, he would have to take another tack. He leaned forward and began to whisper to the Great King, who had slumped back down in his chair. He noted that Highpriest Danthor had moved back out of listening range. "How would your people act if they learned that their Great King dallied with Royal Pages?"

Cleitharses leaned back in his chair and laughed, his toothless mouth and sightless eyes wide open. "Priest, you dare threaten me? Our subjects would be amused at such a trifle in these days of discord. Almtros, bring me the letters."

The Chancellor, who had been lurking in the corner, left the chamber to return a few moments later with a servant carrying a large basket overflowing with parchments and scrolls. "These are all complaints about your Archpriest Roxthar and his Investigation. This is only one of ten baskets, containing more letters than I have received in the past two winters. Rein your beast in, or there will be blood in the streets!"

Anaxthenes leaned in closer. "We are in agreement, Your Majesty. It is Roxthar's plan to join the Grand Host in Hos-Harphax and to take his Investigators with him to rid the false kingdom of Hos-Hostigos of unbelievers."

The Great King slumped down as if his unexpected burst of anger had drained him of all his strength. He was a frail man and naive about the ways of the world since he had spent most of his reign in the Royal Library. "But why should I spend my soldiers to do the Temple's work and thereby aid this madman's desire to ravage Hostigos?"

Anaxthenes leaned in again to make his point. "Because, Your Majesty, it will remove Archpriest Roxthar and his Investigators from Hos-Ktemnos. With the Ktemnoi troops, the Grand Host will be able to defeat the Usurper Kalvan and Roxthar will spend the next few winters Investigating the Hostigi. When he returns, I will be Styphon's Own Voice and there will be no more Investigation in this kingdom—ever. You have my oath."

Cleitharses looked as if he were about to laugh then thought better of it. "Despite all your ruthlessness and scheming, Speaker, I have never heard you called oath-breaker. Still, I hesitate to send my armies to the north against Hos-Hostigos when I now have two new enemies to the west, the Warlord Sargos, who now calls himself the Var-Wannax, and King Nestros, who falsely claims the title of Great King."

"My castellans will guard the borders of Hos-Ktemnos," Soton said, speaking up for the first time.

"With what, Grand Master, after you strip the border tarrs of their Lances to fight Kalvan in Hostigos?"

A brilliant scheme blossomed in Anaxthenes' mind. "What if I could promise you the neutrality of King Nestros, Your Majesty? Would you commit your Army and the princely levy against the Usurper?"

The old king was so quiet that for a few moments Anaxthenes thought he'd fallen asleep.

"That would ease my fears of invasion. Yes, but only if Roxthar and his Investigators also depart."

"There is nothing on this earth, nor in Hadron's realm, that could keep Investigator Roxthar from joining the Grand Host of Styphon. The Investigator is so anxious to Investigate Kalvan and his Queen that he is already sharpening his favorite knives and chisels."

"Then I will agree to join the war against Hos-Hostigos, but only after you bring me proof that King Nestros will not attack or commit any aggression upon Hos-Ktemnos."

"It will be done, Your Majesty. I will conduct the negotiations myself." The situation in Balph was tenuous, with Sesklos at death's gate, but without Cleitharses' support the war against Kalvan would be doomed. It would be up to him to *convince* Nestros to make an alliance with Hos-Ktemnos—for now!

"Very good, Speaker. But, I'm not finished. I also want Highpriest Danthor to represent Us both on the mission to Rathon and in the Inner Circle."

Anaxthenes looked over at Highpriest Danthor who appeared as surprised at the Great King's request as himself. Cleitharses' expression was grim and fixed; Anaxthenes could tell this was not a negotiable point. He knew when to retreat as well as when to advance. "It shall be done. There are two openings in the Inner Circle."

Great King Cleitharses' eyes closed as if the last of his energy had departed with their agreement.

Anaxthenes turned to Danthor and said, "Highpriest, we will meet tonight to discuss the details of both your mission and your new responsibilities as a member-elect of the Inner Circle of Styphon's House."

Danthor nodded, his eyes carefully guarded.

Almost petulantly, the Great King stirred, adding, "I also want Danthor to continue to read my scrolls. He's my favorite reader."

"Of course, as duty permits, Your Majesty," Anaxthenes responded, almost without thought. To be allowed his own ear in Great King Cleitharses' private chambers was too good an offer to refuse. This Highpriest could be a valuable tool, or possibly even an ally. In these troubled times there were only two factions: you were either for Roxthar or against him. And in Balph, if you were against him, you were for Anaxthenes.

III

Verkan was waiting at his desk in the Foundry basement for a call from Danthor Dras, of all people. One of the members of the Balph Study Team had radioed him at his townhouse with a message that the Dean of Aryan-Transpacific Studies wanted to talk with him. A blue light lit up and when Verkan tapped in the proper code, Danthor Dras, calling from the Balph Study Team's office and still wearing the yellow robes of a Styphon's House highpriest, was on the screen.

Danthor looked like a ten-year-old boy who'd just gotten away with pulling his sister's hair. "You won't believe the kind of day I've had today!"

"Yes?" Verkan wondered, by the smile lighting up his face, if the Scholar had been appointed overseer of the Paratime Police.

"For the last moon-half I've been reading chronicles aloud to Great King Cleitharses who suffers from an advanced case of cataracts."

Verkan nodded. It wasn't unusual to see cataract sufferers begging on the streets of Hostigos Town, since there was no known cure at their primitive level of technology. He was hoping that Danthor didn't want to effect a cure—that would be very close to Outtime Contamination.

"You'll never guess who visited the Great King in his private chambers today."

Verkan said, "Archpriest Roxthar?"

"Good guess! No, it was a delegation from the Inner Circle of Styphon's House headed by none other than Speaker Anaxthenes and Grand Master Soton. They were visiting to formally ask for King Cleitharses' military support for the spring invasion of Hos-Hostigos"—Danthor paused to laugh—"or as we're required to call it, the 'false-kingdom of Hostigos.' They were shocked into the last moon when the Great King turned them down. It appears the Holy Investigation has been building a bad name for Styphon's House right in the heart of Styphoni country. Cleitharses, in an unexpected show of strength, told the Archpriests to fight their own war."

Verkan whistled. "Kalvan would love to know about this!"

"Well, he might not be too happy about the conclusion of their chat, Chief. Archpriest Anaxthenes is quite the Machiavellian; when coercion, intimidation or naked threats won't work; he switches tactics and becomes as reasonable as can be. On the Kalvan Control Time-Lines I visited, he is not so self-assured or in charge; there he's more a puppeteer, content to pull strings off-stage. Here Anaxthenes has grabbed the reins of power with both hands: the word on the streets of Balph is that he's to be the next Styphon's Voice after Sesklos dies. Even Grand Master Soton was willing to stay beneath his shadow during the meeting with Cleitharses. Anaxthenes' power struggle with Roxthar over the fate of Styphon's House has made him both a hungrier and more dangerous man. Unfortunately for Kalvan, both Anaxthenes and Roxthar share the same goal: they want to see Hos-Hostigos destroyed."

"Kalvan has his work cut out for him, that's for sure."

"By the end of the meeting, Cleitharses agreed to support the Grand Host, but only if Anaxthenes could neutralize either Hos-Rathon or the Sastragath before this spring."

Verkan smiled. "According to our agents in Xiphlon, Wannax Sargos is secretly in the employ of King RolthoIf of Xiphlon and is planning a major drive into the Sea of Grass to force the southern Ruthani back into the lower portion of the continent, the land they call Mexico on Europo-American. On the way back his army is going to attack the besieging Mexicotál and drive them away from Xiphlon and back to their Pyramid of Skulls."

"That means Anaxthenes doesn't need to bother with winning over Great King Nestros. That little tidbit would earn me a seat in Inner Council if Anaxthenes hadn't all but promised me one anyway—thanks to Great King Cleitharses."

"Come again?"

"I'm a guaranteed Archpriest of the Inner Circle, if I can help Anaxthenes pull off a deal with Nestros."

"Some might say it's awfully close to Paratemporal Contamination, but I think it's within outtime protocol."

"So you know the story."

"Sure, how old Police Chief Zarvan accused you of Contamination on Fourth Level Alexandrian-Macedonia because you were caught by Alexander's guards with a pocket recorder taping The God Alexander CXIV."

Danthor's visage clouded over, as he appeared to mentally replay the sensation and attendant publicity on Home Time Line.

"If it makes you feel any better, I've always thought Zarvan made a mistake. Every good researcher slips up now and then. Isn't that what hypno-mech is for?"

"I'm glad to learn you have a vastly more flexible view of these things, Chief Verkan. I'm afraid I may have judged you too harshly in the past based on insufficient data and my own anti-Paratime police prejudices."

"That goes both ways, Scholar Danthor. I've taken your animosity towards the Force at face value. Zarvan Tharg's problem was that he was a paper pusher who was promoted over his head, and who had spent very little time on outtime investigations. It takes a big man to apologize, Dras, and I not only accept your apology, but also offer one of my own. The entire Balph Study Team and my Police advisors are at your disposal. And, if there is anything I can do to make your job easier, let me know—and it will be done."

Dras smiled. "Thanks, Vall. I'll take you up on that. Archpriest Anaxthenes is going to travel to Hos-Rathon to try to convince King Nestros to forge an alliance with Hos-Ktemnos, which will keep him in Styphon's pocket and his army part of what the Styphoni are calling the Grand Host. I'll keep you informed regarding the outcome."

"What about you becoming a member of the Inner Circle? What deity do we thank for this miracle?"

"No deity. It came about because King Cleitharses doesn't trust Styphon's House to have his Kingdom's best interest in mind. Because he knows I'm new to Balph, he thinks he can buy my loyalty. What he doesn't know is that he already owns it. After Anaxthenes and Soton left, he promised me my weight in silver if I'd act as his eyes and ears in the Inner Council. Of course, like any proper highpriest of Styphon's House, I agreed.

"On my way back from Cleitharses' palace, to my temporary quarters at the Great Temple of Hos-Ktemnos, I was met by two of Anaxthenes' handpicked highpriests and taken to meet the next Styphon's Voice. The Balph

Study Team just learned from an analysis of the sample of Sesklos' hair that someone has been feeding the old man arsenic. I suspect it's his new Healer, who is friends with Anaxthenes concubine, Thessamona. For a Fourth Level middle-aged female, she's very attractive, and quite deadly in her knowledge of indigenous poisons.

"Archpriest Anaxthenes was friendly and forthright. He likes to take you by surprise. He sketched out the competing factions in the Inner Circle, his faction and the Dracar/Roxthar alliance, and gave me a number of good reasons why I should support him. As any proper out-of-town highpriest with the usual ambitions and lust for lucre, I was horrified at the Investigator's effrontery—True Believers in Styphon, how ghastly!—and immediately enlisted myself in the anti-Roxthar cabal.

"Due to Sesklos' faltering health, the Inner Circle has been unable to convene a conclave to replace any absent members; however, as soon as Sesklos' health has 'improved' a Council of Archpriests will be called and the vacant seats will be filled by myself and another of Anaxthenes' supporters, member-elect Highpriest Grythos, a former Zarthani Knight Commander."

"Wasn't there a background check? For all they know, you could be one of Roxthar's sympathizers."

"The Styphon's House's Temple bureaucracy is quite thorough. Anaxthenes had the parchments confirming my appointment as Iylos Temple Archivist and Highpriest, as well as some other biographical information. While I was working with Archpriest Vyros, I planted some documents in the Temple files."

"Will they stand up to Anaxthenes' scrutiny?"

"Yes, I've spent considerable time this past year planting false documents at the Iylos' Temple and have hypno-meched several priests to confirm them."

"Congratulations, Dras. You've cracked the Inner Circle, something I didn't think we'd be able to do for a decade or two. For some reason, not a lot of my people want to join Roxthar's Investigation!"

They both laughed.

SEVENTEEN

I

Anaxthenes counted twenty-seven Archpriests seated in the Innermost Circle, in Styphon's House Upon Earth, the formal meeting place of the Inner Circle. The Great Temple of Styphon was over three hundred years old, the first, and still largest, of the domed temples. Facing them was Styphon's Golden Image, the immense statue of Styphon that was only visible to the public during special occasions or times of great crisis—when it was wheeled out to Temple Plaza. Part of Anaxthenes' job, as Speaker of the Inner Circle, was to provide the voice for the mechanical bellows that allowed the giant idol to mimic human speech and Talk to the people. Usually this chore was the province of Styphon's Voice, but when Sesklos had reached eighty winters many of his duties had fallen upon his own more than ample shoulders. Sesklos was not well enough to attend the Council of Archpriests. Soon, even without another of Thessamona's potions, Sesklos would die. Anaxthenes would be Styphon's Voice, this charade would come to an end, and a new chapter of Styphon's House would begin.

He opened the meeting with the formal Blessing of Styphon and led the ritual chants. When the formalities were complete, all the assembled Archpriests took their seats at the Triangle Table; Anaxthenes sat at the point—Styphon's Voice's seat—since he was speaking in Sesklos' place. He told the assembled Archpriests about the meeting with Great King Cleitharses and how the Great King of Hos-Ktemnos refused to support the War Against the Usurper unless certain conditions were met. He played down the role of the Investigation to save them all from one of Roxthar's interminable harangues. His words were met with stunned disbelief.

Archpriest Bynoss, who filled his robes like a sausage, stood up. "Speaker, Great King Cleitharses has been the pillar of Styphon's House. What could have turned him away from the Temple?"

"I'll tell you," Archpriest Heraclestros said, as they had arranged prior to the meeting. "I was there and heard the words from Cleitharses' own mouth." He turned to point his finger at the whip thin figure of Archpriest Roxthar. "It was *his* doing. The Investigation has turned the Great King and his subjects away from their god!"

Roxthar jumped to his feet, spittle spraying from his mouth. "This Cleitharses has turned his back upon the Temple! Next he will be proposing an alliance with the Usurper. When this War is over, he will feel the fangs of the Holy Investigation—"

Anaxthenes rose up from the Triangle Table and broke into Roxthar's monologue, horrifying the Archpriests sitting to either side. "If we win this War against the Daemon, you mean, Investigator. And, believe me, we won't win it if we cannot count the Sacred Squares of Hos-Ktemnos as part of the Grand Host. That is the truth."

Heads bobbed all around the Innermost Circle. Everyone could see the tension in Roxthar's body as he bit back his response and nodded his head. In a lower voice, he said, "We may have to placate King Cleitharses for the time being."

"Cleitharses' price is the neutrality of the Trygath. I have already informed His Majesty that I will lead a delegation to the false kingdom of Hos-Rathon to negotiate a peace settlement."

Roxthar shot up out of his chair like one of Kalvan's *rockets.* "Nestros is one of the Daemon's allies! Speaker, you are asking the Temple to clutch one of the Usurper's devils to its breast! If we go to Nestros, it should be at the head of a conquering army. The only thing we should be bringing back to Balph is his head on the end of a pole."

Anaxthenes threw his deepest voice at the Investigator. "I am not proposing a permanent treaty, but one that we can break at our convenience. To placate King Cleitharses, we need to neutralize Hos-Rathon until the war with Hostigos is finished. King Nestros is an uncouth barbarian who will be flattered by our overtures and will welcome an alliance that *he* thinks will legitimize his new Great Kingdom of Hos-Rathon."

"Is this Nestros not the false king who destroyed sixteen of our Temples and put many of our highpriests to death, including Highpriest Ullnar of Rathon Town, after he joined forces with the Daemon Kalvan?" Archpriest Dracar asked.

"This is the same Nestros. He will pay for his crimes against Styphon many times over."

"What happens to Nestros after Kalvan's army is destroyed?" Roxthar asked, his voice trembling with barely suppressed anger.

"Former Prince Wygarth of Hythar, who was deposed by Nestros, has told me much about this pretender; Nestros is vain and easily led, but he is also a fierce warrior and commands his people's loyalty. It will not be easy to topple him from his throne from the inside; however, once the Daemon Kalvan has been deposed and slain, we will order our victorious Grand Host into Hos-Rathon. Once Nestros has been defeated, I will hand over this barbarian, who pretends to be a Great King, as a gift to your Office of Investigation."

The smile on Roxthar's face was chilling. "Once we are finished Investigating the Pretender Nestros and his family, we will Investigate the entire Trygath and search out all the Kalvan sympathizers and those unfaithful to Styphon."

Investigating Hos-Hostigos and Hos-Rathon should keep you busy for many winters, thought Anaxthenes to himself with grim satisfaction. "The Temple will rule this new kingdom and Prince Wygarth will act as our administrator."

"What about the treaty?" Grand Master Soton asked.

"Treaties with usurpers are not binding."

All the assembled archpriests nodded sagely at this piece of wisdom.

"I will leave for the Trygath in the morning."

II

Verkan was still blowing on his hands when Tortha opened the thick plank door. "You've got to do something about that knocker, Tortha. It's as heavy as a cannonball and in this cold it just about froze my fingers—through gloves yet!"

"Come on in, Vall. Sit yourself down by the fire." Tortha had a roaring fire blazing in his big flagstone hearth. He passed Verkan a flask of Ermut's brandy.

Verkan took a swig and grimaced. "Very good. Thanks, Tortha, I can feel that all the way to my toes."

"What brings you out on this cold winter night?"

"Inspector Andar Valth just jumped in from First Level. The Prole Protection League has really torn it this time; they've applied to the Council for membership in the Executive Council as a recognized party!"

Tortha nodded. "So the PPL has decided to go from being a gnat to a horsefly. What's the problem? We've been expecting that for decades."

"The problem according to our intelligence is that the Opposition Party has guaranteed their support and the Center Party is leaning in their direction."

"How did all this come about?"

"I don't know. Maybe I have been spending too much time here on Aryan-Transpacific. I'm out of the loop."

"Opposition has been out of power for a long time, but I never thought they'd get desperate enough to seek an alliance with proles."

"They're playing with fireseed, that's what I think. At any given time there are maybe a billion citizens living on First Level, the rest outtime, while the remaining population on Home Time Line are proles, billions upon billions of them."

Tortha shook his head. "It didn't used to be this way. When I was a lad there were very few proles on Home Time Line; almost all of them lived on Fifth Level. It all started with this fad for personal servants, about the time you were born, Vall. I remember Chief Zarvan was opposed to it even then. Robots were plenty good, and they don't talk back or ask for longevity treatments!"

"It started before then. Tortha, how many Home Timeliners live on First Level fulltime? Not many. Most have their own mansions or plantations on Fifth Level like your 'little shack' on Fifth Level Sicily."

Tortha sputtered, "It's my dream home."

"Sure, but who does all the work?" Verkan asked. "You must have three or four hundred proles living on your estate to handle the gardens, to say nothing of the housework. All this started six or seven thousand years ago. There must be a couple hundred proles somewhere on Fifth Level for every Home Timeliner on First Level. And how many of them are really necessary, since we 'import' more stuff from Fourth Level alone than we can ever possibly use?

"The government subsidizes Fifth Level production because we're afraid someday one of these Second or Fourth Level time-lines is going to *discover* the Paratime Secret and put our outtime firms out of business. We've had to turn the moon into a warehouse just to hold all the excess! It's a wonder the proles haven't thrown us off our own time-line."

Tortha sobered up. "They almost have, half a dozen times. And the last time was in my lifetime."

Tortha was referring to the Industrial Sector Rebellion when the proles on about fifty time-lines on Fifth Level had turned on the citizens running the factories and butchered them. The Army Strike Force Teams had flown in and put the revolts down, killing hundreds of thousands of poorly armed proles. A dozen of those worlds had been abandoned because there wasn't enough of the industrial base left standing, after the fires and looting, to be worth rebuilding. The surviving proles on those time-lines weren't living as well as the Zarthani on Aryan-Transpacific.

"I'm surprised there haven't been more revolts," Verkan said. "It must drive a man crazy to have to watch his neighbors live five hundred years or more, while he's doomed to a mere hundred—even with First Level medicine and treatment. Maybe it's time to think the unthinkable and start giving the proles longevity treatments."

"You can't be serious, Vall! There's nothing more inviolate on Home Time Line than longevity, unless it's the Paratime Secret itself. If the Citizens of First Level even *thought* you believed that, you would lose Management support faster than Styphon's House is losing worshippers since Roxthar began the religious murder spree that he calls a *Holy Investigation*!"

"But not fast enough to help Kalvan!"

"True. I can tell Kalvan is really worried about this Grand Host coalition that Styphon's House is supporting in Hos-Harphax. He's putting up a brave front, but he's drinking more and grasping for straws—such as this Hos-Bletha campaign of his."

"Yes. Unlike us, he can't bug out when things go bad."

"That's why it is 'unproductive' to form outtime emotional attachments, as they teach us at the Paratime Police Academy." Tortha paused to re-light his pipe. "Still, thanks to you, I've become friends with Kalvan, Rylla, Harmakros and Prince Ptosphes. So I'm here for the duration."

"What if Kalvan loses to the Grand Host and is forced into exile, or worse?"

Tortha rubbed his jowls in thought. "Then I'll join him. If it's 'worse,' and he's killed or captured by the Investigation along with Rylla—then I'll bug out. Other than that I'm staying. And that's final!"

"I'm not going to try and talk you into leaving. If it weren't for my job—thank you, very much, sir!—I'd be staying myself. I do plan to be here in the spring. I'm not going to miss the next round of fighting like I did this campaign season!"

"I'm too old for fighting, unless they want to make me a Captain-General," Tortha huffed.

Verkan laughed out loud. "If word ever got out, the Opposition Party would drum you right out of the Paratime Commission."

"Let them. I've wasted most of my life fighting politicians. That's what I like about Kalvan's Time-Line; if you want to combat politicians, you take a sword or headsman's axe to them. Which is what I think Kalvan's going to end up doing to King Nestros if he keeps finding excuses not to aid his only ally."

"Nestros may not be Kalvan's ally for long. Prince Ptosphes and Harmakros should be arriving there soon, just in time to meet a delegation from Styphon's House led by First Speaker Anaxthenes and Grand Master Soton."

"Isn't Scholar Danthor Dras part of that delegation?"

"Yes, Dras has been invited. Somehow, within less than a year of arriving at Balph, he's become Great King Cleitharses' trusted reader and advisor, as well as a member-elect of the Styphon's House Inner Circle!"

"I can see his next book already, *Secrets of the Inner Circle*."

Verkan laughed.

"Don't laugh, Vall. It'll probably top the bestsellers lists, too. Does Danthor think the Styphon's House delegation is going to be successful?"

"Actually, he does. Anaxthenes has done his research and is willing to offer Nestros the legitimacy as Great King he's always wanted—recognition of the new Kingdom of Hos-Rathon by the rest of the original Five Kingdoms. And, they're not asking for any military support as Kalvan's delegation is requesting. Finally, they're offering Nestros an opportunity to be on the winning side. If he's not smart enough to realize that the moment Kalvan's gone, it'll be his neck on the chopping block—well, then it's too bad, for him and Kalvan."

III

Soton felt a deep chill that came from more than just the cold stone walls and barrenness of Archpriest Roxthar's cell. Roxthar himself wore little more than his usual thin white robe, and Soton could see the outline of his ribcage where the cloth pressed against his chest. Roxthar's face was as lean as that of a starving wolf, and just as friendly.

"Sit down, Grand Master. I'm sorry I don't have more comfortable furnishings to offer you, but I find they distract me from my meditations with the One God."

Roxthar didn't sound the least bit sorry, but at least he was making an attempt at being civil, which told Soton he was still in the Investigator's good graces—or what passed for them. "I'm an old campaigner, Archpriest. I take comfort where I find it,"

Roxthar nodded.

Soton sat down on a short three-legged stool. He could very easily see how it might discomfort a pampered highpriest. And, thanks to Roxthar, there were fewer of them every day. Next to Kalvan, Roxthar had done more to change the Temple than anyone in the history of the Five Great Kingdoms.

Some of Roxthar's changes are long overdue, thought Soton. *On the other hand, Roxthar's Holy Investigation has everyone in Balph looking over their shoulder.* It was as Archpriest Anaxthenes said: 'Too much of that and everyone might forget who the real enemy was—the Usurper Kalvan.'

"What was it you wanted to see me about?" Soton asked.

"I have a decree from Supreme Priest and Styphon's Voice Sesklos I want you to read."

Sesklos had grown so weak, it was said, that he couldn't lift his hand, much less a quill to parchment. As he and Anaxthenes had suspected, Roxthar had been manipulating the Inner Circle through Archpriest Dracar while they had been attending Lysandros' coronation in Harphax City.

Soton took the parchment from Roxthar with a sinking feeling in his stomach. It was well known in Balph that when Roxthar nodded, Dracar bowed. He took the document as gingerly as one of Kalvan's petards and poured over it. He had been getting instruction on how to read runes from Sarmoth, who was an excellent reader—one of the reasons he'd made him his adjutant. Still, it was slow going as Soton had to sound out each word in his mind. He read each word of the short document with growing disbelief. "By the Wargod's Mace, this is horse droppings!"

"Must I remind you, Soton, to whom you are speaking?"

"I am more than aware of that. Let me remind you that while you might run Balph, when I'm in the field I take orders from no one! To serve under a man who was a mere *captain* in my own command two winters ago—Dralm be damned!"

Roxthar's face turned into an evil mask. "DON'T EVER UTTER THAT NAME IN MY PRESENCE!" Then his countenance returned to its usual lupine state. "No one, including myself, believes that Captain-General Phidestros is a better commander than yourself. Nonsense, of course.

"However, the political situation in Hos-Harphax is very unstable and would be worse yet if not for the debacle in Phaxos and Phidestros' successful storming of Tarr-Veblos. Now, after single-handedly vanquishing Prince Eltar, Phidestros is viewed by the people of Hos-Harphax as a hero."

"That was an act of pure insanity!" Soton said with a snort. "Phidestros is a top-notch cavalry officer, but Eltar was renowned as a swordsman. That gesture could have landed Phidestros in a burial mound and doomed the campaign against Kalvan even before it started."

"This may be true, but it worked. He has won the hearts of the populace. Also, it is also true that certain prominent members of the Harphaxi nobility still hold you responsible for their defeat at Chothros Heights. Is this not true?"

Soton nodded his head in agreement. As much as he didn't like the words, denying their truth would not change the Harphaxi blockheads. "Lackwits, morons, imbeciles, every mother's son of them! They lost that battle through the damned stupidity of their own commanders and the cowardice of their soldiers."

"Your charges ring true, Grand Master. However, this is a political compromise requested by Great King Lysandros to Styphon's Voice Himself to placate his Princes. The Electors of Hos-Harphax are afraid of Styphon's House—as they should be!" Roxthar paused to regain his composure. "And, their Great King, too. We need Lysandros and his Princes support if we are to defeat the Daemon. It has been agreed by Styphon's Voice and the Inner Circle that we will give Lysandros anything he asks us for to aid his fight against the Daemon Kalvan."

"I understand Lysandros' position; it took almost a full season before his Election to Great King. Yet…?"

"Do you doubt this Phidestros' qualifications? It was said that you recommended him to be Lysandros' new Captain-General."

"No. Phidestros is a good commander, and in a few winters he may even become a great one, but for now he is still green."

"Experience may not be what is necessary to stop the Daemon. Look how poorly the gray-beards did at Chothros Heights and at the Battle of Phyrax."

"There is truth in your words," Soton said. "Phidestros has fought the Usurper three times and lived to tell the tale. Let us hope he brings this campaign to a better conclusion than the last."

"If he does not, it will be his fault. After all, no one except the Harphaxi dimwits will blame the True God if the Harphaxi commander leads the Grand Host to defeat…"

"We had best pray to Styphon that Phidestros wins."

"He will win—with your help," Roxthar said as if victory over Hos-Hostigos had already been pronounced as a boon by Styphon. You will be second-in-command. It will be your job to counter Phidestros' inexperience. For your sake, it would be best if we did not have another failure to explain to Styphon!"

"True. If we lose here, the next war might be fought at the gates of Balph herself."

Roxthar's face transformed into one of the fireseed devils that had recently been carved into the façade of Styphon's Great Temple. "That we must not allow! We have to destroy the Daemon Kalvan and all his spawn: Rylla, Ptosphes, Harmakros, Phrames, Chartiphon, and even the baby demon, Demia!"

Soton disagreed with the idea of child murder. He would do what he could for the little child if and when they took Hostigos Town.

"That is why I will accompany the Grand Host in its triumphant march to Hostigos."

While all of Balph knew of the Investigator's plans, Soton had still prayed to all the gods, and even the lesser demons, that Roxthar's mind might be changed. True, Roxthar had accompanied the Holy Host in their first strike against the Usurper Kalvan in the Year of the Wolf, but he suspected that the Investigator would take a much more active role in the Grand Host than he had with the previous force.

Even though Soton knew Archpriest Anaxthenes' plans depended upon Roxthar's presence with the Grand Host, Soton couldn't prevent himself from trying to discourage the Investigator. War was serious business and no place for civilians, especially meddling ones. "A battlefield is not a safe place for someone of your importance to the Temple. Think of the disorder that would occur if some accident of war were to cripple or kill you."

Roxthar's face writhed as he mulled over those possibilities, and for a moment Soton thought he had won his point.

"Styphon will guard me unless it is his Will that I join him at his side. In this world, I will take my own precautions. I will be accompanied by a block of Temple Guardsmen and my own Investigators."

You may be mad, but you're no coward, Soton admitted to himself begrudgingly. "You're not going to bring more civilians along, are you?"

"It is Styphon's Will that the Investigation be brought to Hostigos. We can win the battle against the Usurper and still lose the war against the Daemon's ideas. We must scourge all traces of the Daemon and his spawn from this Earth. It must be done! It will be done! My Investigators will question every living thing in Hostigos, and when we are through there will be no trace, no followers, no children, no memory of Kalvan—it will be as if he had never existed!"

Soton felt goose bumps run up and down his arms. Roxthar was mad, as mad as a Sastragathi snake handler and twice as dangerous. He was screaming now and foaming at the mouth, mouthing obscenities and curses at Kalvan and his followers. What could Soton do to stop Roxthar that Anaxthenes and the entire Inner Council could not? Nothing, it seemed.

"Roxthar, let us win the war and then you can do as you will. But if you continue to—"

"I will brook no further obstacles regarding this matter, Master Soton. Is that understood? If you insist, I may again have to review my List of Investigation for the not-so-Holy Order of Zarthani Knights. Again, do I make myself clear, Grand Master?"

"Completely. Do as you will. But on this I will stand firm. Keep your Investigators out of the way of my troops, or I cannot be held responsible for what happens."

"Do not worry, Grand Master. It is not my plan to usurp your province. Do your job and we will do ours."

The Holy Investigator's final words were measured and without the histrionics of his earlier ravings. It appeared as though he could turn his madness off and on again at will. The thought of that chilled Soton down to the very marrow of his bones.

EIGHTEEN

I

Last night's fine carpet of snow over Harphax City gave a certain dignity to the two and three story ramshackle shops lining Kyros Street that the narrow thoroughfare otherwise lacked. Count Sestembar of Hos-Zygros didn't have to look far to see the One-Eyed Boar, since the cacophony of curses, laughter and music leaving the tavern filled the nighttime air. Outside the grog shop hung a sign showing a one-eyed gray boar with black bristles that stuck out like spears on a white field. It looked like a retired mercenary captain's banner and he wasn't surprised to find a matching shield hung over the doorway.

As he stood under the overhang, Sestembar mulled over the fork in the road that had suddenly risen up before him. In exchange for his help in keeping Hos-Zygros out of the Fireseed Wars, Eylos, the Hostigi agent, had offered to make Sestembar the sole distributor in Hos-Zygros of Ermut's Best. After his second goblet, he knew that he could sell all of the *brandy* that Kalvan could ship him.

For the first time in twenty winters, Sestembar had a real opportunity to get from underneath Duke Eudocles' shadow. Not only would sole distribution rights of Ermut's Best in Hos-Zygros make him a wealthy man; it would give him renown as well, which meant no more running errands from Hos-Zygros to Hos-Harphax. Or dealing with ungrateful whelps like Eudocles' by-blow, Phidestros.

He spat a wad of tobacco on the icy wooden planks and knew his decision was made. As soon as he completed this unpleasant visit, he would return to Hos-Zygros and report the failure of his mission to Eudocles. Then he would begin to plan *his* grand future.

Inside, the tavern was filled with off-duty soldiers and a liberal sprinkling of serving wenches in low-cut dresses that were cinched as tight as saddle belts on horses pulling one of Styphon's House's gold trains. There were roaring fires in both hearths and the room stank of beer and unwashed bodies. It didn't take long to find Captain-General Phidestros—he was at the center of the noise, with his subordinate, Grand-Captain Geblon. Geblon had his head nestled in the bosom of some slattern, while Phidestros was draining the ale from a flagon of heroic size.

Phidestros eyed him and quickly sobered up. "Welcome, Your Lordship."

Sestembar hefted the heavy saddlebag he carried over his shoulder, and motioned to the outside.

Phidestros looked up to the rooms at the top of the leaning banister and nodded his head at the door with an armed guard. The Count fought for calm as he followed Phidestros' arrogant stride up the narrow stairway. He had to keep his jaw from dropping when he saw the nicely furnished room behind the stained and unpainted door. Phidestros took the only chair in the room, facing a large desk with a deerskin map of the Five Kingdoms outlined in black. Sestembar resisted the temptation to remain standing and chose to sit upon one of the three-legged stools.

"Nice desk," Sestembar commented, in an attempt to open their conversation on a neutral topic.

For the first time since Sestembar had arrived, Phidestros smiled. "Yes, I made it myself. The walnut bole was as wide as my arms." He made a circle with both arms as wide as they would go. "Look at the grain."

Sestembar vaguely recalled hearing that Phidestros had once been apprenticed to a cabinetmaker. He stood up and pretended to study the highly polished walnut tabletop. He was far more interested in the muster list of Harphaxi *riflemen* resting on the top parchment than in any wood grain.

Phidestros followed his eyes and his smile disappeared. The Captain-General quickly shuffled the parchments out of sight and indicated that Sestembar should return to his stool by a cool glare and nod of the head.

Now that he was a noble, Sestembar deeply resented inferiors who stepped out of their place; someday he would even this score with Phidestros—royal bastard or not. He didn't like loose ends and Phidestros was a very big one, regardless of what plans his father thought he was weaving for the boy. If Duke Eudocles had listened to him twenty-eight winters ago, he'd have put the baby into a bag right after his entrance into this world and thrown him off the nearest bridge.

"What brings you to Harphax City, Your Lordship?"

Sestembar bit down on his temper and said, "I've come with words of congratulations from your father. He is pleased to see his son rise to Captain-General of the Harphaxi Royal Army."

Phidestros frowned. "His praise has come too late for this son. However, you can give him my thanks."

"I will do that," Sestembar replied with lips frozen into a smile.

"Now I have a request for my father. What I need most are a company of brass-founders and pattern makers for my Artillery Works."

Sestembar's jaw dropped open. "The few brass casters we have are working night and day casting guns and training apprentices. The Grand Duke would rather share his mistresses."

"Well, then why, by the Wargod's Mace, has he shared his brass-founders with the Usurper Kalvan?"

"I know of no such thing." *This is a most interesting accusation,* he thought. *I'll have to investigate it upon my return to Hos-Zygros.*

"It is not common knowledge, this is true," Phidestros said. "At least, not in Hos-Harphax. The brass casters are working in the Royal Foundry of Hos-Hostigos."

Something about Phidestros' guarded expression made him wonder if it was common knowledge among Great King Lysandros' intelligencers. *If not, how did Phidestros find out? Does he have his own 'deal' with Hos-Hostigos?* "Well, the

Ivory Throne knows nothing about it. Furthermore, you must realize that with the Great Kingdoms in the midst of a war we are not in a position to let any brass casters leave Hos-Zygros. Great King Sopharar will not allow it."

Phidestros' large fists clenched and unclenched.

"However, it may be possible that we can arrange a trade." Sestembar's voice lowered to a conspiratorial whisper. "We have heard rumors," Sestembar paused to look over at the parchments, "that the Harphaxi Army has learned the secret of Kalvan's *rifles*. If you could provide me with *rifles* and information on their manufacture, you will be richly rewarded." This offer was a calculated risk; if Phidestros took him up on it, it could very well upset his 'arrangements' with Hos-Hostigos. However, if the Grand Duke ever thought he hadn't done his best to obtain the *rifles*—well, his life wouldn't be worth half-a-phenig.

Phidestros voice rasped like a file over his next words. "I am the Captain-General of Hos-Harphax, not an intelligencer in the pay of my father! These *rifles* you speak of are state secrets, the property of the Throne of Hos-Harphax. Were I stupid enough to trade you one, even for a company of brass founders, Great King Lysandros would have me boiled in oil—and I could not blame him. Yes, I'm a mercenary, but I'm not a harlot who sells her favors to the highest bidder! And you can throw these words in my father's face for all I care. If he wants to show his support, let him send a score of brass founders and fifty companies of Zygrosi soldiers for the Grand Host to use in their war against the Usurper."

"Your father is Grand Duke of a Great Kingdom and don't forget it, Captain. He doesn't make deals with *bastards!*"

"Bastard I am and Captain I was, when last we met in Zygros City. Now, I'm Captain-General and prefer to be addressed as such by those enjoying my hospitality."

Sestembar's hand reached for his sword hilt until he realized where he was. "One day you will go too far."

Phidestros leaned backwards in his highback chair and hooted with laughter.

Sestembar could feel the heat in his cheeks. He lowered his head and thought of the fun he would have breaking this upstart on the wheel in the deep dungeons of Tarr-Zygros. When he felt his composure return, he looked up and calmly said, "It appears we have opened this meeting on the wrong note. If it is my fault, I apologize." The last statement went down so hard he had to gulp back the bile that it brought up.

"I accept your apology, Count. We will not bring up the subject of *rifles* again while you are in my house."

Sestembar gulped again and nodded his head, not trusting his voice. When his composure returned, he said, "I also have very important news to tell you. Your father insisted that I ride all the way from Zygros City to tell you in person."

For the first time tonight, he had the younger man's full attention.

"Your cousin First Prince Pariphon died when he was thrown from his horse."

Phidestros looked thoughtful. "So, the Heir of the throne of Hos-Zygros is dead. Does that make *me* or my father the next heir?"

"Blasphemer! Bastard ingrate! I ought to run you—" Count Sestembar stopped pulling his sword out of its sheathe when Phidestros drew a double-barreled pistol out of a hidden compartment inside the desk and cocked it. Even with death staring him in the face, Sestembar couldn't help but wonder why Phidestros thought his own father might not be the next heir. *Does he know something I don't?*

"Try that again, Count, and I will gladly splatter your tripes all over the wall!" He shot the pistol into the ceiling, filling the room with fireseed smoke and small pieces of falling plaster.

Sestembar carefully put his sword back into its scabbard.

There was a knock at the door. A voice boomed out, "Need any help dragging the corpse out, Captain-General?"

Phidestros' booming laughter filled the room. "The day I can't haul my own dead is the day I retire and run this tavern."

There was the loud stomping of boots walking away on the plank floor.

"Look Sestembar, I've never liked you, or your pretensions. I know all about you and the slum you came from. Don't rise up or I'll shoot! You can give my father his congratulations. Now that Great King Sopharar's only son is dead he is next in line to be the next Great King. If I were Sopharar, I'd hire a regiment of wine tasters."

Sestembar couldn't stop the growl that wrenched from his throat. "You ungrateful, puffed-up popinjay. You will fall soon on Kalvan's blade as fast as you've risen. If you live a hundred winters, you will never be more than a shade of your father's—"

"Please, Sestembar, I weary of your insults. Say what you must and leave before I give you to my men for their sport."

Sestembar bit his tongue until he could taste the salt of his own blood. "As I said before, your father sends his congratulations upon your promotion." He paused to clear his throat to keep from retching. "He also asks that you think well of him and consider accepting this gift—five hundred gold rakmars."

He removed the swollen saddlebag from his weary shoulder and slung it at Phidestros.

Phidestros caught it as if it were a cannonball, then threw it back against Sestembar with such force that it knocked him off his stool and onto the floor, half dazed.

"Tell my father he can keep his blood money! I will not be bought or bribed. He will have to fight his own battles with Kalvan to get one of his *rifles,* if he still has the mettle. And, you old man, come again to Hos-Harphax at your peril."

"You ungrateful whoreson! You've got airs just like your slut mother—"

Phidestros stood to his full height, his big hands clenching and unclenching. "My Mother was a Princess in her heart and in her actions. A Lady, she was—too good for the likes of you or that swine who calls himself my father!"

Phidestros banged his heel on the floor twice.

Sestembar shouted, "You've gone too far—"

The big brown-haired captain opened the door again and marched in with two huge companions.

Phidestros pointed to the Count. "Geblon, take this bag of rubbish and throw it into the alley, before I wring his neck with my bare hands!"

"Gladly, sir. And what about this saddlebag?" he added, hefting it as though it were full of feathers.

"Pass it out among the men—the spoils of war!"

The three men laughed and the Count felt huge calloused hands grab his ankles. Sestembar tried to struggle, but to no avail. The soldiers bounced his head off the stairs as they dragged him down the staircase by the feet. He almost passed out twice. *Have to keep my wits, or I'll never escape.*

Halfway down the stairway, Geblon paused to open the saddlebag and began showering the soldiers below with golden rakmars—enough gold to ransom a baron. In the riot that ensued, Sestembar always thought himself fortunate to escape from the One-Eyed Boar losing nothing more than his hat, jacket and shirt.

Limping away from the alley, Sestembar was bruised from head to toe and promised himself revenge upon the ingrate for each and every insult. *Phidestros, you will pay for this in blood and treasure!* His rage and wounded pride were all that kept him warm until he reached his quarters, with four bruised knuckles and a broken arm—received when a thief attacked him with a cudgel. Sestembar had taken the blow on his left arm, disarmed the thief and beaten him to death with his own crude stick.

For a day that had started off so well, the killing was the only bright spot in an otherwise absolutely horrible evening. Worst of all Sestembar would have to replay it all again in detail to the Duke. Only the thought of all the gold Sestembar would make in his dealings with Hos-Hostigos gave him any solace. Yes, let Kalvan deal with Phidestros; Eudocles' get was lucky, but like all things his good fortune would soon run its course. It was too bad he would not be there in person to savor that comeuppance.

II

Geblon knocked, then pushed the door open. "What was all that about, Captain?"

Phidestros smiled. "Payback. The Count came to inform me that my cousin had died."

Geblon frowned. "Cousin?"

"Prince Pariphon. I'm sure you've suspected that my father is Great King Sopharar's brother, Duke Eudocles."

Geblon shrugged. "I've heard the rumors and the two of you look very much alike...."

"Well, the rumors are true. Grand Duke Eudocles was my father, although I did not learn of it until last winter."

"Not a good father."

"He has helped my career with gifts of gold from time to time through his intermediary, Count Sestembar. All of you must have wondered why the pay-chests were never empty."

Geblon smiled. "Yes, we did. For a while, we thought you were raking in gold rolling bones. But none of the boneshakers knew you."

Phidestros laughed. "But, I want you to keep it to yourself. That's an order."

"Yes, sir."

"I don't want this story on the streets."

"Probably a good idea, since it might give Lysandros reason to suspect your loyalty."

"Exactly. I don't want him to suspect that I'm in my father's purse."

Geblon hooted. "That's a good one. Not after what you did to that Count and his saddlebag!"

"That would read to the Great King as subterfuge. Lysandros doesn't trust anyone because he's a backstabber and a regicide. I suspect he fears that someone might do to him what he did to his older brother, Kaiphranos. I just pray to Galzar he's not an oath-breaker, as well!"

"I haven't heard him tarred with that brush," Geblon said. "Although many a tongue in Harphax City has been wagging over how convenient the old King's death was for Lysandros... But most of the suspicions have been aimed at Styphon's House."

"Always a good target, but maybe not the right one in Kaiphranos' case...."

"Well, like Kaiphranos, young Prince Pariphon, the heir to the Ivory Throne, died a most convenient death—at least, for my father."

"You don't think..."

"Lysandros and Archpriest Anaxthenes aren't the only ones in the Five Kingdoms who know how to use little vials of poison or spook a horse. My father is as ambitious as Lysandros and far less squeamish...." Phidestros let the sentence trail off as he paused to light his pipe with a pine splinter lit by his tinderbox. "Today was independence day. I turned down my father's moneybox because I wanted him to know that I can't be bought and that I'm not about to play lapdog for my father's ambitions—even if he may well be the next king of Hos-Zygros."

Geblon whistled. "Well, after your *heroic* defeat of Prince Eltar you certainly don't lack for willing ladies and well-wishers. As Captain-General of Hos-Harphax, you don't need your father's charity, either. But what about his army?"

Phidestros shook his head. "We have no lack of bodies to throw at Kalvan's guns. And I need no further debts to my father, who only found his son when he proved *useful.* Besides, I had Captain Lythrax follow Sestembar the moment I learned he'd arrived in the City. Lythrax saw him meet with a suspected Hostigi intelligencer."

"Lysandros lets one of the Usurper's agents run free in Harphax City?"

"Yes, it's easier to follow a hawk in the sky than in a forest. My question is: Was this meeting my father's idea, or Count Sestembar's?"

Geblon shook his head wearily. "Things were much simpler before Kalvan came to Hostigos."

"But not so interesting, or profitable. I don't trust either Sestembar or my father; nor, I suspect, do they trust each other. When I return to Hos-Zygros, it won't be to further my father's ambitions."

NINETEEN

This year the snowfall in Hostigos had been heavier than usual so Kalvan was unable to complete the Royal Infantry bayonet training drills. Nor had the War of Three Kings allowed a demonstration of the new massed firepower tactics, since they'd been fighting barbarian armies of combined arms, including chariots, horse archers, lancers and warriors of every stripe, including many that wouldn't have been out of place on the battlefield of France under Edward III and the Black Prince at the Battle of Crécy!

It was the Royal Army pikemen who were giving Kalvan fits. They felt that using an arquebus or musket was a demotion; it was going to take time and success on the battlefield to convince them otherwise.

He'd had more success with the blacksmiths. His new leaf springs had made everyone happy, from the guildmasters to the wagon drivers. The design had been based on the springs of a side-swiped Amish carriage he'd once attended to while a Pennsylvania State trooper. No one had been badly hurt in the accident and he'd had ample opportunity to inspect the buggy's undercarriage.

The leaves of the springs had been easy to duplicate, but it had taken over a year for the Hostigi blacksmiths to figure out how to connect the leaves at the end of the spring. Once they'd solved that problem, the local artisans were soon at work fitting the Conestoga-style wagons they used locally with springs. They'd even installed them on the Royal Coach. The springs would be a good source of export income the day the Fireseed Wars came to an end.

The new semaphore system was up and running, and he was able to send and receive messages to the Royal Army of Observation based in Beshta in less than an hour, instead of a day by way of pony express. Now they could follow the movement of Styphon's Grand Host, as the Harphaxi were calling it now, when the campaign season arrived. The Hostigi army command would have as close to instantaneous communication with the Beshtan border as was possible here-and-now.

Styphon's House had been a faster learner and nastier opponent than he had expected in the military department. Not only did they have good generals in Grand Master Soton and Captain-General Phidestros, but some of the best troops in the Seven Kingdoms in the Order of Zarthani Knights and the Sacred Squares of Hos-Ktemnos. Phidestros' surprise capture of Tarr-Veblos had been a great propaganda victory for the Harphaxi as well as a big morale boost. Suddenly Great King Kalvan didn't look invincible anymore, even though he'd been a couple hundred miles away when the castle had been taken. Of course, since when had truth taken a front seat to the Big Lie....

It didn't help that the war against Styphon's House was taking a lot longer to wrap-up than anyone had predicted, even on the other side of the divide. That Styphon's House had deep pockets, with the Temple Treasury and Styphon's Great Banking Houses, was no surprise. What Kalvan hadn't expected was Styphon's House initiating a Counter-Reformation in the guise of Archpriest Roxthar and his Holy Investigation, a brutal witch-hunt that echoed Torquemada's Inquisition. The rumors were vile enough to make Kalvan and everyone else in Hostigos glad that they lived a long way from Balph.

The recent illness of Sesklos, Styphon's Own Voice, had hit the Inner Circle like bacon fat on a campfire. According to Skranga's spy network in Balph, there was growing resistance to the Holy Investigation among the Inner Circle. Unfortunately, there was little good news for Kalvan with this development as both parties were intent on dismembering Hos-Hostigos and the 'Daemon Kalvan' should he be unlucky enough to survive the defeat of his forces.

The surprising news was reports of growing resistance among the normally placid inhabitants of Hos-Ktemnos towards the excesses of the Investigation. Unfortunately, it was too little and too late to help Hostigos. Great King Cleitharses' reputation as a bookworm meant that he'd rubber stamp any proposal Styphon's Inner Circle proposed regarding the forthcoming spring campaign. It was unfortunate for Hos-Hostigos that the Ktemnoi tercios, man for man, were the best troops in the old Five Kingdoms.

Kalvan was all for the venal and greedy Old Guard; they were easy to understand and counterattack. Reformers like Roxthar bred discontent and fanaticism. The Investigator's excesses were worse than those of Savonarola, and it appeared to Kalvan that he had out-heroded Herod—the tyrant who destroyed all the babes in Bethlehem. Hostigos needed a gung-ho Styphon's House like it needed an outbreak of the Great Pox!

The Plague was another one of his ever-present worries, considering the sorry state of here-and-now hygiene. He had, with Rylla's enthusiastic help, introduced soap to the middle and upper classes, but it was too expensive for the average Hostigi to buy. Once this war was over he was going to see that every Hostigi peasant received ten acres, a plow and a bar of soap.

Outside, the wind howled past the tower. The fire blazed, and in the sudden illumination, Kalvan hefted the chunk of limestone from the nearby Heartridge Quarry and studied its surface as though it might reveal the key as to how it was turned into Portland cement. He'd lived among cement buildings and driven over cement roadways, but he had not given any thought to how it was manufactured. Just a quick trip to the hardware store in Bellefonte to buy a bag of concrete: mix with sand, gravel and water—voila, cement!

He seemed to remember something about baking the limestone, but the new iron smelters had proved too hot. The limestone had to be ground into a powder, but they had gristmills for that. Thankfully, the waterwheel was commonplace here-and-now. Kalvan had given a lot of thought to introducing steam engines, but he had to be careful how quickly he accelerated the pace of mechanical innovation. The last thing he wanted to see was the lovely Pennsylvania countryside filled with smokestacks, sweathouses and tenements like Nineteenth Century London. It could happen—look at New Delhi or Hong Kong.

Maybe concrete wasn't such a wonderful idea after all. Unfortunately, with the introduction of gunpowder and cannon shells he'd already released the Genie of Modern Technology. Maybe he'd have to come up with some kind of atonement, like Albert Nobel with his Peace Prize, after the newspapers confused his brother's death with his own and he got an 'opportunity' to read his own obituary. Somehow the Lord Kalvan Peace Prize didn't have the same ring to it, not with here-and-now armies growing from late medieval miniscule numbers to the massed ranks of the Thirty Years' War—all within the space of a few years!

Kalvan sometimes wondered what would have happened if the sideways time traveling machine had spit him out while he'd been stationed in Germany, during his remaining tour of duty after the Korean Armistice. Judging from the fact that there was no known contact with Europe or Asia, things must have taken a very different turn in Europe from his own world. It was possible that the Indo-Aryans, who'd migrated over the Himalayas through the Gobi desert and across the Aleutians, were the ones who'd settled in Greece—the Dorians. He remembered his freshman history professor telling the class that the Shepherd Kings, the Hittites and even the Medes and Persians were Indo-Europeans. Had the ancestors of these civilizations bypassed the Middle East for a migration route to the New World? If so, how would this have changed the course of European/Middle Eastern history?—profoundly, if the civilization here in North America was any example.

The lack of contact between the Old World and the New World told him, using Occam's Razor, that Europe was still in a pre-industrial state. He had heard rumors of a warlike people who lived in the far north of Hos-Zygros and spoke a strange tongue, which sounded similar to the Norsemen—but it was all hearsay. When the war with Styphon's House was over he meant to travel as far as Labrador and find out for himself.

In his freshman year at Princeton, his philosophy instructor had claimed that without the Greek philosophical and mathematical underpinnings of technology and invention, Western Civilization would have been stillborn and history would have taken a completely different course, more similar to the religious and God Emperor tyrannies of the Middle East and China. There would have been no Macedonian Empire, no Roman Empire, no Middle Ages and no Enlightenment—just an interminable, endless Dark Age.

At best, the Old World nations were probably at the same pre-industrial level of civilization as the Zarthani, who had a civilization with some medieval trappings—castles, pikes, gunpowder weapons—but whose gods and philosophies were little advanced over those of ancient Babylonia. Maybe someday the course of here-and-now civilization would be reversed, from the 'New World' back to the 'Old World.' He wondered if he'd live long enough to see it. He hoped so.

He went to refill his goblet with Ermut's Best and found the flask empty. He used the bell pull to summon Cleon, who arrived, half out of breath, with a small wooden cask and another goblet. "Your visitor just arrived, Your Majesty. I didn't believe a mere flask would do."

Kalvan nodded. Knowing Vanar Halgoth, Cleon was correct. "Send him in."

There was a clanging, stomping noise and the massive Sastragathi headman came into the chamber. Kalvan rose and got a body hug that would have done Freddie Blassie the wrestler proud back on otherwhen. The huge Sastragathi warrior, with his horned helmet, always reminded him of a Viking prince and he almost expected one day to see a dragonship moored in the Harph River.

Then Halgoth started to get down on one knee—Kalvan restrained him as best he could. "No need for that, Vanar. We are friends."

A smile split the big Urgothi's face that would have done a jack o' lantern proud. "We just brought the last wagons of orphans to the Academy. With the fresh teams of horses Your Majesty supplied, we had no trouble following the Nyklos Trail."

"Good. I think the children will do well here in Hos-Hostigos."

Halgoth nodded. "Yes, very well. The Academy is a better home than these children have seen in all their lives."

"We were lucky to finish the Academy dormitories before the first snow. I had the entire Hostigi corps of Engineers and six regiments of regulars building them."

"Sargos is pleased. He asked me to thank you for honoring your word and to tell you he owes you a boon. He was most pleased that you honored the spirit of his request as well as the deed."

Kalvan nodded. He was certain that someday the boon would come in handy. It was unfortunate he couldn't call it in this spring.

"I have also brought the last of your guard."

Not being a dictator, Kalvan had no need for his own Praetorian Guard; not only were they expensive, eating kingdoms out of house and home, but after a while they began to take a personal interest in who was going to be their next paymaster. By the middle of the Roman Empire the Praetorians were changing emperors almost on an annual basis, although a few, like Gaius Julius Maximinus, were among the best Emperors of the period.

Unfortunately, Kalvan couldn't turn down the well-meaning offer from Sargos' best friend and confidant without irreparably damaging relations between the two kingdoms, and offering a deadly insult to Vanar Halgoth—probably the single most dangerous warrior Kalvan had ever met. As a berserker, Halgoth was somehow able to alter his mind and arrive at a state of complete fury and fearlessness. Kalvan had read about such warriors, among the Irish and Vikings, who fought without personal fear and without pain—able to suffer grievous wounds—and still fight on.

It wasn't until the Battle of Spirit Grove that he saw the Urgothi berserkers in action. They were warriors who fought as though possessed, without fear of death and against all odds. Yet, like most primitive warriors, they were emotional, subject to whims and capriciousness. On first reflection they were not an ideal bodyguard for the Great King of an army numbering in the tens of thousands. However, they would die to the last man for their King and with Halgoth in command he knew his orders would be obeyed.

"Good," Kalvan answered. "We have completed their barracks inside the outer bailey. You and twenty of your men who speak our tongue will live with Us inside the Citadel."

Kalvan wasn't exactly sure how Rylla was going to take to this latest development, but Halgoth was certainly pleased.

"Our bodyguard will be called the Tymannian Guard." Kalvan had used the Byzantine's Viking guard, the Varangian Guard, as his model. They had served the Eastern Empire well, far better than Rome's Praetorians. "Your banner will be the Black Raven Hag of War on a white field. I will have Master Cathron, our armorer, design your uniforms."

Halgoth looked worried.

"You will still wear your horned helms and mail hauberks, but we'll add silvered back-and-breasts with my design, the keystone, on the breastplate. Each of you will be issued a regulation sword, two pistols, a powder horn and bullet molds. You can keep your own battleaxes—if you wish. Halgoth, you will be Grand-Captain of the Royal Bodyguard."

Halgoth smiled happily. Kalvan had tried to completely change here-and-now military ranks, but had found considerable resistance to his new order of command, especially among the ex-mercenaries in the Royal Army. So he'd done the next best thing, incorporated them into his own command structure.

Instead of sergeants, he had petty-captains; "sergeants" were common only in the Order of Zarthani Knights and the Sacred Squares so they'd been rejected. "Captain" was the catchall designation for everything from company leader to regimental head. In the Royal Army of Hostigos, captains commanded companies, grand-captains (majors) commanded battalions, while colonels commanded regiments. Hostigi brigades were commanded by generals, while armies were commanded by captain-generals. He'd had to drop the designation "brigadier" as too confusing to the locals. The "Grand Captain-General" of the entire Royal Army was Chartiphon, although in fact it was an honorary post, since Kalvan was the commander-in-chief and Rylla his second.

He poured them both another goblet of brandy and offered a toast to his new bodyguard.

Vanar Halgoth responded with his own toast. "To easy women and good fighting!"

Kalvan laughed. "I don't know about the women of Hostigos, but I can guarantee you all the fighting you can handle—and that's a promise."

Halgoth looked as if he'd just been invited to a feast of all his favorite foods. "My men will do their best to prove themselves worthy of the great honor you have bestowed upon them, Your Majesty." The big Sastragathi warrior re-filled their goblets. "To sharp blades and straight arrows!"

"All right down Styphon's gullet!" Kalvan added, quaffing his drink.

TWENTY

I

Kalvan moved closer to the hearth so he could get a better look at the polished lump of green glass presented to him by Rector Ermut. Outside he heard the whumph of a cannon shot in the outer courtyard as General Thalmoth proof-tested one of the new brass eight-pounders. He could even hear the drill chants in the bailey where, despite the falling snow, the petty-captains were valiantly—and probably vainly—doing their best to combat the low morale of the long and idle winter months.

He imagined his enemies were doing much the same thing in Tarr-Veblos where they were making preparations for the largest invasion in here-and-now history. *Talk about getting the ball rolling!* This was going to be a long and bloody war no matter who won. He wished, for about the thousandth time, that the survival of Hostigos was not totally borne on his own not so wide shoulders.

"Do you see the milkiness, Your Majesty?"

"Yes. It's better than the last lot, but still too cloudy for a lens." Ermut and Kalvan were meeting in the royal bedchamber, since keeping Tarr-Hostigos warm was in the same category as heating a Wisconsin football stadium in the winter. Queen Rylla, wearing a blanket over her lap, was in the corner in her rocking chair—which Kalvan had designed himself as her Name Day present—with little Demia in her arms. It had taken a master wheelwright to cut the runners on the bottom of the chair.

"I can't understand it," Ermut said, tugging at his ginger-colored beard. "I'm at my wit's end. I know how badly you want the farseers for this coming spring."

"It's not your fault, Ermut. There must be something wrong with the sand we're using. We've taken all the lime out of the formula so it has to do with the purity of the sand itself. Let me see the sand you're using again."

Ermut passed over a small leather pouch. Kalvan poured a spoonful into his palm. "It looks like clean quartz river sand to me." He moved his hand closer to the log fire. "Ah Ha! Look at this!"

Ermut pointed to the small chalk pebble. "Limestone!"

"Yes, limestone must be the problem. We'll have to carefully clean the sand we've already collected. Unfortunately, this is no time of the year to go looking for a new source. I should have spent more time on this during the summer."

"But when, Your Majesty? You spent most of the summer fighting in the Trygath."

"I know, maybe next winter I can spend more time at the University."

"Didn't I hear just those words last year?" Rylla asked.

"I'm afraid so. At least our winters are peaceful. Now back to our glass."

"Shall I use the water method to separate out the limestone?"

"No, Ermut. That will take too long and still might not do the job. Limestone dissolves in acid, but we have so little sulfuric acid—"

"What about vinegar, Your Majesty? I have a storeroom full of bad wine we couldn't use for the brandy still."

"Good thinking, Ermut. Vinegar will work just fine. But first, you need to distill it the same way you distill wine to make brandy. Vinegar is a diluted form of acetic acid: it won't work as well as sulfuric acid, but it will do the job.

"Once you have concentrated acetic acid, here is what you do: Wrap the sand in cloth and wash it with the strong vinegar solution. Do it three or four times until the acetic acid has dissolved the limestone. What's left will be mostly quartz sand—"

WHUUMP!

A loud explosion shook the keep to its foundation.

"What the Styphon was that?" Kalvan shouted, as the baby began to cry.

Rylla pulled out a horsepistol from underneath her blankets and said, "It's the Harphaxi! They're attacking Tarr-Hostigos in the dead of winter!"

But how? Kalvan asked himself, as Rylla gave the squalling baby to a nursemaid and proceeded to prime and load her pistol. *Even if by some miracle the Harphaxi were able to move a small detachment over several hundred miles of snow and ice, what could they do to a castle like this? Surely they couldn't bring guns over these roads, not without my getting a message from the Beshtan semaphore.*

Cleon rushed through the door. "King Kalvan, there has been an explosion! One of the guns exploded! Men are hurt."

Kalvan ran to the door only to be met by Captain Xykos and a score of the Queen's Bodyguard. "Follow me, Your Majesty. Make way for the King!"

Xykos led the way down the narrow keep stairway, while Kalvan fought his initial irritation at being nursemaided once again. He was the critical man in a bad situation and nothing was going to change that until either his University started turning out graduates by the hundreds, or Styphon's House fell.

In the Great Hall half a dozen blood-soaked bodies were stretched out, one or two still moving. *Just let Thalmoth be alive and I'll wrestle Styphon himself!*

In the bailey he met a powder-blackened and bloodstained, but apparently unhurt, General Thalmoth being helped by two soldiers. "Are you all right?"

"Curse and blast it! Oh, Your Majesty. I'm fine, but my gun isn't. Must have been an air pocket in the barrel. To Styphon with whomever poured that gun! Where's Captain-General Harmakros?"

"Harmakros?" Kalvan asked.

"Yes, he was with me a minute ago. Then the gun blew and threw me like a bit of wadding cloth. Allos, where are you?"

A thin man with a powder-darkened face ran up to the General. "What is it, General Thalmoth?"

"Find Harmakros for me."

"I saw him back at the courtyard. He was badly hurt and they were carrying him to the Infirmary next to the stables."

"Follow me, Your Majesty. To the stables!"

Kalvan felt his insides drop. *Not Harmakros! My friend, confidant, and finest general.* He pushed his way through the crowd of soldiers to the gate leading to the outer courtyard. Xykos and the Queen's Beefeaters followed close behind.

II

Prince Eudocles, newly elevated to First Prince of Zygros since his nephew had died, was angry—very angry—far angrier than Count Sestembar could remember for a very long time. The Duke was pacing back and forth in front of the flames shooting out of the large hearth, slamming his big fist into the palm of his left hand again and again. "Tell me again what this canker from my privy parts said about me!"

"He said you had Prince Pariphon murdered so you could steal your brother's throne. And other words about how his blood was sick with the fester devils of your ambition." Sestembar had invented a number of vile insults, the better to part father and son. Someday he wanted the personal pleasure of ending Phidestros' life.

"You have been ill used, my friend. Are you sure it was Phidestros who broke your arm?"

"Yes, Your Grace. He grabbed it and snapped it like a twig. He is preternaturally strong. Said he would do even worse should your person ever visit Harphax City."

"Now this happens, just when everything was going so well. It is good that no one but yourself knows he is the sport of my loins. Were he to be making such accusations in Zygros City it would be worth his life!"

"He threw your saddlebag of gold to his men as if it were the shirt off a beggar's back."

"I'm sure his chests are filled with Styphon's gold ingots. Now we know it's the highest bidder who owns his loyalty. Phidestros' temper will cost him and his liege lord more than they know. Had he received you with grace it had been my intention to send him ten companies of horse and twice that of foot for the war against King Kalvan upon your return. Now, he shall receive nothing of his patrimony except my fist in his face when next we meet!"

"I can hardly believe Great King Sopharar would have committed so many soldiers to the Styphoni Army." Ambition, pride and anger were Eudocles' weaknesses, and Sestembar knew better than anyone how to fire these charges. It took all the Count's will power to keep a smile from breaking his lips. Kalvan's agents would pay well for this night's work!

"At this moment, my grief-addled brother would sign any parchment brought before his hand, if he can even read them for all the tears that continue to flow from his eyes." Eudocles snorted as if he couldn't believe what he had seen. "Maybe some night he will drown in all his tears—it would be a boon for Hos-Zygros!

"As for my false son, I renounce him for all time and any claim he shall make upon my person or the Ivory Throne of Hos-Zygros! So I swear to the Twelve True Gods."

III

Lysandros exerted his iron will to quench the anger that burned in his veins, while his hands clenched and unclenched at the side of his chair—out of sight. Archpriest Phyllos continued blathering, blissfully unaware of how close he was to having his neck snapped. When Phyllos finally paused to take a breath, Lysandros interjected, "Am I to understand that the Inner Circle is now telling me who is in command of my army?"

The Archpriest shrugged. "I apologize for contradicting you, Your Majesty, but this army is Styphon's Grand Host. It is our gold which is financing this crusade, and it is our allies who comprise the majority of its forces. Thus, it was decided by Styphon's Own Voice that it would be in everyone's best interest to have a unified command under one general. Captain-General Phidestros was selected by both Grand Master Soton and Speaker Anaxthenes as the best candidate."

As if that should settle the question for once and for all, but what about me, you arrogant imbecile? he shouted silently. It had been his plan from the beginning to command the Grand Host himself; after all, while Kalvan had Captain-Generals at his beck and call, it was the Usurper who commanded his force—not some jumped-up mercenary captain. To Styphon with the lot of them!

It was his late brother's fault he was in this mess, having to feign humility and piety toward a false god and its clutch of priests who weren't worth the fireseed it would take to blow them to Regwarn and back. Kaiphranos the Timid had been everything a king should not be: weak, vacillating, fearful, and worst of all *cheap*. The only good to come of Kaiphranos' reign was the opportunity it had allowed a younger brother to emerge and take charge of the Royal Army, turning it into a force to be reckoned with despite the constant lack of funding.

Unfortunately, Lysandros had been forced to cut deals with Styphon's House to pay his troops and provide them with arms and fireseed. The Harphaxi Army hadn't been a great army, but it had been a good army. Until King Kaiphranos had granted command to that Dralm-damned addlebrained Captain-General Aesthes and his idiot son, Prince Philesteus, who'd at least had the grace to die on the battlefield along with the flower of Harphaxi nobility.

With Lysandros in command, the Holy Host would not only have defeated the Usurper Kalvan and restored the lost lands to Hos-Harphax, but would have had an opportunity to annex new lands in Hos-Agrys. Under the guise of punishing King Demistophon for not supporting the Holy Host, and for permitting the League of Dralm to continue to meet, he would have annexed large chunks of Agrysi territory.

Lysandros ran through a string of vile curses. This plan could not be undertaken unless he was in command of the Grand Host. He didn't trust Phidestros to follow orders that might go against the wishes of Grand Master Soton. He'd picked the young mercenary to command his army, in the first place, because he'd mistakenly thought Phidestros would be easier to bully than those captains with experience and reputations.

Over the years he'd learned to use Styphon's House to further his own ends, even if it had meant bowing and scraping to morons like Phyllos and his predecessor and pretending a piety that he never felt. As Great King of a shattered Hos-Harphax, Lysandros needed the Temple more than ever, first to rebuild the decimated Royal Army and secondly to fight the Usurper and restore his rightful lands. However, the moment Kalvan was defeated and dispatched, Lysandros' autonomy from Styphon's House would begin. It wouldn't be difficult to manufacture some act of treason or treachery on the Temple's part and declare Styphon's House anathema. Then it would be his turn to loot the gold from Styphon's House's temples and Great Banking House.

Now that he'd been *told* he would not be allowed to be in command of the Grand Host it was time to pick a new commander for the Harphaxi Royal Army, one who would be obliged to him—not Styphon's House. He would not allow Phidestros the luxury of twin commands. He'd already promised the mercenary far too much already—the Princedoms of Beshta and Sashta. It was galling enough that he would have to count the mercenary among his Princes, but even more so to know that his loyalty could not be purchased. The real question was: would those lands and title be enough to staunch Phidestros' ambition?

If the mercenary dared to oppose him, he could crush him like a spider under his boots. He was thinking about how much he would enjoy scraping Phidestros off his boot sole, when the Archpriest interrupted his thoughts with a question.

"Your Majesty, His Divinity, Styphon's Voice, believes it would be a fine display of your devotion to Styphon if you were to *require* the nobles of Harphax City to attend devotions at the High Temple each morning. Can we depend upon you to post a notice to this effect in the public square?"

Lysandros reined in his temper before answering. "I believe it is up to each of my subjects to follow his own god, or gods, as well as the manner in which he will display his faith. Already there are many voices in the City that believe I favor Styphon's House above all other gods. To please His Divinity, Styphon's Voice, I have closed several of Allfather Dralm's temples. However, I stop short of telling my subjects which of the Twelve True Gods each must worship."

The Archpriest looked as if he'd just bitten into a crabapple. "I will relay your response to Balph, where I fear it will not be happily received."

Lysandros kept a smile of triumph from appearing on his face. It was a small victory, but a victory nonetheless. He was not going to allow the Inner Circle to continue dictating to him as they did to Great King Cleitharses—not now that *he* was Great King of Hos-Harphax!

IV

The University Hospice was filled with the cries of the wounded and the dying. Kalvan fervently hoped Harmakros was not among the latter. The room reeked of brandy and burning pitch.

The cots were filled with men burnt black by gunpowder and reddened by blood.

Uncle Wolf Tharses saw him and cried, "It's the Great King. Make way for King Kalvan!"

Kalvan was pleased to see the head Uncle Wolf working on Harmakros, but his stomach turned when he came close enough to see the remains of Harmakros' left leg. The Captain-General's face was as white as the snow outside. Kalvan wished he'd thought more about making some kind of primitive blood transfusion device. It was too late now.

He turned to Tharses. "Have you kept his bandages clean?"

"Yes, Your Majesty," the old Uncle Wolf said, looking insulted. "I know your lectures on the fester devils by heart. We have clean bandages and plenty of distilled spirits of wood as an *antiseptic*—isn't that the correct word?"

"Yes," Kalvan said, feeling abashed. "I'm sorry, Tharses. I don't mean to act like an old woman, but Harmakros is a friend. And I'm very worried. I need him; the Kingdom needs him."

Tharses face softened. "We will do the best we can for Harmakros. He has many good friends in Hostigos. I will see that he lives to kill more Styphoni!"

Harmakros' eyelids fluttered and then opened. "I need a spot of brandy, Kalvan."

"Of course." Before Kalvan could give the order Xykos had a flask in his hand.

"Kalvan…I…" Harmakros raised his head and Kalvan gave him a quick sip of brandy. His body shivered but there was a smile on his face. "Cold...so cold. I needed that."

"Want another?"

"No…not for a bit. I just wanted to ask you a favor. Well, just in case."

"Go ahead! Anything you want, friend. Does it hurt?"

Harmakros made a grimace. "Only when I think about it. Actually, I don't feel anything below the knee. It's all right. I saw the leg…before." Harmakros fell back against the cot and began breathing heavily. "Wait…please, don't go…not till I catch my breath."

"I'll stay by you, Harmakros. Don't worry. Maybe another short pull."

This time instead of trying to pour the brandy into Harmakros' mouth, Kalvan took a clean bandage and soaked it with the brandy, putting the cloth into Harmakros' mouth.

"Just like being back in the crib," Harmakros wheezed, and then caught his breath. "I must ask a boon of you, Your Majesty."

"Ask away, old friend. Anything you want that is mine will be yours. Just tell me what you want?"

"It is…my son, Aspasthar. I want you to take care of him like your own son if I…well, if I don't get better."

"Consider it done. I'll make him a Royal Ward and someday he'll be a nobleman."

Harmakros smiled. "Thank you, My King. The boy is rough around the edges, but he means well. He needs a bit more tempering, that boy."

"I know. You've given him a lot to live up to."

"But not too soon…"

"He'll be fine after a tour with the Royal Army."

"I'm glad to hear you say that, because sometimes I'm…not, not so sure… Ahh!"

Kalvan turned to see the Uncle Wolf cutting off the last of Harmakros' breeches. When Kalvan looked back, his friend had passed out.

"I want to speak with you before you cut off the leg, Master Tharses."

The Uncle Wolf nodded. He directed one of his assistants to clean the leg and motioned Kalvan to the foot of the cot.

"How bad is it?"

"The Captain-General, he's lost a lot of blood, Your Majesty. There is no way we are going to be able to save the leg. It must come off. I'm sorry, Your Majesty."

"Legs can be replaced with wood and steel. What I want to know is whether or not he's going to survive the amputation."

"Maybe. He's a strong man, our Captain-General. And he has the will to live, all of which he's going to need."

"Is there anything I can do?"

"Yes, Your Majesty. Please wait out in the ante-chamber while we saw off the leg."

Kalvan nodded. "I'll leave. I'd just be in the way here." He bent over to feel Harmakros' forehead: no fever, but he was still warm.

Out in the antechamber, he finished off Xykos' flask and asked the burly Captain of the Guards if he had another. He did, and the two of them made short work of it. The wait was interminable but Kalvan stopped himself from asking for another flask. He would get good and drunk when he knew how Harmakros was doing, be it for a personal wake or in celebration.

Finally the plank-door opened and Master Tharses, his thin gray hair plastered to his skull with sweat, came out.

"How is he?"

"The leg is off and the wound is cauterized. He never felt a thing."

"He lives?"

"Yes, Galzar be praised! I suspect it will take more than a burst gun to quench the Captain-General's spark."

"Thank you, Tharses! You could have given me no better news." Kalvan turned to Xykos. "Lead me to the nearest tavern, I want to get good and stinking drunk."

A smile split the big man's face. "Better than that, Your Majesty, I know several good taverns."

"To the first then!"

TWENTY-ONE

As Archpriest Anaxthenes walked through the ante-chamber to Great King Nestros' audience room, Archpriest Heraclestros whispered, "Over there, that's Prince Ptosphes of Hostigos."

The Prince, sitting stiffly in one of the marble seats, was making a determined effort not to be intimidated by the large delegation from Styphon's House: six highpriests, three archpriests and the commander of Styphon's Own Guard, High Marshal Xenophes. Prince Ptosphes was a dignified man of some fifty winters with a silver beard and heavily calloused hands. Sitting beside him was a white-haired man who looked like another former soldier, wearing the chain of chancellery, and a handsome young man with a princely crown, said to be Prince Phrames of Beshta.

Interestingly enough, the party from the false kingdom of Hos-Hostigos had arrived a moon-quarter earlier, but Great King Nestros seemed to have gone to great lengths to ensure that both parties would meet before his chambers today. Was this an attempt to intimidate him, or the Hostigi? Maybe Nestros was trying to bargain more concessions from the Hostigi and thought that by letting his party into the King's chambers first, the Hostigi would be willing to increase their earlier offers? From the scowl on Prince Ptosphes face, he was willing to bet that stratagem would fail.

King Nestros was seated upon a throne big enough for two men—big but crude, like his capital, Rathon City. Nestros was a tall, powerfully-built man with ash-colored hair and a well-trimmed beard in the Northern Kingdoms' style. Unfortunately, his attempted sophistication was undone by his underslung chin and puppy dog eyes.

After the lengthy introductions and formal proceedings were finished, Anaxthenes decided the best way to answer Nestros' insult was to address it directly. "Upon Our arrival for a private audience with Your Majesty, We noticed that the emissaries for the Usurper Kalvan and false kingdom of Hos-Hostigos are present and awaiting an audience as well."

Nestros squirmed in his seat. "Well...yes, the Hostigi ambassadors arrived earlier to negotiate an alliance between Hos-Hostigos and Hos-Rathon. We have had several meetings and are giving their offer serious consideration, after taking into account their help against the nomads and the Sastragathi tribesmen last spring."

Not so serious that you were willing to wait a moon-quarter to see what we might offer, Anaxthenes thought. "I did not know that the Usurper Kalvan now desires to extend his dominion into the Trygath. Kalvan's ambitions are legendary, but this effrontery is without precedent."

Nestros face purpled. "Hos-Rathon is a mighty Kingdom, comprised of seven principalities all united under Ourself as one Great Kingdom. In territory, We have more cubits than either Hos-Zygros or Hos-Bletha." Nestros continued in this vein, recounting all the *glories* of his new kingdom.

Anaxthenes had to fight back a yawn.

Nestros finished with, "We are Kalvan's equal—not his vassal."

"Is that what the Usurper told you?" Highpriest Danthor asked, in a moderate tone of voice.

"Well, no. But he has negotiated with Us in good faith and aided Us in our victory over the Warlord Ranjar Sargos."

Anaxthenes nodded almost imperceptibly to Highpriest Danthor and he began speaking again. "Is this the Sargos who also now calls himself Var-Wannax, or Great King, of the Sastragath? The one who is now the Usurper's sworn ally?"

"Yes, but—"

Anaxthenes interrupted, "Now, looking into the future, say after the Usurper Kalvan defeats his rightful liege lord, Great King Lysandros of Hos-Harphax, what's to stop him from turning his army to the west against Rathon? I'm sure his good friend Wannax Sargos would love to annex part of your Kingdom—or split it with the Usurper. With strong allies to protect your flanks, this might be a matter of little concern. However, should you persist in this one-sided alliance with the Usurper, who calls himself a Great King, you could well lose your own throne to him or his ally, the self-proclaimed Great King of the Sastragath."

"Kalvan is a friend and a man of honor, and it is not conceivable that he would act in such a dishonorable manner!"

"Are you a sworn ally of the self-proclaimed Great King Kalvan?" Danthor asked quietly.

Nestor's voice rose. "He has sworn to recognize my title as Great King of Hos-Rathon, but not to aid in the defense of my kingdom. Nor have I sworn to defend Hos-Hostigos."

"My point, exactly. Thus, Kalvan could initiate an attack on Rathon without foreswearing any oath or treaty: is this or is this not true?"

"That is true. He did offer to form an alliance, but I was the one who decided to forbear until after the war against the...the nomads."

Anaxthenes had to bite down on his laughter. Nestros had almost said 'Knights,' which would have opened up a nest of termites upon the fragile structure of this alliance he was putting together.

Highpriest Danthor continued his questions. "Are you sure that was your decision, or was it Kalvan who withheld from any binding agreement? He is known to be a man who takes great pains to present the appearance of great personal honor, while his friends and allies do as they please. Look at the plague his wife unleashed upon Prince Araxes of Phaxos, a man who had once been another ally, an ally who declined to swear fealty to the False Kingdom of Hostigos. A prince who paid dearly for his dalliance with the Usurper Kalvan, not only with his life, but also the lives of all his family and kin. Is this what you are courting here in Rathon?"

Nestros looked perplexed, "Kalvan and I are friends—at least, I think we are."

"Are you willing to wager your title and kingdom on this supposition of friendship with a man of dubious origin, one whose wife willfully attacks princes of another Great King?" Anaxthenes asked.

"I don't know—Kalvan is a great warrior and in all matters that I have observed appears to be a man of honor. However, he did spend a lot of time drinking with the barbarian, Sargos."

"I have heard this Sargos is a man of rude appearance and barbarian demeanor. What nobility could such a man have?"

"He is a man of great strength and fights with honor, but he cannot hold his drink and he listens too much to his women."

"As does Kalvan, who gives the appearance of a household out of order; either that be truth, or he is much more devious and dangerous than he has been credited," Danthor said, as if both statements were the truth and completely obvious.

Danthor would make a good ally and Archpriest, thought Anaxthenes, but one he would have to keep an eye on.

"If I cannot trust Kalvan, who can I trust?"

Anaxthenes held his hands out. "You do have other friends."

Nestros blinked, looking sheepish.

"Before leaving Hos-Ktemnos I had an audience with Great King Cleitharses and he expressed an interest in your welfare. Since both Hos-Ktemnos and your new Great Kingdom of Hos-Rathon share a common border, Cleitharses thought a mutual alliance between both Great Kingdoms might be of mutual benefit."

Somehow Nestros managed to combine the appearance of both being stunned and thoughtful at the same time, which left him looking like the town idiot. "Does this mean Great King Cleitharses would recognize my title?"

"Of course. As allies Great King Cleitharses could hardly refuse to recognize the new overlord of the Trygath. Both kingdoms would be bound by treaty to recognize each other's titles and territorial claims."

Nestros all but jumped up out of his throne and clapped his hands. "This is what I have always dreamed—" Nestros reddened, when he realized what his loose tongue had revealed. He fooled with loading tobacco into his pipe as he attempted to regain his composure. Finally, he nodded, saying, "Yes, I would welcome an alliance with the Great Kingdom of Hos-Ktemnos. Would this mean that my title would also be recognized by Hos-Harphax and Hos-Agrys?"

Archpriest Anaxthenes smiled. "Yes, this would mean recognition by all the legitimate Great Kings of the Five Kingdoms, as well as the Order of Zarthani Knights. However, before we can continue these negotiations, there is a painful subject that we must broach."

Nestros' expression resembled that of a freshly beached fish.

Archpriest Anaxthenes smiled. "Of course, Styphon's House will require compensation for the destruction of sixteen Styphon's House temples, including the High Temple of Rathon Town, which occurred while the Usurper Kalvan used Hos-Rathon to stage his invasion of the Order's provinces. Of course, you will be responsible for the rebuilding and refurbishing of all the destroyed temples as well as replacing their golden domes at a cost of a fifty thousand Rakmars per temple. We will also expect you to help found five new temples. Sadly, the priests who were murdered during the sacking of the temples cannot be replaced; however, a thousand nomad slaves will provide some compensation for the Temple and their families' losses." Anaxthenes continued with a list of conditions, declaration and reparations. "Finally, we will require a declaration from you declaring the Usurper to be an outlaw and voiding any and all earlier treaties and agreements with the false king of Hos-Hostigos."

Nestros was reeling; his ruddy complexion blanched to the color of fresh snow. "What about Prince Ptosphes and his party? What will I tell them?"

"Get rid of them. Send them back to Hos-Hostigos. Or let Styphon's Own Guard place them under arrest." Anaxthenes smiled at the thought of leading a chain of Hostigi notables into Balph headed by Prince Ptosphes, Chancellor Chartiphon and Prince Phrames. Investigator Roxthar would be so busy that the Inner Circle might be spared the Investigator's harangues for a moon-half, at least.

Nestros' shook his head as if he were rising out of a deep pool. "Your blade of negotiations is double-edged. I must meet with my advisors and talk again to the Hostigi delegation. You demand too much, Archpriest! Kalvan has warned me about how you priests speak out of both sides of your mouth. Yet, he has not always been forthright with me, either—I wonder about all those wagon trains going from the Sastragath into Hostigos."

Anaxthenes let his fish wriggle against the hook, then set it. "It's your choice, Your Majesty. You can stay an outlaw and outside of the Five Kingdoms—remaining a provincial lord who *claims* to be a Great King. Or you can join your equals and be one with the Six Great Kingdoms. We will discuss this further after the sun rises."

TWENTY-TWO

The assembled princes, barons, highpriests, kinsmen and captain-generals filled the Great Council Hall at Tarr-Harphax with their fur robes, velvet finery and silvered breastplates. Duke Mnestros noted with interest that the smaller the realm, the larger and more colorful the plumage. He even recognized a few princes from the northern princedoms of Hos-Ktemnos, although the majority of the Ktemnoi nobles, including Great King Cleitharses, were too far away to attend on such short notice.

Most noticeable, however, by their absence were the Great Kings of Hos-Agrys and Hos-Zygros. Of all the Great Northern Kingdoms, only the recently crowned Great King Lysandros was in attendance. The piglet going by the name of Great King Demistophon was still hiding in his palace, blaming his loss in Nostor to Prince Ptosphes on Styphon's House, while the Great King of Hos-Zygros had sent two parchments ripe with excuses why he would not be able to attend the Great Council of the Union of Friends of Styphon's House.

It was a pity about the death of King Sopharar's only son, but Prince Pariphon was doomed at birth. His uncle, now Prince Eudocles, wanted nothing more than to be Great King, and like Lysandros here, only fratricide stood between him and his heart's desire. It was unfortunate for Hos-Agrys, thought Mnestros, that Demistophon was an only son and the issue of a long-lived line.

As the representative of the Princedom of Eubros, Duke Mnestros was here as one of the few pro-League of Dralm nobles in attendance. He had offered to take his father's place to better learn the faces and names of their enemies. Few outside of Eubros knew of his captaincy in Kalvan's army, since the fighting last year had been on the frontier, but he still felt like a plucked turkey dropped into a kennel at feeding time. He was surrounded on all sides by yellow robed highpriests and Styphoni sympathizers.

As the organizer of the Union's first council, Great King Lysandros was seated on a raised dais to the right of Grand Captain-General Phidestros, the commander of the Grand Host. To Phidestros' left were seated Grand Master Soton, who looked as if he'd rather be any place else, and Archpriest Phyllos in the yellow robes with red trim of the Inner Circle of Styphon's House. Phyllos, a great debaucher, was said to be busy concealing both his gold and his mistresses so they would be safely hidden when Investigator Roxthar arrived in the spring.

Grand Master Soton, who was said to have just arrived from Balph by horseback, looked drawn and fatigued. Seated he appeared normal sized, but the Grand Master was reported to be much shorter when standing on his feet.

Great King Lysandros made a chopping motion which stopped the noisy chatter that filled the room. Lysandros, with his short black beard and black hair, now shot with silver since Kalvan's arrival, made an imposing figure as he rose to his feet. "Grand Master Soton," Lysandros paused to give Soton—who was sitting beside Phidestros—a nod, before continuing, "has told us of the preparations the Order and our allies in Hos-Ktemnos have made for the invasion of the False Kingdom of Hostigos. The Grand Host will be joined by eight thousand Brethren of the Holy Order of Zarthani Knights, four thousand Holy Warriors from Hos-Ktemnos and two thousand Order foot. We have been told Great King Cleitharses will be supporting the war with the reformed Royal Square and six of the Sacred Squares of Hos-Ktemnos."

Lysandros went on to name all the Ktemnoi princes and how many additional troops they had promised to send in the spring. Mnestros wondered whether, with all these mouths to feed, there would be a single stalk of barley or cob of corn left in Hos-Harphax before they returned to Hos-Ktemnos.

"Now," Lysandros continued, "I would like to introduce Grand Captain-General Phidestros who will be commanding the Grand Host."

Mnestros couldn't help but notice the way Soton's jaw muscles tightened at that announcement. He wondered if this were a possible fracture in the Styphoni alliance or whether it was just indigestion.

Lysandros continued, "Grand Captain-General Phidestros is the only man alive who has faced the Daemon in three different battles. Under commander, Grand Master Soton, he helped defeat the Usurper Kalvan's army at the Battle of Tenabra. This fall our Grand Captain-General captured a castle right under the nose of the Usurper's murderous wife and two of his best captain-generals. Next spring we intend to take the war into Hos-Hostigos and make Kalvan pay the butcher's bill! I give you the man who will lead the Grand Host to victory—Grand Captain-General Phidestros."

Phidestros, looking martial in a high-combed burgonet helmet with green and black plumes and a battle-scarred but polished steel back-and-breast, stood up, standing half-a-head taller than the Great King. As he looked out over the crowd, Phidestros smiled, like a wolf ready to lunge upon its prey. According to the yarns and minstrel ditties in the Harphaxi wine shops, Phidestros had done just that in the Princedom of Thaphigos where he'd devoured the Thaphigos army and bested Prince Eltar in single-handed combat. His legend was beginning to grow as fast as Kalvan's.

After Great King Lysandros sat down, the Grand Captain-General made his formal address to the assembled dignitaries. He had a gravelly voice that demanded attention—and he got it. Phidestros quickly got to the meat of his speech. "We are in a life or death struggle with the Usurper Kalvan. We have one last chance to stop this devil in human guise from sacking our towns and cities, pillaging our homes and ravishing our wives and daughters. You have all heard how he has made Great Kings out of Trygathi bumpkins and made blood-oaths with Sastragathi barbarians. Is this the same man the peasant priests of Dralm call a Man of Peace? The man who says he wishes harm to no other man?"

Heads nodded their agreement. A voice cried, "Kill the Daemon!"

"His lands are stolen from their rightful overlord, Great King Lysandros. This *Kalvan* is no king, just another ambitious bandit or warlord from the Trygath. The Usurper will not be satisfied until he has deposed all rightful Princes and lords from their hereditary lands and estates."

Phidestros pulled something out of a tall silver urn from behind his chair. Holding it by its hair, he raised up the half-rotted and decomposed head of the Prince of Phaxos. Bits of rock salt fell from the head and rattled onto the marble floor. There were horrified murmurs from the assembled lords. Having just fought the nomads, Mnestros had seen far worse outside Tarr-Ceros, but not at the dinner table—his own stomach lurched.

"THIS IS WHAT HAPPENS TO THOSE WHO OPPOSE THE DAEMON!" Phidestros shouted. "If we do not stop him now, this will be the fate of all of you!"

The assembled lords looked back and forth at each other in horror. Then Phidestros tossed the severed head into the audience.

Prince Mylestros of Balkron tipped back in disbelief as the head landed in his lap. He picked it up by the hair, looked at it and cried, "It is Araxes! May Styphon Be Merciful! Kill the Daemon Kalvan! Kill the Daemon Kalvan!"

Soon the huge hall echoed with "KILL KALVAN! KILL KALVAN! KILL KALVAN!"

Mnestros noted with interest the frown that crossed Lysandros' brow as he watched his princes and noblemen fall under Phidestros' sway. Mnestros would not want that malevolent gaze aimed in his direction.

When the room had settled, the Grand Captain-General went on to detail his plans for the invasion of Hos-Hostigos, but not in enough detail to provide any intelligence to the few members of the League of Dralm who'd dared attend, or secret Kalvan sympathizers. He did emphasize the part the Royal Army of Hos-Harphax would play in the proceedings.

"In previous battles, we have left it up to the Usurper to pick the battle-field. This spring we will take the war to Kalvan and to the False Kingdom of Hos-Hostigos. Our target is the Usurper and his army—not Hostigos Town. We will take our united command and fight this false king on *our* terms. With the help of our friends from Hos-Ktemnos and Hos-Agrys and Hos-Bletha our army will be great in number and stouter in heart than the False Army of Hos-Hostigos. It's time he tasted *our* steel!"

There were shouts of agreement from the assembled nobility.

"Our friends in Styphon's House have promised their full support and will provide all the victuals and fireseed we will need. Those of you who are vassals of Hos-Harphax are sworn to bring your standing armies, but we are going to ask for more. In addition, we want you to muster a levy of every man-jack of fighting age in your Princedoms to come to the aid of your Great King and your god, Styphon!"

Prince Mylestros rose to his feet again. "I pledge not only my Princely army of three thousand horse and two thousand foot, but I will lead my own bodyguard and another two thousand cavalry, if I have to drag every nobleman in Balkron and his retainers behind me!"

There was a thunderous applause and suddenly almost every lord and Prince in the Hall was on his feet with his own pledge, trying to outdo his neighbor. The only silent ones were those, like Eubros, sworn or sympathetic to the League of Dralm.

The Harphaxi princes were oath-bound to provide their standing armies, although some would be ill-armed and poorly trained. Mnestros saw that both Lysandros and Phidestros had more eyes for those who were quiet than for those Princes who shouted out their contributions to the Grand Host. He decided that this would be a good time to make his exit.

TWENTY-THREE

I

Kalvan was pacing back and forth in front of the blazing fireplace while he waited for Prince Phrames' briefing on the negotiations with Great King Nestros. Word had just arrived that Phrames—far in advance of the rest of the expedition—had just arrived at Tarr-Hostigos. Kalvan suspected that it wasn't good news that brought the Prince home so quickly. Something must have gone badly awry in Hos-Rathon. *But what?*

Has something happened to Ptosphes? The Prince was clearly unwell and the only reason he'd asked him to lead the expedition was that Nestros would have been insulted if anyone of lesser rank had headed the party. Nestros was too much in awe of titles, and not enough of the people who bore them. Maybe it was part of Nestros' inferiority complex, stemming from the fact that he was the self-proclaimed king of a hick kingdom—at least, that's the way the Northern Kingdoms' viewed him. And possibly how he viewed himself. Nestros certainly took a lot of pains to ape Northern manners.

Of course, it was also true that Ptosphes would have been insulted if *he* hadn't been invited to head the expedition to Hos-Rathon. Kalvan had purposely sent Prince Phrames along to keep an eye on Ptosphes. His father-in-law had many of the symptoms, shortness of breath and chest pains, of some sort of heart ailment. There were no cures here-and-now for heart disease and Kalvan saw no benefit to having the Prince spend his last years as an invalid—even if Ptosphes would let him, which he doubted. The Prince could be as stubborn and headstrong as his daughter.

There was a knock at the door.

"Enter."

Prince Phrames, his face and clothes travel worn, walked into the audience chamber. "Your Majesty."

"Have a seat Phrames. Would you like some of Ermut's Best?"

"Please, sire."

While Cleon came and filled two goblets with brandy, Kalvan noticed that Phrames was clearly agitated.

"What's wrong?"

"It's Nestros." He looked sick. "Your Majesty, he's turned down the alliance with Hos-Hostigos."

"Really? He needs the alliance more than we do. It's not as if I was ordering him to attack Hos-Ktemnos next spring! At the very least, I was hoping for at least five thousand Rathoni troops for next year's campaign."

Phrames took a long drink, shuddered and said, "No, we'll be lucky if we're not fighting the Rathoni right along with the Styphon's Grand Host."

"How could this be?"

"From the first day we reached Rathon City, it was obvious that Nestros was trying to avoid meeting with our party. There was delay after delay. In our talks he was distracted and making unrealistic demands, such as Your Majesty sending him a flying battery and a hundred rifles with riflesmiths."

Kalvan whistled, then lit his pipe. "He must have known those requests would never have been granted."

"Exactly. Then a big delegation from Balph arrived, headed by Archpriest Anaxthenes and the Commander of Styphon's Own Guard."

"Ouch! Nestros must have been waiting for them. Maybe he was planning to play both sides off each other?"

Phrames nodded. "We were in Rathon Town almost a moon-quarter and Nestros wouldn't grant us even a perfunctory audience—until after the Styphoni arrived. At the meeting Nestros was very distant and it was apparent he'd already made his decision to ally himself with Styphon's House. At a later meeting, when Chartiphon accused him of being dishonorable, Nestros blew up and told us that it was only because of his honor that we weren't already in chains being marched to Balph. He then stated that our alliance with his enemy Sargos had freed him from any obligations to either Hos-Hostigos or Your Majesty. We were then ordered to leave Rathon with all due haste."

Kalvan shook his head; this was completely unexpected. Nestros had sold out to Styphon's House for something—but what? "Do you have any idea why Nestros is allying himself with our enemies?"

"Prince Phosphro of Distros, a man who fought alongside Your Majesty, gave us some information. It appears that Styphon's House has bought Nestros' loyalty with the promise that he will be *recognized* as Great King by all the *legitimate* Great Kingdoms. The Prince claims that the Archpriests have promised Nestros military aid in his war against the Sastragath as well as an alliance with Hos-Ktemnos, which Nestros believes will give Hos-Rathon true legitimacy as the Sixth Great Kingdom. That's what Nestros is telling his princes."

Kalvan laughed bitterly. "Until Styphon's House doesn't need him any longer. Is he going to be attacking us in the spring?"

"No, Nestros told Ptosphes, as long as we recognized his territory and made no claims upon Hos-Rathon, he will continue to remain neutral in the Fireseed Wars."

"The silly bugger! If anything happens to Hostigos, the Styphoni will dismember Hos-Rathon, enslave his people and eat him alive."

"True, Your Majesty. If the Styphoni win, Roxthar will feast upon his corpse. The stink of his betrayal will reach up to the Sky-Throne of Dralm!"

II

As Anaxthenes entered the ornate private chamber of Styphon's Voice On Earth, his eyes traveled over the room's décor: fine paintings, with depictions of Styphon throughout the centuries by the Five Kingdom's greatest artists; elegant wall hangings; the wall-sized Fireseed Tapestry, displaying the struggle between the fiend Dralm and Styphon, as he struggled to steal the Fireseed Mystery from the Palace of the Gods on Mt. Vynarth after the Trickster had stolen it from Ormaz's Pit; and thirty-six cast gold images of Styphon, each with upraised hand to hold a candlestick. *One day soon this will all be mine,* he thought.

Sesklos had not regained his full health since ingesting small portions of Thessamona's poison throughout summer and fall, and Anaxthenes was the first visitor to enter this chamber in over six moons. Other Archpriests had attempted to visit Sesklos since his recovery, especially Dracar, but all audiences had been refused. He wondered if Sesklos had figured out that he'd stopped the poison not out of loyalty, but because the timing for his death was not right.

Sesklos, wearing the red robe of primacy, was sprawled on a large purple velvet divan. His bald head peeped out of his robe like a dead turtle's skull stretching out of its shell. Sesklos lifted a frail hand and waved him to sit down upon an ornately carved highback chair.

"Speaker, your poison has not yet killed me, as you can see."

Anaxthenes sat still as a stone. "I do not know where you get such ideas, but—"

"Do not attempt to cover your deeds with lies. You have used your little vials too many times at my bequest. Make no denials. Just be careful that you do not put any of your other mistresses above the Lady of Death who shares your chamber. For who knows where her fangs may strike next…?"

Sesklos pointed his skeletal finger at his face. "Next time make sure the poison works. I am tired of this life and all its travails. Archpriest Roxthar sent me a missive from Harphax City reminding me to appoint Dracar as my successor."

So Roxthar is already in Harphax City. Since his leaving, the City of Balph had let out its collective breath and a celebratory air had blown through the City. *The Investigator is mistaken if he believes all of Balph will jump at his commands while he is in Hos-Harphax.*

"After my most recent illness, death holds few terrors for me. Of course, I will do no such thing—I'd as soon appoint Roxthar my successor, as Dracar. Don't look so anxious, old son. After all, everything you know, you learned at my knee. One does not blame the panther for its sharp claws."

"This was not—" Anaxthenes sputtered.

"Don't interrupt—let an old man have his last words. I have made many mistakes in my long life, but entrusting the fate of Styphon's House into your stewardship was not one of them."

Anaxthenes forced himself to contain his sudden glee and put on a solemn face.

Sesklos lifted up from the divan. "Don't waste your pity or guilt on this old man. I have committed many sins in the name of Styphon because of my own ambition and lust for power—too many for me to be in a position to judge anyone else. But during my reign, Styphon's House flourished and grew prosperous, and made its first real advances into the Northern Kingdoms. We now have our own Great King in Hos-Harphax. This is my legacy. I had always thought when I died, all would pass with me. But I know now that I was wrong.

"A vision came to me while I was ill: an image of a great black raven, with a man in its beak, which flew around Balph. I was that man, but the black bird did not hurt me. Instead it cradled me in its beak and flew over hill and valley until it came to a great Temple, mightier than Styphon's Own Temple in Balph. I watched as a great army descended upon this fortress and shot all manner of big guns at its walls. Still, despite all their efforts, the walls of the Temple held. Finally, the Temple door was opened and hundreds of white rats scurried out of the Temple. The army chased after the rats, stabbing and clubbing them until they were all dead. I *know* this was Styphon's Own Message to me that Roxthar and his Investigators will be driven from Styphon's House!"

No, thought Anaxthenes, *not another true believer!*

"Now more than ever, I know the Temple will not share my fate. Save it, Anaxthenes, save Styphon's Own House from Kalvan and from Roxthar. That is my *last* request." Then the old man fell back down on the divan, panting.

Tears began to leak from Anaxthenes' eyes.

"Ah, real emotion. There is still flesh inside that heart of stone. I have made the right decision."

Anaxthenes tried to keep the smile, which followed those words, from cracking his lips. Little did the old man know that those were but tears of relief upon learning Sesklos was not going to denounce him to the Inner Circle for attempted murder. And, possibly, from relief that he did not have to strangle the old lizard inside Styphon's Inner Sanctum—after all, he would be living there soon, after the anterooms were rebuilt and expanded.

It would have been difficult to explain Sesklos' death, even with the Investigator absent from the Holy City. Now, if the old man would only die before Roxthar returned from the campaign against Hostigos.... Well, if he didn't—

III

Phidestros stood up carefully from his worktable to greet Great King Lysandros and his party. He tried to keep the growing anger he felt inside off his countenance. He was wasting too much of his time answering Lysandros' interminable questions. Lately, Lysandros had been asking why Great King Demistophon was refusing to join the Grand Host in the war against the Usurper. Lysandros' greatest fear was that Demistophon was planning a sneak attack on his vassals while the Harphaxi Army was in Hostigos—'it would be just like the cowardly swine!' the King had declaimed.

As long as Lysandros didn't ask him to leave half the Royal Army behind, Phidestros didn't care what either of the Great Kings did. Once the Grand Host defeated Hos-Hostigos, they could easily make hash out of Hos-Agrys, if the sausage who called himself King Demistophon was stupid enough to attempt a land-grab in Hos-Harphax while they were fighting Kalvan.

Lysandros was accompanied by two gray-bearded men with obvious military bearing. *Is one of these graybeards my replacement?* he thought. *Did I say something I shouldn't last night?* He thought back to the previous night, the formal celebration of his swift victory and duel with Prince Eltar. It had been well over a moon since his return to Harphax City and there had been rumors in the taverns and wine shops about the long-delayed victory celebration, saying that all was not well between him and the king.

No, he had not done anything obvious to incur Lysandros' displeasure. Unless being given cheers by the King's Lifeguard were grounds for dismissal—?"

He bowed deeply and then Lysandros introduced the other two members of his party. The one with protruding teeth was the newly arrived Lord High Marshal Zythannes, the new commander of the Royal Army of Hos-Ktemnos. The previous one, Leonnestros, had died at Phyrax Field.

The second was Captain-General Antaphon, a broad man with a stubborn tilt to his jaw, who smoked a corncob pipe. Antaphon was a distinguished former Harphaxi mercenary general who had fought in scores of battles but never against Kalvan.

When Lysandros was sure that he had his attention, he said, "Captain-General Antaphon is the new commander of the Royal Army of Hos-Harphax and your second in command."

"A pleasure to meet you at last, Grand Captain-General."

It was an uncomfortable situation for both of them and Phidestros was pleased that Antaphon was wise enough to know that it wouldn't better his standing to snub his superior commander before the king. It was obvious that Lysandros was not taking any chances regarding the future of his new realm.

Phidestros didn't know whether to be relieved or angry. He had assumed that he would resume command of the Royal Army as soon as Kalvan was vanquished. On the other hand, he would now be able to devote his full energies to the new territories that he had been promised if he defeated Kalvan and conquered Hostigos.

After seeing that everyone had a full goblet of winter wine, Phidestros asked, "What is it that has brought Your Majesty so far from the warmth of the castle hearth?"

"Now that the Lord High Marshal has arrived, I want him to be briefed on your plans for the invasion of the false kingdom of Hos-Hostigos. If things were more secure in the Kingdom, I would take command of the Grand Host myself."

If Styphon's House wasn't opposed to your being commander, that is, Phidestros thought. *I smell a skunk.* He was about to be brought up to a review and he was certain if there were any questions about his campaign plans he would be unceremoniously relieved of his command. Why now, when the hard work was done and everything was going so well? Well, why not? Now that he had reorganized and rebuilt the Royal Army there were probably dozens of generals who believed they could do a better job of invading Hostigos. What he needed were some allies.

"If I'm going to explain the invasion thoroughly, I will need my commanders. Do I have Your Majesty's leave to call them?"

King Lysandros made a brushing motion with his slender left hand. "Of course, Captain-General."

Phidestros called in Knight Commander Orocles of the Zarthani Knights, one of Soton's underlings, three of his top generals and General Geblon, commander of his bodyguard the Iron Band. When he introduced his young generals, he could see a sneer of disapproval on Antaphon's face and even Marshal Zythannes looked mortified.

"I do not understand this title of general," the Marshal said. "One is either a Captain-General or a Captain. These new ranks are confusing and smack of Hostigi heresy!"

"Let me explain, Lord High Marshal Zythannes. Before the Usurper Kalvan arrived to snatch western Hostigos from its rightful rulers, armies were not very large, numbering only in the thousands, and there was no need for ranks other than those of Captain and Captain-General. Yet even so, there was enough confusion that the titles of Grand-Captain and Petty-Captain arose. I now have under my command blocks of men numbering upwards of four thousand, each under a General, ten Grand-Captains and forty Captains. What was I to do: create more Captain-Generals until they become as common as captains?"

Both commanders looked horrified. Lysandros fox-like face appeared amused.

"No, of course, not. Instead I appointed my ablest commanders, all of them veterans in the war against Kalvan, as Generals." *That covers a multitude of sins,* thought Phidestros. *Now let me hear from these men, who have never tasted Hostigi steel, make an issue of their youth.*

Captain-General Antaphon took out his pipe, sputtered, then put it back in his mouth.

"Your words are convincing, Grand Captain-General," Marshal Zythannes said. "We no more need a plague of Captain-Generals than we need more of Ormaz's demons!"

King Lysandros nodded his agreement. "What are your invasion plans?"

"This time we will fight as one Host, rather than several armies as was done under the late King Kaiphranos. Grand Master Soton will join us from the south. Knight Commander Orocles will brief you on the Grand Master's plans."

Orocles stood up and began to speak. "Grand Master Soton will be leading seven Lances, four thousand Holy Warriors of Styphon, seven thousand mercenaries, and three thousand light Sastragathi cavalry. Many have already arrived and will be wintering in Hos-Harphax." He went on to break them down by unit and troop type.

Lord High Marshal Zythannes broke in to say he would be commanding eight Sacred Squares, the rebuilt Royal Square, the Royal Cavalry, and almost ten thousand mercenary horse and foot. "With the Ros-Zarthani mercenaries, Grand Master Soton and I will be leading more than sixty-five thousand soldiers to join the Grand Host."

Even Great King Lysandros was impressed by those figures. "By Styphon's Great Beard, this will truly be a Grand Host. With both armies joined we will have more than a hundred thousand men to ravage the false Kingdom of Hostigos. What are your estimates of the Usurper's forces?"

"The False King's army has grown rapidly this past year, but even with all his levy he will be lucky to match our numbers by half."

Captain-General Antaphon looked disappointed; it appeared that this meeting was going in every direction but the one he'd envisioned. "We have outnumbered the Daemon Kalvan before, but to no avail. Why should the Grand Host win any successes the Holy Host was unable to garner?"

"Before we were divided, now we are one host," Phidestros answered. "Also, we are more experienced in the Usurper's tactics and strategy."

Phidestros diplomatically restrained from mentioning that they were also rid of several idiotic Captain-Generals, such as Prince Philesteus who had died at Chothros Heights with most of his equally thick-headed Royal Lancers.

Antaphon looked like a man who had just sucked a lemon dry. "Are you implying that because I have never fought personally against the Daemon King that I could not defeat him?"

Phidestros paused to tap the tobacco out of his pipe, thinking *if the boot fits, pull it on!* However, one did not maintain command of the Grand Host by insulting his Great King's favorites to their face.

Before Phidestros could speak, Knight Commander Orocles butted in. "The Grand Captain-General is too much of a gentleman to give a candid answer. I, however, answer to no one but my god and Grand Master Soton. King Kalvan devours inexperienced commanders much like the Daemon Ormaz eats the dead in Regwarn. To defeat Kalvan we must remain united among ourselves under commanders, such as Captain- General Phidestros and Grand Master Soton. To do anything else would be sheer folly, one that the Order may well decline to participate in."

Following that pronouncement was dead quiet. Orocles was known to have the Grand Master's ear and wouldn't be speaking thus unless he were reflecting Soton's own thoughts.

Antaphon, his face flushed, rose to his feet with his hand grasping his sword hilt. Orocles stood to his full height, half a head taller than the burly Captain-General.

Lysandros, obviously not wanting an incident that could splinter the Grand Host, put his hand on Antaphon's sword arm with such pressure the Captain-General's hand turned the color of chalk. "Sit down, Captain-General, or your next rank will be that of Grand-Captain of Latrines!"

White-faced, Captain-General Antaphon sat back in his seat.

"Grand Captain-General Phidestros, I would like to compliment you on your success. You have gathered the greatest force in the history of the Five Kingdoms and appear to be firmly in the saddle. We have complete faith and confidence in your abilities to command the Grand Host. We pray for your continued success in Hostigos. To Grand Captain-General Phidestros, a toast!"

Servants quickly brought everyone at the table a goblet of potent winter wine.

Phidestros diplomatically countered, "To a noble and wise Great King!"

Lysandros, who knew how to lose gracefully, nodded ironically. But the message in his eyes was crystal clear. Defeat Kalvan and glory is yours. Lose and you will spend eternity in the deepest pit in the Cavern of the Dead.

TWENTY-FOUR

I

As a pile of parchments slipped off his desk and fell to the stones floor, Phidestros watched them fall in disgust. Requisitions and muster lists were still piled chin-high, and he was spending more time scheduling wagon trains of provisions and fireseed than working out a strategy for the coming spring campaign. Worse, he lost yet more precious time jawing with the Holy Investigator, who kept sniffing around the Grand Host for heretics. He was coming to the conclusion that Grand Master Soton was right about appointing junior officers to take care of the detail work.

The Harphaxi arm of the Grand Host was stalled outside, while the remainder wintered in Tarr-Harphax and several other nearby tarrs. He couldn't wait until they entered Hostigi territory so Roxthar would stop peering over his shoulders.

He was still beating his head against his desk trying to figure out how to break into Tarr-Locra, the most fiendishly designed castle he'd ever encountered. The tarr was built in the shape of a multi-pointed star, with long killing lanes for gunfire that would decimate any siege train that approached the walls—another of Kalvan's innovations, he was sure. Sometimes he thought he was fighting on the wrong side in this war.

If the Grand Host couldn't get past Tarr-Locra they'd have to go around through the rolling hills of Beshta to the steep and high ridges of the Besh Valley, Sashta, Sask and Hostigos, which would be expensive in both men and animals. He was pushing his hand through a pile of parchments to find his tinderbox when he heard a knock at the door. "Come in," he responded.

General Geblon came into the room leading a haughty man in the fur-lined robes of a nobleman. Geblon winked and said, "I'd like to introduce Baron Sthentros, late of Hos-Hostigos, and the cousin of Prince Ptosphes. He has come to share his knowledge of Kalvan's army, fortifications and weapons."

Phidestros bolted upright in his chair. "Your Lordship, I'm pleased to meet you."

The Baron looked at Phidestros as though he were looking down rather than up. "Yes, I'm sure. I'm no traitor, I want you to know that. I've only come to you because I believe that this man who calls himself Great King Kalvan is a fraud, and not of noble blood. He has bewitched my uncle, Prince Ptosphes, and married my cousin under false pretenses."

Phidestros watched as Sthentros actually sniffed in disdain, then he paused to remove something from inside his robe—a move that had Phidestros grabbing his hideaway gun. He only stopped when he saw that it was a snuffbox. The Baron never noticed.

Geblon looked flustered, then quickly made the motions of patting himself down behind the Baron's back, letting Phidestros know the Hostigi had been frisked. Phidestros let out a deep breath.

"Would you like a drink, Your Lordship?"

The Baron nodded, while Phidestros motioned for Geblon to bring some winter wine. Geblon might be a general in the Harphaxi Army, but he was still Phidestros' right-hand man and understood that Phidestros didn't trust, or feel comfortable, around civilians, one of the reasons that he still resided at the One-Eyed Boar rather than a manor in Harphax City—despite his new wealth and position.

Phidestros used the interruption to pull out his tinderbox and light his burl pipe. After drinks had been served, he asked, "Why do you believe that Kalvan has risen above his station, Your Lordship?"

"When King Kalvan arrived in Hostigos, calling himself Lord Kalvan—Lord of what, I ask you?—he refused to give me any information on his lineage save that he was a 'Blue Blood' and born with a 'Silver Spoon.' What kind of nonsense is that?"

Phidestros didn't bother to reply: the fool didn't know when he was being given wet powder. Still, Sthentros might prove to be the best door out of the blind alley he found himself in. "Maybe you can answer some questions for us?"

"Of course, why else do you think I'm here? However, I would like to ascertain what my position will be after the war is concluded."

Phidestros clenched and unclenched his hands, while putting on a false smile. "I'm sure a suitable position will be found for you within Hostigos after the war."

"Good. Since I am a member of the princely family, I suggest that I would be the ideal candidate to rule as Prince of Hostigos."

Lysandros had even less love for traitors than Phidestros. But Phidestros had no trouble letting this treacherous swine believe whatever he wanted to think. "I personally could promise you a title of nobility equal to your own in Beshta after the war, providing your information is of value. Anything beyond Baron is the province of Great King Lysandros; however, I can promise to arrange a Royal Audience."

Sthentros looked smug. "I thought so. My wife didn't want to leave Hostigos, but I told her that the information here," he paused to point to his skull, "was worth its weight in gold. I also want to assure you that I've always been a follower of the True God, Styphon, despite the persecution we believers have suffered in Hostigos."

Phidestros struggled to keep a smirk off his face. He couldn't wait until he introduced Sthentros to Roxthar.

"Now you can ask me any questions you have about Hos-Hostigos and the Royal Army and I will do my best to answer them."

"How many men has Kalvan mustered out for his armies?"

"Thousands upon thousands. They crowd us out of Hostigos Town. It's a crime. It's getting so that one can't even find a willing wench who will take less than three pieces of silver. The taverns are so crowded that everyone has to sit together!"

Phidestros reined in his temper. "What I need to know are troop depositions, how many musketeers, how many pikemen, how many cavalry, those kinds of things."

"I don't know anything about the military—I served as an officer before Kalvan arrived, and fought in the Battle of Fyk. Once I realized that my cousin favored this outlander, I resigned my position. My son took over my squadron and led it faithfully until the disaster at Tenabra, when Prince Ptosphes foolishly defied the Holy Host of Styphon. This mistake on his part cost me my son and several score of troopers." His face scrunched up. "I will never forgive Ptosphes for leading my son into a trap that cost him his life! I've told him this to his face several times."

Phidestros shook his head in disgust. *It's Styphon's Own Miracle that his overlord didn't take this fool's head. A mistake that may both cost him and profit us.*

Sthentros continued, "I fear my talent is in leading men, not armies. I do know that Kalvan has abolished the pike; that's all his soldiers talk about at the Silver Stag. I also know the Royal Army is the biggest army I've ever seen."

Obviously, Kalvan not only mistrusted the Baron, which was no surprise, but found him incompetent as an officer. Ptosphes, being blood kin, had to provide him a proper position; Kalvan was under no such obligation to marriage kin.

The fact that Kalvan had done away with the pike was very interesting intelligence. Soton had mentioned that Kalvan's infantry had been carrying firearms during the Siege of Tarr-Ceros, but pikes were not the weapon of choice when going up against nomad cavalry, as Kalvan had done at the Battle of Spirit Grove. He tried to envision what Kalvan was up to: if you converted all your pikemen to arquebusiers then you could double your fire, which would be devastating to an army expecting half that firepower! But what about cavalry? How did Kalvan expect to stop heavily armed cuirassiers, or fully armored Knights? Yes, the Baron was a fool, but he was a useful fool.

"We have heard that Kalvan has a secret technique for getting messages to the borders so quickly. Do you know how he does this?"

"He uses his *semaphores.* Kalvan's dotted the countryside with those wretched huts. I can't begin to tell you all the things he's done to Hostigos since he arrived from the gods only know where."

Phidestros rose to his feet and began to pace. "Do you know how Kalvan uses these 'huts' to send messages?"

"He's put one of those huts right in my barony. He has troopers waving flags and flashing lights back and forth. I can see the ugly thing right out of my window. I had to order that glass special from Agrys City, and you wouldn't believe how much it cost…"

The chief Harphaxi Intelligencer had received reports that Kalvan was building a series of watchtowers, but no one had been able to discern their use since they weren't placed at the usual watch points. Phidestros had wondered if they were to be used for sending smoke signals, but no one had seen trails or puffs of smoke. However, flags and light signals were faster and more reliable than smoke signals. This sounded important.

"What about Kalvan's guns?"

"The Royal Foundry, yes, Kalvan makes all these noisy big guns there. He imported the most awful foreigners, from Greffa and Hos-Zygros, to tell by their accents—you know what hicks the Zygrosi are, don't you?"

Phidestros nodded, barely trusting himself to keep a straight face. Could the Baron be so ignorant—even being a Hostigi—not to know that he was a former Zygrosi? Killing was too good for the man. Fortunately, for the rest of his body—since it wouldn't live long without the head—Sthentros was providing the most valuable intelligence of the war. Lysandros would be beside himself when he learned that the Baron was kin to Ptosphes and, by marriage, to Kalvan, himself!

"The Foundry women are doubly strange, and take more liberties—of course, it helps that they're Royal Wards—than any decent women I've known. I've heard tales about Grefftscharrer women, but these are strange fowl indeed. This one old bird—Lala, what kind of proper name is that, I ask you?—argues with everything she's told, gabbling like an old goose." Sthentros made a grabbing and jerking motion with his hands. "It took all my willpower to keep from wringing her neck the one time we met."

"I understand, your feelings Your Lordship, I truly do. Did you get an opportunity to observe the brass-founders at their work?"

"What, me stay in a smelly, noisy foundry to watch a gang of foreigners and artisans? I should say not. That's another thing that's wrong with Kalvan. He spends too much time at common places like the Royal Foundry and that *University* of his talking to riffraff and giving them airs. One of them, Ermut is his name—the Usurper even named a new potable after him—was a former Temple-farm slave. Now he's a Master and it's rumored that Kalvan offered him the position of Rector at the University. Posts like that should only be held by those of noble blood!

"The same with his Captain-General Harmakros—his parents were merchants, ran a vegetable stall in Hostigos Town, if you can believe it! The Captain-General even has a bastard that Kalvan's made a Royal Page—the illegitimate get of vegetable merchants parading up and down the halls of Tarr-Hostigos and in the Royal Audience Chamber. I'd rather see Styphoni—I mean worshippers of the True God—in Tarr-Hostigos than lowlife townies and peasant scum."

Phidestros gritted his teeth so hard they ached. This was his penance for losing his temper with Count Sestembar. But when he'd talked about his mother as if she were some drab that had tainted his father's saintly blood—well, enough was enough. This rattlehead would have to be coddled until his wits were poured out, then he could be tossed to Roxthar and Investigated.

But first, there was much to be learned about Kalvan's underlings and the political situation in Hostigos.

"Now, tell me more about his *University*."

II

No matter how hard he tried Count Sestembar couldn't remove the smile of satisfaction from his face. He had just finished questioning the last of the brass-founders in the dungeon of Tarr-Zygros and the stink of the man's fear still clung to his clothes like bad perfume. What he had learned from the founder was worth far more than all the whale ambergris in the kingdom.

"What are you smiling about, Sestembar?" Prince Eudocles asked.

"Here we went all the way to Hos-Harphax for a treasure that was resting in our own backyard," he answered smugly.

"Enough of your riddles, old friend. I just returned from a lengthy visit with my brother's latest charlatan, a self-proclaimed wizard dressed all in black topped with a pointed hat, who claims the voice of the dead Prince speaks through his tongue. My brother had me sitting in a dark chamber for the entire afternoon while this man threw his voice about the room, an instrument that sounded to these ears no more like Prince Pariphon's voice than my own!

"His obsession with the deceased Prince grows so desperate that it's bandied about in all the wine shops on the waterfront. He will make us all a laughingstock."

Not all, thought Sestembar. No subject who valued his life would ever consider joking about Eudocles, who was notorious for both his quick temper and his lack of humor, especially about his own person.

"Your brother will grow tired of his weeping, maybe sire another child. Your sister-in-law is still fertile, is she not?"

"Who knows, she's so ugly no other man will look at her. Now she cries both day and night with such emotion one would think the Daemon Kalvan was perched on the city gates."

"More evidence that the kingdom needs a new ruler."

Eudocles frowned. "Be careful where you speak such thoughts. Although I will admit there is a great deal of truth to your words. Now, what is this about a treasure?"

"When I talked to the One Who Shall Remain Nameless—"

"Spit it out, Sestembar!" he growled. "I know the ungrateful whelp of whom you speak."

"During our meeting at the brothel he frequents, he asked me to have you send some of our brass-founders like those employed by the Usurper Kalvan in his Royal Foundry. The other day it struck me that if Kalvan is using our founders, he may have actually visited Zygros Town before or after his sudden appearance in Hostigos. Since so little is known about this Kalvan, I decided to visit all the foundries in the area and talk to the founders myself. It was a most enlightening visit."

Eudocles leaned forward. "Go on, old friend."

"I visited six different foundries, all of which are most busy. It was not always such before Kalvan's arrival."

Eudocles spat a string of curses. "These Dralm-blasted dogs of Styphon never let us have enough of their fireseed." He laughed maniacally. "Now their Fireseed Mystery is known to every woodcutter and charcoal burner in the Five Kingdoms!"

"We do owe Kalvan a debt of thanks for removing Styphon's chains," Sestembar added, careful not to offend his lord. When the First Prince was in his dark place, his moods could spin like a coin. And one never knew what side would land face up.

"I will thank him even more if he leaves us in peace," Eudocles said.

"I may have uncovered the means to ensure that he does just that."

"Enough mystery, Count. Talk on."

Sestembar nodded. "Three of the founders remember a tall stranger, who may or may not prove to be Kalvan, who called himself Verkan the Greffscharrer."

"I've not heard of any Verkan. But we get visits all the time from Greffscharrer merchants."

"I talked to some former mercenaries who took wounds while fighting for Kalvan, and several of them recognized the name—one called him Colonel Verkan of the Mounted Rifles."

"Then there is such a man. How is this important to me?"

"I wanted to learn more about his visit and what he asked for. Memories differ on the facts—after all, this visit occurred over three winters ago—but two casters remember this Verkan well; he was quite generous with his purse and paid in gold. It was said that he left town with five brass-founders and some pattern makers."

"Yes, yes!"

"Before leaving he taught two of these gunsmiths the secret of *rifling*."

"*Rifles!* Kalvan's far-shooting muskets? The ones we've been searching high and low for?"

"Yes."

"Why has this not come to our attention?"

"Because, Your Highness, we were looking in all the wrong places, and certainly not right under our noses. Two gunsmiths have been selling these *rifles* as fowling pieces for hunters. One, a Master Ptoythos, showed me his rifling bench and explained that it takes considerable effort to carve the inside of the barrel with the right grooves. Far too expensive a piece to waste on the battlefield, he said. The other gunsmith was most reluctant to tell me of his secrets until I talked with him in our dungeon. He's now anxious to cooperate and *share* his knowledge."

"You have taught him wisdom and saved his head. To keep secrets from the Throne is a capital offense. He can teach the rest of the Gunsmiths Guild the secrets of making *rifles*. Inform Master Ptoythos that We have found a new place for his talents. He will be elevated to Royal Gunsmith, and if he can makes us *rifles* we will elevate his station as well."

"Ptoythos will be most pleased, Prince. He is a master artisan and has the arrogance of the best of that breed. He will be a suitable tool to provide us with our own *rifles*."

"Sestembar, I must say I am most pleased about your part in this discovery. It is time you received a proper reward."

Sestembar felt his heart hammer, as he contemplated how many ounces of gold he would be gifted.

"I need more faithful retainers and you are a good example for them. I will raise you to duke—yes, that would be a proper payment for all your services."

Sestembar felt light on his feet and had to sit down, or risk stumbling. This wonderful a reward he had never expected.

"You are a little rough in the graces, but too many of the Zygrosi nobility are too fine for the kind of work that may lie ahead. There are no suitable positions for your rank at present; however, Duke Phremnos has no heirs and is approaching sixty winters. Sadly, he and his wife are both in good health. A stout fire might not only cleanse that ruin of a tarr they inhabit, but solve your problem as well."

"It will be done," Sestembar said with a big smile. "But isn't Phremnos close to Great King Sopharar?"

"True, one of his biggest supporters. Unfortunately for him, my brother's grief is such that his passing will be as little noticed as the death of one of the palace pigeons caught in a stableboy's trap."

Sestembar nodded eagerly. Arson was an art he'd perfected during his days as a mercenary captain.

Eudocles rose up and put his hand on Sestembar's shoulder. "Once the King has finished grieving for his friend I will place your patent before him. Then the Throne will build you a new castle, one worthy of your station. You will need an emblem."

"A *rifle*, Your Highness."

The Prince laughed. "A most appropriate choice. With our own *riflemen* the Zygrosi Royal Army will be a force to be reckoned with."

Spring

TWENTY-FIVE

I

Captain Jarask shaded his eyes from the sun as he tried to peer through the dust clouds to determine just how many men were approaching the Nolvos Gap from the top of the watchtower. *From here, they look like a carpet of ants. Too many to count,* he decided. *It must be the Grand Host on the move. I need to get word to Tarr-Beshta at once.*

He turned to one of his guardsmen. "Yannos, what was the last message we got from the Almyros semaphore station?"

"Weather's fine, no enemy in sight, Captain."

"That's just plain wrong," Jarask said, letting loose with a string of curses. "Dralm-damnit, they should have seen this many men from there. Something's gone wrong, very wrong."

"You think the enemy's captured one of the stations, sir?" Yannos asked.

"Maybe, or they've broken our code or something…I don't know." He paused to put his thoughts in order. "I don't trust sending anymore messages by semaphore. I need you to ride to Tarr-Beshta and tell Prince Phrames that the Grand Host is coming."

The young trooper looked excited. "What about the townspeople and villagers?"

Jarask remembered the last time the Styphoni had marched through Beshta and how they'd stolen everything that wasn't nailed down in Nolvos Town, killing any peasant who dared to protest. "Tell them to leave. And the same to any other villages and towns you pass through."

"For Tarr-Beshta?" Yannos asked.

"No. That old tarr is not going to hold out for long against this crowd. Tell them to take everything they can carry and make way to Hostigos. They need to bring all their animals and foodstocks as well. Anything they can't take with them, tell them to destroy. Otherwise, we'll just be provisioning our foes."

Yannos reared back. "They're not going to like that!"

"If our intelligence is correct, the Holy Investigation will be following in the Grand Host's trail. Anyone stupid enough to stay can take their chances with Archpriest Roxthar and his butchers. Tell them that and, if they still won't go, leave them behind and may Dralm have mercy on them."

Yannos nodded. "What about you, Captain. What are you going to do?"

"First, I'm going to block the trail. Then I'm going to send the rest of the guards off to warn the farmers and villagers to the south and west that the Styphoni are coming. After that's done, I'll ride like the wind to Hostigos and to the Great King's headquarters. If they don't know that the semaphore stations are in enemy hands, the whole Kingdom could be lost."

Yannos nodded. "Go with Appalon's speed, Captain."

The Captain followed him down the stone staircase to the common room where three other guards were lounging around drinking chicory and sassafras tea. Seeing the expression on his face, one of the guards rose up. "What wrong, Cap'n?"

"The Harphaxi are on the move. We need to go to the deadfall right now!"

Yannos was already out the door and heading for his mount.

One of the other guards pointed to him, asking, "Where's Yannos going, Cap'n?"

"To Tarr-Beshta to warn Prince Phrames. The rest of you are going to help me release the deadfall."

Outside the watchtower, they went to their horses which were tied to posts near the front portal. "How long do we have?" one of them asked.

"About a quarter candle. Let's go!"

They quickly rode to the top of the Nolvos Trail where Phrames had ordered a deadfall to be built and where another party of guards was waiting. The deadfall was a patchwork abatis of large trees woven together to make a damn holding back a great mass of huge rocks and boulders, some of them the size of a small hut. Normally merchants and travelers would have been up in arms against this wall of trees and stones blocking their trail, but there had been no traffic between Beshta and Hos-Harphax since last summer. Even the smugglers avoided the main trails and paths.

The Grand Host was moving quickly, most of their light cavalry were already a quarter of the way up the trail. Jarask nodded and the guards holding slow matches made their way down the hill and found their places in front of the fuses running to six large fireseed pots located in strategic spots at the foot of the deadfall. The fuses were timed to go off in one-twentieth of a half candle.

Jarask waited patiently until all the guards had reached their pots. When the van of the Grand Host had reached the twin oaks, his marker telling him they were three-quarters of the way up the trail, he dropped his arm and the guards lit the fuses at the same time. The instant the fuses were on fire the guards ran back up the hill as if a pack of Styphon's fireseed devils were on their trail.

Jarask nodded his approval as he moved back himself and quickly scrambled up the side of the hill to his viewing spot, where he watched the Styphoni cavalry ride up the rail. Unfortunately, the trail was only wide enough to allow three or four horses at a time which would limit the number of casualties.

In his mind, it seemed to take forever before the first pot blew up. The logs teetered and jostled back and forth, then the other five fireseed pots exploded and the abatis disappeared in a cloud of gray smoke and an avalanche of stones. Between the explosions and the cascade of falling rocks, he went completely deaf for a few moments.

The falling rocks took everything down in their way, from small trees to big boulders. A few of the larger rocks bounded out of the avalanche and bounced their way through the Grand Host, smashing and scattering men and horses alike. Horns were sounded as men scrambled out of the way, but many were too late, too slow or had no place to go. The broiling scree of dust and rock washed over the enemy van like an ocean wave. Even from his watch point, Jarask would hear the screams of wounded men and horses.

His guardsmen stood down below with their mouths open.

Jarask turned to them, shouting, "GO NOW! Follow your maps and warn everyone in your path that the Styphoni are coming. Tell them to leave Beshta and Sashta for Hostigos. There's no place in either princedom that will be safe from the Grand Host, not after this!"

"Yes, sir!" one of them called out as they turned and ran down the hill as fast as they could towards the trees where their horses were tethered.

Jarask waited until the dust rose and he could better estimate the number of casualties. Scores of bodies littered the hillside and much of the trail was clogged with rocks, bodies, dead horses and debris. Some of the van had moved out of the way or had been spared when the avalanche's fury was spent, but he estimated some two thousand casualties, many of whom might still live but would not fight this season—if ever again.

II

Prince Phrames was seated at his table pouring over his map of Beshta in the candlelight as he tried to figure out where the Great Host of Styphon's House was going to attempt a break through. At first, he'd thought that Grand Master Soton might come up through the south mountains by way of the Pirsystros Valley, like he'd done two springs ago. But that idea had been squelched when he learned the Soton had joined Grand Captain-General Phidestros in Hos-Harphax. Instead of a divided force, his subjects were going to be facing Styphon's best commanders and the largest army ever assembled in the Five Great Kingdoms, or anywhere else he knew about.

Maybe they had larger armies in the Cold Lands, as Kalvan intimated, but this Grand Host was the whale of Seven Kingdom's pond.

There was a loud knock at the door.

"Who is it?" he demanded.

"Your Highness, we have a trooper from Nolvos. He has an urgent message."

"Bid him enter," Phrames replied. "And bring him a tankard of ale. I'm sure he's thirsty after such a long ride."

The scout, his leathers covered with dust and reeking of sweat and horse lather, came bursting into the chamber. "Your Highness, please excuse me, but I bring urgent news from Captain Jarask."

Phrames directed him to a seat and tried to slow down his own thumping heart. By his appearance and weary face, the trooper did not appear to be the bearer of good news. Phrames personal servant brought in the ale and the young man gulped it down as if it were the first thing he'd drunk in days.

As soon as the scout caught his breath, Phrames asked, "What brings you to my chamber with such urgent news?"

"It's the Grand Host of Styphon, Your Highness! They're on the march. When I left the Nolvos Gap watchtower, they were already a quarter of the way up the divide."

"Did the deadfall slow them down any?"

The scout shrugged. "I didn't wait around to see. The Captain sent me straight to Tarr-Beshta to give you the news."

"If the Grand Host is on the way, why weren't we warned by the semaphore stations?"

The scout shook his head. "I don't know, sire. But my Captain thinks that they've been taken or the code's been broken."

Phrames reared back in shock. *Those stations were our first line of defense! Kalvan needs to know about this immediately.*

"I'll send a messenger off to Hostigos," Phrames said.

"Captain Jarask told me that he would go to Hostigos to warn the Great King. And to warn everyone I passed on my way here to leave for Hostigos. He said no place in Beshta is safe from the Grand Host."

"Your Captain is a wise man," Phrames said. *I'll have to promote him if he survives the coming battle. I'll have to make a note of his name.*

Phrames turned to his Chancellor and the other notables who'd pushed their way into his chamber. "We're going to have to evacuate the castle along with Besh Town."

"What?" the elderly Chancellor squawked.

"We haven't finished the rebuilding yet, but even if we had, it wouldn't hold out long against the Host's guns. Maybe a quarter-moon at best."

Turning to his captain-general, he ordered, "Start the evacuation at once, as per our plans, but don't force anyone to leave. We'll have enough trouble shepherding the ones who want to go, much less the ones who don't."

"What'll happen to those who stay behind?" the Chancellor asked.

"Nothing good, I believe. If the rumors from Balph are true, anyone picked up by the Investigation is in serious trouble."

III

A loud scream was the first indication of the attack on the small village of Crynn. Moments later the stableboy heard the bark of small arms, more screams, then the sound of horses galloping down the small town's main street. Gryon peeked out of the stable to see a dozen horses with Styphon's Own Guard, their red capes whipping in the wind, riding down the street. He hadn't seen any of Styphon's Red Hand since the death of Balthar the Black, before Prince Phrames the Good took the chain of office. Styphon's Red Hand were firing indiscriminately at anyone on the street, including women and children. He saw one ginger-haired boy dodge a Guard's saber slash, only to be ridden into the dust by the following horse.

The sight of six of the white-robed priests, with Styphon's black sun-wheel on their chests, following behind the Temple Guard and a squad of soldiers in the red and yellow colors of Hos-Harphax, holding a banner with a green hawk, sent him scurrying back into the stable and hunting for cover. Styphon's Investigators! Rumors had filled the streets of Crynn for days, ever since the Grand Host had come into Beshta, about Styphon's Holy Investigation and the terrible tortures undergone by those Hostigi unfortunate enough to be taken prisoner and Investigated. Over half of the villagers had left when Prince Phrames' outriders had told them the Prince was fleeing to Hostigos. Now he wished he'd left with them, but his master, the innkeeper, had told him that even Styphoni devils like a clean bed and a place to rest their horses.

Working in the stable was the best job Gryon had held since his father died in the war and his mother had turned to wine and the streets for solace. The innkeeper was a good boss and he didn't want to leave for Hostigos where he'd be just another homeless boy underfoot. At least here in Crynn he held a job and had a space in the inn's attic to sleep.

As he exited the back of the stable, the boy saw the town's priest dragged behind a horse with a rope around his chest, his blue robes slashed and blood running down his blond beard.

He'd been a lot younger when the Hostigi army had advanced through Beshta over two winters ago, but it had been a far different invasion. Great King Kalvan's soldiers had left the townspeople alone, only killing soldiers of the old regime and Styphon's false priests. The rumors said the Grand Host had come to scour the subjects of Hos-Hostigos and the followers of the Allfather from the very earth!

Gryon hid under some hay behind a broken windmill blade at the northernmost corner of the stable. Outside he heard more shots and screams and cries. After about a candle's wait in the darkness, he heard the screech of hinges and a big bang, as the front doors were forced open. "I saw one of the Daemon's mice run in here," said a voice.

Through the blade Gryon saw a big soldier in leather armor, wearing a yellow and red sash and a green helmet, pick up a pitchfork and begin to punch half-heartedly through the piles of hay. "This is a waste of time. I'm a soldier, not a child murderer."

A tall beardless priest in white robes was laughing. "You're just pissed because you got the short straw for the maidens. These Beshtan's are well fed, but not for long. Your commander has given you first rights, but when you're through they will all belong to the Investigation—Styphon help the lot of them!"

The big trooper turned around and spat a wad of tobacco on the floor. "Shut your gab-hole priest, before I shut it for you!"

"You are here to aid Styphon's Work, not give orders! The Investigation did not begin in Hostigos, nor will it end there."

"It will end here for you!" The soldier slammed the pitchfork into the priest's stomach, staining his white robe red. The priest fell to the ground twitching and writhing, with the pitchfork standing upright. The Harphaxi soldier yanked the tines out and stuck it into the hard-packed earth floor, as easy as sticking it into a block of butter. Then he pulled out a knife and slit the priest's throat.

Gryon watched transfixed as the soldier removed a long pistol from the yellow and red sash around his middle and in about five strides, as quick as a rattlesnake strike, stood over his hiding place, aiming the pistol at his head.

"Boy, come out now! With your hands open."

The stableboy slowly pushed the hay aside and crawled out from behind the windmill blade. He was shaking like a leaf in a stiff wind.

The soldier stuck the pistol back into his sash. "Don't be afraid of me, boy, I'm saving your life. I'm a Green Hawk and our company still follows Galzar's Way. It's these dung worshippers of Styphon that you need to be scared of. I've been watching them torture women and children for days now, and I've had it up to here." He held his hand way over his head.

"I don't think the Grand Captain-General knows what's happening in these small towns and villages. But, you and me, we're going to tell him."

The boy nodded.

"Now, help me hide this miserable piece of crow bait in the back of the barn. Or, better yet, where's the town's privy pit?"

TWENTY-SIX

I

Kalvan gave Rylla a reassuring hug as thunder battered the walls of the keep like a battery of Styphoni guns. Rain was falling from the sky in sheets and he wondered how long a reprieve the rains would give Hos-Hostigos from the coming campaign. This year he needed more time, since some ten thousand reinforcements were strung out over the Nyklos Trail between Ulthor and Hostigos Town. His army was badly out-numbered by the Grand Host so Kalvan needed every allied trooper he could find. Yet, even as he waited, more enemy soldiers were pouring into the staging areas for the Grand Host of Styphon. Even figuring that each Hostigi trooper was worth two Styphoni, it was a Mexican standoff.

The real question was: *Should I attempt a battle of maneuver, or spit into the breach?* The terrain was in his favor, mostly mountainous with cornrows of high ridges that could break an army's back. *Easy to defend if you didn't have to worry about the homes and the lives of the people who lived there.* One of the reasons he preferred to take the war to the enemy.

The Russians had made a defensive weapon out of their own country, but the Appalachians were not wide enough to break Phidestros' heart like the steppes of Russia had broken Napoleon's. Maybe it would be smarter to pick a spot to defend, bunch up the Grand Host, and make them come to him. Maybe, maybe not. He did know that sitting in Tarr-Hostigos mulling over alternative strategies with Harmakros and Rylla for another moon wasn't going to leave him fit for much more than a straitjacket.

There was a loud knock at the door.

"Yes!"

Cleon stuck his gray head into his private chamber. "Sire, Captain-General Hestophes here to see Your Majesties."

"Tell him to come in."

Captain-General Hestophes was still dressed in soaking wet traveling leathers and smelled like horse. Kalvan and Rylla let him sit by the hearth, while they returned to their chairs.

Kalvan held aloft the first glass bottle of Ermut's Best. "Would you like a drink?"

"Yes, but only if Your Majesties drink with me." Cleon brought fresh goblets and topped them.

"How was your journey?"

"Slow, wet, and miserable, Your Majesties. A raft would have been faster than my horse."

After more pleasantries, Kalvan asked, "What is the situation at Tarr-Locra?"

"Prince Phrames sent a replacement to relieve me of my command, as ordered. Morale was high considering that the Grand Host has started its advance from Tarr-Veblos."

"Tarr-Veblos! What did you say?" Kalvan rose to his feet without a thought, while Rylla appeared to be searching her gown for a sword. That Hestophes was known for understatement only made his announcement that much more astounding. "When did this happen? Why wasn't I notified by semaphore?"

"You don't know? Why I've sent a dozen messages. Your orders were that I was needed in Hostigos and relieved of command, and to return immediately to Tarr-Hostigos."

"No such message was ever sent from Us, or from Tarr-Hostigos. I know nothing about the invasion of Beshta."

Hestophes lowered himself into a chair and dropped his head into his hands.

Rylla shook her head along with Kalvan's. They'd been snookered. Somehow Phidestros had learned about the semaphore stations—where, when or how were the questions…?

"Hestophes, it's worse than you think. For the past week all the semaphore messages received at Tarr-Hostigos have been fakes, telling us that the Styphoni forces were gathering to besiege Tarr-Locra." The reason Kalvan had spent so much of his precious Beshtan resources building the massive fortifications at Tarr-Locra was that the fort blocked the eastern entrance, from Hos-Harphax, into the west bank of the Harph to the Besh and then up the Besh Valley. The Styphoni had to take Tarr-Locra to reach the Harph River, or else they would have to enter Hos-Hostigos the rough way, through the mountains of Beshta and Sashta, the route Soton had taken to the Phyrax battlefield two years ago.

Tarr-Locra was a tough nut to crack and could hold out for moons; if Phidestros had realized that and just put a token force there, he could have easily hit Beshta unaware from one of the gaps with only Prince Phrames and his Besthan Army to block him. Meanwhile, the Army of Observation was sitting on its thumbs guarding Tarr-Locra from a detached force, while Phidestros was advancing through Sashta and Sask toward Hostigos. It was a brilliant plan, Kalvan marveled, worthy of the man who made the legendary mad ride to join the Holy Host after Chothros Heights.

"Your Majesties, I thought you knew. A large portion of the Grand Host entered Beshtan territory just after I left Tarr-Locra. I thought this was why I had been recalled to Hostigos Town. I was about to tender my resignation."

"No. You were recalled because Harmakros' wounds have not improved. His leg is still infected with fester devils so he will not be able to ride or lead the army. I needed you here to take over as Grand Captain-General of the Royal Army."

Hestophes' eyes grew wide. "Me! Why not Prince Phrames or someone of noble blood?"

"Because you are the best man for the job. Phrames has his own duties as Prince of Beshta. Ptosphes is needed as First Prince of Hos-Hostigos. There are no others but my wife. And she is needed to care for our child."

Kalvan was just glad he was out of elbow distance when he made that last statement. As it was, he got the grandmother of all dirty looks.

"We've agreed that you are the best man for the job," Rylla added. "You have Our faith."

Hestophes bowed his head and when he looked up again there was a steely look of determination on his face. "I will not fail Your Majesties. This is a post to which I never dreamed to ascend. I give you my life."

"That will not be necessary, Hestophes. Just fight to the best of your ability. No one expects miracles. Although if Father Dralm should strike the entire Styphoni Grand Host with the pox We would build him the greatest Temple ever seen!"

Rylla let forth an exaggerated sigh. "Allfather Dralm, please forgive my husband, he does not mean these words."

"Now, tell us more about the invasion of Beshta."

"Yes, Your Majesty. The weather along the border has been unseasonably good and at first, when the Styphoni advanced, we thought it was another feint by the Grand Host to test our resolve. Our light cavalry have been attacking their scouts and supply trains all winter.

"When they easily repulsed our first attacks, I began to realize the entire host was on the move. That is when I sent the first message to warn Your Majesty. As soon as my replacement arrived, I left immediately for Hostigos."

Kalvan slumped down in his chair. "We need more information. I'll send someone to fetch General Klestreus and see what he knows."

II

Prince Phrames, who had arrived in Hostigos a moon-quarter after Captain-General Hestophes, gave his rulers a quick briefing. "The Grand Host was held up at the Nolvos Gap for several days as they had to clear it of their own dead and the boulders and rocks the deadfall had left in its wake. The early warning given us by Captain Jarack allowed us to evacuate most of the nearby villages and towns.

"Despite the mud and rain of the next few days, the Grand Host advanced quickly and overran most of our border forts and two tarrs. The Styphoni have many large siege guns with huge crews to man them and captured Beshtans to move them into position. Unfortunately, some of my subjects did not take our warnings to leave seriously enough."

"Already, they're taking revenge upon Our people," Kalvan said through pursed lips, as he visualized hundreds of captives using ropes and pulleys to manhandle the massive two-hundred pound bombards up and down hills. While this tactic might save a few teams of horses for other chores, it wasn't really cost-effective—more a terror tactic. It would force the Hostigi defenders to fire upon their own people, or take fire from these huge guns.

"Worse than revenge, Your Majesty. Archpriest Roxthar, the Holy Investigator, is Investigating all captured Hos-Hostigi. I am told that those who immediately recant their faith in Dralm are allowed to haul the guns. The rest, including women and children, are best not seen again."

"How do you know?" Kalvan asked.

"Before we left Tarr-Beshta," Phrames said, "my men captured a small party of Investigators and their victims. The poor wretches had been so badly abused it was merciful to grant them death. The Investigators were taken to Tarr-Beshta, put into the large guns, and shot over the walls."

The look of horror that crossed Phrames' face made Kalvan burn with fury. "Here we are planning our attack while they bring the war to us. Now it is my duty as Great King to bring it to them!"

"But Kalvan," Rylla said. "If we move now, we are but marching to Phidestros and Soton's drumbeat. Let us wait and meet them in Hostigos, now that Phrames has drawn their blood."

Like most Zarthani who had never experienced or known the horrors of religious wars, Rylla had no idea of how thoroughly zealots could scour a land of its people. King Henry's armies had killed tens of thousands of Huguenots, including women and children, in their desire to rid France of Protestant heresy. "No, we cannot wait. With Roxthar's Investigation leading the Grand Host, there will be no people to rule even if we win the war. In my homeland the histories tell of a General Sherman who burned the land to the ground; he was a man of peace in comparison to this bloody butcher who calls himself an Investigator."

"You are more knowledgeable in matters of war, my husband, than I am. However, let us wait at least until the roads are no longer running like rivers."

Rylla was right. To march the army in this weather would leave their troops weakened and scattered long before they reached the enemy. "We'll wait until the rain has stopped. Then we must leave. When we learned that Lysandros had promised Captain-General Phidestros the Princedoms of Beshta and Sashta, I had hoped the Captain-General's self-interest would protect our people. Now I see behind King Lysandros' generosity. Give Phidestros lots of land, but turn it into a desert before he gets it."

"I fear you are right, my husband. In any case, Phidestros will be too busy worrying over his soldiers to protect civilians he may, or may not, one day rule. You are right in this thing, too: without our people, we have no Kingdom."

And I have brought to this fair land that which I had most hoped to leave behind, a religious war. One that may quickly prove to be as bad, if not worse, than those of my own world.

TWENTY-SEVEN

Phidestros cursed the fog, the drizzling rain, the mud and the weather goddess all in one sentence as his horse plunged up to her fetlocks in what had looked to be firm ground. Some of the mud splashed on his gilded armor and he cursed the custom which required army commanders to wear equipment more suited to a pavane in Harphax City than a march across hostile terrain. Not that his mud-splattered armor and red and yellow plumage looked all that glamorous at the present moment.

A petty-captain reined up next to him. "The Grand Master's temporary headquarters draws near, sir. I will ride ahead and let him know you are coming."

Phidestros nodded his approval. The Host's temporary headquarters were not too grand, a confiscated farmhouse, but as long as it was dry and warm, he'd be happy. The first units of Kalvan's van had been spotted earlier in the day and a council of the Grand Host's commanders was needed.

Phidestros' horse stumbled again, almost pitching him head first into the mud. He tightened his grip on the pommel and let loose a litany of curses so vile his bodyguards gave off a cheer when he was finished.

So legends are made, he thought wryly. If the truth were known, he'd much rather be commanding the Iron Band and searching for Kalvan's outriders.

This grand commander business was harder on both head and arse than honest soldiering—and a lot less fun.

At the farmhouse Phidestros was gratified to find both a roaring fire and most of the Grand Host's senior commanders. Grand Master Soton was seated at the head of the long plank table, seated on both sides were the captains-general of Hos-Bletha and Hos-Ktemnos. Sitting by himself with the junior commanders at the other end of the table was Stratego Zarphu, the Ros-Zarthani commander.

Zarphu was a true enigma. He appeared to be more interested in the Grand Host's weapons and tactics than he was in Great King Kalvan's army. Phidestros had to admit with some admiration that Zarphu kept his soldiers on a short rein. Also, despite their archaic weapons, the Ros-Zarthani gave the impression of being the kind of men you would want under your command were you to try and storm Regwarn, the Caverns of the Dead. Now if only they were as good as they *looked* upon the battlefield...well, if it turned out they were, Kalvan had better hold onto his throne with both hands.

After touching palms, Phidestros sat opposite Soton while the generals and grand-captains scurried around for maps and oil lamps. When all were seated, he turned to General Kyblannos. "How are your guns traveling?"

Kyblannos took out his pipe. "Better than I prayed for. The two mobile batteries are keeping pace with the rearguard. We should have no trouble moving them into place, unless it's up a cliff face, within a few hours. I only wish I had more. The siege guns are about two days behind the main battle. *Magal,* our three hundred pounder, is out of action for the time being. It slipped off its carriage on one of the passes and took out about a dozen wagons before it came to a halt. We should have it moving again in time to invest Tarr-Hostigos."

"Excellent!"

Phidestros turned to Uncle Wolf Olmnestes. "How are the wounded doing?"

The Uncle Wolf shook his shaggy gray-haired head. "We left almost over a thousand dead at Nolvos Gap and three hundred and twenty more men have died of their wounds since we departed. Most of the survivors are recovering, although more than a few will have to be mustered out due to missing limbs or other injuries."

He nodded. The Nolvos deadfall had been a disastrous opening to the campaign. If the Hostigi had had their main army there, the Host would have been in trouble. As it was, they lost far too many irreplaceable light cavalry and skirmishers. "We'll have to keep the wounded and maimed with us. We can't afford the men it would take to sent them back to Syriphlon and if we leave them behind the Hostigi will kill them."

"Can you blame them?" the Uncle Wolf asked. "Look what that butcher in white is doing to the farmers and villagers here in Beshta."

Phidestros ignored him since he agreed, but his complaints fell upon deaf ears. Soton had his orders and Archpriest Roxthar was not moved by entreaties. If he had his way, he'd have left the Archpriest behind or had one of his men cut his throat.

"How are we on provisions, Master Jomnocles?"

Jomnocles was Master Sutler of the Grand Host, a position Phidestros had created to make sure his huge army had enough to eat and wear. It was Soton who'd taught him the value of delegating authority. When commanding well over a hundred thousand men, a commander could only attend to certain affairs. He wanted to be sure those were matters dealing with strategy and military preparedness, rather than muleskinners and foraging expeditions.

"Despite this abominable weather, Grand Captain-General, we have on hand better than fourteen days' victuals, with more arriving every day. Praise Styphon and the generosity of the Inner Circle! If tonight's soup is short on cabbage, you can all thank General Kyblannos' *Magal.* Those six wagons that his gun knocked off the road held half our cabbages!"

"I think we can survive the cabbage shortage, Master Jomnocles. The important question is: will we have enough victuals to reach Hostigos without running out of food?"

"Yes, if we can keep those Ros-Zarthani barbarians from eating us out of bottle and barrel!"

Arch-Stratego Zarphu shot the Master Sutler a look that left the smaller man quaking in his boots. "My men have not been getting their fair share of victuals, Captain-General Phidestros. When they do, they will no longer find hunger driving them to take what is rightfully theirs."

"Is there any truth to these charges, Jomnocles?"

"Is it my fault these barbarians eat the barrels right down to the staves?"

"Do not refer to our allies as barbarians again, or I will make you chief potato peeler of the Grand Host. Is that understood?"

"Yes, Grand Captain-General, Sir."

"Good. Now see to it that our allies have their proper proportion of victuals so we will not have to put one half of the Grand Host guarding supplies from the other half. I do not want to discuss this again. If I do, it will be your head! Now, please answer the question. Do we have enough provisions to feed the Grand Host should we have to chase Kalvan over every hill and ridge in these Dralm-cursed mountains?"

Jomnocles voice trembled. "Yes, Grand Captain-General. With Styphon's ships and caravans bringing supplies from all over the Five Kingdoms, we will have all the victuals we need as soon as the roads dry up. Styphon Be Praised!"

"That was all I wanted to know."

Grand Master Soton asked, "What do we know of Hos-Hostigos?"

Phidestros nodded and a petty-captain brought up a thin aristocrat with a haughty face. "This is Baron Sthentros, kin to Ptosphes and, by marriage, to Kalvan himself. He is accompanying my headquarters and acting as my informant in matters of Hos-Hostigos."

Everyone in the farmhouse looked impressed.

"Sthentros is a believer in Styphon, and claims to have left Hostigos to escape the clutches of Kalvan and the idolaters of Dralm. It was through his services that we were able to spoof the Hostigi semaphores." Even Phidestros had been impressed with the Baron's guile when he returned to his castle and used his daughter to help suborn the local semaphore station. If nothing else, Sthentros' aid in disrupting semaphore communications and the intelligence he'd provided on the Hostigi forces and countryside had changed the course of the war. Although, at this point, only the gods knew if it was enough to ensure their victory. Personally, he knew the Grand Host would have fared far worse without the traitor's help.

Phidestros continued, "The Baron has offered to share everything he knows about Kalvan's army and his fortifications. Sadly, he knows less than the usual foot soldier. But his eyes have grown sharper since his last visit to Hostigos."

The other generals looked at Sthentros with growing respect. The Baron did everything but preen. As useful as this fool was, Phidestros had to resist the temptation to stick the Baron in the side with his poniard. Besides, the Investigator had taken great interest in their turncoat and was busy converting his eager student into a disciple. Phidestros vowed to keep a close eye on the Baron, since anyone who could convincingly mislead Roxthar was a rare bird indeed. It was an art he had certainly not mastered.

Baron Sthentros spent the next candle describing the roads and byways of Hostigos, including Kalvan's new Great King's Highway. He also told them about the changes in the Royal Army, which favored the common soldier at the expense of their captains, such as those in terms of punishment. All the generals looked disturbed but Soton, who soaked up the Baron's words, and Phidestros, who privately agreed with Kalvan's reforms. Many were similar to the reforms he had instituted for the Royal Army of Hos-Harphax and he saw several sideways glances directed in his direction.

When Sthentros had finished, Grand Master Soton spoke up. "Captain-General, I take it you expect Kalvan to evade us rather than stand and fight?"

The Baron nodded.

"That's what I would do in his boots," Phidestros added. "Either that or force us to attack him where he can limit our mobility and neutralize our greater numbers."

"How do you plan to counter that?" the Grand Master asked.

"By not letting Kalvan call the shots," Phidestros answered. "First I'm going to send a large force of cavalry and mounted infantry into Sashta to try to outflank Kalvan's army. It will require the Usurper to divide an army that is already much smaller than our own. Plus, it will force him to march to our cadence.

"The Usurper's men know these mountains and hills as well as they know their privy parts. They also know, thanks to Archpriest Roxthar, that this is a fight to the death. Under these conditions and on their terrain, they will try to bleed the Grand Host until it is one big bloated corpse. What I want to do is play Kalvan's game, let him lead us on a merry chase through the Pyromannes. Then we will feign exhaustion and when Kalvan is lulled we will make a forced march and make him fight or run."

"It might work," Soton said, as he tugged on his goatee. "But won't our own men be disheartened by not coming to grips with Kalvan's army?"

"We will feed them well and half-march them. Keep them busy enough looting and foraging so they don't have time for trouble or talk, but rested enough so they can give Kalvan their best. Kalvan cannot afford to let us march over his lands forever. Every rod of Hos-Hostigos we take hurts him and his cause. If we chase him long enough, we will be in the Princedom of Hostigos and he will have no choice but to fight."

"An excellent case, Phidestros," Soton replied. "You have taken time to study the man as well as the army. Kalvan, if the truth be spoken, is an honorable man."

There was an audible gasp of breath at this heretical notion, but no one there was about to upbraid Grand Master Soton in his own headquarters. Phidestros was glad that Roxthar was not present to overhear Soton's words.

"Despite all words to the contrary, a study of Kalvan's actions since he has been in Hostigos will bear this out. Because he does care so much—possibly too much—for his subjects and their welfare, he cannot stand by and watch them suffer or be destroyed. This is his greatest vulnerability, one that our Grand Captain-General is attempting to use against him. You young generals and grand-captains, pay attention here; this is how wars are won!"

Phidestros made a slight bow to Soton, somewhat taken aback by his uncharacteristic praise.

"Remember, this war against Kalvan is a new kind of war. A war not only against Kalvan, but Hos-Hostigos as well. We must not rest easy because a battle or a siege is won. This war is *not* over until Kalvan and every member of his court is defeated and destroyed."

"Praise Styphon!" a grand-captain shouted. His voice was echoed by the assembled generals.

As the meeting broke up a high-ranking officer wearing yellow and blue Blethan colors came into the room to confer with Captain-General Lykron, commander of the Hos-Bletha contingent. A few moments later Lykron motioned Phidestros over.

"Is there trouble, Captain-General Lykron?"

"Worse than you know, Grand Captain-General." He lowered his voice to a whisper. "There has been a revolt in Hos-Bletha. Bletha Town is under siege. Great King Niclophon has ordered me to return to Hos-Bletha at once!"

Phidestros first reaction was to cry "impossible," but he stilled his voice, and slowly took out his tobacco pouch to cover sudden silence.

There were less than twelve thousand regular Hos-Blethan troops under Lykron's command and, to tell the truth, they were over-armored and under-armed. They were certainly no match for Kalvan's regulars. In addition Lykron commanded three or four Sastragathi and Ruthani light cavalry companies that might be put to good use, especially if taken away from Blethan command and put under an officer who knew how to get some real use out of his auxiliaries.

"Captain-General Lykron, you know I have the authority to order you and your troops to remain with the Grand Host?"

"Yes, but—"

"No, I do not intend to force you to make such a choice. You have my permission to remove yourself and most of your men and return to Hos-Bletha."

Relief was openly visible on the Captain-General's face.

"I just have one request. I have need for some of your men."

The Captain-General's expression changed to that of a farmer about to make a deal with a shifty horse-trader.

"You are free to leave with all your regular troops, but I would like your light cavalry to stay with the Grand Host. I have something special in mind for them."

"You have my blessing, Captain-General Phidestros," Lykron said, looking visibly relieved. "I have many more back in Bletha. They are yours. Styphon be praised! I have many preparations to make. May I leave now?"

"Of course, Lykron. You are dismissed."

Soton had drifted over to pick up the last part of the conversation. "Trouble in Hos-Bletha?"

"Yes, although this is one disaster that can't be laid at Kalvan's table. For a long time, King Niclophon has more misruled, than ruled. Now it appears that even his long-suffering Blethans have grown weary of it."

"I owe him little good will," Soton said. "His weak hand has long made the Order's job of guarding the marches more difficult. But little good is to be gained by the loss of his troops from our Host."

"Maybe, maybe not. Do you have someone you trust who can speak the Blethan Sastragathi and Ruthani tongues?"

"Yes. Heron, my oath-brother."

"Could I borrow him to command a little expedition?"

"Of course, but what do you plan?"

"Kalvan has some Sastragathi allies, does he not?"

"Yes."

"What if a large party of them were to be seen looting his pay wagons during the battle… What then?"

Soton's open hand fell on Phidestros' shoulder like a hammer. "You never cease to surprise me! At the right moment, such a move could prove disastrous for Kalvan. I will tell Heron your plans. He was born in the Magaouisse Swamps. He winters in Hos-Bletha and speaks the local dialects. I will put him in command of the Blethan Ruthani light cavalry. Heron has learned much by my side, and has taken several wounds meant for this old hide; he is the man for this job."

TWENTY-EIGHT

I

At the top of the ridge, Verkan and his Mounted Rifles were waiting in ambush for an advance wing of the Grand Host. According to Kalvan's scouts, there was a large detachment of Harphaxi cavalry, some three to four thousand, which were attempting to circumvent the Army of Hos-Hostigos by way of the northeastern Sashta. Kalvan had sent Verkan and the Mounted Rifles, along with two other brigades of Hostigi cavalry, to stop their advance. Whichever detachment ran into the enemy first was to send messengers to bring the other force on the run.

Verkan, as he checked the priming pan of his new 8-bore Hostigos rifle, scanned the opposite ridge for the first sign of the enemy. According to his scouts, a combined Harphaxi and Ktemnoi cavalry force was within three and a half marches, as the Hostigi called it. He wished he could consult Kirv, but local spy-eyes were out of the question due to the clear weather, which was ideal for contrails. This was no time for transtemporal contamination, not with so many Hostigi running over Sashta. All the Paratimers needed was for some cavalry officer to tell Kalvan about the strange trails he saw in the stark blue sky.

Verkan was under no illusions about outtimer inferiority; the men of the Royal Hostigos Mounted Rifles were just as savvy and intelligent as any squad of Paratime Police. The Zarthani might be less educated and technologically backward, but never inferior.

As much as he enjoyed a good fight, this time Verkan had hoped that it wouldn't be the Mounted Rifles who would make first contact. Verkan had placed his command at a critical juncture, the last mountain pass before the Kythros Valley, the one Kalvan—when he was in his cups—called the Nittany Valley. If the Styphoni took this pass they could overrun the Foundry, along with the First Level Study Team, and cut Kalvan off from Hostigos Town. Both would result in a disaster; one a political bomb for Verkan back on Home Time Line, the other a major setback for Kalvan's beleaguered army.

Verkan had been a student of military history since his first posting as a Paratime Police cadet over a hundred years ago when the War Between the States was raging on time-lines throughout the Europo-American, Hispano Columbian Subsector. For a few decades he'd read everything he could find on warfare, until he met Dalla—then his life took a much more interesting and less predictable turn. Still, he was very aware of the challenge posed to Kalvan by this Grand Host, the largest army ever raised on any Aryan-Transpacific, Styphon's House Subsector.

The Hostigi were in an ordered retreat after rushing into eastern Sashta only to find the Grand Host deep inside the princedom, less than twenty miles from the border of Hostigos. Instead of fighting a pitched battle against an overwhelming force, Kalvan had chosen to fall back. Verkan was well aware just how much that had rankled Kalvan and the Hostigi regulars who were used to setting the pace and forcing opposing armies to dance to their tune.

The Grand Host was even larger than the first estimates compiled by Hostigi intelligence; anywhere from one hundred thousand to one hundred and twenty-five thousand men were the numbers that had been bandied around at Kalvan's War Council. Overhead surveillance and some groundwork by the Harphax City Study Team had given him an estimated figure of one hundred and thirty thousand combatants. The army of sutlers and camp followers following the Grand Host was estimated to be twice that number.

One of his sergeants came by and offered him a canteen of winter wine. Verkan took a deep drink. All this waiting was thirsty work, not to mention time consuming. And time was something he didn't have a lot of these days, especially with all the work he had left waiting back at Paratime Police HQ. This year's Year-End Day riots had been the worst in a millennium. The radical wing of the Prole Liberation Movement was claiming credit, while the establishment center of the PLM was decrying the riots and blaming them on citizen anti-prole prejudice.

There was still no sign of Dalla's brother, Hadron Tharn, on First Level or any of his other regular haunts. Tharn had, however, stripped several of his holding companies of their assets through intermediaries, causing turmoil in the Home Time Line stock market. He was now the Number One fugitive topping both the Dhergabar Metropolitan Police and Paratime Police's most wanted lists.

Verkan's thoughts flashed back to the here-and-now when he spotted a small cloud of dust and half a dozen Hostigi scouts rode over the ridge and down into the valley. The scouts reached friendly lines and were tucked out of the way before the twenty-five to thirty enemy cavalry, with red and yellow helmet-plumes, following behind came into view. Verkan signaled his men to hold their fire. Not only was the Harphaxi detachment out of rifle range, but moreover he didn't want to warn the main body of the Mounted Rifles presence.

"Sergeant Ryff, bring these troopers to my tent at once!"

After Ryff left at a fast trot, Verkan gave a First Level hand signal to Captain Dalon, who was his Paratime Police assistant in this battle, now that Ranthar Jard was in Hos-Bletha with Kalvan's Insurrection Group. Dalon Sath had fought with Colonel Ranthar in the Army of the Trygath and had distinguished himself enough to win the rank of captain—Kalvan was very generous at rewarding faithful and decisive subordinates. Dalon was a master tech and in charge of the Beshtan observation sky-eyes.

Even though they were out of voice range of the locals, Verkan spoke in First Level, assuming that anyone who overheard them would presume it was his native Grefftscharrer tongue. "Sath, I want you to change the setting on the sky-eye; I want to know what's coming over that ridge. Then contact Kirv at the Foundry and tell him to batten down the hatches."

Dalon Sath shook his head. "That's going to be tough, Chief. We've got the anti-gravity spotter almost within visual range now—"

"I don't care anymore. Our need for information overrides any transtemporal violation. If any indigenes see the satellite they'll just assume it's a portent of the coming battle. We need to know what's coming over those ridges. I'm not worried about some dirt farmer talking about Styphon's Eye in the Sky! Just do it!"

"Yes sir, Chief."

When the Harphaxi scouting party reached the valley bottom they stopped to water their horses and fill their water flasks. Two of the enemy scouts threw off their buckskins and jumped into the creek, shouting and whooping it up. The Mobile Force sergeants ran up and down the line of riflemen making sure no one took a pot shot.

When Ryff returned with the scouts, Verkan debriefed them.

"Sir, there's about ten thousand Harphaxi horse and infantry—even a band of Red Hand—coming our way."

After squeezing the scouts dry of what little information they had, he returned to the ridge to wait for the Harphaxi. The wait seemed interminable, but Verkan knew only ten or fifteen minutes had passed when the main body topped the rise and rode over the crest. As the Harphaxi cavalry moved into the valley the horsemen kept coming and coming and Verkan realized they were facing close to twelve thousand horse. Many of the forward horsemen were light cavalry, with breastplates or leather jerkins, javelins and swords; but the majority wore the three-quarter-lobster armor of the cuirassiers. Verkan wished he had a small battery of the heavy sixteen-pounders with explosive shells; they could have harvested a bloody crop on the Harphaxi force.

Verkan had organized his Mobile Riflemen into three battalions, each containing three one-hundred man companies. The battalions were to fire in rotating volleys while the remaining HQ Company of sharpshooters fired at targets of opportunity—mainly officers and pockets of resistance.

He shouted, "ONE!" A single boom rolled through the valley, ripping through the Harphaxi men and horses alike. Taken by complete surprise, the

Harphaxi detachment boiled, musketoons and pistols firing in every direction. Horses dropped and men spilled to the ground. "TWO!" Another volley, followed by a third, fourth and fifth, tore through the mass of enemy horsemen. His riflemen were using the new Minié balls and paper cartridges, which gave them the fastest rate of fire this time-line had ever seen.

The Harphaxi horsemen, with their red and yellow plumes, began to re-form—even under the withering fire of the Mounted Rifles—and began to ride up the ridge. Still more riders came over the far ridge. Now Verkan could make out their shouting, "Down Kalvan! Down Kalvan!"

Verkan signaled his sergeants to stop firing and prepare for a single volley. The volley tore through the Harphaxi lines like a reaper through a fresh field. Suddenly, the wind changed and everything was obscured by swirling smoke. When the air cleared, the Harphaxi were half again as far up the ridge. The Mounted Rifles fired another volley and the leading riders went down en masse, the survivors jumping off their horses and scrambling close to the ground. Then the wind changed direction again and all he could see was roiling gray gunpowder smoke.

By the time the air had cleared again, a trooper had scrambled up the ridge and was pointing a bell-mouthed musketoon in his face. Captain Dalon shot him point-black in the face with his horsepistol—even before Verkan could flinch.

"FIRE!" shouted Sergeant Ryff. The falling trooper and his companions, who'd lost their mounts and fought on foot, disappeared in a wash of red blood and swirling gray smoke. Verkan ran his sword point past the nasal guard and into the eye of one trooper trying to liberate a rifle from a fallen officer. The next volley fired through a scrum of patchy smoke and attacking cavalrymen. It took three more ragged volleys to clear the ridge and force the dismounted Harphaxi troopers into a retreat, signaled by the bellow of Harphaxi war horns.

Verkan had the healers, sawbones and Uncle Wolfs brought to the front lines to remove the wounded and dead Hostigi on litters made of poles and blankets. Friendly casualties were surprisingly light. The enemy dead and wounded lay strewn over the hillside by the hundreds. The screams of wounded men and horses split the air.

The retreating Harphaxi reformed out of rifle range on the opposing hillside. Enemy reinforcements continued to join the main battle in small and large groupings, many of them dragoons. This was going to turn into a real rough-and-tumble if some Hostigi reinforcements didn't show up soon.

He walked down the line talking to his troopers, giving them encouragement, and making jokes at Styphon's expense. "How many Styphoni does it take to fire a musket?" he asked. "You don't know, do you? Five: one lowerpriest to fill the pan with fireseed, one temple highpriest to push down the striker, one Archpriest to put fireseed and drop the bullet down the barrel and use the rammer, one Red Hand to fire it, and one Holy Investigator to hold the target!" It hadn't been half so funny back in camp, but here it drew gales of laughter.

He had time to smoke and refill his pipe twice before the Harphaxi cavalry formed up for their second attack.

II

The rain had finally letup and beams of golden sunlight were lancing through the trees of their makeshift council site. For an army on the move, it was not an unusual place to hold a Council of War—the nearest town was five miles away and in ruins. The arching trees overhead gave it the interior spaciousness of a cathedral. Instead of a Catholic bishop or priest giving the sermon, it was Uncle Wolf Tharses, who was wearing his official uniform, a wolf's head hood and wolfskin cape over a mail hauberk.

His usually open and placid face was a mask of fury. "It is wrong, what the Styphoni are doing in Sashta, wrong in the eyes of Galzar Wolfshead, the God of War, and wrong in the name of all the other true gods. War is to be fought among men, not helpless women and children." There was a chorus of agreement from the assembled princes and commanders of the Army of Hos-Hostigos.

This is all true, thought Kalvan, but where were Galzar's priests from Hos-Ktemnos and Hos-Bletha? *On the other side, saying most of the same things about Kalvan and Hos-Hostigos,* he told himself cynically.

"Galzar is Judge of Princes and the Wargod will judge both the devil-worshipping Styphoni and the bootlicking Harphaxi, who use Styphon's gold to wage this unjust war against the subjects and people of Hos-Hostigos. It is the field of battle, not the nursery, that is the courtroom of Galzar. Styphon's House has not only declared war against Hos-Hostigos, but also the Sky-Thrones of the Gods. I have sent Rynnos, Highpriest of Xyphos Town, to Galzar's High Temple in Agrys City to seek a Ban of Galzar on all the armies of Styphon's House!"

That, here-and-now, was an unprecedented declaration of war upon Styphon's House by the only other temple in the Six Kingdoms that had any teeth. Under the Ban of Galzar, any mercenaries fighting for Styphon's House would have to renounce their colors and retire from the field of battle. Kalvan wasn't sure just how many mercenaries were included in the Grand Host, but it had to be a quarter to a third of their force. The only problem was no single highpriest of Galzar could declare the Ban; it had to be decided upon by the Temple Highpriests. It might be a moon or two before Highpriest Rynnos traveled to Agrys City, presented their case against Styphon's House, the case was adjudicated and word sent to all the Six Kingdoms.

Of course, Styphon's House would renounce it and say it was a vicious smear campaign against Styphon's House by the Daemon Kalvan and Tharses himself would have to appear before the High Temple, with his witnesses, and the whole thing would drag on until the war was over, or until no one cared anymore. No one was more concerned about their virtue than the schoolyard bully, and Styphon's House was the Great King of all bullies!

"This is a war against all the gods, by the foul brood of the false god Styphon. When we destroy the army of Styphon, we shall not only kill his evil spawn, but also save our lands from this vile plague that threatens all of the Six Kingdoms. Kill the False Styphoni!"

There was a chorus of "Down Styphon!" and the meeting began to break up. Kalvan motioned Prince Ptosphes over.

"Prince, I have a favor to ask."

Ptosphes' face looked drawn and his color was bad. Camping out in the night air after riding eight to ten hours, day after day, was taking its toll. "Anything you ask that is mine to give is yours, Your Majesty."

Kalvan prepared himself for an explosion. "I want you to return to Tarr-Hostigos. Wait, let me explain, before you speak! It's been over a day now and we still haven't heard back from General Verkan or any of the other Mobile Force. We have too much territory to protect and not enough men to cover it all. I believe we can still beat the Styphoni, but it could be close, very close."

Ptosphes nodded tiredly, not even trying to interrupt.

Kalvan wasn't sure whether if that was a good or bad sign. "In case—and I'm only trying to prepare for the worst possible outcome—should we lose the upcoming battle I want someone back at Tarr-Hostigos whom I can completely trust. True, Harmakros is still at the castle, but he's in no condition to act as the commander of our rearguard. And I need someone to keep an eye on Princess Demia."

The First Prince nodded. "With his leg gone, Harmakros can no longer sit on a horse. I will do as you ask, Kalvan. I am a stubborn old fool—no, don't protest. But I am not blind or addled. My body has slowed down and it needs more time to rest. Some days my breath is so short, it is hard to breathe. So, I will return to Tarr-Hostigos and prepare for the grand victory celebration for when you return with the head of Arch-devil Roxthar mounted on a pole!"

Surprising himself, Kalvan gave his father-in-law a big bear hug. "Thank you, Ptosphes. I will miss your wise counsel."

"I see Rylla over there. It's best that I tell her myself."

"Of course."

He heard the shouting and suddenly everyone within sight quickly drew a sword or pistol—or both. Kalvan relaxed when he saw it was Prince Sarrask of Sask, leading at pistol point a reluctant and fully armored Prince Balthames into the clearing. Three of Sarrask's Bodyguard with halberds at port arms followed behind.

Prince Balthames, who was dressed in silver plate more appropriate for a parade than a field of battle, was shaking badly. The visor to his armet helm was up and Balthames' handsome face was beet red, although it was hard to tell if it was from being roughed-up, anger or embarrassment.

Sarrask spoke first, "I thought it was odd when I noticed Balthames was not at the meeting, since earlier I had seen this popinjay put on his fancy armor."

Kalvan could remember a day when Sarrask's Bodyguard wore more silver than Styphon's Temple Guard. These days they dressed in good Arklos plate and their armor was rain-proofed with liberal smears of sheep tallow and pig fat.

"So I had one of my guardsmen follow him and he found this traitorous swine with his guardsmen trying to loot our paychests! He reported back to me and I took my Guard. We killed Balthames' henchmen and brought him back for Your Majesty's Justice."

There was more to this than met the eye; Kalvan knew that for certain. Sarrask's daughter Princess Amnita and Prince Balthames had been married in an arranged dynastic marriage; it was one of convenience, since she liked dashing cavalry captains while he preferred boys. Last spring she had become with child and Balthames had banished her from Sashta, after beheading her current lover. Now, the Princess was under-foot, pregnant, miserable and making Sarrask's life "like that of a manure shoveler in a bull's pasture," as Sarrask so colorfully put it.

"The uppity bugger has run through the Sashta treasury, giving patents to all his boyfriends. Now, he wants our gold and silver!" Sarrask's last words came out in a snarl.

Balthames wore a petulant sneer. "It's only your word against mine! You're an even bigger liar than that harlot you call a daughter!"

It took Vanar Halgoth to hold Sarrask back from tearing his son-in-law limb from limb. While he had lost a lot of weight, the Prince of Sarrask was still a big man, only now it was muscle, not fat, he was carrying.

Kalvan made a calming motion with his hands to Sarrask. He turned to the Prince's Bodyguards. "What did you men see?"

"It's like the Prince says," the tallest Bodyguard answered. "We saw this character steal away from camp with a score of his men-at-arms to the baggage train and try to take the paychests! We didn't have to hear 'kill them' twice before we ran 'em down and cut 'em to pieces. After all, that's our silver they're takin'!"

The other bodyguards nodded in agreement. One of them stepped forward and said, "I was one of the paychest guards. Prince Balthames took us by surprise and had his men aim their pistols at us. Told us 'we'll kill you if you move.' Then they used hammers to knock the locks off. They were stealing Your Majesty's gold and silver, all right."

"I believe these men have given a brief but accurate account of what just transpired," Kalvan stated. "What's your story, Balthames?"

"You'd take the word of these, these…commoners?"

"Yes, now give me your account before I make my judgment."

Prince Balthames looked wildly around him for a sympathetic eye or friendly face. He found neither. His face fell. "Look, King Kalvan, everyone knows that the Styphoni outnumber us better than two to one—this war is hopeless. In another night or two they will be fighting in Sashta Town. I just wanted what was mine; I wouldn't have taken it all. I wanted enough gold to go to Agrys City and live like a Prince, not some pauper—is that so wrong?"

Kalvan nodded to Vanar, who released Sarrask from his hold. He turned to Captain Simodes, "Take my Bodyguard and round up all the nobles within a candle from the camp."

"Yes, sir." Simodes mounted his horse and rode off to the temporary headquarters.

Kalvan knew what had to be done, but he wanted witnesses. It wouldn't do to have rumors running about the camp about why Balthames was executed. It was bad enough he had to deal with this mess just before a major battle.

When enough nobles had gathered, including Prince Ptosphes, Prince Pheblon and Tythanes, Prince of Kyblos, Kalvan recounted Balthames' treachery. Before he was finished, there were shouts of "behead him" and "shoot him out of a cannon!"

Balthames face was as white as a sheepskin.

Prince Sarrask looked at Kalvan and said, "King's Justice."

Kalvan nodded.

Sarrask pulled a pistol out of his green and gold sash, while Balthames looked on in disbelief. "I'm a Prince…"

Sarrask raised the pistol up, as a paralyzed Balthames watched it like a pigeon hypnotized by a snake. He quickly marched over to the Prince, slammed down his visor, put the gun barrel to the eye slit and fired.

There was a sound that reminded Kalvan of a car backfire. The suit of armor danced spasmodically a few times, then fell into a quivering heap. Blood dripped out of the airholes and visor slit.

Sarrask squatted down over Balthames and pulled a long, thin boning knife out of his right boot, which he stuck through the helmet's eyehole. "Let no one say he did not die like a Prince." He pulled out the bloody knife, with a sucking sound, and wiped the blood on his dun-colored breeches.

The Prince turned to his Bodyguards. "Take this piece of offal to the nearest privy pit and bury him."

"What about his armor?" the tall one asked.

"Strip him naked," Sarrask said. "Anything you find is yours."

The guards left with grins, telling all and sundry what a grand prince they served.

Kalvan's stomach felt queasy, but military justice had to be quick, irrespective of rank, firm and cruel—or the result was anarchy. They had hanged three rapists the day before and Balthames hadn't even blinked. Well, what's fair was fair—equal justice under the law. And one less Quisling—like his brother Balthar of Beshta who turned coats in the middle of the Battle of Tenabra—to worry about.

Sarrask approached him with a pewter mug of brandy for him and one for Halgoth. "Let's make a toast, Your Majesty."

One of the Prince's Bodyguards rushed up with another mug, which the guard proudly gave to his prince. "To thieves and cowards, may Hadron feast on their bones!"

"Hear, hear!" Kalvan answered.

TWENTY-NINE

Verkan walked along the Mounted Rifles' files, patting shoulders, stepping over bodies, passing out tobacco and giving encouragement to the wounded. "We'll send these godless Styphoni bastards right back to Balph!" he told one helmetless young man with straw-like hair. His morion helmet was lying on the ground with a bullet hole in the comb. The boy had an awful belly wound that meant certain death on Aryan-Transpacific, considering the dismal state of the healing arts.

The man-boy's feverish eyes lit up and he smiled, saying, "You show 'em, Colonel. I'm going to take a little nap and then I'll be right back in the fray." Then dropped dead as a stone.

A tiny drop of moisture beaded up in one of Verkan's eyes. He shook his head and mentally disciplined himself. He'd grieve for this boy and the other brave Hostigi of his command when this battle was over and he could afford to relax his First Level mental controls.

Verkan, as a drummer boy, had observed some of the bloodiest battles of what was known across most of Fourth Level Europo-American as the Civil War, but he had never been in a fracas where the combatants were so determined to fight to the last man—which he'd always thought was a cliché until now.

The hillside below him was littered with what had to be around fifteen hundred dead horses and some two thousand dead and wounded Harphaxi regulars. From the way they were forming up, he decided the Harphaxi were gathering steam for another charge!

His Mounted Rifles had stood off eight determined attacks, exhausting both their powder kegs and ranks—at last count over a third of the Mounted Rifles were dead or mortally wounded. Still the Harphaxi Army came on. Verkan wasn't sure if it was courage or sheer blockheadedness on the enemy's part for being held up by such a small force.

He would have ordered retreat, but there was nowhere to go. He certainly didn't want to bring the Harphaxi into the Foundry's backyard. For the first time since arriving on Kalvan's Time-Line, he was seriously considering asking for First Level back up! There was no way he could leave *his* Rifles on their own.

Sergeant Ryff came running over, favoring his right leg. He'd taken a flesh wound from a lance in the upper thigh. Verkan noted that the blue halberd of Hostigos and the Rifles own banner, two crossed rifles on a green field, were flying proudly. "At last!" the Sergeant puffed. "Reinforcements! The Second and Third Royal Dragoons. They just arrived."

"Praise the Allfather!" Verkan said, and meant it. "First, tell them, we need more fireseed."

Ryff nodded. "I've already got the petty captains passing out fireseed horns and gathering the rifles we no longer need." He didn't need to expound on the fact that their owners were soon to be a part of Sashta's soil.

"Good thinking, pass the extra rifles out to the dragoons!" He was so busy berating himself for not thinking of the rifles, he barely noticed the smile that lit up the sergeant's face. "There's not enough rifles for all of them," he added, "so put the dragoons in the first rank where their smoothbores will do some good. It looks like our friends are buying courage for another charge."

"For Styphoni, they are right brave. *Almost* as good as Hostigi."

Verkan found himself in reluctant agreement. "For Styphoni without the Red Hand to stiffen their courage, they fight and die well." There, that was as much as he would give them.

It wasn't long before the Dragoons' horns were sounding the 'take formation' tune that Kalvan had taught them. Verkan noticed that the Harphaxi were still reordering their lines. The Mounted Rifles were back to full strength, but with significantly less firepower as the smoothbores were inaccurate at distances over a hundred paces and a growing number of rifles were fouled or damaged.

Verkan felt a vibration against his chest, where his communicator hung from a chain—disguised as a golden image of Galzar. He looked down at the ground and brought the small emblem of Galzar Wolfhead to his lips. He wasn't worried about attracting attention since it was not uncommon to see soldiers talking to Galzar's image on a battlefield just before an engagement.

It was Kirv's voice from the foundry. *"Big trouble coming your way, Chief. We just got a good peek at your area from the sky-eye: it looks like an entire army is headed to your little dustup. Actually, a really big detachment. Our estimate is twenty to twenty-five thousand effectives tops. Half cavalry and half infantry. It appears Phidestros is trying to out-flank Kalvan. He takes your boy most seriously."*

Verkan sucked wind through his cheeks. "Sweet Styphon!"

"We'd like to pull you out of there now, Chief. Let the locals think Allfather Dralm's Chariot came to take you away! By the time this fracas is over, there aren't going to be many witnesses."

"No. I'm not leaving my Rifles."

"Chief, be reasonable—they're just outtimers!"

Verkan held back from releasing a string of Second Level curses that would have left Kirv's ears flaming red.

"I'm staying, and that's final."

"But it's hopeless, Chief. I could have a small anti-gravity personnel lifter over there in twenty minutes—Here's Dalla, she wants to speak to you."

"Kirv, you Styphoni sucking—"

"Hi, Vall. I see you've picked up some more colorful Aryan Transpacific idioms. It's not Kirv's fault I'm here; I was tired of all the Study Team bickering and came down here to watch my husband's last stand."

"Hi, Dalla. Don't try and talk me out—"

"I wouldn't dream of it Verkan. I know you too well to demand that you do something you'd never forgive yourself or me for. I just wish I was there."

"I'll be back, love."

"I hope so," Dalla answered, with a muffled sob. *"I'll miss you—my only love."*

"Love you too!" Then he flicked the com off—before he agreed to take a lift back to the Foundry.

It took the Styphoni main body another twenty minutes to reach the opposite slope. Even Verkan had to admit they arrived with panache, flags and banners of every color and stripe flying, dominated by Styphon's black sun-wheel on yellow, white and even red, which meant there was at least one band of Styphon's Own Guard—so either Phidestros or Soton took them seriously indeed.

Verkan stood up and used a disguised Kalvan farseer, which was augmented by First Level tech into a very high quality imager. Yes, he could see several Harphaxi squadrons dressed in silvered armor at the fore with their musketoons and flowing red and yellow capes. No, those weren't musketoons, they were aiming—they were rifles! And they were about to fire a salvo.

"GET DOWN!" he shouted, as a hail of lead flew across their lines. Twenty or thirty troopers took shots, but they were mostly dragoons who hadn't reacted fast enough. The Mounted Rifles had learned to expect just about anything. He was so proud of them his chest swelled.

Verkan didn't need to repeat himself as the Hostigi lay in their trenches, loading rifles and priming pans. He noticed that many of the dragoons in the forward line had several flintlock pistols and arquebuses, taken from the dead troopers, lined up so they could use them at clash of arms. They were learning. Sergeant Ryff and his petty-captains were passing out pouches of fireseed and Minié balls to the Mounted Rifles. He called Ryff over to make certain there was lead shot and fireseed for the dragoons, who wouldn't know what to do with the Minié balls.

Kalvan didn't have enough Minié balls for everyone, but he made sure his Mounted Rifles had them. He wished his friend were here by his side to take his place in Verkan's Last Stand, because that's what this was shaping up as. Not a bad way to end a long life. It could have been longer, and Dalla would miss him—but there were a lot of worse ways to leave this fleshly shell. And, as Dalla kept telling him, maybe there was something to reincarnation; too bad he wouldn't be able to tell her in person....

This time when the Styphoni charged up the slope it looked as if a multi-hued carpet had come to life and was creeping up the hillside. "Fire!"

The first salvo shook the front line, but only for a moment. On the opposing slope he could see the Harphaxi riflemen aiming their rifles, looking for targets of opportunity. "Stay down! Fire Two!"

They got off four salvos before the wave of soldiers and slashing hand weapons reached their line. In that tightly bunched up mass of humanity, he guessed the casualties were at least one to two thousand. Gunshots were crackling like firecrackers and the screams of dying and wounded horses ripped the air. With the lines this blurred, Verkan dropped two or three Harphaxi. Then his rifle jammed; he bent the barrel over a foe's helmet and smashed the stock into a big mercenary's face. Then he pulled out his needler and began to open up a pocket. Then his charge was on empty and he was using his sword to fend off three slashing sabers.

Verkan took one trooper out with a slash to the eye, another with the heel of his left hand and the third with the point of his blade into his armpit, where there was only thin chain mail. Before he could disengage, he saw the barrel of the biggest pistol barrel he'd ever seen—then an explosion. He fell to the ground with a thud. *I'm fine,* he told himself, as a searing, tearing pain ripped apart his chest. Someone's booted heel gouged his cheek and then the wave of troops passed over him. He heard shouts of "Down Styphon!" and screaming cries of "Kill Kalvan" and then it all faded into oblivion….

Verkan awoke to someone slapping his face. "Chief, can you hear me?"

He groaned, which was answered by a sigh of relief that he recognized as coming from Dalon Sath. Or, as Kalvan would have said, it looked as if the Marines had landed after all…

"Don't pass out on me, again, Chief. This is going to hurt." Verkan could feel him struggling at the straps on his back-and-breast. He couldn't catch his breath and his chest hurt worse than the infected tooth he'd gotten back on Alexandrian-Roman when he'd been stranded there for three years….

"How are my Rifles?"

Sath shook his head. "We'll talk when you're feeling better."

That was not the answer he'd wanted to hear. Verkan felt his head swim and moaned. Then a pain, like that of a tomahawk striking his chest, jerked him back to reality as Sath tried to un-hook his breastplate. Looking down, he noticed a strange rip in the metal of his chestplate, with pieces of steel bent every which way. He saw a red bubble and almost fainted. *No time to pass out, old boy,* Verkan told himself.

He exerted his First Level mental controls to pinch off the flow of blood to his pectoral muscles. Unfortunately, while he could also dampen the stabbing pain of ripped lung and broken ribs, he could not make the wound go away. "Medpack!" he stammered.

"Quiet, Chief! I have it right here, disguised as a lead bullet mold box. Every trooper should carry one…."

"Now, who's panicking?"

"Sorry, Chief—I'm not used to this. And if I screw up, I get to tell Dalla! Besides, this damn breastplate doesn't want to come off, not without taking two of your ribs with it."

Verkan winced. He felt a stinging hypospray shot in the arm. Moments later the pain disappeared and his head began to clear.

Finally Dalon Sath ripped the breastplate off; it had been caught on the flak jacket underneath, which was supposed to protect him from this kind of wound.

"I don't know what kind of big game gun you were shot with, Chief, but it tore the Styphon out of this plastisteel!

"I saw it, just before it went off—the biggest pistol I've ever seen, 12-bore, maybe bigger."

"You're lucky that breastplate was reinforced with plastisteel, or he would have put your breastplate through your spine."

"Thanks for the comforting words, Sath!"

"Sorry, Chief. This is going to hurt. Here's another shot for the pain. Now, I've got a single-cell membrane bandage and I'm going to lay it over your chest. First, I'm going to put this stick between your teeth. It'll take about a minute before the membrane joins with your skin."

The mono-skin was an import from a Second Level world where the emphasis had been on biological science rather than the mechanical arts.

Suddenly Verkan felt a searing pain, as if a pot of hot oil had been tossed on his naked chest. Nothing he'd ever felt had prepared him for this kind of pain! His teeth sank into the wood and he was covered in a cold sweat by the time the sheer agony receded, but he noticed that he could breathe easier.

"What happened?" he asked as soon as the pain was at a tolerable level, using self-hypnosis exercises to calm his adrenalin charged body.

"The Styphoni rode right over us, Chief. We took a lot of them with us, but in the end they passed over the crest and right now they're chasing what's left of our friends."

"What about my Rifles?"

Dalon shook his head. "Sorry, Verkan. It doesn't look good. Maybe a few of them will get away, but most of them died right here." There were Hostigi and Harphaxi bodies three deep all over the ridge. "It was the dragoons who broke—not that I blame them! When you're out-numbered ten to one, out-sabered, out-gunned and facing the Investigation if you surrender—well, running seems like a pretty good option."

"How did you…?"

"Make it?" Sath finished. "I got this cut," he pointed to a superficial blade slash over his eye. "Which put me out for a few minutes. When I came to there were half a dozen dead Styphoni and Hostigi covering me. I saw a couple of scouts cutting throats and stripping the dead so I kept quiet. Some Temple Guards came along, the Red Hand with those bell mouthed muskets and pole arms of theirs. They chastised the looters. Several of them were shot right where they stood. Seems the Red Hand doesn't believe in stripping the dead until after the enemy is defeated. First time I ever felt like saluting those bastards!

They left a couple of Harphaxi soldiers behind as observers; I managed to use my needler to good effect and took them all out—it took a while though. Mostly re-shooting their corpses with muskets so they looked like 'typical' battlefield casualties."

Verkan nodded. "Good thinking under pressure. We don't want to contaminate a battlefield which Kalvan might possibly visit. Did you find the bodies I left…."

Dalon Sath nodded. "I prettied them up, too. Then I went looking for you, Chief. You had me worried there for little bit. At least, till I saw you were still breathing."

"We're still not in the clear. We need to find a place to hole up until nightfall."

"I agree. Think you can walk now? I can help."

Verkan groaned, but made it to his feet. Not even the drugs could keep the stabbing pains in his chest at bay. "Let's go. Have any plans?"

"Yes, according to Kirv there's a small cave three ridges over. I've got a global nav on me and he's given me the coordinates. We should be able to hole up there until nightfall when Kirv can bring a lifter in."

Verkan felt a wave of pain—either physical, mental or both. His bloodstream was filled with too many drugs to tell. Whatever happened, he knew he wouldn't forget this battle for the rest of his life—no matter how long he lived. What would Kalvan and Rylla think? No one had anticipated the Grand Host tossing a small army this way. Kalvan was going to have to sink or swim on his own for now....

The stabbing pains in his chest were hitting him like blades every time he lifted his right leg. Something was wrong with his leg, too. "Sath, I need more support!"

"Here, put your arm around my neck. I'm not big enough to carry you, but that should take some pressure off your right leg. I forgot to mention, someone shot you there but it's only a flesh wound. I bandaged it while you were out."

A cavalryman with a bloody sword in his hand rode out of some bushes. "Kill the Hostigi! Prepare to meet your comrades in Hadron's Hall!"

"You talk too much," Sath replied, as he calmly shot the trooper out of his saddle with his needler.

Verkan felt his head begin to swim from loss of blood.

"Chief, pull yourself together! You're too Dralm-damned big for me to carry!"

After that all he remembered was the steady rhythm of one-step, two-step, three-step, four—

THIRTY

I

Sirna found herself mindlessly pacing back and forth before the locked metal door that led to the Hostigos Paratime Transposition Depot.

"Stop that infernal pacing, Sirna," Professor Lathor Karv said. "You're going to wear ruts in the floor stones! How will we explain *that* to the Foundry workers?"

Sirna bit back a sarcastic rejoinder. She wasn't sure in her own mind why she was so concerned about Chief Verkan, except that she liked him. To her he'd always been the most competent and strongest man in any room. To know the Chief was lying in the depot with a sucking chest wound only demonstrated how vulnerable all the timeliners were, trapped in the middle of a war, on a time-line millions of parayears from First Level. Not only was outtime work hard and messy—but dangerous, too.

The only other member of the University Team who seemed concerned about the Chief was Aranth Saln, who had pulled up a chair and was waiting for news patiently. She wished she shared his First Level mental discipline.

Finally, Captain Skordran Kirv—the latest Paratime Police babysitter—came through the door. Colonel Ranthar had taken Eldra with him when he'd left for his secret mission for Kalvan in Hos-Bletha. Sirna was convinced the only reason Eldra had gone along was that she'd been exiled by Chief Verkan for approaching Kalvan at the University party and trying to seduce him in public. It was a stupid thing to do, especially with Rylla waiting in the wings. She missed Eldra, but not the air of danger the older woman carried around with her like a scarf.

"How is our Chief?" Saln asked, finally breaking the silence.

"Dalon Sath saved his life," Kirv answered. "Quick thinking on his part to use the monocell membrane to cover Verkan's chest wound. He wouldn't have lasted long without it."

Sirna saw the wince that Aranth made upon hearing about the monocell treatment. It was supposed to be very painful; she wondered if he had direct experience with it during his time in the military.

Kirv continued. "We just sent him back to the Fifth Level Police Terminal for treatment. He should be back in four to five days."

They'd probably graft him a new lung and use cellgrow to repair the tissue damage, she thought. His wounds must have been serious or he would have been back in a day. Now they were really alone.

"Is he badly hurt?" she asked.

"Yes and no. They're mortal wounds for Aryan-Transpacific. Minor for First Level; he wants to stay at the Terminal and study the battle reports, as well as catch up on some of his backlog, until the battle's settled. It's too soon for him to make an appearance in Hostigos—win or lose."

"What about Kalvan?"

Captain Kirv looked at her thoughtfully.

"I mean, what's the Chief's cover story?"

"Badly wounded and left for dead. We'll leave some pretty nasty 'scars' to show the locals and Kalvan when the war is over. There's tremendous variability in trauma survival anywhere medicine's in its infancy. Here one can just as easily die from a rusty wire as a chest wound. 'It's all up to the gods,' is the local healers' disclaimer. I don't think anyone here will be suspicious unless the Chief returns too soon."

"When do we leave?"

Talgan Dreth, the Study Team Director, who'd just entered the foundry, looked at her as if she were one of Styphon's minions.

"Only when—and if—Kalvan evacuates Hostigos Town. Otherwise, we'll stay put. I'll not be made a laughingstock by the media again!"

The previous year someone, maybe one of the Paratime Policemen, had smuggled out a recording of the original Study Team hastily deserting the Foundry based on false reports of a Hostigi defeat from some Ulthori deserters. Most of the Team, as they struggled through their chaotic evac- uation, had come off as amiable idiots—at best. Sirna, Eldra and Aranth Saln had received all the good press, since they'd stayed behind and helped to aid the Hostigi wounded. Neither Lala nor the rest of the Team had expected their hasty exit to be viewed on Yandar Yadd's news show.

When she heard about it, Lala had thrown a fit, letting off a stream of curses that any of Kalvan's troopers would have been proud to claim as their own. Talgan had just sulked for almost an entire ten-day.

Sirna hoped Talgan's pride wouldn't get in the way of an orderly evacuation, if it looked as if the Grand Host were about to besiege the Foundry. The horrible things she was hearing about the Investigation had her edgy and worried sick, and not just about herself. Some of the atrocities that had been committed on innocent civilians had left her stunned and frightened for both herself and the Hostigi people.

II

Rylla watched lovingly as Kalvan pored over his maps in the sputtering lamplight while she scrambled turkey eggs for their breakfast omelet. They were billeted in a small manor house outside Ardros Field, a large cattle ranch, whose titled owner had fled upon learning of the Styphoni invasion. It was such an ordinary domestic setting that for a few moments Rylla was able to imagine they had nothing more pressing to worry about than the best time to plant their vegetable garden.

She had missed last night's grand strategy meeting since she'd been in Hostigos Town visiting her father and Harmakros for the past quarter-moon.

Her party had left Hostigos Town two days ago and she had arrived at Ardros Field in mid-morning to find her husband fast asleep.

Rylla was making a determined effort to be quiet; Kalvan, Prince Phrames, General Hestophes and the newly arrived Duke Mnestros had been celebrating the arrival of three thousand League of Dralm 'advisors' the day before far into the night. Since the Covenant of Hos-Agrys, passed by the Council of Dralm, forbade the League's Princes to give any direct material support to Hos-Hostigos, Mnestros and some other Hostigi sympathizers had put together their own army to aid in the war against Styphon's House. From Agrys City there wasn't a Dralm-damn thing Xentos could do about it either.

Phrames, Hestophes, Mnestros and Kalvan had spent most of the evening studying maps and discussing battle plans, as well as drinking the best part of a cask of Ermut's Best. Kalvan, still nursing a hangover, was making a valiant attempt to show only his best humor. Despite the revels of the evening, she was determined to find out what they'd accomplished before every general and busybody in the army wanted their piece of the Great King's time.

The Army of Hos-Hostigos had spent the last moon quarter in Sashta retreating, winding back and forth over hill and dale until now, until they were only a day's ride from the Hostigos border. There wasn't any place left to run and Kalvan's worried expression showed traces of every acre they had lost to the Grand Host.

With more than twice as many men as the Army of Hos-Hostigos, the Grand Host had been able to put the Hostigos Army into a wearing retreat. Their greater numbers were forcing Kalvan into a position where he would have to make a stand here in Sashta or fight in Hostigos itself. Already the roads were lined with throngs of refugees and it was growing increasingly difficult to feed them and the huge army, even with all the depots that Phrames and Hestophes had put in place last year throughout Sashta and Beshta. Praise Dralm for last season's bumper harvest!

When Rylla had finished cooking her turkey egg, cheese and onion omelet, she added some cornbread to the plate and brought it over to the table.

"Thank you, darling," Kalvan said, pushing aside his maps to make room for his breakfast. "I've gone over these maps until my eyes ache and I still can't see a better place to make a stand than right here. You know the creek that runs down the hill?"

"Yes, it allows our army a good supply of fresh water."

"True, but more than that we're going to use it against the Grand Host."

"How, my love?"

Kalvan stopped eating and said, "See this hillside." He snatched a parchment of Ardros Field drawn by his own hand out of the pile of maps, and pointed to the hill. "We're going to build a dam right below where a small spring is running. I hiked up there yesterday with Hestophes and he agrees it's a perfect spot for a small lake. If I know Hestophes, he's already got a team of engineers working on the dam."

"How will that stop the Grand Host?"

"The Johnstown Flood that's how." He pointed at the map again. "When the Styphoni left wing approaches this point, we'll blow up the dam and the resulting flood will completely disorganize the Styphoni left wing."

"I like that! Then Hestophes' right wing can smash the survivors like we did at Phyrax."

Kalvan nodded. "This depression won't hold enough water to wash the entire Grand Host away, but it should scatter and soak most of the left wing. Then it'll be up to Hestophes to pull them down from the trees and wring their necks!"

"That will be something to watch. But, my husband, you're not eating!"

Up close Rylla could see bruise-colored bags under Kalvan's eyes that hadn't been there two moon quarters ago. Her heart went out to this man, who only a few years ago was a stranger to this land. Yet, who had almost single-handedly saved her homeland and made her his wife, giving her the happiest times of her life—until this war.

Kalvan put the Ardros Field map away and returned to attacking his plate.

The next few days, Rylla thought, would determine not only the course of her future, but its duration as well.

"You are right to stop the Grand Host now. Look at what the Styphoni dogs have done in Beshta and Sashta—trampled fields and burned farmhouses; looted towns and torched villages and driven off or killed most of our subjects. We can't let them destroy Hostigos, too."

"They've done everything but poison the wells and salt the fields," Kalvan said. "That's probably next, if I know Roxthar. We have to stop them here."

A knock at the door interrupted Rylla before she could respond.

"Let me answer the door, Kalvan. You finish your first meal. It may be the only one you take out of the saddle today."

Aspasthar, Kalvan's page, was at the door. He was smiling for the first time Rylla could remember since Harmakros' amputation. He looked older, too. She was learning war did that to people, especially children.

"Some good news, at last, Your Majesties!"

"What?" Kalvan asked. "Has Roxthar's horse thrown him and broken his head on a rock?"

"Not nearly that good, Your Majesty. But good, nonetheless. One of General Klestreus' intelligencers has just reported that the entire Army of Hos-Bletha had to retire from the Grand Host because of a revolt in Bletha Town."

"Skranga's work, Dralm be praised!" Kalvan shouted. "I told you that old horse-thief knew what he was doing, Rylla."

She rolled her eyes. They'd had their first argument since the Phaxos incident when Kalvan had let Skranga and several hundred valuable troopers leave on his crazy mission. She had thought then, and still did, that it had been hatched more to save Skranga's bacon than cause any inconvenience to the Styphoni. That it had worked probably had surprised Skranga as much as herself.

"You were right, dear. I'm still amazed that Skranga didn't run off to the nearest tavern and spend every gold piece you gave him on drink and worse."

"Skranga may be as crooked as the Nyklos Trail, but he does have loyalty and keeps his word. If he keeps this up, I'll make him Prince of Arklos after I hang King Lysandros from the battlements of Tarr-Harphax."

"If his work in Hos-Bletha makes that day one hour closer, I myself will weave the gown for Skranga's coronation!"

Kalvan laughed. "Atta girl. Now, Aspasthar, go get Captain-General Hestophes, Prince Phrames, General Alkides, and the rest of the general staff."

"Yes, Your Majesty."

"Before you leave, any word on General Verkan and the Mounted Rifles?"

"Not yet. At last report, the Mounted Rifles were holding off a large body of Harphaxi cavalry waiting for reinforcements. Enemy casualties were heavy."

"That sounds like one of Verkan's dispatches. I'm sure there was a lot of blood spilled. Have any of the other units reported in?"

Aspasthar looked crestfallen. "Not yet, Your Majesty. The courier who brought this had to fight his way to our lines. I'll be back as soon as there's any news. These dispatches are over a day old."

Kalvan shook his head and gave a guarded look to Rylla.

"Thanks, Aspasthar. How is your father?"

He brightened up. "I just received a letter this morning from his scribe. He's feeling much better and wishes he were back in the saddle."

Rylla noticed her husband kept his thoughts about Harmakros' health to himself, since there was no sense in worrying his son anymore than he already was. She doubted that Harmakros would sit in a saddle this season, or next. The infection that had set in after the amputation had been bad—serious enough it would have killed a lesser man. His stump was still as sensitive as a baby's rump. Harmakros was one of Hostigos' best generals and Kalvan needed his expertise and command skills now. They missed him a lot.

"Now get my generals," Kalvan ordered.

"Yes, Your Majesty!"

After his young page scampered off, Kalvan filled his pipe with fresh tobacco and turned to Rylla. "I'm worried about Verkan. I don't like that his dispatcher had to fight his way out of Styphoni lines to reach our forces."

"I agree. I will say a prayer to Allfather Dralm for his success."

Kalvan nodded. She knew he only gave "lip service," as he called it, to the True Gods, but in all other ways he was a good husband. Until he found his faith she would continue to pray to Dralm, Galzar and Yirtta for the both of them.

"Before they get here, let me run over my plans with my favorite general."

"Flattery will get you everything."

"I know, my love. My plan is to command the center, with half the Royal Army and the Princely Army of Sashta—where I can keep an eye on it."

Rylla nodded. "I don't trust Balthames' nephew anymore than I trust my cousin Sthentros."

"Have you located him or his daughter?" Kalvan asked.

Rylla shook her head in the negative. "I had his friend Baron Euklestes questioned; he knew nothing except that Sthentros and Lavena disappeared almost a moon ago."

Kalvan gave her one of those questioning looks she so hated. At times, it was almost as if he were a stranger, judging her. "No, I didn't torture him—well, not very much."

He cleared his throat. "I'm sure Euklestes knew nothing of importance, or you would have wrung it out of him."

She shrugged her shoulders. "The Baron still has his life." *More than the dog deserved,* she thought. Euklestes had to have known his old friend was up to something untoward, but kept his worries to himself. This made him a traitor, too—in her eyes. He should have known something was up when Sthentros went off on his own without his usual boasting and attention seeking."

In General Klestreus' dispatch, their head of intelligence informed them that the Baron had infiltrated the Tyros semaphore station with his own men and, once they were familiar with its operation, permanently silenced the regular crew.

"We should have kept better track of the traitorous dog," Kalvan said. "It was not like Sthentros to disappear without a word to anyone."

"You don't think he's with the Styphoni?" she asked.

"Of course, where else would he get his reward for suborning the semaphore station? I should never have put so many locals into the stations."

"You were trying to keep the veterans close to their families, my husband. Most of our Hostigi soldiers would die for the throne. How could you have known that Sthentros had his own traitor's nest in Tyros? For a moon-half all we got were false messages from the Beshtan border."

"If I ever see that traitor," Kalvan said, "I'll geld him first, then I'll—"

"How do you think I feel? I've known Cousin Sthentros all my life! I never liked him, but he shares my Mother's blood…."

"I know. Don't take it too hard. I'll have to tell you about the Borgias sometime—maybe not."

"It doesn't help that your best spy master is off fighting in Hos-Bletha, either."

Kalvan nodded. "I never thought I'd say it, but I miss that old turkey-thief Skranga."

"Still," added Rylla through clenched teeth, "Dralm help Sthentros, if I ever get my hands on that spineless pigeon-brained cousin of mine…."

Kalvan cleared his throat. "Anyway, as I was saying. I'm going to keep Duke Euriptos and the Army of Sashta right under my nose; that way, if he tries to bug out I can turn my Tymannian Guard on him."

Rylla laughed. "He turned beet red when you told him that! I've heard ducks that gabbled less than Euriptos. After what happened to his Uncle Balthames, he's frightened to death by the tame Sastragathi of yours, Vanar Halgoth!"

"Which only goes to show Euriptos has more brains than either of his uncles! But getting back to business, I'm also going to add the Army of Nyklos, the Army of Ulthor, and all twelve thousand mercenary horse and foot to the center where I can keep an eye on them."

"Is it best to put all our softest eggs in one basket, my husband?"

"Yes, if you've got half the Royal Army to prop them up with. I don't want anyone else to have to wonder if Duke Euriptos will change sides and join the enemy at the last minute like his Uncle Balthar did at the Battle of Tenabra, or loot our baggage. With some thirty-five thousand troops, the center will be the anvil for Hestophes and Phrames to hammer the Grand Host."

"What about me?"

"I haven't forgotten you, kitten. You'll be in command of the rearguard. I want you where you can do the most good."

Yes, and you'd whisk me right off the battlefield, my dear husband, if you thought you could get away with it! It was hard not to love a man who had your best interest at heart, even if his opinion of that *best interest* disagreed dramatically from your own. This time, however, she was going to bite her tongue and let Kalvan have his way without a quarrel. From the looks of things, he was going to need every bit of strength he had for the upcoming fight with Styphon's Grand Host.

"If that is where you want me, that's where I'll be."

Kalvan looked so flustered at her acquiescence she went over and nuzzled his beard. *How sickening,* she thought to herself. *I wasn't like this before the baby was born.*

"I'll give you all five thousand men of the Mobile Force and the Hostigos cavalry."

She was sure he added the last to show her how pleased he was. The Princely Army of Hostigos had taken a bad beating during the past few years and it was nice to see that Kalvan recognized their sacrifice. "What about the Mounted Rifles and the Hostigi Carbineers?"

Kalvan said, "I'm going to use the Mounted Rifles to stiffen the center. That'll leave you with the Carbineers."

Rylla nodded. That was fair.

"Prince Phrames will command the left wing. I'm going to give him the remaining six regiments of Royal Foot, including the Hostigos Rifles. Plus four regiments of Royal Horse, his own Army of Beshta, the Ulthori infantry, and three thousand heavy horse. That will give Phrames almost twenty thousand men, two-thirds of them good infantry, except for the Ulthori foot who are fighting mostly with crossbows and spears."

Kalvan paused to eat some more of his breakfast, giving Rylla a chance to comment.

"What about the Hostigi foot? Phrames could use them to stiffen his Ulthori levy."

"Good thinking. Done. That will leave four regiments of Royal Horse for Hestophes on the rightward. I'll also give him the Princely armies of Nostor, Kyblos and Sask. Sarrask's Army of Sask is now the largest and best trained army we have, other than the Royal Army itself."

"I agree. But do you think we should use Sarrask as a sub-commander under Hestophes."

"You're right, it might ruffle his feathers. Sarrask works so well with you, I'll let him and his army join you in the rearguard and post Phrames with his Beshtans and the Army of Nyklos."

Rylla made a face. "Sarrask is going to be 'ticked off,' as you put it once he finds out he's in the rearguard! He wasn't very happy when you left him to go fight Soton in the Trygath."

"Actually, as hard as this is to say, Sarrask's the only Prince other than Phrames or your father whom I'd trust at my back."

"Then you tell him that. The only thing Sarrask likes better than fighting is flattery, especially when it's true and it comes from you."

"Good idea, I will. Besides, everyone will get their fill of fighting in this battle, I promise."

"What about the Ulthori cavalry?"

"I'll give those iron-hats to Hestophes. Maybe he can come up with something to keep them busy. They're not as elegant as the old Harphaxi Royal Lancers, but they'll fight until they drop or die. I have a feeling that is the way this battle is going to go."

"That will make Sarrask a happy man!"

"What will make me happy?" Sarrask asked, as he barged into the room. He looked hungrily at Kalvan's half-finished plate of eggs and cornbread.

Rylla went over to the hearth and built a plate for Sarrask.

His eyes lit up when she handed him his plate, along with one of the *forks* her husband had introduced. It was hard to believe now, but a few years ago that *fork*, along with any other weapons she could lay her hands on, would have been sticking out of Sarrask's throat had they met like this.

"Thank you, Rylla!"

"Kalvan was just saying there would be lots of fighting in the battle and certainly enough to make you happy."

Sarrask nodded his head in between bites; he was eating noisily, with both hands, the fork fallen forgotten to the baked tile floor. "Swearing fealty to Kalvan was the smartest decision I ever made. There hasn't been a year since I swore my oath without one, two or three great battles!"

There was shouting outside the farmhouse. Plates dropped from both Kalvan and Sarrask's laps and in their places were pistols. Rylla was holding the frying pan with one hand like a shield and a knife in the other.

Moments later Aspasthar came running into the farmhouse, followed by General Hestophes and Chancellor Chartiphon, who looked stricken.

"What is it?" Rylla demanded.

Chartiphon moved the boy aside and began to speak. "Curse and blast them! The Styphoni out-maneuvered us."

"What do you mean? Are they here now?" Kalvan demanded.

"Not that bad," put in Hestophes. "They must have expected a flank attack and laid a trap for us. The Mounted Rifles are no more!"

Kalvan growled out loud.

Rylla cried out, "Oh no! General Verkan—is he all right?" *How could she ever face Dalla again if anything happened to Verkan?*

Chartiphon came over and took her into his arms. She tried to push away, but they encircled here like two steel bars. "Quiet, little one. We don't know what happened to General Verkan. Only a few stragglers have returned to camp." He paused to wipe off her tears with a cloth from his jerkin.

Hestophes continued, "According to Sergeant Ryff, Verkan made a valiant last stand against an army ten times the size of his detachment. The last he saw of Verkan was when a Harphaxi trooper shot him in the chest. The Styphoni overran his position and he never saw the General again. Ryff himself is badly injured; he took a bullet in the thigh and a sword took off one hand."

"How many Riflemen returned?"

"Less than fifty and maybe twice that number of dragoons. They say the rest of the survivors, many of them wounded, will return to camp before nightfall."

"Send outriders to help the wounded and those without mounts."

"What about the rifles?"

At first she thought Kalvan might berate her, but he looked as interested in the answer as she felt.

Hestophes hung his head, shaking it from side to side. "Half the riflemen who returned came back with rifles with fouled locks or bent barrels. They say many of them surrendered; those who didn't were slaughtered—the Styphoni rode them into the ground. Even worse, Ryff reports there was a troop of Royal Harphaxi troopers who had their own rifles!"

Kalvan shook his head like a dog throwing off water from its fur. "What's done is done. I'm surprised we haven't had to face rifles before now. Chartiphon, and you too Hestophes, gather the other generals. We need to meet for a Council of War!"

They couldn't get out of the room fast enough. Sarrask walked over to Kalvan and threw his arm over his shoulders. "Verkan was a good friend, Your

Majesty. I've always been jealous of your friendship. But I liked him—even admired him. I know that a warrior with his prowess dispatched many Styphoni to Regwarn—which is as it should be. He died as a great captain. Now, let us make a mountain of Harphaxi corpses to do his bidding in Galzar's Great Hall!"

Rylla smiled at Sarrask, thanking him with her eyes. "Yes, my husband, let us kill many Styphoni and dedicate their funeral pyre to Verkan and all the other Hostigi dead!" *And to my friend, Dalla, who will mourn her man as I would.*

THIRTY-ONE

I

Phidestros peered across the low-lying valley to study the Hostigi troop disposition upon the opposite hillside. There was some low-lying morning fog, but not enough to obscure the landscape. It was mostly farmland, but most of the rye and corn had been trampled into the ground. The weather had held for the past several days and the mud had mostly dried up so it wouldn't prove to be a hazard.

He was using a captured Hostigi 'farseer' as one of the prisoners had called it. This magnifying tube had been discovered by one of his soldiers and brought to him by Geblon, who had been forced to finish a bloody engagement on the northern flank started by an impetuous Prince who had never fought in a Kalvan-style battle. The Hostigi position had been overrun and the enemy routed, but at a horrendous cost. Too many more such victories would cost them the war.

It was obvious that Great King Kalvan had selected his ground with care. He'd picked a position on a long hillside with gentle slopes, facing a similar but lower ridge. His center battle sat higher than his left wing, while the right flank was forward.

Kalvan's army was divided into three divisions, with the Great King's maroon standard at the center. There was a small reserve behind the center. A fortified manor house and outbuilding rested in front of Kalvan's center battle and Phidestros could see emplaced guns at the front and on both sides of the manor. It was a position that slightly favored the Hostigi, since Kalvan had a fortified defense, but not enough that it would abort an attack by the Grand Host.

The Grand Host had chased Kalvan for a moon-quarter and now were only a day's march outside the Princedom of Hostigos. Phidestros wondered if it were wise to follow in Kalvan's footsteps. True, the Grand Host had the superior force in terms of manpower, but Kalvan wouldn't have picked this valley to make a stand unless he perceived some strategic advantage.

However, to take the war into Hostigos, rather than fighting the battle here, would give Kalvan the advantage because his soldiers would know there could be no retreat or escape from Hostigos—not with the Investigation in full rampage. On his part, Phidestros had too many squabbling princes and captain-generals who debated his every move. It was becoming more and more difficult to hold the 'Unwieldy' Host, especially the Investigator, Archpriest Roxthar, to one purpose. Once they reached Hostigos proper, Roxthar would want to 'borrow' entire companies to pursue fleeing Hostigi.

If they didn't strike soon, the Grand Host would begin to split apart. Already desertions were becoming a problem; enough that he'd been forced to place two Temple Bands of Styphon's Own guard behind the rearguard.

No, the coin was tossed for better or for worse. Besides, he might never be able to position the Blethan irregulars so advantageously again for their surprise attack on the Hostigi baggage train. To say nothing about their desertion problem, which had grown worse daily, ever since their comrades had left to return to Hos-Bletha. As light cavalry, the Blethan irregulars didn't have much of a problem evading Styphon's Own Guard.

Over the winter, Phidestros had heard stories of the Investigation and put them down as child's tales, told to scare youngsters into behaving. Then the Grand Master had acquainted him with tales of the Investigation's excesses in Balph. So far he'd manage to keep the Investigators on short reins until they'd left Tarr-Veblos and crossed into Hos-Hostigos territory. Then Roxthar's Investigators had begun their 'work' on the enemy prisoners and peasants.

Phidestros had tried to ignore the Investigation; the war against Kalvan was enough to occupy any general's mind. But this morning a Beshtan trooper from the Green Hawks, a mercenary company that had changed sides at the Battle of Tenabra, had brought a young boy whom he'd saved from one of the Investigators to tell his tale. The story he told was a perversion of the Code of Galzar, and not the first such story he had heard. Killing innocent civilians, especially women and children, was against all of Galzar's teachings.

As soon as the Wargod's highpriests in Agrys City learned about the Investigation's civilian atrocities in Hos-Hostigos, the Grand Host would be put under the Ban of Galzar. Maybe he'd get lucky and Roxthar would catch one of Kalvan's *rifle* bullets.

But the mercenary had also presented him with a new worry: the possibility that his own soldiers might mutiny against the civilian depredations of the Investigation and rise up and kill the Investigators. This might leave his army fighting both the Hostigi and Styphon's House! With Great King Lysandros still anchored in Hos-Harphax, lest one of his princes revolt while the Royal Army was fighting in Hos-Hostigos, Phidestros would have to find a way to rein in the Investigator—or failing that, find a way to silence him for good.

There was a loud boom as one of Kalvan's big guns fired a ranging shot from the opposing hill. The shot went wide and to the right of the packed Ros-Zarthani wing. There was some movement among the front line of Ros-Zarthani archers as they broke ranks and reformed. Phidestros prayed to Galzar that Arch-Stratego Zarphu had more control over his soldiers when the battle was actually joined.

Grand Master Soton, accompanied by Marshal General Albides of Styphon's Own Guard and Knight Commander Orocles, rode up alongside Phidestros. "Phidestros, when do we start this bloodbath?"

Phidestros grimaced. "General Kyblannos said he would have his mobile guns in position in another candle."

"Good. The sooner we come to the clash of arms the better. We do not want to give Kalvan's big guns a chance to disorder our ranks before we've joined in battle. By Galzar's Mace, I just hope those western barbarians fight as well as they brag."

Phidestros nodded. Soton was in command of the right wing, to the rear of the Ros-Zarthani. He had a Wedge of Knights and 2,000 light cavalry to ride over the Ros-Zarthani if they showed signs of faltering before Kalvan's veterans. Phidestros himself was in charge of the Center, although it was really Geblon his subordinate who was in command since Phidestros was charged with directing the battle from the hilltop.

Phidestros had always been a front line commander and did not take to the idea of being out of the thick of things. But, as Soton had pointed out, in a battle where the wings were larger than the armies at Chothros Heights and Phyrax, *someone* had to direct the Grand Host. Soton had gone so far as to extract an oath out of him—never again!—not to join in the fray unless there was no other recourse.

So here he was to sit out the battle with the reserve, his own bodyguard the Iron Band, the Royal Dragoons and the Harphaxi Royal Lancers. The Lancers, if possible, were even more disconcerted about being out of the battle than he was. But he had wanted the Lancers where he could keep an eye on those iron-headed blockheads.

If this battle was to be lost, it would be through his stupidity—not theirs.

"Remember your promise," Soton said echoing his thoughts.

"Dralm blast it! I made a promise and by Galzar's Mace I'll keep it!"

"See you do! If I'd stayed out of the front lines so that I could see what Kalvan was doing at the Battle of Phyrax, we wouldn't be fighting here today."

Soton's words served to remind Phidestros that despite his title of Grand Captain-General he wasn't completely in charge of the Grand Host. Regardless of what King Lysandros desired, this was Styphon's army paid by Styphon's gold and run by Styphon's generals. Of course, he'd rather be upbraided by Soton, a military commander he admired, than Great King Lysandros who believed himself to be the greatest commander in the Five Kingdoms. May Galzar bless the Hos-Agrysi inspired unrest in Argros that had kept Lysandros penned Harphax City with the city bands.

"I will stay here. I'm just worried about Marshal Zythannes."

"Zythannes is a good commander and he has some of the best soldiers in the Five Kingdoms under his command with the Holy Squares. All he has to do is keep the Hostigi right from outflanking our center. Great King Cleitharses would have taken it as a deadly insult if we had not put him in command of one of the wings."

Phidestros had to choke back an insult to Zythannes, whose idea of military tactics was forming his men into giant squares, or tercios, which might have been good tactics before Kalvan, but now it bordered on suicide.

It appeared that ten thousand reinforcements had bought Zythannes more say in the Grand Host than Phidestros owned. Yet there was no denying that the arrival of the Holy Squares, delayed by a peasant revolt in Hos-Ktemnos, had raised the Grand Host's morale as well as Zythannes' stature.

"Let us hope Zythannes' deeds match the ferocity of his words."

"Nobody's that good!"

They both sniggered.

"On the other hand," Soton added, "if they don't, well, accidents have been known to happen in the midst of battle."

They both grinned at each other.

"I'm off, Captain-General Phidestros. May Styphon's Will be done."

"So be it, Grand Master. Kill some Hostigi for me!"

Captain-General Albides pulled up beside him as Soton wheeled and rode down hill. Styphon's House had been generous, not only with food and gold but with Styphon's Own Guard as well. Almost half of all the Temple Bands, about nine thousand men in all, were under Albides' command. Another eight bands accompanied Roxthar's Investigators, which were now acting as a rear-guard. If the Grand Host lost here, there wouldn't be enough military might left to stop Kalvan from marching straight to Balph.

Phidestros grinned, since he liked playing for big stakes.

"Not that I would question the wisdom of your orders, Grand Captain-General, but is it wise to place my entire command at the center behind the Sacred Squares? Might they not be better employed supporting the Grand Master or as an anchor for Marshal Zythannes' wing should his resolve melt in the heat of battle?"

Phidestros carefully studied Albides' face for duplicity. Unlike Grand Commander Xenophes, he had served in the ranks as a mercenary for twelve winters and risen as high as Captain-General on his own merit before committing to the Temple Guard. However, like Xenophes, he was known to have Roxthar's ear and should this battle be lost his support might be all that would save him from the Investigation. Phidestros judged him sincere.

"I have complete confidence the Sacred Squares will hold the center. On the other hand, I am concerned about the steadfastness of these Ros-Zarthani, who have little experience facing cannon and salvo fire. I would like Styphon's Own Guard to be near at hand should their courage leave them in the heat of battle."

Albides answered him with a toothy smile. There was little love shared between the Temple Guardsmen and the Holy Order of the Zarthani Knights, since both bodies viewed themselves as the martial arm of Styphon's House on Earth. Albides would pray on his knees all day for a chance to save Soton's bacon from Kalvan's troopers.

"You may well prove to be the right foil for the Daemon's witchcraft."

Phidestros took that as a high compliment, coming from the commander of the Red Hand. He pointed down at the forlorn hope, the forward arquebusiers and skirmishers, who were already within range of Kalvan's army. "As long as they are properly used, it is the common soldiers who will win this war for us."

THIRTY-TWO

I

General Hestophes bit down on the end of his pipe as he watched the three Hostigi batteries tear gaping holes in the advancing Styphoni horse. For a moment his view was obscured as the wind changed and a cloud of gray smoke drifted between him and the front lines. Then just as quickly it was tossed aside by the wind and he could see a banner-bearer, with the Princely flag of Arklos, blown off his horse.

One of the commanders, smarter than the others, had sent mounted arquebusiers and some of them dismounted and began shooting at the Hostigi gunners. A score of Hostigi riflemen returned fire with a vengeance and within moments most of the Harphaxi dragoons were down. One forward surge of mercenary cavalry swarmed over a four-pounder and its crew, then everyone disappeared in a great cloud of smoke as someone blew up the gun.

"By Styphon's Beard, there's a gunner who should have been a cavalryman!" Captain-General Pylonnos shouted. Pylonnos was commander of the Kyblosi Army since Prince Tythanes had never fully recovered from the gut wound he suffered at the Battle of Chothros Heights.

Quickly, he said a prayer to Galzar, asking that the valiant Hostigi gunners, who had blown up their own gun to keep it from being captured, be given a place of honor in Galzar's Great Hall.

"When do we sound the retreat, General?" asked the head musician.

The Royal Batteries were firing irregularly now, but they still tore ragged gaps in the swirling Styphoni cavalry.

"Not yet, but soon." Hestophes turned to one of his aides. "Colonel Sythros, fire the *rocket.* It's time for our surprise!"

"Yes, sir!"

The rocket banged and sputtered upward in a zigzag.

"Now!" he cried, and his trumpeters sounded retreat.

The Hostigi infantry and cavalry of the right wing beat a hasty retreat. Only the officers knew about the 'surprise,' but Hestophes suspected, by the way the troopers wheeled their horses, that most had learned of the plan. He didn't really care, since it was obvious by the way the Styphoni were beginning to boil after the retreating Hostigi that they didn't have a clue as to what was coming.

The big guns were quiet. The artillerymen had been given orders to halt firing and run for cover upon hearing the trumpets call. For the first time in a candle, the swirling white and black smoke began to clear.

Suddenly there was a great boom, as if someone had smashed a war hammer into his helmet. The earth shook! Water and earth exploded over the top of the hill.

Hestophes had to grip his reins with all his might to keep his horse from bolting. Others weren't so lucky and found themselves heading directly toward the descending wall of mud, rolling trees and raging water. He said a quick prayer to Galzar when he saw the muddy wave slam into the Styphoni line, throwing horses and men aside like tiny dolls. Many of the men went down to stay, weighted by heavy armor or pinned beneath their horses. Others climbed trees or drug themselves up out of the muck that was left behind by the quickly receding wave of muddy water.

Almost as fast as it had begun the flood passed, leaving the ground a sodden mess of dead, wounded and dazed troopers. The waters lost most of their force by the time they reached the Holy Squares, sowing more disorder and confusion than death. However, at least a third or more of the entire Styphoni wing was either dead or down.

Hestophes dropped his arm. Trumpets shrilled and the ground trembled to the drumbeat of thousands of galloping horse hooves. The iron men of Ulthor and Old Hostigos on their beer-wagon destriers were in the front rank and they smashed into the churning mass of panic stricken Styphoni horse. Men cried, horses shrieked, pistols banged.

The Ulthori heavy cavalry, followed closely by the King's Heavy Horse, the Royal Lancers and the Nostori Princely Bodyguard, smashed like a hammer into the fleeing Styphoni light cavalry. The Styphoni horse tried to turn and retreat only to find themselves forced into the muddy ground, riding over their own wounded and dead, or pinned by the front ranks of their own infantry battle-line, the Holy Squares.

The only way out for the cavalry was to the left, skirting the edge of the Styphoni flank. Those soldiers who were at the flanks tried to move aside. Most of the infantry, however, were trapped between the retiring horse and their own advancing ranks: a vice grip pressed tight by the slowly advancing juggernaut of Hostigi men-at-arms.

In the ongoing melee the Styphoni horse, most armed with empty pistols and swords, were severely out-weaponed and out-armored by the Hostigi, who had lances, big sabers, maces, hammers and full or three-quarter armor. This was the kind of fighting these armored lobsters were designed for and the Styphoni retreat quickly turned into a full rout. Hundreds of Styphoni troopers were spitted or thrown from their saddles as they turned and tried to follow their fellows in escape.

Soon there was a steady stream of riders moving to the left flank and escaping. Hestophes was appalled when the Ulthori iron hats followed in pursuit. Hestophes signaled the trumpeters to call a halt.

The Ulthori heavy cavalry acted as if they were deaf and continued their pursuit. The Royal Heavy Horse appeared to halt momentarily, but were spurred on by the charging Ulthori Bodyguard, resplendent in their silvered armor and green plumes.

"Pylonnos, stop those iron heads! Bring them back here where they can do some good."

Captain-General Pylonnos smiled, as if he wished he were at the head of his charging Lifeguard, running down the routing Harphaxi horse. "I will try and regroup them. Then, by Galzar, we'll hit the Styphoni curs on the flank!"

"Not unless you catch those fatherless sons of a Beshtan harlot! I fear the Styphon's Own Lot of them will be in Hostigos before nightfall." This was exactly the kind of disaster that Kalvan was always warning about. Now it had happened to him, and despite the destruction of the Styphoni left wing, he knew he'd hear about it for years to come. The only good news was that almost all the cavalry of the Styphoni left wing were either dead or in an uncontrolled rout.

At least Hestophes still had one Royal regiment, the First Royal Carabineers, and three thousand Nostori and Saski cavalry in reserve; more than enough cavalry to hold off the Styphoni reserve and to keep the remaining Harphaxi horse from out-flanking his infantry.

The Ulthori skirmishers were already busy cutting the throats of fallen Styphoni and stripping the bodies for loot. The foot of the Holy Squares were milling in confusion as their petty-captains tried to reform ranks, which had been disordered by the flood, wounded horses or panic stricken troopers who had preferred riding down their own men to facing the Hostigi devils.

One Ktemnoi band, flying red and black colors, reformed and fired a half-hearted salvo at the Hostigi looters. Hestophes gave the trumpeter the signal to recall the skirmishers to their ranks. After an eighth of a candle, the call for General Advance was given.

Most of the arquebusiers had returned to their ranks, but some were too blood-crazed or greedy and were churned into the ground by thousands of their own charging pikemen.

It was a tactic Hestophes wouldn't have even considered with Kalvan's Royal Musketeers, with their puny bayonets. The push of pike was a tried-and-true tactic Hestophes knew and trusted. Let the others try their luck with dagger-pointed muskets. It wasn't for him and he was glad that Great King Kalvan had put the Royal regiments of foot at the center and left wing.

If Hestophes had been the Styphoni commander, now would have been the time to commit his reserve; instead, the Ktemnoi commander turned with his bodyguard, joining the retreating cavalry and jamming his own lines!

Hestophes punched the air with his fist. The Ktemnoi Captain-General either distrusted his own reserve, or was reacting in blind, cowardly panic. The Ktemnoi, before Kalvan's arrival, were considered the best soldiers—man for man—in the Five Kingdoms; it appeared their commanders were only good when winning. Losing was a new lesson they were learning the under the tutelage of the Hostigi hammer.

The Ktemnoi Holy Squares, unaware that behind them their own commander was fleeing from the battle, fired a few very ragged salvos at the charging Hostigi and then attempted an undisciplined countercharge with their own bills. The two lines met with a shock of impact that jarred the very ground. But, when push came to shove, pikes had the advantage over bills as long as they kept advancing. If the two lines came to a halt, the billmen had the advantage since they could run down the files and attack the front lines of pikemen with their billhooks. Here at Ardros Field the disordered Ktemnoi were unable to halt the Hostigi pikes and were ground into hamburger by a forest of unstoppable pike heads.

As the center of the charging Hostigi pikemen began to push into the Ktemnoi center, Captain-General Hestophes ordered his remaining cavalry to swing around the Styphoni left wing, to encircle the center and force the enemy right to flee. With Hestophes and his bodyguard at the fore, the Hostigi horse thundered down the hill running down fleeing enemy foot soldiers, suddenly catching up with the retreating Hos-Ktemnoi commander as he tried to escape. Hestophes and his bodyguard were the first to reach the enemy commander; they pulled out their horsepistols and sabers and charged into the retreating enemy leader's party. He had the joy of shooting the Ktemnoi popinjay in the back of his silvered and brocaded armor, knocking him off his mount. *If Kalvan can hold the center,* Hestophes thought, *this battle is as good as won!*

II

Phidestros watched with shock as the hillside exploded and a huge brown wave of mud and death washed over his left wing. Entire regiments disappeared beneath the boiling wave never to appear again. Some survivors clung to trees or tried to bull their way out of the mud. Three or four thousand men and twice that number of horses, dead—in the blink of an eye! The entire battle could be lost if the Hostigi could fully exploit the collapse of the left wing's forward elements.

With mounting frustration he watched as the Hostigi heavy horse followed the mudslide with a charge into the chaotic melee, destroying the surviving regiments in detail as they tried to flee from the field of battle. Kalvan's flood had broken their morale and it would take a miracle to save the left wing from a complete rout.

His first thought was to commit his own cavalry reserve. Then his better judgment prevailed. The most his reserve would accomplish would be to pad the butcher's bill.

The Royal Lancers demonstrated no judgment at all when they saw their fellows being ridden down by the Hostigi cavalry. Only Phidestros' threat to have Albides' Temple Guardsmen shoot them out of their saddles had kept them from rushing pell-mell down the hillside to a vainglorious death. Being shot by mere *infantry* qualified neither as glorious nor a grand gesture. So the Lancers had stayed put under loud and strenuous objection. After the twentieth complaint by some minor Harphaxi noble, Phidestros almost wished they had forced his hand.

While the Grand Host's left battle was in serious trouble, the same could not be said about the center or right wing. At the center the Sacred Squares of Hos-Ktemnos held Kalvan's musketeers at bay despite grievous wounds made by continuing Hostigi artillery fire. Phidestros' own two batteries were still returning fire at twice the rate of the Hostigi, but they were outnumbered by the Hostigi guns at better than three to one.

Phidestros had been forewarned that Kalvan had eliminated most of the pikes in the Royal Army. He had tried to take advantage of that by having the

Ktemnoi and mercenary horse charge the Hostigi center. Kalvan's artillery had performed as a meat grinder on the charging cavalry and Phidestros had been forced to recall the charge before more than a handful had reached the enemy musketeers. Still, he had a hunch that Kalvan's over-reliance on his musketeers was a vulnerability he could exploit. First, he had to somehow neutralize Kalvan's big guns. To do that, Phidestros was using the best infantry he had, man for man, as cannon fodder. The ground gained by the Sacred Squares was costing hundreds of lives, but if he could force Kalvan to withdraw his mobile batteries, or even better let the Sacred Squares overrun them and then turn them on the Hostigi—this battle could be won.

On the right wing the Ros-Zarthani had been slow to start, but now it appeared their cavalry was making real progress. Their mounted archers had already neutralized about ten of Kalvan's guns. The foot, behind two-man shields, were moving slowly and inexorably, despite horrible losses from cannon fire, toward Kalvan's forward mobile guns.

Phidestros watched through the *farseer* in amazement as one troop of silver-scaled cavalry advanced obliquely on one of Kalvan's mobile field pieces. Ignoring heavy musket fire, the *Kataphracti* (as Zarphu called them) threw javelins at the gunners who were trying desperately to slew the gun around. The *Kataphracti* were the Ros-Zarthani light cavalry and each one carried a sword and four javelins. He watched as the forward regiment threw flight after flight of javelins at the Hostigi gunners, finally killing most of them and forcing the rest to retreat under a hail of spears. Moments later the *Kataphracti* dismounted and, despite heavy musket fire, destroyed the wheels of the artillery carriages with sledgehammers and set the carriages on fire with turpentine.

Phidestros hooted with amazement as he watched Kalvan's gunners turn tail and run!

A guard unit of halberdiers countercharged the Kataphracti and were sent scattering by a squadron of the Ros-Zarthani heavy cavalry, the *Klibanophoru.* The *Klibanophoru* wore scaled armor, as did their horses, and fought with bows as well as lances. A nearby gun took out half a dozen *Klibanophoru,* but they quickly regrouped and charged the firing gun. This artillery piece was much closer to the Hostigi forward line and the charging Ros-Zarthani disappeared into a churning sea of muskets and halberds never to reappear.

By Styphon's Beard, maybe we can win this battle!

"How fares Styphon's Battle, Captain-General?" asked a familiar rasping voice.

He turned to face Archpriest Roxthar with three of his white-robed Investigators and a score of red-caped Temple Guardsmen.

"Grand Master Soton told me you would not be interfering in this battle, Your Holiness."

Phidestros could hear the sound of Roxthar's grinding teeth over the battle clamor.

"I am not here in an advisory position, Captain-General, but only to witness Styphon's great triumph." His eyes told a different story.

Keeping his temper under tight rein—after all, it did not pay to antagonize the most powerful priest in Styphon's House—Phidestros bit his tongue. "As Styphon Wills. We are all his tools against the Usurper Kalvan and his minions." *Tools* he thought to himself, *who will fight much better and more effectively if they don't have to deal with fools in white bedsheets.*

The Investigator gave him a look as though he could see behind Phidestros' eyes and read his thoughts. "Captain-General we will stay here to watch the battle's progress while you deal with the unbelievers. We wish you great success in Our endeavor."

Phidestros nodded.

"What is happening to the Holy Squares?"

Phidestros saw the Holy Squares, the Royal troops of Great King Cleitharses, of the left wing begin to buckle as a mass of Hostigi pikemen pushed them aside. *Where did these pikemen come from? Didn't Kalvan disband his pike units for musketeers? That's what Baron Sthentros and Lysandros' intelligencers claimed.*

Then he caught sight of the infantry flags; these were Kalvan's princely levy, not his Royal regiments. The cavalry who were supposed to support the flanks of the Holy Squares were being chased from the battlefield by Kalvan's heavy horse, leaving behind the unprotected infantry. He would have Marshal Zythannes head on a pike before this day was over!

"You must do something!"

"This is High Marshal Zythannes doing. See his flag there. He's turned his tail to the Hostigi!"

Roxthar let forth with a string of curses that would have been the glory of any veteran petty-captain. "Are you going to let this coward give Kalvan the field of battle?"

For a moment Phidestros toyed with the idea of ordering Royal Lancers to charge over this mass of human excrement but squelched it. "No. Nor am I going to commit my reserve when they may be needed elsewhere. Look over there!"

Phidestros pointed to where three of Kalvan's guns were being overrun by the Ros-Zarthani *Klibanophoru.* A big band of Hostigi cavalry rode up to protest and the two units disappeared in a swirl of smoke and dust.

III

Rylla watched with growing anxiety as the scaled horsemen overran three more field guns. Now their heavy infantry was approaching the Hostigi lines. She was more than tempted to run the reserve down the hill to plug the line, but would Kalvan approve? What was it he had told her this morning:

"If one side or the other doesn't blow it during the first few candles, then whoever can hold their reserve the longest will probably take the field."

"Look at that!" Sarrask of Sask cried out.

Rylla looked down to see that Phrames—at long last!—had sent the Royal horse out front to deal with the heavy barbarian cavalry. She watched as the Third Regiment of Horse smashed into several squadrons of very heavy Ros-Zarthani cavalry. At close range the Hostigi horsepistols decimated the barbarian heavy cavalry. For a while it looked as if the Ros-Zarthani cavalry were about to break, then the Hostigi troopers expended their guns.

On foot the long horsepistols could be primed and loaded in a fortieth of a candle. But in the midst of a melee on horseback that time could be multiplied by ten or twenty, which was why most troopers carried all the pistols they could beg, buy, or steal and stuck them into saddle holsters, sashes, and boots. In the rear ranks some would have time to re-load and shoot again, but in the front ranks, pressed horse-to-horse with friend and foe, a saber or pistol butt were the only weapons they could use.

With the ranks closed, the barbarian heavy armor became an important factor, where a man sometimes couldn't find room to lift his sword arm. Suddenly it was the Hostigi cavalry that appeared to be giving way.

Rylla was about to send down a regiment of dragoons to reinforce them when she heard the sound of gunfire from behind Hostigi lines. She turned from her vantage point at the top of the hill to see fighting around the baggage train. Camp followers, men, women and children, were scurrying every which way.

"It's Harmakros' Sastragathi!" Sarrask shouted, pointing at the attacking horsemen. "The Styphon spawned buggers are attacking *our* baggage train!"

"Dralm damn them!" she said, when she saw they were wearing Hostigi colors. Without Duke Harmakros here to lead them, his Sastragathi light cavalry had been restive, some had deserted and more than a few had been hung for horse stealing or disobeying orders. To turn allegiance in the midst of battle was the kind of tactic these barbarians cut their teeth on. She should have anticipated something like this! Kalvan hadn't lived here long enough to really understand barbarian ways.

Rylla soundly cursed herself and Sastragathi nomads in general until she realized she was wasting precious time. *Form ranks?* "Sound the trumpets. Charge!"

Rylla followed the charge from the rear surrounded by her bodyguard as she had promised Kalvan. Prince Sarrask led from the front, with a score of his Princely Bodyguard, followed by the Hostigos Horse. The dragoons were in the rear and dismounted as soon as they reached the baggage train and began to shoot their arquebuses and rifles.

The traitorous Sastragathi scattered like seeds in the wind before the heavier Hostigi cavalry, but those burdened down by food, blankets, and coins were quickly run into the ground and dispatched. The dragoons took a fearful toll of the remaining Sastragathi until the raiders were out of gun range.

Rylla was busy trying to reform the dragoons and to assess the damage to the camp when Prince Sarrask rode up like a madman with his horse blown and all lathered up. "Queen Rylla! It was a ruse! These are not our Sastragathi."

"What do you mean, ruse?"

"Petty-Captain Zarnos, a former Blethan mercenary, was examining some of the Sastragathi prisoners when he heard them talk in the tongue of the Blethan border! He checked their saddlebags and found other items of Blethan origin."

"Blethan? You mean we were tricked!"

"Yes, these Sastragathi are Blethan auxiliaries draped in our colors. By Styphon's Brass Balls, I fell for it too!"

"Don't blame yourself, we all share the guilt. How long will it take you to reform the Hostigi horse?"

"About half of them are well on their way to Hostigos Town, the rest I can call in about a candle. Curse and blast it!"

"Recall everyone you can and meet me on the other side of the hill. I'll take the dragoons and the Queen's Lifeguard. I have to know what's been going on in our absence."

Sarrask ground his teeth, then dismounted, jumped on a fresh horse, and took off with the nearest trumpeter, his Bodyguard galloping behind.

THIRTY-THREE

I

Stratego Donos wheeled up to Arch-Stratego Zarphu and saluted. He paused to remove his silver facemask. "Arch-Stratego, I believe we have now crippled enough firetubes to call for a general advance."

Zarphu turned as a firetube exploded in a burst of light, rocking the front lines. It was useful to know the Hostigi would blow their own tubes if they could take enough enemies with them. Zarphu appreciated such acts of heroic folly. This battle would already be over were the Hostigi as worthless as much of this so-called Grand Host. The insults his soldiers had been subjected to ever since they'd entered this cold land had almost been beyond endurance, even from barbarians. Were it not for duty…

The Hostigi firetubes had inflicted heavy casualties, far more than the firetubes they had encountered at the Iron City. King Kalvan had several times the firetubes of the Grand Host. Truly, Kalvan was a great Stratego—even though he was a barbarian.

The firetubes were deadly, as this army had learned on the Iron Trail. Still his iron-hearted soldiers had proved that the firetubes could be silenced if the men who fed them their fireseed were killed. It was easier to silence the firetubes since Stratego Phidestros had taught his soldiers to destroy their wheels and burn their wooden frames, which kept the enemy from recapturing them and turning them back on his troops.

Less than a dozen of the Hostigi firetubes were still firing upon his men. Even so a direct charge into the Hostigi front would result in thousands of casualties. To wait would also be a disaster. The Hostigi were bringing up more and more of their firesticks to replace the lost firetubes. While the firesticks were not as deadly as the bigger tubes, *en masse* they were as dangerous as arrow flights. The time had come to take the fight to the enemy.

"It is time to move, Donos. Sound the horns!" The great battle horns sounded and the entire army began beating spears and lances against shields and body armor. The noise was deafening to him and even more terrifying to those hearing it for the first time. He would not have been surprised had the entire Hostigi flank collapsed. That it did not showed that his men's steel was being whetted on worthy foes.

II

"Fire!"

Syllon pulled the trigger and felt his musket buck. He didn't hear it fire, not with hundreds of smoothbores firing to either side. All he heard was an ear-pounding roar. Then everything was obscured in a fog of gray-streaked white smoke.

"First rank, fall back! Fourth rank, forward!"

The wind lifted the smoke for a moment as he turned to fall back through the files, and Syllon saw scores of writhing horses and men in iron scales being ridden over by their own men. He shuddered despite the intense heat that left rivers of sweat to run beneath his boiled leather jack.

Syllon was no coward; no man who had survived the Battles of Fyk, Chothros Heights, and Phyrax could be called such. Yet, in those battles he had fought with his pike, a pole of ash, six rods long, topped with a frog's-mouth of sharp steel, not a stubby musket with a knife at the end! *Some pike.*

As he walked back through the ranks, he passed by the Second Royal Regiment's banner: Styphon's head impaled on a red axe head on a blue field. He reached the rear rank and took his position, while his petty-captain began the familiar litany. "Up flint!"

Syllon raised the striker. The rest of the drill was so familiar he did not even have to listen to the commands, just the cadence of his petty-captain's voice. He removed one of the new paper cartridges from his bandolier, tore it open with his teeth, and put a pinch of fireseed in the pan. He then lowered the striker. Next, Syllon set the musket butt on the ground with the gun barrel angled so he could quickly pour the fireseed down the muzzle.

"Pour charges!"

He then poured the remaining fireseed from the paper cartridge down the barrel, followed by the lead ball and the wadded up paper cartridge. He used his ramrod to ram the ball and paper well down into the breech.

"Raise muskets!"

Syllon took a quick look at the battle again; for an instant he saw a moving wall of Ros-Zarthani, then another cloud of gray smoke obscured everything but the rank of soldiers directly in front of him. He watched as they advanced to the front. There was another roar and then he heard the order, "First rank, forward!"

He noticed the files and ranks of the Regiment were growing ragged. Bodies stitched with arrows and javelins littered the ground, making walking difficult. There was a bone-jarring clang as an arrow bounced off his morion helmet; he stopped to shake his head and was almost pushed aside by the man behind him.

"You Dralm-damned fool! Keep moving."

Syllon stumbled forward, somehow keeping his balance. He had a feeling in the pit of his stomach that if he lost his footing and fell he would never get up again. Pushing through the smoke and over fallen bodies, he reached the front. He lifted his musket and pulled down the striker, set the flint down and squeezed the trigger. He was shocked to discover that the Ros-Zarthani had advanced to within fifty paces of the Hostigi line. One of the lancers was coming straight for him so instead of waiting for the command to "fire" he shot the rider's horse in the chest. The horse stumbled, catapulting the lancer out of his saddle. The lancer rolled to the ground and bounced up, to Syllon's great surprise.

A ragged volley followed the command to 'fire,' but it only dropped a few handfuls of the enemy.

Meanwhile, the barbarian lancer had dropped his lance, instead of searching for it, he drew a wicked hand-axe from a loop at this belt and ran straight at Syllon! Syllon dropped his useless smoothbore and from his blue sash pulled the pistol he'd taken from a dead cavalry officer at Phyrax Field and shot the lancer at point-blank range.

The lancer staggered backwards and dropped to the ground. The polished iron scales over his breast were bent and splayed, but not penetrated. Syllon said a short prayer to Galzar as he stuck the unloaded pistol back in his sash and pulled out his sword. He stuck the lancer, who was starting to rise, in the mouth—unleashing a fountain of blood. The lancer fell back to the ground, twitched a few times and lay still.

"To Regwarn with you!" he cried, hoping this time the lancer was truly dead.

A quick look to either side showed that the entire Hostigi line was collapsing, some of the musketeers were dropping their weapons and running. Syllon felt his own heart leap. It took all his willpower to keep himself from turning to join the runners; instead, he remembered Captain-General Harmakros' words, "Most of the dead and dying on any battlefield are shot or stabbed in the back while fleeing." It was as if Harmakros were speaking into his ear and he felt his pulse grow calm. Syllon would not go to Hadron's Realm so easily!

He heard a petty-captain shout. "Mount bayonets."

Syllon would have obeyed, but he'd dropped his musket and was too busy using his sword to fend off a charging lancer to search for it. He managed to knock aside the lance, but when the horse reared he fell under its slashing hooves and the world went black—

Suddenly Syllon was in a white tunnel, seeing friends and family long dead. "Where am I?" he asked. They smiled, patted him on the back, then took him before a huge hearth, made of rich marble with gold veins; it was grander than any hearth had ever seen—even greater than Prince Ptosphes' great hearth at Tarr-Hostigos. A giant with a wolf's head turned away from the fire, haloed by the light, and toasted him with a huge flagon of ale. His eyes burned like embers. Then soldiers came from everywhere, some in armor unlike any he had ever seen, some who had fought at his side. 'So this is Galzar's Great Hall,' he told himself. He took an offered flask and began to drink…

III

Phidestros watched with an exhilaration bordering on glee as the Hostigi left wing began to waver and then fall back. Arch-Strategos Zarphu had used his heavy cavalry to batter and pin the flank of the Hostigi left wing, while his light cavalry and heavy infantry mounted a determined frontal assault. The result was that the *entire* left wing of the Hostigi army was falling back. If Kalvan didn't counterattack immediately, he might find himself out-maneuvered as the Ros-Zarthani swept through the ranks of the Hostigi left flank, wheeled and hit his center from behind! Most of the Hostigi right wing was off the battlefield, chasing the collapsed left wing of the Grand Host. He hoped they stayed in full pursuit.

The Blethan ruse must have worked since he had seen nothing of the Hostigi reserve for over half a candle. He suspected it was now too late for them to make any difference to this battle. As to his own left wing, Phidestros had to assume the worst. After the horse had gone into retreat, the Hostigi foot had pressed his left wing so strongly they had been out of visual sight for over a candle and a half. The last scout report had said that, other than the Harphaxi Royal Foot Guard, the entire left wing was in full rout and Marshal Zythannes, who had reportedly run from the battlefield, was mortally wounded.

Zythannes had better be dead before this battle ends, otherwise he will be the subject of an 'investigation' by his own Grand Captain-General!

Phidestros left four companies of dragoons to protect the baggage train and sent the rest of his reserve downhill to a place where there was a natural ridge that he could use to his advantage should the Hostigi right turn and try to outflank his own center.

Now, if only he could break through the logjam in the center of Kalvan's battle line! Most of Kalvan's guns were still firing and the Sacred Squares were stymied between them and the forward musketeers. It was time to send Alkides and the Red Hand into the gap left by the advancing Ros-Zarthani.

IV

Kalvan watched with growing apprehension as his aide-de-camp beat the rear of his horse with the flat of his saber to get him to the top of the small hillock where Kalvan was perched above his army. What additional bad news did Colonel Kronos bear now? The entire Hostigi left wing was being held together, and kept from out-and-out rout, by Phrames' cavalry, who had just pinned the flanking Ros-Zarthani heavy cavalry so the infantry could retreat in formation. Now the Red Hand was joining the fray against the Royal Batteries at center of his battle line; what else could go wrong?

"King Kalvan! King Kalvan! The mercenaries have learned our baggage train has been attacked. They are threatening to retire *en masse*!"

"Those milk-sucking dogs! To Styphon with them!" Kalvan caught his breath and quickly reviewed his remaining options. Rylla—he assumed she still had the reserve committed to saving the baggage train from the traitorous Sastragathi—was out of the picture. Damn her pride! She should have let the Sastragathi take the wagons; they could have recaptured them later. Or, if worst came to worst, they wouldn't have mattered anyway. Yet, would he have done any different, facing an attack from behind? He shook his head.

If the mercenary cavalry retired *en masse* it would leave the already heavily pressed infantry and Phrames' regiments unsupported. Then it would be every man for himself. If only General Hestophes would return with the right wing. Where in the Sam Hill was he?

Probably chasing Styphoni over hill and dale all the way into Sask. He couldn't expect any help from there. Kalvan had a sinking feeling that he was about to lose everything. As he had told his own generals countless times: *The general who commits his reserve first is the one most likely to lose.*

With Rylla Dralm-only-knew-where, his single guard cavalry regiment and the Urgothi Tymannian Guard were the only reserve left to the entire Hostigi army.

"What do we do? Where do we go, Your Majesty?"

Kalvan turned and peered at Colonel Kronos; his helmet gone, his face streaked with black powder, blood and grime.

Kalvan turned back to face his mounted Lifeguards and addressed them with what he thought might be valuable advice—at least it had done old Cromwell some good. "Put your trust in Dralm, and keep your fireseed dry!"

He doubted that one in ten could have heard his words, over the din of battle and thunder of guns, but they raised their pistols and cheered anyway. His Tymannian Guard hoisted their battleaxes and boar spears, looking for all the world like the Vikings of Harold Hadrada. The Urgothi battle horns began to bellow and the Guard spurred their horses. The Raven Banner was hoisted by one of the Guardsmen following Vanar Halgoth, who was so tall his warhorse looked like a pony.

Kalvan raised his saber and cried, "Lay on, McDuff, and damned be him who first cries, 'Hold! Enough!' CHARGE!"

Kalvan led his men straight into a clot of several hundred Ros-Zarthani cavalry, who had circled around the center, and were about to launch an attack on the Hostigi rear. The mercenary horse, which was on the verge of retreat, suddenly stiffened and Kalvan heard them chant. "King Kalvan! For King Kalvan! Down Styphon, too!" A moment later he had fired the pistol in his left hand, bowling a lancer in scaled armor out of his saddle, and was swinging his saber at a helmless Ros-Zarthani man-at-arms.

Vanar Halgoth's massive battleaxe split the helm of a Ros-Zarthani who was about to throw a nasty looking dart at Kalvan. He nodded his thanks, and Vanar's face split in a grin that showed a mouthful of jack-o'-lantern teeth. Then Kalvan was too busy exchanging sword blows with a fully armored Agrysi knight to notice anything but the red splatter in the air as his saber split the man's armet helm in twain.

V

White and gray smoke swirled around Vanar Halgoth like the early morning fog broiling around the banks of the Great River. The stench of fire and brimstone filled the air. A breeze came up and blew the fireseed smoke into tatters and he could see a sea of soldiers moving towards their position. The big guns went off again and a thunderclap smote his ears. The Tymannian Guardsmen moved uneasily, but he knew they would hold against anything this world had to offer. They were still not used to seeing and hearing so many guns at once. More fireseed had been burned in that salvo than all the fireseed used in the Sastragath for a generation.

Great King Kalvan had provided the Guard with horses, but they fought better on foot, so most had dismounted and formed a line six men deep. Only Vanar and a dozen handpicked Guardsmen were on horseback, since it was the Great King's way to ride off into battle, often ahead of his Lifeguard. Vanar had given Queen Rylla his oath that he would not let Kalvan get farther than two horse lengths away from his Guard.

The Urgothi warriors who made up the Bodyguard were not accustomed to holding a formation in the midst of battle so there was a lot of uneasy movement back and forth. These men were not fearful, just anxious to join in battle against their foes. Traditionally, the berserks would spend two or three ritualized sleepless evenings, drinking, smoking pipes, dancing to the drums and shouting until they felt the very blood in their veins boil. Some of the warriors were anxious and even angry at foregoing their battle rituals, but Vanar had explained this was a new type of warfare and the old ways did not always work, especially against the fireseed devils.

He watched as a load of case shot tore through a troop of enemy cavalry, shredding armor, men and horses with impartiality. Already the scent and excitement of battle must have put some of the Bodyguard into the battle-rage, he could tell by their eyes and how some of them were chewing the edges of their shields. If they broke out of line, battle-rage or no, they would answer to him!

His own mouth was dry as dust and he felt the accelerated pulse of the rage as it coursed through his body. Vanar pulled a piece of jerky out of his pouch and began to chew. He fought down the urge to yank out his sword and charge into the enemy lines. He did not like this new way of fighting, but it was King Kalvan's way and the path his overlord had ordered him to follow.

He watched as one of Kalvan's aides galloped up and talked hurriedly to the Great King, pointing furiously at the Hostigi left wing. Vanar gave the hand signal for the Guard to mount up on the double. Before the last of his men had taken their mounts from the horse handlers, Kalvan had signaled him and his regular cavalry guard to follow. He heard the Great King shouting, but all he could understand was the last word, "Charge!"

Kalvan was headed straight into a group of cavalry with iron scales. He made a quick prayer of thanksgiving to the Raven Hag of War and jumped into the fray behind his overlord. One of the scaled Ros-Zarthani cavalry aimed a wicked looking barbed dart at the Great King, but before he could throw it Vanar's battleaxe cleaved his helmet, leaving a trail of blood and brains. Moments later he was at his King's side, wrestling a lance out of a cuirassier's arms. He looked over at Kalvan and smiled—life didn't get much better than this!

Suddenly a company of Styphon's Guard, wearing fancy red capes and silver armor, surrounded the King. Vanar usually only had contempt for soldiers who spent money on fancy armor and weapons, but these red birds appeared to have sharp beaks and talons as well as finery. He couldn't wait to test their claws against his battleaxe!

"To the King!" he shouted, as he bashed his battleaxe into the shoulder of a Red Hand, taking the man's entire arm off. Then all was lost in a red haze of killing and battle lust.

THIRTY-FOUR

I

Rylla turned quickly in her saddle at the sound of someone running and raised her horsepistol. She quickly lowered it as she recognized green and gold plumes and the gilded armor of Prince Sarrask of Sask, moving with surprising quickness for someone so big. When Sarrask reached her horse, he paused to remove his gilded and engraved burgonet and catch his breath.

"Your Majesty, these slime-sucking Styphoni have broken our right wing! And the entire left is gone!"

Rylla felt her stomach fall. Would the right wing have broken had she held her position? "Dralm-damn that baggage train!" *How would she ever explain this to Kalvan?* She thought quickly, *What to do? What to do?* It had taken what seemed to be a complete candle to reassemble the reserve from the baggage train botchery. All the dragoons were here and about two-thirds of the regular cavalry.

The rest were still chasing the false Sastragathi. With growing apprehension, Rylla led her command back up the hillside. At the top her worst fears were confirmed.

The entire right wing was gone, no sign of Hestophes or any of his troops. Kalvan's flood was supposed to kill only the Styphoni, but it appeared from the number of bodies that much of both armies had died in what was now a muddy swamp. What remained of the Hostigi left wing was retreating through a defile ahead of several thousand Ros-Zarthani cavalry. A lane of dead and wounded marked their passage. Only the center was still holding and it was about to be encircled by the Red Hand.

Rylla stifled a sharp sob, grasped the hilt of her saber so hard she could feel the metal cut her hand, then raised her sword and shouted, "Charge!"

She didn't wait to see if anyone followed but charged blindly down the hillside with Prince Sarrask at her side toward the hated Red Hand. She looked for her husband's banner but it was nowhere to be seen. *Had she lost her only love as well?*

She felt her horse stumble and would have fallen from the saddle but for Sarrask's firm hand. His face was a terrible mask of anger and vengeance and she was truly glad he was on her side. She knew her own face mirrored Sarrask's.

When they reached the Red Hand, her sword fell and slashed until it was as dead of feeling as her heart. She must have killed a dozen Temple Guard before they realized that they were being attacked from behind. Suddenly glaives were falling like scythes at harvest time and Rylla's saber was knocked out of her hand. She pulled a loaded pistol out of her sash and shot the silver helmeted Guardsman in the mouth. Then she heard her horse scream, threw her pistol at another red-cloaked Guardsman, and wrestled two more pistols from her saddle holsters.

Rylla looked around and saw she was separated from the rest of her command by an inlet of red. She dodged a glaive thrust and used one of her boot guns to shoot the Guardsman in the face. Something hard struck her breastplate, and for a moment, she thought she was going to be knocked off her horse. Then she caught her balance, righted herself and used her last bullet to take out another Guardsman. Finally, Rylla grabbed the pistol by the barrel and began to use it as a club.

She would take as many of these red devils with her as she could. Yes, there would be fine company this eve in Galzar's Great Hall!

II

A miasma of anxiety and worry lay over the Foundry quarters like a thick blanket of fog. The sky was filled with broiling dark clouds, and every few minutes sheet lightning would light up the sky. In the far distance Sirna could hear the distant roll of cannons, or maybe thunder—she couldn't be sure.

The normal clanging, banging and thrumming of the Foundry were absent. Many of the workers belonged to the Hostigos Militia and were off to fight the Grand Host; others had sons or brothers who were off to war and might not be coming home. Even the Study Team members were sticking to their quarters, avoiding the common rooms of the two-story stone manor.

Sirna put down the sweater she'd been knitting to relieve the tedium, and went downstairs to the first floor dining area. Mrytta, the housekeeper, usually kept a pot of sassafras tea on the stove. Everyone but Varnath Lala allowed Mrytta to clean their rooms; the famed Metallurgist refused to promote sexual stereotyping "in any of its myriad of corrupting guises" and as a result her personal quarters looked like a pigsty. The only person sitting at the long plank table was Aranth Saln who was busy taking apart a long flintlock pistol and cleaning it.

"Do you mind?" she asked, pointing to a seat.

"No. Could use the company. This waiting is hard on everyone. I'd be down in the basement with Kirv watching the fighting on the sky-eye feed, but I'm not cleared for access. Although to be fair to Kirv—who's really a decent sort—if he let me into the basement, he'd have to let everyone else on the Study Team—"

"And that would be a disaster!" they both said in unison, laughing afterwards.

"What do you think of Kalvan's chances?" Sirna asked.

"He's got the advantage of fighting in his own backyard and the best man-for-man army in the Six Kingdoms. His biggest problem is sheer numbers. Kalvan wins one battle and Styphon's House throws twice as many troops at him on the next go-around. See, they know they can lose a hundred battles and still be in the game, but the moment Kalvan loses once—" Saln threw out his hands and brought them together with a loud bang! "Well, that's the end of Hos-Hostigos. Problem solved."

"Didn't he lose once already, at Tenabra?"

"Technically, but it was his father-in-law, Prince Ptosphes, who lost that battle—and it was a 'relatively' small skirmish compared to the fight that's going on in Sashta right now. Every time Kalvan commits his army there's a chance he might take it on the chin. Don't get me wrong; with the Fireseed Mystery out in the open, Styphon's House only has a limited time to marshal their forces before their house of cards collapses, to use an appropriate Europo-American cliché. I learned a lot of them working undercover at the Missouri *Independence* newspaper with young Sam Clemens.

"Until then, Styphon's House has all the power and men that gold and silver can buy. And someone over there in Balph—Archpriest Anaxthenes, according to our inside source, Danthor Dras—is smart enough to know it and he's not afraid to spend whatever it takes to defeat Kalvan. In three years there won't be a Styphon's House if they don't eliminate Kalvan and consolidate their power militarily. Even if they do win it's going to be an uphill fight to maintain a church without a constituency."

"Isn't that what Roxthar's revolution is all about, putting the true believers back in control of Styphon's House hierarchy, including the Inner Circle?"

"That's what Archpriest Roxthar thinks it's about, Sirna. I've seen this before. Fourth Level Macedonian-Imperial has this wonderfully fragile system of government run by the God Alexander. Everyone on the inside who runs things knows that Alexander is really just a mortal man and the god designation is purely traditional and ceremonial; it went along like this for millennia—until God Alexander CXII came to power. A true megalomaniac, he actually believed—just as Roxthar believes that Styphon is an actual god—that he was a *God*, and by Alexander's Ghost, he was going to act like one. Are you familiar with Macedonian-Imperial at all?"

"No, Saln," she said.

"It's was a small subsector only about ten or twelve parayears wide," he replied. "Its divarication point was Alexander of Macedonia surviving the illness that killed him at age thirty-two on all other Europo-American subsectors. He went on to conquer the known world at that time, whopping the Styphon out of anyone who objected. By the time of his death at the ripe old age of eighty-eight he'd not only cowed all his opponents but created, in typical Mediterranean-style, a cult of god worship in his image. He went from a cultural innovator—even bringing his tutor Aristotle along with him to do 'research'—to a typical Persian god king. A perfect example of a Fourth Level quote that's been popular on First Level for some time; 'Power corrupts; while absolute power corrupts absolutely.' Of course, we Home Timeliners have seen this all over Second Level, Third Level and numerous times on Fourth Level.

"To make a long story short, Alexander created the longest-lived and most peaceful dynasty of that entire Sector. Unfortunately, his legacy has not only been peace, but cultural and scientific stagnation. They're still mired at the pre-mechanical stage of development and only recently discovered gunpowder."

"What happened to the God who thought he was a god?"

"Since he was the heir apparent and the closest living descendant of Alexander the Great, the oligarchs who rule in his name did their best to put up with his antics, such as having everyone in Alexandria dress in yellow, no stepping on cracks every odd day of the month or killing all the one-legged children in the Empire. It didn't take long before his demands tried the patience of even his true worshippers, of which there were a surprising number! At first they tried to find a double to act in his place, but he had peculiarly wide eyes and without advanced cosmetic surgery there was no way they were going to find a twin to double for him. They couldn't publicly admit their God Alexander CXII was insane and that he didn't yet have any heirs with whom they could replace him.

"So one of the councilors came up with a devilishly evil idea of putting him into a permanent coma and telling the people he was communicating with his godly ancestors."

"How did they do that?"

"One of them must have been in the holdup trade at one time because he came up with the idea of hitting the Emperor's skull with a leather sandbag."

"That's awful!"

"Yes, but it doesn't leave any lasting marks and turns the brains underneath to jelly. Of course, if the beating is too severe it's fatal. They were very careful in their execution. Once the bruises went away they were able to display him in a crystal crypt, keeping him alive for over forty years. It made everybody happy."

Sirna shivered. "But didn't that end the line?"

Aranth smiled. "No. The rest of his body worked just fine. They bred him like a paralyzed sheep."

Sirna shuddered. "Some of the things that are business as usual outtime make you long for Home Time Line. But getting back to Aryan-Transpacific, if you're saying that Roxthar has the same take on reality as Alexander CXII, then why hasn't anyone slipped a blade between his ribs?"

"Because he's Styphon's House's best weapon in the war against Kalvan; look at how quickly he's been able to mobilize the Inner Circle and Temple bureaucracy. I doubt the Grand Host would have ever come into being without Roxthar's backing. Without Roxthar to mobilize and scare them, the Inner Circle would still be worrying over how to maximize their kickbacks from their suppliers of war materials and transportation.

"But, once the war against Kalvan is finished, Roxthar will then become their greatest liability. In addition, Roxthar also has an important ally, High Marshal Xenophes, the commander of Styphon's Own Guard."

Aranth paused while he finished cleaning his flintlock pistol, when it was ready to reassemble, he continued. "First Speaker Anaxthenes has been mobilizing all his Temple resources against the Investigator, but he may still not be able to stop Archpriest Roxthar, who has built a sizable faction and not just among his own Investigators. The Roxthar/Anaxthenes struggle may be as important to this time-line as the war between the Styphon's House and Kalvan."

Sirna heard shouting coming from outside the Foundry quarters. Aranth Saln motioned her to shush and put his half-assembled pistol back together faster than she would have believed possible, priming, loading and cocking it almost in a single motion. He tiptoed over to the door, his pistol barrel down at his side. The shutters were open and he carefully pulled back the scraped cowhide shade to show the outer courtyard and Foundry building. There were four towers at each corner of the compound and the guards at the front were waving and shouting to someone out on the Great King's Highway.

Aranth used his pocket phone, disguised as a powder horn, to call Captain Kirv and tell him there was some commotion going on outside the gates. He talked quickly and sub-vocally so Sirna was unable to hear his half of the conversation. When he was finished, he put away the phone, saying, "Kirv says it looks safe for the moment. He's already at the stable; he was contacted by one of the lookouts. Let's go outside and see what the hoopla is all about."

Sirna grabbed a flintlock musket out of the gunrack next to the door, loaded and primed it before following Saln into the courtyard. She noticed that Aranth was still holding his cocked pistol by his side. It hit her that Saln was also wearing his back-and-breast and that she'd never seen him outside the Foundry without it, which bespoke of long service outtime on primitive worlds like Aryan-Transpacific, where being prepared meant living to see another day.

Captain Kirv rode up on his horse and indicated for the guards to open the gates. Sirna moved to where she could see out the gate doors, while Saln scaled a ladder and got up on the outer walls catwalk. She could see a crowd of heavily armored men, all of them with raised visors and pennants flying. One of the flags was the Hostigos standard, a blue halberd on a red field. A lot of the armor looked dented and banged up; one shield appeared as if it had been chewed by giant rats. Several of the men-at-arms had impromptu bandages and missing armor. One of the knights shouted, "Hail Kalvan! The Styphoni have broken—Down Styphon!"

His cry was echoed by a score of voices both inside and outside the courtyard.

One of the officers rode through the gate and into the grounds. He recognized Kirv as the man in charge and asked, "Have you seen any of Styphon's curs today?"

Kirv shook his head. "No, you're the first soldiers we've seen coming from Sashta in days."

"Today we feasted upon the Styphoni soldiers. A great victory! We broke through the Styphoni lines at Ardros Field and have been chasing them down, killing all the cowardly swine that turned their hindquarters and ran."

Kirv looked worried. "How has the rest of the battle gone?"

The commander looked back and forth. "A victory, what else with the Styphoni leftwing fleeing the field? Tell your people about our Great King's destruction of the cowardly Host!"

"I will, Grand-Captain."

The knight turned and rode away, while Kirv rode over to Aranth Saln. "I felt like telling that Ulthori idiot he'd be better off supporting his Great King than chasing down strays, but I don't think he'd have taken it well."

Saln nodded. "We'll know soon enough if there's a victory to celebrate, but don't break out the victory wine just yet, Captain."

III

Sarrask watched with mounting horror as Queen Rylla pushed her way through the Styphoni ranks. Her big bodyguard, Xykos, was slashing everything in sight with his great sword but was still several horses removed from his charge. Moving his horse through Styphon's Temple Guard was like navigating a fast moving stream over cobblestones. Sarrask swung his saber to cleave a passageway until it lodged in a Guardsman's shoulder so firmly he couldn't remove it. Then he dropped it and used his mace.

Rylla was now only two or three bodies away, using her guns like clubs until one was knocked out of her hand. The Red Hand appeared to know who Rylla was and now only hands were tearing at her. Quite a few got bruised knuckles and broken fingers as a result. Xykos and the Queen's Beefeaters were caught in the tide of battle and were two horse-lengths removed from their Queen.

Sarrask knew he had to reach her before Guardsmen tore her from her horse and all was lost. How could he face Kalvan if he returned with Rylla missing, or worse, a prisoner of the Red Hand and Roxthar's Investigators? Sarrask literally pulled one Guardsman off his horse, silencing him with a smack of his mace.

About half a dozen of his own Guardsmen and two of Rylla's Beefeaters were at his side when he reached the Great Queen. She was half off her horse, but still fighting like a she-panther. Sarrask saw one Red Hand take a kick to the jaw that must have loosened every tooth in his head. Then Sarrask had the Queen by the back of her back-and-breast, and yanked her onto his own horse. He took a couple of hard elbows to the breastplate before she recognized him for a friend. He wasn't surprised to see dents the size of fists in his breastplate when he got her situated behind him on his mount.

"Why did you save me?" Rylla screamed.

Sarrask turned and slapped her hard across the face, hard enough to send her helmet with the white owl plumes tumbling.

She reddened and then straightened up. "You have saved me from an honorable death. Why?"

"There is no honor on Roxthar's racks or in his hot irons. Did you think they would just kill you? No, your death would to be slow, horrible and with no honor."

Rylla shook her head, her blonde hair cascading over her shoulders. "I am sorry. You are right, Sarrask. I don't know what possessed me. Find me a horse so I can kill more of our enemies."

"Of course, Your Majesty," Sarrask answered. Not that he had the slightest intention of letting Rylla out of his sight, or off his horse, until this Ormaz-spawned battle was over. The Saski bodyguard and her Beefeaters had now formed a circle around Sarrask and their Great Queen and for the first time in a quarter candle he could afford to take a deep breath.

Xykos rode up on his lathered horse, his face dripping with sweat. His great sword was battered and covered with gore. "Praise Dralm and Yirtta Allmother—the Queen lives!"

One of the Queen's Beefeaters cried, "I saw Sarrask single-handedly rescue Great Queen Rylla from the Red Hand!"

Xykos made a quick bow. "Prince Sarrask, I owe you my honor!"

Queen Rylla grabbed his cheek and bussed him, crying, "My paladin!"

Heads turned as the combined Queen's and Saski bodyguard cheered.

Sarrask lowered his face so no one would see how inflamed his cheeks had become. Someday he would savor this moment, but not now. He had to find

Great King Kalvan and help him salvage what could be saved from this disaster.

From the looks of things, Sarrask would not be returning to Sask and his current sharp-tongued mistress, who was beginning to leave him longing for his late wife—something he had never dreamed possible. *Things could be a lot worse! As long as Kalvan was alive and healthy, Praise Galzar, there would be many more battles and much glory to be won—that is, so long as they found their way out of this great murthering mess!*

IV

"By Styphon's Beard, those Ros-Zarthani barbarians ran down four Temple Bands of Styphon's Own Guard! They must be punished!" Marshal Albides cried, punctuating his words with his fist against his saddle pommel.

Phidestros groaned. He had a massive headache and his ears were ringing from standing too close to one of the Grand Host's big guns. He was on the verge of the greatest victory in history and this Holy Butcher wanted him to punish those most responsible. Until he'd taken command of the Harphaxi Army he hadn't realized how much more there was to being a general than fighting wars and winning battles.

"I talked to Stratego Donos and he claims it was an accident. His men were counter-attacking the Hostigi left when they encountered the Guard bands and because they were wearing red the troopers mistakenly thought it was a Hostigi flank attack." Phidestros had also seen a twinkle in Donos' eye that told him that it wasn't all that much a mistake, but having dealt with the Red Hand for the past several moons he was more than a little sympathetic to the Ros-Zarthani commander.

"We must make an example of them! What if others think they can get away with dishonoring Styphon's Own Guard?"

"By the Mace of Galzar, we are in the middle of a battle! At the moment we are winning, but it could all change in the wink of an eye. If we turn on our own, like starving wolves, we may well lose the war and everything with it. How would you like to explain that to Styphon's Voice or the Inner Circle? Or better yet, Holy Investigator Roxthar!"

The usually implacable Temple Guardsman actually blanched. "I will hold my hand for now, Grand Captain-General, but there will be no guarantees if we are put on the same field again with these western barbarians." Albides' face was beet red and Phidestros knew he was deadly serious. He spat a wad of tobacco on the ground and rode off with his Bodyguard in a swirl of dust.

This battle was even more precarious than Albides knew. True, the Hostigi left wing was broken and in full retreat, chased by the Ros-Zarthani horse and Soton's Knights. The center was surrounded by the Ros-Zarthani foot, Styphon's Own Guard, and the Sacred Squares of Hos-Ktemnos. However, there was no sign of the victorious Hostigi right, which had devoured the Holy Squares and the Princely cavalry of Hos-Ktemnos. At any moment fifteen thousand Hostigi cavalry could come back over the rise and all there was to stop them was his small reserve.

It might be a good time to slowly disengage the Ros-Zarthani foot, which would also keep them and the Red Hand from going at each other's jugulars, as well as give him a strategic reserve to deal with any returning Hostigi force.

Also, it might be politic to split the Ros-Zarthani off from the rest of the Grand Host after the battle and have them act as a rearguard. He didn't need his army torn apart by internal dissension. It would also help with the supply problems they would soon encounter as they chased the remnants of Kalvan's army through the false-Kingdom of Hos-Hostigos. There would be no more supply depots from here on out; they would be covering ground already foraged by Kalvan's retreating troops.

Phidestros lowered his head reflexively as the internal pounding rose in volume. *By Styphon's Brass Balls, I wish I were down on that field bashing in someone else's brains, rather than using my head as a battleground for thoughts.*

THIRTY-FIVE

I

Kalvan drew in a deep ragged breath. He was in the eye of the storm; all around him battle raged, but for the moment he was shielded by his Tymannian Guard and had his first opportunity in an hour to catch his breath. Halberds, poleaxes, glaives, bills and polearms of every description were tilling the human soil, spilling a river of blood and gore upon the ground. His arms were so numb from hacking at enemy foot soldiers that he couldn't trust them to reload his pistols. Pistol, he should say. Somewhere in the heat of battle, he had thrown away or lost four pistols.

If that were all he lost today, it would be a miracle!

His left wing was in retreat, his right wing was lost, and meanwhile the center was getting the stuffing kicked out of it. He had heard that Rylla had rejoined the battle, but hadn't seen any sign of her. Their only hope was that Hestophes would return and save the day. Had he been a praying man, he would have fallen down upon his knees to Dralm for that miracle.

Suddenly there was a commotion and he saw a helmet-less Colonel Kronos trying to work his way through the tightly packed horses to his side. Kalvan helped by turning his own horse and pressing toward his aide.

When Kronos was within hailing distance, he began to shout. "Part of the enemy is breaking off the attack."

"Is it Captain-General Hestophes?"

"I don't know."

"Let's pray to Dralm that it is. Men, it's time to give our friends some help. Down Styphon! Down Styphon!"

A thousand voices quickly took up the chant. He took a moment to reload. Kalvan didn't know where he was, only that he was somewhere inside the Unholy Host. It reminded him of Fyk, the Dralm-damned Battle, where everyone was lost in the fog. Kalvan guessed it didn't matter where they struck so he pointed his pistol at the nearest concentration of Hos-Ktemnoi and shouted, "Charge!"

The troopers around him moved, sluggishly at first, but slowly picking up momentum. *It's like fighting through quicksand!* Kalvan thought. He just hoped Hestophes was somewhere on the other side of this mass of Ktemnoi billmen.

The Hostigi hit the Ktemnoi line like a bulldozer running into a stone wall. Suddenly, as the battle surged around him, Kalvan found himself at the front. He used his pistol at point-blank range to kill a Ktemnoi petty-captain, then drew his nicked and bloodied saber. One of the Ktemnoi recognized him, starting a counter-chant of "Kill Kalvan! Kill Kalvan!"

He looked all around for his Guardsmen. Within an instant Kalvan found himself fighting half a dozen billmen and musketeers for his life. He slashed one in the face, opening the cheek to the bone beneath, and chopped off a falling billhead. Then a bill sliced through his guard and he felt it slash through his steel tasses and cotton breeches into the muscle underneath. A groan slipped through his teeth. He could feel sharp, hot pain, wetness on his right thigh. Suddenly, his head grew light.

Kalvan grabbed on to the pommel with all his strength; if he fell right here he would be finished. Then what would happen to Rylla, his daughter, Ptosphes, and so many friends? As if the enemy sensed his weakness, the attack against him grew in fury. It was all he could do to beat off the falling billheads and swords. Then he was propped up from behind by a hand so strong it could only belong to Vanar Halgoth.

The rest of his Tymannian Guard raced to his side, many diving off their horses to fight their enemy on foot with their axes. The billmen scattered before their concentrated fury. The enemy pulled back and Kalvan found he could breathe again, but his head was growing lighter…

Suddenly, he began to fall. It was only Vanar's grip that kept him from falling to the ground.

"The Great King's hurt! We must get him to safety."

Kalvan tried to straighten up. "It's just a flesh wound!" His breeches were soaked with blood, but the bleeding appeared to have been staunched—for the moment. He still felt lightheaded, but he could ride.

"Vanar, I need to get back to the top of the ridge so I can see the course of the battle. Can you get me there?"

"Of course, Your Majesty. And kill more of Styphon's servants on the way."

II

Syllon took a moment to catch his breath and drink some warm wine from his flask. He was in a little pocket a ways back from the front line. He had someone's red sash wrapped around his head; his morion was long lost. He had lost his helmet when he was struck in the head. If he put his fingers over the wound, he could feel a rakmar-sized depression where a portion of his skull had caved in. It didn't hurt much, but it made him sick to the stomach even to think about it. At least it had stopped bleeding….

Syllon found another helmet on the ground, a burgonet to protect his head.

He was still dizzy when he moved too quickly, but that didn't happen often on this floor of death, littered with broken corpses and discarded weapons and armament. He knew he'd come close to death when he'd been struck by a warhammer. He remembered a vision of blinding light and something about

Galzar's Great Hall—but already the memory was fading. It was good; men weren't supposed to know their gods' will.

If the battle current hadn't passed away from him, he might have been trampled or had his throat slit by Sastragathi robbers or Harphaxi camp followers. Whether or not he had visited Galzar's Hall, he owed the Wargod his life and he would make the proper sacrifices at the next temple he visited.

Once again Syllon began to move through the press of bodies. He realized the movement away from the frontline was like a slow river current; you could push against it, but it would still have its way. The entire Hostigi center was moving back up the hill, pressed upon the front and both sides by the Grand Host. The guns were silent; the smaller ones had been moved while the bigger ones were spiked or now in the hands of the godless Styphoni.

The few Hostigi who broke ranks and tried to run were shot dead by their fellow soldiers. Better a bullet from a friendly gun than the agony of the red-hot branding iron of the Holy Investigation of Styphon's House. It wasn't just former Captain-General Harmakros' warning either; it was the stories everyone had heard from the refugees fleeing Beshta and Sashta that had convinced every man jack of the Hostigi Army that if they broke formation they would die—and die horribly. "No quarter, no mercy from Styphon's House!"

Galzar the Wargod and Judge, despite Syllon's vision, was not at Ardros Field today!

His musket was a memory, but Syllon carried a pistol he'd ripped out of the hands of a dead Harphaxi cavalryman. What he needed was a pike! He searched the battleground, careful to maintain his footing. The dead and the wounded covered the ground like boulders in a rapid stream.

At last, he spotted an unbroken pike, dropped by one of the Nostori soldiers. He held the ash stock lovingly; it was as smooth as a whore's cheek.

Syllon raised the pike to high port and began to push his way to the front. Other pikemen in Nostori green and black saw him and followed his lead. A few musketeers dropped their muskets to pick up abandoned Harphaxi and Hostigi pikes.

One of the petty-captains took up the cry, "Hedgehog! Pikes forward!" Other captains joined the cry.

Soon the pikes reached the front of the battle-line, forming at first one thin rank, then two and suddenly three and four ranks. The arquebusiers and riflemen began to fill the files. A huge grin split Syllon's face. This was the natural order of warfare.

"Pikes down!"

A group of Harphaxi lobsters, in three-quarters armor, slowed as their horses fell back from the sudden forest of pikes. Several of them were shot out of their saddles by the musketeers in the files. Syllon pushed his pike head into the face of an unarmored horse, which reared up and threw a cuirassier off his saddle. After a short pause, the line started to fall back again, but this time it was at a measured cadence—the Styphoni press had relaxed.

III

Soton watched through one of the captured Hostigi *farseers* with mounting fury as the Grand Host smashed the Hostigi center with wave after wave of attackers and still the Hostigi battle-line held. The Army of Hostigos was slowly retreating up the hillside away from Ardros Field. What magic did Kalvan possess that turned mere soldiers into statues? Did Kalvan have his own Red Hand willing to shoot their comrades who broke and ran? Or was there more here than met the eye…?

Most of the Grand Host's small guns, the four and six-pounders, had been dispersed throughout the left wing. All had been swept away by the flood and subsequent Hostigi advance that took the Styphoni left wing off the battlefield, and only Styphon knew where they were now—since only a few loiterers had been seen since. General Kyblannos had mounted two batteries with the new Kalvan-style carriages and trunnions and used them to anchor the center. The heavier bombards were all carried on carts or wagons and strung out over the road between Ardros Field and Tarr-Veblos—they had as much mobility as the burnt-out manor house that was now at the center of the Hostigi ordered retreat. With those guns he could have forced the Hostigi to break ranks or scythed them down as they stood. Kyblannos himself had disappeared in the confusion—where was he? Probably, at Phidestros' rear like any other well-heeled dog.

Any man who produced such loyalty among his subordinates had to be watched carefully; he made a mental note to mention this to Great King Lysandros.

Sergeant Sarmoth, who rode at his side, asked, "Why are the Hostigi holding firm? It is not natural for soldiers to stand in the face of certain death. Are they demons, too?"

"The Hostigi are men and die as such," Soton pronounced. "I have fought them before, but this fortitude in the face of defeat is unusual—even for Kalvan's troopers. There are other fears than death."

Soton pointed to one of the Temple Bands as it attacked the slowly moving Hostigi hedgehog. Suddenly he knew exactly why the soldiers of Hostigos were not surrendering or crying 'Oath to Galzar!'

"There is the Hostigi courage! The Red Hand of Styphon's House and Roxthar's Dralm-damned Investigation!" The Hostigi knew that if they ran or surrendered they would be given over to Styphon's Arch-Butcher and it was not only more honorable, but much safer, to fight than surrender. Soton let off a stream of oaths that would have startled a petty-captain and turned any matron close enough to hear them bright red.

Sarmoth raised his helm and peered at the distant tableau. "These are the Temple Bands, but they are not Roxthar's bands."

"No, but try telling that to the Hostigi! I fear they will not see any difference; although, if truth be told, there is little since these bands will be set loose on the Hostigi once we cross the border into Hostigos."

"Won't the Grand Captain-General have anything to say about that?"

Soton smiled at the younger Knight. "Phidestros will bluster and threaten, for all the good it will do. His heart's in the right place, but the Grand Host's paymaster is still Styphon's House and Roxthar has the authority of the Inner Circle and his Investigation. And the Temple Bands to make his will felt."

Roxthar's Investigation had turned this war against the Usurper into a war unlike any Soton had ever witnessed in all his fifty winters. He had heard the stories about atrocities committed against the Hostigi population by Roxthar's

Investigators. At first, he hadn't wanted to believe them, even though he knew better from the Investigation's depredations in Hos-Ktemnos. But repetition and eyewitness accounts were impossible to refute. To commit such acts of cruelty on a vanquished population struck him as madness, or bloodlust, like that of a pack of wolves slaughtering a herd of sheep inside a corral.

Uncle Wolf Olmnestes, the Host's Highpriest of Galzar, had veritably blown the wax out of his ears with his heated words about the Investigation. Already word had been sent by Olmnestes to the High Temple of Galzar in Hos-Agrys and any day a delegation might appear placing the Grand Host under Galzar's Ban. It appeared that Roxthar's excesses would cost the Temple a complete victory over the Usurper Kalvan, and maybe lead to a war with Galzar afterwards. He suspected that the latter would not cost Roxthar any sleep, but then the Archpriest's military knowledge could be contained in a thimble.

He suspected the Grand Host would face the Ban of Galzar before a moon quarter had passed—he'd even said as much to Phidestros. This would make it impossible for Styphon's House to hire any mercenaries in the Five Kingdoms until it was rescinded, which would not happen until Roxthar and his Investigators stopped looking for heretics under beds and in chamber pots in every man's cottage in the Five Kingdoms. The Ban would also mean that all mercenaries currently under oath to the Grand Host would be obliged to fore-swear their oaths and retire from the field, which would be disastrous.

If word reached Roxthar's ears of Olmnestes' words, he would not be surprised if the Highpriest were murdered in his sleep. He would have to put a guard of Knights around the Highpriest of Galzar—the murder of the popular Highpriest could tear the Grand Host asunder—Ban or no Ban!

The Grand Master watched in surprise as the Hostigi suddenly formed into a hedgehog formation. *Phidestros' spy had claimed that Kalvan had relinquished pikes for his Royal Army?* Then it hit him, of course! Kalvan may have done away with pikes, but not his Princes. He gnashed his teeth in anger at the thought that Kalvan might exit this battlefield with a crippled, but intact army.

Once again, Soton upbraided himself for swearing an oath to Anaxthenes that he would aid Roxthar in every way, as long as the Investigator stayed out of Balph until winter. Yet, Soton knew full well the Speaker was correct; if

Roxthar were away from Balph, it would be possible for Anaxthenes to claim Sesklos' chair as Styphon's Own Voice. Too many of the Archpriests, despite their loathing of him, were too frightened to take a position against Roxthar in person. Oh, but were they brave when the Investigator was out of Balph!

Soton set off another string of curses, this time against Temple politics and all the compromises that came with them. He turned to Sergeant Sarmoth. "Sound the battle horns!"

"Yes, sir!" The tone of his voice said, 'it's about time.'

Soton hoped his large subordinate was right.

He had a Wedge of Knights behind his point; maybe they could break through the hedgehog. At least, Kalvan's soldiers were men he could fight and kill—not Temple upperpriests who hid behind words and bloody white robes.

With Soton at the head, the Wedge of heavily armed Knights and Sergeants came down the hill like an avalanche of steel, which unfortunately slowed to a crawl as they crossed the valley and then rode uphill to meet Kalvan's retreating center. The shock of impact when they struck Kalvan's hedgehog was not enough and the Knights were unable to break through the forest of pikes aimed at their mounts. The lead destriers were trained to charge into pike heads, but that only worked if they were galloping, since at slower speeds the horses' instincts rebelled against what appeared to be certain death.

Within moments, the Knights were stalled in front of Kalvan's center, with pikes impaling screaming horses and Hostigi muskets barking confusion and death. The Order used their horsepistols in return, but they didn't have enough firepower to break the hedgehog.

"Curse and blast them!" Soton cried, as the Hostigi formation not only held, but gave the Order more casualties than it was taking. Slowly and inexorably Soton's Knights were pushed back as the Hostigi pikemen opened more files for the musketeers and arquebusiers to shoot. Halberdiers and two-handed swordsmen began to run through the pike files, attacking isolated Knights and Brethren.

Soton found himself fending off one attacker with his mace, while his armored horse reared and started walking backwards, trying to stay away from the stinging pikeheads.

Reluctantly, Soton gave the signal for retreat.

Sarmoth looked at him in surprise.

"We are taking too many casualties. Let us pull back and let the light cavalry and skirmishers harass this porcupine of Kalvan's. We have won the battle, now we must win the war."

IV

Phidestros' victory joy turned to dust when he saw who was at the forefront of the party coming to meet him. Leading the delegation was Archpriest Roxthar, followed by Grand Master Soton, Captain-General Antaphon and Captain-General Albides, commander of the Temple Guard. He dismissed all his aides but Kyblannos.

"Congratulations, Captain-General," Roxthar said, with a smile that would have looked more natural on a ravenous wolf. "You have done well for the One God."

Phidestros' attempt to look appropriately humble at Roxthar's words put a smile on Soton's face. "Yes, Your Holiness, we have struck a great blow for Styphon."

Roxthar nodded as if Kalvan's defeat had been preordained. "The victory is not complete as long as the Usurper still lives."

"Kalvan still lives? I heard he'd been gut shot."

"We have no proof other than words as to whether or not the Daemon is alive. Until I see his corpse, I will believe he is alive."

"Have you seen the Daemon in the flesh, Your Holiness?"

"Of course not. But I will *know* him, Styphon be praised!"

"Your Holiness, there are as many rumors as truths on the battlefield. I agree that the only way to be certain Kalvan is dead is to find his body. This we will attempt to do." Phidestros left out the unspoken part of the sentence, that he would do his job best if unhampered by Archpriests, Albides and other meddlers.

Roxthar looked at him sharply. "There are other important duties that lie ahead, such as our Holy Investigation. Hostigos overflows with every brand of heretic and infidel: all must be put to the Investigation."

Phidestros suppressed a burst of anger. Killing civilians was not the job he'd signed on for. "There are military matters that have to be undertaken first. Isn't that right, Grand Master?"

Soton nodded, but looked as if he would rather be taking his dinner with his Knights than attending to this foolishness.

"What matters are these?" Roxthar asked.

"For one," Albides interjected, "we have to punish the Western barbarians for their traitorous attack upon my Guardsmen. They must pay and pay mightily."

Phidestros stared Albides down, forcing his gaze to the ground.

"We had already agreed that it was a mistake to punish—"

"No, that was *your* conclusion, Phidestros, not mine. I want those godless swine punished!"

Phidestros gritted his teeth. "I believe the Holy Investigator will agree that it is more important to crush Kalvan than it is to punish mercenaries who have fought and died well for Styphon. As I told you before, Captain-General Albides, I will order the Ros-Zarthani to remain in the rear to secure our supply trains. To do more would be most unwise."

"Captain-General Phidestros is following the path of Styphon," Roxthar pronounced. "You will continue to answer to him in all things military."

Albides looked as if he'd just swallowed a crabapple, but he kept his mouth shut.

"Our duty here is clear," Roxthar continued. "Before all else, we must annihilate the Daemon and his followers. To this end, I will send mounted troops of my Investigators, with Temple Guards, ahead of the Host. They will capture the Daemon's subjects before they can flee and detain them for the Investigation."

Now it was Phidestros' turn to choke. "But, but... Our first priority must be to pursue the Hostigi Army so they cannot reform and counterattack." The Hostigi had left behind a rearguard that was blocking the valley from both sides. He had sent out detachments to either flank, but it would take time before they would be able to climb the mountains on either side of the valley and force the Hostigi rearguard to abandon its position. Phidestros saw finding a way to advance the Grand Host out of this valley quickly, not harass civilians, as the first order of business.

"Destroying the Daemon's army is just part of our work," Roxthar proclaimed in a tone that brooked no argument. "The Grand Host shall have its turn. But first we must scour Hostigos of all traces of the Daemon and his corrupt teachings. Nothing else is as important to the Great God Styphon."

This is Hadron's own way to run an army, thought Phidestros. The only way he could ignore Roxthar's orders and live to tell about it would be to have his men behead Roxthar with the nearest sword and put his Investigators and Albides' Temple Guardsmen to death. Of course, he'd have to go through Soton first, and—even if he won—well, there would go his Princedom...

"Your word is my command, Your Holiness."

Phidestros noticed that he wasn't the only soldier biting his tongue. Captain-General Antaphon was so green he looked about to spill his tripe.

"As for you, Captain-General Albides, I order you to stop wasting heat on our allies that could be used to scorch our enemies. Round up horses for those of your men who are on foot and break them up into tens to escort my Investigators."

"Yes, Holy Investigator," Albides replied, then left as though Kalvan's fireseed demons were scorching his hindquarters.

"Grand Captain-General, why is the rest of the Grand Host milling around here like sheep who've escaped their pens?"

"My captains are trying to reorganize the units that have become disorganized and scattered. The Hos-Ktemnos Captain-General not only managed to get himself killed for his poor generalship, but cost me a quarter of the Harphaxi Army in casualties and all the Ktemnoi cavalry!"

"How could this be? Are we not the victors?"

"Yes, but only just barely. When Marshal Zythannes' cavalry regrouped after running from Kalvan's men like curs, they discovered their commander was dead. The captains held an election and decided to return *en masse* to Hos-Ktemnos."

"The cowards!" Soton boomed, as though releasing all the pent-up anger he had been carrying since arriving with Roxthar. "They ran from the battle like dogs and now they've put their tails between their legs and gone home! At least they didn't take the Sacred Squares with them."

Phidestros nodded in agreement; the Ktemnoi cavalry were nothing to brag about, but the Sacred Squares were the Host's best infantry. Nobody, except maybe his mistresses, would miss Zythannes.

"Styphon shall punish them in due time," Roxthar said, as though he had just received this word direct from the Styphon's Sky-Throne. "How long will it take to gain command over your army again?"

"About a half sun. There will be no moving them until the corpses are stripped and the seriously wounded given Galzar's Grace. Remember, Your Holiness, we are dealing with soldiers, not temple priests."

Roxthar's eyes grew hard. "Yes, but it is your duty to see they do Styphon's Will. Remember *your* place."

"The Grand Host has taken many casualties, Your Holiness: some eight to ten thousand Hos-Ktemnoi of the Sacred Squares are dead and dying from the Hostigi guns, twelve, maybe as many as fifteen thousand of my own Harphaxi gone, and only Hadron knows how many dead mercenaries. Soton, how many of your Knights remain here on Ardros Field?"

"Too many! Two or three thousand casualties, maybe more. We have not had time for a full muster."

"Once our soldiers have stripped the dead, gathered their wits, filled their stomachs and slaked their thirst, they will be ready to drive Kalvan's army to the Great River, if need be."

"We shall drive the Daemon and his impious minions from this land," Roxthar pronounced, "water the land with their blood, strip the very flesh off their bones and feed the wolves with their leavings. We will chase the Daemon and his army to the very end of the world. They will die, all of them."

Phidestros felt the chill of Roxthar's words cut right through his buffalo skin jacket. He would not want to be in Kalvan's boots at this moment. His earlier victory joy was all gone and the only taste in his mouth was of ashes.

THIRTY-SIX

The sounds of gunfire filled the night air, waking Sirna from a sound sleep. *What's happening?* she asked herself, rubbing the sleep out of her eyes. The shouts grew louder and she heard what sounded like fireworks going off in the Foundry courtyard.

Sirna, who'd been sleeping fully dressed ever since the invasion of Sashta, rose up off her straw tick. She hadn't been sleeping very well ever since word had come from a ragtag gang of deserters that Kalvan had been defeated and the Army of Hos-Hostigos was in retreat. She picked up a musketoon from beside her bed.

Professor Aranth Saln's had strongly suggested that they leave the Foundry and return to Fifth Level Police Terminal, or even Home Time Line. His had been the only voice of reason as the Hostigos Study Team elected to stay in Hostigos instead of leaving the Foundry for a safer harbor.

Varnath Lala was convinced she could negotiate with the Styphoni and sell the Study Team's skills to the invaders, thereby learning invaluable information about the inner workings of the newly reformed Styphon's House. Talgan Darth, who had run before from the Styphoni to universal derision, said, "I'm not running. Not again!"

The rest of the Team echoed one viewpoint or the other in a marathon gab session that tried Sirna's patience to the breaking point.

Captain Skordran Kirv, the Paratime Police operative, had been just as stubborn; if the Kalvan Study Team wouldn't evacuate the Foundry, then neither he nor his men would leave. "Nobody will take it amiss if we post a few extra sentries on the towers, Dralm damnit! If we don't we'll look like fools to the Styphoni and traitors to the Hostigi."

"Treason? Are you mad?" Talgan Dreth asked.

"Great King Kalvan's last words to me at Tarr-Hostigos, before he left for Beshta, were: 'If things go badly, be sure to evacuate the Foundry in a timely fashion. Whatever the cost, do *not* let the masters be captured by the Grand Host!' Would you like to explain to Duke Harmakros why you attempted to keep me from observing the Great King's orders?"

"Harmakros is—"

"Not dead, yet. Until he is, he'll be watching over Hostigos Town and everything nearby. Which includes us."

Harmakros was probably already seething. Word had come from Tarr-Hostigos yesterday to start evacuating the Foundry. The horns of Skordran Kirv's dilemma were: first, neither he nor the Paratime Police dared let the University Study Team go into exile with Hostigi refugees for fear they would blow their cover under the adverse conditions they'd encounter; second, the Paracops couldn't evacuate the Foundry until such time as the Grand Host were near enough that the Styphoni could be blamed for the disappearance of the Zygrosi brass-founders and their helpers.

What the Paratime Police didn't want was some refugee telling Kalvan the Foundry had been evacuated a day before the Grand Host had even arrived! Kalvan had proven he could add and even multiply on a number of different occasions. The last thing anyone wanted was to have Kalvan start adding up his strange journey and the peculiar habits of the Zygrosi Foundry workers.

What evacuation meant to Sirna personally was the end of her assignment on Kalvan's Time-Line. Kalvan would write off the whole Study Team as 'lost in action,' which meant Sirna would be returning to Home Time Line—for good. She'd greeted this possibility with both regret and anticipation. Regret that she would have to leave this bustling time-line when things were going very badly for people she had grown to know and admire. Anticipation at leaving some of the more unpleasant University faculty for the peace and quiet of the library where she would write her thesis, and at living again where civilized amenities were taken for granted. Regret at having to confront Hadron Tharn and having to explain why she had not provided the information she had been charged with obtaining.

Well, if there is one thing I've learned from living here, it's to confront problems directly. If Tharn makes any threats, I'll just tell him to desist, or I'll have a polite chat with Paratime Police Chief Verkan Vall. That should shut Tharn up like nothing else.

"I still think there is enough time," Talgan Dreth continued. "Every hand we set to watching for enemies, still hours or days away, is one less we have to move things to safety."

Sirna smiled. Talgan Dreth had to be overwrought indeed to come that close to breaching Paratime security. She rather wished he'd come closer. *Anything* to make sure the Kalvan Study Teams wouldn't be encumbered with him when they returned to Home Time Line.

"You are gambling too much on your notions of what the Styphoni *might* do," Kirv replied. "I say they could be here much sooner than that. We need to guard against what the Styphoni can do, not what they might do."

The old argument of capabilities versus intentions. Three years ago Sirna had barely heard of it. Two years ago it was still a theoretical question, even if Aranth Saln could talk about it for hours. Now it was a life-and-death matter.

"Captain Kirv," the Study Team Director said using his most formal classroom voice. "We not only have a large number of computers and recording machines to remove, but also a number of priceless tools that were obtained from other time-lines at great expense. I would like to transport as much of this material as possible to Fifth Level so that future Kalvan Study Teams will have a chance to become familiar with these tools and not waste time importing them from the Kalvan Control Time-Lines.

"I'll hold off posting the sentries for another half-day," Kirv said reluctantly. "We still have a number of charges to set around the Foundry. Kalvan does not want the Foundry to fall into Styphoni hands. We can deal with the *protected* conveyor-head depot later; after a war like this what will one more big explosion mean to the survivors? But hear this, Talgan: get your people organized for the moving party at once! I'm posting sentries where they're needed, and may Galzar's Mace strike anyone who argues."

"You start posting sentries without my orders and I'll report you to General Verkan!"

"I don't care if you report me to Great King Kalvan. Anything they'll do to me for disobeying your orders isn't half what they'll do if I neglect my duty!"

Kirv turned away from Talgan Dreth and walked straight past Sirna without seeing her. As he passed, he muttered in a voice obviously not meant to be overheard, "If any of us live that long."

Sirna was about to hurry after him and ask for an explanation when she sensed someone behind her. She turned, to see Urig, the senior warehouse foreman.

"Mistress Sirna. I thought I'd best warn you. Some of the lads—they're talkin' about makin' off with the horses on their own."

"Thank you for the warning, Urig. We're going to want everyone to help move equipment for at least two or three candles; what can be moved goes into carts. What can't be moved goes into the warehouses, with tar and fireseed laid ready. Then we'll be dividing up the extra horses, food, money—everything. Those who have given good service won't be forgotten. And who knows? Even if Kalvan loses this battle, he may win the next."

Urig's look told her that the last sentence had been a waste of breath, but he jerked his head. "I'll give 'em your words, Mistress Sirna. It's grateful they'll be. The lads trust you, you're not like some of them—" He made a pointed glance over at some of the senior faculty.

Sirna didn't know if that was the actual plan, if indeed Talgan Dreth had any plan at all. His habit of being close-mouthed made it impossible to tell. Sirna only knew she was going to see that *something* was done for the Foundry workers—even if it meant defying the Director.

She could be sure of trouble back at the University if she did. But here-and-now, she could be sure of help from Aranth Saln and Captain Kirv, at least. And, when he recovered his health, Chief Verkan.

Sirna jumped again as a soft footfall sounded behind her. It was Aranth Saln, who greeted her outraged look with a soft laugh.

"If you can find anything to laugh at in this—!" Words failed her. She took a deep breath and added more gently, "At least try not to sneak up behind me."

"I wasn't sneaking. I've just been trying not to be noticed by our dear Director, and I guess the habit stuck."

Having a potential ally on hand made Sirna breathe easier. "Will you help me keep my promises to Urig? If he begins to doubt me, we'll have a mutiny on our hands right when we least need it."

"I will, Sirna. But I'm going to spend the next few hours on the roof of the main forge. One extra pair of eyes on sentry can't hurt. If I know Kirv, he will have his men on sentry duty, but they'll have to stay hidden. I'm not one of Skordran's people, so Talgan can't fume at him over me."

Sirna's mouth went dry. "Are the Styphoni that close?"

"The main body, no. They'll be coming on in a day or two. Phidestros is a damned good general, but he's working with a divided command, Archpriests up to his bellybutton and an army that's taken a pounding. What I'm worried about is his sending parties of Investigators ahead of the Host. We've heard rumors that armed bands of Roxthar's torturers are taking hostages and killing peasants—in fact, Kirv showed me a few pictures of the Investigators in action."

"Can I see?"

He shook his head. "You don't want to see these pictures! They're not for civilians."

Sirna felt a shiver run its way up her spine.

"The cavalry we don't need to worry about," Saln continued. "But a few regiments from Phidestros' reserve could raise havoc in Hostigos Town. At least among those stupid enough to dally this long."

It was a physical impossibility for Sirna's mouth to go drier. Her knees couldn't decide between knocking together or folding under her.

"Come on. I'll walk you over to the forge. Tandar Volth is inside making sure what we can't move is melted down. Varnath Lala tried to stop him, but Tandar had two of the smiths throw the old crow out and bar the door against her."

"Pity I didn't see that."

"You'll see even more entertaining things before you get to Home Time Line, I'd wager."

"Dinner at the Constellation House?"

"Done."

It had still been a stalemate and she'd gone to her bed, long before Captain Kirv and Talgan Dreth's arguments had wound down. From the sounds of fighting outside it appeared they all might have to pay for the ritual antagonism between University and Paratime Police.

There was a loud WHUMMPH! which shook the old manor like an earthquake. She peered out the window and saw the foundry building was now a fiery ruin! *How are we going to escape now,* she asked herself? Had Kirv set off the demolition charges without warning anyone to beat Talgan at his own game? No, that didn't sound like the Paratime Policeman. Maybe his sentries had spotted a major force of Styphoni coming toward the Foundry.

There was another loud explosion, as though someone had set off a casket of fireseed; only this one was right below her and she felt the floor underneath shiver and then collapse, sending her downward in a tangle of bed, furniture and stones. She landed in a sprawl and was hurting all over, but everything was still working—even her fingers.

She heard someone shout, "Capture the foreign dogs. Roxthar wants to investigate them himself. Beware of all demonic arts!"

"Dear Father Dralm!" Sirna whispered, as she tried to compress herself into a tiny little ball amongst the rubble and ruin of the second floor. There was something wet running down her arm and she was certain it was her own blood. She felt around and winced as her fingers found a deep scratch in her upper arm.

She heard Lala screech, "We can talk about this! I demand to see your superior. I am an important personage. I know things the Inner Circle wants to know. I order—"

Lala's words were cut off by a gunshot and a shrill scream.

She saw a big figure, which she recognized as Aranth Saln, moving through the rubble toward the back door. She tried to call out, but all that came out of her mouth was a croaking noise. Then Aranth was gone into the shadowy night.

There were more screams and the sounds of fists hitting flesh. "Take this fool in chains. He will answer to the Investigator for killing the woman." Suddenly there was a fusillade of shots and more screams.

A voice that sounded like Captain Kirv's said, "Move back, away from the Styphoni, so I can get a good shot!"

There was another barrage of gunfire and she heard Kirv's voice turn into a womanish scream. Her heart dropped into her stomach. She was alone!

There were more screams and cuffs, she recognized the voice of Talgan and said a quiet prayer.

"Please don't hurt me!" Talgan shouted, his pleas cut short by a wet thud. She had never liked the administrator, but no one deserved to provide sport for the Investigation!

Sirna felt around in the dark and found her musketoon. She'd heard too many stories about Roxthar and his Dralm-damned Investigation. Holy torture was what it was. It was no wonder that on Home Time Line religion was considered a plague on mankind, a verbally transmittable mental illness.

Sirna had never felt so alone in her life.

Suddenly some men entered the room with bright torches and burning sticks covered with tar. They were searching through the rubble for survivors. Several of the men were mercenaries, but one wore the white robe of the Investigation and she saw several Temple Guardsmen in their shiny armor and red capes. *The Red Hand, isn't that what the Hostigi call them?*

Kirv hadn't been prepared for a Temple band of Styphon's Guardsmen. She held her breath and squeezed against the wall as though she could will herself to disappear.

She watched as a soldier found a leg under some fallen masonry. It took three men to drag the body of a woman out of the rubble; it was Mrytta the housekeeper. "By Galzar's Teeth, she's an ugly one! Almost as old and withered as the hag the Captain shot."

"And just as dead," someone else finished.

"Shut up," another soldier commanded. "There's somebody else in here, I can feel it."

Suddenly a light flashed in her eyes, temporarily blinding her. Sirna heard a shout. She closed one eye and aimed the musketoon at the priest in the white robes, hoping that all the shooting lessons Aranth had given her had taught her something.

Her shot was deafening in the quiet tomb of what had once been a prosperous manor. The priest screamed and clutched his stomach. *Good*, she thought, *he's gut shot!* There was a salvo of returning fire and something struck her head like a hammer—

THIRTY-SEVEN

I

"Chief! I think you'd better see this now," Paratime Police Inspector Andron Veral said as he bulled his way into the Chief's office.

Verkan looked up from his screen, saw the message ball in Andron's hand, and thought, *what now?* His chest was still a mass of bruises from where the gunshot had struck him, but fortunately the lung graft was fine and his ribs had already knitted back together. An occasional sharp pain would remind him that he'd come awfully close to termination in an anonymous mass gravesite a few days ago. Dalla had been hovering over him like a mother cat tending a wounded kitten ever since they'd arrived on First Level. He'd forced himself to come to work today just to escape her well intentioned but smothering concern.

Andron first handed Verkan the data wafer that was held in his other hand. "Chief, this just arrived from Aryan-Transpacific, Kalvan's Time-Line. It was red flagged. I just got through running it in my viewer."

Verkan felt his stomach sink. In his mind an army of doubt and uncertainty attacked his mental wall of control. The years of training took command and Verkan remained impassive. He pushed the wafer into his desk viewer.

"This is their last feed."

It was a feed from the sky-eye above Hostigos. He could see the two armies poised on either side of the valley in almost perfect geometric precision, like toy soldiers or a computer battle simulation. It was hard to think of them as real men, some friends, many of whom were about to die or be horribly maimed for life.

The camera showed a close-up and he could see the Royal Banners of Hos-Hostigos blowing in the wind, a dark green keystone on a maroon field. The picture was too grainy to identify faces but he could discern individuals. The next shots showed the two armies' opening moves, with Kalvan's field artillery tearing holes in the front ranks of the Grand Host.

He watched as the Hostigi right wing moved forward and chased the Styphoni out of the valley and into the next. Meanwhile, the two centers were locked in an embrace of death. Then he watched in surprise as the Hostigos left wing gave way to a determined attack from the Grand Host's right wing and was enveloped by the Styphoni cavalry, who looked remarkably like the Roman *cataphracti* he had once seen close up on Fourth Level, Alexandrian-Roman. *They must be the Ros-Zarthani I've heard so much about.*

Fortunately, the left wing's reserve was able to stop the envelopment long enough to allow a retreat that took them out of the valley, but no longer supporting Kalvan's center.

While the Grand Host's right wing cavalry chased Kalvan's left wing, the infantry turned and joined the assault on the Hostigi center, already under heavy attack. The camera sped up to cover action that must have taken hours. The two armies were locked in hand-to-hand combat. For a while it looked as if the Hostigi were surrounded until a reserve force joined the main body. For the first time it looked to Verkan as if Kalvan had a chance to push the Styphoni back.

The camera moved to the next valley where the missing Hostigi right wing was thrashing the remnants of the Styphoni left wing's foot. Both armies were devoid of cavalry support and he suspected the troopers were chasing each other over the ridges of the mountains that were called the Appalachians on Europo-American.

Like most pre-mechanical armies, where command depended upon line-of-sight, the Hostigi right wing did not realize the rest of the army was in dire peril. Verkan wished he were there, instead of here shuffling papers; he would have found some way to warn them.

He watched as the camera returned to the main battle and saw part of the Styphoni army break off, probably to prepare for the return of the missing Hostigi right wing. Too bad! Someone in the Grand Host camp knew what he was doing—either Grand Master Soton, or that mercenary Grand Captain-General Phidestros.

While hundreds of smaller actions took place unnoticed, the two centers pushed back and forth strewing the ground with piles of their dead. He estimated the casualties in the tens of thousands: not atypical in this kind of engagement when one side or the other did not break off. Some of the Hostigi field artillery guns were still firing, inflicting scores of casualties with each shot in the tightly pressed ranks.

Then he saw the Hostigi right wing return to where the Grand Host's right had once been where it was met by the Ros-Zarthani reserve. The Hostigi still had most of their mobile artillery and, without cavalry support, their guns tore the Ros-Zarthani infantry apart.

For a moment, Verkan began to believe in miracles. Then he watched in disbelief as the Zarthani Knights, who'd just returned from pursuing the Hostigi center, slammed into the fray. Surprisingly, the Hostigi right wing, now hit on the flank, did not break. It was hard to imagine the thousands of heroic acts that made for such resolution.

Yet, it wasn't enough to save the day. The right began to slowly wheel and then continue its march around the entire Grand Host!

With the support of the Temple Guard, the Styphoni suddenly seemed to redouble their battle against the beleaguered center. A few small bands of Hostigi soldiers began to break off and Verkan suspected they were mercenaries who had given their oath to Galzar. There was to be no grace for the Hostigi regulars, only Roxthar's Investigation, and they fought on as though they understood exactly what that meant. Then suddenly, on the fast motion feed, the center re-formed itself into a hedgehog, with pikes all around the perimeter holding the Grand Host at bay.

Slowly the center began to retreat. Verkan wondered if Kalvan was still alive. Probably, or the entire center might have broken, with each man for himself. Certain suicide. But Kalvan had taught his men well; they were leaving with an intact battle-line.

Verkan shut off the viewer. "That's enough! Veral, is there anything we can do to help Kalvan and Rylla."

"How could we find them? They'd be impossible to locate, Chief. There must be two or three hundred thousand Hostigi refugees, and that's not counting the Hostigi Army. The roads have been clogged for days with fleeing Beshtans and Sashtans. Once word reaches Sask and Nostor there will be a half-million refugees fleeing Hos-Hostigos. Kalvan's subjects are *that* scared of Styphon's revenge squad and Arch-Butcher Roxthar! Anyone with half a brain is taking whatever he can carry and bugging out.

"But Chief, that's not our problem."

"What are you talking about?"

"This battle took place yesterday! The inspector who was supposed to scan these tapes was a day behind. When he saw this he moved like a bee-stung grizzly."

Verkan threw his left hand up to his forehead "What about the Kalvan Study Team?"

"That's what I'm worried about, Chief. There hasn't been a conveyer out of the Foundry in days. I don't even know if they've received word about Kalvan's defeat."

Verkan shook his head. *One way or another, they know.*

Andron handed him the message ball. "Take a look. It's a day old, but it's our most recent communication."

Skordran Kirv's wan face filled the viewer. "Chief, it looks like your friend Kalvan was killed, at least that's what the rumors are saying. But then, according to rumor you're dead, Rylla's dead and Galzar's Great Ghost has been seen walking through the battlefield."

Kalvan! No, it couldn't be true. Verkan needed hard data and he needed it now.

Kirv continued. "The Study Team is all in an uproar. Lala wants to try and negotiate with the Styphoni. Talgan Dreth wants to leave, but he still remembers the joshing he got when the entire team deserted the Foundry after Kalvan's victory at Phyrax. The others are torn between these two competing personalities. And I can't get either side to listen to reason. I'm all for getting everyone the Regwarn out of there!

"I've stationed perimeter guards and nothing short of a regiment and a battery of guns will pry us out of the Foundry so I'm not worried about security. Still, if Kalvan loses this battle we're in big trouble.

"Will keep you posted. Skordran Kirv, Inspector, signing off."

"That's all there is, Chief. I'm putting a team together right now here on Fifth Level to return to the Foundry."

Verkan thought of the political fallout if something happened to the Kalvan Study Team. "Let me know when you're ready. I'm going along and am personally taking charge. This is not only a major screw-up, but political dynamite!"

II

"Make Way! Make way, for Great King Kalvan!" Colonel Kronos shouted at the top of his lungs. The sky was dark and a light drizzle, the last of the morning rain, was falling. Kronos' voice penetrated through the din of milling refugees and soldiers making their way along the series of switchbacks leading up to Tarr-Hostigos. The slippery road was alive with people, wagons, carts, litters and wounded of every description on makeshift stretchers and travois. The din was that of a madhouse—mothers calling out for children, widows crying out in grief, soldiers cursing the crowds, draymen shouting at animals and above all, the injured shrieking in pain.

Rylla, her patience long exhausted, used the flat of her sword to make a path for her husband's litter. A moment later, Captain Xykos joined her efforts with Boarsbane and suddenly the way to the gate was cleared.

Kalvan, just coming out of the fog of unconsciousness, saw all of this as though it were happening long ago and far away. Then a peasant woman jostled the litter and a lightning bolt of pain brought his attention back to here-and-now. "Ah!"

Rylla halted the procession and put a damp cloth on his forehead. It was as cool as if it had just left the Big Spring, which told him he was suffering from a fever as well as a concussion. He tried to sit up. "Rylla, we have to talk."

"Not now, my love. First we must get to the gate and into Tarr-Hostigos. Then we will have all the time we need."

"Did we lose...?"

"Yes, my husband. The Styphoni devils drove us from Ardros Field, but not without paying a stiff butcher's bill." There was a tiny lilt of pride in her voice, but her face was haggard and her blue eyes bloodshot. For the first time, Kalvan had a good idea of just how Rylla would look as an old woman. He only hoped he would live long enough to see it.

"The last I remember: I was surrounded by the enemy. How did I get away?"

"Your Tymannian Guard, they fought like wolves against the Styphoni until your Lifeguard arrived and escorted you to safety."

Kalvan fell back on the litter and rested for a moment. Then he rose up again, his flushed face creased with lines. "Where is my army?"

"Prince Phrames is in command. He has sent the wounded to Hostigos Town, while the rest of the Army is helping the refugees cross Tynn River. The rains have swelled the rivers and only a few fords are passable."

"Any sign of the Grand Host?"

"Not yet. Hestophes is in command of the rearguard. From his most recent report, he has the Grand Host pinned at the Argos Gap. The rains have slowed them, too. Hestophes has promised to delay the Styphoni by at least a moon quarter."

"Good. Hestophes always keeps his promises—usually with interest."

"Now lie down, my love," Rylla said. "You need your rest."

"Yes, yes..."

The next time Kalvan came to he was in his own bedchamber, being attended by Uncle Wolf Tharses. Tharses was busy putting some kind of mustard and cobweb pack on Kalvan's right thigh. The wound itself was wide rather than deep, but he did not like the livid red color along its lips. If only he'd had the time and the means to reinvent penicillin....

After Tharses finished packing the wound, Kalvan asked, "Can I get up now?"

"I would advise against it, Your Majesty. If you move around too much, it will leave you open to an attack by the fester devils."

"That's a chance I'm going to have to take. Where are Rylla and Prince Ptosphes?"

"Down the hall in the audience chamber with Duke Harmakros."

Kalvan asked Tharses for help with pulling his breeches over the bandages and tying up his doublet. Thankfully the Uncle Wolf, a former military man himself, didn't attempt to talk him out of his decision. Kalvan would have liked nothing better than to lie in bed for three or four days, but there were too many things that *had* to be done and most of them should have been done yesterday.

Rylla and Ptosphes were studying the deerskin map of Hostigos, pointing to some place in the Lystra Valley when Kalvan entered the operations room on a chair carried by two of Rylla's Beefeaters.

Rylla turned in surprise. "Should you be leaving your bed already?"

"Tharses brought me this chair. He thinks I should stay in bed, but Styphon's House isn't going to permit me that luxury."

"He is right, my daughter," Prince Ptosphes said. "The enemy draws near."

"How long have I been asleep?"

"Since yesterday," Rylla answered.

Kalvan moaned. "How far away is the Grand Host?"

Harmakros pulled out his pipe and said, "Two, maybe three, days. Hestophes is still holding them at the Argos Gap; we can count on Hestophes to make them pay in blood for every march of Hostigos they cross."

"Good. How many men has Phrames moved across the Tynn River?"

"About half the army, or what's left of it. The rest are with General Hestophes."

"Good."

"I have a question," Ptosphes said, looking a little sheepish. "What happened to the children?"

Kalvan looked questioningly at him for a moment, then it hit him. "The cadets!"

"Yes. The Ruthani children."

"I vaguely remember sending Vanar Halgoth to escort them to safety, as soon as we quit the Ardros Field." There he said it, quit the field. *It didn't hurt that much did it? Yes it did, but you'll get over it.*

"Kalvan, I was wrong," Ptosphes said. "I admit it now. You did a wise and good thing by permitting those children to come into Hostigos. I am proud to have you as my son."

Kalvan didn't know what to say; he felt his face flush. He just nodded his head.

"I went to the Academy just before we left to fight the Grand Host to see them for myself." Ptosphes smiled. "They were so proud to have their Prince visit! Someday they will be good subjects. They marched on their parade ground and did drills in their tiny uniforms! They made me feel good about the future. You were right, they are tomorrow's hope; someday they will be a big part of the legacy of Hostigos."

"What time is it now?" Kalvan asked. To himself, he added, *there won't be much of a legacy unless we get out of here soon.*

"Noon."

"Then we don't have much time left. I expect that Phrames has emptied Hostigos Town of supplies and wagons."

"Yes. He sent Chartiphon to organize the supply train. We've given him all the food, weapons and fireseed we can spare from the castle's storerooms," Ptosphes said. "The defenders will need the remainder."

Tarr-Hostigos was the key to the entire range of the Bald Eagles or the Tyrgros Mountains as they were called here-and-now. There were other passes, like Esdreth Gap, Tynath Gap, Vryllos Gap and Dombra Gap, but only a fool would leave a stronghold as powerful as Tarr-Hostigos at his rear; and neither Soton nor Phidestros would be considered fools in any army Kalvan had ever fought in.

Kalvan's biggest problem would be in transporting as many of the survivors of his army and refugees as he could over the Great King's Highway to the Nyklos Trail and into the Middle Kingdoms. Once he was there he'd worry about the little things such as where they were going to winter, what they were going to eat, and most of all how they were going to re-take Hos-Hostigos. Nothing like being a king without a kingdom—and he'd thought he'd had problems before!

But first things first. "Prince Ptosphes, who are we going to put in charge of Tarr-Hostigos?"

Kalvan saw Rylla's eyes film, then she turned away. Obviously, this was not the first time the subject had been broached.

Prince Ptosphes crossed his arms over his tarnished breastplate and said, "I do not intend to leave Tarr-Hostigos at Arch-Pimp Roxthar's insistence. I myself will defend Tarr-Hostigos against the Styphoni, or anyone else who wants to take it."

"Father, as strong as these walls are, they will not hold forever against so many," Rylla answered, doing her best not to cry. "Nor will Tarr-Hostigos hold all our army, nor feed and water it."

"I am not asking you or anyone else to stay, little one. In fact, I order you and your husband to leave these walls before nightfall."

Kalvan rose from the chair he'd been sitting in. "Prince Ptosphes, it is I as your Great King who order you to leave. There is no need for you to die protecting this castle; there are many who would volunteer to stay and see that these gates never open to Styphon's soldiers."

"I for one," Harmakros said from his chair. He pointed to his stump. "Tharses says that if I ride before another moon this leg will never heal and he will have to remove it at the hip. Let me stay and barter this useless hulk for some of Soton's teeth."

Prince Ptosphes gripped the pommel of his sword so tightly that his knuckles whitened. "He who comes for my Hall, first must take it."

Tears streamed down Rylla's face as she walked over to her father and tugged on his sword arm. He remained as immobile as a statue. "Kalvan, order him to change his mind!"

Kalvan stared into Ptosphes' eyes and realized he'd have a better chance single-handedly moving the solid limestone mountains on which Tarr-Hostigos rested than changing Ptosphes' mind. "I'm sorry, Rylla. It is your father's decision and I'm in no position to make him do anything he doesn't want to do."

"Father, if you stay you will never see your granddaughter take her first steps, lose her teeth, wear her first bonnet—" Rylla stopped when she saw the look of pain on Ptosphes' face.

"I do this so that my granddaughter may live to do all those things."

"Darling, he's right." Kalvan knew the people of Hostigos would do anything to please their beloved prince, even die with him. Not Kalvan, not Chartiphon, not even Harmakros owned their hearts as Ptosphes. Only Rylla—and that was unthinkable. "No, your father is right."

"Then to Hadron with you both!"

"Hush, my daughter. You don't mean that. These are things that must be done. It will give me no pleasure to stall Styphon's Host, if you and Kalvan do not use my gift wisely. You, Kalvan, and Princess Demia are my future. Now, let us get back to work and plan your leave-taking so my death will not be spent in vain."

Tears coursed down Rylla's cheeks. "Father, do not speak as if your death is already ordained! These walls are thick and rest high above where Styphon's soldiers will have to fight. Maybe they will not have the heart to pay the price for their taking."

"Yes, all things are possible," Ptosphes said with a gravity that belied his words. "Take the Old Stone Bridge over the Athan River, then blow it up after you cross. That will slow the Styphoni devils for a few days."

Harmakros added, "I will send engineers to blow all the bridges along the Harph for two hundred marches in either direction. The Harph is still swelled by runoff, enough that the Grand Host will have to use Syrax Ford. That will cost them days in doubling back and forth along the river."

Kalvan watched as everyone got into the discussion of how to delay the Grand Host. Everyone but Rylla; she stood frozen, her face a tragic mask. Neither of them would ever forget this terrible day.

THIRTY-EIGHT

Paratime Police Chief Verkan Vall watched as Fourth Level farms, airports, cities and battles flickered overhead through the paratemporal silver mesh as the conveyer approached Fourth Level Aryan-Transpacific, Kalvan's Time-Line. Maybe Kalvan's Time-Line was a misnomer after the events of the past ten-day. Styphon's House's Grand Host, at the Battle of Ardros Field, had broken the outnumbered army of Hos-Hostigos and possibly killed Kalvan along with his friends and dreams. Dalla had wanted to accompany him, but the ominous silence from the Foundry paratemporal depot convinced him it was too dangerous, the probabilities too fluid, to risk her life.

Verkan had been by Kalvan's side less than a ten-day ago, before he'd lost the Mounted Rifles, and almost his life, to an overwhelming force of Styphon's cavalry. Dalla was calling it Verkan's Greatest Folly; it had almost been his last. His chest ached every time he thought of the gaping wound he'd taken from a point-blank pistol shot by some enraged Harphaxi trooper. Thanks to the miracle of First Level medicine he was feeling as well as ever, with only an occasional nagging chest pain to remind him of his lung wound and the wait for the med team.

Unfortunately, he had more to worry about than the fate of his friends and the dismemberment of Hos-Hostigos and Hostigos Town. The biggest of those headaches was the Dhergabar University Kalvan Study Team caught in the rout of the Hostigi army. Like all outtime researchers, they worked under the Paratime Police umbrella. That might not be enough to protect them on the kind of Fourth Level time-line where civilians were likely to end up a part of the body count when a victorious army swept through hostile territory.

The entire University Team was unaccounted for and every casualty among them would be a gift to the Opposition Party.

Kalvan would have to fight his own battles for a while, against much longer odds than before. It would take all of Kalvan's skill, as well as luck, to save his life and Queen Rylla's, never mind saving his empire.

Already the Grand Host's cavalry scouts had raided almost to the outskirts of Hostigos Town. Its main body could hardly be more than a day or two behind. One of Kalvan castellans might be able to hold Tarr-Hostigos for a few days. If the Grand Host had to stop and lay siege to the castle, Kalvan still might escape. While he would never rule a kingdom again, he and Rylla could flee westward to sell the services of their army in the Middle Kingdoms.

The conveyer dome shimmered into material existence inside the Foundry basement. The sensors read that it was empty of life and everything was in its place. Nevertheless, Verkan checked his personal equipment, pulled his pistol out of his sash and headed for the hatch. Somehow four Paracops reached it before him, all with drawn pistols and palmed First Level sigma-ray needlers.

"Sorry, Chief," Kostran Garth said. He didn't sound sorry. Garth was his brother-in-law, and one of a handful of good friends and completely reliable Paracops. Like Skordran Kirv, Andron Veral and Ranthar Jard. Verkan looked behind and sighed. The other eight men of his personal guard had closed tightly around him from the rear. Swaddled in bodyguards like a baby in cloth, Verkan stepped out into a large basement, where there was a large wall screen at one end showing an overhead of Hostigos Town. The streets were uncharacteristically empty and Verkan could see no sign of either the Hostigi army or Styphon's Grand Host. The rest of the conveyer-load of Paracops followed, lugging sensor gear or pushing anti-grav lifter pallets to ferry the dead.

The room before them held a desk, some First Level monitoring equipment, racks of muskets, barrels of unopened fireseed and hundreds of baskets of barley and corn. No sign of the small Hostigos Paratime Police garrison, five men—including his friend, Inspector Skordran Kirv.

No good to anybody except maybe the Grand Host, was Verkan's thought as he strode across the room. Like the other Paracops, he held a flintlock pistol nearly two feet long, loaded and cocked. On his head he wore a high-combed morion helmet; his clothes were a sleeveless buff jack, dark blue breeches, a bright blue sash, and thigh-high boots. Nobody from Kalvan's Time-Line would have thought him anything but a Hostigi light cavalry officer—"General Verkan of the Hostigos Mounted Rifles, at your service, sir."

He opened the keyed magnetic lock to the door that led to the Royal Foundry of Hos-Hostigos, stepped back, let the four point men go first, then followed at their hand signals of "All clear."

The door was intact, as he had expected. Under local oak planking, it had a collapsed-nickel core. Nothing local could dent that, not even a two-hundred-pound iron ball from a big bombard. The door at the other end of the short stone stairway was similarly protected. It opened to the inside to show a shifting pile of stones, timber and metal rubble. While Paracops skipped out of the way, stones and timbers tumbled down the stairwell. Suddenly patches of sunshine were breaking through the upended timbers. Outside he could hear the chirping of birds, but no human noise.

The rubble was a nuisance, but nothing that could stop five determined Paracops. So where were they?

"Step back, Chief," one of his protectors ordered.

The debris was quickly shifted aside and a passage was made through the wreckage into the badly damaged Foundry. Forges were overturned and big anvils squatted like toadstools amongst the rubble. Two walls were gone and the roof was mostly on the floor. The Paratime Police, with guns drawn, carefully navigated their way out of the Foundry into the courtyard.

Nothing else in sight had been as lucky. The main storerooms had all been demolished, as if someone had set charges—maybe Kirv. *Had things gotten that bad?* Some had collapsed. Most of the outer buildings also showed battle scars, and bodies lay everywhere. A flock of birds, mostly ravens and vultures, and one eagle, squawked angrily and glided into the air, only to hover over their heads.

The Study Team's headquarters had fallen in on itself, the upper floor and roof gone. Not even a slight wisp of smoke still rose from their former quarters. That confirmed Verkan's guess that the attack had come at least two days before. There didn't appear to be any survivors. The dead had already been stripped, not only of valuables and weapons, but their armor as well. The birds had removed eyes and other soft tissue.

Several of the dead still wore the red cloaks of Styphon's Own Guard; no one wanted those telling garments, although their silvered armor was fair game.

"Too many tourists," a Paracop said.

Verkan nodded. The University had insisted on doing its own study of Kalvan's Time-Line. Short of imposing quarantine, there'd been no way to stop them. For a moment Verkan wished himself back as Chief's Special Assistant, where he could do the sensible thing without having a dozen political potentates baying at his door.

The Paracops spread out, leapfrogging from building to building, covering one another until they'd reached the edge of the Foundry on all sides. Then they posted sentries, sent a miniature sky-eye to hover a thousand feet up and began the grisly task of recovering the bodies.

Verkan turned over the nearest civilian casualty with his sword. It was the Team's expert on pre-mechanical sociology, Professor Lathor Karv. He had a gaping hole in his forehead and several stab wounds in his torso, but no signs of torture.

First good news all day.

No signs of torture meant that none of Archpriest Roxthar's 'Holy' Investigators had ridden with the cavalry, or not enough to conduct one of the torture fests they called an Investigation. Hypno-mech conditioning or not, it was asking a lot of anyone to resist the kind of torture the Investigators handed out. Not that they were as efficient as the Second Level priests of Shpeegar or some Europo-American secret police agencies, but they would improve with time and practice. The Grand Host's victory had bought them the time, and Roxthar's fanatical determination to find and extirpate heresy everywhere would guarantee the practice.

"Chief—over here!"

Verkan walked back to the ruined manor that had served as the Foundry's headquarters. One of the men was dragging out a horribly mutilated body in what appeared to be the remains of a white robe.

"The scavengers didn't like this one at all!"

"It looks like one of Roxthar's Investigators. Can you find the killing wound?"

"No. The body's all sliced up—payback. I guess word about the Investigation has spread throughout Hos-Hostigos."

"Like a foul odor," Kostran Garth added.

Of the sixty-odd bodies in the open, some were here-and-now Foundry workers; others house servants—the proverbial innocent bystanders. About thirty were mercenaries or undercover Paracops, the rest members of the University Team.

'Fiasco' is a mild term for this was Verkan's thought. *Nobody is going to be happy about it.*

"Chief!" Kostran called. He ran up and lowered his voice. We've found Inspector Kirv. Over here by the manor fireplace."

Nobody, starting with me.

Kirv's dead mouth was twisted into the parody of a smile, but it looked as if he'd fought as well as he'd lived. Five troopers in yellow Harphaxi sashes and lead-splattered back-and-breasts lay dead and bloody around him.

Verkan cursed out loud. There went an old friend and one of the few Paracops he could still trust absolutely.

The lifter teams started loading bodies for shipment back to First Level, while the rest began the house-to-house (or ruin-to-ruin) search. In spite of the danger from smoldering embers and falling beams, they turned up twelve more Paratimer bodies, three of them Paracops. Seven skeletons too badly burned for field identification made the last load before the conveyer headed back to Fifth Level. Paratime Police Fifth Level HQ had a full-medtech team on standby, for DNA identification.

Verkan spent most of the time before the conveyer's return wandering aimlessly among the manor ruins. Every Paracop on this team knew when to steer clear of the Chief, who knew he was being guarded but so tactfully that he couldn't complain.

One thought dominated Verkan's mind. He'd thought he had a crisis, with an alliance of Opposition Party chiefs and outtime traders after his scalp over the anticipated closing of Fourth Level Europo-American. He had a good case—too many nuclear, biological and chemical weapons in the hands of national and rogue governments. Still he and Dalla would live through it, even if he couldn't persuade anyone else to shut that profitable subsector down.

Kalvan and Rylla were running for their lives, which might not be very long if his castellans couldn't hold Tarr-Hostigos for at least a few days.

As the day wore on, Verkan began to hope that the Grand Host's scouts would reappear. It was out of the question to seek the main body and tear it apart with First Level weapons. A few hundred dead cavalry troopers, however, could be labeled 'non-contaminating self-defense' in an Incident Report. Their demise would make the Grand Host only a little less strong but a lot more cautious.

Or it might make people genuinely believe that demons fought for Kalvan, and create enthusiastic support for Roxthar's fifty-times-cursed Investigation! That was the problem with contamination—you couldn't control how people would interpret your intervention. Good Paracops always remembered that.

Verkan Vall gritted his teeth and decided to be a good Paracop again. He hoped his present set of teeth would survive the experience!

"Vall?"

He started to glare at the interruption, and then recognized Kostran. The conveyer must have returned with the lab test results—although from the look on Kostran's face, he was not the bearer of good news.

"What are the autopsy results?"

"No Police survivors."

"Damn this bloody Styphon's House crowd! This must have happened fast, or Kirv wouldn't have been caught out in the open like this…."

"I'm sorry, if that helps any," Kostran said.

"Some. Better security would have helped more. Dralm-damnit, we should have had it!"

"By Xipph's mandibles, Chief, you did all you could!" He added several more curses from a particularly vile Second Level timeline where spiders and beetles were sacred fetishes. "The damned Study Team sabotaged every security measure you and Kirv tried to establish. Ten good Paracops died trying to defend this cock-up!"

"The Study Team paid for it, too." But keeping that from happening was ultimately the Chief's responsibility. *My* responsibility. Verkan managed a wry grin. "Wasn't it Kalvan's own Great King Truman who said, 'The buck stops here?'"

The grin faded, but Verkan managed not to sigh. "All right. Who else among the Study Team did the lab find?"

"Lathor Karv and Sankar Trav, the Team medic."

"We found Varnath Lala and Voldon Andar. That leaves Danar Sirna, Gorath Tran and Aranth Saln unaccounted for." The two Paracops' eyes met. If the missing people were prisoners, they were probably on their way into the hands of the Investigation. Then they'd soon wish they had burned to death instead.

Kostran whistled. "Gorath Tran, the nervous Assistant Director. Too slight for the slave auction block. Maybe he got lucky and bugged out with Kalvan's refugees."

"Danar Sirna. Doctoral candidate in outtime history?" Verkan asked.

Kostran nodded. "Right. Tall woman, good figure, auburn hair. The one Eldra identified as Tharn's patsy."

"Wish her better luck in her next incarnation," Verkan stated. "The soldiers here-and-now have rough-and-ready notions about dealing with female enemy captives. What about Aranth Saln?"

"He's ex-Strike Force, one of the few Team people with survival skills. He was their expert on pre-mechanical military science." Kostran hesitated. "I wonder if he was forced to try putting some of his skills into practice?"

"You mean, take an unscheduled field sabbatical?"

"Exactly. His cover is an artillery officer from Hos-Agrys and you can bet he won't break it by accident. If he catches Phidestros' eye, he may even be safe from the Investigation."

The possibly of owing anything to the man principally responsible for Kalvan's defeat rubbed Verkan the wrong way. Still, if Aranth had survived and was masquerading as a native, Verkan could only wish him luck.

It was time to return to Fifth Level Police Terminal, Kalvan's Time-Line Depot to try and make sense out of this mess. No time for him to resume his cover as General Verkan; he'd have his Paratime HQ brain trust figure out a cover story that would convince Kalvan, if and when he had time to visit here again. With the political fallout this debacle threatened, it might be a while.

He suspected Kalvan would be so busy he wouldn't have time to send out a search party for missing officers, even friends. He wondered how Tortha was doing. *Well, the old dog was a survivor and if anyone could come out of this disaster smelling like a rose in a manure pile, it was ex-Paratime Police Chief Tortha Karf.*

THIRTY-NINE

I

Word of Great King Kalvan's defeat and expulsion from Hos-Hostigos reached Agrys City by Styphon's relay riders four days after Kalvan's army was defeated at Ardros Field. It was trumpeted at the High Temple of Styphon's House in Agrys City as a great victory for Styphon and his followers. "The Daemon Kalvan is vanquished! Praise Styphon the True God!"

Crowds filled the streets, some in jubilation for the True God's victory, but most in anger or fear that an army was already on its way to punish Hos-Agrys for not contributing to the Grand Host. Others passed on rumors about the Investigation, which so angered the crowds that two of Styphon's House's lower priests in white robes were beaten to death in the city streets and a stone and brick throwing mob attempted to break into Styphon's House's Great Temple. In response Styphon's Own Guard had to post armed guards on the Great Temple both day and night.

After threats of retaliation against the High Temple of Dralm, Lord Vythos, who was the town's richest merchant and a follower of Dralm, put his personal guardsmen to watch the Temple portals. Inside the High Temple the priests were virtual prisoners as the city seethed with anger and fear. Riots and fights in the taverns and streets of Agrys City were a common occurrence; the followers of Styphon wore red armbands of Primacy, while the Dralm and Kalvan sympathizers wore blue. The underpaid and undersized City Watch was unable to control the crowds or stop the looting.

News from Hos-Hostigos was sporadic and often conflicting—at first, the Daemon was dead, next he had escaped the Grand Host, then was said to be in exile. Other stories had him in Greffa assembling an army with the aid of King Theovacar, or returning to the Cold Lands for divine assistance.

Great King Demistophon was said to be hiding in the palace basement, for fear of Styphon's House's retribution. When the rioting got serious and spread to King's Island, Demistophon moved into Tarr-Agrys and called out the army, ordering a sunset to dawn curfew.

Xentos was praying in the rear chapel when he received word that a delegate from the League of Dralm had come for a conference with the Council of Dralm. Ever since Styphon's House had bandied the account of Kalvan's defeat, he'd been heartsick. In his mind he could already envision the tortured bodies of Kalvan, Rylla and their tiny daughter, Demia, named after Rylla's beautiful mother, who had been the love of his life. Had he been prince, she would have been his wife, not Prince Ptosphes'. Rylla was the very image of her mother which was why they all had spoiled and protected her.

Xentos had his first spiritual crisis when Demia and her unborn son died in childbirth. Prayer and fasting had cured him of his soul sickness and given his faith a real strength, a resiliency he prayed would sustain him through this latest crisis and the doubts that assailed him. *Was it possible all this would have been averted if he'd supported Kalvan instead of putting the Temple ahead of his friends and home?* He would never know the answer to that question, but he was sure that he would think about it many times before he arrived at Dralm's Sky-Palace.

There was a hesitant knock at the door. "There's a visitor to see you, Primate."

"Bid him enter."

A young and very big man, wearing his dusty riding cloak and riding boots, came stomping into his private chamber. His eyes blazed and his huge frame shook with controlled fury.

"Who are you?" Xentos demanded, with all the authority of his office. He asked knowing full well no enemy of the Temple would ever be granted entrance to the High Temple unless things were so bad that the Styphoni had breached the temple gates.

"Duke Mnestros of Eubros, Your Sanctity."

Xentos' memory identified the heir of Eubros at once. The son of Prince Thykarses, a young hothead who loved to fight and wench, and showed little reverence to the Temple of Dralm. "You're the one who accompanied Kalvan's Army to the Trygath in violation of the Covenant of Dralm!"

Mnestros sneered. "I was there as a volunteer. If you have a complaint to make, tell it to the League Council, I don't expect they'll be very interested at the moment."

Xentos looked away; the boy was right. After Kalvan's defeat, there was little stomach for the Covenant in Hos-Agrys and some were saying the strictures of it had aided Styphon's House's conquest of Hos-Hostigos.

"What you don't know is that I have just returned from Hostigos where I was fighting alongside your friends and overlord against the godless Styphoni."

"This is news to me! How are Ptosphes and Rylla?"

"Ptosphes is well, organizing the defense of Tarr-Hostigos against the Grand Host; I would imagine the Grand Host's siege guns will be at the walls within a few days."

Xentos winced. "How are Rylla and Kalvan?"

"They are fleeing Hos-Hostigos with the remnants of the Hostigos Army. Hostigos is a wasteland. Archpriest Roxthar and his Investigators are tilling the soil of Hostigos with the blood and bodies of its people. None are exempt—from the youngest child to the oldest crone. The Arch-Fiend Roxthar is determined to root out every trace of Kalvan and Dralm from every Princedom in the former Kingdom of Hos-Hostigos. And from all I saw, he is achieving his heart's desire."

Xentos looked down at the stone floor. "Why have you come to see me?"

Mnestros held up a huge hand showing all his fingers. "First, I want you to declare a Ban on Styphon's House. Next," he ticked off, "I want you to put the full weight of the Temple behind your friend, Kalvan. Then I want you to call a crusade to drive Styphon's wolves from Hostigos. Then, I want you to empower the League of Dralm—"

"Enough! You speak like one of the City's rabble-rousers. If I were to do as you asked, Great King Demistophon would have the High Temple walls pulled down around my ears!"

"Primate, listen to me! Right now if we act quickly we can hit the Styphoni while they are at their weakest, attacking Kalvan. We could separate the serpent's body from its head, and with its body gone—Balph is ours!"

Such is the rashness of youth, thought Xentos, *act now, think later.* It would take a moon or two, at least, to raise a sizable army and meanwhile the Grand Host would have Kalvan in its grasp, and his army wiped out. Then this victorious army would destroy the untested troops of Hos-Agrys. Those who weren't killed would scatter with Styphon's House's blessing. Then the Grand Host would seize Agrys City and the High Temple of Dralm.

"It is too late, young duke. The Styphoni are already victorious. Now, we must prepare for the defense of the true faith of Allfather Dralm, the God of Peace. In the words of King Kalvan, "The best offense is a good defense."

Duke Mnestros shook his head. "You have a fine way of twisting words, priest. But you know little of warfare, or of Styphon's House. They plan to make slaves of all of us and you and your kind only prepare their siege train."

Xentos felt the old pressure inside his head grow. "I suggest you leave this temple, boy, before I have to call the guards and have you pitched out by your ears!"

Mnestros laughed. "Those old men you call guards would have Hadron's own time pitching me anywhere, priest! I will leave now before I say things that may cause my father pain upon their retelling. But mark my words, the Temple of Dralm will rue the day it turned its back on Kalvan, whose only sin was that he was the Temple's greatest champion!"

Mnestros spat on the floor, spun around and stalked out of the chamber.

The moment the door closed half a dozen lower priests scurried into the chamber asking if Xentos was all right. "I don't know. We have either done what was wise, or we have committed the gravest error in the history of the Temple. Only time will tell."

The priests looked at him in confusion.

Highpriest Davros, who must have been waiting outside the door, entered saying, "We have only done what we must to preserve the Allfather's High Temple."

Xentos nodded, but could not still the voice asking in the back on his head: *But have we done what we must to preserve Dralm's people?* He had no answer to that question, most especially for the faithful of Hos-Hostigos.

FORTY

I

The climb to the gun platform on top of the north tower of Tarr-Hostigos left Prince Ptosphes unpleasantly short of breath. Old age had been pursuing him for a long time. Now it had finally caught him. Under other circumstances he would have been angry at the prospect of not seeing his grandchildren grow up, but that matter had been taken care of a moon quarter ago at Ardros Field.

"Should we summon an Uncle Wolf for you, my Prince?" the gun captain asked.

Ptosphes shook his head. "No. Just let me sit down and catch my wind."

He lowered himself onto an upended fireseed barrel and was about to light his pipe when he remembered what he was sitting on. The gunners and sentries, he noticed, had returned to their work as soon as they knew he didn't need their help.

Good men, and more than ever a pity that they had to stand here and face certain death even if most of them were, like him, a bit long in the tooth. At least they were the last good men he'd be leading to their doom. No more battles like Tenabra, to haunt him during the long winter nights. Kalvan wouldn't be so lucky; he would just have to endure Rylla's tongue on the subject, as Ptosphes had endured Demia's.

Ptosphes chuckled, as he thought of Rylla's mother for the first time in nearly a moon. Rylla had much of her mother in her; the great beauty, the strengths, the tongue and temper. Ptosphes remembered Demia asking (at the top of her lungs) whether he was afraid of war too much to hold even the little Princedom of Hostigos. He hadn't been afraid of a war with Nostor, Sask or Beshta; only afraid for his vassals, outnumbered and out-gunned by ambitious neighbors on every border.

Well, Demia had been right in a way. He would have lost everything to Gormoth of Nostor if the gods hadn't sent Kalvan. *Why, then, have those same gods turned their faces away when I needed their help most?* What had he or Kalvan done to earn their wrath?

Great Dralm, I ask nothing for myself. Let your wrath fall on me, and spare Kalvan, Rylla and my granddaughter Demia.

Ptosphes's breath came more easily now, and he badly wanted that pipe. He rose and was turning toward the stairs when he saw a horseman riding uphill toward the castle. He wore armor but no helmet, and a sash with Prince Phrames' colors. Probably one of Phrames' loyal Beshtans.

"Ahooo! Prince Ptosphes! I am Captain Jarask. Prince Phrames has sent me back to warn you. The Styphoni are on the march once more. Their scouts are barely a candle from Hostigos Town!"

"Thank you, and carry my thanks to Prince Phrames." *So the siege begins even sooner than we expected.*

The trooper made no move to turn his mount; Ptosphes glared down at him. "No, you can't come into the castle. Your Prince and your Great King need you more than I do."

"Prince—"

"Now, Dralm-damn you, turn that horse around and get it moving! If you're not gone before I count to ten you'll be the first casualty of the siege of Tarr-Hostigos."

Ptosphes drew his pistol but his roar had already startled the horse into movement. It whickered and suddenly wheeled, nearly losing its footing on the rocky apron, then broke into a canter. By the time Ptosphes had counted to five, the Captain was out of pistol range. He was still looking back at the castle. Ptosphes hoped he would turn around and look where he was going before he rode off the side of the road and down the hill.

Once his pipe was drawing well, Ptosphes walked around the walls to where he had a good view to the southeast. That was the likely direction for the Grand Host; or at least where he hoped most to see them. Anyplace else would mean they had a too-godless-good chance of cutting off at least Kalvan's rearguard.

The southwest was empty of smoke clouds, and so were all the other directions. Were the Styphoni advancing along roads where there was nothing left that even a fanatical believer would consider worth burning? Or was the Grand Host already thinking of having roofs over their heads and food in their bellies during the siege?

Tarr-Hostigos should have a bit of time before its walls *had* to be kept manned until the Styphoni stormed them. Plenty of time for what Ptosphes intended.

He pointed the stem of his pipe at the nearest sentry. "Take a message to Captain-General Harmakros. Summon everyone in the castle, except the sentries, to the outer courtyard."

"Every—?" the man began, and then broke off at Ptosphes' look. "Everyone. Captain-General Harmakros, too."

"Yes, my Prince."

The soldier hurried off, as if he wanted to open the distance between himself and his Prince before Ptosphes showed any more signs of madness.

Ptosphes followed at a more leisurely pace.

II

By the time the garrison was gathered in the outer courtyard, the sun was high overhead. Even the twenty-foot walls cast short shadows. Ptosphes sweated in his armor, wishing the laggards would hurry, and rested his hand on the hilt of his sword. It was a newly forged Kalvan-style rapier, balanced for fighting on foot but quite long enough for his purposes now. The Great Sword of Hostigos, which he'd belted on the day he was proclaimed Prince, was on its way westward with Kalvan and Rylla. His grandson would need that Sword some day, when he ruled a realm so huge that Old Hostigos would barely rank as a respectable Princedom.

If the gods are merciful.

Ptosphes saw no more men joining the crowd. He drew the sword and raised it overhead in both hands. Sunlight blazed from the steel.

"Men of Hostigos. You all know why you are here. You all were told, when you offered to hold Tarr-Hostigos until our Great King and his family might reach safety. Every one of you has already earned honor in the eyes of Allfather Dralm, Galzar Wolfhead and the other true gods, and the gratitude of your Prince and Great King and the goodwill of your comrades.

"Styphon's Grand Host is approaching faster than we thought. Within a half-candle or less, this castle will be surrounded by the mightiest army in the history of the Great Kingdoms. For every one of us, there will be a hundred of the enemy. When they camp, a mouse won't be getting out of this castle.

"Any man who wants to leave can still do so. I'll say nothing against him nor let anyone else say a word. He'll have to hurry to catch up with our rear-guard before nightfall, but there's still an open road for any who wants to take it." He pointed toward the castle gate with his sword.

"For those who stay, you all know what kind of quarter Styphon's dogs gave us at Ardros. The lucky ones will have a quick death. The rest will have an appointment with Roxthar's Unholy Investigation."

A few hollow laughs sounded from the ranks; most faces were set and pale. All knew what had happened to the Hostigi prisoners after Ardros Field; almost all had lost kin or friends in that butchery. Most of the prisoners not slaughtered outright were in the hands of the Investigation, doubtless envying their dead comrades.

Ptosphes lowered his sword and strode to the door of the woodshed on one side of the courtyard. Then he drew a line with the sword's point—like the one in the story Kalvan had told him about when he was in his cups one night—through the dirt and straw covering the flagstones of the courtyard, from the woodshed to the blacksmith's forge on the other side. He then took a deep breath, sheathed his sword, and turned to face his men.

"All who want to stay cross over this line and join me. Those who want to die somewhere else—stay where you are!"

Silence. Ptosphes could hear the stamping of horses from the stables on the far side of the courtyard. An unnaturally complete silence to be hanging over five hundred men. No one coughed, no one shuffled his feet. Ptosphes could have sworn some had ceased to breathe.

A thickset man in battered armor pushed his way from the rear into the open. Ptosphes tried not to stare too hard. It was Vurth.

Vurth, the peasant who'd been Kalvan's first host in this land, who devoted his life and his family's to Kalvan's fighting skill. His son-in-law, Xykos, was Captain of Rylla's Own Guard. It was he who'd sent word of the Nostori raiders to Tarr-Hostigos, so that Rylla could lead out the cavalry who cut off the raiders and found Kalvan.

Vurth, a peasant who might really be called Dralm's first chosen tool for bringing about everything which had happened since that spring night almost four years ago. Ptosphes wondered briefly what Primate Xentos would have to say about the theological propriety of that notion—if presiding over the squabbles of the Council of Dralm in far-off Agrys City left him any time for such matters.

I'd like to be in Dralm's Great Hall when Xentos has to explain to the Allfather why the Council and League of Dralm sent only words of condolence, instead of soldiers and muskets, to aid those who fought His battles against Styphon.

Ptosphes examined the gray-haired peasant. His clothes and face were caked with mud and powder smoke, one shoulder was bandaged and he limped. He wore the breastplate of some Harphaxi nobleman, once etched and gilded, now hacked and tarnished, over his homespun smock. On his head was a battered morion helmet, on his feet cavalry boots from two different corpses. He still carried the Nostori cavalryman's silver-butted musketoon he'd acquired the night of Kalvan's coming, and both it and the horn powder flask at his belt were clean.

"First Prince, Captain-General Harmakros, people," Vurth began. "This isn't really a Council, so maybe I don't have the right to start off, as if I was

Speaker for the Peasants like Phosg, may Dralm protect him. I think I've a right to be heard, though."

Ptosphes would have cut down anyone who disagreed. The men saw this, and Vurth went on.

"Prince, most of us here either can't run, don't want to run or don't have anywhere to run to. My farm has burned, my wife is dead and one son too. The other son's off with King Kalvan, in the Royal Dragoons, and my son-in-law Xykos is Captain of Queen Rylla's Beefeaters. Dralm keep all the daughters who ran off with mercenaries.

"Styphon's House has taken or chased off everything I had except my life. All I want to do with what's left of it is kill Styphon's dogs until they kill me. I'm too old to go climbing trees or hide in caves like a thief. I'd rather sit here and kill the bastards in comfort!"

Vurth shouldered his musketoon and stepped forward across the line before anyone could cheer.

Ptosphes felt his eyes burn and quickly blinked back the threatening tears. He stepped up beside Vurth and put his arm around the peasant's shoulders. Any land that bore men like these would be barren ground indeed for Styphon's House. Such men could be killed; they could not be frightened.

Harmakros' voice cut through the new silence.

"Lift that litter, you fools! You don't have to stay yourselves!"

The bearers' reply was nearly inaudible and totally disrespectful. They had the Captain-General across the line before Ptosphes stopped grinning.

Another man stepped out, then two more, then five, then a band of ten, then a band too numerous to count, and after that it was a steady stream.

Ptosphes saw one gray-haired man telling a club-footed boy no more than ten to stand where he was, then step out himself. The boy looked sullenly after his grandfather until he was sure the man couldn't see him, then slipped across the line.

Ptosphes turned his back on the men. He didn't want them to see his face until he could command it as a captain and a Prince ought to.

By the time he turned around, the space on the other side of the line was empty.

Ptosphes ran his eyes over the garrison, with the care of a man trained at the quick counting of large masses of men. There'd been just over eight hundred before. No doubt a few had slipped off, perhaps as many as a man could count on his fingers and toes. Call it seven hundred and eighty left behind, quite enough to do all the work Styphon's Grand Host would allow.

Ptosphes was fumbling for words of thanks when a sentry with one of Kalvan's farseers on the keep tower shouted. "Prince Ptosphes! Enemy scouts in Hostigos Town! On the Great Kings Highway, cavalry with two guns."

Guns up with the scouts meant they had orders to fight instead of hit and run. Who would have such orders? Perhaps the Zarthani Knights…

Ptosphes swallowed; the lump in his throat twitched but remained where it was. "What colors?" he managed to shout.

"Great King Cleitharses and a mercenary company's. Looks like a rearing white horse on a blue field."

The lump shrank. Regulars wouldn't burn a town they expected to provide them with dry beds and hot food, unless they had other orders—nor would they let mercenaries. Such orders might not be obeyed, either, unless the man who gave them was watching.

With Grand Butcher Soton not up yet and Phidestros himself—although a mercenary—the commander of a Great King's army, there might be no such man here. If Soton arrived after the Grand Host's advance guard had settled in well, making mercenaries in another king's pay burn their own shelter and food was a task Ptosphes wouldn't wish even on Soton.

FORTY-ONE

I

The Holy Investigator's Inquiry Chamber, a former smokehouse outside the burned-out shell of a Hostigi farm, was unnaturally quiet, which worried Investigator Kynnos far more than the usual cries and sobs that had poured out of the thin walls when he had arrived late last night. Even the slave pens, filled now with hundreds of crowded peasants, were still. Only the occasional cry of a babe broke the early morning stillness.

He remembered some Hostigi merchant asking him, as he ransacked the man's house, what made one Hostigi a slave, while his neighbor was targeted for the Investigation. "The possession of the heretic's image," had been his answer. "But every house and hut in Hostigos has images of Allfather Dralm!" "Yes, but mercy is given to those who can buy their freedom."

Kynnos had left that household with three gold rings, two silver coins and a tiny golden image of Dralm that he kept safely tucked into his boot. As soon as he was safely alone, he would start a fire and melt it down.

Kynnos had shared half his booty, except the golden image, with the Guard Captain. They had then escorted the merchant and his family to the slave pens. The last thing they wanted was the merchant to talk about he gold he'd spent to save his miserable hide under one of the Upper Investigator's

'Blades of Truth'—especially if that Investigator turned out to be His Holiness, Archpriest Roxthar! Killing the merchant outright would have been easiest, but Roxthar frowned on killing peasants and commoners before they had been judged by the Investigation. And no one, least of all Kynnos, wanted the Holy Investigator's eye turned in their direction—no indeed!

Which was why he'd asked the Guard Captain to come with him, while he told Archpriest Roxthar about the botched takeover of the Royal Foundry. The Captain had laughed in his face. "You tell the Holy Butcher whatever you want, but leave my name out of it. Or taste my sword, underpriest!"

Kynnos rued the day he joined the Investigation. Like most underpriests new to Balph he had not liked what he had found upon his arrival at the Holy City: too many underpriests competing for too few jobs, too many upper-priests who viewed their underlings as little more than personal servants and too many older highpriests. He hadn't joined the Temple to fetch and carry. Since childhood he'd dreamed of becoming a highpriest with his own retinue and large estate.

Many underpriests were able to curry favor with one of the highpriests, or even an archpriest, and use the favor to rise through the Temple hierarchy. He was not so blessed. His wife blamed this on his lack of ambition; yet how could he earn respect from those above him if all they saw was his arse as he scraped and bowed?

Kynnos missed those carefree days of visiting the Great Temple of Styphon in Balph, watching the dignitaries and every so often being ordered to run an errand, usually to inform some mistress or wife that some Sanctity or other was delayed. Then Archpriest Roxthar had begun his Investigation of corruption within Styphon's House. In the early days, the Investigation had been exciting, pulling superiors from their night chambers and torturing them over heresies for which, not surprisingly, they all were found guilty. There were few believers of Styphon, even amongst the most rabid of the Investigators, so why should highpriests be any different? Along the way, he'd been able to pocket gold coins and other valuables, some from bribes, others 'discovered' during the course of the Investigation.

What profit was to be found in the hovels of Hostigi peasants, for Styphon's sake? The merchant had provided his first good haul since he'd arrived in Hostigos.

A moon quarter ago, he had taken a wound in the arm from a knife thrust during the fight at the foundry, saw his superior killed, been lost in the burning wasteland of Hostigos and finally, after days of wandering through this deserted land, located the Holy Investigator at this blasted ruin of a farm. The truth was that none of the party, including the Guardsmen, had wanted to return to face Roxthar's wrath. When he had awoken in the morning, it was to learn that all had fled—leaving him to face the Investigator with their lone, crazed prisoner. He would not have been surprised had the madman turned into a bat and flown away during the night with the rest of them, leaving him alone to face the Holy Investigator.

In the false kingdom of Hos-Hostigos without the Inner Circle to distract him and rein in his powers, Roxthar was like a blood-crazed wolf loosed upon the countryside. Styphon's Temple Guard was in mercenary heaven with whole towns to loot, ravage and pillage with no accountability; it was Styphon's Own Work, as Roxthar blessed it! Kynnos found little sport in murdering helpless serfs and freedmen, or the drabs they were married to. Not for a few coppers and bits of colored glass.

Any comely wench the Investigation happened upon too quickly disappeared into the clutches of Styphon's Own Guard. It was Balph all over again, only bloodier and dirtier and far less profitable! When he'd first heard about the expedition to Hos-Hostigos, he'd dreamed of untold riches and unheralded glory. Instead, he was sleeping in wet byres and herding frightened peasants. The only profit in this accursed land—unless a miracle occurred and Kalvan left his paychests in Hostigos Town—was in the slave pens. Already the Five Kingdoms' slave dealers were gathering, like the birds and flies above the dead littering Ardros Field, as they made their way to Hostigos Town. And none of that gold would ever weigh down his purse.

The ambush of the Hostigos Foundry had been the biggest disaster of all. Roxthar had ordered them to take it at night before the Grand Host arrived; the Holy Investigator was worried that Grand Captain-General Phidestros would reach it first and take the Hostigi gunners captive and protect them from the Investigation. The plan had been that Kynnos and Gyff were to lead an attack on the Foundry under the cover of night and take them all prisoners, whereupon Roxthar would Investigate all those involved with the Daemon Kalvan's impious arts.

Unfortunately, the Foundry had been well guarded and even better booby-trapped, for when they went to fire the outbuildings many of them exploded or burned as if covered in pitch. Investigator Gyff had been killed while capturing the main outbuilding along with several Guardsmen and mercenaries. Who had expected outlanders to fight so fiercely? As the only surviving Investigator he knew the blame for this misadventure would fall upon his head.

He hadn't had a good night's sleep for almost a moon quarter. Now his sliced arm burned so badly he couldn't sleep even were he to be cradled in Styphon's Own Hand!

Roxthar's frightened little scribe, Myros, came out of the shed, saying, "The Holy Investigator will see you now, Investigator Kynnos."

Roxthar held court in the darkest corner of the shack, where lay blackness so dark even the flickering candlelight couldn't pierce it. The reason for the quiet was apparent in the broken body lying on the floor, the back encrusted with gore.

"Where have you been?" Roxthar asked. "Does it take six nights to bring back a few prisoners?"

Kynnos cringed. "Your Holiness, the Hostigi put up a fierce resistance, killing Investigator Gyff and many of our party. They used demonic arts to fire their own buildings and thus protect their secrets. I was bitten in the arm by one of their devils!"

He pulled up his robe to show his fiery knife wound, which now looked as if the Hadron's Hounds had been chewing upon it.

"The Daemon's work!"

"Yes," said a relieved Kynnos, knowing he'd chosen the right scapegoat. "The Royal Foundry was a veritable nest of unclean beings. They fought with great cunning and supernatural strength, unlike any creatures of this world. I fear they also put a spell upon us so that we could not find our way in this realm of the damned."

"Unclean beings, truly. What about the women?"

"Even the women were possessed, Holy Investigator. Several of them flew up into the air and disappeared! They are all gone, as well."

"Witchcraft, too! It is worse than I feared. The Daemon's foul work has infected all the people in Hos-Hostigos. Our work here will take a long time. Baron Sthentros is right, the Daemon who calls himself Kalvan has taken captive the very spirits of the people of the False Kingdom of Hos-Hostigos'."

"We only took one man captive—all the rest are dead. Or disappeared!"

"A captive. Excellent, is he one of Kalvan's lesser demons?"

Kynnos tried to envision the pathetic Gorath Tran, as he called himself, as a demon and found it difficult. The poor Zygrosi was so addled he'd even begun to believe he was one of Kalvan's devils, threatening his captors with dire words about flying boats with lights and pistols that spit bullets as small as needles.

Since Kynnos was having such great success laying all his ills at Kalvan's feet, he was not inclined to abandon this approach. "Yes, he is one of Kalvan's lesser devils. He speaks in strange tongues and talks of all manner of demonic devices. He is an artificer out of Regwarn's Caverns. I will bring him to your Chamber for Investigation."

Roxthar, as he made washing motions with his hands, gave him a smile that chilled him to the bone. "At last, one of Kalvan's lesser demons to question. You have done well, Kynnos."

He nodded, not daring to speak. While Kynnos was not happy to be in Hostigos, it was much safer to be one of the Investigators than among the investigated—as all those Hostigi unfortunates were learning to their sorrow.

"Captain Asthos, come here!" Roxthar called out.

The Guardsman came into the Chamber at a run. "Yes, Your Holiness."

Kynnos was finally going to get a reward. He wondered if it would be a comely wench or a fat purse of gold.

"Take this priest," Roxthar said, pointing to Kynnos, "to my Healer." Roxthar pulled up the sleeve of Kynnos' robe. "See this wound—he claims it is a bite mark from one of Kalvan's devils. Tell the Healer to amputate the arm before it inflames the body."

Kynnos blanched and his head started to reel.

He watched in shock as Roxthar gave him an imitation of a gentle smile. "We will save your life, Kynnos. And your spirit. But we will not be able to save your arm."

Kynnos fainted dead away.

When he awoke, he was tied to a cot in a dark tent. His arm was throbbing in pain. He went to move his finger, but they would not move. Why was he tied to the cot? He suddenly remembered Roxthar's words and looked to the side in horror, knowing full well what he was about to see—a bandaged stump.

He screamed and screeched until Captain Asthos came barging into the tent. "Shut up, heretic!"

"Heretic? What are you saying? Did you see what they did to my arm! I believe in the True God, the only god, Styphon!"

Asthos reached into his belt pouch and pulled out a small figurine of Dralm, a very familiar golden idol.

"That's not mine!"

"It was discovered in your boot, where you had hidden it, turncoat." Asthos smiled slyly. "I suppose you'll claim one of Kalvan's evil fireseed devils planted it there."

Kynnos was about to reply in the affirmative, when he realized that Asthos was a soldier, not a brain-addled highpriest. "You're a fighting man. You'll understand. I was given that little figurine in exchange for a Hostigi merchant's life—I took him to the slave pens instead of to the Investigator."

Asthos gave a cat-like grin. "Taking bribes, betraying the Investigation—His Holiness will love to hear this story! Archpriest Roxthar has far too many heretics in this foul land; he will enjoy Investigating a thieving priest for a change."

"I've got other pieces to trade—"

The Guardsman used his knife to cut off Kynnos' leather belt purse, removing the rings and coins inside. "Not anymore. Save your words, thief, for His Holiness. I also suggest you start formulating your apology to Styphon as well; you will be seeing him soon—or will it be Hadron?"

Kynnos started to protest, but the Guardsman silenced him by making a hand slice across his own throat. "Enough of your lies. Any more talk, any more screams, any more cries"—he paused to waggle his knife blade—"and I will cut your tongue out at the root!"

II

Phidestros felt his guts twist as the vanguard of his Iron Band rode by a burning farmhouse. A child lay on the steps, his skull smashed in and still bleeding.

In the farmyard itself, three of Roxthar's Holy Investigators were "questioning" a Hostigi woman, no doubt the child's mother. The Investigators wore hooded white robes with Styphon's red sun-wheel over the breast. The robes were well stained with mud and blood—some of the bloodstains old and dried on.

"They can fight women and children well enough!" growled Geblon. "Where were Styphon's swine when we charged Kalvan's artillery batteries at Ardros Field?"

Phidestros leaned out of his saddle to grip his friend's hand before he could draw a pistol and do something foolish. Most of the soldiers in Iron Band and Grand Host felt the same way; professional soldiers didn't deal in torture and murder. Phidestros shut his ears against the woman's screams. *At the very least: Why in the name of the Twelve True Gods couldn't the Investigators find private places to torture and maim their victims?*

It was Archpriest Roxthar, of course: Roxthar, with the fanatic's blindness to the opinions of others and total belief in his own righteousness. *Roxthar had better learn discretion before the Grand Host began hunting Investigators, instead of Hostigi.*

Phidestros led hardened veterans, men accustomed to anger, violence, wounds, and death in all its myriad of forms. But, in the end, they were professional soldiers who didn't shirk from their duty, no matter how onerous. What they were not were butchers who reveled in killing like weasels among goslings.

Curse and blast the Holy Investigation and its heinous works! They were dragging honorable soldiers down into the same kind of pigsty they enjoyed, without doing Styphon's House on Earth all that much good. These priests needed to learn what his soldiers had learned in this campaign, if they wished to grow old: men made desperate by fear will fight to the last.

Phidestros twisted his head and flexed his shoulders as much as his armor would allow, easing his stiff muscles. He should be the happiest man in the Great Kingdoms; instead he felt more fear of the future than he felt of Kalvan and his Army of Hos-Hostigos.

Kalvan was not invincible. Ardros Field proved that. The greatest victory since Simocles the Great defeated the Ruthani Confederation at Sestra more than three centuries ago; won by a mercenary commander who three years ago was lucky to count two hundred soldiers under his banner. A victory so great that Styphon's House had sent out messengers to every temple of Styphon in the Five Kingdoms with orders to celebrate this triumph with a feast of thanksgiving in every village, town and city.

The Grand Host had already sent men to garrison captured tarrs. Fifteen thousand of the best were hard on the heels of the fleeing Royal Army of Hos-Hostigos. Phidestros knew he should be riding with those men instead of playing steward to Archpriest Roxthar and his Investigators. But two days earlier a letter had arrived from Great King Lysandros saying that he was on his way to Hostigos and there was to be a victory celebration in Hostigos Town with the investiture of the new Prince of Greater Beshta, "which includes the lands falsely claimed as the Princedom of 'Sashta' by the Usurper," and the "new Prince to be in attendance." *So Lysandros was a man of his word. Good. Now, my first proclamation as Prince of Greater Beshta will be a complete ban of the Investigation in my territory. And woe to the fool that tries his hand at Investigating my subjects!* As for his investiture as Prince, not even Hadron's Hounds could keep him away.

His first act would be to send someone to his new princedom to insure the Investigation was shut down. *Whom do I trust: Kyblannos, but I need him to run the Royal Artillery. Geblon is one of my best generals. Hmm. How about Captain Cythros of the Blue Moon Company? He's not the most imaginative of captains, but he's as loyal as a wolfhound.*

He'd also learned from the letter that traveling with Lysandros was the new and rightful Prince of Hostigos, the newly crowned Prince Sthentros! Phidestros' head was still swimming with that news. Some reward for a traitor, who should have his neck stretched, since an oath-breaker could never be trusted—at least, in his experience.

He had even heard rumors, before leaving Hos-Harphax, about the Baron's daughter and Lysandros, but had thought them malicious gossip at best. Maybe not? The wench did have a way about her and was comely indeed. As to whether or not Lavena was the spitting image of Great Queen Rylla—he would leave that to those who had seen them both. True, he'd been less than a horse length away from Great King Kalvan, but had never seen the Great Queen up-close.

After the investiture, let Grand Master Soton besiege Tarr-Hostigos while Phidestros pressed the pursuit until the Usurper Kalvan was no more. The Grand Host was large enough for two main bodies; one to besiege Tarr-Hostigos, the other to run down Kalvan and his army.

As long as Kalvan was alive, he might rise again. A man who could conjure a Great Kingdom out of not much more than the gods' own air was no ordinary foe.

But try telling that to anyone else, including Grand Master Soton, who ought to know better. Phidestros could not understand why Soton deferred so much to Roxthar. The Grand Master was not only the highest-ranking soldier of Styphon's House, he was an Archpriest in his own right, the Investigator's equal in priestly rank. It would not be an answer easily come by, either. Undue curiosity about the affairs of the Investigation was a short road to a charge of 'heresy' and a nasty, brutal death.

The Iron Band started down the last slope into Hostigos Town, laid out in alternating hills and dales. In the distance, Phidestros saw the Hostigos Gap, with Tarr-Hostigos perched atop two spurs of the formidable hill to the right of the Gap.

The first prong held the main castle surrounded by walls and gun towers. The second and higher spur held the great keep and tower with its own walls. Removing Tarr-Hostigos from the path of the Grand Host was not going to be as simple as taking a splinter from a child's foot, regardless of what Roxthar thought. If Phidestros had his choice, he would leave a large detachment to blockade the castle and let starvation do the rest.

But he was merely a Grand Captain-General, in a war run by priests. Also a Royal Captain-General who answered to a Great King who'd mortgaged everything but his concubines' shifts to Styphon's House.

It was time to send the priests back to their temples and the counselors back to their castles so his soldiers could get on with the business of finishing off Kalvan.

As they rode down the Great King's Highway toward Hostigos Town, Phidestros was pleased to see only two columns of black smoke rising from the heart of Hostigos. Two years earlier, there wouldn't have been a third of the town left untouched by fire and looters. Now, many of the former mercenaries had been brought into the Army of Hos-Harphax, or were well on their way to becoming 'regular' soldiers—four winters of hard war could do that.

General Geblon said, "There'll be dry beds in Hostigos Town."

"You don't sound surprised."

Geblon sniggered. "Not after what you told the Grand Host the morning after Ardros Field." In mock stentorian tones, he said, "'We need all the buildings we can get for living quarters, so no arson when you reach Hostigos Town. We can always burn the place down when we leave.'"

A rider galloped up, shouting for Phidestros, saving him from a reply. From the rider's silvered armor and black-caparisoned horse with a silver sunwheel on each quarter, he was a Knight of the Holy Order of Zarthani Knights. *Soton is nearby,* he thought.

"Hail, Grand Captain-General Phidestros! I am Commander Lythar of the Holy Lance, with a message from Grand Master Soton."

Most of the Lances had numerical designations. The Holy Lance was the Grand Master's personal bodyguard. "Greetings, Commander Lythar. What is your master's pleasure?"

"The Grand Master requests your presence upon yonder hill. The Commander raised his visor and pointed to a nearby hill. A Blade of sixty Knights stood in attendance to the diminutive figure of the Grand Master, whose blackened armor made a stark contrast to their polished finery.

Phidestros nodded to Geblon. The General told off sixty of the Iron Band and placed them around his Captain-General until Phidestros felt like a babe in its nurse's arms. He held his peace; Geblon would be like a she-wolf with one cub toward his captain until the day he died.

It took a few moments for the horses of Phidestros' party to get used to rough ground again, after several candles on the smooth paving of Kalvan's Great King's Highway. *Kalvan is a hard man not to respect, even in defeat,* Phidestros thought. *Many saw the wisdom of such roads. None were built, until Kalvan came.*

If these be demonic arts, let me see more of them!

A quarter-candle took Phidestros up the hill to Soton's outpost. Phidestros dismounted and advanced to greet Soton, as General Geblon arrayed the Iron Band facing the Knights.

The two commanders touched palms. Soton pointed to Tarr-Hostigos.

"A hard nut to crack, aye, Captain-General?"

"One to give even a red squirrel a bit of quarrel. It's big enough to hold fifteen thousand men and supplies for a year, if they don't mind horseflesh. We may see snow before we see a breach in those walls."

"Rest easy, Captain-General. We've interrogated some prisoners—*not* as the Investigation does it, but by the old ways. Kalvan's left only a skeleton garrison, less than eight hundred men and some of those wrinkled like crab apples. We should have the castle invested in a few days. Then we can see about tracking Kalvan all the way to the Sea of Grass, if we must!"

Phidestros wanted to sing, dance, and embrace Soton, but dignity and caution shaped his tongue to a question. "Will His Bloodiness let us show such wisdom?"

"Guard your tongue, Phidestros. Great King Lysandros will be here soon; let him wrestle archpriests while we tend to our wounded."

"Yes, Grand Master. I have seen the fate of the wounded Hostigi women and children who defy the Holy Investigator."

Soton's face paled and he looked away. "It is our duty to obey the Temple's will," he muttered. "This war against women and babes is not my choice, either, Phidestros. There are changes taking place in Balph you know nothing about. When the Hostigi heresy is scourged from the land, the Investigation will be corralled."

If you believe that, Phidestros thought, *you aren't half the man I'd thought.*

Phidestros lowered his voice so the guards could not overhear. "It's not just innocent blood we have to wash from our hands. This archfiend Roxthar with his sermons of One True God has the priests of Galzar so stirred up you'd think they had wasp nests under their wolfheads! There's talk of a Ban of Galzar and rumors of Highpriests on their way from Agrys City—did you know that?"

"Yes, the Holy Investigator lacks tact."

"He lacks humanity. He is a fiend in human guise with a taste for human flesh. Rein him in or I cannot guarantee that my troops will not do their own investigation. Already several companies of mercenaries have resigned their contracts, saying this is an unjust war. Highpriest Olmnestes has given them his Blessing. Now, unless this torture is halted, he threatens to leave with all the priests of Galzar—that would bleed this army worse than horse leeches or Kalvan's *rifles.*"

Soton's face hardened. "There will be no more desertions. I have sent a detachment of four Temple Bands of Styphon's Own Guard act as a rearguard to the Grand Host. Those who lack the mettle to fight this war will taste Styphon's Own steel!"

Phidestros couldn't keep the distaste he felt off his face. He spat on the ground.

"My young friend, when you war against Daemons, you use the finest weapons you can find. Roxthar has tempered Styphon's House and brought a unity of purpose no one else could have forged."

Phidestros let the Grand Master have the last word, but this argument was a long way from being finished.

"The commanders are to be billeted at Ptosphes' summer palace in Hostigos Town," Soton continued. "I'll be going there myself, as soon as we finish this drawing of Tarr-Hostigos."

He pointed at a Knight sitting on a stump with a slate and charcoal in hand. Phidestros peered over the man's shoulder, to see a fine rendering of the castle, with every tower, battlement and gate clearly shown.

I'd best round up Kalvan's mapmakers as soon as we're settled in. Some may have fled, and doubtless Soton will want his share. I'll have the Iron Band search them out. But, please

Galzar, let this be something soldiers can settle between themselves without listening to priests babbling about demonic arts.

A hundred petty matters kept Phidestros and his Iron Band out of Hostigos Town for much of the morning. By the time they'd covered the last march of Old Tigo Road, the fires were out. The streets were deserted, except for soldiers and chain gangs of prisoners, led by Roxthar's Investigators and Styphon's Own Guard, resplendent in their silvered armor and red capes.

The chain gangs all seemed bound for Hostigos Square, which Phidestros found already half-filled with slave pens bursting with Hostigi prisoners. The palace itself was garrisoned by Guardsmen standing practically shoulder-to-shoulder, with Investigators darting in and out like rats from a half-eaten corpse. Phidestros led the Iron Band toward the palace, ignoring the curses and threats of Styphoni brusquely pushed aside.

The Iron Band replied only with silence, and occasionally with a hand rested lightly on a pistol butt. Before they reached the palace, the Styphoni were giving way without protest.

As Phidestros dismounted, he knew one thing. He'd be damned if he billeted any of his men in this nest of temple-rats. He'd say that the siege demanded all his attention and find quarters elsewhere. Let the unholy butchers do their investigation outside town, or better yet not at all. Otherwise, the Iron Band would begin a war against the Investigators right here-and-now, and, afterwards, he'd be lucky to end up back commanding a company of every other captain's leavings.

FORTY-TWO

I

Danar Sirna's first thought on waking up was to wish that she hadn't. Being dead or at least asleep seemed the best solution to quite a number of her problems, starting with her crashing headache.

The first thing Sirna saw clearly was a dead man. Beyond him lay two more dead men, one with half of his face blown away. Was she in what passed for field hospitals on Kalvan's Time-Line?

She was lying on a straw pallet, with a wood-beamed roof over her, white-washed plaster walls around her and a window in one of those walls. The warped wooden shutter was ajar; through the gap she could see what looked like a cobblestone street in Hostigos Town.

She must have been picked up and brought in by one side or another and put in here because she looked dead or dying. The whole left side of her head not only throbbed horribly but was caked and stiff with dried blood. A scalp wound like that could make you look dead to people in a hurry.

Who pulled me from the manor? And where are Chief Verkan and the Paratime Police—they wouldn't abandon her, even if my colleagues at the University would? In her mind's eye, she could still see Aranth Saln slipping out of the Foundry quarters. Had Saln come back and rescued her? *Or is this a holding pen for the Investigation?*

Sirna had just decided that sitting up was a bad idea when a board creaked behind her. She decided to face her visitor sitting.

She struggled upright, groaned, and turned to see a woman well past middle age. With a woman in attendance, this must be a Temple of the local mother goddess, Yirtta Allmother. Any temple to Dralm would already have been pulled down and burned to the foundation.

"So you're alive," the lady said.

Sirna nodded.

"You've been laid out like a corpse for over a moon quarter." The lady pointed to a squat girl in a loose shift. "If it hadn't been for Cryissa there, we'd have tossed you into the lime pits days ago. Those dead soldiers are waiting for a proper send off to Galzar's Great Hall."

"Yeah, and we pay good coin for you to keep the bodies," said one of the soldiers angrily.

"Hey! This is our work; we minister to men in life and in death."

Sirna tried to say her thanks to the squat girl with ringlet curls, but the only sound she could make came out like a frog's croak. Cryissa brought Sirna a wet cloth and let her squeeze some watered wine into her mouth. She tried to thank the lady with her eyes, but they felt too heavy....

It was evening when Sirna awoke the second time. The moment her eyes opened, Cryissa called to the older woman. "She's awake."

"They call me Menandra. What's your name, sweetheart?" The older woman's voice was gruff and coarsened by alcohol, but not unfriendly.

Better say something. Sirna didn't dare nod, but her mouth was still so dry that only a croak came out.

Menandra bawled something in a voice that would have rallied a cavalry regiment. Sirna winced. One of the house women appeared with a jug and a cup.

"Drink this."

Sirna rinsed her mouth out, and then swallowed. It went down, heavily watered wine with some herbs in it. When she thought it was going to stay down, she said, "My name is Sirna. Thank you."

The woman who called herself Menandra looked embarrassed, as if she wasn't used to kind words. "Praise Yirtta Allmother, it was She who brought you back from Regwarn."

"Are you a priestess?" It was surprising how ignorant she still was about Zarthani religion, but religious inquiry had been squelched by the Study Team as detrimental to their cover as craftsmen. However, Sirna did know from her studies at the University that in some cults the priestesses engaged in ritualized prostitution.

Menandra laughed so loudly the walls rang. "I minister to men's bodily needs, not their spirits. But thank you kindly for asking. What accent is that?"

"Grefftscharri. I was working at the Royal Foundry as a pattern maker when Styphon's Red Hand came."

"Say no more—they're demons in human form, the red bastards! You can't walk down the street without being kidnapped or raped by one of Styphon's Guardsmen."

Sirna took another drink and asked, "What's been happening since Ardros Field?" She realized she was very lucky to be alive.

Menandra looked at the ceiling as she spoke. "Well, King Kalvan is on his way west with what's left of his army. Prince Ptosphes is holding the castle, to let him get away. We're playing host to Captain-General Phidestros' Iron Band. Does that answer your question, girl?"

"What's Phidestros doing here?" Sirna asked, her heart beating wildly. *Is he as bad as the Hostigi claim?*

Menandra's reply was a hoarse whisper. "I hear that the Captain-General's not too pleased with how Roxthar's Investigators are tearing up this town. He's supposed to be staying over there at the big headquarters in what used to be Prince Ptosphes' palace. But he spends most of his nights here, or over by the siege works." She grinned. "Once he sets eyes on you, he won't be staying anywhere else."

Sirna strangled another groan. Menandra shrugged. "War's like that. Now, the next question is, what do we do with you now? Some peasants picked you up, thought you fit for selling. They ran you on into town on a cart; face down on top of a load of squash with your skirt up to your arse. They brought you here, thinking to earn some coppers. But when I saw how ill you were I sent the peasants on their way with a good buffeting."

"With my skirt up?"

The picture made Sirna giggle, then laugh. Once she started laughing she couldn't stop, although it made her head hurt even worse. It also shook her stomach, which finally rebelled.

When Sirna stopped retching, Menandra was still standing over her, trying to look stern but not entirely succeeding. "Nothing but bile, girl. Cryissa, make some turkey broth for Sirna here."

She nodded her thanks.

"As I said, what about you, girl? You're a long way from Greffa and your friends at the Foundry are either dead or run off, the true gods alone know where."

The sounds of gunfire and screams in the Foundry quarters came rushing back. "Run off?"

Menandra couldn't give many details, but what she said told Sirna very clearly that the survivors of the University Study Team had left her for dead. It took all of her First Level mental discipline not to breakout weeping. She not only felt sick, she was frightened.

"Not good for you, the more so since the Styphoni will be looking for people from the Royal Foundry. Outlanders especially. I can probably protect you here at the Gull's Nest, if you're willing to work."

This was more than Sirna could digest in one gulp. It suddenly dawned on her that Menandra was the owner and Madam of the Gull's Nest (and why that name, this far from the sea?) and was quite willing to let her earn her keep, sick or not.

"No!"

"That's how I started out in Agrys City, girl. More years ago than either of us wants to think about. There's worse things than making a living on your back. Gives you a new view of the world, you might say."

Sure, there probably were worse things here-and-now than making a living as one of Menandra's whores. But, right now Sirna couldn't think of them. She shook her head slowly.

"Well, you're handsome enough for it, and to spare."

Sirna shook her head again.

"I'll leave it be, then. Just remember, though—anything you make in the house, half goes to me. Or you go to the soldiers."

The matter-of-fact way Menandra said the latter made a believer out of Sirna. She closed her eyes and wished it all away. The smoke-blackened timbers were still there when she opened them back up. She really was in a situation where she could be turned over to a band of mercenaries and passed from man to man until she died or they got tired of her. It was a long way from reading or even writing about 'the inferior position of women' to experiencing it.

Deliberately, she closed and locked a door in her mind, on First Level and all the pleasures and privileges she had there, even on her chances of ever seeing it again (which were slim enough at best, with Kalvan defeated and her left for dead). She would look forward, look this Styphon-cursed time-line squarely in the eye, and dare it to do its worst.

Not that it hasn't already given me its best shot. She came back from this mental exercise to see Menandra looking positively concerned. "That crack on the head didn't addle your wits, did it?"

"I don't think so. I must have slept off the worst of it. I was just thinking about what I'm going to do to those sons of the gods-only-could-count-how-many-fathers who ran off and left me."

That was no lie, either. She now understood emotionally as well as intellectually the concept of the blood feud. If she ever caught Outtime Studies Director Talgan Dreth alone in a dark place—

"By Yirtta's dugs, girl, I can't give charity! Phidestros' men may pay me if Styphon's House ever pays them. Then again they may not. If they don't want to and I ask, they may burn the place down!"

And pass the women around among themselves, Sirna added mentally. Somehow the idea was no longer so paralyzingly frightful, now that she'd closed that door to First Level.

"If you know anything about healing, even the smallest bit, you might make yourself useful. Phidestros is going to be sending his sick and hurt here. The Iron Band's Uncle Wolf was killed in the battle, and there aren't so many priests of Galzar that even a Grand Captain-General can conjure them up. You help patch and purge Phidestros' men, and there won't be any trouble keeping you."

"Help those damned filthy Styphon's sons of—" Sirna began. Gently but emphatically, Menandra slapped her. At least it was probably intended as a gentle slap. Sirna had to shake her head a couple of times, to make sure her neck wasn't broken. Through the ringing in her ears, she heard Menandra warning her against saying anything less than complimentary about Styphon.

"Archpriest Roxthar's here with his Investigators. Anyone who blasphemes Styphon within a day's ride of him will wish she *had* been turned over to the soldiers. Yes, and the stallions and the draft oxen too!"

From what she'd heard of Roxthar, Sirna saw no reason to argue the point. "I'm sorry, Menandra. I'm still a little confused." *Make that a lot confused*, she said to herself.

"Well, un-confuse yourself, girl. You might start with that head wound. Clean it up, and I'll think you're good enough to turn loose on Phidestros' men."

Menandra bawled for scissors, a mirror, hot water, and bandages, while Sirna took off her mud and blood-smeared clothes and examined her body for other injuries. A prize collection of black-and-blue marks was all she turned up. Her anger toward the people who'd abandoned her grew. If they hadn't been too panic-stricken to spend ten seconds examining her, they'd have learned she was alive and fit to be moved.

Or was it possible that she and Aranth were the only survivors? No, the rest of the Team must have used the conveyer in the Foundry basement to flee. They were the least heroic people she'd ever met. They probably lit out of the Foundry like a gaggle of geese fleeing a fox.

The head wound was a long shallow gash, probably from the gunshot. She must have picked up the concussion when she fell. No signs of infection, but she made a thorough job of cleaning the wound, starting with cutting off the hair all around it. It was bleeding again by the time she was finished, and so was her lower lip where she'd bitten it. She finished by trimming her hair all around.

"You're cutting off one of your best parts, you know that, girl?" Menandra said.

Persistent, aren't you? "I'll be hard to recognize with my hair short. Maybe they'll even think I'm too ugly to bother."

"With a figure like yours? You've got a lot to learn about men, girl. Somebody's going to want what you've got if you shaved yourself bald! Best arrange to give it to a man big enough to fight off the rest. Or else you'll wish you'd taken my first offer."

What am I, a mare to go with the strongest and fiercest stallion in the herd?

Exactly.

Sirna sighed and stood up, swaying slightly but not really wanting to lie down again. That was one good sign. Another was that she was hungry.

"Is there anything to eat around here?"

Menandra chuckled. "You'll do, girl. Come on down to the kitchen and I'll see if the bread and tea are ready."

II

This was only Phidestros' second visit to Kalvan's former palace, both times under duress. The first time had been for his investiture as Prince of Greater Beshta, where he'd felt like the country cousin to the groom at a village wedding. (Being a prince was going to take more getting used to than being great captain-general.) Nor had sharing the dais with his co-prince, Sthentros, made it any easier. This visit, however, was for a council of war led by Great King Lysandros with both the Princely commanders and their Captain-Generals, Prince Sthentros of Hostigos, Grand Master Soton, Prince Valthames of Xanx, Archpriest Phyllos, Prince Epiclytis of Arklos, Investigator Roxthar, Prince Karmanes of Hyphax and Xenophes, Commander of Styphon's Own Guard. He was certain he would be the one getting the orders, not giving them.

Before he reached the private audience chamber, he was motioned aside by Chancellor Lyphannes, Great King Lysandros' chief advisor.

Lyphannes, a tall wispy man with a receding hairline, whispered in his ear, "The Great King wants to meet you in private, Your Highness, before he meets with the others."

Phidestros shook his head. This being called "Your Highness" would take some getting used to.

The Chancellor escorted him into a small handsomely appointed study.

Lysandros saw his eyes examining the room and answered, "This was Kalvan's study." He pointed to the deerskin map on one wall, with the boundaries of Hos-Hostigos marked in red ink. "The Usurper left in too much of a hurry to pack. Unfortunately, he did take time to empty the treasury. Prince Sthentros finds that impossible to accept and has his men poking their way into every palace nook and cranny looking for Kalvan's moneybox."

They both exchanged grins, leaving Phidestros feeling reassured; he hadn't been sure if Lysandros had been completely taken in by Sthentros—or his daughter.

Lysandros suddenly sobered. "There are things we need to discuss before meeting with the others. I've just received an urgent dispatch from Count Hythar. The Highpriests of Galzar have been meeting at the High Temple in Agrys City and have decided to place the Grand Host under Galzar's Ban"

Phidestros expelled a large breath, and began coughing. "I was afraid of this."

Lysandros nodded. "Styphon's House has rather more enemies in Hos-Agrys than in Harphax or Hos-Zygros. Archpriest Phyllos suspects the League of Dralm is behind this; not that Roxthar and his Investigation have made these charges difficult to justify."

"I warned Roxthar not to Investigate the Hostigi prisoners of war—at least, not where Uncle Wolf Olmnestes could learn of it."

Lysandros struck his fist on the stone wall. "These walls listen better than the Investigator. Why do you think I followed the Army so quickly? Be still, Captain-General, I know you think it was to snatch your mantle of command and put it on my own shoulders, but my real concern was to put some curbs upon the Investigation. I had heard about the rumblings in Hos-Agrys from my intelligencers a moon-quarter before I left Hos-Harphax. The Council of Galzar would have moved faster with their Ban had I not sent a large number of purses to my envoys; they spent them well, or this Ban would have been pronounced a moon half ago."

Phidestros nodded. That was gold well spent.

"Also, I wanted to Invest you as Prince of Greater Beshta as quickly as I could arrange so that you were able to issue an edict banning the Investigation from Beshta."

"Thank you, Your Majesty! I am most happy with your command."

Lysandros grinned, "As I expected. You will like the next one even better! I will transfer all the mercenary units in the Grand Host to the Army of the Princedom of Greater Beshta."

Phidestros was completely taken aback. "But why?"

"I want all the mercenaries in the Grand Host, almost all of whom are loyal to Galzar, mustered out and put into your army."

Phidestros shook his head in puzzlement. "I don't understand."

"According to my most recent dispatch, the Council of Galzar has publicly cleared you of all charges of torturing prisoners. Thus, Beshta—and you—are not under the Ban, since the government of Greater Beshta did not exist when the Ban was ordered."

"Roxthar will be livid!"

"I do not need his permission. All of Styphon's House's soldiers, including the Zarthani Knights are under the Ban of Galzar."

"Does Soton know this?" Phidestros asked.

"No, not yet; nor does Roxthar, nor even Archpriest Phyllos."

"How is this possible, Your Majesty?"

"It is We who control the roads through Hos-Harphax into the False Kingdom of Hos-Hostigos—not Styphon's House. I have had my men waylay Styphon's messengers, claiming they carry the plague. We will release them when it is to Our advantage. I will do likewise with the highpriests of Galzar, but there is no guarantee that my men will capture them all."

Phidestros nodded his agreement. Lysandros was far more devious than he had suspected; he would have to be even more careful about his plans now that he was a Prince and under the Great King's eye.

"Thanks to the Investigator's excesses, the Royal Army of Hos-Harphax is also under the Ban." Lysandros face was red and he was breathing faster. "If only I had my— Enough, I cannot change what already is." He took a few deep breaths and continued, "Furthermore, I will open negotiations with my princes and vassals to transfer any of the Galzar faithful, who so request, from the Royal to the Princely armies."

"Excellent idea, Your Majesty! That will buy us time and help convince Uncle Wolf Olmnestes that you are acting in good faith and are not connected to, or in support of, the atrocities the Investigation has committed in Styphon's name—not yours! In addition, it will take moons to transfer that many soldiers, complete with pensions, to the Princely armies."

Unspoken was the fact that it would also reduce the power of the Iron Throne and make Phidestros the most powerful military man in Hos-Harphax, if not the Five Great Kingdoms. Now, having actually seen firsthand Lysandros at work power brokering, Phidestros suspected the Great King might be just as formidable on the battlefield as he was in the field of statecraft. As one of Lysandros' princes, it was now to his advantage to help weaken the Royal Army in whatever way possible. This was a good start.

Plus, he could see another advantage to Greater Beshta from Lysandros' plans: Once word got out that the Investigation was not allowed in Beshta, the remaining Hostigi from all the other Princedoms would flock to Greater Beshta. Phidestros could see all manner of ways to take advantage of this flood of skilled artisans, road builders, mapmakers and former Hostigi soldiers.

"Now," the Great King continued, "We have another reason for not wanting to have the Grand Host chasing the Usurper Kalvan all the way down the Nyklos Trail into Ulthor Port. As you are no doubt aware, while We are preoccupied with the war against the Usurper, several of the member princes of the Agrysi League of Dralm would like nothing better than to march into Ulthor and add it to the Great Kingdom of Hos-Agrys. We must not allow this to happen.

"I want to completely destroy the Usurper's military forces in Hostigos before the Grand Host follows after him, wherever he goes. Once Tarr-Hostigos falls, and fall it *will*, there will be no distractions or possibilities of any further uprisings in this blighted princedom. Thus, the Grand Host will be in a position to not only destroy the Usurper and his army, but drive the Agrysi

League of Dralm out of Hos-Harphax should they be so foolish as to move into Our realm with their army. Finally, it is Our will that all those lands that were once part of Hos-Harphax, until the Usurper Kalvan's arrival, shall once again be brought to their rightful place in the order of things. Do I make myself clear?"

"Yes, Your Majesty. You have my complete and unwavering support both as one of your princely vassals and as the Grand Captain-General of the Grand Host."

"Good. Now that's settled, I want you to tell this council of war that you believe that it is best to root out the Hostigi resistance at Tarr-Hostigos, rather than hare off after the Usurper."

Phidestros had to bite his tongue. He most certainly did not agree, but, on the other hand, he was now a prince and his overlord's vassal, thus he would have to do as he was ordered. "Yes, Your Majesty, I will make such a presentation, even though it goes against my better judgment."

Lysandros allowed himself a small cat-like smile. "Good. Remember, this war is not just about the Usurper Kalvan and the conquest of the False Kingdom of Hos-Hostigos. There are other matters afoot, including Styphon's House's wish to put all the Great Kingdoms under its heel. You will do better as a prince than my courtiers and your fellow princes expect. We have chosen well. Let us now put these words into action."

III

As Phidestros entered the audience chamber from the rear portal at the side of Great King Lysandros, he couldn't help but notice the frowns and looks of disapproval on the faces of all the assembled dignitaries, except for that of Grand Master Soton. *They probably think we were making a backroom deal before they could present their cases, or, even worse, that I'm now one of Lysandros' favorites.* He intentionally kept his face a blank mask, *let them read upon it what they will.*

While the Chancellor went through the opening formalities and ritual, Phidestros studied Archpriest Roxthar. The Holy Investigator was seething underneath his rigid exterior, releasing enough steam to raise the temperature inside the audience chamber. Roxthar, who was accustomed to Balph temple politics where he always got his way, appeared not to be used to waiting on his *betters.* According to the rumors Phidestros had heard, Great King Cleitharses of Hos-Ktemnos would sacrifice the life of his youngest granddaughter to appease the Investigator. Fortunately for the Great Kingdom of Hos-Harphax, as he had just learned, Lysandros was made of stronger metal.

Archpriest Phyllos, the Highpriest of Harphax City, was trailing Roxthar like a puppy—it appeared he had a new master. Phidestros doubted Phyllos was making any points with Lysandros.

The moment Lysandros gave his permission, the Investigator began to speak through clenched teeth, "Your Majesty, I have learned Captain-General Phidestros has requested your permission to take Styphon's Own Grand Host and chase Daemon Kalvan and his false army into the frontier. While this work must be done, make no doubt of that—Styphon be Praised!—our first job must be to eliminate all heresy in the False Kingdom of Hos-Hostigos, beginning with the Daemon's nest, Tarr-Hostigos."

Roxthar's possessive use of 'Styphon's Own Grand Host' told both Lysandros and Phidestros that with or without Lysandros' blessings, the Styphoni-paid-portion—the majority—of the Grand Host would stay in Hostigos despite what they wanted, or ordered. If it were possible for the diminutive Grand Master to shrink, he appeared to be doing thusly.

Phidestros spoke up. "Your Majesty, may I have permission to speak?"

Lysandros nodded with perceptible relief.

Despite his own misgivings, Phidestros stated: "Let it be said that I, Grand Captain-General Phidestros, believe that the Investigator is correct and that we must wrest control of Hostigos from its defenders before we send our main force to chase the Usurper Kalvan." Everyone looked at him as if seeing him for the first time; his view of the Investigator was well known among the Grand Host. Even Roxthar, for once, appeared to be speechless.

Grand Master Soton was shaking his head. Soton had to know that it was a huge military blunder not to follow the Usurper Kalvan and drive him and his forces into the ground until the army of the False Kingdom of Hos-Hostigos was defeated, or demolished in such a manner that it was no longer able to function as an army.

Now that control of the war council had been decisively wrested from Roxthar and his supporters, Lysandros went on to inform the council of the Ban of Galzar; it was as if one of Kalvan's 'shells' had dropped through the roof. Phidestros relaxed to watch a master politician at work; Roxthar didn't stand a chance, not with this crowd.

FORTY-THREE

I

Three tiny clouds of white smoke rose from the Styphoni siege battery. Ptosphes started counting. At 'five' the three shots crashed into Tarr-Hostigos. One struck the face of the outer wall; the others hit the left side of the breach. Rock dust as white as the powder smoke whirled up, carried down toward Ptosphes on the morning breeze. He tasted the grit on his tongue and teeth; it was a familiar taste by now, with the siege into its tenth day.

The Hostigi men working on the barricade rising inside the breach barely looked up from their work. The barricade was made of heavy timbers from the buildings of the outer courtyard, flagstones from the courtyard itself and dirt from the floor. The men at work were lacing the timbers together with ropes and strips of leather, while others stood by, ready to haul a cannon onto the top of the barricade.

"The Harphaxi are beginning to master King Kalvan's way of doing things," said Master Gunner Thalmoth, who was standing beside Ptosphes. He pointed to the Styphoni siege battery. "Some of those Harphaxi guns have trunnions and many of the guns look like ours."

"Some are," Ptosphes answered gruffly, "as are those slaves they're using to haul them up."

Thalmoth was old enough to remember standing in the crowd with his father to see the newborn Ptosphes presented to the people of Hostigos as their future Prince. Too old to take the field, he'd taught at the University as well as lending a lifetime of artillery experience to testing the new Hostigi guns.

Ptosphes wondered if Thalmoth had volunteered to remain behind entirely because of his age. (He'd been seen to lift powder barrels and wield handspikes on balky guns.) Or perhaps he held himself responsible for the proof-testing explosion that killed four men and took off Captain-General Harmakros' leg.

Thalmoth owed an answer to that question only to Dralm or Galzar, not to an overcurious Prince.

"It's their first big siege," Ptosphes said tolerantly. "No doubt they'll do better next time."

This morning he felt almost benign even toward the besieging Styphoni. It was a beautiful day, and not too hot. He'd eaten a good breakfast. The garrison's wounded were doing as well as could be expected. Best of all, the men of Tarr-Hostigos now knew they'd won the victory they had to win.

Last night a party of picked men had slipped into the besiegers' forward positions. Their score was twenty-eight taken prisoner, more than fifty killed, a magazine blown up, and three bombards wrecked, all for the price of one man dead and four wounded.

All the prisoners said that Kalvan hadn't been overtaken. Some added that the men chasing him had been ordered back to join the siege. One said he'd heard a whole band was wiped out in an ambush by Kalvan's rearguard. Ptosphes suspected that the last man was trying to please his captors, who had nothing to lose by blowing him from a gun. The last stand at Tarr-Hostigos was not going to be a waste of lives. If that wasn't worth celebrating, then nothing was.

Of course, the odds against the besieged would rise still higher now that the Grand Host was bringing back their vanguard. Since those odds were already over a hundred to one, who cared? Ptosphes rather liked Harmakros' way of putting it:

"Aren't we lucky? We'll *never* run out of targets now!"

That might have been Harmakros' fever speaking. In spite of his stump having been cleaned to drive out the fester devils, Harmakros had been working far too hard for a man so badly hurt. However, most of the rest of the garrison seemed to feel the same way.

Ptosphes continued his walk around the castle walls, Thalmoth following ten paces behind. The riflemen in the towers encouraged enemy musketeers to stay beyond accurate range, and the besiegers didn't waste cannon shot on single men. Ptosphes suspected that they were short of fireseed and saving what they had for the storming. No trouble of that kind for his people, even without the reserve of over twenty tons of Styphon's fireseed in the cellar of the keep.

He inspected the Styphoni gunners at the battery at the top of the draw leading up to the gate. The battery had been laid out by someone who knew his business, which was also why it had no guns in it as yet. They would be needed for the storming, to keep the Hostigi on the gates from having target practice on the men coming up the draw. Until then, they would simply be on the wrong end of plunging fire from the gate towers.

Another hundred paces along the walls, and some of Ptosphes' good mood evaporated. On this side Archpriest Roxthar had his prison—really more of a stock pen for the people he was Investigating. Like most of the besiegers' works, it was walled in timber and stone carted by slave gangs from Hostigos Town, but lacked their roof of old tents. At the rate the besiegers' works were swallowing the town, it soon wouldn't matter if it burned or not.

A long line of gallows rose by the gate of the prison pen, most of them dangling bodies, and continued on down the road all the way down the hillside and down the Old Tigos Road into Hostigos Town. Ptosphes could smell the bodies that'd been dangling more than a couple of days, even over the stable-and-powder-smoke reek of the siege.

The gallows seemed to be more burdened now than even a few days ago. No doubt the Styphoni had finished with many of their Hostigi slaves after they'd sweated and bled to haul the captured sixteen-pounders up the slope to the siege battery. That whole affair had been as bloody in itself as some of the battles of the days before Kalvan.

The Styphoni had even killed a fair number of their own men, hammering footholds and passageways in places where his grandfather had carved the slopes into vertical faces. Then Ptosphes' men had also had to kill some of their own folk, weeping and cursing, as they raked at the gun teams with case shot and rifles.

The end of it was what had to be, when one side could spend men like water. The guns were in place and hammering at the walls of Tarr-Hostigos in a way even those ancient stones could not endure forever. Many of the guns were ancient bombards, most likely dragged all the way from Tarr-Harphax and other Harphaxi forts; one huge bombard was even mounted on its own carriage! Hostigi guns, too, even some of Alkides' prize sixteen-pounders. No surprise that, considering that all of the big guns except *Galzar's Teeth* had been lost at Ardros Field.

No surprise, and therefore something Ptosphes *should* have been able to do more about. He'd forgotten Kalvan's advice, given late one night when they'd all been emptying a jug of Ermut's brandy.

"Always plan against the worst thing your enemy can do. That way you'll be safe, no matter what he does. If he doesn't do his worst you'll win more easily."

Wise words. Truly the army of the Great King Truman taught its captains well.

Ptosphes shook his head and lit his pipe. There was no call to feel sorry for himself. He had done too much of that. Besides, while he might not be fit for service in the hosts of Great King Truman, he was no bad captain for Tarr-Hostigos when every day it held out was another victory over the Styphoni.

II

The screeching ravens overhead darkened the sky and drowned the cries of the babies and wounded trailing the retreating army, as the Hostigi made their way along this Trail of Tears. Kalvan's mount whickered as they passed another horse. He gouged its flanks with his boot heels to keep his horse's head forward. He was riding, with a small escort of Lifeguards, back along the Hostigi train to get a better idea of just how many refugees and supplies accompanied the retreating army. Actually, they were no longer an army but a folk migration—like the Zarthani immigrants of half a millennium ago, only traveling west instead of east.

They had just crossed the Nyklos/Ulthor border and were now following the Nyklos Trail across the Princedom of Ulthor. The Ulthori border guards had glared at them sullenly as the endless train of soldiers and refugees passed into their Princedom, probably thinking about the Grand Host following behind. Prince Kestophes, his head heavily bandaged from a sword blow, was leading the van with Rylla and Prince Sarrask. The border guards had joined the column reluctantly after Kalvan had reminded Kestophes of his duty.

Only Prince Sarrask was in good humor. Kestophes acted as if he'd already lost his Princedom and was only waiting for an audience with Investigator Roxthar. Rylla was stiff as a board, rejecting everyone's sympathy and concern. Kalvan had wisely left her to herself and to Lady Eutare, worried sick over Prince Phrames who had taken a gunshot wound to the shoulder. Brother Mytron was hovering over all of them like a mother hen with her chicks.

As his party made its way around a tall stand of trees, mostly first stand walnuts and hemlocks, they ran into another Hostigi party bearing Baron Hestophes' banner, a black boar's head on a yellow field. Kalvan gave orders to halt and waited for the Captain-General to appear. What was Hestophes doing here when he was supposed to be with the rearguard holding back the Grand Host's pursuers?

Hestophes, riding a huge black destrier and wearing armor that appeared to have been beaten by baseball bats, pulled up short when he saw the Great King's banner. "Your Majesty!"

"Captain-General, where is my army?"

Hestophes turned and looked over his shoulder. "Behind the rearguard. The Styphoni have broken off, but not without heavy casualties. But I fear it was not our stout defense that caused them to turn back. A captured mercenary captain told us that the Grand Host is preparing for the final attack on Tarr-Hostigos and have recalled their advance army to join the attack."

Kalvan shook his head and pulled out his pipe. Ptosphes had bought them breathing room; he just hoped he could capitalize on his father-in-law's dearly purchased gift. His biggest problem was where to go. He knew that as soon as Tarr-Hostigos fell the entire Grand Host would be on his trail, and without an endless stream of refugees to slow them down. It was fortunate for all involved on the Hostigi side that the Grand Host had taken the bait of Tarr-Hostigos and stubbed their toes on it. He suspected the siege was more a priestly decision than a military one, which meant Archpriest Roxthar was running the show and not just the Investigation.

"The Agrysi captain brought us more news. The High Temple of Galzar in Agrys City has proclaimed a Ban on the Grand Host because of their mistreatment of Hostigi prisoners. Great King Lysandros, who is now in Hostigos Town, has tried to circumvent their Ban by enlisting most of the Host's mercenaries into his Princely armies. Some of the more devout followers among the mercenaries, like our Agrysi captain, have deserted their posts in protest."

Kalvan snorted. "Or, not wanting to be regulars, are bugging out. There must be a way we can use the Ban to our advantage." Kalvan suspected Roxthar was more interested in killing heretics than in winning battles. What he needed was a good diversion to buy him more time. Then it hit him in the face. It was time the League did *something* useful, even if it were only acting as a ruse.

"Hestophes, what do you think Captain-General Phidestros would do if word arrived that an invasion force from Hos-Agrys was imminent?"

"Hos-Agrys!" Hestophes grinned, and shook off his fatigue like a dog ridding itself of fleas. "Has the League of Dralm finally moved off its rump and come to our aid?"

Kalvan paused to light his pipe with his tinderbox. "No. But rumors know no boundaries. And, with the Grand Host, now under the Ban of Galzar, anything is possible. What if Phidestros and Soton learned of a large Agrysi force coming south through Eubros and into Nyklos?"

"They would have to answer it, of course, Your Majesty." Hestophes smiled. "Are you thinking what I'm thinking?"

Kalvan exhaled a small cloud of smoke and smiled. "Yes. We'll dress up our own League Army and send them against the Grand Host. Maybe that will buy us some time." It was unfortunate that Duke Mnestros had lost the better part of his army at Ardros Field; the Duke's force had taken over fifty percent casualties when the left wing had collapsed. At that point, he had agreed there was little more the Duke could do and had sent him back to Hos-Agrys. He hadn't missed the extra mouths during the retreat, but the Duke would have been the perfect foil for this gambit.

"When, Your Majesty?"

"I'll give you the Army of Observation and you can lie in wait until their siege is over. Then I want you to hit the Grand Host's van as hard as you can."

Hestophes straightened up in his saddle. He'd been in low spirits ever since the Battle of Ardros where his wing had charged out of control off the battlefield. It hadn't been his fault, when those heavies got moving not even their Great King could have stopped them. It was the inherent problem commanders historically ran into when they used fully-armored noble cavalry. They were easy to wind up and hell to stop, especially when they smelled blood or spoils.

"Your Majesty, I would like the honor of leading the Army of Observation against the Unholy Host."

"The honor is all yours, Captain-General Hestophes." All the other commanders Kalvan might trust for such a perilous and important mission were wounded, dead or missing in action. "Now, round up General Klestreus—you should be able to find him at the nearest chuck wagon. First, I want him to gather every former Agrysi mercenary in the army. Then, tell him I want a list of every Agrysi prince, duke and baron he can think of that's in sympathy with the League of Dralm. I will also need a list of all their colors, devices and banners. If we're going to make this invasion real, we are going to need the right window dressing."

III

To impress his guest, Captain-General Kyblannos fired off the entire big siege battery, six giant bombards lugged all the way from Tarr-Harphax and four of Kalvan's thirty-two pound brass guns from Ardros Field and Tarr-Sashta. The resulting *whumph* shook the valley like one of Endrath's earth-quakes. Even the Holy Investigator was impressed by the cloud of gray smoke and noise, although not so impressed with the results. The smaller iron cannonballs just bounced off the stone outerworks of the castle, and slammed back down into the defensive breastworks.

One spectacular ricochet bounced back from the wall and into a clump of sentries and guards, sending body parts flying, killing half a dozen men and wounding even more.

Kyblannos shook his head in dismay. If that continued, he'd have the Grand Host's own sentries storming his batteries before long!

The huge granite balls smashed into the outer wall of Tarr-Hostigos and exploded into thousands of deadly fragments that didn't appear to do much damage to the walls, but would have been devastating to any Hostigi standing nearby—had there been any quite that foolish.

Roxthar gave Kyblannos one of his "there'd better be a good explanation for this looks," which made his skin crawl. "Your Holiness, the walls of Hostigos are not only strong, but thick as well—almost twice the height of a man at the base. Our guns are penalized by having to shoot uphill against Endrath's grasp."

Roxthar frowned at the mention of the god of the earth and Kyblannos wondered if he had committed heresy by mentioning the name of any god other than Styphon. *How was a simple solider supposed to do his job with priests and Archpriests underfoot? And why did Galzar continue to let this Styphoni foolishness continue?*

"See that big crack there next to the watchtower," Kyblannos said, using his finger to point out the fissure in the outerworks. "That's the breach that we're trying to open up for tomorrow's sortie. And, over there, the facing is splintered and beginning to crumble. We are making progress, but it is slow. *Magal,* our biggest siege gun, can hurl a stone ball the weight of two men!"

Roxthar didn't appear impressed. He was watching the men swabbing out the barrels of the big siege guns. "How long before you shoot again?"

A band of litter carriers and priests of Galzar pushed past them, running to where the cannonball had struck the sentries.

"Half a candle." Sometimes it took longer, but with Investigator Roxthar watching over their shoulders the artillerymen were working like madmen.

"A half candle! No wonder there is so little progress. I command you to shoot every quarter candle."

Kyblannos shook his head. "It can't be done. First, we have to cool off the gun barrels, or the fireseed will explode while we load it. There are no wells nearby so the water has to be carried by cart in barrels uphill from the Hostigos springs. Then we have to clean the fireseed fouling from the inside of the gun barrels."

"I want to see how this is done." Roxthar demanded.

Kyblannos paused to wipe the sweat from his brow. "Follow me." He led the Investigator and his party of Temple Guardsmen to one of the big siege bombards. Roxthar waited impatiently while the barrel was swabbed, which was slow work since every time the pole-mounted swabs went into the barrel a cloud of steam erupted, forcing the swabbers to jump back from the gun or have their faces scalded. At long last the barrel was cool, the touchhole plugged and the breech was opened.

"Why is that plug put into the base of the gun?" Roxthar asked.

This was safe territory and Kyblannos' usual confidence reasserted itself. "See those braziers, we use those to light the wires that fire off the guns. If a spark should enter the touchhole before we're ready, the fireseed would explode—killing anyone nearby."

One of the artillerymen took a large ladle of fireseed and placed it into the breech. Once the breech was closed, a rammer placed a wooden disc into the barrel and used his ramrod to push it tightly against the fireseed inside the breech. "The fireseed explodes with more force if we use a disc." He was careful not to mention that this was another of Kalvan's innovations; previously they had used cloth or other wadding; the fireseed discs worked much better.

Next a lift was brought over to raise the huge stone cannonball and place it into the bombard's barrel. The ball was nested inside a net of ropes and pulled up by winches and pulleys. A winch party of several artillerymen lifted the ball and positioned it over the barrel. At a signal from Kyblannos the granite ball was dropped from the net into the bombard where it fell with a resounding thud against the disc.

One of the rammers used his ramrod to insure the ball had positioned itself tightly against the wooden disc. Some powder was poured into the touchhole and everyone moved back except the Investigator.

"I want to set off the gun."

Kyblannos knew he was on slippery ground, but this was his bailiwick and no one—Holy Investigator or not—was going to tell him how to do his work.

"No, Your Holiness. It is a job for well-trained artillerymen. They are trained to know how and where to move after they light the fireseed. Please step back, this is dangerous! You can watch from here."

Roxthar slowly moved away from the guns, with obvious displeasure; the Investigator was used to giving orders, not taking them.

There was a quarter of a candle wait while the rest of the guns were loaded and ready to fire.

"Fire in the hole!" Kyblannos yelled, who was so focused that he lost sight of the Investigator.

An artilleryman took a red-hot piece of wire off the brazier, where he'd set it moments before, and jammed it into the touchhole. There was a bright flash and then the ground shook as the fireseed inside the breech exploded, shooting out the huge stone ball. Roxthar jumped back two rods after the flash singed his robe.

The other guns began to go off —and suddenly the very earth rocked from a tremendous explosion, knocking Kyblannos right off his feet and on top of Roxthar.

Moments later a hat-sized piece of gun barrel flew right over the very place they had been standing—clearly the Investigator was under Styphon's protection!

"What was that?" Roxthar exclaimed, pushing Kyblannos off as though he were tainted by heresy.

Kyblannos, who could just barely hear, wobbled to his feet. He pointed to one of the big siege bombards, which had up-ended; its breech split. Half a dozen broken artillerymen lay strewn over the hard ground. One rammer whose tunic had been burned off his body was wandering around with his mouth open in an O and his hands over his ears. Miraculously, there wasn't a single cut or burn on his naked torso.

"The Daemon Kalvan's work!" Roxthar shouted.

Or so Kyblannos thought, since everything sounded like it was at the bottom of a deep well. He made his way over to the up-ended bombard. Fortunately, the fireseed barrel was set a ways back from the gun and was still intact. If it had gone off, the damage would have been much greater. He checked the proof stamp at the bottom of the barrel—it was the keystone of Hos-Hostigos. He motioned Roxthar over, saying, "It *was* the Daemon's work! Someone must have mixed this confiscated barrel of Hostigi fireseed up with Styphon's fireseed."

"I don't understand."

"The Hostigos fireseed has twice the blast effect of Styphon's fireseed."

"Are you saying it is better?"

"I'm not saying anything, just reporting what I know with these ears and eyes, Your Holiness. I know guns and fireseed like you know heretics, and Hostigi fireseed is twice as powerful as the Temple's fireseed."

"I had given orders that Styphon's new fireseed was to be shipped from Balph."

"It was, Your Holiness. However, there wasn't enough for both the Grand Host's firearms and the siege guns. So we were given the old fireseed. Somehow a barrel of Hostigi fireseed got mixed up with our magazine."

"Treachery!"

"No, just carelessness." He pointed to the unmoving artillerymen. "Someone in this gun crew didn't check the barrel's proof mark so I lost a crew and one of my guns. They lost their lives and Tarr-Hostigos just gained more time."

His ears were clearing enough that he could hear the grinding of Roxthar's teeth.

FORTY-FOUR

There was the sound of the big siege guns firing at Tarr-Hostigos, then an explosion that shook the room, knocking plaster and cobwebs from the ceiling. The man on what had been Menandra's best table writhed and twisted, and almost but not quite screamed. The four mercenaries holding him strained to keep him still.

In the other room Menandra screamed, "Curse this Dralm-blasted war! How's a proper house to work with all this noise? And who in Bloody Regwarn is going to fix my mucking door?"

"What happened?" Sirna asked.

A petty-captain, with a wounded arm in a cloth sling, hurried out of the room. He returned shortly to report: "A fireseed wagon exploded half a block down Tigo Street and blew the Nest's door off its hinges. Praise Galzar, we were lucky! Another hundred paces—" He paused to rub the image of the Wargod he wore on a gold chain around his neck. "It took out five or six buildings!"

"Do you think it was meant for us?"

The petty-captain looked thoughtful. "If the Hostigi thought they could take out the Grand Captain-General's headquarters, they'd do it in an eye wink. So would the Red Hand. And there are more than a few Captain-Generals unhappy with his success—"

"'Tis the Daemon's work," muttered the wounded soldier.

"Lie quiet," Sirna muttered. "You lie quiet, or I'll have to use a sandbag on you. I don't want to do that. You may have already hurt your head, when the tunnel caved in." She wasn't really mad at the poor hurt soldier, but at her own fear. She not only had the wounded, Roxthar's Investigators and the Red Hand to worry about, but now Hostigi saboteurs—what next?

The soldier on the table sank his teeth into his lower lip. Blood came, but he lay still as Sirna cut open the flesh of his cheek over the finger-length splinter there and drew out the bloody wood. More blood flowed freely. Sirna let it flow while she picked out the last bits of wood, then bound up the wound in a dressing of boiled rags. By the time she'd finished the bandaging, the soldier had fainted, but he came awake as his comrades lifted him off the table.

"Sorry to be so much trouble, girl," the soldier said between clenched teeth. "But I wanted to look at something pretty."

Sirna grinned. "With the gods' favor and no fester devils, you'll have two eyes to look at pretty girls. And a fine scar to attract the ones you want."

The scar would be a lifelong disfigurement—no reconstructive surgery here-and-now. Still, if the soldier was able to contemplate life with it....

She'd thought she'd been used to what people on Fourth Level could face, after almost three years with the University Team. It was a lot different to live alone among such people, with the nearest person who would have ever heard of First Level at least a hundred miles away—farther if Saln had kept on running. Not to mention the possibility of spending the rest of her life on Aryan-Transpacific.

On top of everything else, Styphon's soldiers! It wasn't easy to accept that men who fought for something as silly, irrational, even barbaric, as Styphon's House could be like other men. But they fought just as bravely; cried out just as loudly for their mothers when they hurt and made just as many bawdy jokes that could still turn her face brighter than her cropped hair.

Or rather, it hadn't been easy to accept this at first. Now it sometimes seemed that she'd never believed anything else.

No more sick or wounded seemed to be coming, so Sirna sent one of the women with the knife and the salvaged bandages off to the kitchen to boil them clean. She also made at least her twentieth mental memo: *Borrow some better instruments from a priest of Galzar, or have the Iron Band's armorers make them.*

Another woman, face streaked with makeup, wiped down the table with a bucket of boiling water. Menandra herself brought Sirna a cup of hot turkey broth. "You'd better eat something solid, you know," the madam said. "Even if it's only an omelet. Won't do, having you faint on top of men too hurt to enjoy it."

"Oh, I'll eat something tonight." At the moment, the mere thought of solid food made her gag.

"Tonight..." Menandra began, then lowered her voice to a whisper so that none of the wounded on pallets along the other side of the room could hear. "The talk in town is that it's tomorrow they go for the castle. So you'd better eat and sleep tonight, or by Yirtta's dugs I'll turn you over my knee and spank you!" She ruffled Sirna's hair with one large greasy hand.

Sirna gulped her broth with both hands clasped tightly around the cup so Menandra wouldn't see that they were shaking. Seventeen wounded men in one day was bad enough. If they stormed the castle, it could be more like seventy or seven hundred! Although she might have more help from the priests of Galzar if the promised reinforcements came up. Had they? She was trying to think of a tactful way to ask when the door to the street opened and a suit of armor wearing dusty leather breeches and boots strode in.

The suit of armor also had a brown beard and wide gray eyes, but it wasn't until the high-crested helmet came off that Sirna realized there was a man inside. When she saw that the man had a high forehead and a long scar across his right cheek, she knew who'd come to visit his wounded. She'd seen his picture often enough at the Foundry, during their briefings.

Grand Captain-General Phidestros waved the men trying to rise back onto their pallets with his free hand, set his helmet on the table and took off his mud-caked gloves. Then he grinned at Sirna.

"You randy bastards! You've been keeping secret the best thing this wreck of a town has to offer. Where's your loyalty to your commander, you—?" The term would have been insulting as well as obscene in any other tone. The men replied in kind, except for General Geblon, on light duty today because of an attack of dysentery.

"She is Menandra's healer, Captain-General," Geblon said, trying to look and sound innocent. "She has been marvelously chaste."

"I'm sure she has," Phidestros replied. "But has she been caught? If she hasn't, you aren't the men I thought you were!"

Sirna stopped blushing and started giggling. Phidestros bent down and gripped her by one arm, pulling her to her feet as easily as if she'd been a child. His long face showed deep lines, apparently gouged with a blunt chisel, then filled with dust. Upon closer view, he was much younger, late- twenties or early thirties, than he appeared from a distance. *He's probably quite handsome when rested and bathed,* popped into her head. Then she put her hand over her mouth before realizing the words were unspoken.

By the time he'd led her into the hall where no one could see her, she was trying to stop giggling. Somehow she wanted to impress him favorably, and not only because he had the power of life and death over her.

"To speak plainly—what is your name, by the way?"

"Sirna."

"Speaking plainly, Sirna, I owe you for a good thirty of my men helped and at least two saved outright. Where did you learn to treat burns like Aygoll's?"

"My father had some skill in healing; and I was always quick to learn anything someone else would teach. One year we lived not far from a smithy. They knew how to heal burns from molten metal."

"Curious. What you did for Aygoll is very much like what Kalvan is said to have taught, about driving out the fester demons."

"Is it not possible that the gods can send wisdom to both good and evil men, and leave it to them how it shall be used?" She looked up to meet his eyes as she spoke, and she thought she kept her voice steady.

"It's not only possible, it happens all the time," Phidestros said. "Only don't try arguing the point with Holy Investigator Roxthar. He's threatening to purge the hosts of Styphon once he's finished with Hostigos."

"Aren't you speaking a little freely, if he's that suspicious?" she asked. Like most of the surviving population of Hostigos Town, Sirna had stayed indoors. Those whom urgent business or the search for food drove outside too often found themselves confronted by white-robed Investigators or squads of Styphon's Red Hand. Few of those returned. Now only soldiers, rats and fools strayed outside; rumor had it that the Investigators were making house-to-house searches in east Hostigos Town.

"Afraid you won't be paid, Sirna?"

"That's not it at all! I just—I'm not like Menandra, you know. I'd feel sorry for a thrice-convicted rapist facing the Investigation."

"So would I, believe me." He grinned, displaying a mouthful of almost intact white teeth, which meant not only good health but good luck in battle.

"Menandra is no worse than the gods made her, but they were drunk that day and perhaps a little careless. No, Sirna. I'm in no danger. Not unless the Archpriests decide they don't need good soldiers anymore. That won't be until Kalvan's dead, and somehow I think that man is going to take a lot of killing."

Sirna would have kissed Phidestros if she hadn't known he would misinterpret the gesture. "I wouldn't be at all surprised if he did," she said.

"Which means that Roxthar is going to be dealing lightly with soldiers for a while. Healers who may be tainted with heresy aren't quite as indispensable. Remember that, and you may live to be paid for your work with the Iron Band. Fifty silver rakmars, is that enough?"

Fifty ounces of silver! she thought, that would be enough to set her up in a small business as a seamstress, or pattern maker—there'd be a lot of those jobs until the war was over. "Yes, and thank you, Captain-General!"

"Call me Phidestros," he said with a wink. "Its fair pay for good work. Oh, and I'll pay it right into your hands. And two gold pieces, if the Styphoni pay their victory bonus. If Menandra asks for a single brass piece, tell me. We'll roast our victory ox over her furniture."

The way Phidestros' voice and face changed in those last words made Sirna want to flinch away from his touch. She forced herself to stand still as he put a hand behind her back and urged her back toward the main room.

"Let's join the men, before they gamble away all their money wagering which one of us was on top!"

FORTY-FIVE

I

The moonlit clearing was empty of everything but spring flowers and two frisky rabbits. Tortha Karf brushed the sleep out of his eyes and leaned back on the trunk of a sycamore that was as wide as he was tall. He'd been awakened from a sound sleep by the vibration in his dagger. After putting the handle next to his ear, he was given a set of coded instructions to leave the bivouac and walk a half-mile to the northeast where he would meet a vehicle.

It had taken him almost five minutes to explain to the guards picketing the camp that he was searching for mushrooms for his breakfast omelet. There was a long wait while the sentry sent for his captain, who sleepily vouched for Tortha, having seen him in the Great King's company. While Tortha mentally lauded Kalvan for his tight security, he also cursed him for making him have to wait out in the wet night air for the captain of the guard. Of course, had the captain not identified him he might have been forced to spend the night in a makeshift cell in protective custody—so things could be a lot worse.

Who and where is my contact? I'm getting too old for this cloak and dagger stuff, Tortha decided.

A few minutes later there was a gentle whoosh and an anti-gravity lifter dropped soundlessly into the clearing.

Out of the cab stepped the familiar form of Verkan Vall, wearing a back-and-breast and his uniform.

"Vall! I didn't expect to see you," Tortha exclaimed. "Last I heard you were shot dead."

"I took one point-blank in the chest; it was bad. Another hour—" He thumped the chestplate opposite his heart "But I'm not that easy to kill."

"Don't I know it; after all we've been through together. Still, if you ever needed a good excuse to take care of business back on First Level, a sucking chest wound qualifies as about the best excuse you can get here-and-now!"

Verkan winced. "It was the worst experience I've had since I joined the force. I wanted to talk with you firsthand and let you know I was all right."

In actuality, the reports of Verkan's death had upset Tortha more than he liked to admit, but he certainly wouldn't let Vall know—he'd think he was turning into a silly old woman. "Thanks, I was wondering…."

Now that the unpleasantness was over Verkan brightened up. "Tell me, Tortha, how are our friends Kalvan and Rylla taking all this?"

"Rylla's not doing so well. Her father's back at Tarr-Hostigos on a suicide mission and she knows it. She also knows he's unwell, but that isn't helping. Ptosphes has always been both mother and father to Rylla and she is having a difficult time coming to terms with his death."

"You mean she's blaming Kalvan?"

"To a degree, probably less than if they hadn't just patched things up after the Phaxos Incident. We had a talk yesterday—no it was *her* idea, Vall!"

"I believe you. I'm just glad you're here for her, with Xentos in Agrys City and her father back in Hostigos, she really doesn't have anyone but Chartiphon."

"Chartiphon's a mess. He thinks his place is at Prince Ptosphes' side and he's acting as though it's his fault he didn't stay behind for the defense of Tarr-Hostigos. Kalvan's really hoping he'll snap out of it, because with Harmakros gone he's short staff generals for that army of his."

"How is Kalvan taking the defeat?"

"Kalvan's like a cat, always lands with feet firmly on the ground—no matter what! He sees his biggest problem as the refugees that have followed the army into exile. A quarter of Beshta, likewise for Sashta, a half of Nostor, half of Sask, two-thirds of Hostigos: I'd estimate half to three-quarters of a million refugees stretched between Tarr-Hostigos and the Saltless Seas. The army of Hos-Hostigos is in better shape than Styphon's House realizes; otherwise they wouldn't have let that butcher in the bedsheets stop the Grand Host dead in its tracks to take Tarr-Hostigos. Kalvan still has about half of his original military force—a more than respectable number of men. Enough that he should be able to topple any of the local despots in the Upper Middle Kingdoms, or what Kalvan calls the 'Great Lakes' area."

Verkan shook his head. "Not unless he wants a war with Grefftscharr. Theovacar is no more anxious to have Kalvan in his neighborhood than Kalvan would have liked Theovacar to set up shop in Hos-Agrys!"

"Isn't Theovacar hamstrung by his nobles?"

"In most cases, but a so-called invasion by Kalvan could tip the scale and have Theovacar's nobles and merchant princes offering their support in a bid to stop Kalvan before he establishes a staging ground in the Middle Kingdoms. Kalvan will have to be very careful before he commits himself."

"Enough of Kalvan's problems. I understand we have a big one of our own. One of Kalvan's scouts reported the massacre at the Foundry—did we lose any of the Study Team?"

Verkan filled him in on all the details of arriving to find the Foundry a burnt-out hulk with bodies littering the courtyard. "We lost the whole Team except for those missing in action."

Tortha whistled. "What about Kirv?" Skordran Kirv was one of the top Paratime Police Inspectors as well as one of Verkan's right-hand men. Tortha had liked him a lot, even had him over for half a ten-day at his villa on Fifth Level.

"Kirv was killed, along with five good patrol officers." Verkan shook his head. "I'm losing friends faster than I can replace them. He could have left—should have bugged out, as Kalvan would put it. But the Study Team refused to budge. He was afraid if he left it would discredit the force—I've got it all on a recording. Kirv recorded everything, Praise Dralm!"

"What do you mean? The Paratime Commissioner isn't blaming you, is he? If he is, it's time I got back to First Level and kicked some—"

"No, the Commissioner backed me all the way. It was the University Director—"

"Old Zyldor himself—I'm not surprised."

"The Commissioner suggested that Director Zyldor Uln and his team meet with me and listen to Kirv's recordings before they did anything stupid."

Tortha laughed. "Zyldor must have loved that!"

"No, he came in looking for a fight and left like a paratemporally displaced outtimer. Especially after he listened to half an hour of Varnath Lala's ravings about negotiating with the heathen Styphoni, who would need good brass-casters to ensure that Kalvan never returned to Hos-Hostigos. Talgan Dreth actually flat out refused evacuation when Kirv pressed him on leaving. He'd been made to look the fool in Dhergabar after the last evacuation, and he wasn't going to travel that road twice—regardless of what Kirv said. No, if those recordings were to surface, it'd be the University that would take a black eye, not the Paratime Police.

"The missing Study Team members are another problem—one that's not going away. Three of them: Aranth Saln, Danar Sirna and Gorath Tran. Our agents haven't been able to find a trace of Aranth or of Danar, who's striking enough to leave a trail. It's like they've fallen off the face of the earth."

"What about Roxthar's Investigation?"

"I don't think so. We have a Paracop that's infiltrated Roxthar's gang—there are so many Investigators now not even Roxthar knows them all. I suspect more than a few are former highpriests who are using the white robe of the lower priesthood as camouflage. Anyway, our imposter hasn't found any trace of Aranth or Danar, but he has found Gorath Tran. He ended up in one of Roxthar's slave pens, telling tales of transtemporal conveyers and Paratime Police—to Investigator Roxthar, of all people! Fortunately, Roxthar put his own spin on it; now he's convinced that Kalvan is leading an invasion of demons from Regwarn into the Five Kingdoms. He's keeping Gorath the Demon as his personal pet."

"That's the Paratemporal Secret he's running off at the mouth about! What if Kalvan gets word of this?"

"Our agent managed to talk with Gorath—he's completely mental. Doesn't even remember his name; a ten-day with Roxthar has pushed him completely over the edge. No one, other than Roxthar, would take anything he says seriously."

"What does the University say?"

"They're embarrassed. They want him back for a visit to the Bureau of Psy-Hygiene before some newsie catches word about all this. We'll pick him up when Roxthar tires of him and dumps him at one of his slave depots. If we took him now, it might convince Roxthar that there was some truth to his words—the poor bastard."

"His troubles make Kalvan's look small. It looks like the political fallout from the Study Team's fiasco has been minimal. So, Vall, why do you look so miserable?"

"There's some dustup on the Europo-American, Islamic Kaliphate Subsector; it appears that India has just fallen to the Communists and the entire subsector is on red alert. The Commissioner wants me to visit personally and decide whether to quarantine the entire Kaliphate Subsector or just one of the belts."

"Isn't the Hartley Belt part of that subsector?" Tortha asked. "The one where the Hartley kid, now President Allan Hartley, claimed to have visited the future and witnessed World War III?"

"Yes, it's the same one Dalla and I visited to track down the Wizard Traders a few years back. Allan Hartley was our first psychic time traveler…or, at least, that was our conclusion. The Organization was illegally shipping yellow cake out of that Belt. We shut that operation down and since then have kept a hands-off policy regarding the Hartley Affair."

"Okay, now I remember," Tortha said. "This Hartley Belt is part of the Kaliphate Subsector, which divaricated from Europo-American over twenty years ago. It seems like most of Hartley's attempts to stave off the war have created more problems than they've solved!"

"That's the problem," Verkan said. "It appears that the Hartley Belt is closer to a nuclear meltdown than any other belt or sector throughout the entire Kaliphate Subsector. What do you think we should do about it?"

"It's a pretty open-and-shut case; if they're about to go nuclear, you shut down our operations throughout the belt, or the entire subsector if necessary. Fortunately, we don't have any commercial establishments to shut down, just some observational posts which means minimal political fallout. Vall, you're a realist and a historian as well as a Paracop. You know what to do. What's really bothering you?"

"Tortha, you know how to get to the heart of the matter. Maybe I will, too, after I've sat at the big desk another century or so."

Not much chance of that if you keep taking every outtime friend's bad luck so personally. It was a shame because, apart from this Kalvan problem, Verkan showed every sign of being an above-average chief for the Department. "Now, once again. What's eating at you?" he asked.

"This Hartley assignment is going to keep me away from Kalvan's Time-Line and up to my elbows in work for the next four or five ten-days. I need to be here, helping Kalvan find a place to winter his people. I have all this power and I can't do a Dralm-damned thing to help my friends without upsetting some bureaucrat or breaking some Paratime reg."

"Vall, let me give you some good advice. Take care of your First Level problems first, then worry about your outtime hobby—if that's what it still is. If it isn't, then maybe it's time to change jobs."

Verkan winced as if he'd been slapped, then laughed. "Maybe you're right. Maybe I'm not cut out for Chief."

"I didn't say that. You have the potential to be a good Chief, but you've got to learn to put your priorities in the proper order. I suggest you think about that all the way to the Hartley Belt."

II

Phidestros awoke the instant a hand pressed hard over his lips. Instinctively his right hand snaked underneath the bedroll on which his head rested to grasp the handle of the poniard.

Now another hand gripped his right wrist. Phidestros used his left hand to reach for the single-shot widow-maker he kept in a pouch next to his heart.

"For Galzar's sake, sir! It's me, Kyblannos."

Phidestros stopped struggling when he recognized the voice, but didn't let go of the still un-drawn widow-maker.

"What in Regwarn's Hidey-hole is up now?"

"A parley, sir. Some of the mercenary captains would like a private word with you before the storming—out of Arch-Torturer Roxthar's hearing."

"By the Wargod's Mace, couldn't they pick a more civilized hour?" Phidestros groaned.

At least the captains had picked the right place. The tent Phidestros used when he spent the night in the siege lines was a thousand paces from the nearest other camp. Men like Geblon guarded it, men who had been with Phidestros in the days of the Iron Company, men who had no fear of priests or torturers. Men who had guarded him with their lives and would go on doing so.

Phidestros cursed again and sat up. "Who wants to talk with me?"

"Grand-Captains Brakkos, Demmos and Thymestros; Captain Phidammes; Highpriest Olmnestes and three other captains I did not recognize."

Included were some of the best freelances in the Grand Host, leading about a sixteenth of its strength. Now that he was awake enough to think clearly, Phidestros found himself not altogether surprised.

The first attempt to storm Tarr-Hostigos had been a disaster. The attack up the mountainside at the breach and up the draw toward the gate had been bloodily repulsed. The Hostigi had thrown everything from explosive shells to ordinary rocks at the storming parties, reducing them to bloody rags fifty paces from the walls.

In the northern works, a handful of Hostigi had slaughtered twenty besiegers for every man they lost before the scaling ladders finally reached the walls. The Hostigi might have held as firmly as they had in the main castle, if it hadn't been for the newly arrived rifle companies back from the vanguard under Captain-General Antaphon.

Once in action, they pinned even a Hostigi rifleman perched on a tower. Two companies of them had given the Grand Host the northern work of Tarr-Hostigos. Five might have given them the main castle.

At least they now had a place where heavy guns might play against the keep, once they were hauled up there. Given time, those guns would finish the work with no need for another attack.

Time, though, is exactly what I won't have. If the free company captains don't take it away, Roxthar will. He knows only one way of solving this problem, and it's always the bloodiest. Does he plan to bleed the Grand Host to an empty husk so it cannot turn against him after Kalvan is overthrown?

Phidestros began pulling on his breeches. "Kyblannos, what do they want? More gold?"

"I don't know, sir. Truly."

"Help me get my breastplate on, then let them in."

The captains slunk into the tent like foxes into a turkey yard. Uncle Wolf Olmnestes was in the lead, chief among the Host's Uncle Wolfs and formerly a freelance Captain-General of some note in his own right. His hair was almost white and his beard iron gray, but his face was still ruddy and his back straight as a musket barrel.

When everyone was inside, Phidestros rose. "I won't apologize for poor hospitality. It's too late for that. What can I do for you gentlemen?"

Olmnestes spoke first. "In the name of Galzar, can you bring this mad siege to an end?"

"Not without putting my privy parts between the blades of Roxthar's clipping shears."

Nervous laughter skittered around the tent.

Grand Captain Brakkos spoke up next. "I thought you led this army, Grand Captain-General, not Roxthar's regiment of bedgowns."

"I command, but only so long as I do nothing to offend Styphon's House or Great King Lysandros. Where do you think I would be now if we had lost at Ardros Field? In chains, I tell you! Even now, I have Grand Master Soton, Roxthar, and would-be successors all tugging at my sword arm—especially Captain-General Antaphon, Lysandros' pet lapdog. The real commander of this Host is the one who fills your paychests with gold and you damn-well know it."

"Isn't there some way you can stop this senseless assault on Tarr-Hostigos?" Olmnestes asked.

"No, Uncle Wolf. Were it up to me I'd leave a blockading force with our heavy guns, to starve the Hostigi out of their fortress or knock it down upon their thick heads. I would take the rest of the Host after Kalvan until I caught him, and then pickle his head as a gift for Lysandros.

"But our Holy Investigator decrees otherwise. And, since I would like to survive this siege, I am not going to disobey."

"May Thanor strike that blasphemer of Galzar dead with a lighting bolt!" Captain Brakkos shouted.

"Hush, man! Here even the trees have ears," a captain urged.

"Curse and blast Styphon and all his Archpriests!" Brakkos raved. "This isn't the only gap in the mountains, for Galzar's sake. None of the others are half so stoutly defended. Let us push through one of them and fight Kalvan's fugitives, not sit here like owls in a thunderstorm!"

"Silence, Brakkos," Olmnestes snapped. "Your flapping tongue is a danger to us all." His steely gaze finally reduced Brakkos to muttering.

The Uncle Wolf turned to Phidestros, "Grand Captain-General, you are the leader of this Host, and that is a sacred trust given by Galzar. It is your duty to stop this madness."

"If I had Galzar's hand to guide mine, I would. But I do not. Only Styphon's branding iron and the headsman's ax rule here. I say again, and I hope for the last time, if I order the Grand Host to do anything whatsoever that displeases Roxthar or Soton, my life will be forfeit and the Host will be under the command of Grand Master Soton or Great King Lysandros."

"Then stay and be Roxthar's slave if you will," Grand-Captain Thymestros snapped. "We shall do otherwise."

"Do anything else and your life won't be worth a bent phenig." Phidestros answered. "Roxthar has a memory like Galzar's Muster Book."

"Styphon's tentacles do not cover the earth," Demmos replied. "King Theovacar is always ready to hire freelances, and I've word of a revolt in Thagnor with a prince taking oaths. There are no Investigators in the Upper Middle Kingdoms, nor in Hos-Zygros or Hos-Agrys."

"Not yet, my friends," Phidestros said, wearier than even the hour and a moon of killing could account for. "I have known you, Demmos, for six winters have I not?"

Grand-Captain Demmos nodded.

"We have fought side by side in four wars. I consider all of you my friends, as well as companions at arms. I fear for your lives. If you leave, it is at your own risk. The day is Styphon's and his sun burns hot and scorches everywhere. If you must leave, do so at night, without a word to anyone. If Roxthar hears of your plans, the Red Hand will drown you in your own blood. Marshal Xenophes has bands of Red Hand watching all the roads out of Hostigos Town—so beware. Also let it be said that this is oath breaking and I speak against it. Uncle Wolf, what say you?"

Uncle Wolf Olmnestes sighed. "There are reports of a Ban of Galzar against the Holy Host, specifically Styphon's Own Guard and the Investigators who have murdered and tortured Hostigi prisoners of war. But until I receive the Ban itself from the Council of Galzar, I am unable to put it into force and can do nothing to stop Roxthar or the Grand Host. If any of you free company captains break your oaths, you will also be under the ban and no reputable lord will be able to hire your services. This is the Law."

Brakkos cried, "By Styphon's Brass Balls, you are as weak-spined as our Grand Captain-General! Don't any of you see what's going on? The moment Roxthar and his butchers are through with Kalvan, they will next turn on All-father Dralm, then Tranth, then Yirtta Allmother, finally on Galzar himself! Fight before it is too late. We betray our oaths, but not our god!"

Demmos shook his head. "Uncle Wolf Olmnestes speaks words of truth. Any of you who desert this siege without his permission will be under Galzar's ban. Captain-General Phidestros has publicly offered us a position in his own Beshtan Army; I for one will take him up on his offer. I fear the time of the free companies is over. The Fireseed War has changed our lives; we are no longer free."

Phidestros, who knew full well when the time to strike was before him, said, "I will guarantee your ranks in the Army of Beshta. In these times, I can also guarantee you plenty of work with your swords, as well."

Captain Demmos rose up and touched his heart with his hand. "Both I and the White Company swear to faithfully serve Prince Phidestros of Beshta, obey his orders and commands. I give my blood oath. It is done, before Galzar and my new commander."

Phidestros gave him the ring off his finger, saying, "By this token, I take your oath."

The other captains looked at each other nodding their heads. Thymestros came forward to give him his oath.

In a thunderous silence, Brakkos left the tent.

It was Olmnestes who broke the silence. "Captain Brakkos and his men will be gone before dawn." The priest intoned in a hushed voice, "By Galzar's Mace, they are doomed. Yet I fear Brakkos may well be right."

FORTY-SIX

I

Ptosphes looked around him at the battle-strained faces on the keep's roof. At dawn they would face the twenty-first day of the siege; almost certainly they would face the second storming attempt. The first storming attempt over a quarter moon ago had gained the enemy the north tower, but shellfire from the keep had kept them from mounting guns there.

The first had cost the garrison of Tarr-Hostigos a hundred men, the Styphoni three thousand. Another prisoner raid had yielded them that intelligence. To strike back and take Styphoni prisoners had helped boost sagging morale.

The second storming would be more dangerous. The enemy would certainly have some tactics devised to meet shells. Those rifles would come into play against the Hostigi marksmen who had butchered the mercenary captains. He would have to order his riflemen to the upper floors where they could fire behind the protection of arrow slits and battlements.

Worst of all, this time Styphon's Red Hand would be clutching at Tarr-Hostigos. The Temple Bands had been gathering along the Old Tigo road all day. Would they lead the assault, or bring up the rear to remind the vanguard that there was something to be feared more than Hostigi shells?

Two men carrying Captain-General Harmakros' chair set it down with a thump. The two men carrying Harmakros himself gently lowered him into the chair, arranged the cushions behind him and stepped back.

Even in the twilight, Ptosphes could see that Harmakros' cheeks were too flushed for a man who was supposed to be healing well.

"Did you have wine at dinner?"

"Why not, Prince? It will take more wine than we have in Tarr-Hostigos to kill me before Styphon's House does."

Ptosphes sighed. With variations, he'd heard this at least twenty times today, since it had become obvious that the Styphoni were gathering again. No one expected to see tomorrow's sunset. Nobody appeared to care either, so long as they could take a proper escort to Galzar's Great Hall with them. To be sure of doing that, everybody had worked all day as if demons would pounce on them the moment they dropped their tools or even stopped to take a deep breath.

Ptosphes looked the length of what was, for another night at least, his castle. The work done to protect the *mortars* showed most clearly. The four small ones now had stones banked around them, so that the shells bursting outside wouldn't do so much damage. The three larger *mortars* were back on their field carriages. They could move to prepared positions all over the courtyard as fast as the men on the ropes could pull them, then fire again almost as soon as they stopped.

The four biggest *mortars* were still in the pit in the outer courtyard. They were really just an old twelve-pounder and three eight-pounders, with their breeches sunk into the earth and their muzzles raised. They were too heavy to move or mount anywhere else, and in any case they could reach everywhere around Tarr-Hostigos from the inner courtyard. Their crews were finishing a magazine of timbers covered with stones, to protect their shells and fireseed.

"Prince Ptosphes!" One of the riflemen on sentry duty was pointing toward the siege lines on the west side of the castle. "They're starting to move around before the light goes. Think they'll come tonight?" He sounded almost eager.

Ptosphes stared into the dusk through his *farseer,* wishing for the hundredth time in the last four years that he had one of the far-seeing glasses of

Great King Truman's army that his son-in-law talked about. They were like Kalvan's old pistol—the Great King couldn't even teach his friends how to make the tools to make the glasses.

Yet those skills *would* be learned. Ermut had made six or seven of the long *farseer* tubes that brought far away closer. Kalvan had praised Ermut, but the truth was they were only two or three times better than the naked eye—not like the far-seers Kalvan talked about. Yet, what the gods had taught once, they could teach again—and more easily, because they would be teaching men who were trying to learn and knew what power the new knowledge might give them.

If Kalvan's luck continued to hold, his children might live to look at a battlefield through farseers, or even ride into battle aboard one of those armored wagons that moved without horses and carried guns that fired many times while a man was drawing a deep breath.

Ptosphes put aside thoughts of the future he wouldn't live to see and looked to where the rifleman was pointing. The man was right. Things that looked vaguely like enormous carts were rolling slowly along behind the trenches. It was too dark to make out more, but they must be heavy. The wheels of the carts looked to be solid wood and as high as a man.

"Should we try a few ranging shots, just to remind them that we're awake?" Harmakros asked.

"Not with the mortars. We want to save their shells."

"That little rifled bronze five-pounder on the inner gate, though it might not have the range."

"Kalvan said we shouldn't use case shot with rifled guns," Ptosphes said. "It damages the rifling. With solid shot, that five-pounder will do more good up here."

Harmakros' face asked what he was too tactful to put into words: 'how likely is it that any gun in Tarr-Hostigos will last long enough to damage itself, once the Grand Host advances?' Perhaps he was chafing at having to wait like a bear tethered in a pit, as the dogs circled just out of reach.

The hoisting tackle on the keep easily hauled the five-pounder up to the roof, but not before darkness fell. Half a dozen shots produced a satisfactory outburst of shouts and curses from the Styphoni, but otherwise they seemed to have fallen off the edge of the world. After the half dozen failed to start a fire, Ptosphes ordered the gun to cease fire.

He made a final inspection, counting with special care the torches and tar-pots laid ready, in case the Styphoni came at night. It wasn't likely; the chance of hitting friends in a night attack would not please the mercenary captains. It wasn't impossible either, and Ptosphes was determined to follow Kalvan's teachings to the end (not far away now): prepare for *everything* that isn't impossible.

At last Ptosphes returned to the Great Hall, to find Harmakros asleep in the chair of state and snoring like volley fire from a company of musketeers. Ptosphes rolled himself in his cloak without taking off his armor, on a pallet as far from Harmakros as he could find.

He'd thought he might be too tired or uneasy to sleep, but instead he drifted off into oblivion almost as soon as he stretched out his legs and lowered his head onto the dirt-stiffened cloth.

II

Phidestros brushed the sleep out of his eyes and stared through the valley's early-morning shadows at the Grand Host's encampment. A splendid sight with its thousands of campfires—until one remembered that all these tens of thousands of men were chained to this desolate valley by a castle held by three or four hundred old men and walking wounded. Meanwhile, the Usurper Kalvan continued to flee into the wilderness.

As it was, he was chief over the Grand Host only in name. In truth, he was first among equals, all of them hamstrung by Archpriest Roxthar—including Great King Lysandros who was in debt to Styphon's House up to his eyebrows. The Investigator was utterly convinced that the root of Kalvan's heresy was to be found in the Princedom of Hostigos and equally determined to extricate it if he had to Investigate every man, woman and child still remaining in the Princedom. Roxthar would not allow any stone to be left unturned, including that mother-of-all-stones, Tarr-Hostigos. Against that particular stone the Grand Host had bruised its foot for the best part of a moon, while Kalvan's real army slipped away. But, with Galzar's blessing, today that was about to change.

A small forest of poles already held the bodies of about a fifth of Hostigos Town's townspeople, those who had failed the Investigation. Add to that number those who fled with Kalvan, and by spring there would hardly be enough Hostigi left to bury their dead.

If the Investigation came to his lands again, Phidestros resolved it would not be *his* new subjects who decorated the gallows. He doubted the Investigators would do as well with their hot irons and boning knives against soldiers as they did against women and children. It might cost his own head to take Roxthar's, but at least he would have the pleasure of harvesting the madman's first.

The shadows began to fade. From his vantage point, Phidestros saw the camps coming to life, like kicked anthills. He'd wanted to lead the Iron Band in the first assault himself, but Soton insisted that Phidestros keep himself safely in the rear. Captain-Generals, Soton stated emphatically, were *not* meant to be fired off like Kalvan's *rockets*.

Soton was right, of course. Had Phidestros been in the vanguard during the first storming attempt, he might be dead along with so many others from Ptosphes' exploding cannonballs.

It still rankled, though, to be leading from behind. One more thing he would have to get used to, he supposed; along with asking who had married whom *before* he swore unquestioning obedience. Great King Lysandros' support was reluctant because the Great King owed his throne to Styphon's House and knew that Roxthar and the Inner Circle had to be placated before he could allow his commanders to do their jobs. At least Lysandros had shown the good judgment to forestall Galzar's Ban and ride to Hostigos Town to recast the Grand Host in such a manner that when the Ban was made public it would not lose most of its mercenaries.

Phidestros cupped his hands around a wood splinter and used the tinderbox to get a spark. When the pipe was drawing, he blew out a long plume of smoke, watching the rising morning breeze chase it away.

"Please, Captain-General," Geblon said. "Would you get down? Otherwise the Hostigi will aim at your smoke."

Phidestros doubted that in this breeze even a Hostigi rifleman could hit a man at this distance, but obeyed anyway. He could see as well, and make Geblon happy to boot.

The guns newly emplaced in the battery at the foot of the draw thumped. Their shots tore masonry from a gate tower. Another salvo followed, and white smoke rose in place of the morning mist.

Phidestros puffed on his pipe and prayed to all the true gods that today the butcher's bill would be a light one.

III

Kalvan watched as Xykos, Captain of Rylla's Beefeaters—in polished silver dinner plate yet—opened the tent flap so that he could enter the makeshift Council Hall. Rylla walked beside him, her face set like stone, careful not to accidentally brush up against her husband. She had been frozen like this ever since she had been unable to talk Prince Ptosphes out of leaving Tarr-Hostigos. Possibly she blamed herself for this, or her father—or him.

With all that was going on with their exodus from Hostigos, Kalvan had neither the time nor the patience to draw it out of her. Rylla was too proud to talk about her problems without a struggle. A fight between the Great King and his Queen, with no privacy and things so uncertain, would be bad for army morale. Still, he should be doing something, but what? Nothing came to mind so he squeezed her arm affectionately. That she didn't shake his hand loose, he took as a good sign.

All the surviving Princes of what was once the Great Kingdom of Hos-Hostigos, and most of the generals, were seated upon barrels, boxes and chests facing the Fireseed Throne, which had been shipped out of Tarr-Hostigos by wagon at no small cost in space. Kalvan knew that it had displaced a load of foodstuffs, but symbols were as important as food—maybe in cases like this, more important. His people needed a visible reminder that their *homeland* was not forgotten and that their migration was temporary—not permanent.

Kalvan grimaced in pain as he limped over to his *ad hoc* throne with the aid of a panther-headed cane. His wound was no longer inflamed, but it still ached. Willow bark tea made the pain endurable.

No longer Great King Kalvan of Hos-Hostigos, but Great King in exile. Great King of all the land his army occupied and overlord to only those he surveyed in their encampments and inside this *faux* council hall: Prince Pheblon, formerly of Nostor, head swathed in bandages courtesy of an axe blade; Prince Sarrask, late of Sask, looking disgustingly hale and hearty; Prince Tythanes of Kyblos, who looked as if he didn't know who or where he was; and Prince Kestophes of Ulthor, whose face showed he knew his reign in Ulthor was coming to an end. Prince Phrames of Beshta, his face still pale, was leaning on a cane of his own.

Well, no matter how disgruntled the assembled Princes were they were better off than the rest; Prince Balthames of Sashta was no longer of this world, courtesy of a bullet to the head—payment for his treachery, Prince Armanes of Nyklos had died in his saddle at Ardros Field from a halberd blow and Prince Ptosphes, still—he hoped—holding Tarr-Hostigos, would soon join the ranks of heroes in Galzar's Great Hall. Certainly without Ptosphes and Harmakros' valiant stand at Tarr-Hostigos they would not be here today.

After Kalvan sat down, Chancellor Chartiphon opened the meeting with the traditional ceremonial remarks and flourishes; in times of trouble these rituals and customs were more important than when times were good. "All ye rise, Great King Kalvan will now speak!"

Kalvan rose to his feet, paused to light his pipe and then said, "Now to business. As you all know the Great Kingdom of Hos-Hostigos has been displaced along with Our person. As far as We can determine, Styphon's armies occupy the Princedoms of Beshta, Sashta and Hostigos. Nostor's days are numbered, as are Sask's. Nyklos' too, once Phidestros clears the Gap. However, it will take time to conquer and occupy those Princedoms—" He paused to look over at Rylla, who was sitting rigidly at her Throne. "Time we have, thanks to First Prince Ptosphes' noble sacrifice. Let us all Praise Allfather Dralm."

There were murmurs of "Praise Dralm and Ptosphes." All of the assembled bowed their heads in silent prayer after Kalvan's example. He felt like the worst sort of hypocrite, but it was the least he could do for the man who had treated him as a son, rather than son-in-law, and given the ultimate gift of his life to his people—time.

"As Great King in exile and no longer being able to offer the protection We have sworn to give, We will release Prince Tythanes of Kyblos from homage. He is free to return to his lands with any and all sworn subjects who wish to return with their overlord."

Despite everyone else's shock, Kalvan hoped they took him up on his offer. He already had more mouths than he could feed as well as more soldiers than any sane ally would welcome.

Prince Tythanes' look of relief was so genuine and heartfelt, he looked as if he were about to breakout in tears. "Thank you, Your Majesty. I withdraw any and all oaths to Your Majesty and the Throne of Hos-Hostigos." He continued on in this vein for almost ten minutes with a litany of praise regarding his former king and fellow princes.

"We will return to Kyblos and await each candle until Your Majesty returns to his rightful place on the Fireseed Throne of Hos-Hostigos. Upon that moment I shall pay my homage, thus I swear."

"I shall remember your loyalty and wish you Dralm's grace," Kalvan intoned. "You may leave now." As Tythanes and his entourage left the big tent Kalvan thought, the Prince might miss Styphon's noose this time, but it would yank him out of his saddle the following year. He was doing Tythanes no favor: a fact not missed by Prince Sarrask, who muttered under his breath yet loud enough that Kalvan could hear, "Styphon's own fool!"

"It is settled. Chancellor Chartiphon, will you give Us a report on the status of the subjects of Hos-Hostigos?"

Chartiphon, his formerly silver hair turned white, rose to his feet. While still fleshed out, Chartiphon carried himself like an old man. Leaving his home and friends to die, had taken most of the starch out of his step. Kalvan was glad he'd taken the initiative to remove him as captain-general last year. It suddenly hit him full force just how alone he was without Ptosphes, Harmakros and Verkan. *Damn Styphon's House all to Hell! What am I going to do without them?*

"Your Majesty, I have attempted to make an accurate census of the refugees, but it has proven impossible. New parties join us every day, while others drift away or leave for Hos-Agrys or Hos-Zygros. Some return to be counted again." Chartiphon shook his head.

"I don't need an exact answer, Chancellor. A good guess will do."

"Four hundred and fifty to six hundred thousand men, women and children is my estimate."

There was the sound of indrawn breath from among the assembled nobles.

Chartiphon, oblivious to the reaction of his words, continued. "The refugees are strung out behind us for two hundred and fifty marches. Impossible to count them all. Many more are just arriving from Sask, Nostor, Sashta, Ulthor and even Kyblos. A Nostori party of two hundred and fifty soldiers arrived yesterday with ten times that amount of civilians, by way of Glarth. They told tales of brigandage and starvation that would melt even Styphon's brass heart."

For about the hundredth time in the last moon, Kalvan wondered if it wouldn't have been better for everyone if he'd just stayed where he belonged in his own world. *Stop feeling sorry for yourself! What's done is done, damnit; now get back to the job at hand.*

"Then we will be running out of food even faster than I had thought. Uncle Wolf Tharses, We are going to put you in charge of victuals as well as medicine."

"But, Your Majesty—"

"Tharses, there is no one else. You are the only person *everyone* trusts. Starting tomorrow, everyone—including Ourselves—will be going on half-rations. Also, We want you to double the number of hunting parties. And continue to burn anything and everything we cannot take with us, including crops and orchards. This is total war and anything that we cannot use we will kill, destroy or torch! "

The majority of the assembled councilors and princes drew back in horror, while many drew the circle of Dralm upon their breasts. It was time to give his allies the unvarnished truth; they were going to need it if they were to survive.

"Now, Prince Phrames will give us a report on the active status of the Army of Hos-Hostigos. General."

Phrames stood up stiffly from too many days on horseback. Despite his youth, Phrames was a first-rate field general as well as chief of staff. These days he and Captain-General Hestophes were the strongest shoulders Kalvan had to lean on now that Harmakros was gone.

"As of this morning, our muster book shows thirty-six thousand, five hundred and sixty-two active soldiers, including those wounded expected to return to active duty. About twenty-six thousand of these are on the muster rolls of the Royal Army of Hos-Hostigos. The remaining soldiers are members of Princely retinues or mercenaries. Many are short on armor and helmets, but all have weapons and at least one firearm. Our supply of fireseed is adequate and we have ample supplies of shot and lead for casting."

"How many of these are mercenaries?"

Hestophes winced. "Many of the mercenaries have deserted. We are still carrying over two thousand."

"We cannot afford to feed unreliable troops. Give them a choice: either they join the Royal Army or we muster them out."

"What about back pay?"

"Pay them whatever we owe, not a phenig more." The treasury of Hos-Hostigos was in a small baggage train of fourteen wagons. They were not impoverished, not yet, but that gold could disappear faster than an ice cream cone on a hot day if he wasn't careful. However, it was important to maintain the reputation of a King who always paid his debts.

The big question was: what to do next? He was faced with an alarming number of choices: he could return to the Princedom of Nyklos and attempt to hold off the Grand Host until winter when the change of seasons would provide some breathing room. Of course, by that same token it would have been smarter to try to hold Tarr-Hostigos and wait the Styphoni out. But, with the Princedom occupied by hostile troops, he would have been unable to protect or feed his people. Moving lock, stock and barrel into Nyklos would only postpone the inevitable.

Or, he could make nice with King Theovacar and hope that he needed a vassal punished or removed. In other words, sell the army to the highest bidder, knowing that Styphon's Grand Host would think twice about going up against the combined armies of Hos-Hostigos and Grefftscharr. But, as Tortha had pointed out in their talk last night, that was another temporary solution to a permanent problem. In the end, it still would not provide Kalvan and his people with a home base from which to operate.

Tortha had agreed to travel to Greffa and see if Theovacar could come up with a better solution because right now Kalvan was fresh out of ideas. At least when Napoleon was exiled to Elba he didn't have a half a million or more mouths to feed.

FORTY-SEVEN

Ptosphes was leading a cavalry charge at the climax of a great battle. The guns thundered and something else was growling like a whole forest full of hungry bears.

He looked down again. He wasn't riding a horse, but standing on top of one of Great King Truman's wagons with its strange gun. Except that the wagon wasn't quite as Kalvan had described it—it had the head and tail of a horse, the mane flying into his face. As they rode downhill toward the lines of an enemy flying the colors of Styphon's Red Hand, the wagon-horse turned its head to look at Ptosphes.

Its eyes glowed a sinister green, and he knew he was riding a creature possessed by demons.

He clawed for reins he couldn't find, trying to turn the creature so he wouldn't have to look into those eyes. No matter how desperately he groped, he couldn't find the reins. At last his fingers closed on something that felt like woolen cloth, which was a strange thing to make reins out of—

"Prince Ptosphes! Prince Ptosphes! Wake up!"

Nobody should be telling him to wake up in a dream and this was still a dream. He could still hear the thunder of guns, even if he couldn't hear the bear-like growling of the iron wagon.

"Prince Ptosphes! The Grand Host is coming!"

"Hu-rrrupppp!" Ptosphes lurched into a sitting position before he realized that he was awake and clutching his blanket.

He heard guns thundering and someone shouted in his ear that the Styphoni were attacking. The window showed gray instead, of black. Two men ran toward it, carrying heavy rifled muskets, nearly tripping over Ptosphes as they came.

Ptosphes threw off the blanket and stood. The air of the keep already held a sodden heat. He felt obscurely resentful that so many men should have to fight their last battle on a miserably hot day.

Someone was pushing a cup of tepid sassafras tea into his hands. He emptied it in three gulps and held it out again for more. The second cupful was half Ermut's brandy. He set the cup down on the nearest chest, retrieved his sword and buckled it on.

Harmakros was sitting in the chair of state, wide-awake and barking orders. His stump was propped up on a pillow-padded stool and two pistols hung from the arm of the chair.

"Good luck, Prince."

"The same to you, old son."

That was all the speech Ptosphes allowed himself, even if it was probably the last time he would see Harmakros. If the riflemen were taking position before the arrow slits, there was hardly time to talk.

Chroniclers a hundred years from now will probably make up fine farewell speeches for both of us. Tutors will torment children by forcing them to learn those speeches.

As Ptosphes passed through the keep door to the outer stairs, the gunroar doubled, then doubled again. The mortars had opened fire. Whatever was coming at Tarr-Hostigos was now within their range.

Ptosphes hurried down the stairs as fast as he could without appearing uneasy. At the bottom he saw that the guards who saluted him were also busily piling tar-soaked brushwood under the timbers of the stairs. One torch and the easy way into the keep would go up in flames, making another line of defense for the last of the garrison.

From the tower over the gate between the courtyards, Ptosphes could see everywhere except directly behind the keep. In the last attack, they had given the Styphoni dogs heavy casualties with case shot and supporting rifle fire, but in the end he had ordered the last of his command back to the keep in the inner bailey, where they could maximize the firepower of Tarr-Hostigos' small garrison. He hadn't the heart to call muster, but a lot of familiar faces, like Vurth's, were missing.

Three large storming parties were advancing, one toward the breach made by the siege guns, one by the main gate, and one holding well back on the northeastern side. At a single glance, Ptosphes knew that nearly half the Grand Host must be hurling itself at the castle. It would take all they had to stop the Styphoni now. It was Dralm's own miracle they'd held out as long as they had, he admitted to himself. Kalvan, Rylla and the baby should be well into Ulthor. *Now, let's go out in a blaze of glory!*

The northeastern column was in fact so far away that Ptosphes wondered if they were the reserves, until he saw what was slowing them down. They had last night's mysterious wagons with them, except that they weren't wagons. They were stout-timbered wooden platforms mounted on immense solid wheels, each pushed by a hundred men with poles and pulled by hundreds more with ropes.

Except some of the 'men' wore skirts, and some were too small to be adults. Men, women and children from Hostigos Town, forced to haul the platforms forward until they reached the moat. The platforms would fill the moat most handily, offering a firm base for ladders. Of course the castle's defenders wouldn't fire on their own people to keep the platforms from reaching their destination....

This had to be the Arch-Butcher Roxthar's work! Behind the platforms marched a large body of infantry with pikes, halberds and glaives, leading ten bands of musketeers, each a thousand strong or more—the last, a Temple Band of Styphon's Red Hand, held aloft the Guard's black pinion with a red sun-wheel. Scores of two and three-man teams carried scaling ladders, while others carried coils of rope. Once the wooden platforms were in place, the Styphoni would pour into the castle like a mountain stream swollen by floodwaters.

Ptosphes used the name of every god he'd ever heard of but couldn't find words to describe the habits of Soton and Roxthar in this world or the fate he wished for them in another. To set women and children as targets—and to fight behind their skirts!

He started to add Phidestros to the cursing, then halted. After all, one does not swear at the whip when it strikes, but at the hand wielding it.

Ptosphes gripped the railing until his nails gouged the wood, and then shouted, "Gunners! Open fire on those platforms! Round shot, and aim at the wheels." Styphon himself couldn't start those landbound rafts moving again once their wheels were wrecked.

The gunners looked at each other, then at their Prince. They'd seen who was out there in front of their guns, maybe even seen their own kin. Thalmoth shouted, "Better clean Hostigi cannonballs than the Investigator's rack!" Then they began slewing the guns around. Ptosphes heard most of them cursing and praying, one or two weeping.

Three siege guns were now firing from the Host's battery in front of the main gate, over the heads of the column marching to the gate. Big guns, too. Ptosphes saw half the main gate flung backward off its hinges into the portcullis, which bent ominously.

A less well-aimed shot ploughed through the infantry of the storming column. They halted, giving the guns and riflemen and musketeers on the gate towers an even better target. Their firing sounded like a single volley, and they fired three more times before the enemy column moved again. It moved more slowly now, leaving behind a trail of writhing, bloody bodies, like a dying animal dragging its guts behind as it sought to close with the hunter.

The column coming at the breach was taking the most punishment from the mortars, whose crews were firing much too fast to be concerned with safety. Ptosphes saw one man knocked down and crushed as a mortar shifted on its base, and a shell with a fuse cut too short blew up just above the walls. A dozen defenders went down. The ones who rose again shook their fists at the mortar crews.

Now the guns beside Ptosphes were shooting at the wheeled platforms. The first shot flew high, glancing off the heavy timbers and soaring over the heads of the Harphaxi infantry directly behind the platform. Another regiment was coming into sight behind the first one—armored men in blackened armor, marching under a black banner with a silver sun-wheel. Soton's Knights were fighting on foot today.

The second shot bowled into the prisoners hauling the platform. The third chewed splinters from its edge. Before a fourth could hit, the people in front of the platform dropped their ropes and ran.

The infantry charged forward, though the gaps between the platforms. The fourth shot smashed the head of a company of arquebusiers, halting it. The rest of the company reached open ground. The pikemen picked up the fallen ropes, while others leveled musketoons, arquebuses and pistols, firing at the fleeing Hostigi rushing towards Tarr-Hostigos. A few of the townspeople tried to run back behind the platforms, but were cut down by the swords and maces of the advancing Knights.

Ptosphes had long given up hope of adequately cursing Styphon or his servants. He merely shouted, "Change to case shot!" Those platforms weren't going to be smashed or stopped, but they could be made useless by killing enough of the Grand Host ready to pull them into place and climb from them up the walls.

Forget the Hostigi prisoners. They were doomed.

So was the garrison of Tarr-Hostigos. Not that there'd been much doubt about this since they'd refused Soton's latest offer of terms. (And what terms—death for all the captains and the rest to be at the mercy of Roxthar's Investigators!) The last quarter-candle had just made an existing certainty more certain still. Men who stormed a castle after this kind of punishment would be half-mad and totally deaf to requests for quarter, which they wouldn't give anyway.

The siege guns aimed at the main gate were firing higher now, trying to silence the guns in the gate tower. One of them was disabled, but the other two were still hurling case shot straight into the column, inflicting hideous losses. Guns from the other towers were now hammering at the column as well, scything down entire companies like farmers harvesting wheat.

Smoke gushed up from the enemy battery, more than one could expect from the discharge of even the largest gun. Ptosphes saw men flying into the air and others running with their clothing on fire. He heard the thump of an explosion—someone careless with fireseed—as the rate of fire increased.

More Hostigi case shot tore into the column then, suddenly, it was breaking up and the men were running back down the draw in a futile effort to find shelter, some of their officers beating at them with halberds and swords, others joining the rout. From the walls of Tarr-Hostigos, cheers joined the gunfire.

Ptosphes had a moment of thinking that perhaps their doom wasn't so certain after all. One column broken, its men looking as if they would be hard to rally for another attack. If the defenders could do the same with the other two columns, the mercenary captains might have the same second thoughts they'd had during the first storming attempt. If they had second thoughts and let Styphon's House know them, the False God himself couldn't keep the Archpriests from having to listen. And if the Archpriests chose to turn the Red Hand loose on the mercenaries, the Grand Host's war against Hostigos would become a civil war within its own ranks—

Ptosphes' moment of hope ended as he saw the column approaching the breach suddenly sprout scaling ladders. They were going to get in or at least close; the heavy mortars had fired off all their shells and round shot wouldn't do so well even against packed men.

The twelve-pounder on top of the barricade let fly with a triple charge of musket balls. "I told you it wouldn't blow!" Thalmoth cried. Like a volley from a massed regiment, it smashed into the column. Already ragged from climbing the slope, the column now barely deserved the name.

Hard on the twelve-pounder's heels came point-blank musketry that melted away more of the column. Every musketeer within range had six or seven loaded weapons ready to hand for just this moment. For a brief space, they could fire as fast as the rifles of Great King Truman's host with their 'magazines' of eight rounds.

These foes had their blood up though, or maybe better captains. Then Ptosphes saw blue and orange colors and recognized the Sacred Squares of Hos-Ktemnos, the reputed *best* infantry in the Seven Kingdoms. They rose across the rubble before the breach like a blue wave, with clumps of musketeers on the flanks firing over the heads of the storming parties to keep down Hostigi fire. The crews of the useless heavy mortars drew swords and pistols and joined the mass of men struggling in the breach. Ptosphes drew his own sword, ready to join them if they showed signs of flagging.

Two of the three platforms were still closing on the walls, a third had put one wheel through the roof of a sinkhole and was defying all efforts of the men on its ropes to get it moving again. Around the others was a mob of Hostigi prisoners, Zarthani Knights and mercenary infantry being hit every minute by case shot and rifle bullets but coming on nonetheless—

One of the overheated four-pounders beside Ptosphes recoiled so violently that it snapped its breechings and knocked down Thalmoth. He laid with his thigh a mass of blood, white bone shining through the torn flesh, cursing the gun crew for not remembering what he taught them and asking for a pistol. Ptosphes gave him one of his own pistols.

The first platform rumbled up the last few paces of the slope and crashed across the moat, which ran some ten rods wide and eight rods deep. Soldiers on the top of the platforms began to hoist ladders. The Hostigi riflemen firing inside the castle's towers thinned their ranks.

The first ladder rose up on the platform, and then flew to pieces as a shot from nowhere split it from top to bottom. At least it came from what seemed like nowhere to Ptosphes, although he knew that the part of the battle he could see and hear must be rapidly shrinking. This storming of Tarr-Hostigos was already making every other battle he'd fought sound like a mother's lullaby.

Off to the left of the platform, Soton's guns were finally coming into action. One was firing from an incline, with dead gunners around it showing that the Hostigi riflemen hadn't overlooked this new target. The other guns were being emplaced on the open hillside by men working in frantic haste, obviously eager to start shooting before the battle ended and they lost their share of glory. Ptosphes wondered what share of glory they would have if they hit more of their own men than the enemy's. Their share of broken bones and heads, more likely.

The second platform was in place now, ladders rising on it. The men on these ladders must be some of the southern swampmen Soton had brought north, or the Blethan Ruthani who had raided their baggage train at Ardros Field. They carried no armor, no clothing except leather leggings and breechcloths, and no weapons but hand axes and long wicked knives. If the men in the mortar pit could start hitting the wall in time, there was still a chance—

The Hostigi mortar emplacement spewed flame, smoke, slabs of stone, and flying timbers. An enemy shot or a stray spark had touched off the remaining fireseed in the magazine. Most of the men in or around the pit went down where they stood.

Flying debris scythed into the rear of the Hostigi infantry holding the barricade at the breach. Their line wavered. Some charged forward, grappling with Styphoni and rolling down the rubble to die in the moat with them. Others gave way, and a volley of musketry cleared a path through the ones who stood. Across the dying and the dead of both sides, the Sacred Squares poured over the barricade and down into the outer courtyard.

It seemed to Ptosphes that the Styphoni reached the gatehouse where he stood in the time between one breath and the next. Bullets whistled around him; the men atop the keep were now firing on the inner wall without caring much who was there. His reluctance to turn his back on the enemy gave way to an indignant refusal to be shot in the back by his own men. He ran to the edge of the gun platform, sheathed his sword, and made his way down the rope ladder, with both hands until he was sure his arms would pull out of their sockets. The rope ended about two rods above the flagstone paving of the inner courtyard.

It was a long drop for an armored man no longer young. Ptosphes went to his knees and was quite sure all his bones were jarred loose from one another. Thankfully, all of them seemed intact when he stood. Smoke was rising from the base of the stairs to the keep. He sprinted for them without stopping to take a breath.

A bullet tore through his jack and glanced off his breastplate, while another clipped his beard and seared one hand. At first they came from both sides, then he heard a shout from above, "That's Prince Ptosphes, you wolf's bastard!" and the bullets from the keep stopped. A moment later a crash like the end of the world sounded from behind, followed by screams and curses that penetrated even the ringing in Ptosphes' ears, and a choking wave of fireseed smoke. Some Styphoni with more zeal than sense must have used a petard on the inner gate, no doubt blowing it open but also demolishing a good many comrades as well!

Two of the swamp warriors reached the foot of the stairs before Ptosphes. He cut one down with his sword, knocked the ax out of the other's hand, leaped on to the stairs, and dashed up them. By the time he reached the top, the blood pounding in Ptosphes' ears drowned out every other sound. He leaned against the wall beyond the doorway, feeling the cool stone against his forehead and not hearing the outer door being shut and bolted behind him.

By the time he'd been led to a chair and had a cup of wine thrust into his hands, Ptosphes had enough of his wits back to think about what to do next. This was no normal siege, where the garrison of the keep was always given one last chance to surrender. This one would end with the Styphoni trying to bury the Hostigi under a pile of their own dead flesh if they couldn't finish the battle any other way.

If Phidestros and Soton and their captains had the wits the gods gave to fleas, they would launch the last attack as soon as they could, before their men had time to lose their battle-rage. Otherwise those men might start thinking of the kind of fight waiting for them behind the walls of the keep.

When Ptosphes had drunk the wine and could stand, he walked over to Harmakros in the chair of state. He had to walk carefully, to avoid stepping on exhausted men catching their breaths, cleaning their weapons or just lying staring at the ceiling. The lightly wounded were taking care of each other; the badly wounded hadn't reached the keep.

"I lost sight of the column on the ridge. What of them?"

"They started to close when the column at the main gate ran. Then the breach fell, and the ridge fighters drew back. Not without leaving a good many men behind, to be sure."

"What do we have left?"

Harmakros' shrugged. "A hundred, maybe a few more. That's all, unless we get some through the underground passage from the outer courtyard."

"It's being watched?"

"Of course!" Harmakros wasn't going to take accusations of carelessness lightly, even now. "Three men, with a barrel of fireseed to blow it up if the bastards try to come through."

"They'll come soon, wherever they do it." Ptosphes leaned against a stone archway and propped himself up with his sword. By the Twelve True Gods, he was getting old!

"I have men watching on the roof, and more men on the stairs relaying messages, my Prince. They won't catch us napping."

"Unless they kill the men on the roof."

"With Soton's cannons? Not without shells, and maybe not even with them. Anyway, I'll wager a cask of Ermut's Best they don't have any shells."

"Done," Ptosphes said. "But just in case they do..."

"I've had the men on the roof build themselves a shelter, with chests and rolled-up tapestries."

Some of those tapestries, Ptosphes realized, were probably part of his wife's dowry. Not that anybody except Rylla would be left to care before long, of course, and this was a better end for the tapestries than being looted or burned, eaten by vermin or left to rot in the crumbling shell of the keep.

Ptosphes forced his mind away from such thoughts and climbed the stairs to the roof.

FORTY EIGHT

Seeing the Styphoni swarming over the shambles that had been his seat and home didn't improve Ptosphes' mood. It helped to see the men on the rifled five-pounder actually smiling as they carved notches in the smoke-stained oak of the gun carriage.

"The big one's for smashing the wheel of one siege gun. Didn't hit any of our people either," the gunner added. "The four little ones are banners we knocked down. The circle is one of the guns. We might have got ourselves a second, but the Styphoni were too cowardly to man it again and by then we'd run out of shot and we're firing broken pottery and chunks of masonry."

One of the swabbers laughed. "Styphon's bully boys didn't like eating our stones!"

Never mind that the gunners probably hadn't done half the damage they thought they had. If they spent the last candle of their lives grinning and the last moments killing more Styphoni, what did anything else matter to them now?

Ptosphes had just descended to the keep hall when a messenger followed him down the stairs. "They're moving a heavy field gun into the inner court-yard. One of theirs, though, from the number of men they've put to hauling it."

"Everyone to your places, men," Ptosphes said. He hesitated; adding, "It's been an honor to be your Prince and captain."

A ragged cheer rose, then outside the musketry began again with heavy, rapid fire. The expected message came down from the roof—the bullets were mostly coming up, to keep the gun up there out of action. Even a three-pound ball could wreck a gun carriage.

He saw a black-faced and bloodied Vurth crouching with a musketoon. "I thought you were dead!"

Vurth smiled, his crooked yellow teeth grinning like a death's head. "It'll take more than a Styphoni musket ball to take my life—Down Styphon!"

Ptosphes grinned as a score of harsh voices echoed with "Down Styphon!"

"Wait until they attack," Ptosphes ordered. "Then they'll have to cease fire or have spent bullets falling back on their friends." He doubted that the mercenaries or even the Knights would care to risk much of that. It had been a bad day for self-inflicted casualties on both sides; for the Styphoni it was about to get worse.

Galzar's muster-clerks are going to be working long hours today, Ptosphes thought.

Chrunngggg!

Something struck the outside of the wall—a solid shot, the report of its firing lost in the roar of musketry. "Not bad," Ptosphes said. "Sounds as if they hit just to the left of the door."

It took three more shots before the smashing of wood and the ringing of iron signaled a direct hit on the outer door. Two more shots completed the work. A rifleman crept up the stairs and into the doorway, peering through the wreckage.

"They're reloading, but they've lined up a storming party too. They can't be going to fire right over—here it comes—ahhhh!"

The pieces of the door flew into the keep chamber hall. So did the pieces of the rifleman. A cannonball rolled in after them, making the Hostigi do sprightly dances to avoid it.

Harmakros unhooked his pistols from the arm of the chair of state, cocked them and laid them in his lap, then raised an empty wine cup in salute to

Ptosphes. "I'll claim that brandy, Prince. If they had shells, they'd have used one then."

"So it would seem."

Then, from all the firing slits, the sentries shouted that the storming party was on the way. The gun on the roof let fly, although no one bothered to tell Ptosphes if it hit anything. It fired a second time…a third.

As the fourth shot went off, a score of Styphoni burst into the chamber hall.

A ragged volley of pistols and muskets half-deafened Ptosphes. He saw the leading rank of the enemy stagger and go down, but realized the men behind them now had shields of once-living flesh. He drew his own pistol and fired it over the heads of the six men who'd appointed themselves his last bodyguard. Then the Styphoni were everywhere.

Ptosphes decided that if demons ever really came into the world, they might look like Styphon's soldiers. The attackers wore every sort of armor and clothing except for those who wore little of either. They were black-faced, red-eyed, stinking, shrieking cries in no language intended for human ears, and waving strange weapons in more arms than the gods gave men.

The massed Styphoni gave Vurth a fine target for his musketoon. He shot one man, smashed in a second's face, then got a third in a wrestler's headlock and broke his neck before someone else ran him through. Vurth's diversion let Ptosphes break away from his bodyguards toward the fireplace and the concealed ladder leading down to the cellar. He had to be down there to do his last duty as Prince of Hostigos—not the last Prince; the gods grant it!—and knew he might have already waited too long.

Four of the bodyguards stayed alive to reload their weapons and see that their Prince no longer needed them. They fired into the Styphoni, and then closed with steel.

The first man to make a way past them Harmakros shot in the head. The second man ran Harmakros through the stomach; the Duke returned the compliment with his second pistol. A third man hesitated, uncertain whether to help his comrades or see if Harmakros was dead. Harmakros snatched the pistol from the man's belt, rammed the muzzle up under its owner's jaw, and pulled the trigger. The chair of state fell over, spilling out Harmakros' body as Ptosphes swung himself into the chimney.

The room was filling with Styphoni, many of them Temple Guardsmen with dented plate and fouled capes. Ptosphes forced himself to go down the iron rungs of the ladder one at a time. It would help nobody except Styphon's House if he failed in his last duty by falling down the chimney and dashing out what the siege had left of his brains.

By the time he reached the bottom, he knew that if he had to climb back up again his heart would burst before he finished the climb. He'd been right; he would not have lived to see his grandchildren grow up even without this Dralm-damned war! However, this way he was at least spared years of listening to old Tharses and Rylla fussing at him, making him eat and sleep and rest as they thought proper and generally trying to turn him into a corpse while he was still alive.

The blessed coolness of the cellar revived him a little. He found that he'd brought his pipe, tobacco and tinderbox with him, started to light up, stopped as he remembered the ironclad rules about smoking near fireseed, then laughed. It made precious little difference what anybody did down here now.

Ptosphes found the fireseed intact, all twenty tons of it minus a barrel or two. He also found the last of the magazine-keepers sitting at the foot of the stairs, along with his clubfooted grandson. The keeper was an old soldier past campaigning, with the grandson to support and no other kin. Ptosphes had given him the magazine by way of a pension.

"What can we do for you, my Prince?"

"If you have pistols—?"

The keeper showed an old cavalryman's matchlock. The boy produced a heavy-barreled boar-hunter's pistol.

"Good. Keep watch on the stairs."

With his pipe in his mouth, Prince Ptosphes walked over to a row of small barrels, chose one from the top, cracked it open, and then laid a trail of fireseed a thumb wide and a finger deep to the center of the larger barrels. Just to be safe, he borrowed one of the keeper's handspikes and knocked in the head of one of the larger barrels. Fireseed cascaded out until a helmetful lay waiting at the end of the train, with the twenty tons waiting beyond.

By the time Ptosphes was finished, fists were hammering on the outside of the cellar door. Then he heard the more solid sounds of a chest or bench being swung against it. Wood cracked and metal pulling out of stone screeched as a hinge gave way. The door half-swung, half-fell inward.

All three Hostigi fired together at the first silhouettes to appear. The answering volley sent bullets spanging around the cellar. One hit the boy in the stomach. The Styphoni drew back except for the one who fell forward and rolled down the stairs to land at Ptosphes' feet.

He was as filthy as all the others and no more than eighteen. He was crying for his mother as he clasped his hands over a belly wound that under other circumstances would have killed him slowly over the next few days. Well, he'd be spared that and he'd already lived longer than the keeper's grandson would, or Harmakros' son would—if the Grand Host overtook Kalvan.

Except that the Styphoni wouldn't. Ptosphes knew this although he couldn't have explained how he knew it. He was sure it was true knowledge, not a dead man's dreaming to make his death easier.

My mind is wandering, he thought. He was having trouble breathing, too.

Since he was dead, why wait any longer, in case one of those Styphoni cursing so loudly at the top of the stairs wanted to come down and argue the point?

Ptosphes finished tamping the ball and wadding of his new load, checked the pan, then rested the pistol on one knee as he knocked the live coal from his pipe into the trail of fireseed.

FORTY-NINE

I

Soton cursed Roxthar and his stubbornness that was costing the Grand Host so many lives. A quarter of the storming party was inside Tarr-Hostigos, swarming over it like bees. Both courtyards were littered with bodies, most of them Styphoni. Clouds of smoke wreathed the keep, but before they rose Soton had seen, even from his distant post, the savage struggle to enter it.

Why in the name of all the gods hadn't Phidestros held back, instead of closing the breach? True, it was such reckless abandon that had built Phidestros' reputation at the Battle of Phyrax, when he and his Iron Band had made a suicidal ride to join the battle after the calamity of Chothros Heights. Soton had even ordered him not to fight; if only his rash commander had listened, then there would have been someone to go down and put matters in order.

Instead Phidestros was wounded—badly, the tales ran. Small loss, with the last defenders of Hostigos dying even now and Kalvan fleeing toward the Saltless Seas. If Phidestros were going to make a habit of such follies, perhaps it would be best if he stormed Regwarn's Caverns. If he didn't, Soton would make him wish he had!

The smoke around the keep eddied. Soton turned to summon a messenger.

He never completed the turn. Instead, something as invisible as the air but as hard as stone flung him to his knees. Thunder swelled until it seemed that someone was beating on his helmet with his own warhammer. Three Knights flew off the hill, along with a shower of rocks. Soton knew he cried out at that sight, but couldn't hear his own voice.

He lay, gripping the rocky ground as closely as he ever gripped a woman, until it stopped shaking. Then he rose to his knees, and when they did not betray him, to his feet.

The air was filled with acrid smoke and fine ash. Looking toward Tarr-Hostigos, he saw only a vast swirling cloud of smoke. Somewhere in that smoke was the entire storming party—one man in six of the Grand Host's strength.

One of the Knights was shrieking. "It's the Daemon Kalvan! He's come to save his people! Great Styphon, save us!"

Soton smashed his gauntleted fist into the Knight's face. The man fell as if poleaxed. Soton didn't know what he was really smiting, the Knight or his own fear.

Slowly, the air around what had been Tarr-Hostigos cleared. The slopes around it were alive with men, thousands of them all streaming away from the castle. Soton let out a deep breath he hadn't even known he was holding.

Another quarter-candle showed him what was left of Tarr-Hostigos. The keep was only a pile of smoking rubble, the towers had mostly lost their tops, and the walls looked to have been chewed by monsters. How many of their soldiers lay there under the fallen stone or in fragments strewn across the hillside? The Grand Host would be far less grand by the time they were all counted—of that Soton was sure.

Yet this should not have been a surprise. Desperate men will take desperate measures. Who had more experience fighting the desperate than Soton, Grand Master of the Zarthani Knights?

Soton smashed his fist against his armored thigh, insensible to the pain.

"Roxthar!" he shrieked. "Investigator, you will pay for this! By Styphon's Wheel, I swear it!"

II

"Damn you, Sirna! What are you using in the wound? Galzar's Mace?"

Sirna ignored Phidestros' blustering. She knew she must be causing him agony, probing his wounded thigh with her limited skills and instruments improvised by the Iron Band's armorers from Menandra's kitchen utensils. He'd refused a sandbag, though, and she had to go on and extract that last piece she felt in the wound. Otherwise he would certainly lose his leg and probably his life. Then what would happen to her? Sirna told herself that her concern was thoroughly practical and continued digging.

Finally the probe clicked on the fragment again, this time loosening it until she could grip it between two blood-slimed fingers. It was a piece of stoneware, sharp-edged but solid. It wouldn't leave any more fragments in the wound (or so she told herself, because she knew that her hands would start shaking uncontrollably if she had to burrow back into that mangled flesh).

She held up the stoneware. Phidestros managed a grin. "So that's why they didn't run out of bullets. They saved up their last moon's trash and shot it at us!" Phidestros made a face and groaned.

"That's not all the trash I'm going to get shot at me when Soton learns I got this kiss from Galzar rallying his musketeers not a hundred paces from the breach! My ears will hurt worse than this leg."

Petty-Captain Hellos lifted Phidestros' leg so that Sirna could bind it in the boiled remains of a shift. Hellos' wrenched knee made him slow, but as long as he could stand he felt that he had to be on duty. Certainly he'd had more experience dealing with battle wounds than any of Menandra's girls, and he didn't mind taking orders from a woman who knew her business.

At last, Phidestros was bandaged. Sirna came as close as she could to offering a prayer for his recovery. She could no longer tell herself that her wish was entirely practical, either. Phidestros was too good a man to die, even if he was serving a particularly murderous brand of superstition.

"Sorry to give you such a bad time," she said, as four of the hastily recruited orderlies lifted Phidestros off the table. Half the Captain-General's bodyguard had escorted him to the Gull's Nest after he fell. She'd drafted most of them into helping with the wounded who'd been streaming in since dawn. And this was only one of the besiegers' hospitals! Galzar's Great Hall was going to be crammed to the rafters tonight.

"Menandra runs a fine whorehouse, but it's not much of a hospital," Sirna went on. "If I had some proper tools, or the help of a priest of Galzar—"

Phidestros sighed. "My lovely Sirna, if I knew where to find an Uncle Wolf who didn't already need two heads and six hands, I'd have him dragged to you. You're going to be all we have for today. When they carted me off, I heard we already had five thousand men down."

"Five thousand!" Sirna shuddered at the implications. Phidestros had been hit early enough to reach the Gull's Nest before the storming of the keep. Five thousand men down in the time it took the Styphoni to close the walls. How many more had died in the fighting since?

Thunder battered at her ears and the floor quivered and bounced. The door and all the window shutters banged wildly and dust rose until the room looked as if someone had fired a cannon inside. Sirna looked frantically out the window, saw nothing but people gaping idiotically—knew she must be doing the same—and dashed out the door.

A vast cloud of gray smoke towered over Tarr-Hostigos, blotting out the entire hilltop and slowly swallowing the hillside below it. The top of the cloud was already several thousand feet high, spreading into something dreadfully like a fission bomb's mushroom. Sirna lived a moment with the nightmare that Kalvan had done the impossible, taking his time-line from a poor grade of gunpowder to fission bombs in four years.

Then she remembered there had been no pre-explosion lightning flash of gamma ray radiation, and she breathed more easily. Sirna watched as the mushroom shape started to blur; the top of the cloud was simply spreading in a breeze not felt here in the lee of the hills.

Ptosphes had given himself and the last of his men over to a quick death, destroying Tarr-Hostigos and more of his enemies than anyone would ever know.

Sirna wanted to weep, scream, pound her fists against something. For a moment she even wanted to die herself. There had to be something wrong with her, if she was still alive with so much death around her. The battle, the flight, her surgery at Menandra's, Roxthar's Investigation, and now the storming of Tarr-Hostigos—dead men and women and children were everywhere.

Sirna didn't die. She didn't even have hysterics. Instead she gripped the porch railing until she knew she could stand without help. Around her Hostigos Town awoke from a stunned silence into a hideous din of bawled orders, howling dogs, shrieking women and children, horses neighing or galloping wildly about in panic and an occasional pistol shot.

Menandra was standing in the doorway when Sirna turned. "Better come in quick, girl," she said. "The soldiers who lost comrades up there—they'll be wanting someone's blood for it. Can't keep it from being yours if you stand out there."

Sirna followed the older woman inside. She wasn't afraid of death itself. After today she never would be again. Ptosphes had shown her that death could sometimes be your best friend.

He'd also shown her that there were good and bad ways to die. No, not good and bad. That implied a simple moral distinction. If there was anything simple about death, Sirna hadn't seen it.

Wise and foolish ways? Better, but still an oversimplification.

Useful and useless? Yes. That wasn't a universally sound way of distinguishing kinds of death, but there probably wasn't any such thing. It certainly made sense here.

Staying outside to be shot or raped by soldiers mad with rage or wine would be a useless death. She wouldn't risk it. What she would do another time, she would decide when that time came.

A phrase from one of Scholar Danthor Dras' seminar lectures came back to her: *The only universal rule of outtime work is that there are no universal rules.*

III

Verkan Vall finished lighting his pipe with a Kalvan's Time-Line silver and ivory inlaid tinderbox, then turned back to the data screen and its display of information on one Khalid ibn Hussein. The second cousin of a minor Palestinian prince assassinated a year earlier on his subsector branch, Khalid had brought together a new bloc of Arab states which he had named the Islamic Kaliphate, outmaneuvering Abdel Nasser of Egypt, by co-opting the emerging Republic of Egypt into the Kaliphate.

The Kaliphate, with its pro-Western leanings, was tipping the balance between Communism, that strange atheistic quasi-religion, and the so-called Free World. In what direction no one knew, since India had just fallen to an internal Communist takeover. The Hartley Belt was even more unstable than most of the Kaliphate Subsector, due to President Allan Hartley's attempt to *fix* the problems that he had experienced in his previous life that would lead to a Third World War. The problem was—as it almost always was when one man believed he alone knew the answers—that many of his so-called fixes were actually making things worse and ratcheting up the growing tension between the Free World and the Communist Empire.

Another case of the inherent instability of the entire Europo-American, Hispano Columbian Subsector.

Verkan made a note to send out some investigators to see if this Khalid ibn Hussein was another transtemporal hitchhiker, like his friend Kalvan, or if he was another one of the great men of history, like John F. Kennedy or Adolph Hitler. Of course, the men who changed the course of history were not always good men, or even nice ones, many like Genghis Khan, Stalin, Sennacherib, Hitler and Atilla the Hun were little better than mass murders.

One of the biggest problems with transtemporal history was that it was always easier to spot the important historical divarication points after the damage was done. There was that Paracop chief, over two thousand years ago, who hadn't paid any attention to an anonymous carpenter's son until the religion in his name shattered the Europo-American Sector into several new subsectors.

The red light on Verkan's horseshoe desk lit up, announcing an important visitor. He looked up to see Kostran Garth enter. Kostran's face was flushed from exertion, his breath came short as if he'd been running, and he was holding out a data-storage wafer in one hand.

"What is it?"

"This just arrived from the Hostigos spy-eye. I scanned it briefly—Dalla had it red-flagged—and I knew you'd want to see it right away."

From the look on Kostran's face, Verkan knew the wafer did not contain good news; only bad news ever traveled that fast. Verkan slipped the wafer into his viewer and watched the wall visiplate light up.

The views began with a sky-eye scan of Hostigos and the surrounding Princedoms, from an altitude that made them all look deceptively peaceful. The next shots were close-ups of Tarr-Hostigos. Verkan sighed with relief; at least he wasn't going to watch Kalvan and his remaining soldiers caught like fish in a net. Without noticing, he began to rub the spot where he'd taken that musket ball to the chest.

The camera panned in closer, suggesting manual control of the cameras (*remember to commend Dalla, who was running things back in Harphax City, for that precaution*). A human wave was approaching the beleaguered castle; almost the whole Styphoni host seemed to be on the move; closer still, and Verkan saw whole units going down under Hostigi shells and musketry.

Verkan hit the fast-forward. Whatever was coming, he wanted to get it over with.

The attackers poured into the castle like ants over leftover dog food. Muzzle flashes showed that the keep still had some live defenders. Were Ptosphes and Harmakros among them—Ptosphes who'd refused to leave his home, and Captain-General Harmakros, still worth any three men with two legs?

Suddenly everything vanished in a cloud of smoke. Verkan held his breath until the smoke began to clear. Slowly Tarr-Hostigos reappeared—or what had been Tarr-Hostigos.

A few stubs of the former walls still stood, battered and leaning. Otherwise Ptosphes' seat was a pile of smoking rubble. Verkan saw where one aircar-sized chunk of stone had crushed an entire company of Styphoni. The slopes around the castle were covered with more Styphoni—lying still, crawling, stumbling, a few lucky enough to be able to run.

Verkan's fist slammed down on his desk. "By Dralm, Ptosphes did it!"

"What?"

"The old man did what even Kalvan couldn't do. He stopped the Grand Host in its tracks! Look at that mess! The bastards must have taken ten, maybe fifteen thousand casualties. That, my friend, is no longer a Grand Host. By the time Soton and Phidestros sort things out, Kalvan will be safe in Grefftscharrer territory."

Verkan rummaged for a flask of Ermut's Best and two cups out of a drawer. "A toast, Kostran. A toast to the memory of a valiant Prince and his last and greatest victory!"

Kostran gagged at the taste of the brandy, but he was smiling as he said, "To Prince Ptosphes!"

FIFTY

Considering the Hostigi resistance, the five thousand casualties taken in entering Tarr-Hostigos surprised no one. From the stories brought in during the day with the wounded, Sirna concluded that another ten to twelve thousand must have been casualties of the keep's explosion. That made roughly seventeen thousand casualties. More than half were dead, and half the wounded wouldn't fight again this year, if at all. Sirna would have liked more accurate figures, but she was relieved to know that she could go on doing a University outtime observer's work even in the middle of a battle.

It would be embarrassing if she ever returned home and had to confess that she hadn't taken advantage of her "unique opportunity" to observe historically significant Fourth Level events. It would probably cost her that doctorate.

Sirna told herself this over and over again, to keep some grip on her sanity, as the wounded poured into the Gull's Nest. It was the first time she'd allowed herself to think of Home Time Line since the day she woke up in Menandra's back bedroom. Somewhat to her surprise it helped.

Having some extra hands helped even more. More of the lightly wounded men turned to changing bandages or helping comrades to the privies. Menandra rolled up her sleeves and went to work setting bones, a skill she'd acquired in her younger days from cleaning up after tavern brawls in Agrys City. She also turned out most of her girls who could be trusted to know a clean bandage from a dirty one, which was a larger number than Sirna had expected.

Another of Scholar Dras' bits of wisdom kept running through Sirna's mind: "The danger of paratemporal contamination doesn't come from the stupidity of outtimers. It comes from the fact that they're inherently just about as smart as we are. Once they've been shown that something is possible, you would be surprised how fast they can pick it up and even start filling in gaps on their own."

Sirna knew that the problem-solving abilities of outtimers would never surprise her again.

By the time the western sky turned an appropriately bloody color, the flow of fresh wounded had stopped. A little later the sky darkened and rain began to fall. The crash of thunder resounded inside the Gull's Nest, reminding her of Soton's guns. She trudged through the house on feet that felt shod in lead boots, checking splints and dressings she hadn't put on herself.

In the pouring rain outside she heard shouts and screams. Men, drunk or avenging dead comrades or simply celebrating being alive when they'd expected to be dead, were sacking Hostigos Town. The hard-eyed mercenary guards from the Iron Band kept the noise and the noisemakers safely outside.

At least she didn't hear the sinister crackling of flames she'd heard the night the Royal Foundry was sacked. The Styphoni weren't going to burn the town as long as they needed its roofs over their heads.

Sirna felt like a deer that'd somehow managed to be adopted by a pack of wolves. The Captain-General's men would protect her against all the other packs as long as she did what they expected. But that didn't make her a wolf. Somehow it was no longer hard to take for granted a situation she would have found unbelievably degrading two years ago. Not hard at all, when she listened to the screams outside.

She was changing the bandages on the stump of a man's arm when someone banged on the door to the street, loud enough to be heard over the din outside and the cries of the wounded inside. One of the house women looked through the peephole. Then she unbarred the door and jumped aside, with a look on her face that brought every fit man in the room to his feet.

Two of Styphon's Own Guardsmen strode in, their red cloaks flapping dramatically. Behind them came a tall man in a white robe. Two more of Styphon's Red Hand followed their white-robed charge inside, and then stood flanking the door. Sirna saw hostile glances flicking over the Guardsmen's clean clothing and silvered armor.

At least Holy Investigator Roxthar looked as if he'd worked today, and worked hard. His long hollow-cheeked face was coated with dust and soot and his robes were bloodstained and frayed. He reminded Sirna of a Fourth Level Christian representation of the Devil.

For a moment she wondered if Kalvan was the only cross-time hitchhiker on Styphon's House Subsector. Then she remembered the file she'd read on the Kalvan Control Time-Line equivalents to the major Archpriests. On one group of time-lines, possibly the beginning of a new paratime belt, Archpriest Roxthar was purging Styphon's House almost as spectacularly as he was here. On several others he'd died mysteriously, no doubt courtesy of one of Archpriest Anaxthenes' handy little vials. On the rest Roxthar was ignored, or shunned by the rest of the Inner Circle.

Phidestros struggled to a sitting position and raised a hand in greeting. "Welcome, Your Holiness. Today Galzar's Hall is filled to the bursting, but the strongest and vilest of the Daemon's nests has at last been burned out."

Roxthar nodded, as though acknowledging a remark about the weather, and then looked around the room. His nostrils flared.

"So this den of flesh-selling has served as the Captain-General's lair. I wondered why we had so often lacked your esteemed company at the Palace."

From the Grand Captain-General's face, Sirna knew his patience was strained nearly to the breaking point.

"I must admit, Your Holiness, that I much prefer the cries of honest passion in this house to the constant uproar in former Prince Ptosphes' Palace basement. No offense meant, of course. Let Styphon's Will Be Done!"

Roxthar's face paled. "Do not presume, Captain-General, or you may yet find yourself enjoying the hospitality of my Investigators."

"I also suspect they might find a soldier too much work, after so many women and children."

Roxthar's gray eyes turned into steel ball bearings. "Enough of this babble. We have the God of Gods to serve today. The Daemon Kalvan has fled, and with him the remnants of his host. The land he left behind is tainted with the evil he wrought; the servants of his devils lurk everywhere. Let the Investigation of Styphon finish its work, then we can attend to lesser duties."

It was just as well Roxthar didn't smile. If he had, Sirna knew she would have laughed out loud, hoping to wake up on the other side of the abyss between her and the sane reality of Home Time Line, where people didn't blow up castles in wars over non-existent gods. Instead she bit her lip and unwound the last strip of bandage, then stood up to take the sterilized fresh dressing from the soldier holding the basin.

The movement drew Roxthar's eyes. Sirna felt their hard, unclean gaze on her all the time she was binding on the dressing, emptying the water into the slop bucket and putting the old bandages into the empty basin to be returned to the cauldrons boiling in the kitchen. She was proud that her hands didn't tremble once.

At last there was nothing more to do except stand up and face the Investigator. He was now smiling, an expression to which his gaunt features hardly lent themselves. Sirna decided that she much preferred him expressionless.

"Those bandages have been boiled to drive out the fester demons, have they not?"

"That is so, Your Holiness." Sirna was relieved that she'd kept all traces of a tremor out of her voice.

"That is knowledge given by the lord of demons, Kalvan. Do you know that?"

You're not afraid of death anymore, Sirna reminded herself. *Besides, Roxthar won't spare a heretic even if she goes down on the floor and kisses his feet. Do as you please and at least you can hope to go out with dignity, like Ptosphes.*

"That is so, Your Holiness. Yet the new compounding of fireseed was also brought by Kalvan. With the blessing of Styphon's holy priests, the new fireseed has been used in the guns of Styphon's Grand Host to smite Styphon's enemies. Is it not possible that the knowledge of smiting the fester demons may also be used to aid Styphon's cause?"

Roxthar's vices did not include being at a loss for words. "This may be so. Yet I see no priests of Styphon's House here to bless your work, so that it may drive out devils and demons instead of letting them in. Also, it is too soon to tell what may come of this day's work. Not all demons leap forth at the wave of their servants' hands. Some bide their time."

If it weren't that her life was at stake, Sirna would have believed this conversation about demons and their servants totally absurd. "In your own words, Your Holiness—that may be so. Yet I have been healing the men of the Iron Band since the siege began. In all of them, the wounds are cleaner than they would have been without my work. Ask the Grand Captain-General or the men themselves.

"As for there being no priest here—today there were many wounded and few hands to heal them. Should I have let men who shed their blood for Styphon die, their wounds stinking and festering, because there is no priest to bless work that I know is wholesome and good? If I did that, then you would have good cause to bring me before the Investigation. I think what I have done is good service to the God of Gods, and I will pray for his blessing and also for his mercy on you if you falsely accuse me."

She knew that the last sentences must have been audible on the street outside, from the way the door guards were looking behind them. Roxthar's smile froze, and then he shrugged.

"As Styphon Wills. I only know what I must do in his service and I pray for his mercy if I misjudge what that is. You must come with us before the Investigation and hope that witnesses may be found in your behalf."

Sirna knew that her last moment was close at hand, and also that she was going to spend it as a woman of this time-line rather than as a scholar of First Level. Her right hand was at waist level, closing around the hilt of a non-existent dagger and she'd shifted her footing to open the distance between her and Roxthar. One of the Temple Guards stepped forward—

—and stopped a yard from Sirna, as a dozen mercenaries drew entirely real swords and daggers. Two more armed with halberds appeared on the stairway and a third in the door to the hall, with a pistol.

"Archpriest Roxthar," Phidestros said, in a tone that reminded Sirna of a baron she'd once heard sentencing a poacher. "There is nothing but truth in what this woman says. This I swear, by Styphon God of Gods and Galzar Wolfshead, as well as by Tranth who blesses the hands of the craftsman. My men will swear the same."

"How many of them?"

"As many as needed to make it unlawful for this woman to go before the Investigation, and ten more besides. The Iron Band knows good healing when it sees it."

One of the Temple Guardsmen started to draw his pistol at Phidestros' tone. An imperative and slightly frantic gesture from Roxthar stopped him. The Archpriest's good sense clearly extended to recognizing when he saw a situation where one false move would leave him and his guards dead on the floor and the Investigation of Styphon's enemies in chaos.

"We value your judgment and honor you for your good work in the Holy Investigation," Phidestros went on, as big a lie as Sirna had ever heard anyone deliver with a straight face. "Therefore we will also swear to watch this woman day and night and bring word to the Investigation of any evil effects from her healing."

Phidestros paused, then fired his final shot. "And is not one of Styphon's own signs of his presence among us his gift of healing?"

Roxthar's head jerked, but to Sirna's relief he stopped short of smiling. "As you wish, Captain-General. Clearly Styphon's favor is with you today, but this may not always be so. I shall return tomorrow, to see those wounded who have been healed in days past and to take the oaths you have promised."

The Investigator whirled and strode out so fast that the Guardsmen had to scurry to catch up with him. A chorus of harsh laughter and obscene remarks about why the Guardsmen had un-battered armor, after a battle as bloody as this one, hurried their departure. Sirna also heard a few bawdy remarks about who would have the job of watching her by night.

Sirna remembered nothing afterward until she found herself in a chair, her head pushed down between her knees and Menandra and Grand-Captain Geblon chafing her wrists so vigorously that they felt ready to catch fire. She kept her head down and let the chafing go on until the giddiness and the urge to vomit on an empty stomach passed.

"Sirna—"

"Get back down on that pallet, Grand Captain-General!"

"I need to talk—"

"When you're down on the pallet. Not a word until then!"

Sitting cross-legged by Phidestros' pallet, Sirna could hear him without anyone else being able to eavesdrop. Geblon made sure of that, with help from Menandra.

"I'm sorry if I put you in danger," she began. "But I couldn't—"

"And you didn't, and there's no need to apologize," Phidestros interrupted, with a grin. "We are the Iron Band, and we can do nicely without temple-rats chittering in our ears in our own quarters. You, on the other hand…."

Phidestros reached over and put a hand on her knee. "As I told you before, you've got a petty-captain's share of pay for this past campaign coming, and more if Styphon's House pays any of the victory gift they've promised. That's enough to be a good dowry for you, or buy you a horse and cart with traveling rations and servants to take you home—if you have any home left."

"Or you could stay here and buy into a partnership with me," Menandra said, who had quietly moved beside Phidestros' pallet. "I'm not as young as I once was. Somebody I could leave the place to would be a comfort to me now."

Phidestros gave Sirna a smile that showed what he thought of the Gull's Nest's prospects after the Grand Host departed.

"A partnership," Sirna began, and then pressed her palms into her eyes until the pain and the swimming red fire killed the desire to laugh. She owed Menandra too much to ridicule the idea of staying in Hostigos Town and becoming assistant madam of a bordello!

"I don't advise any of those," Phidestros went on. "Roxthar can't try anything with us, or at least anything the rest of the Inner Circle or Grand Master Soton won't stop, as long as I'm Grand Captain-General of the Grand Host of

Styphon. Soton and Anaxthenes both know good captains are valuable, as long as Kalvan's still on the loose.

"You, on the other hand, Roxthar will snap up like a weasel grabbing a new-hatched duckling the moment you're out of our protection. You've humiliated him before men he distrusts. He'll forgive that the day Queen Rylla begs on her knees for a pardon from Styphon's House."

Phidestros was making sense—too much sense—but not telling her what to do. Or perhaps he assumed she already knew, and was waiting for her to offer it freely.

"I...I suppose I could ride with the Iron Band, that is, if you've a place for a healer. I'd like to train some of your men to help me, if that could be arranged, because I really can't do it all myself—"

Phidestros was kissing her eyelids and cheeks as well as her lips. Sirna wasn't quite ready to kiss him back, but she didn't stop him, either. She managed to be deaf to the new chorus of cheers and bawdy remarks around her.

"Some of my girls may want to come with you," Menandra added. "Hostigos Town may not be the most comfortable place for a while. I've three or four who've earned out their time and may want to travel on. If you could train them too—"

It's insane! Here she was, planning to live as the healer to a band of Fourth Level mercenaries and madam to their field brothel. Not to mention, probably, mistress to their Captain-General—an idea that now left her feeling curious rather than degraded. *Although please, don't let the contraceptive implants run out before I find a way home!*

It was insane—and it would keep her alive. If Roxthar's Investigators had to fight the Iron Band to reach her, they probably would give her up as not worth the trouble. If she had to sleep with Phidestros to keep his favor, she would at least be sleeping with an interesting man—and not interesting in a purely academic sense, either.

She would go with Phidestros and his men. She would do what they wanted her to do, and they would keep her alive until Great King Kalvan returned and took vengeance for this day and all the other crimes of Styphon's House.

Sirna was sure that day would come. It would be worth enduring much to be there to see it, and maybe, Dralm willing, help bring it about.

FIFTY-ONE

I

There was dancing in the streets of Balph. Hostigos was an abattoir and the renegade Prince Ptosphes was dead. The Daemon Kalvan was fleeing for his life and the mighty fortress Tarr-Hostigos had fallen to the Grand Host of Styphon's House. The war against the Blasphemer was over! "Styphon Victorious" rang out throughout the Holy City. The only dark cloud on the horizon was the unasked question: How long before Archpriest Roxthar and his Investigation returned?

That was the question that had weighed heavily on the mind of Archpriest Anaxthenes for the last moon as he pondered the future of the Temple's hold over the Five Kingdoms. Today, he had gotten an answer. Soon he would attend a meeting with the rest of his co-conspirators at Relic Tomb deep underneath the Great Temple of Styphon. Now he was meeting with Highpriest Danthor in the Speaker's private chamber. Danthor had just returned from Hos-Rathon and Anaxthenes was anxious to learn if he had any news of Usurper Kalvan.

After the Highpriest was brought into his chamber, Anaxthenes dispensed with the usual ritual greetings. "Have a seat, Highpriest."

"Your Eminence be praised."

"Yes, yes… Let us dispense with the formalities today. I invited you to my chambers to learn firsthand of your time in Rathon Town."

Danthor laughed nastily. "The Trygathi call it Rathon City these days. These bumpkins will rue the day their king sold them out so he could pose as Great King—Ha! Great King Cleitharses has plans for the Holy Squares to deal with these upstarts as soon as they return from Hos-Hostigos."

Now it was Anaxthenes turn to laugh. "Return—not this winter! Ho! Ho! Maybe not the next, either."

Danthor looked at him in curiosity.

"Not a word of this to Old Rat's Nest. He will learn in Our time. The Holy Squares were massacred by the Hostigi Army; less than half will return to Hos-Ktemnos."

"The Great King will be inconsolable. They were the elite of the Sacred Squares of Hos-Ktemnos! How did this happen? I thought we won."

"Yes, we won, but the butcher's bill was high. Unfortunately for the Holy Squares, Marshal Zythannes turned and ran from his post, when the Hostigi attacked, thereby leaving the Holy Squares without a commander. Many more were lost when Prince Ptosphes blew up Tarr-Hostigos."

"Cleitharses will be sick when he learns of this disaster."

"That's not all. The Grand Host will not be disbanding, or rather most of it will not. Great King Lysandros is willful and thinks of his own gain, rather than the Temples."

Danthor nodded. "Like an Archpriest."

They both laughed.

"For our safety, the Grand Host will continue its work. Also, Soton does not trust the Host's commander, Grand Captain-General Phidestros. He is by far too ambitions; somehow he convinced Lysandros to have all the Host's mercenaries swear oaths of fealty to him, as Prince of Greater Beshta! This was supposedly done to forestall the Ban of Galzar, but not even Styphon himself knows what plots are hatching in Phidestros' or Lysandros' skulls! Nor does Soton trust subordinates who disobey his orders, as Phidestros did by leading the siege party to Tarr-Hostigos himself."

"If he did this contrary to the Grand Master's personal orders, he is not to be trusted."

Anaxthenes nodded, "My thoughts exactly. Of course, with Roxthar still in Hostigos, the problem may resolve itself with Phidestros under Investigation. However, Roxthar is a dangerous tool—like one of Kalvan's swords which I have heard has a deadly point as well as a sharp blade."

Danthor added, "Truly, Roxthar and his Investigation are now endangering the Temple. With Hos-Hostigos conquered and the Usurper gone, does Styphon need Roxthar?"

"Ha! Better yet, does Styphon's House need the Investigator and his Investigation? Yes, this is the sticking point for the Inner Circle—most of whom wet themselves upon hearing the Investigator's very footsteps!"

Danthor nodded solemnly. "Fortunately, Speaker, there are those among the Inner Circle who still have backbones."

Anaxthenes smiled, but refrained from comment. This Blethan Highpriest appeared to be a good prospect for the new Inner Circle. At the next session of the Inner Circle, he would have Archpriest Heraclestros put Danthor's name up for investiture. He knew that he'd promised King Cleitharses he'd have Danthor elevated as Archpriest, but he could have stalled until Old Rat's Nest died, had he not sensed a kindred soul.

Now, he needed information. "How did our new Great King take to Kalvan's troubles?"

"Not well, Speaker. When I last saw Nestros, before my departure to Balph, he was cradling his head in his arms as though in great pain. I fear the new Pretender, of the soon-to-be shortly lived Kingdom of Hos-Rathon, is beginning to doubt the wisdom of his agreement to ally himself with us. As well he should. I spent half of his treasury building new Temples and shrines to Styphon!"

Anaxthenes hooted. "Very good, he will have little gold to spend on troops and weapons. New taxes will turn his friends into enemies and embolden those who already despise him. I hope you thought to bring some of this gold home to Balph with you."

"Of course, Speaker...the other half!"

They both howled!

"I brought back four wagonloads of valuables from Hos-Rathon, everything that wasn't tied down."

"How come I haven't heard about these wagons?"

"What Speaker, and have every temple rat between here and Rathon stealing the scraps? No, I used handpicked men from my bodyguard to protect the treasure. I ensured the teamsters' silence by having their tongues cut off. Of course, the teamsters will be suitably rewarded now that the treasure has arrived in Balph. Maybe Styphon will grow them new tongues!"

Despite himself, Anaxthenes chuckled. "We need more highpriests with your wit, and foresight." *I'm going to have to keep an eye on this one,* he thought. Then his curiosity got the best of him, "What have you done with the treasure?"

"With Styphon's own coffers already so over-burdened with gold and other riches, I thought this wealth might be more valuable as a private Inner Circle treasury, for those deeds that are wont to be kept secret."

Oh, you are good! thought Anaxthenes. "Most perspicacious of you, Highpriest. I will see that you are personally given one tenth of all the treasure." He failed to mention that he would personally take a third for himself. Of course, if Danthor were half as smart as he came across, he would have already taken his own third. Too bad he couldn't question those drivers himself…

"That is more than fair, Speaker." Danthor replied.

"Did you hear any word of the Usurper's plans while you were in the False Kingdom of Hos-Rathon?"

"No. I left just after news of the Battle of Ardros Field reached Rathon 'City.' There was no joy in the streets of Rathon, nor any on Nestros' face at word of Styphon's great victory. Kalvan was only in Hos-Rathon for a short time, but he made many friends among the commoners and soldiers there."

Anaxthenes shrugged. "Kalvan's victory over the Order of Zarthani Knights did not tarnish his reputation, either. Still, if Kalvan had not wooed Ranjar Sargos so ardently, we would have never been able to convince that blockhead Nestros that Kalvan was untrustworthy."

"It was Nestros' ambition that was his undoing. He desired to be what he could not be and will never be—a Great King."

"Most true. He is the Great King of Swine of the Trygathi Pigpen. But what of Ranjar Sargos? There could be danger for all of us if Kalvan were to join with the nomads and then worry our borders."

"Xiphlon has hired this Warlord who deems himself Great King, like Nestros, under the Urgothi title, Var-Wannax. It is said that Sargos has taken a great army to the Sea of Grass to subdue the Ruthani and Mexicotál who besieged Xiphlon. Win or lose, Sargos will be in no position to help Kalvan."

"You have brought us much good news, Danthor. Now it is my turn to give you some; I will sponsor your investiture as Archpriest at the next Council. In return, I expect your complete loyalty and that you will act as my ear in Great King Cleitharses audience chamber and library."

Danthor bowed his head. "Your wish is my command, First Speaker."

II

Heraclestros, holding a torch, was the first to arrive at the Tomb after Anaxthenes, and was quickly followed by the other seven Archpriests who were the core of the Inner Circle cabal against Roxthar. The Relic Tomb was damp and cold despite the heat outside above the streets. At the center of the Tomb were the sacred bones of Tythos, the priest of Styphon who had discovered the true value of the Fireseed Secret. The bones were covered in gold leaf and placed in a glass coffin edged with gold and silver.

"The Usurper is vanquished!" Heraclestros announced.

"Not truly, he still breathes," Anaxthenes said.

"As does Sesklos," someone else intoned.

Anaxthenes ignored the jibe; Sesklos would dwell in Regwarn's Caverns shortly—as would Kalvan. "The Grand Host will bring the Usurper to heel soon enough, if the Inner Circle stays out of the commanders' path. I have more interesting news to impart.

"Today Sesklos received a post from the Holy Investigator," Anaxthenes paused to pick up a parchment filled with runes that looked like they'd been burned into the sheepskin. "Let me read Roxthar's own words:

Styphon's Voice On Earth,

Tarr-Hostigos, the last symbol of the Daemon's rule over this accursed land, was destroyed today. The siege under Grand Master Soton and Grand Captain-Phidestros took a moon to conclude. All of Kalvan's minions and imps died today when Styphon caused the tarr's fireseed stores to explode—ending this blasphemy against the True God for all time. Let all of Balph rejoice in His victory—All Hail Styphon!

Our mission here is not complete, as heresy is deeply rooted in the blighted lands of the False Kingdom of Hos-Hostigos. We are resolved to Investigate every man, woman and child in this Styphon-forsaken kingdom until we have ended Kalvan's pestilence for all time.

The omens have augured well for the Investigation; the skies have opened and voiced their displeasure upon the False Kingdom, deluging the earth with water in an attempt to scour the very memory of Hos-Hostigos from the land.

We will not be returning to Balph until winter at the earliest. Grand Captain-General Phidestros, who has proven unworthy of the trust we have placed in his hands, will shortly be dismissed as Commander of the Grand Host. Great King Lysandros has invested him, in reward for his service to the Iron Throne, as Great Prince and Elector of Greater Beshta, which is comprised of two Princedoms of the former False Kingdom of Hos-Hostigos. He refuses our offer of Investigation, for now. We will deal with Prince Phidestros and his heretics when our more pressing duties have been completed.

Anaxthenes tried to remember the chain of command of the Grand Host. Grand Captain-General Phidestros had been forced by Lysandros to relinquish his command of the Royal Harphaxi army to become overall commander of the Grand Host. Regardless, Phidestros was oath-sworn to Lysandros so, despite Roxthar's pronouncement, Phidestros could only be dismissed by his Great King. Both, of course, in actuality were in the pay of Styphon's House. Still, they believed themselves free men and would continue to act in this manner, despite Roxthar's wishes, until Balph cut off the flow of gold—which as long as Anaxthenes had a say in the matter was not going to happen until Kalvan was dead.

Roxthar appeared to be taking over the duties of the Host's paymaster and commander in chief. He hoped Soton would be able to rein him in. Anaxthenes could not foresee Great King Lysandros firing the one man, both because of his popularity with the soldiers and his military prowess, who could protect him from the Holy Investigator. Clearly, Archpriest Roxthar was out of control, after his rampage in Hos-Hostigos, and was now a danger not only to himself and those around him, but to Styphon's House, as well.

It had been their pact that Soton would keep the Investigator out of Balph until winter to give him time to dispose of Sesklos and win election as Styphon's Voice. Sesklos had just survived another winter, his ninety-third. He would not survive another summer, even if Anaxthenes had to pillow his face himself.

About Phidestros he didn't care a bent phenig. He'd been a useful tool in the war against Kalvan, a tool whose usefulness was coming to an end.

Grand Master Soton will leave in Our hands those forces necessary to continue Styphon's Work among the heretics and unbelievers of the False Kingdom of Hos-Hostigos. Meanwhile, the Grand Master will continue to pursue the Daemon Kalvan until he is vanquished. When the Usurper's army is destroyed, I will forsake my work here and Investigate all Hostigi captives until I have convinced them of the error of their ways so that their spirits will be free of the taint of heresy when they leave this world.

Your Obedient Servant in Styphon's Work,
Roxthar
Holy Investigator

One of the Archpriests said, "Does this madman actually believe the Highpriests of Galzar will sit there quietly while he brazenly kills prisoners taken in battle? His actions have already brought Galzar's Ban upon the Grand Host."

"He believes what he wishes, I fear," Anaxthenes said.

"Stop Roxthar!" Archpriest Zemos exclaimed. "Only death will stop that madman. Does Roxthar not realize the consequences of the Interdict: no Uncle Wolfs to tend the wounded, no rites of Galzar for the dead and dying, no parley or surrender and all god-fearing men's hands turned against them. No believer in Galzar or the gods will fight in an army under Interdict—not even the soldiers of the Sacred Squares. Can we not have the Grand Master remove the Investigator or put him in exile?"

"As long as Roxthar has the Temple Guardsmen to enforce his edicts, they will be obeyed. The Guard will kill Uncle Wolfs as easily as wringing turkey necks. The last thing we can afford is a war between Styphon's Own Guard and the Zarthani Knights, who still hold Galzar in high esteem. The political ramifications would shake the Temple to its foundation!"

"How is it that this wolf in human guise gained such loyalty among Styphon's Own Guard?"

Anaxthenes smiled. "I worried over that bone myself until I learned the answer; Roxthar gives the Guard one third of all monies and properties seized by the Investigation."

One Archpriest whistled. "No wonder Xenophes bought a new palace last winter!"

"Captain-General Xenophes is no fool. He shares half the proceeds with the Band captains and troopers."

"Where does the rest of the plunder go, Anaxthenes?" Heraclestros asked, as if he wanted his share. Having met Heraclestros' new wife, a tavern singer with airs, he suspected the Archpriest needed all the gold he could find.

"One third to the Temple Treasury and the last third to the Investigation. Our Roxthar is quite generous with other people's wealth. The Investigators themselves are given a third of the Investigation's share, but each Investigator can only collect his own share when he's mustered out of the Investigation—and who knows when that will be!"

"Ahh. I wondered how Roxthar held their loyalty. I know it's not out of love!"

They all laughed.

"What will happen to the Grand Host after Kalvan is defeated?" Archpriest Lymachor asked.

"That is why I called this meeting. Even with our success on the battlefield Styphon's House faces a crisis unlike any in the past, one that threatens the very existence of the Temple."

"The Fireseed Mystery."

"Yes. It is no longer a secret and dung-rakers all over the Five Kingdoms are building their own fireseed mills, with their Princes' and Kings' complete support. Thus, in a blink of an eye Styphon's House's greatest source of income is gone. True, our cotton plantations, our sugar trade, tobacco fields and Great Banking Houses will continue to bring us gold, but now we will face increased competition from other trading houses. Soon even the Middle Kingdoms will vie for our markets. Our political power and domination over the Five Kingdoms will only last to the day that the first Great King decides to tax our collections or temples. Then our favored status will not even last our lifetimes.

"Therefore, we must act in all haste. After Kalvan has been defeated or chased into Grefftscharr, we will use our Grand Host to bring to heel the Northern Kingdoms and consolidate our control over all the Five Kingdoms before it disbands."

"How do we get Soton to go along with this?"

"Much of this is the Grand Master's own scheme. He enjoys his power, which is greater than even the most powerful of Great Kings, because of the Temple. Soton does not want to see the Order dissolved or crippled by the collapse of Styphon's House. He will plant the idea of Investigating the Great Kings and Princes of Hos-Agrys and Hos-Zygros who did not support our war against the Usurper—how could Roxthar resist such bait?

"The Grand Host will bring the Great Kings of Hos-Agrys and Hos-Zygros to heel, and even Lysandros should he object. When all the Northern Kingdoms are under our domination, we will truly rule all the Five Kingdoms and enjoy even greater wealth than we possess today!"

Someone broke out a cask of mead and golden goblets were passed around.

"To Styphon's Great Victories—may they never end!"

"To First Speaker Anaxthenes, may he soon be Styphon's Voice!"

"Aye, aye," they agreed.

"We need his hand on the rudder of our ship of state," said Archpriest Zemos, who had been the former head of Styphon's Great Fleet.

"And around Roxthar's neck!" someone else shouted.

They all laughed. Anaxthenes smiled; it was a pleasant image.

Heraclestros added, "And a toast to the Daemon Kalvan and a quick death! Only Dralm himself can save him from the fate rushing his way."

True, thought Anaxthenes. *But there's no Dralm to help Kalvan, and most of all—no Styphon to help Roxthar!*

FIFTY-TWO

The Hostigi host had been camped outside Ulthor Town for almost a moon quarter. Prince Kestophes had offered Kalvan the use of his own palace to use as his personal quarters and command post, but Kalvan had turned him down. His people needed him here. Rumor had it that Nestros the False had brought a large army to the south to prevent the Hostigi from foraging or settling within the borders of Hos-Rathon. Kalvan found himself in the position of a missionary whose first convert had just invited him to dinner—as the main dish.

It was tempting to conquer Hos-Rathon, which was both poor in firearms and skilled captains. Unfortunately, that would leave Kalvan sharing borders with both the Zarthani Knights and Hos-Ktemnos, neither of whom could be expected to welcome their new neighbor with anything but the family shotgun.

Maybe they could settle in the border areas of Grefftscharr, Dorg or Wulfula and sell their swords as mercenaries. The real problem was that there were just too Dralm-damned many Hostigi soldiers and refugees to make any king comfortable.

He could, like Moses, lead them to the Promised Lands of California or Florida, but Hos-Bletha (Florida) was too close to Balph for comfort and mostly swamp land. He'd already had enough experience fighting the Ros-Zarthani of the Pacific coast to know they were no pushovers either—

He wished Verkan were here, but he was either holed-up or dead. So, instead, he'd sent Master Trader Tortha and Chancellor Chartiphon to lead a delegation to talk with King Theovacar; he was still waiting to hear back from them. The Upper Middle Kingdoms were the only place he had left to go. And he was either going to go into them, or through them.

With more than a half million refugees from Hos-Hostigos to feed and cloth and prepare for next winter, he was either going to take someone else's lands or move into Ulthor—lock, stock and rifle barrels. Holding Ulthor would encourage Roxthar and the Grand Host to continue their pursuit. Then, he might find himself in the same position as in the Princedom of Hostigos, where staying would have resulted in a fight to the death with the Grand Host. Defeating the Grand Host in Hostigos would have left him ruling a kingdom comprised of ruins and starving subjects, while losing would have meant certain death and slavery for all his people.

As far as going down the Samnos River was concerned, there weren't enough boats on all the ports of the Saltless Seas to transport this Hostigos crowd.

Kalvan stared into the glowing embers of the dying campfire, wishing he were anyplace but here. As if he didn't have enough problems on his plate, he was waiting for Aspasthar to arrive so he could tell him that his father had died. This was the toughest duty Kalvan had to face in a year that had cost him just about everything dear to his heart—and cost his subjects even more.

This great king business isn't all that it's cracked up to be, he thought.

It had been about two years ago, after the death of his mother, that Harmakros and his son had been reunited. There had been some problems at first, not surprisingly, but lately the two of them had been growing close….

As Aspasthar approached the orange glow of the fire, he saw the apprehension on the young page's face, a countenance that was beginning to resemble his father's. "Sit down, here on this log."

"Yes, Your Majesty," Aspasthar said, trying in vain to keep a slight tremor out of his voice.

The whole camp knew something was up, ever since the messenger had arrived on a half-dead horse just before sunset asking to speak to Great King Kalvan. There was an unnatural quiet in the air over the camp; only the soft creaking of leather, the neighing of horses and distant crying of babies broke through the stillness. Some of the soldiers must have recognized the messenger as one of the rearguard assigned to Hostigos Town. The news had been bad, very bad, but not a surprise. Having been a noncom in Korea himself, Kalvan wouldn't be the least bit surprised if most of them already knew as much as he did about the fall of Tarr-Hostigos.

Kalvan could tell from the young page's composure that Aspasthar hadn't heard the scuttlebutt about the fall of Tarr-Hostigos, but he certainly had a premonition that something bad had happened—bad enough for his Great King to call him for a private audience in this forest glen.

"There's no easy way, to tell you this, son. So I'll give it to you straight."

Aspasthar rose up off the log, standing parade-ground still.

Kalvan felt a stab of guilt that this defeat was all his fault, but he shook it off. Truthfully, the people of Hostigos were doomed the moment Styphon's House had decided it needed Wolf Valley sulfur springs for a temple farm. For many of his subjects, the arrival of the 'Gods-sent Lord Kalvan' had given them 'interesting times' and a few more years of life. Of course, he had worked hard for better things for his people than this Trail of Tears out of Hos-Hostigos and into the wilderness of the Middle Kingdoms to who knew what kind of reception from King Theovacar and his vassals. But, even the best magician could only pull so many rabbits out of a hat and this time when Kalvan had reached down to the bottom of his hat, well, that hat had been empty.

He was no longer the infallible Great King Kalvan and his subjects—and his wife—were just going to have to get used to it. Kalvan would do his best to find them a new home and someday lead them back to Hostigos, if he could.

"Your father, Aspasthar, was a brave solider and my friend."

Aspasthar nodded, his eyes welling.

"He gave his life so that we would gain ours. His valiant stand with Prince Ptosphes and the Hostigos Veterans gave us time to escape the Grand Host."

The boy crumpled and Kalvan caught him as he fell. He held the boy tight and fought his own faltering emotions as Aspasthar sobbed into his shoulder. Harmakros had been his best friend here-and-now and a fine man. "You could have had no better father."

"I will try to live up to his memory," Aspasthar sputtered. He pulled back and dried his eyes with his sleeves. "I apologize, Your Majesty—"

"Do nothing of the sort. You only have one father and he deserves to be mourned. Do not be ashamed of honest feelings."

The young page nodded.

"I made Harmakros a promise, after he demanded to be allowed to stay behind at Tarr-Hostigos and help his Prince and Our people."

For the first time, Aspasthar perked up.

The resiliency of youth, thought Kalvan. "I promised your father that if anything happened to him that Your Queen and I would become your Guardians." Adoption, no matter how much he liked the boy, was out of the question; he didn't want any dynastic squabbles after his death. He had to choke back the laughter that welled up inside—what dynasty? Right now calling the stragglers and dispossessed that followed him anything more than refugees or displace people—even if they were the Great Kingdom of Hos-Hostigos in hiding—had to be presumption!

"Thank you, Your Majesty. I was wondering what would happen after my father—" He began to tear up again.

"You will be under Our protection. When you have reached your maturity, you will receive your father's title of Duke, and his lands." Young people here-and-now grew up fast and reached their legal age at sixteen. He could see the boy mature right before his eyes.

"Yes, Your Majesty."

"We also have a very important Crown position We would like for you to fill."

Aspasthar brightened up.

"We want you to be Commandant of Cadets of the Hostigos Royal Academy."

Kalvan wasn't sure of what reaction Aspasthar would show upon hearing this news, what he didn't expect was near jubilation.

"Do you mean it?"

"Yes," Kalvan answered with a smile.

"This is—I mean, would be—the happiest day of my life, if it weren't for the news about my father."

"Take whatever joy you can find, son. Tomorrow morning I want you to meet with Colonel Tyral and help reorganize the cadet regiments. The cadets did an excellent job of protecting the women and children during the retreat out of Hostigos and many of them will receive medals from Ourselves, after we get settled."

Aspasthar nodded as if it were a given. The cadets, under the watchful eye of Vanar Halgoth and the Tymannian Guard, had been one of the last lines of defense between the Grand Host and the retreating Hostigi civilians. Even Chartiphon had commented on what a great job they'd done. They'd also taken several hundred casualties during the Retreat.

No Hostigi who lived through the Retreat would ever look upon the Ruthani cadets again as anything but worthy subjects of the Kingdom. Making Harmakros' son, and his ward, their commander would cement their position as loyal subjects of Hostigos-in-Exile for all time.

After telling Aspasthar the sad news of his father's death, Kalvan returned to their campsite. He had yet to face Rylla since the news arrived about Ptosphes; instead he walked back and forth before his tent, digging a trench in the wet soil with his boots. Every time he passed the flap he could hear Rylla crying inside. Prince Ptosphes had been both mother and father to his daughter, and maybe too lenient for all intents and purposes. Still, he had raised her with love and she had returned it in full measure. Now, she was coming to terms to living life without it.

His own father's death had been easier on Kalvan; the Right Reverend Morrison had died while he was off fighting in Korea—presumably from a broken heart, after his son had dropped out of Princeton and abandoned all pretense of becoming a clergyman. They had never been close, so to Kalvan his father's death had been like the closing of a familiar book.

He had thought consoling Aspasthar was tough duty, but it paled in comparison to comforting Rylla over the greatest loss of her life. One which she believed was mostly his fault. Well, Rylla hadn't come out and said that, but that's the feeling he'd had in his gut ever since they'd left Hostigos with their tails tucked firmly beneath their bellies.

With trepidation, Kalvan slowly pulled back the tent flap. He would have rather faced a Temple Band of Styphon's Red Hand unarmed.

The End

www.ingramcontent.com/pod-product-compliance
Lightning Source LLC
Chambersburg PA
CBHW030827310726
48980CB00006B/669/J

* 9 7 8 0 9 3 7 9 1 2 1 8 8 *